The Writer's Handbook

EDITOR
Barry Turner

M
MACMILLAN
REFERENCE
BOOKS

First published 1987 by
THE MACMILLAN PRESS LTD
London and Basingstoke

Associated companies in Auckland, Delhi,
Dublin, Gabarone, Hamburg, Harare, Hong
Kong, Johannesburg, Kuala Lumpur, Lagos,
Manzini, Melbourne, Mexico City, Nairobi,
New York, Singapore, Tokyo

British Library Cataloguing in Publication
Data
The Writer's handbook.
  1. Authorship
  I. Turner, Barry
  808'.02   PN145

  ISBN 0–333–46382–X
  ISBN 0–333–4456–8 Pbk

Typeset by August Filmsetting, Haydock,
St Helens
Printed by The Bath Press Ltd, Bath

Contents

US Publishing

INTRODUCTION

This book owes much to three organisations—**PEN, The Society of Authors** and **The Writers' Guild of Great Britain.** Officers and members have given help and advice unstintingly. I am grateful to them and to many other professional bodies, notably the **National Union of Journalists**, who have provided valuable information not easily available from other sources.

The brunt of the research has been carried by Andrea Gillies who, a year ago, had no idea that *The Writer's Handbook* was to take up such a large share of her waking hours. Her patient interrogation of publishers, producers, agents and other reticent characters turned up a wealth of interesting material. Andrea was assisted, at various times, by Paul Ryan and Jill Fenner who made manageable the awesome task of compilation. For any errors or omissions that might be spotted, the Editor alone takes responsibility.

We are already at work on the next edition of *The Writer's Handbook*. We would like to hear from writers on any item or subject they think should be included. Words of warning or advice will be treated with the strictest confidence.

Publisher's Note

The directory sections have been arranged alphabetically by company name or by town, as in the case of *Regional Newspapers* and *Local Radio*. Where the company name is that of a person, it is ordered by the surname. The television stations have been ordered regionally by areas which are headed as, e.g. Midlands, South East and Scotland.

Since compilation some organisations have ceased to exist. These are indicated by vertical lines on either side of the relevant entry e.g.

The Press Club
76 Shoe Lane, London EC4A 3JB ☎01 353 6207
Subscription £27.60–£66.70 (plus entrance fees)
FOUNDED 1882. Membership is open to both men and women in journalism, publishing and allied professions.

So You Want to be an Author?

First write your book. Now that's the easy part out of the way. Well, no, it's not quite as bad as that. But there are authors of fame and distinction who argue that the hardest time of their lives was trying to persuade publishers to take them seriously.

Frederick Forsyth, one of the most successful writers of our time, had his first novel, *Day of the Jackal*, rejected by four publishers before it was picked up by **Hutchinson**. David Storey's *This Sporting Life* was returned by fifteen publishers and Richard Adams was given the thumbs down by just about everyone in the business when he first submitted *Watership Down*.

There are authors who have struck lucky first time but most build up a collection of rejection slips before experiencing the pleasure of seeing their names in print. A typical case history was provided recently in an article by Jeremy Cooper, whose first novel, *Ruth*, taught him all there is to know of the tribulations of the author as salesman. Rejected by Michael Joseph ('To be absolutely truthful, I do not think you are a fiction writer') the manuscript passed rapidly through the front doors and out the back of **Quartet** and **Chatto**. **Hutchinson** showed an interest but lost it again when **Century** took over. **Faber** too expressed interest. The trouble there was that Robert McCrum, senior editor, was on sabbatical. After correspondence, meetings and an eight months' wait, the manuscript was returned. **Heinemann** said 'No'; so did **Penguin** after seeing a revised version. As a last throw, Jeremy Cooper went to Richard Cohen, the new fiction editor at **Century Hutchinson**. After that it was relatively plain sailing though it took another year to get the book into the shops.

For the author who is just starting out there is everything to be said for studying form. Our own publishers' list gives much of what the beginner needs to know but it helps to talk to other writers in clubs, societies or unions. Because links between writers are traditionally weak, the same mistakes tend to crop up time and again. If for no other reason than self interest, writers should take more trouble to learn from the experience of their peers.

As a general rule go first for publishers who are growing and who, by definition, are most likely to take on new writers. Admittedly, these characters are not always easy to spot. Publishers are cautious by nature. Like farmers who complain when the rain devastates the crop and complain even more when a fine harvest creates a glut in the market, publishers are never entirely happy with their lot. But despite recent talk of unsettled economic conditions, library cuts, decline in educational standards and even competition from the record industry made buoyant on compact discs, all the signs are that publishing is doing quite nicely.

True, retail sales have dropped some twenty per cent over two years but this must be set against an across the board price increase on books of fifteen per cent in 1980 and seventeen per cent in 1986, which leaves room for a healthy return on capital.

New bookshops are springing up, three new major publishers have come on the scene and the takeover mania, though worrying for those who are made nervous by impersonal conglomerates, suggests another push for expansion.

For the aspiring author, there is everything to play for.

So, having spotted the publishers that look set for a bright future, narrow the list to those who are likeliest to share your interest. There is not much point in sending a children's book to **Kogan Page** who specialise in business and management, or a novel to **William Kimber** who are strongest on military history. Yet it is staggering how many writers aim at totally unsuitable publishers, relying presumably on pot luck. Or maybe they think it wise to steer away from publishers who bring out a lot of titles which sound curiously like their own. Isn't this where the competition is toughest? But publishers who do well in one area, are usually keen to exploit their editorial and marketing expertise. They want more of the same.

For the most part, an unsolicited manuscript is less welcome than a synopsis and a sample chapter. Even with a novel, a publisher is more likely to be enthused by a slim file which he/she can read and assess fairly quickly than by a solid manuscript which requires hours of study. With non-fiction the case for involving the publisher at an early stage is even stronger. His advice on how best to tackle the subject could be invaluable.

If the publisher is at all interested in the material you send in, sooner or later (usually later) he will suggest a meeting. Don't be impatient. Writers are often sinned against but they can be unreasonable in their assumption of a quick decision on what, after all, is a risky investment.

If after three or four weeks, nothing is heard, a telephone call is justified. But a polite inquiry is more likely to get results than a demand to know 'what the hell is going on'. It helps to have sent material to a named editor. That way you avoid the risk of being sucked into the whirlpool of internal company communications which can delay it ever reaching the right person.

If the outcome of a first meeting is encouraging, the next discussion should focus on the size of the advance. Any author who wants to make a living by writing must establish early on that his publisher is prepared to make a substantial down payment on account of royalties. The bigger the advance the more likely the publisher will be to put his back into the marketing effort. Even if he winds up hating the book, he will want his money back.

Ideally, the advance should be paid whenever it suits the author best, e.g. on signature of the contract or part on signature, part on delivery of the script, and part on publication. *Except in the case of a bestselling author, it is difficult to secure an advance much above the equivalent of 60% of the royalties likely to be payable on the first edition.*

The advance may be on account of royalties on the publishers' own editions or on account of all income, including subsidiary rights. The former arrangement is preferable, but where the advance is substantial, it may be reasonable for the publisher to recoup his outlay from, say, the proceeds of a US or paperback deal. In either case the advance should be non-returnable except when the author fails to deliver the manuscript.

And so to the contract. Contracts vary significantly from one company to another and since they are all hideously complicated the differences do not always show up to the unpractised eye.

This is where an agent can be invaluable. But the writer who handles his own affairs is not entirely alone. Having campaigned vigorously for ten years or more, the writers' unions have hammered out a minimum terms agreement (MTA) which has met with the approval of several leading publishers.

Hamish Hamilton was the first to sign. That was in 1978. Then came **W. H. Allen** (after a strike by an important group of Allen authors who were also members of the Writers' Guild) and **BBC Books** (after the threat of a strike). **Faber** signed up on their own volition and **Century Hutchinson** followed after lengthy negotiations. This was reckoned to be the turning point though to date **Headline** is the only other publisher to fall into line. As with **Faber**, support from **Headline** came out of the blue, the directors having decided independently that the MTA is just and equitable.

Many hold out against the MTA and no doubt will continue to do so, arguing for the special relationship between the writer and his publisher which does not allow for standard terms. Or as **Weidenfeld** put it, 'All responsible and self-respecting publishers do offer fair terms.' Writers who have suffered the cavalier treatment on matters ranging from unexpected costs for illustrations to delayed royalty payments, have a thing or two to say about the difference between offering fair terms and abiding by them. But publishers retain a strong regard for their own sense of fair play. Misplaced, maybe, but there it is. Authors who are not already members of the **Society of Authors** or the **Writers' Guild** are urged to join if only to be kept up to date on the MTA negotiatons.

A copy of the MTA, which can be obtained from either of these organisations (free of charge to members who send a stamped addressed envelope), is a useful standard against which to judge the virtue of a publisher's offer. When it comes to signing on the bottom line, you may feel you have had to give way on a few points, but if the general principles of the MTA are followed the chances of securing a reasonable deal are much enhanced.

Probably the most important break from tradition contained in the MTA is the clause allowing for the length of licence granted by the author to the publisher to be negotiable. The custom is for the licence to run for the duration of copyright (i.e. the author's lifetime plus 50 years). Originally the writers' unions pressed for a maximum of 20 years but have since compromised on a review procedure which permits the contract to be revised every ten years. This gives the author the opportunity to claim, for example, improved royalties if the book has been a success.

The latest MTA agreements with **Century Hutchinson** and **Headline** confirm the extent to which authors should be involved in the publication of their books. For example:

● There will be full discussion prior to signing the contract of illustrations,

quotations, etc., the costs thereof, and the party responsible for paying them. Normally the publishers will pay some or all of the costs involved.
● There will be full consultation on any changes to the text (with the author seeing the final edited script before it goes to the printers), and consultation on all the illustrations, the jacket, blurb and publication date.
● The author will be invited to make suggestions for publicity, and will be shown the proposed distribution list for review copies.
● The author will be fully consulted before any major sub-licences are granted by the publishers (e.g. paperback, American, film, television and merchandising deals).

On the touchy question of royalties:

● The basic hardback scale will be 10% to 2500 copies, 12½% on the next 2500 copies and 15% thereafter – on the published price (home sales) or the publisher's receipts (exports). On certain small reprints the royalty may revert to 10%.
● On home paperback sales the minimum royalty will be 7½% of the published price, rising to 10% after 50,000 copies. On exports the minimum royalty will be 6% of the published price. If paperback rights are sub-licensed, the author will receive at least 60% of the income, rising to 70% at a point to be agreed (50,000 copies in **Headline**'s case).
● The author will receive 85% of the income from the sale of American rights and 80% from translations.
● The author will receive 90% from first serial rights, TV and radio dramatisations, film and dramatic rights, etc. Other percentages to the author include: anthology and quotation rights, 60%; TV and radio readings, 75%; merchandising, 80%.

But bear in mind that the royalty percentages do not necessarily apply to all books. For example, heavily illustrated books are excluded and there are certain exceptional circumstances in which publishers may pay lower royalties (for example, long works of fiction published in short print-runs for libraries).

As a spot check on the acceptability of a contract confirm three essential points before finally adding your signature.

1 There should be a firm and unconditional commitment to publish the book within a specified time, say twelve months from delivery of the typescript or, if the typescript is already with the publisher, from signature of the agreement. It is also as well for the approximate published price to be specified.

The obligation to publish should not be subject to approval or acceptance of the manuscript. Otherwise what looks like a firm contract may be little more than an unenforceable declaration of intent to publish. It is equally important to watch that the words 'approval' or 'acceptance' do not appear in the clause relating to the advance payment. For example, if the advance, or part of it, is payable 'on delivery and approval' of the script, this might qualify the publishers' obligation to publish the work.

This point about the publishers' commitment to publishing a book is of vital importance, particularly since publishers' editors change jobs with increasing frequency. An author who has started a book with enthusiastic support from his editor may, when he delivers it, find he is in the hands of someone with quite different tastes and ideas. The publishers should satisfy themselves at the outset that the author is capable of writing the required book – if necessary by seeing and approving a full synopsis and sample chapter. Provided the book, when delivered, follows the length and outline agreed, the publishers should be under a contractual obligation to publish it (subject possibly to being entitled to ask the author to make reasonable and specified changes to the typescript before publication).

However, even when the contract contains a firm undertaking to publish, the publishers cannot be compelled to publish the book. But should they fail, the author is legally entitled to compensation for breach of contract.

2 There should be a proper termination clause. This should operate when the publishers fail to fulfil or comply with any of the provisions of the contract or if, after all editions of the work are out of print or off the market, the publishers have not within six months of a written request issued a new edition or impression of at least 1500 copies.

When, in any of these circumstances, rights revert to the author, this should be without prejudice to any claims you may have for monies due. Occasionally termination clauses state that if the publishers fail to reprint a new edition after due notice from the author, the agreement shall terminate provided the author refunds any unearned balance of the advance and buys back blocks, stereo-plates, etc., at a proportion of their original cost. You should insist on the deletion of such a proviso.

3 There should not be an option clause that imposes unreasonable restrictions on future work. The best advice is to strike out the option clause but if this proves impossible, an option should be limited to one book on terms to be mutually agreed, (not 'on the same terms'). The publishers should be required to make a decision within, say, six weeks of delivery of the complete work in the case of fiction, or of submission of a synopsis and specimen chapter in the case of non-fiction. (An option clause which provides for publication 'on the same terms', or that the author shall grant 'the same rights and territories' as in the original agreement, can be most disadvantageous to the author and should certainly be altered or deleted.)

It is as well to specify the type of work covered by the option, for example, your next work of fiction, non-fiction or children's books, since you may want to publish different types of book with different publishers. Another wise precaution is to exclude works you may be invited to write for a series published by another firm. Very occasionally, in the case of a new author, the publishers may try to obtain a two-book option. If you accede, it is important to provide that, if the publishers reject the first option book, they should automatically lose their option on the second.

After all the effort of getting into print, the actual appearance of a book can be an anticlimax. Unlike the playwright or screenwriter who quickly knows if he is on to a winner, an author, unless he is very well known, can wait for weeks or months before the critics take notice (if they ever do) or the sales figures are divulged. By then, if he wants to pay the mortgage, he will be on to the next project.

But what about those authors who are for ever being invited on to chat shows or to speak at literary lunches? Not all of them are establishment figures; newcomers do occasionally get a look in. True, but they are a small minority. Some fifty thousand titles a year are published in Britain, about the same as in the United States. It is a crowded industry with not much room at the top.

On the other hand, you do not have to be famous to make money as an author. Some of the wealthiest are virtually unknown to the general public; the writers of popular textbooks, for example. Then again, the mere fact of writing a book can lead on to other money-making activities such as lecturing or broadcasting. There is a popular illusion that he who manages to have a book published must know what he is talking about. Naturally, authors are the last to think of disabusing their paymasters.

While it is extremely rare to hit the jackpot with a first or second book, a modest run of success in an area where there is the potential for big sales can lead to what the publishers call the break-out book. This puts the author into the select company who benefit from marketing hype. It can and does work wonders. Carefully leaked stories of genius soon to be revealed, talk of large sums of money offered and accepted, and cleverly staged promotions can propel a writer up into the bestseller lists. But he will stay there only if the product matches the promise. A year or two on, the question most frequently asked of hyped authors is 'Where are they now?'

On the more mundane level of promotion, the growing sophistication of marketing techniques should be an encouragement to all authors. In the days when publishing was a gentleman's profession the only contact the author had with the commercial world was via his editor. This could lead to a critical failure in communications. Nowadays there are opportunities at sales conferences and other meetings to talk directly with those who are responsible for promoting and selling books. The opportunities should be taken. No-one is better than the author at explaining what a book is trying to achieve and where it is likely to make its impact. Armed with this knowledge the sales effort can be properly targeted and the promotional budget allocated to best effect.

Publishers

AA Publishing

The Automobile Association, Fanum House, Basingtoke, Hants RG21 2EA

☎ 0256 492929   Telex 858538

Managing Director *Peter Tyer*   **Approximate Annual Turnover** £9.6 million

Publishes Atlases and maps; crafts and hobbies; guide books; scientific and technical, travel and topography. 60 titles in 1986.

Editorial Director *J. B. Doyle* Unsolicited mss not welcome.
Royalties paid annually.

Authors' Rating Tendency towards weighty popular reference books inspired in-house. Not much opportunity for outsiders unless directly commissioned.

AB Academic Publishers

PO Box 97, Berkhamsted, Hertfordshire HP4 2PX   ☎ 04427 74150
Managing Director *E. Adam*

Mainly a publisher of journals with only a few books. *Publishes* Learned journals and books in the fields of materials science and metallurgy, mathematics, agriculture, forestry, nutrition, medicine, education, economics and related subject areas. Unsolicited synopses and ideas for books are welcome provided they are of a high academic level.
Royalties paid annually.

Abacus Kent Ltd

Abacus House, Tunbridge Wells, Kent TN4 0HU   ☎ 0892 29783
Telex 957137 Abacus G

Chairman & Managing Director *N. A. Jayasekera*
Approximate Annual Turnover £1.15 million

The company was established in 1970. Its first titles were translations of advanced scientific technical material from Eastern Europe. Since the late 1970s the emphasis has switched to British, American and European authors, mainly academic/high level titles. *Publishes* Computer Science, Information Technology, Systems Science, Energy and Engineering Science, Natural Science and Maths. Future plans include publishing books for a much wider readership, branching out into Social Science, Management, Business and Current Affairs. 12 titles in 1986.

ABACUS PRESS
Editorial Head *Mark Bicknell* Unsolicited mss, synopses/ideas for books welcome. *Royalties* paid annually. *Overseas associates* Abacus Press, Cambridge, Mass., USA.

Authors' Rating After a period of financial difficulty, when there were complaints of slow payments, the company now seems to be in much better shape and ready for expansion.

Aberdeen University Press
Farmers Hall, Aberdeen AB9 2XT   ☎0224 630724   Telex 739477

Managing Director *Colin Maclean*

FOUNDED in 1840, the company was restricted to printing until 1979. Owned by **Pergamon Holdings**. *Publishes* academic and general, principally Scottish with particular interests in dictionaries, Scottish history and Scottish literature. 22 titles in 1986.

Editorial Head *Colin Maclean*   TITLES *Concise Scots Dictionary; Dictionary of Scottish Biography; Popular Literature in Victorian Scotland.* Unsolicited mss will be considered if they fall within AUP's categories of interest. Synopses and ideas for books welcome.
Royalties paid annually. *Overseas associates* Distribution overseas, as in the UK, by Pergamon.

Harry N. Abrams Inc.
43 High Street, Tunbridge Wells, Kent TN1 1XL   ☎0892 45355   Telex 957565

Publishes architecture and design; cinema and video; cookery; wines and spirits; fine art, art history; history/antiquarian; photography. 45 titles in 1986.

Editorial office in America. See *US Publishers*.

Absolute Press
14 Widcombe Crescent, Bath, Avon BA2 6AH   ☎0225 316013
                                                    Telex 449212 LANTEC G

Managing Director *J. M. Croft*

FOUNDED in 1980, the company brings out up to 10 titles a year. *Publishes* Food and Wine related subjects.

Editorial Director *J. M. Croft* Unsolicited mss not welcome, though synopses and ideas for books are.
Royalties paid twice yearly.

Abson Books
Abson, Wick, Bristol, Avon BS15 5TT ☎027582 2446

Partners *A. Bickerton, P. McCormack*

FOUNDED in 1970, **Abson** publishes original paperbacks, but no fiction. National and European representation. 3 titles in 1986. *Publishes* English language glossaries, literary puzzle books, West Country, general information.

Editorial Head *A. Bickerton*   TITLES *American English; Cockney Rhyming Slang; Jane Austen Quiz and Puzzle Book; Get Squash Straight; Job Hunters' Work Book; Correct Way to Speak Bristol; Resolving Rubik's Magic Cube.* Unsolicited mss welcome if with return postage.
Royalties either once or twice yearly.

Academic Press Inc. (London) Ltd
24–28 Oval Road, London NW1 7DX   ☎01–267 4466   Telex 25775 Acpres G

Managing Director *J. Fujimoto*

Part of **Harcourt Brace Jovanovich Inc., USA.** Now also own **Holt, Rhinehart & Winston; W. B. Saunders & Co.** *Publishes* academic, agriculture, animal care, archaeology, bibliography, biology, chemistry, economics, educational, engineering, geography, geology, history and antiquarian, languages, law, mathematics and statistics, medical, natural history, physics, politics and world affairs, psychology, reference books, scientific, technical, sociology, veterinary. Over 200 titles in 1986.

Editorial Director Dr Conrad Guettler

DIVISIONS
Academic Press   Medical Books   Mss, synopses and ideas welcome.
Royalties paid annually for **Academic Press** titles, twice yearly for **Holt Saunders** titles.

Authors' Rating A good, solid list, which puts to shame some of the university presses. But lots of modest sellers at high prices.

Academy Editions
7 Holland Street, London W8 4NA   ☎01–937 6996   Telex 896928 Academ G

Managing Director *Dr Andreas C. Papadakis*

FOUNDED 1967. Belongs to the **Academy Group Ltd.** *Publishes* books and magazines on art and architecture, architectural design, art and design, *The UIP Journal.* 18 titles in 1986. Owns The London Art Bookshop in Holland Street, London W8, and The Art Shop at the Royal College of Art (selling art objects and materials).

Editorial Director *Dr Andreas C. Papadakis*   TITLES *Post Modernism* Charles Jencks; *Glass – Art Nouveau To Art Deco* Victor Arwas. No unsolicited mss but welcome unsolicited synopses and ideas.
Royalties paid annually.

Authors' Rating Lavish with production but not with advances.

Acair Ltd

Unit 8a, 7 James Street, Stornaway, Isle of Lewis, Scotland ☎ 0851 3020

Manager/Editorial Director *Agnes Rennie*

Publishes academic, biography and autobiography, children's, educational and text-books, history/antiquarian, military, music, poetry, reference books and dictionaries, religious, sports and games, transport, Gaelic adults' and children's books, titles on Scottish culture. 10 titles in 1986. Unsolicited mss welcome.
Royalties paid twice yearly.

Addison-Wesley Publishers Ltd

Finchampstead Road, Wokingham, Berkshire RG11 2NZ ☎ 0734 794000
Telex 836136 ADIWES G

Chairman *Don Hammonds*   **Managing Director** *Peter Hoenigsberg*

Part of **A-W Publishers Inc.**, Mass., USA. Established over 40 years ago, it is now a major publisher of scientific, technical, academic and senior school books, and one of the largest computer science publishers in the world. *Publishes* Educational books and material covering science, maths and computer studies, academic, scientific, technical and general interest. Several series cover computer science, micro-electronics and international business, for an international market. 300 titles in 1986.

Head of Acquisitions *Sarah Mallen* Unsolicited mss, synopses and ideas for books welcome.
Royalties paid twice yearly, in March and September.

Authors' Rating Steady and reliable.

Adlard-Coles Ltd

See **William Collins Sons & Co. Ltd**

Airlife Publishing Ltd

7 St John's Hill, Shrewsbury, Shropshire SY1 1JE ☎ 0743 235651
Telex 35161 HOGROB G

Chairman/Managing Director *A. D. R. Simpson*
Approximate Annual Turnover £500,000–£1 million

Established to publish specialist aviation titles, Airlife is gradually broadening its list. *Publishes* technical and general aviation, military and maritime, travel and adventure, country pursuits and local interest. 17 titles in 1986.

Editorial Head *A. D. R. Simpson*   TITLES *Open Season; Flying The Big Jets; They Gave Me A Seafire; The Trees of Shropshire.* Unsolicited mss, synopses and ideas for books welcome.
Royalties paid annually, twice by arrangement.

Ian Allan Ltd
Coombelands House, Addlestone, Weybridge KT15 1HY ☎0932 585511
Telex 929806

Chairman Ian Allan **Managing Director** David Allan

Publishes atlases and maps, aviation, auto/biography, crafts and hobbies, guide books, military and war, nautical, reference books and dictionaries, transport, travel and topography. 100 titles in 1985.

Editorial director *Michael Harris* Unsolicited mss considered.

Philip Allan Publishers
Market Place, Deddington, Oxford OX5 4SE ☎0869 38652

Chairman *Philip Allan* **Approximate Annual Turnover** £50–60,000

FOUNDED 1974. Primarily publishers of economics but expanded into accountancy, business and finance. In spring 1988 will be launching a politics list. Four years ago launched *Economic Review*, a magazine issued five times per year with a circulation of 31,000. In 1985 launched *Social Studies* with a circulation of 9000. April 1987 launched *The Contemporary Record* and in May 1987, *Geography Review*. 14 new titles in 1986.

DIVISIONS
Business *Philip Allan* TITLES *Current Issues in Accounting* Bryan Carsberg & Tony Hope. **Economics** *Philip Allan* TITLES *Modern Economics* David Heathfield. **Finance** *Philip Allan* TITLES *Multinational Finance* Adrian Buckley. **Politics** *Philip Cross* TITLES *British Party Politics* Gillian Peele (Spring 1988). Almost all titles are commissioned; do not welcome unsolicited mss. Unsolicited synopses and ideas for books are welcome.
Royalties paid annually.

Allardyce Barnett Publishers
14 Mount Street, Lewes, East Sussex BN7 1HL ☎0273 479393

Publisher *Fiona Allardyce* **Managing Editor** *Anthony Barnett*

FOUNDED 1981. Strong interest in modern English poetry. *Publishes* Literature, art and music with emphasis on substantial collections by current English language poets. 2 titles in 1987 (none in 1986).

Editorial Head *Anthony Barnett* TITLES *Poems* J. H. Prynne; *All Is Where Each Is* Andrew Crozier; *Kind* Douglas Oliver; *The Resting Bell* Anthony Barnett.

IMPRINT
Agneau 2 *Anthony Barnett*
Unsolicited mss or synopses not encouraged.

W. H. Allen & Co. plc
44 Hill Street, London W1X 8LB   ☎01–493 6777   Telex 28117

Chairman *Bob Tanner*   **Approximate Annual Turnover** £7 million

Established in the early 1800s. Recently acquired **Virgin Books**. *Publishes* art, biography & memoirs, practical handbooks, current affairs, educational, fiction, films, general history, humour, reference, sociology, television, theatre, ballet, travel. Approx. 300 titles in 1986.

DIVISIONS
W. H. Allen *Mike Bailey* General hardbacks   **Comet** *Nigel Robinson* General, biography, paperbacks   **Crescent** *Joe O'Reilly* Large print hardbacks & paperbacks   **Mercury** *Robert Postema* Business books   **Planet** *Pat Hornsey* Illustrated books   **Star** *Joe O'Reilly Paperbacks*   **Target** *Nigel Robinson* Children's, TV & film tie-ins, Dr Who   **Virgin** *Cat Ledger* General, music & film   Unsolicited mss, synopses and ideas for books welcome.
Royalties paid twice yearly.

Authors' Rating After trouble in the 1970s, when it acquired a reputation for publishing third-rate biographies, W. H. Allen has recovered strongly. A varied output allows plenty of room for new ideas.

Allison & Busby
A little short of its 20th birthday, went into receivership on 24 April 1987. Saved from extinction by **W. H. Allen** who took over an 'extensive and varied book list' with a turnover of about £500,000. TITLES include the recently reissued *Absolute Beginners* by Colin Macinnes, *Black Jacobins* by C. L. R. James and *The Worst Witch* by Jill Murphy.

Authors' Rating Often guilty of haphazard accounting and a notoriously slow royalty payer. Allison and Busby have always been known as better list-builders than business people. Likely to disappear in **W. H. Allen**.

Alphabooks
Church House, Half Moon Street, Sherborne, Dorset DT9 3LN   ☎0935 814944
Telex 46534 Alphab G

Managing Director *Tony Birks-Hay*   **Editorial Director** *Leslie Birks-Hay*

Taken over by **A. & C. Black** in March 1987 but continues to operate from Sherborne. *Publishes* illustrated books on ceramics, horticulture, architecture and genealogy.
Royalties paid twice yearly.

Amber Lane Press

9 Middle Way, Summertown, Oxford OX2 7LH ☎0865 51045

Chairman *Brian Clark*   **Managing Director** *Judith Scott*

FOUNDED in 1979 to publish modern play texts. *Publishes* Plays and books on the theatre. 12 titles in 1986.

Editorial Head *Judith Scott*   TITLES *Children of a Lesser God; Who's Life is it Anyway; Another Country* (play texts); *Playwrights' Progress* Colin Chambers. No unsolicited mss. Synopses and ideas welcome.
Royalties paid twice yearly.

Andersen Press Ltd

62–75 Chandos Place, Covent Garden, London WC2N 4NW   ☎01–240 8162
Telex 261212 Litldn G

Managing Director *Klaus Flugge*

FOUNDED in 1976 by Klaus Flugge and named after Hans Christian Andersen. *Publishes* children's hardcover fiction. 75% of their books are sold as co-productions abroad. 36 titles in 1986.

Editorial Director *Klaus Flugge*   Best selling titles include *Not Now Bernard* David McKee; *A Dark, Dark Tale* Ruth Brown; *King Rollo* David McKee. AUTHORS Christine Nostlinger, Tony Ross, Michael Foreman, Hazel Townson, Satoshi Kitmura. Unsolicited mss are welcome, providing they fit the 32 page format.
Royalties paid twice yearly.

Angus & Robertson (UK) Ltd

16 Golden Square, London W1R 4BN   ☎01–437 9602   Telex 897284

Managing Director *Barry Winkleman*

Bought by Bay Books in 1981. Part of **Times Books**. FOUNDED over 100 years ago in Australia. *Publishes* Biography & autobiography, children's books, cinema & video, cookery, wines & spirits, fiction, humour, illustrated & fine editions, natural history, photography, sports & games, theatre & drama, travel & topography. 100 titles in 1986.

Senior Editor *Valerie Hudson*   TITLES Cinema & Theatre *Golden Turkey Awards* Medved Brothers; Humour *The World's Best Jokes Series*; General Non-fiction *Pavlov's Heirs* Steven Schwartz, *The Formative Years of Australian Cricket* Jack Pollard; Adult Fiction *The Sugar Factory* Robert Carter; Children's Non-fiction *Activity Books Series: Fun With Kites, Tricks & Games With Paper*; Design *The Designer's Guide to Color Series*; Health & Self Help *Dr Claire Weekes' Self-Help Series*; Wine *Halliday's Australian Wine Compendium*. Welcome unsolicited mss, synopses and ideas for books.
Royalties paid twice yearly.

Authors' Rating Up and down. A small publisher ten years ago, then expansionist, now slipping back again. Low brow non-fiction written to order. Author enthusiasm closely tied to size of advances. Heavily weighted towards Australian market.

Antique Collectors' Club

5 Church Street, Woodbridge, Suffolk IP12 1DS   ☎03943 5501

Telex 987271 Antbok G

Joint Managing Directors *John Steel, Diana Steel*

FOUNDED 1966. Has a five figure membership spread throughout the world. It was in response to the demand for information on 'what to pay' that the price guide series was introduced in 1968 with the first edition of *The Price Guide to Antique Furniture*. Club membership costs £14.95 per annum. Members buy the Club's publications at concessional rates. *Publishes* Specialist books on antiques and collecting. Subject areas include furniture, silver/jewelry, metalwork, glass, textiles, art reference, ceramics, horology. Also books on architecture and gardening. 12 titles in 1986.

Editorial Head *John Steel*   TITLES *The English Garden in Our Time* Jane Brown; *The Book of Wine Antiques* R. Butler & G. Walking; *The Price Guide to Antique Furniture* John Andrews; *English Country Houses* (3 vols) C. Hussey; *Popular 19th Century European Painting* Hook and Politmore; *The Dictionary of British Watercolour Artists* (2 vols) H. Mallalieu. Unsolicited mss, synopses and ideas for books welcome. *Royalties* paid quarterly as a rule, but can vary.

Anvil Press Poetry

69 King George Street, London SE10 8PX   ☎01–858 2946

Managing Director *Peter Jay*

FOUNDED 1968 to promote contemporary English and foreign poetry (in translation). English list includes Peter Levi and Caroline Duffy, and has now developed to the point at which most of Anvil's new titles are new volumes by their regulars. Only one or two first collections by new writers a year.

Editorial Director *Julia Sterland* Welcome unsolicited mss.

Appletree Press Ltd

7 James Street South, Belfast, Co. Antrim, Northern Ireland, BT2 8DL

☎0232 243074/246756   Telex 42904 Books G

Managing Director *John Murphy*

FOUNDED 1974. Currently have about 100 books in print. *Publishes* Irish interest non-fiction. 18 titles in 1986.

Senior Editor *Douglas Marshall*   TITLES *Irish Touring Guide; Faces of Ireland; Caught In the Crossfire – Children and the Northern Ireland Conflict*. Welcome unsolicited mss and synopses.
Royalties paid twice yearly.

Aquarian Press Ltd
See **Thorsons Publishing Group Ltd**

Aquila Publishing UK Ltd
PO Box 418, Leek, Staffs ST13 8UX   ☎0538 387368   Telex 8954958

Chairman/Managing Director *James Green*   **Editorial Head** *James Green*

FOUNDED 1968. Aquila remained Scottish based until it became part of the Johnston Green group in the 1970s. James and Anne Green took over the company in 1986, moving it to Staffordshire where it now operates as a wholly independent concern. *Publishes* Poetry, fiction, biography, critical studies, essays, guides for businesses. 43 titles in 1986.

IMPRINTS
Aquila Poetry; Aquila Fiction; Aquila Essays; Aquila Critical Studies; The Phaethon Press; The Wayzgoose Press; Moorlands Press; Moorlands Mini Books; Aquila Pamphlet Poetry; Aquila Guides; Aquila Books; Iolaire Selection. Enquiries preferred to unsolicited mss. Unsolicited synopses and ideas for books welcome. 'We often commission books from ideas, and indeed from essays submitted to our magazine, *Prospice* (editor James Green).'
Royalties paid twice yearly. *Overseas associates* Aquila Publishing Ltd, Dublin; Aquila America Inc., Washington, USA.

Arcady Books Ltd
2 Woodlands Road, Ashurst, Southampton, Hampshire SO4 2AD ☎042 129 2601

Managing Director *Michael Edwards*   **Approximate Annual Turnover** (small)

FOUNDED 1981. *Publishes* second editions; general non-fiction, literature, the outdoors, and books about the New Forest. Has published eight books. 1 title in 1986 *The Family Outdoors*.

Editorial Director *Anne Edwards* TITLES *The New Forest Companion* Anne Edwards. Unsolicited mss and synopses welcome.
Royalties paid twice yearly.

The Architectural Press
9 Queen Anne's Gate, London SW1H 9BY   ☎01–222 4333   Telex 8953505

Managing Director *Colin Urquhart*

Publishes Technical and professional books on architecture (mainly 20th century), and design; telecommunications. 40 titles in 1986.

Commissioning Editor *Maritz Vandenberg* TITLES *The Decorative Art of Today* Le Corbusier; *A Guide to the Built Works of Le Corbusier* Andrea Filippone; *Michael Graves Buildings and Projects 1982–1986* Karen Nichols & Patrick Burke; *Acoustic Design* Duncan Templeton & David Saunders.

IMPRINT
The Telecommunications Press Welcomes unsolicited mss.
Royalties paid twice yearly.

Argus Books Ltd

1 Golden Square, London W1R 3BB   ☏01–437 0626   Telex 8811896
Chairman *T. Gold Blyth*   **Managing Director** *Peter Welham*
                                            Approximate Annual Turnover £600,000

The book publishing division of **Argus Specialist Publications**, magazine publisher. *Publishes* modelling, woodwork, crafts, field sports, new technology, wine & beer making, leisure and hobbies in general. 35 titles in 1986. Prefer to see synopses rather than complete mss.
Royalties paid twice yearly.

Aris & Phillips Ltd

Teddington House, Warminster, Wiltshire BA12 8PQ   ☏0985 213409

Managing Director *Adrian Phillips*

FOUNDED 1972, publishing books on Egyptology. A family firm which has remained independent. *Publishes* Academic, classical, oriental and hispanic classics. 21 titles in 1986.

Editorial Director *Adrian Phillips* **Classics Editor** *Philip Mudd* **Hispanic Classics Editor** *Lucinda Phillips*. With such a highly specialised list, unsolicited mss and synopses are not particularly welcome, although synopses will be looked at.
Royalties paid twice yearly.

Arlington Books Ltd

Kingsbury House, 15–17 King Street, London SW1Y 6QU   ☏01–930 0097
                                                        Telex 896616 Sendit G

Chairman *Desmond Elliott*

FOUNDED 1960 by Desmond Elliott. Has remained independent. *Publishes* Biography & autobiography, cookery, wines & spirits, crime, fiction, health & beauty, humour, illustrated & fine editions. 18 titles in 1986.

Editorial Director *Penny Smart*   TITLES *Brief Lives* Suzanne Foster & Pamela Smith; *The Memory Man* Derek Lambert; *Pacific Clipper* Richard Doyle; *Spiral* David Lindsey; *The Closet Hanging* Tony Fennelly; *How To Slim Your Waist and Flatten Your Stomach and Trim Your Thighs In Thirty Days* Katy Parks; *The 200 Calorie Solution* Dr Martin Katahn. Welcome unsolicited mss and synopses/ideas for books.
Royalties paid twice yearly.

Authors' Rating Ticking over and has authors Jilly Cooper and Leslie Thomas. As a former publicist, Desmond Elliott is clever at spotting chances for book promotion.

Arms & Armour Press Ltd

Link House, 25 West Street, Poole, Dorset BH15 2SS   ☎0202 671171
Telex 418394 Linkho G

Managing Director *Philip Sturrock*

Part of **Cassell plc**. *Publishes* Military, aviation and naval books.

Editorial Director *Rod Dymott*   TITLES *Top Gun – The U.S. Navy's Fighter Weapons School* George Hall; *Weapons and Equipment of Counter-Terrorism* Michael Dewar; *Britain's First War Planes* Jack Bruce; *Argentine Air Forces In The Falkland Conflict* S. M. Huertas & J. R. Briasco. Unsolicited mss and synopses welcome. *Royalties* paid annually.

Alan Armstrong & Associates Ltd

72–76 Park Road, London NW1 4SA   ☎01-258 3740

Managing Director *Alan Armstrong*   **Annual Turnover** £3 million

FOUNDED 1977 as business and technical booksellers. Now geared to the information market place; runs courses for librarians and information officers. *Publishes* mainly business directories and annuals. 6 titles in 1986.

Editorial Director *Mark Rasdall*   TITLES *The Top 3000 Directories and Annuals; Inside Information; Directory of Management Consultants in the UK; Management Training Directory; The International Directory of Information Products on CD-Rom; 5001 Hard-to-find Publishers and Their Addresses; AEBIG Membership Directory.*

Edward Arnold (Publishers) Ltd

41 Bedford Square, London WC1B 3DQ   ☎01-637 7176

Managing Director *Anthony Hamilton*

Fully merged in Spring 1987 with **Hodder & Stoughton's** educational publishing. *Publishes* educational, academic and medical books.

School Books *Brian Steven*   **Tertiary Publishing** *John Wallace*

Authors' Rating Sound achievements in medical and educational publishing were not enough for Edward Arnold to escape their lacklustre image. Authors should benefit in every respect from the merger with **Hodder & Stoughton**.

Arnold-Wheaton. (E. J. Arnold & Son Ltd)

Lockwood Distribution Centre, Parkside Lane, Dewsbury Road, Leeds LS11 5TD
☎0532 772112   Telex 556347

Managing Director *Chris Bundy* (Group)

Owned by the **Pergamon Group**. *Publishes* atlases and maps, biology and zoology, chemistry, computer science, computer software (educational), economics, educational and textbooks, geography and geology, history and antiquarian, languages and linguistics, mathematics and statistics, music and physics. 120 titles in 1986.

Publishing Director *Stan Sharp* Unsolicited mss considered.
Royalties paid twice yearly.

Artech House

28 Eaton Row, London SW1 0JA   ☎01–235 8121   Telex 885744 MICSOL G

Managing Director (in USA) *William Bazzy*

Approximate Annual Turnover £½ million

FOUNDED 1970. The European office of Artech House Inc, Boston. *Publishes* Electronic engineering. 20 titles in 1986.

Editorial Head *Daniel Brown* Will consider unsolicited mss and synopses.
Royalties paid twice yearly.

Ashford Press Publishing

1 Church Road, Shedfield, Hants SO3 2HW   ☎0329 834265   Telex 261412

Chairman *Clive Martin*   **Managing Director** *Jane F. Tatam*

Approximate Annual Turnover £750,000

FOUNDED 1984 and taken over by **Martins Printing Group** in 1987. Published 35 books in the first year. Starting with reprints such as a limited edition of the 1902 *Lawson History of the America's Cup* and Charles Dickens' long forgotten *The Life of Our Lord*, they have now turned their attention to new mss, many of them unsolicited. New titles include the biographer of publisher Michael Joseph. *Publishes* Non-fiction, nautical, sports, education, business. 40 titles in 1986.

Editorial Head *Jane F. Tatam* Unsolicited mss welcome if return postage included. Synopses and ideas for books considered.
Royalties paid twice yearly.

Authors' Rating An exciting young company with a strong sense of good marketing and promotion.

Ashgrove Press Ltd

19 Circus Place, Bath, Avon BA1 2PW   ☎0225 25539

Chairman & Managing Director *Robin Campbell*

FOUNDED 1980. Originally published local history but moved more into 'alternative' lifestyles. *Publishes* health, healing & diet, psychology, metaphysics, countryside, regional and local subjects. 10 titles in 1986.
   Unsolicited mss welcome, preferably after initial letter. Synopses and ideas for books welcome.
Royalties paid twice in the first year; thereafter annually.

Associated Book Publishers

11 New Fetter Lane, London EC4P 4EE   ☎01–583 9855   Telex 263398

Chairman *P. H. Allsop*   **Managing Director** *Michael R. Turner*

Approximate Annual Turnover £85 million

Bought by **International Thomson** in 1987, ABP is the parent company of: **Chapman & Hall, Eyre & Spottiswoode, Methuen, Routledge & Kegan Paul, E. & F. N. Spon Ltd, Stevens & Son Ltd, Sweet & Maxwell Ltd, Tavistock Publications Ltd** and **Croom Helm** (see separate listings for details).

Authors' Rating
An extraordinary conglomerate run with great skill by Michael Turner who somehow manages to inspire a sense of company unity while encouraging writing and editorial talent. One of the few big publishers where authors are not made nervous by political tensions. But all this could change with the takeover by the **Thomson Organisation**. Wide scale rationalisation may be necessary to justify the £210 million price tag, over two and a half times the company's pre-bid market value. Of the individual companies, **Eyre & Spottiswoode** has long since lost its general publishing to **Methuen** and now hardly counts as an identity. Will the same happen to **Routledge & Kegan Paul**? Norman Franklin, Chairman of **RKP** has a good reputation with authors, though some shrink from his blunt talking.

Athlone Press

44 Bedford Row, London WC1R 4LY   ☎01–405 9836/7   Telex 261507 ref 1334

Managing Director *Brian Southam*

Established in 1950 as the publishing house of the University of London, after University of London Press was sold to **Hodder**. Now wholly independent, but preserves links with the university via an academic advisory board. Anticipated developments in the near future: more emphasis on women's/feminist studies and environmental/'green' issues, including medicine. *Publishes* archaeology, architecture, art, economics, history, medical, music, Japan, oriental, philosophy, politics, religion, science, sociology, zoology, women's/feminist issues. 35 titles in 1986.

Editorial Head *Brian Southam* Unsolicited mss welcome. Synopses/ideas for books considered.
Royalties paid annually/twice yearly by arrangement. *Overseas associates* The Athlone Press, Atlantic, New Jersey, USA.

Attic Books

The Folly, Rhosgoch, Painscastle, Builth Wells, Powys LD2 3JY   ☎04975 205

Managing Director *Jack Bowyer*   **Editorial Head** *Jack Bowyer*

FOUNDED in 1984 by its architect owners. Publishes books on building crafts and architecture, technical books for the industry mainly dealing with restoration and conservation. 3 titles in 1986.

IMPRINT
Orion Books *A History of Building* Swillerton & Toomer. Unsolicited mss, synopses and ideas for books welcome.
Royalties paid annually.

Aurum Press Ltd
33 Museum Street, London WC1A 1LD   ☎01–631 4596   Telex 299557 Aurum G

Chairman *Timothy J. M. Chadwick*

FOUNDED 1977. Committed to producing high quality illustrated non-fiction. Now developing Aurum Books for Children. 15 titles in 1986.

Editorial Director *Michael Alcock*   TITLES *The Americas Cup – The Official Record* Bob Fisher & Bob Ross; *Quisine Fraicheur* Jean Conil; *Wales: The First Place* Jan Morris & Paul Wakefield; *Angelina Ballerina* Catharine Holabird & Helen Craig. Prefer to see a synopsis before considering completed mss.
Royalties paid annually.

Bachman & Turner
9 Cork Street, London W1X 1PD   ☎01–439 3806

Sales & Publicity *Mike Green*   **Approximate Annual Turnover £50,000**

FOUNDED 1973. *Publishes* Biography & autobiography, fiction, peripheral medicine, psychology. 4 titles in 1986.

Editorial Director *Marta Bachman*   TITLES *Let The Petals Fall* Countess Long; *Orgasmus* John Gartland; *Beyond the Brief* Odette Tchernine; *Artist Unknown* Robert Rubens. Future titles include a biography of Nijinsky and an illustrated book on the work of the sculptress Karin Jonzen. Unsolicited mss and synopses welcomed but must always be accompanied by return postage.
Royalties paid twice yearly.

Badger Books Ltd
Lenches Press, Hill Barn Orchard, Church Lane, Evesham, Worcestershire
WR11 4UB   ☎0386 871035

Managing Director *Marlene Badger*

FOUNDED 1980. *Publishes* children's books, humour. 3 titles in 1986.

Editorial Director *Marlene Badger*   TITLES *Matt and the Mermaid* Chris Skelton & Ron Smith. Do not welcome unsolicited mss but will consider synopses.
Royalties paid annually.

Bailey Bros & Swinfen Ltd

Warner House, Bowles Well Gardens, Folkestone, Kent CT19 6PH

☎0303 56501   Telex 96328 Bailey G

Chairman & Managing Director *J. R. Bailey*

Approximate Annual Turnover £5 million +

FOUNDED 1929. In 1967, to accommodate the expanding business in educational and trade publishing, they moved from London to Folkestone. Now cover distribution for book publishers, subscription processing for journal publishers, and a mailing and publicity service. Part of Bailey & Swinfen Holdings. *Publishes* General, children's and reference. 6 titles in 1986.

Editorial Director *J. R. Bailey* TITLES *The Data Book For Pipe Fitters and Pipe Welders* E. H. Williamson; *The Basic Gurkhali Dictionary*; *White Tie Tales* John Moorecroft. Do not welcome unsolicited mss but will consider unsolicited synopses and ideas.

Overseas associates in Australia and New Zealand.

Howard Baker Press

27a Arterberry Road, Wimbledon, London SW20   ☎01–947 5482

Chairman/Managing Director *Howard Baker*

FOUNDED in Bloomsbury in 1968 and moved to Wimbledon in 1971. *Publishes* general non-fiction, political science, autobiography, de-luxe editions, biography, maps, reference books, specialist facsimile editions.

IMPRINTS

Greyfriars Press   Greyfriars Book Club

No unsolicited mss. Synopses welcome if accompanied by s.a.e.

Royalties paid twice yearly.

Barny Books

The Cottage, Hough on the Hill, nr Grantham, Lincs NG32 2BB   ☎040050 246

Managing Director *Molly Burkett*   **Approximate Annual Turnover £10,000**

Recently founded with the aim of encouraging new writers and illustrators. *Publishes* Children's books. 3 titles in 1986.

Editorial Head *Molly Burkett* Too small a concern to have the staff/resources to deal with unsolicited mss. Writers with strong ideas should approach Molly Burkett by letter in the first instance.

Royalties Division of profits 50/50.

Barracuda Books Ltd (Quotes Ltd)
Meadows House, Well Street, Buckingham MK18 1EW   ☎0280 814441/2

Managing Director (Barracuda) *Clive Birch*   (Quotes Ltd) *Carolyn Birch*

Barracuda was formed in 1974, and its sister company **Quotes** in 1985. The Sporting and Leisure imprint was launched in 1976. Now moving into co-publishing ventures in the general interest field with particular emphasis on Heritage-based books. *Publishes* local and natural history, county and sporting life, military and genealogical histories. 35 titles in 1986.

DIVISIONS
Barracuda Books *Clive Birch*   TITLES *Nature of Derbyshire & the Isle of Wight; Yesterday's Town: St Albans; The Book of Shrewsbury.* **Quotes Ltd** *Carolyn Birch*   TITLES *Leicester in Camera; Lincs Railways in Camera.* Unsolicited mss, synopses and ideas for books welcome if relevant.
Royalties paid annually.

John Bartholomew & Son Ltd
12 Duncan Street, Edinburgh EH9 1TA   ☎031–667 9341   Telex 728134

Chairman *George Barber*   **Managing Director** *David Ross Stewart*
Approximate Annual Turnover £7 million

Established over 150 years ago. Produces everything from town plans to world atlases including the cartography for the *Times Atlas of the World* (**Times Books** is now its sister company). Family owned until eight years ago, when it was sold to *Reader's Digest*. Bought by **News International** in 1985. Sixty titles in 1986.

DIVISIONS
Bartholomew *Colin Kirkwood*   TITLES *Road Atlas Britain; Walk the North Downs; Children's World Atlas.*

IMPRINTS
Geographia *Colin Kirkwood* Street atlases.   **J & B Maps** *Colin Kirkwood*   TITLES *Touring Map of Scotland; Irish Family Names Map.* No unsolicited mss. Letter essential in the first instance.
Royalties paid twice yearly.

B. T. Batsford Ltd
4 Fitzhardinge Street, London W1H 0AH   ☎01–486 8484
Telex 943763 CROCOM G

Chairman *A. G. Cox*   **Managing Director** *P. A. J. Kemmis Betty*
Approximate Annual Turnover £4 million

FOUNDED 1843, as a bookseller; started publishing in 1874. An independent company which has become the world leader in books on chess and lacecraft. Acquired the **Dryad Press** in 1983. *Publishes* Non-fiction: academic & scholarly; animal care/breeding; archaeology; architecture and design; cinema and video; crafts/hobbies;

educational/textbooks; fashion and costume; history and antiquarian; languages and linguistics; literature & criticism; photography; sports & games; theatre & drama; transport; travel & topography; vocational training/careers. 138 titles in 1986. Generally, they publish 150 non-fiction titles a year, with a backlist of 1200. **Dryad** publishes 40 titles a year.

DIVISIONS
Academic/Educational *Peter Kemmis Betty* TITLES *Mitchell's Building Construction; Batsford Chess Openings; Living Through Nazi Germany; Understanding Archaeological Excavation.* **Trade** *Tim Auger* TITLES *Inspiration for Embroidery; The Lilies of China; The Illustrated Dictionary of Film Stars; The Encyclopaedia of World Costume.*

IMPRINTS
Dryad Press *Bill Waller* TITLES *Complete Book Of Tatting; Acid Rain.* **Mitchell Publishing Company** *Tony Seward* TITLES *Maintaining Building Services; Auditoria.* This imprint specialises in building and architecture. Welcomes unsolicited mss and synopses/ideas for books.
Royalties paid twice in first year, annually thereafter.

Authors' Rating A quaintly old-fashioned publisher with one of the most imposing addresses in the business. Does well by sticking to what it knows best. New ideas often mooted but usually dropped before they become expensive.

BBC Books
35 Marylebone High Street, London W1M 4AA ☎ 01–743 5588

Editor in Chief *Tony Kingsford* **Editor, BBC Books** *Nick Chapman*

BBC Books, a division of BBC Enterprises, is expanding its list to the extent that it now publishes books which, though linked with BBC television or radio, may not simply be the 'book of the series'. An example of this is the publishing of cookery books by past television cooks who no longer have series running. 80 titles in 1986.

  Books with no BBC link are of no interest, and unsolicited mss (which come in at the rate of 15 weekly) are rarely even read. If books are not commissioned, they are packaged and devised in consultation with known writers, or through known agents. Having said that, strong ideas well expressed will always be considered, and promising letters stand a chance of further scrutiny.
Royalties paid twice yearly.

Authors' Rating Until recently the surprise about BBC Books was the number of opportunities they turned down. With a TV tie-in, how could they fail? Now more adventurous, an encouragement to authors to try their luck with the broadcasters.

Bellew Publishing Co Ltd

Nightingale Centre, 8 Balham Hill, London SW12 9DS ☎01–673 5611
Telex 8951182 GECOMS G

Chairman & Managing Director *Ib Bellew*

Approximate Annual Turnover £250,000

FOUNDED 1983 as a publisher/packager. *Publishes* Illustrated non-fiction, craft books, general interest. 7 titles in 1986. Welcomes unsolicited mss and synopses.
Royalties paid annually.

Berg Publishers Ltd

24 Binswood Avenue, Leamington Spa, Warwickshire CV32 5SQ
☎0926 29470   Telex 312440 PBSSPA G

Chairman/Managing Director *Marion Berghahn*

Approximate Annual Turnover £200,000

West German parent company in Hamburg. *Publishes* scholarly books in the fields of history, economics and other social sciences, also books in German. Scholarly and general titles in literature and the arts, biography and current affairs published under the recently acquired imprint **Oswald Wolff**. Specialises in translations into English. 25 titles in 1986.

Editorial Head *Juliet Standing*   TITLES *The Americanisation of West German Industry; The Railway Journey.*

IMPRINTS
Oswald Wolff Books *Juliet Standing*   TITLES Coupe: *Germany Through the Looking Glass*. No unsolicited mss. Unsolicited synopses and ideas for books welcome.
Royalties paid annually.

BFI Publishing

81 Dean Street, London W1V 6AA ☎01–437 4355   Telex 27624

Head of Publishing *Geoffrey Nowell-Smith*

Approximate Annual Turnover £100,000

FOUNDED 1982. Part of the British Film Institute. *Publishes* film- or television-related academic books which other publishers are unwilling to do. Six titles in 1986.

Editorial Head *Geoffrey Nowell-Smith*   TITLES *All Our Yesterdays: 90 Years of British Cinema,* Charles Barr (ed.); *Home Is Where The Heart Is: Studies in Melodrama and the Women's Film,* Christine Gledhill (ed.); *Sex, Class and Realism: British Cinema 1956–1963,* John Hill. Prefer unsolicited synopses/ideas rather than complete mss.
Royalties paid annually.

Bishopsgate Press Ltd
37 Union Street, London SE1 1SE ☎01–403 6544

Chairman & Managing Director *Ian F. L. Straker*

FOUNDED 1800. Since then has been mainly producing financial books for the City but for the last four years has developed into general publishing. *Publishes* General books, biography, non-fiction, crafts, arts & crafts, religious books, poetry, children's books. 12 titles in 1986.

Publishing Director *Austen Smith* TITLES *Small Hands Big Ideas* Tony Hart; *Old Garden Flowers* Brian Halliwell; *Just Like You and Me* Johnny Morris; *New Foods for Healthy Eating* Liz Brand; *Hyperactive Children: A Parent's Guide* Shirley Flack. Softcover series *Practical Guides series*. Unsolicited mss and synopses welcome. *Royalties* paid twice yearly.

Bison Books
176 Old Brompton Road, London SW5 0BA ☎01–370 3097 Telex 888014

Chairman *S. L. Mayer*

BOOK PACKAGERS Part of Bison Books Corporation, Connecticut, USA. *Publishes* large format, illustrated books on history, transport, travel, cookery, militaria and art. 56 titles in 1986.

Editorial Head *Jane Laslett* TITLES History *Hitler's Propaganda Machine* Ward Rutherford; Transport *Encyclopaedia of Sports Cars*; Art *Masterpieces of American Painting* Leonard Everett Fisher. Unsolicited mss not welcome. The vast majority of titles originate by commission but synopses/ideas are considered. *Royalties* by arrangement.

A. & C. Black (Publishers) Ltd
35 Bedford Row, London WC1R 4JH ☎01–242 0946 Telex 32524 Acblac

Chairman *Charles Black* **Joint Managing Directors** *Charles Black and David Gadsby*

Publishes Academic, agriculture, antiques & collecting, archaeology, architecture & design, aviation, children's books, crafts & hobbies, educational & textbooks, fashion & costume, fine art & art history, geography & geology, guide books, history & antiquarian, medical, music, nautical, reference books, dictionaries, sports & games, theatre & drama, travel & topography, veterinary. 150 titles in 1986. TITLES *Writers' & Artists' Yearbook; The Blue Guides Travel series*.

IMPRINTS
Alphabooks Autobooks John Baker Publishers Ltd Ernest Benn Adam & Charles Black E. P. Publishing Lepus, F. Lewis (Publishers) Ltd Welcome unsolicited mss and synopses/ideas for books. *Royalty* payments vary according to each contract.

Authors' Rating After years of dozing on a substantial backlist, A. & C. Black have rediscovered their energy. Recent staff appointments and acquisitions (**Nautical Publishing** is the latest) promise a more aggressive style of publishing. Well regarded in education and children's books.

Black Spring Press Ltd
335 Kennington Road, London SE11 4QE   ☎01–587 0331

Managing Director *Simon Pettifar*

FOUNDED 1986. *Publishes* Fiction, literary criticism, theatre, cinema studies, popular music. 1 title in 1986.

Editor *Simon Pettifar*   TITLES *The Paris Olympia Press: An Annotated Bibliography* Patrick J. Kearney. Paperback *D. H. Lawrence, An Unprofessional Study* Anais Nin. Prefer to see a proposal rather than completed ms.
Royalties paid twice yearly.

Blackie & Son Ltd
Wester Cleddens Road, Bishopbriggs, Glasgow G64 2NZ   ☎041–772 2311
Telex 777283 BLACKI G

Chairman & Managing Director *R. Michael Miller*

FOUNDED 1809. Still independently owned. Educational and Academic divisions based in Glasgow. Children's division in London (see below). *Publishes* educational textbooks (*Modern Maths for Schools*), children's books (*Flower Fairies*), academic and professional. 140 titles in 1986.

DIVISIONS
Academic *A. Graeme Mackintosh*   **Children's** *A. D. Mitchell* located at 7 Leicester Place, London WC2H 7BP   **Educational** *A. Rosemary Wands*   TITLES **Academic and Professional** animal behaviour; plant biology and agriculture; aquatic biology; biochemistry; developmental biology and genetics; environmental biology/ecology; microbiology; neurobiology; physiology and immunology; instrumental analysis; food science and technology.   **Children's** Picture books for the very young/older children; *Topsy & Tim*; *Flower Fairies*; general fiction; fairy tales; folk tales and anthologies; non-fiction. Unsolicited mss, ideas and synopses welcome.
Royalties paid yearly/twice yearly.

Authors' Rating Not the most exciting publisher but a good children's list and a steady provider of school texts within the core curriculum. Own **Abelard Schuman** (children's books).

Blackstaff Press Ltd
3 Galway Park, Dundonald, Belfast BT16 0AN   ☎02138 7161/2

Chairman *Michael Burns*   **Managing Director** *Anne Tannahill*

FOUNDED 1971 by Jim and Diane Gracey and bought by Michael Burns and Anne Tannahill in 1980. *Publishes* mainly but not exclusively Irish interest books, Fiction, Poetry, History, Politics, Natural History and Folklore. 17 titles in 1986.

· **Editorial Head** *Michael Burns* Unsolicited mss, synopses and ideas welcome. *Royalties* paid twice yearly.

Authors' Rating One of the best of the small publishers, led by Anne Tannahill, a forceful personality who scored a remarkable double first in 1984 when she became the first woman president of the **Irish Publishers' Association** and the first president from Northern Ireland.

Basil Blackwell Ltd
108 Cowley Road, Oxford OX4 1JE   ☎0865 722146   Telex 837022

Chairman *Nigel Blackwell*   **Managing Director** *David Martin*

Part of the **Blackwell Group**, 50 Broad Street, Oxford. Founded in 1922 as an academic and educational publishing house; the early list included fiction, poetry and (curiously) Enid Blyton. Expanded into journals and now owns more than 50. Rapid growth in the 1970s and 1980s included the establishment of a wholly-owned distribution company and the takeover of **Martin Robertson**. *Publishes* academic, humanities, social sciences, primary and secondary schoolbooks, books for teachers, general books. 300 titles in 1986.

DIVISIONS
Academic & General *John Davey*   **Schools** *James Nash*

IMPRINTS
Shakespeare Head Press *David Martin*   **Raintree Press** *James Nash* Unsolicited mss welcome, but prefer synopses with specimen chapter and table of contents. *Royalties* paid annually. *Overseas associates* Basil Blackwell Inc., New York.

Authors' Rating Still family owned, with all its attendant benefits and frailties. The personal service is encouraging but recent cancellation of some contracts has been reported. Strong in school publishing.

Blackwell Scientific Publications Ltd
Osney Mead, Oxford OX2 0EL   ☎0865 240201   Telex 83355 Medbok G
Deputy Chairman *Robert Campbell*
          Approximate Annual Turnover £10–15 million

FOUNDED 1939. Part of the **Blackwell Group**. Growth in the 1960s led to a move to Oxford. In 1987 the company broadened its base by buying **Collins'** professional list. *Publishes* Medical, professional and science. 230 titles in 1986.

Editorial Director (acting) *Robert Campbell* TITLES *Textbook Of Dermatology* edited by Rook et al; *Essential Immunology* Roitt; *Lecture Notes in Clinical Medicine* Rubenstein. Unsolicited mss and synopses welcomed.
Royalties paid annually. *Overseas associates* **Blackwell Scientific Publications Inc.**, USA; **Blackwell Scientific Publications Pty Ltd**, Australia.

Authors' Rating A tightly organised, highly competent publisher. Rewards may not be madly generous but they do get paid on time.

Blackwood Pillans & Wilson

61 North Castle Street, Edinburgh EH2 3LJ ☎031–225 8282

Chairman/Managing Director *Graham Wilson*

Did not publish any books in 1986 and are now concentrating on printing rather than publishing. Do not welcome unsolicited material.

Blandford Publishing Ltd

Link House, 25 West Street, Poole, Dorset BH15 2SS ☎0202 671171
Telex 418304 Linkho G

Managing Director *Philip Sturrock*

FOUNDED 1919, the company took its name from the location of its first office in London's West End. Taken over ten years ago by Link House and three years ago by United Newspapers. Recently acquired by **Cassell** who plan a rapid programme of expansion. *Publishes* Animal care & breeding, art & graphics, aviation, aviculture, bodybuilding & sport, crafts & hobbies, do-it-yourself, fashion & costume, gardening, humour, magic & the occult, military & war, natural history, photography, popular music, sports & games, theatre & drama, transport, woodworking. 150 titles in 1986.

Editorial Director *John Newth*

DIVISIONS
Art & Graphics *Watercolour Painting* Ron Ranson **Aviculture** *Parrots, Their Care and Breeding* Rosemary Low **Bodybuilding** *Hardcore Bodybuilding* Robert Kennedy **Crafts** *China & Porcelain Painting Projects* Sheila Southwell **Gardening** *Fuchsias In Colour* Brian and Valerie Proudley **Military** *War At Sea 1939–1945* John Hamilton **Music** *New Rock Record* Terry Housome **Natural History** *Wildest Britain* Roland Smith. Unsolicited mss and synopses/ideas for books are welcome. Mass-market paperback imprint Javelin covering wide ranging subjects. **Editorial Director** *Jonathan Grimwood*.
Royalties paid twice yearly.

Authors' Rating A curious transition over the years from moral re-armament publisher to light non-fiction with pop music in the lead.

Bloodaxe Books Ltd

PO Box 1SN, Newcastle upon Tyne, NE99 1SN ☎091–232 5988

Managing Director *Neil Astley*

Publishes poetry, literature and criticism, photography, literary fiction, theatre and drama, women's studies. 25 titles in 1986 (9 in 1985). 90% of their list is poetry.

Editorial Director *Neil Astley* Unsolicited mss welcome.
Royalties paid annually.

Authors' Rating One of the best of the small publishers; enterprising and imaginative.

Bloomsbury Publishing Ltd

4 Bloomsbury Place, London WC1A 2QA   ☎01–636 0336

Chairman & Managing Director *Nigel Newton*

One of the three major new imprints set up in 1986. **Bloomsbury** was launched in a glare of publicity which made much of its radical manifesto: the attempt to bring authors into far greater involvement with the machinery of publishing, and the setting aside of a share of the company's equity for division among its authors. **Bloomsbury** was founded by Nigel Newton (ex-**Sidgwick & Jackson**) together with David Reynolds (ex-**Shuckburgh Reynolds**), who then headhunted Alan Wherry from **Penguin** (marketing) and Liz Calder from **Cape** (editorial). How many authors would leave **Cape** with Liz Calder became a common topic of trade gossip in early 1987; 3 of the 25 titles launched between April and July were by novelists who did.

Editorial Head *Liz Calder*   TITLES *Trust* Mary Flanagan; *Anywhere But Here* Mona Simpson; *A Warmer Season* Joseph Olshan; *Coming First* Paul Bryers; *Temporary Shelter* Mary Gordon; *The Land That Lost Its Heroes* Jimmy Burns; *Look Homeward: A Life Of Thomas Wolfe* David Donald; *Blundering Into Disaster* Robert McNamara; *Nostradamus & The Millenium* John Hogue; *Natural Parenting* Peter and Fiona Walker; *Marilyn Among Friends* Shaw and Rosten. Welcome unsolicited mss and synopses.
Royalties paid twice yearly (April and October).

Authors' Rating Too early to be dogmatic but early signs are encouraging even if first titles did not quite live up to their promotion. With young leadership (Nigel Newton is only just into his thirties) and a dedication to energetic marketing, **Bloomsbury** is not likely to be short of good writers. The shares for authors scheme will be worth watching though at the time of writing the details are unclear.

The Bodley Head Ltd

32 Bedford Square, London WC1B 3EL ☎01–631 4434   Telex 299080 CVBCSE G

Chairman *Max Reinhardt*   **Managing Director** *David Machin*
                      Approximate Annual Turnover £3 million

Taken over by **Random House Inc.**, New York. Formerly part of the **Chatto, Virago, Bodley Head and Jonathan Cape** group. FOUNDED in 1887, and run by John Lane for the first 31 years, The Bodley Head remains editorially inviolate. Its early list included H. G. Wells, Arnold Bennett, Saki and later Agatha Christie. Allen Lane, John Lane's nephew, left the company to found **Penguin**. Max Reinhardt acquired the firm in 1957; authors who subsequently joined the list include Graham Greene, Alistair Cooke, Georgette Heyer, Solzhenitsyn, Muriel Spark and William Trevor. A strong children's list was developed, with writers such as Maurice Sendak, Pat Hutchins and Shirley Hughes. *Publishes* General non-fiction (biography, history, travel, current affairs); fiction; children's (fiction, non-fiction, picture). 107 titles in 1986.

DIVISIONS
Adult *Chris Holifield* TITLES General *The Baader Meinhof Group* Stefan Aust, *Iceland Saga* Magnus Magnusson, *Kobbe's Complete Opera Book, Stranger on the Line* Fitzgerald and Leopold; Fiction *Sandmouth People* Ronald Frame, *The Stories of Muriel Spark, I Am England* Patricia Wright, *Knots and Crosses* Ian Rankin. **Children's** *Margaret Clark* TITLES *The Fisherman and the Cormorants* Gerald Rose, *Rightway Jack* David Cox, *Dr Jekyll and Mr Hollins* Willis Hall; reprints *I Capture the Castle* Dodie Smith, *An Overpraised Season* Charlotte Zolotow (ed.). Unsolicited mss welcome if they include return postage. Synopses and ideas welcome.
Royalties paid twice yearly.

Authors' Rating A dear old thing. Thought by some to be a bit staid for these tough times but authors appreciate the personal touch and the strong sense of loyalty. The children's list is outstanding and a firm favourite with librarians.

The Book Guild Limited
Temple House, 25–26 High Street, Lewes, East Sussex BN7 2LU
☎0273 472534   Telex NOSLIP VIA 987562 COCHAS

Chairman *Gerald Konyn*   **Managing Director** *Aimee Konyn*
Approximate Annual Turnover £500,000

FOUNDED 1982. *Publishes* General, Fiction, Juvenile. 40 titles in 1986.

DIVISIONS
Biography *Carol Biss* TITLES *The Walpoles of Wolterton* Nancy Walpole; *The Consul's Memsahib* Masha Williams; *Teacher Extraordinary* Mora Dickson.   **Fiction** *Carol Biss* TITLES *Beirut, The Shadow Dancers* David Creed; *Koyama's Diamond* Adrian Berry; *Tar & Cement* Martyn Goff.   **Religion & Philosophy** *Carol Biss* TITLES *God and Human Chance* Bishop Paul Burrough; *God in Everything* Donald Neil; *Everyman Revived* Drusilla Scott.

IMPRINTS
Temple House Books *Carol Biss*   Paperback TITLES *Breaking The Ice* Ian Crichton; *Selling: How To Succeed In the Sales Arena* David Baldwin; *The Leap From Doubt To Faith* Canon Reginald Dobson. No unsolicited mss. Ideas and synopses welcome.
Royalties paid twice yearly.

Authors' Rating An efficient and competently run small publisher but with a tendency to drift over into vanity publishing. In all cases of vanity publishing, would-be authors should take independent advice before committing their own money.

Bookmarks Publication

265 Seven Sisters Road, Finsbury Park, London N4 2DE   ☎01-802 6145

Managing Director *Peter Marsden*   **Approximate Annual Turnover** £75,000

FOUNDED in 1979 to project the international socialist movement. Linked with the Socialist Workers Party and its internationally related organisations. *Publishes* Socialist books on politics, economics, labour history, trade unionism, international affairs. 12 titles in 1986.

DIVISIONS
General Publishing *Peter Marsden*   TITLE *The Revolutionary Ideas of Karl Marx* Alex Callinicos. **Revolutionary Classics** *Charles Hore*   TITLE *Labour in Irish History* James Connolly. Unsolicited synopses and ideas welcome as long as they are compatible with existing policy. No unsolicited mss.
Royalties paid annually. *Overseas associates* Chicago, USA; Melbourne, Australia.

Bookward Ltd

10 Mandeville Road, Aylesbury, Bucks HP21 8AA   ☎0296 435418

Managing Director *John Goodchild*

Publishes children's, crafts and hobbies, fiction, humour, literature and criticism, military and war, nautical, science fiction, vocational training and careers. Forty-eight titles in 1986.

Consulting Editor *Margaret Crash*

IMPRINTS
John Goodchild children's books. Unsolicited mss considered.
Royalties paid twice yearly.

Bounty Books

59 Grosvenor Street, London W1X 9DA   ☎01-493 5841   Telex 27278

Managing Director *Jonathan Goodman*

Part of the Octopus Publishing Group. FOUNDED in 1981 as the Bargain Reprint Division of Octopus. *Publishes* out of print titles only; general interest, cookery, gardening, natural history, sport, antiques, militaria, humour, children's, facsimiles, fiction. 100 titles in 1986.
No unsolicited mss, synopses or ideas for books.

Authors' Rating Some complaints of reprints appearing without full credits.

The Bowerdean Press
85 Battersea Business Centre, 103–109 Lavender Hill, London SW11 5QF
☎01–223 7870

Managing Director *Mr R. H. Dudley*

FOUNDED 1986 as a packager of illustrated non-fiction. Interested in books on royalty, architecture, gardening, wine, sport, humour. 2 titles in 1986.

Editorial Director *R. H. Dudley* Unsolicited mss and synopses are welcome.
Royalties 'does not apply'.

R. R. Bowker UK Ltd
Borough Green, Sevenoaks, Kent TN15 8PJ   ☎0732 884567   Telex 95678

General Manager Philip Woods

Part of **Butterworths**. *Publishes* biography and library service; biography and auto-biography, politics and world affairs. 54 titles in 1986.

Editorial Director t.b.a. Unsolicited mss considered.
Royalties paid twice yearly.

Boxtree
25 Floral Street, Covent Garden, London WC2E 9DS   ☎01–240 7419

Chairman *Hugh Campbell*   **Managing Director** *Sarah Mahaffy*

FOUNDED in April 1987 to publish books related to television programmes primarily in the areas of current affairs, children's, leisure and general interest. No fiction. TVS (Television South) is the major shareholder in the company. Around twenty titles by the end of 1987, more for 1988.

Editor *Sarah Mahaffy* Unsolicited mss not welcome; because the company publishes tie-ins with television, close consultation with writers well in advance of the writing of mss is essential. However, synopses and ideas welcome.
Royalties paid twice yearly.

Authors' Rating One of the few hopeful signs of intelligent and constructive co-operation between publishing and commercial television.

Marion Boyars Publishers Ltd
24 Lacy Road, London SW15 1NL   ☎01–788 9522

Managing Director *Marion Boyars*

FOUNDED 1975. Formerly Calder & Boyars. *Publishes* Academic & scholarly; architecture & design; biography & autobiography; business & industry; economics; fiction; health & beauty; law; literature & criticism; medical; music; philosophy; poetry; politics & world affairs; psychology; religion & theology; sociology & anthropology; theatre & drama; travel; women's studies. 25 titles in 1986.

Editorial Director *Arthur Boyars*   **Editor-in-Chief** *Marion Boyars*   **Non-fiction Editor** *Ken Hollings*   **Iris Series Editor** *Stephanie Lewis*.   TITLES *Taking It All In* Pauline Kael; *State of the Art* Pauline Kael; *Potboilers* Charles Marowitz; *Memory Gardens* Robert Creeley; *X: Writings '79–'82* John Cage; *The Flood* John Broderick; *Marat/Sade* Peter Weiss; *Selected Letters* Federico Garcia Lorca; *Cathy Come Home* Jeremy Sandford. Unsolicited mss welcome for fiction. Unsolicited synopses and ideas welcome for non-fiction.
Royalties paid annually. *Overseas associates* **Marion Boyars Inc.,** 26 East 33rd Street, New York, NY 10016, USA.

Authors' Rating A publisher of independent judgement with an eye for talent that others might overlook.

Boydell & Brewer Ltd
PO Box 9, Woodbridge, Suffolk, IP12 3DF   ☎0394 411320

Managing Director *Mr R. W. Barber*

Publishes Animal care & breeding; archaeology; architecture & design; bibliography & library service; crafts & hobbies; history & antiquarian; languages & linguistics; literature & criticism; military & war; natural history; theatre & drama.

All books commissioned. Most definitely do not welcome unsolicited material.

Authors' Rating An introspective publisher, best left to make their own decisions unhindered by authors or agents.

Brentham Press
40 Oswald Road, St Albans, Hertfordshire AL1 3AQ   ☎0727 35731

Director *Margaret Tims*

FOUNDED 1974 by three people with professional publishing experience. Now run mostly by editorial director. The aim is to publish material of literary merit and social value which falls outside the commercial mass market. 'Such a press is not economically viable and cannot be run as a source of income!' *Publishes* Poetry, criticism, essays. 1 title in 1986.

TITLES Series *Poet's England*, Lawrence and Murry; *A Twofold Vision* E. A. Lea; *Art and Society: Ruskin in Sheffield 1876* Robert Hewison. Do not welcome unsolicited mss but welcome synopses and ideas if relevant to programme and interests, i.e. verse, mainly topographical, local history, art and society, environment.
Royalties paid annually.

Breslich & Foss

Golden House, 28–31 Great Pulteney Street, London W1R 3DD

☎01–734 0706   Telex 264188 Bresl G

Director *Paula Breslich*   **Approximate Annual Turnover** £350,000

Started with a reprint list but now mainly packagers of a wide variety of non-fiction subjects. *Publishes* Art books, music, gardening, crafts, sport and health.

Unsolicited mss are welcome although synopses preferred. Always include stamped addressed envelope with submissions.
Royalties paid twice yearly.

Brimax Books Ltd

4–5 Studlands Park Industrial Estate, Exning Road, Newmarket, Suffolk CB8 7AU

☎0638 664611

Managing Director *Patricia Gillette*

Old established publisher specialising in children's books. Some educational; reading books for young children up to the age of 13; board books for very young children. All fully coloured and illustrated. Now part of **Octopus**. 40 titles in 1986.

Editor-in-chief *Trevor Watson* Unsolicited mss will be considered but would prefer to see synopses.
Royalties paid twice yearly.

Bristol Classical Press

Dept of Classics, University of Bristol, Bristol BS8 1RJ   ☎0272 214187

Managing Director *T. A. G. Foss*   **Approximate Annual Turnover** £150,000

Offshoot of Chapter & Verse Bookshops Ltd. Founded 1977 to attempt to revive the study of classics in schools and colleges by producing cheap texts. *Publishes* Academic & scholarly, archaeology, educational & textbooks, English literature, languages & linguistics, literature & criticism, philosophy, classics textbooks. 30 titles in 1986.

General Editor *John H. Betts* Unsolicited mss and synopses welcome.
Royalties paid annually.

The British Academy

20–21 Cornwall Terrace, London NW1 4QP   ☎01–487 5966

Publications Officer *J. M. H. Rivington*

Approximate Annual Turnover £80,000

FOUNDED 1901 to promote Humanities. Most of the work published comes from inside the Academy. *Publishes* Art, archaeology, classics, history, music, numismatics, philosophy, poetry, economics, social anthropology, jurisprudence. 15 titles in 1986.

Editor *J. M. H. Rivington*. *Publishes* numerous series including *Records Of Social and Economic History; Oriental Documents; Classical and Mediaeval Logic Texts; Corpus of Anglo Saxon Stone Sculpture; Auctores Britannici Medii Aevi*. Unsolicited mss will be considered but synopses preferred.

The British Academy more or less publish at a loss, so payment of *royalties* only occurs if a title does particularly well.

Lewis Brooks Ltd
2 Blagdon Road, New Malden, Surrey, KT3 4AD ☎01–949 4699

Telex 24667 Impemp G

Chairman *John M. Verge*

Publishes Academic & scholarly, architecture & design, engineering, reference books & dictionaries, scientific & technical. 1 title in 1986.

Editorial Director *John M. Verge*

Brown Watson (Leicester) Ltd
55A London Road, Leicester LE2 0PE ☎0533 545008 Telex 342678 BWL G

Managing Director *Michael B. McDonald*

FOUNDED 1982. Part of the **Peter Haddock Group**. *Publishes* Children's books. 80 'series' in 1986. Most books are commissioned and therefore unsolicited mss and synopses are not welcome.

Authors' Rating Children's books for the cheaper end of the market. Not in itself a bad thing but authors need to sell a lot to make money.

Buchan & Enright Publishers Ltd
53 Fleet Street, London EC4Y 1BE ☎01–353 4401

Chairman *R. V. Rhodes James* **Joint Managing Directors** *J. W. Buchan and Dominique Enright*

FOUNDED 1982. Planning to expand operations in the near future though not intending to be a big publishing house. *Publishes* Biography, history & antiquarian, humour, military & war, country pursuits, sports & games. 12 titles in 1986.

Editors *J. W. Buchan and Dominique Enright*. TITLES *Shooting From Scratch* Michael Paulet; *Mutiny* Lawrence James; *Never Such Innocence* ed. Martin Stephens; *Land Fit for Heroes?* Christopher Grayling. Prefer to see synopses and ideas rather than unsolicited mss.
Royalties paid twice yearly.

Burke Publishing Co. Ltd

Pegasus House, 116–120 Golden Lane, London EC1Y 0TL   ☎01–253 2145

Telex 27931 Burke G

Chairman *Harold K. Starke*   **Managing Director** *Naomi Galinski*

FOUNDED 1935 to publish general books and children's fiction and non-fiction. Reconstituted in 1960 to concentrate on education. *Publishes* Children's books, educational & textbooks (all levels), medical, reference books & dictionaries. 30 titles in 1986.

Editorial Director *Naomi Galinski*   TITLES *Headstart Books*; *Read for Fun*; *Sparklers*; *Animals and their Environment*; *Encyclopaedia of Psychoactive Drugs*; *World Leaders*; *Young Specialist*; *Wake Up to the World of Science*. Welcome unsolicited mss and synopses/ideas but require return postage or s.a.e. *Royalties* paid annually.

Authors' Rating Tight on money but open to ideas.

Burke's Peerage Ltd

104 New Bond Street, London W1Y 0AE   ☎01–385 4206

Publishing Director *Mr H. B. Brooks-Baker*

Have not published anything for the last two years. Hope to commence publishing again in 1988.

Graham Burn

28D High Street, Leighton Buzzard, Bedfordshire LU7 7EA   ☎0525 376390

Telex 825562 Chacom G Burnpub

Concentrate on the overseas market with books written by authors in other countries. Emphasis is presently more on printing, however.

Business Education Publishers

Leighton House, 17 Vine Place, Sunderland, Tyne & Wear SR1 3NA

☎091–567 4963

Joint Managing Directors *P. M. Callaghan and T. Harrison*

Approximate Annual Turnover £150,000

FOUNDED 1981. Currently expanding into further and higher education, computing and books for the Health Service. *Publishes* Business education, law, economics. 4 titles in 1986.   TITLES *BTEC National Course Studies* Paul Callaghan, Tom Harrison & John Ellison; *Law For Housing Managers* Tom Harrison; *The Abbotsfield File* Paul Callaghan & John Ellison. Welcome unsolicited mss and synopses. *Royalties* paid annually.

Butterworth & Co. Ltd
Borough Green, nr Sevenoaks, Kent TN15 8PH   ☎0732 884567   Telex 95678

Chairman *W. Gordon Graham*   **Managing Director** *G. R. N. Cusworth*
Approximate Annual Turnover £70 million

FOUNDED 1818 by Henry Butterworth. Now part of **Reed Publishing**. By the turn of the century **Butterworth** was publishing many of the legal titles familiar today. The Bond family bought the company at that time, and added to its list such classics as *Halsbury's Laws of England* and *Encyclopaedia of Forms and Precedents*. Publishes legal, medical, scientific, technical, bibliographic books and journals. 200 titles in 1986.

DIVISIONS
Butterworth Law Publishers Ltd *D. L. Summers*. Located at 88 Kingsway, London WC2B 6AB ☎01–405 6900   TITLES *All England Law Reports*; *Stones Justices Manual*; *Simon's Taxes*; plus full legal, tax, banking textbook lists. **Butterworth Scientific Ltd** *E. J. Newman*. Located at Westbury House, Bury Street, Guildford GU2 5AW ☎0483 31261   TITLES *Operative Surgery*; *A History of British Architecture*; *General Anaesthesia*. **Focal Press:** *Techniques of TV Production*; *Basic Photography*.   **Bowker UK Ltd** *P. W. Woods*   TITLES *Books in Print*; *Ulrich's International Periodicals Directory*. Unsolicited mss welcome, but preliminary letter preferred. Synopses and ideas for books should be addressed to the relevant publishing director.
Royalties paid twice yearly. *Overseas associates* in Australia, New Zealand, Singapore, South Africa, Canada, USA.

Authors' Rating Shares with **Sweet & Maxwell** the highly profitable market for law books. But while classics like *Halsbury's Laws of England* ensure a sound base income, the scientific and medical lists are coming up fast. A highly efficient enterprise.

Byway Books
Unit 2, Tweedbank Craft Centre, Haining Drive, Tweedbank, Selkirkshire TD1 3RJ
-   ☎0896 57869

Managing Director *W. F. Laughlan*

FOUNDED 1981. Small publishing house now concentrating on children's books. *Publishes* Children's picture books in paperback series: *Byway Bairns*. 8 titles in 1986.

TITLES *A Furl of Fairy Wind*; *Hi Johnnie*; *The Brownie*; *The Enchanted Boy* – all by Mollie Hunter. Prefer synopses to unsolicited mss.
Royalties paid twice yearly.

Cadogan Books Ltd

16 Lower Marsh, Waterloo, London SE1 7RJ   ☎01–633 0525   Telex 917706

Chairman *Frank Rice-Oxley*   **Managing Director** *Paula Levey*

Approximate Annual Turnover £320,000

Part of **Metal Bulletin plc**. The company was once called **Gentry Books**, and published motor titles, anthologies and guide books. In 1985 they decided to concentrate solely on guide books. 5 titles in 1986.

Editorial Director *Rachel Fielding* TITLES *Cadogan Guides*. Unsolicited mss not welcome; introductory letter and synopsis essential. Unsolicited synopses/ideas for books welcome.
Royalties paid twice yearly.

John Calder (Publishers) Ltd

18 Brewer Street, London W1R 4AS   ☎01–734 3786

Chairman and Managing Director *John Calder*

A publishing company which has grown around the tastes and contacts of its proprietor/manager/editorial director John Calder, the iconoclast of the literary establishment. *Publishes* fiction (literary), poetry, biography, autobiography, drama, playscripts, music, opera, literary criticism, politics, sociology.

Editorial Head *John Calder* TITLES include all Beckett's prose and poetry; William Burroughs; Marguerite Dumas; P. J. Kavanagh; Alain Robbe-Grillet; Nathalie Samante; Claude Simon; Howard Barker (plays); ENO and ROH opera guides. No unsolicited mss. Synopses and ideas for books welcome.
Royalties paid annually. *Overseas associates* Riversun Press, New York.

Authors' Rating A brave publisher who has often ventured where others feared to tread, John Calder is as independently minded as the authors he brings to print. This leads to reports of eccentric behaviour such as mss returned without covering letter, plus complaints of overdue payments.

Caliban Books

17 South Hill Park Gardens, Hampstead, London NW3 2TD   ☎01–435 0222

Managing Director *Peter Razzell*

FOUNDED 1977. *Publishes* Sociology, social history, autobiography, academic, history of exploration, psychotherapy. 12 titles in 1986.

TITLES *Bhagwan, The God that Failed* Hugh Milne; *The Lonely Soldier – The Autobiography of a Polish Soldier* Yan Maslamy. Do not welcome unsolicited mss but will consider synopses.
Royalties paid twice yearly.

Cambridge Learning Ltd
9 Hills Avenue, Cambridge CB1 4UY ☎0223 242794

Managing Director *Sue Ecob*   **Approximate Annual Turnover** £30,000

FOUNDED 1972 as an offshoot of **Cambridge Communications**, then publishing purely computing and electronics texts. In the early 1980s moved into English books and other subjects for schools. *Publishes* Educational textbooks and kits. 1 title in 1986.

Editorial Director *Sue Ecob*   TITLE *Moonstone* Jan Jones. Welcome unsolicited mss and synopses.
Royalties paid quarterly.

Cambridge University Press
The Edinburgh Building, Shaftesbury Road, Cambridge CB2 2RU
☎0223 312393   Telex 817256

Chief Executive *Geoffrey A. Cass*   **Managing Director (Publishing Division)** *A. K. Wilson*

The oldest press in the world, and still part of Cambridge University. Recently the company has diversified into reference publishing, ELT and software and expanded its activities in Australia and the USA. 1988 will see the establishment of a joint publishing imprint for reference titles with **W. & R. Chambers Ltd**. *Publishes* Academic and educational for international English language markets, at all levels from primary school to post-graduate. Also publishes bibles and academic journals. Approx. 800 titles in 1986.

DIVISIONS
Bibles *R. Coleman*   **ELT** *A. du Plessis*   **Humanities/Social Science** *R. J. Mynott*
Journals *D. Forbes*   **Schoolbooks** *R. Davidson*   **Science** *S. Mitton*

Authors' Rating Smaller than its younger Oxford counterpart (no children's list, for example) but recent changes bode well for a publisher with such an eminently marketable name. Not given to offering big advances.

Canongate Publishing Ltd
17 Jeffrey Street, Edinburgh E1 1DR   ☎031–556 0023   Telex 72165 Canpub G

Managing Director *Stephanie Wolfe Murray*
Approximate Annual Turnover £150,000

FOUNDED 1973. *Publishes* books by Scottish authors and of Scots interest. Some plays. 20 titles in 1986.

Editorial Director *Fiona Mackenzie King*. Paperback series *Canongate Classics*. 8 titles per year.   TITLES *The Quarry Wood* Nan Shepherd; *Imagined Corners* Willa Muir; *Consider The Lilies* Iain Crichton Smith; *The Story of My Boyhood and Youth*

John Muir; *Island Landfalls* Robert Louis Stevenson; *Land of Leal* James Barte. Prefer to consider synopses rather than unsolicited mss.
Royalties paid twice yearly.

Authors' Rating One of the best of the small publishers. Highly imaginative within their specialist area.

Jonathan Cape Ltd

32 Bedford Square, London WC1B 3EL   ☎01–636 3344   Telex 299080 Cvbcse G

Chairman *Tom Maschler*   **Managing Director** *Graham C. Greene*

Taken over by **Random House** in May 1987, along with its partners, **Bodley Head** and **Chatto**. *Publishes* Academic & scholarly, archaeology, architecture & design, children's books, economics, fiction, fine art & art history, history & antiquarian, humour, illustrated & fine editions, literature & criticism, natural history, philosophy, poetry, politics & world affairs, psychology, reference books & dictionaries, sociology & anthropology, travel & topography. 100 new titles in 1986.

Editorial Director *Frances Coady*   TITLES Fiction *Love and Shadows* Isabel Allende; *Einstein's Monsters* Martin Amis; *Bluebeard's Egg* Margaret Atwood; *The Songlines* Bruce Chatwin; *A Sport of Nature* Nadine Gordimer; *The Counterlife* Philip Roth. Children's *Cyril of the Apes* Jonathan Gathorne-Hardy; *Kelpie* William Mayne; *Fred* Posy Simmonds. Non-Fiction *Land of the Snow Lion* Elaine Brook; *Greetings From the Fast Lane – 32 postcards for the Post-Modern World Chix Pix*; *The Political Diary of Hugh Dalton* Ed. Pimlott; *Bob Dylan Lyrics 1962–1985*; *The Secrets of the Service* Anthony Glees; *A Share of Loving* Han Suyin; *Rab: The Life of R. A. Butler* Anthony Howard; *Sex Within Reason* Anne Kelleher; *Gabriel Garcia Marquez* Stephen Minta; *The Traveller's Guide to Malta and Gozo*. Will consider unsolicited mss for fiction and synopsis with sample chapters for non-fiction.
Royalties paid twice yearly.

Authors' Rating Chances of success are heavily dependent on the judgement of Tom Maschler, the second biggest shareholder in the former **Cape**, **Virago**, **Bodley Head** and **Chatto** group, and probably the best-known editor in the country. Once London's most prestigious publishing house, Cape has lost its cutting edge of late. The departure of Liz Calder, one of the best editors, to Bloomsbury was judged by some writers as the last straw.

Carcanet Press Ltd

208–212 Corn Exchange Buildings, Manchester M4 3BQ   ☎061–834 8730

Chairman *Robert Gauton* (proprietor)   **Managing Director** *Michael Schmidt*

Carcanet has grown in 15 years from an undergraduate hobby into a substantial venture. Anglo-European in orientation, they are Manchester based, with a Mexican M.D. Robert Gauton bought the company in 1983. *Publishes* fiction, memoirs, translations, academic, biography, educational and textbooks, but mostly poetry. Success has led to tie-ins with **Grafton**. Some **Carcanet** titles now appear in **Paladin** editions, and **Grafton** will soon start its own poetry list in association with **Carcanet**. 45 titles in 1986 (and 6 issues of *P.N. Review*).

Editorial Director *Michael Schmidt* **Fiction Editor** *Michael Freeman* AUTHORS John Ashbery, Edwin Morgan, Elizabeth Jennings, Iain Crichton Smith, Natalia Ginzburg, Stuart Hood, Leonardo Sciascia, Christine Brooke-Rose, Pier Paolo Pasolini.

Authors' Rating A small publisher of high repute. One of the most imaginative lists; very strong on poetry.

Cargate Press
25 Marylebone Road, London NW1 5JR ☎01–935 2541

Part of the Methodist Church, Overseas Division. No longer publish books, but leaflets for use internally by the Methodist Church. Do not welcome unsolicited material.

Frank Cass
Gainsborough House, 11 Gainsborough Road, London E11 1RS ☎01–530 4226
Telex 897719

Managing Director *Frank Cass*

Publishes History and antiquarian, politics and world affairs, Africa, Middle East, development/strategic studies, education, literature. 25 titles in 1986.

Editorial head (books) *Margaret Goodare* TITLES *Dilemmas of Nuclear Strategy* ed. Roman Kolkowicz; *Looking Back on India* Hubert Evans; *From Fair Sex to Feminism* ed. Mangan & Park; *Studies in Public Enterprise* V. Ramanadham; *Wilfred Owen – Anthem for a Doomed Youth* Simcox; *Special Needs in Ordinary Schools* Neville Jones; *Party Politics in Contemporary Western Europe* ed. Bartolini & Mair; *New Perspectives in Scottish Legal History* ed. Kiralfy & MacQueen. Although unsolicited mss will be considered, a synopsis with covering letter is preferred.
Royalties paid annually.

Cassell plc
Artillery House, Artillery Row, London SW1P 1RT ☎01–222 7676
Telex 9413701 CASPUB G

Chairman/Managing Director *Philip J. Sturrock*
Approximate Annual Turnover £10 million

FOUNDED 1848 by John Cassell; acquired **Studio Vista** in 1969; bought by **Collier Macmillan** the same year, sold to **CBS Publishing Europe** in 1982, and finally achieved independence in 1986, as **Cassell plc**. In its first year of operations, **Cassell** has acquired the book publishing division of **Tycooly Publishing Ltd** and **Link House Books**, which has been renamed as **Blandford Publishing**. *Publishes* General non-fiction, business, education, religious, primary and secondary school books, English language teaching. 120 titles in 1986.

DIVISIONS

Blandford *John Newth* TITLE *Animal Folklore, Myth & Legend.* **Cassell Business and Accounting** *Stephen Butcher* TITLE *Managerial Finance.* **Cassell Education** *Juliet Wight-Boycott* TITLE *Psychology and the Teacher.* **Cassell ELT** *Simon Nugent* TITLE *Exploring English.* **Cassell Trade** *Barry Holmes* TITLE *Brewer's Dictionary of Phrase & Fable.* **Cassell Tycooly** *Francis O'Kelly* TITLE *Industrial Water Use and Treatment.* **Geoffrey Chapman** *Robert B. Kelly* TITLE *Pope John XXIII.* **Studio Vista** *Barry Holmes* TITLE *Coloured Pencil Drawings.* **Wisley Handbooks** *Barry Holmes* TITLE *Plans for Small Gardens.* Unsolicited mss welcome. Non-fiction only. Synopses/ideas for books also welcome.
Royalties payment depends on the title.

Authors' Rating Flying high twenty years ago, **Cassell** suffered a crisis of identity when it joined the CBS conglomerate. A sign of decline was the loss of its once sizeable fiction list. Now back on its own, Cassell has still to develop a clearly identifiable publishing policy.

Godfrey Cave Associates Ltd
42 Bloomsbury Street, London WC1B 3QT ☎01–636 9177 Telex 266945

Chairman *John Maxwell* **Managing Director** *Geoffrey Howard*

No new books. The list consists entirely of reprints of illustrated books where rights have reverted and the re-issue of out-of-print titles. Fourteen of these were published in 1986.

Centaur Press Ltd
Fontwell, Arundel, Sussex BN18 0TA ☎024–368 3302

Chairman & Editorial Head *Jon Wynne-Tyson*

FOUNDED 1954. A one-man outfit which adds only 1–3 new titles a year to its list of biography, literature, philosophy, reference, environment, and education. No unsolicited mss. **Centaur** is not currently seeking new books.

SUBSIDIARY IMPRINT
Linden Press

Central Books Ltd
14 The Leathermarket, London SE1 3ER ☎01–407 5447

Managing Director *William Norris*

Approximate Annual Turnover £1 million

FOUNDED 1939 principally as book distributors. Importing, chiefly from Eastern Europe, came to dominate, but now also distributes books from small presses and originate some titles. *Publishes* Scientific & technical, politics, history, economics, children's books. 200 titles (mostly imported) in 1986.

Editorial Director *William Norris*. As (mainly) book importers they do not welcome unsolicited mss, but will consider synopses and ideas.
Royalties paid annually.

Century Hutchinson
Brookmount House, 62–65 Chandos Place, London WC2N 4NW ☎01–240 3411
Telex 261212 Litldn G

Chairman *Anthony Cheetham*   **Managing Director** *Peter Roche*

Publishes antiques and collecting; aviation, biography, autobiography; business and industry; children's books; cinema and video; computer software (business/entertainment); cookery; wines and spirits; crime; crafts and hobbies; DIY; fashion and costume; fiction; fine art and art history; gardening; guide books; health and beauty; humour; illustrated and fine editions; magic and the occult; military and war; natural history; photography; poetry; politics and world affairs; reference books and dictionaries; sports and games; theatre and drama; travel and topography. 500 titles in 1986.

DIVISIONS
Arrow Books *Peter Lavery* **Children's** *Susan Hook* **Fiction** *Rosemary Cheetham* **Hutchinson** *Richard Cohen* **Non-fiction** *Gail Rebuck* **Stanley Paul** *Roddy Bloomfield* *Publishes* Fiction: general, women's, crime, science fiction and fantasy, war, horror and the occult, thriller/suspense. Non-fiction: general, humour, war, health/self help, poetry and anthologies, astrology, travel, true crime, biography/autobiography. Children's books. 250 titles in 1986.

ARROW BOOKS IMPRINTS
Arena *Peter Lavery* *Publishes* international contemporary fiction. **Beaver** *Alison Berry* *Publishes* children's paperbacks, humour, activities, picture books.

Century Hutchinson welcome unsolicited mss and synopses/ideas for books. *Royalties* paid twice yearly. *Overseas associates* Century Hutchinson Australia/New Zealand/South Africa.

Authors' Rating Good news for the likes of Frederick Forsyth and Len Deighton when **Century** took over sleepy **Hutchinson**, now fully absorbed into the parent company. Under Anthony Cheetham's command best sellers sell even better. Writers with modest ambitions are less likely to feel at home. It's the same with paperbacks. There are authors who can remember the days when **Arrow** was a highminded list in rivalry with the classier **Penguins**. No longer. Today, mass marketing is the guiding principle. The ideas that are likeliest to take hold are those with stunning popular appeal. Not in the first flight of paperback publishers. Closer to **Star** or **Futura** than to **Penguin** or **Pan**.

Ceolfrith Press

Northern Centre for Contemporary Art, 17 Grange Terrace, Sunderland, Tyne & Wear SR2 7DF ☎091–514 1214

Sunderland Arts Centre was founded by Chris Carrell whose original connection with the arts was a second-hand bookshop. Premises were obtained at Grange Terrace and development has led to a concentration on visual arts and crafts exhibitions. *Publishes* Visual arts, visual poetry, criticism, design, general. 4 titles in 1986.

Editorial Director *Tony Knipe* Not particularly keen to receive unsolicited mss but will consider synopses.
Royalties paid twice yearly.

Chadwyck-Healey Ltd

Cambridge Place, Cambridge CB2 1NR ☎0223 311479
Telex 265871 MONREF G

Chairman *Sir Charles Chadwyck-Healey*
Approximate Annual Turnover £500,000

FOUNDED 1973. **Chadwyck-Healey Inc.**, New York followed the next year, and Chadwyck-Healey France in 1985. *Publishes* mainly on microform with a few reference works and guides for microform collections. Occasionally publishes monographs on fine art and architecture. 12 titles in 1986.

Editorial Head *Alison Moss* TITLES *The English Satirical Print*; *Theatre In Focus*; *Index of Manuscripts in The British Library*; *Government Documents*; *Bibliographies*. No unsolicited mss. Synopses and ideas for books welcome.
Royalties paid annually.

W. & R. Chambers

43–45 Annandale Street, Edinburgh EH7 4AZ ☎031–557 4571 Telex 727967

Chairman *A. S. Chambers* **Managing Director** *W. G. Henderson*

The company was established in the early 1800s to publish self-education works, but soon diversified into dictionaries and other reference works. *Publishes* reference, school and college textbooks, Scottish non-fiction, self-help guides in medical, social, language subjects. 22 titles in 1986. Now commencing co-publication of major reference works in association with **Cambridge University Press**. Prefer synopsis accompanied by letter to unsolicited finished mss.
Royalties paid annually. *Overseas representation* by Cambridge University Press, among other agents/publishers.

Authors' Rating Until recently a rather sleepy family firm best known for out of date reference works like the once marvellous *Chambers Encyclopaedia*. Latest developments suggest a revival of energy. Brought off the neatest promotional trick of this year's Bookseller Conference when delegates were presented with a beautifully bound do-it-yourself *Chambers Dictionary*. The pages were blank.

Geoffrey Chapman

Artillery House, Artillery Row, London SW1P 1RT ☏ 01–222 7676
Telex 9413701 Caspub G

Managing Director *Philip Sturrock*

Part of **Cassell**. *Publishes* Educational & textbooks, philosophy, religion & theology, liturgy, including music.

Editorial Director *Robert B. Kelly*   TITLES *Studies in the Synoptic Gospels* series. Prefer to see sample chapter and synopses rather than unsolicited mss.
Royalties paid annually as a rule.

Chapman & Hall

11 New Fetter Lane, London EC4P 4EE ☏ 01–583 9855

Chairman *Richard Stileman*

Parent Company **Associated Book Publishers (ABP)**
FOUNDED 1832. *Publishes* scientific, technical and medical books. Ninety-five titles in 1986.

Editorial Head *Phillip Read*   TITLES *Spon's Price Books*; *Dictionary of Organic Compounds*. Welcome unsolicited mss and synopses.
Royalties paid twice yearly.

Authors' Rating Literary fame as the original publisher of Evelyn Waugh. But he was the odd man out. Technical writers give high marks to Chapman & Hall.

Chappell Plays Ltd (formerly English Theatre Guild)

129 Park Street, London W1Y 3FA ☏ 01–629 7600   Telex 268403

Managing Director *Jonathan Simon*
Approximate Annual Turnover (new company)

Editorial Head *Adline Finlay* Part of the Chappell group which includes the literary agency of the same name (see *Agents*). *Publishes* Theatre playscripts in paperback form.   TITLES *Crown Matrimonial* Royce Ryton; *Arsenic & Old Lace* Joseph Kesselring; *Now Now Darling* Ray Cooney and John Chapman; *Bouncers* John Godber; *Mumbo Jumbo* Robin Glendinning (winner of the Mobil Playwriting Competition). Preliminary letter essential.
Royalties paid twice yearly.

Chatto & Windus Ltd/The Hogarth Press Ltd

30 Bedford Square, London WC1B 3RP ☏ 01–631 4434   Telex 299080 Cbcser G

Chairman *John Charlton*   **Managing Director** *Carmen Callil*

Taken over by **Random House Inc.**, New York in May 1987. Formerly part of the **Chatto, Virago, Bodley Head and Jonathan Cape** group. The original Chatto was founded in 1855, and took over **The Hogarth Press**, which had been founded by

Leonard and Virginia Woolf, in 1946. It was relaunched as a paperback imprint in 1984. *Publishes* academic & scholarly; archaeology; architecture & design; autobiography; business & industry; cookery; crime; fiction; fine art & art history; gardening; health & beauty; history & antiquarian; humour; illustrated & fine editions; literature & criticism; military & war; music; natural history; nautical; philosophy; photography; poetry; politics & world affairs; psychology; science fiction; sociology & anthropology; theatre & drama; travel & topography; women's studies. 105 titles in 1986.

Chatto & Windus Editorial Director *Andrew Motion* AUTHORS include Iris Murdoch, A. S. Byatt, Angela Carter, Timothy Mo, Blake Morrison.

The Hogarth Press Ltd (Hardbacks) **Editorial Director** *Andrew Motion* TITLES include works by Virginia Woolf, Sigmund Freud and others in the International Psycho-Analytic Library. (Paperbacks) **Editorial Director** *Christine Carswell* Fiction; lives & letters; crime; travel; poetry; critics. Unsolicited mss, synopses and ideas for books welcome if sent with return postage.
Royalties paid twice yearly. *Overseas associates* Australasian Publishing Co. Sydney; Book Reps Ltd, New Zealand.

Authors' Rating Once the preserve of Norah Smallwood, the most formidable lady in publishing, Chatto is now led by Carmen Callil who continues in the tradition of forceful opinions and tough negotiating. Described by a newspaper as the 'hand grenade of British publishing' and by one of her former authors as 'the headmistress I had hoped never to have', Carmen Callil had a difficult time re-establishing Chatto as a profitable enterprise while in partnership with Cape, Bodley Head and the company she founded, Virago. It is too early to say if the Random House takeover will ease her problems.

Chivers Press (Publishers)
Windsor Bridge Road, Bath, Avon BA2 3AX ☎0225 335336 Telex 444633

Chairman *G. M. Nutbrown* **Managing Director** *Roger H. Lewis*

Part of **The Gieves Group**. Originally part of **Cedric Chivers**; known as **Chivers Press** since 1979. *Publishes* Mainly reprints for libraries. Biography & autobiography, children's books, crime, fiction, large print editions, spoken word cassettes. 400 titles in 1986.

IMPRINTS
Atlantic Large Print Firecrest Books Gunsmoke Westerns Lythway Children's Large Print Lythway Large Print New Portway Facsimile Reprints New Portway Large Print Swift Children's Books Windsor Large Print. Do not consider mss or synopses as concentrating on reprinting for the time being. *Royalties* paid twice yearly.

Churchill Livingstone

Robert Stevenson House, 1–3 Baxter's Place, Leith Walk, Edinburgh EH1 3AF
☎031–556 2424   Telex 727511

Managing Director *Andrew Stevenson*
Approximate Annual Turnover £10 million

Part of the Longman Group. Founded in early 1970s from two originally private companies, E. & S. Livingstone and J. & A. Churchill, which had earlier become separate parts of Longman. *Publishes* medical; nursing; medical journals. 182 new titles in 1986. Do not welcome unsolicited mss. Welcome synopses/ideas.
Royalties paid annually. *Overseas associates* Churchill Livingstone Inc., New York; Longman Cheshire Pty Ltd, Melbourne.

Authors' Rating The best of the medical publishers.

Churchman Publishing Ltd

117 Broomfield Avenue, Worthing, West Sussex BN14 7SF   ☎0903 692430

Chairman and Managing Director *E. Peter Smith*
Approximate Annual Turnover £250,000

Specialist publishers who pursue the 'small is beautiful' concept. *Publishes* religion and theology (ecumenical), travel, psychology, autobiography and biography, history, social science and education. 30 titles in 1986.

IMPRINTS
The Lantern Press *B. P. Smith*   **Landmark Books** *B. P. Smith*
Unsolicited mss welcome in all non-fiction subjects. No fiction. Very little poetry. Unsolicited synopses/ideas for books welcome.
Royalties paid annually. *Overseas associates* in Canada, Australia and New Zealand.

Authors' Rating Vanity publisher. The usual warnings apply: authors should take independent advice before handing over money.

John Clare Books

106 Cheyne Walk, London SW1O 0JR   ☎01–352 7521/7333

Proprietor *Bryan Breed*

FOUNDED 1979. Started with a wide general list and became increasingly specialised. *Parent Company* **Interpress Features**. *Publishes* Non-fiction with an educational bias, social education. 12 titles in 1986.

TITLES *Music Therapy* Juliet Alving; *Social Drama* Bert Amies. Prefer synopses and ideas for books within their specialist field.
Royalties paid twice yearly.

T. & T. Clark Ltd
59 George Street, Edinburgh EH2 2LG   ☎031–225 4703   Telex 728134

Chairman *David Ross Stewart*   **Managing Director** *Ramsay Clark*
         Approximate Annual Turnover £500,000

FOUNDED 1821. Acquired by **John Bartholomew & Son Ltd** in 1974. *Publishes* religion, theology, law, philosophy, (all academic). 24 titles in 1986.

Editorial Head *Geoffrey Green*   TITLES *Church Dogmatics* Karl Barth; *A Textbook of Christian Ethics* Robin Gill ed.; *Sources of Law, Legal Change and Ambiguity* Alan Watson. Unsolicited mss, synopses and ideas for books welcome.
Royalties paid annually.

Clematis Press Ltd
18 Old Church Street, Chelsea, London SW3 5DQ   ☎01–352 8755

Chairman & Managing Director *Clara Waters*

Clematis Press act as distributors of imported books and have no editorial facilities. No unsolicited mss.

The Cleveland Press
1 Russell Chambers, Covent Garden, London WC2E 8AA   ☎01–240 9849

Managing Director *A. R. Powell*   **Approximate Annual Turnover** £150,000

FOUNDED 1984 *Publishes* Mostly railway histories. Also travel, historical, political. 8 titles in 1986.

No editorial director.   TITLES *Down The Line* series; *Metro* series; *Settle to Carlisle, A Tribute*. Welcome unsolicited mss and synopses.
Royalties paid annually.

Clio Press Ltd
55 St Thomas' Street, Oxford OX1 1JG   ☎0865 250333   Telex 83103 Clio G

Chairman and Managing Director *John Durrant*
         Approximate Annual Turnover £2 million

Part of **ABC-Clio Inc.**, Santa Barbara, California. Founded in Oxford in 1971 to publish academic reference works. Now also publishes art reference and large print titles for both children and the elderly. *Publishes* social sciences and humanities; general fiction and non-fiction in large print. 87 titles in 1986.

DIVISIONS
Isis Large Print *V. Babington Smith*   TITLES *Know Your Medicine; Charles & Diana*. **Windrush Large Print** *V. Babington Smith*   TITLES *Charlie and the Chocolate Factory*. **Clio Press** *A. J. Sloggett*   TITLES *World Bibliographical*

Series. **Art Bibliographies** *A. J. Sloggett* TITLES *Artbibliographies Modern.* Unsolicited mss welcome. Synopses/ideas for books considered. *Royalties* paid twice yearly.

Frank Coleman Publishing

Maulden Road, Flitwick, Beds MK45 5BW ☎0525 712261   Telex 825115

Managing Director *Neil Goldman*

Approximate Annual Turnover under £100,000

Publishes children's books. Six titles in 1986. Unsolicited mss welcome. Synopses and ideas for books considered.
Royalties paid annually.

Rex Collings Ltd

6 Paddington Street, London W1 (formerly)

Defunct. Sad demise of original publisher of *Watership Down* – a book rejected by more famous publishers.

Collins Publishers

8 Grafton Street, London W1X 3LA ☎01–493 7070   Telex 25611 Colins G
PO Box, Glasgow G4 0NB ☎041–772 3200

Chairman Ian Chapman   **Group Managing Director** (*Publishing*) *G. D. S. Blunt*

Approximate Annual Turnover £144 million

After troubles in the early 1980s, when Rupert Murdoch bought a minority share in the company, Collins goes from strength to strength. 1986 raised company turnover (including bookselling) by 19.1% with publishing turnover up by 5.9% to £67.8 million. This success has been consolidated by bookshop acquisitions; Claude Gill was bought in 1985 and there is rapid growth in the Collins-owned Hatchards chain. Good news on the overseas front too, with recovery in Australia, and optimism for Collins USA, where the ground has been prepared with the acquisition of the *A Day in the Life of . . .* series. 1429 new titles in 1986.

DIVISIONS

Collins General Division *M. Chapman, A. McKillop, C. O'Brien, H. Fraser* TITLES Recent non-fiction: *Time & Change* James Callaghan; *Made in Japan* Akio Morita; *Baldwin* Roy Jenkins; *The Illustrated Kipling* Neil Philip (ed.); *Leonardo's Kitchen Notebooks* Routh (ed.). Recent fiction: *Herself In Love* Marianne Wiggins; *Red Storm Rising* Tom Clancy; *Strangers* Rosie Thomas; *The Janus Man* Colin Forbes; *The Golden Bird* Edwin Mullins; *The House on Moon Lake* Francesca Duranti. 340 new titles in 1986.   **Collins Children's Division** *L. Davis, R. Sandberg, A. Sheehan* TITLES Fiction: *Little Grey Rabbit* books; *Paddington*; *Wil Cwac Cwac*. Classics: Narnia stories; Noel Streatfeild novels. Non-fiction: *Technology and Science – Inside Story* series; Nature, History, Prehistoric World, Hobbies, Dictionaries and Language; *Help Your Child* series. 300 new titles in 1986.   **Adlard Press** Sailing books only. **Collins Educational, Reference and Professional Division** ELT *R. Thomas* **Liturgical** *G. Chapman* **Technical** *D. Fulton*. Also **Bibles** *A. Watson* **Maps & Atlases** *D. Thompson* **Reference** *A. Macfarlane* located at the Glasgow office. 480 new titles in 1986. **Collins Grafton** (see **Grafton**) **Collins Special Interest Division** *J. Clibbon*. 86 new titles in 1986.

Authors' Rating Raised from the doldrums some four years ago by Ian Chapman's strong leadership, there was some unhappiness among authors as familiar figures in editing and marketing disappeared in a succession of staff upheavals. But the good effects of change are undeniable. As a quality publisher with a talent for mass sales – an unusual combination – Collins is a natural target for top writers and agents. Lately splashing out on big contracts (e.g. £500,000 to Fay Weldon for three books). Can afford to be choosey but for the right talent investment and returns usually match expectations.

Columbus Books Ltd

19–23 Ludgate Hill, London EC4M 7PD ☎01–248 6444   Telex 28673 CONSOL G

Chairman *Eric Dobby*   **Managing Director** *Medwyn Hughes*
Approximate Annual Turnover £3 million

FOUNDED in 1980 as a subsidiary of **Transatlantic Books Service Ltd**. Taken over in 1985 by Stancroft Trust, the majority shareholder is **Harrap Ltd**. *Publishes* Biography & autobiography, cinema & video, cookery, crafts & hobbies, guide books, health & beauty, photography, travel & topography, vocational training & careers, women's studies. 100 titles in 1986.

DIVISIONS
Columbus Books *Gill Rowley*   TITLES *The World of Marathons* Sandy Treadwell; *Help Yourself to Mental Health* Mary Manning; *Luchino Visconti* Claretta Tonetti; *The Duffer's Guide* series; *Country Inn Guides* Karen Brown; *British American Football League: The Official Rule Book* Radcliffe Phillips. **Harrap Columbus** *Medwyn Hughes*. Welcome unsolicited mss and synopses/ideas for books.
Royalties paid twice yearly.

Constable & Co. Ltd

10 Orange Street, London WC2H 7EG   ☎01–930 0801   Telex 27950

Chairman & Managing Director *Benjamin Glazebrook*

FOUNDED in the 1890s by Archibald Glazebrook. Published George Bernard Shaw and Katherine Mansfield, Muriel Spark has recently joined the list. *Publishes* Archaeology, architecture & design, biography & autobiography, cookery, wines & spirits, fiction, guide books, history & antiquarian, natural history, psychology, sociology & anthropology, travel & topography. 69 titles in 1986.

Editorial Director *Robin Baird Smith* TITLES *Twilight of the Ascendancy* Mark Bence-Jones; *A Girdle Round the Earth* Maria Aitken; *Istanbul, A Traveller's Companion* Laurence Kelly; *Ancient Places, The Prehistoric and Celtic Sites of Britain*

Glyn Daniel, Paul Bahn & Anthony Gascoigne; *The Old Lie, The Great War and The Public School Ethos* Peter Parker; *No Flowers By Request* June Thomson; *The Levels* Peter Benson. Unsolicited mss and synopses/ideas for books welcome.
Royalties paid twice yearly.

Authors' Rating Sound backlist but nothing spectacular in recent years. Nice people to deal with but is niceness enough in these hard times?

Countryside Books
3 Catherine Road, Newbury, Berkshire RG14 7NA   ☎ 0635 43816

Chairman *D. Chamberlain*

FOUNDED 1978. *Publishes* Mainly paperbacks on regional subjects. Pictorial and local history and leisure. 80 titles in 1986.

Commissioning Editor *Ron Freethy*   Welcome unsolicited mss and synopses.
Royalties paid twice yearly.

Croom Helm
Burrell Row, Beckenham, Kent BR3 1AT   ☎ 01–658 7813
Telex 24274 CROOMH G

Chairman *Alan Miles*   **Managing Director** *David Croom*
Approximate Annual Turnover £3.7 million

Part of **ABP**. Founded in 1972 by Christopher Helm and David Croom, and sold to ABP in May of 1986. *Publishes* Academic and Professional titles on social sciences, biology and health sciences and the humanities. 365 titles published in 1986.

Social science *Peter Sowden*   TITLES *The Future of Land Warfare*.   **Biology/health science** *Tim Hardwick*   TITLES *Incontinence and its Management*.   **Humanities** *Richard Storeman*   TITLES *Law and Society in Classical Athens*.   **Reference** *Jonathan Price*   TITLES *The World's Major Languages*. Unsolicited mss, synopses and ideas for books welcome.
Royalties paid annually.

Authors' Rating Great improvements since ABP takeover. They started on a shoestring and for several years managed to turn a profit on academic books rejected by other publishers. Christopher Helm has now departed to set up his own imprint.

The Crowood Press
Crowood House, Ramsbury, Marlborough, Wiltshire SN8 2HE   ☎ 0672 20320
Telex 449703

Chairman and Managing Director *John Dennis*
Approximate Annual Turnover £1 million

FOUNDED 1982 by John Dennis as a one man concern, **Crowood Press** has grown steadily to employ more than twenty people. *Publishes* sport & leisure. Branching out into cookery, gardening and health in the near future. 80 titles in 1986.

Editorial Head *John Dennis*   Preliminary letter preferred in all cases. Synopses and ideas for books welcome. *Royalties* paid twice yearly for initial year, annually thereafter.

Curzon Press Ltd
42 Gray's Inn Road, London WC1   ☎01–242 8310

Managing Director *John F. Standish*

Scholarly and specialised publishing house with imprints on Asian and African studies. *Publishes* academic and scholarly, archaeology, history and antiquarian, languages and linguistics, philosophy, religion and theology, sociology and anthropology, Oriental and African studies. 17 titles in 1986. Unsolicited mss considered. *Royalties* according to contract.

Dalesman Publishing Co. Ltd
Clapham, Lancaster LA2 8EB   ☎04685 225

Managing Director *Dennis Bullock*

Also publishers of the famous country magazine of the same name. *Publishes* crafts and hobbies, geography and geology, guide books, history and antiquarian, humour, transport, travel and topography. 26 titles in 1986.

Editorial Director *David Joy*   Unsolicited mss considered in all subjects. *Royalties* paid twice yearly.

Darf Publishers Ltd
50 Hans Crescent, London SW1X 0NA   ☎01–581 1805

Chairman *M. Fergiani*   **Managing Director** *M. B. Fergiani*
                              Approximate Annual Turnover £500,000

Formed in 1982 to publish and republish books on the Middle East, theology and travel. Strong emphasis on students' books. *Publishes* travel, history, language, religion, theology, geography, politics, oriental, literature. 50 titles in 1986.

Editorial Head *M. Fergiani*   TITLES *The Historical Geography of Arabia, vols. 1 & 2; Let's Learn Arabic; Spoken Arabic: Self Taught; The Life of Mahomet; Carthage and her Remains.* Unsolicited mss, synopses and ideas for books welcome. *Royalties* paid twice yearly. *Overseas associates* Dar Al-Fergiani, Cairo and Tripoli.

Darton, Longman & Todd Ltd
89 Lillie Road, London SW6 1UD   ☎01–385 2341

Chairman *Derek Stevens* (non executive)   **Managing Director** *Ronald Chopping*
                              Approximate Annual Turnover £1 million

Founded by Michael Longman, who broke away from Longman Green in 1959 when that publisher decided to stop its religious list. First major publication was the

Jerusalem Bible. On the death of Michael Longman in 1978, the company became a common ownership business. *Publishes* Christian books of all types. 42 titles in 1986.

Editorial Head *Miss L. J. Riddle*. TITLES *Jerusalem Bible; God of Surprises*. Unsolicited mss, synopses and ideas for books welcome.
Royalties paid twice yearly.

David & Charles Ltd
Brunel House, Forde Road, Newton Abbott, Devon TQ12 4PU ☎0626 61121
Telex 42904 BOOKS G

Chairman *David St John Thomas* **Approximate Annual Turnover** £4.5 million

FOUNDED 1960 as a specialist company. Still family controlled. *Major subsidiary* the Readers' Union Book Clubs for Enthusiasts. *Publishes* Practical: crafts, gardening, hobbies, travel; wide-ranging non-fiction. No fiction, poetry, memoirs or children's. 120 titles in 1986.

Editorial Head *Michael de Luca* TITLES *Knitting in Vogue; Sunday Times Travel Book; Great Days of the Country Railway; Complete Book of Microwave Cookery*. Unsolicited mss, synopses and ideas welcome. '*Authors' Guide*' available on receipt of a first class stamp.
Royalties paid annually; twice yearly in first two years on request.

Authors' Rating Strong name in leisure and hobby books but not seen as particularly helpful or friendly to authors. Go in with a tough agent. Readers' Union is among the leading non-fiction book clubs.

Christopher Davies
PO Box 403, Sketty, Swansea, West Glamorgan SA2 9BE ☎0792 48825

Managing Director *Christopher T. Davies*
Approximate Annual Turnover £100,000

The company was founded in 1949 to increase the output of Welsh language publications, and by the 1970s this had reached the level of over 50 titles a year. The drop in Welsh sales in that decade led to the establishment of a small English list, which has continued. The company now publishes around 6 Welsh language titles and 12 English titles annually. Plans are in hand to beef up its marketing and promotions. *Publishes* fiction, general, sport, biography, history, cookery and literature. 12 titles in 1986.

Editorial Head *Christopher Davies* TITLES *Guide to Rugby Union World Cup; Dylan Thomas's Places; Celtic Cookery; One Increasing Purpose – The UN Since 1945; English/Welsh Dictionaries*. Unsolicited mss welcome only if relevant to their field. Synopses and ideas for books welcome.
Royalties paid twice yearly.

Authors' Rating A small publisher with all the attendant problems of living up to authors' ambitions.

Debrett's Peerage Ltd
73–77 Britannia Road, London SW6 2JR   ☎01–736 6524/6

Chairman *Ian McCorquodale*   **Managing Director** *Geoffrey Fox*

FOUNDED 1769. Main publication *Debrett's Peerage* every five years. *Publishes* books on sporting subjects, etiquette, modern manners and correct form, royalty. Eight titles in 1986.

Publishing Manager *Kitty Hunter*   Welcome unsolicited mss and synopses. *Royalties* paid twice yearly.

Dennys Publications Ltd
2 Carthusian Street, London EC1M 6ED   ☎01–253 5421

Chairman *P. P. Maher*

FOUNDED 1976. Part of the Dennys Group. *Publishes* academic books.

Editorial Director *A. Maher*   TITLES *The Handbook of Mathematical Formulae For Scientists and Engineers*. Welcome unsolicited mss and synopses. *Royalty* payments vary from contract to contract.

J. M. Dent & Sons Ltd
33 Welbeck Street, London W1M 8LX   ☎01–486 7233

Chairman *V. F. Chamberlain*   **Managing Director** *Peter Shellard*

FOUNDED 1888. *Publishes* all kinds of books, except poetry, technical and scientific, law, business and accountancy. Best known for the *Everyman* list of classics. 100 titles in 1986.

DIVISIONS
Children's *Vanessa Hamilton*   Picture books in full colour: *The Boy With Two Shadows* Margaret Mahy; *There's An Alligator Under My Bed* Mercer Mayer; *Storm Bird* Elsie McCutcheon.   **Fiction** *Imogen Taylor*   TITLES *God, Spartacus and Miss Emily* Christopher Leach; *Do Lord Remember Me* Julius Lester.   **General** *Peter Shellard*   TITLES *The Stonehenge People* Aubrey Burl; *Power From the Earth* Thomas Gold; *That's Not What I Meant – How Conversational Style Makes or Breaks Your Relations With Others*.   **Music** *Malcolm Gerratt*   **Everyman** *Judy Tagg*   TITLES Fiction: *Stalin's Shoe* Zdena Tomin; *Seeing Things* Frances Thomas; Classics: *Travels In West Africa* Mary Kingsley.   **Phoenix House** *Bill Neill-Hall*   Recently revived hardback imprint publishing history, biography, literature, travel, sport, current affairs.   TITLES *The Englishman's Flora* Geoffrey Grigson; *Straight From the Bench* Judge James Pickles.   **Healthright** *Jocelyn Burton*   TITLES *The New Organic Food Guide*; *F For Fish*; *Holistic Living*. Unsolicited mss, synopses and ideas for books welcome.
Royalties paid twice yearly. *Overseas associates* J. M. Dent (Pty) Ltd, Australia.

Authors' Rating After floundering on a disastrously expensive encyclopaedia, Dent was refloated on a management buyout. Now all it needs is to re-establish its sense of direction.

André Deutsch

105–106 Great Russell Street, London WC1B 3LJ ☏ 01–580 2746
Telex 261026 ADLIB G

Chairmen and Managing Directors *André Deutsch, Tom Rosenthal*

FOUNDED by André Deutsch in 1950, the original list included *Books are Essential, To Live in Mankind* and *Jewish Cookery*. A major fiction list followed, with writers like V. S. Naipaul, Philip Roth and Norman Mailer. *Publishes* Adult fiction, general books (particularly history, politics, current affairs, biography), art, illustrated, photographic, children's picture books, fiction and non-fiction. 120 titles in 1986.

DIVISIONS
Adult *Diana Athill* AUTHORS John Updike, Paul Erdman, Penelope Lively, Carlos Fuentes, William Gaddis, Gore Vidal, Dan Jacobson, Gerald Priestland, Malcolm Bradbury, Dale Spender, Julian Critchley. **Children's** *Pam Royds* TITLES *Postman Pat; You're Thinking about Doughnuts; Different Friends; The Tooth Ball; The Story of a High Street; House Inside Out.* Unsolicited mss, synopses and ideas welcome.
Royalties paid twice yearly.

Authors' Rating An idiosyncratic publisher led by two notables who have firm ideas on what makes a good read. One of the best children's lists on the market. Ideas are taken seriously but do not expect a quick response or an open chequebook.

Diploma Press Ltd

76 Shoe Lane, London EC4A 3JB ☏ 01–583 8888

Have not published anything since 1981 and do not intend to publish anything in the immediate future.

Distropa Ltd

3 Henrietta Street, London WC2E 8LU ☏ 01–240 0856

BOOK IMPORTERS ONLY

Dobson Books Ltd

Brancepeth Castle, Durham DH7 8DF ☏ 0385 780628

Managing Director *Margaret Dobson*

Stopped publishing books two or three years ago and at present have no plans to recommence publishing.

Dolphin Book Co. Ltd

Tredwr, Llangrannog, Llandysul, Dyfed SA44 6BA ☎023978 404

Managing Director *Martin L. Gili* **Approximate Annual Turnover** £5000

FOUNDED 1957. A small publishing house specialising in Spanish and South American academic books. 1 title in 1986. TITLE *Mediaeval and Renaissance Studies in Honour of Robert Brian Tate* Ian Michael and Richard A. Cardwell. Unsolicited mss welcome but prefer them to be preceded by a letter.
Royalties paid annually.

John Donald Publishers Ltd

138 St Stephen Street, Edinburgh EH3 5AA ☎031–225 1146

Managing Director *Donald Morrison*

Publishes academic and scholarly, agriculture, archaeology, architecture and design, business and industry, economics, educational and textbooks, guide books, history and antiquarian, languages and linguistics, military, music, religious, sociology and anthropology, sports and games, transport. 30 titles in 1986.

Editorial Director *John Tuckwell* Unsolicited mss considered.
Royalties paid annually.

Downlander Publishing

88 Oxendean Gardens, Lower Willingdon, Eastbourne BN22 0RS ☎0323 505814

President *Nora Potter* MBE

Publishes Poetry. 10 titles in 1986. Downlander is a non-profit-making organisation aiming to bring poetry of real literary merit into print. Not vanity publishing, but a joint venture by the author and publisher, with any profits shared.

Editorial Director *Derek Bourne-Jones* Unsolicited mss not welcome. Preliminary letter with 5–10 poem sample and SAE essential.
No royalties.

Richard Drew Ltd

6 Clairmont Gardens, Glasgow G3 7LW ☎041–333 9341 Telex 777308

Managing Director *Richard Drew*

Publishes Fiction, general non-fiction, travel, children's books, Scottish books. Approximately 30 titles in 1986.

Editorial Head *Richard Drew*

IMPRINTS (Paperback & Hardback)
Businessmate French & German **The Scottish Collection** TITLES *The Lost Glen* Neil Gunn; *The Bull Calves* Naomi Mitchison. **Swallows** TITLES *The Flute in May-*

ferry Street Eileen Dunlop; *The White Nights of St Petersburg* Geoffrey Trease. **Travelmate** French & Italian. Welcome unsolicited mss and synopses/ideas for books.
Royalties paid twice yearly.

Gerald Duckworth & Co. Ltd
The Old Piano Factory, 43 Gloucester Crescent, London NW1 7DY
☎01–485 3484   Telex 896827 Tacs G

Managing Director *Colin Haycraft*

FOUNDED 1898. Authors on their early list included Hilaire Belloc, August Strindberg, Henry James and John Galsworthy. *Publishes* Mainly academic with some fiction. Approximately 50 titles in 1986.

Editorial Head *Colin Haycraft*   TITLES *Philoponus and the Rejection of Aristotelian Science* Richard Sorabji (editor); *Imperial Patient, The Memoirs of Nero's Doctor* Alex Comfort; *More Home Life* Alice Thomas Ellis; *The Good Book* Brian Redhead & Frances Gumley; *On Birth & Madness* Eric Rhode; *Men Change Too* Stuart Sutherland; *Good Retirement Guide 1988* Rosemary Brown; *Grammar of the Yiddish Language* David Katz.

PAPERBACK IMPRINT
Paperduck Welcome unsolicited mss and synopses/ideas for books.
Royalties paid twice yearly.

Authors' Rating A cosy publisher of the old school. Nice to know but lacking punch in the market place.

The Dunrod Press
8 Brown's Road, Newtonabbey, Co. Antrim BT36 8RN   ☎02313 2362

Managing Director *Ken Lindsay*

FOUNDED 1979. *Publishes* children's books, politics and world affairs. 6 titles in 1986.

Editorial Head *Ken Lindsay* Preliminary letter essential. Synopses and ideas for books welcome.
Royalties paid annually. *Overseas associates* The Dunrod Press, Irish Republic.

Ebury Press
Coloquhoun House, 27–37 Broadwick Street, London W1V 1FR   ☎01–439 7144
Telex 263879

Publishing Director *Roger Q. Barrett*
Approximate Annual Turnover £4.5 million

The book publishing imprint of the National Magazine Company. Founded in the early 1960s by Marcus Morris, and grew out of the successful range of Good House-keeping books. *Publishes* GH cookery and related homecraft subjects, health, beauty, photography, humour, crafts, gardening, natural history, biography, film.

Also publishes books linked in to the journals *Good Housekeeping, Cosmopolitan, Harpers & Queen, She, Country Living*. 54 titles in 1986.

Editorial Head *Roger Q. Barrett.*   TITLES *The Good Health Kit; The Better Pregnancy Diet; Quantum Carrot; Country Living Country Cook; Test Your Executive Skills; The Goldcrest File; Painting in Watercolour; The British Art and Antiques Directory 1987.* Unsolicited mss, synopses and ideas for books welcome.
Royalties paid twice yearly.

Economist Publications Ltd
40 Duke Street, London W1M 5DG   ☎01–493 6711

Managing Director *Hugo Meynell*
                              Approximate Annual Turnover (books) £500,000

Owned by *The Economist. Publishes* Business & industry, computer software (business), economics, educational and textbooks, finance, guide books, politics and world affairs, reference books. 6 titles in 1986.

Editorial director *Sarah Child* Unsolicited mss considered.
Royalties paid twice yearly.

Authors' Rating Powerful marketing via *The Economist* distribution network. Strong on direct sales.

Edinburgh University Press
22 George Square, Edinburgh EH8 9LT   ☎031–667 1011   Telex 727442 Unived

Publishes Academic & scholarly, archaeology, biology & zoology, computer science, history & antiquarian, Islamic studies, law, literature & criticism, music, philosophy, physics, religion & theology. 20 titles in 1986.

Would prefer to be approached with a letter or synopsis rather than unsolicited mss.
Royalties paid annually.

Authors' Rating One of the smaller university publishers drawing mainly on local talent.

Element Books Ltd
Longmead, Shaftesbury, Dorset SP7 8PL   ☎0747 51339

Chairman/Managing Director   *Michael Mann*
                              Approximate Annual Turnover £1.5 million

Founded by John Moore and Michael Mann in 1978. *Publish* 30 of their own titles annually, and in addition represent and distribute for over 60 publishers from the UK, USA, Australia and Europe, bringing the present list to over 700 titles. An increase of new titles to around 60 per year is anticipated. Fifteen titles in 1986. *Publishes* philosophy, mysticism, religion, art, psychology, complementary medicine and therapies, astrology and esoteric traditions.

DIVISIONS
Element Books Ltd *Michael Mann* **Broadcast Books Ltd** *Laura Sanderson*

IMPRINTS
Nadder Books *Michael Mann* Unsolicited mss, synopses and ideas for books welcome.
Royalties paid twice yearly.

Elliot Right Way Books
Kingswood Buildings, Lower Kingswood, Tadworth, Surrey KT20 6TD
☎0737 832202

Managing Director *Clive Elliot, Malcolm G. Elliot*

FOUNDED 1946 by Andrew G. Elliot. All the early books were entitled *The Right Way to . . .*, but this format became too restrictive. However, most books are still *How To* titles, instruction books illustrated with line drawings, published in **Paperfronts**. *Publishes How To* books on: cooking, motoring, car repairs, fishing, DIY, family health and fitness, looking after pets and horses, popular education, family financial and legal matters, quizzes, puzzles and jokes. 12 titles in 1986.

Paperfronts *Clive Elliot*
Unsolicited mss, synopses and ideas for books welcome.
Royalties paid annually.

Aidan Ellis Publishing Ltd
Cobb House, Nuffield, Henley-on-Thames, Oxon RG9 5RT
☎0491 641496   Telex 825751 JMDENT G

Chairman *Lucinda Ellis*   **Managing Director** *Aidan Ellis*
Approximate Annual Turnover £250,000

Publishes Fiction and general trade fiction. 12 titles in 1986.

Editorial Heads *Aidan Ellis, Lucinda Ellis* Unsolicited mss, synopses and ideas for books welcome.
Royalties paid twice yearly.

Elsevier Applied Science Publishers
Crown House, Linton Road, Barking, Essex IG11 8JU   ☎01–594 7272

Managing Director *Hans Gieskes*   **Parent company** **Elsevier Science Publishers, Amsterdam.**

Publishes Scientific and technical books. 90 titles in 1986.

DIVISIONS
Applied Biosciences *Norman Paskin*   **Applied Sciences** *Robert Lomax*

Welcome unsolicited mss and synopses/ideas for books.
Royalties paid annually.

Authors' Rating One of the two leading Dutch academic publishers and may soon reign alone if the bid for **Kluwer** comes off. Refreshingly honest with authors in the tradition of northern European publishers – early news on print-runs and sales and royalties paid promptly.

Elvendon Press
The Old Surgery, High Street, Goring on Thames, Reading RG8 9AW
☎0491 873003   Telex 849021

Founded nine years ago. *Publishes* food, drink, nutrition and cookery, but is branching out into other areas and will consider all general subjects except fiction. Also expanding its packaging operation. 10 titles in 1986.

Editorial Head *Mr R. Hurst* No unsolicited mss. Preliminary letter essential. Synopses and ideas for books welcome.

Enitharmon Press
22 Huntingdon Road, East Finchley, London N2 9DU   ☎01–883 8764

Chairman/Managing Director *Alan Clodd*

A one-man publishing house, founded in 1969. *Publishes* poetry and literature. Three titles in 1986.

TITLES *Selected Poems*, Frances Bellerby; *Selected Stories*, Frances Bellerby.

Do not welcome unsolicited mss or synopses.
Royalty payments vary according to contract.

Epworth Press
Room 195, 1 Central Buildings, Westminster, London SW1H 9NR
☎01–222 8010 ext. 234

Chairman *John Stacey*

Publishes Humour, philosophy, religion and theology. 10 titles in 1986, 12 in 1987.

Editorial Director *John Stacey*

IMPRINTS
Epworth Press   Cell Books Unsolicited mss considered.
Royalties paid annually.

Evans Brothers Ltd
2a Portman Mansions, Chiltern Street, London W1M 1LE   ☎01–935 7160
Telex 8811713 EVBOOK G

Managing Director *Stephen Pawley* **Approximate Annual Turnover** £2 million

Founded by Robert and Edward Evans in 1908. Originally published educational journals, books for primary schools and teacher education. But after rapid expansion into popular fiction and drama, both lists were sacrificed to a major programme of educational books for schools in East and West Africa. A new UK programme launched in 1986. *Publishes* UK children's and educational books; adult travel; educational books for Africa, Caribbean and Far East. 25 titles in 1986.

DIVISIONS
Overseas *F. J. Austin*   TITLES *Effective English for Junior/Secondary Schools*.   **UK Publishing** *F. J. Austin*   TITLES *Ready Steady Go; Foundations of Geography; Kenya – A Visitor's Guide*. Unsolicited mss, synopses and ideas for books welcome.
Royalties paid annually. *Overseas associates* Kenya, Hong Kong & Pacific. *Overseas associates* Evans Bros (Nigeria Publishers) Ltd.

Authors' Rating A company which has suffered more than most from the vagaries of African currencies. From being one of the leaders in educational publishing in the 1960s, Evans all but disappeared in the late 1970s. Now well on its way on the long haul back to prosperity but publishing mostly for overseas education.

Exley Publications
16 Chalk Hill, Watford, Hertfordshire WD1 4BN ☎0923 48328/50505

Managing Director *Richard Exley*

FOUNDED 1976. *Publishes* humour, gift books, general non-fiction. In 1988 will have a very substantial children's non-fiction list and cartoon list, with turnover forecast at £1 million. Fourteen titles in 1986.

Editorial Director *Helen Exley* Do not welcome unsolicited manuscripts but will consider synopses if accompanied by an s.a.e.

Authors' Rating On expansionist course; open to ideas.

Eyre & Spottiswoode (Publishers) Ltd
11 New Fetter Lane, London EC4P 4EE ☎01–583 9855

Chairman *Christopher Falkus*   **Managing Director** *A. Holder*

Parent Company **Associated Book Publishers** *Publishes* bibles, prayer books and religious books. No unsolicited mss. Will consider synopses/ideas for books.
Royalties paid twice yearly.

Authors' Rating *See* **Associated Book Publishers**.

Faber & Faber Ltd
3 Queen Street, London WC1N 3AU ☎01–278 6881   Telex 299633 Faber G

Chairman & Managing Director *Matthew Evans*

Geoffrey Faber and Richard de la Mare founded the company in the 1920s, with T. S. Eliot as an early recruit to the board. The original list was based on contemporary poetry and plays (the distinguished backlist includes Eliot, Auden and MacNeice). *Publishes* in addition to poetry and drama, art books, a children's list, fiction, nursing and medical, music, specialist cookery, and a growing number of miscellaneous one-offs. The new blood of recent years including Pete Townshend (of *The Who* fame) has led to Faber looking to new areas, though it remains in most respects deeply conservative, with hotspots of street-credibility.

Art *Giles de la Mare*   **Children's** *Phyllis Hunt*   AUTHORS Gene Kemp, Helen Cresswell, Errol le Cain.   **Cookery** *Rosemary Goad* Specialist titles only: *The Vegan Cookbook*; *The Student Cookbook*.   **Fiction** *Robert McCrum*   AUTHORS P. D. James, Lawrence Durrell, William Golding, Milan Kundera, Mario Vargas Llosa, Caryl Phillips, Rachel Ingalls.   **Music** *Patrick Carnegy*   **Nursing & Medical** *Paddy Downie* Specialist titles, and popular books; e.g. physiotherapy, general health.   **Plays** *Frank Pike* AUTHORS Samuel Beckett, David Hare, Sam Shepard, Tom Stoppard.   **Poetry** *Craig Raine, Chris Reid*   AUTHORS Seamus Heaney, Douglas Dunn, Tom Paulin. TITLES include the *Hard Lines* anthology of street poetry.   **Others** *Will Silkin*   TITLES *Not 1983/4 calendars*; *Tooth and Claw – Inside Spitting Image* (Entertainment); *The Hip-Hipsters, Jazz and the Beat Generation*; *Sex, Drink, and Fast Cars* (Street Culture). Unsolicited mss will be considered; synopses and ideas for books welcome.
Royalties paid twice yearly. *Overseas offices* Boston.

Authors' Rating Applause for one of the original signatories of the *Minimum Terms Agreement* (MTA). Heavily dependent on its dealings with the literary establishment, **Faber** is not in the game to lead fashion. Notwithstanding its much vaunted younger image, new ideas are still thin in the list. Writers who are not already big names are unlikely to be taken up unless their subjects are mainstream and uncontroversial. Excellent nursing and children's lists. Prompt payers.

Falling Wall Press Ltd

75 West Street, Old Market, Bristol, Avon BS2 0BX   ☎0272 559230

Managing Director *Jeremy Mulford*

FOUNDED 1971. *Publishes* non-fiction, politics, history, biography, autobiography. One title in 1986.

Editorial Director *Jeremy Mulford*   TITLES *The Disinherited Family* Eleanor Rathbone (with introductory essay by Suzie Fleming); *Wonderful Adventures of Mrs. Seacole in Many Lands*; *Black Women and the Peace Movement* Wilmette Brown; *Ask Any Woman – A London Enquiry into Rape and Sexual Assault*.

IMPRINT
Loxwood Stoneleigh   *Publishes* high quality new fiction and poetry.
Prefer to see synopses and ideas for books, plus s.a.e.
Royalties paid twice yearly for the first year and then annually.

Falmer Press
Rankine Road, Basingstoke, Hants RG24 0PR   ☎0256 840366   Telex 858540

Managing Director *Malcolm Clarkson*

Publishes Educational: books about education, educational materials for all levels. Largely commissioned.

Editorial Director *Malcolm Clarkson* Unsolicited mss considered.
Royalties paid annually.

Floris Books
21 Napier Road, Edinburgh EH10 5AZ   ☎031–337 2372

Managing Director *Christian Maclean*
                    Approximate Annual Turnover £120,000

A Christian community publishing house, previously trading as **Christian Community Press** from its inception in 1929 to the birth of **Floris Books** in 1977. *Publishes* books related to the Steiner movement, including religious, Christian community, history, science, social questions, arts & crafts, children's. 16 titles in 1986.

Editorial Head *Michael Jones*

IMPRINT
Floris Classics *Michael Jones* No unsolicited mss. Unsolicited synopses and ideas for books welcome.
Royalties paid annually.

Fountain Press Ltd
45 The Broadway, Tolworth, Surrey KT6 7DW   ☎01–390 7768   Telex 4107

Managing Director *Mr H. M. Ricketts*
                    Approximate Annual Turnover £1 million

FOUNDED 1923 when it was part of the Rowntree Trust Group. Owned by the **British Electric Traction Group** until four years ago when it was bought out by the present Managing Director. *Publishes* Architecture & design, British history, children's books, crafts & hobbies, do-it-yourself, medical, photography, veterinary. 15 titles in 1986.

TITLE *Photography Year Book*. Unsolicited mss and synopses are welcome.
Royalties paid twice yearly.

W. H. Freeman & Co. Ltd
20 Beaumont Street, Oxford OX1 2NQ   ☎0865 726975   Telex 83677

Chairman *Linda Chaput* (New York office)   **Managing Director** *Graham Voaden* (Oxford)

Part of **W. H. Freeman & Co., USA**. *Publishes* academic, agriculture, animal care and breeding, archaeology, biology and zoology, chemistry, cinema and video, cookery, wines and spirits, economics, educational and textbooks, engineering, gardening, geography and geology, mathematics and statistics, medical, natural history, photography, physics, politics and world affairs, psychology, sociology and anthropology, veterinary. 55 titles in 1986 (both UK and USA).

Editorial Office in New York (Oxford is a sales and marketing office only), but unsolicited mss can go through Graham Voaden, who filters out the obviously unsuitable and passes the rest on to America.
Royalties paid annually.

Samuel French Ltd

52 Fitzroy Street, London W1P 6JR   ☎01–387 9373

Chairman *M. A. Van Nostrand*   **Managing Director** *John L. Hughes*

The company was founded in 1830 with the object of acquiring acting rights and publishing plays. Part of Samuel French Inc., New York. *Publishes* Plays only. 50 titles in 1986.

Unsolicited mss welcome and should be addressed to The Performing Rights Department. No synopses or ideas.
Royalties paid twice yearly.

Authors' Rating Unlike some drama publishers which limit themselves to critically approved plays, Samuel French takes a more liberal view of what makes a publishable text. A boon to playwrights and amateur dramatic societies alike.

Ginn & Company Ltd

Prebendal House, Parson's Fee, Aylesbury, Bucks HP20 2QZ   ☎0296 88411
                                                        Telex 83535 GINN G

Chairman *Nicolas Thompson*   **Managing Director** *William Shepherd*
                                Approximate Annual Turnover £7 million

Part of the **Heinemann Group**. Though started in Boston, USA, in 1867, Ginn & Co. now has no US connections, except through the Heinemann Group, who acquired the company in 1978. *Publishes* Educational books for primary school and home use. 40 titles in 1986.

Editorial Head *Olga Norris* Almost all titles are commissioned. Unsolicited mss will not be considered. Synopses and ideas for books are welcome largely as a means of introduction to potential authors. *Royalties* paid annually. *Overseas* various agency and representative arrangements.

Authors' Rating With the decline of the *Janet and John* readers, Ginn was a sad little company when it was bought by Heinemann. It is now busily trying to re-establish its credentials in the educational market.

Mary Glasgow Publications Ltd

Avenue House, 131–133 Holland Park Avenue, London W11 4UT ☎01–603 4688

Managing Director *Alfred Waller*

Part of the **Wolters Samson Group**. Mary Glasgow founded **Mary Glasgow & Baker Ltd** in 1956 with the publication of her first French magazine, *Bonjour*. Her objective was to provide a service for teachers and learners of languages, aiming to make their work more effective and more enjoyable. The company changed its name in January 1970 and published under its present title. Apart from a regular output of magazines, there is a steadily growing list of main course, text and audio-visual materials not only in the area of foreign languages but also English, social studies, religious education and media studies. *Publishes* mainly language magazines, catalogues and books.

DIVISIONS
Books *Nick Hutchins* TITLES *Eclair*. **Magazines** *Neil Durham* TITLES *Bonjour*; *Hoy Dia*; *Das Rad*; *Catch*. No unsolicited mss. Will consider synopses/ideas for books.

GMP Publishers Ltd

PO Box 247, London N15 6RW   ☎01–800 5861

Managing Director *Aubrey Walter*

Publishes biography and autobiography, children's books, cookery, wine, fashion and costume, fiction, fine art and art history, guide books, health and beauty, history and antiquarian, humour, illustrated and fine editions, literature and criticism, photography, poetry, politics and world affairs, psychology, sociology and anthropology, theatre and drama, travel and topography, women's studies. Twenty-seven titles in 1986.

Editorial Director *Richard Diddle*

IMPRINTS
Heretic Books Unsolicited mss welcome.
Royalties paid twice yearly.

Golden Cockerel Press Ltd

25 Sicilian Avenue, London WC1A 2QH   ☎01–405 7979   Telex 23565

Chairman/Managing Director *Thomas Yoseloff*

Set up in London in 1980 to distribute the books published by its overseas associate company, Associated University Presses Inc., New Jersey, Golden Cockerel Press now acts as a full publishing house, with its own editorial function. *Publishes* Literary criticism, film, music, art, history, philosophy, Judaica, sociology, collecting, special interest. Approx. 100 titles in 1986.

Editorial Head *Sarah Manson*

IMPRINTS
AUP member presses include **Fairleigh Dickinson, Bucknell, Delaware, Folger Shakespeare Library.** *Publishes* scholarly, academic. **Cornwall books** *Publishes* trade hardbacks. Unsolicited mss, synopses and ideas for books welcome.
Royalties paid annually.

Victor Gollancz Ltd
14 Henrietta Street, London WC2E 8QJ ☎01–836 2006   Telex 265003

Chairman *Livia Gollancz*   **Managing Director** *Stephen Bray*

Founded as a general publishing company by Victor Gollancz in 1928, and famous for its political books during the 1930s and 1940s (Left Book Club). It has continued as an independent company ever since. *Publishes* general fiction, science fiction, music, children's, detective stories and thrillers, natural history, mountaineering, current affairs, sociology, travel, biography and memoirs, history.

DIVISIONS
Children's *Chris Kloet* **Fiction** *Joanna Goldsworthy* TITLES *Summit* D. M. Thomas, *Investing the Abbots and Other Stories* Sue Miller, *Bluff* Jeremy Leland, *Deception* Joan Aitken, *In the Middle of the Wood* Iain Crichton Smith **Music and Mountaineering** *Livia Gollancz* **Non-fiction** *David Burnetts* TITLES *Onassis and Christina* L. J. Davis, *The Dali Scandal* Mark Rogerson, *Marilyn* Gloria Steinem, *A Book of Sausages* Hippisley Coxe, *Historic Towns of South East England* David Lloyd, *Stravinsky* André Boucourechliev **Paperbacks** *Liz Knights* **Science Fiction** *Malcolm Edwards* **Thrillers** *Julia Wisdom* Prefer typescripts to be preceded by descriptive letter. Unsolicited synopses and ideas for books welcome.
Royalties paid twice yearly.

Authors' Rating Until recently, thought to be too closely tied to the eccentric ideals of their founder. But the old-fashioned image is fast disappearing and authors are even reporting (with some surprise) acceptable advances.

Gordon & Breach Science Publishers
1 Bedford Street, London WC2E 9PP ☎01–836 5125   Telex 23258 SCIPUB G

Managing Director *Alan Davies*

FOUNDED 1962. *Publishes* science with a number of music and dance titles.

IMPRINT
Harwood Academic Publishers *Publishes* science books. Welcomes unsolicited mss and synopses.
Royalties paid annually. *Overseas office* **Gordon & Breach Science Publishers Inc.,** New York.

Authors' Rating Had troubles in the late seventies. Now keeping a lowish profile. Apparently unable to say how many titles published last year.

Gowan Publishing Ltd

24 Freemount Drive, Beechdale, Nottingham NG8 3GL   ☎0602 292995

Managing Director *Joan Wallace*

FOUNDED 1983, initially to help and encourage new writers. *Publishes* Fiction. Particularly interested in showbiz books, both fiction and non-fiction. Published 3 books since 1983.

Editorial Head *Joan Wallace*   TITLES *Independent Street At War* Joan Wallace. Welcome synopses and ideas for books.
Royalties 'not applicable'.

Gower Publishing Group Ltd

Gower House, Croft Road, Aldershot, Hampshire GU11 3HR   ☎0252 331551
Telex 858001

Chairman/Managing Director *Nigel Farrow*

Founded 1967 by Nigel Farrow, formerly of Academic Press. *Publishes* Professional and academic books in business, social sciences, the professions, the humanities, and technology. 250 titles in 1986.

DIVISIONS
Avebury Press *John Irwin* Research monographs on the social sciences.   **Gower** *Malcolm Stern* Business, professional and academic books and journals.   **Scolar** *James Price* Quality produced hardbacks on art, architecture, books and illustration, cinema/photography, music, history, biography, literature, medieval studies, social sciences.   **Technical Press** *John Hindley*   TITLES *The Applied Information Technology Series; Chemical Synonyms and Trade Names.*   **Temple-Smith** *John Irwin* General academic books on political and social issues, economics, sociology, history and the environment.   **Wildwood House** *John Irwin* The paperback imprint of the group. Unsolicited mss welcome. Unsolicited synopses and ideas for books considered.
Royalties paid as per contract. *Overseas associates* USA, Australia, Hong Kong, Singapore.

Authors' Rating Growing fast in that hazy but obviously profitable area extending from academic to quality non-fiction for the general reader.

Grafton Books Ltd

8 Grafton Street, London W1X 3LA   ☎01–493 7070   Telex 25611

Chairman *F. I. Chapman*   **Managing Director** *Jonathan Lloyd*

Part of Collins. Formerly known as **Granada Publishing**, the company was sold by Granada Television in 1983. Name changed to **Grafton Books** in 1985. *Publishes* general trade hardbacks, fiction, non-fiction, paperbacks, sailing books. 364 titles in 1986.

DIVISIONS

Grafton Hardbacks *John Boothe* TITLES Non-fiction: *The English: A Social History 1066–1945; The Punch Book of Health; Tycoon – The Life of James Goldsmith; Without Conscience – Charles Manson in His Own Words; Alan Sillitoe's Nottinghamshire; The Value of Dreams.* Fiction: *Shah* Eric Van Lustbader; *Reckoning* Michael Pye; *The Seventh Sanctuary* Daniel Easterman; *Act of Will* Barbara Taylor Bradford.   **Grafton Paperbacks** *Nick Austin* TITLES Non-fiction: *Punch* books; *The Complete Upmanship; The Genius of the Place; Turner; AIDS The Story of a Disease; A Dictionary of Superstitions; Eating for Health; The Cuisine of Paul Bocuse; Britain's Heritage.* Fiction: *Daggerspell* Katherine Kerr; *The Dalkey Archive* Flann O'Brien; *Woman of Substance* Barbara Taylor Bradford; *Spider World – The Tower* Colin Wilson; also books by Arthur C. Clarke, Ray Bradbury, William Goldman, Robert Ludlum.   **Adlard Coles** *Janet Murphy*   *Publishes* sailing books on technical, instructional, building and design, and travel subjects.   **Paladin** *Nick Austin.* Accepts unsolicited mss. Welcomes synopses and ideas for books.

Royalties paid twice yearly. *Overseas associates* see **Collins**.

Authors' Rating Tightly organised, commercially sharp company not given to oversensitive relationships with authors. Healthy rewards for those who can stand the pace.

Graham Cameron Publishing

10 Church Street, Willingham, Cambridge CB4 5HT   ☎0954 60444

Editorial Director *Mike Graham-Cameron*   **Art Director** *Helen Graham-Cameron*

FOUNDED 1984 mainly as a packaging operation. *Publishes* books for children and for institutional and business customers. Also publishes biography, social history and educational materials. 10 titles in 1986, of which 8 were packaged.   TITLES *Up From the Country* (children's); *Anglo-Saxon Households* (educational); *In All Directions* (biography). Unsolicited synopses and ideas welcome.

Royalties paid annually.

Graham & Trotman Ltd

Sterling House, 66 Wilton Road, London SW1V 1DE   ☎01–821 1123
                                                     Telex 298878 GRAMCO G

Chairman *Dr F. W. B. van Eysinga*   **Managing Director** *Alastair M. W. Graham*

FOUNDED 1974. Part of the **Kluwer UK Group** from 1986. *Publishes* books, looseleaf directories and journals, international business finance, law, earth sciences and environmental sciences. There are plans to increase output. 50 titles in 1986.

DIVISIONS

Business *A. M. W. Graham*   **Law** *A. M. W. Graham*   **Technical** *D. N. Smith* Unsolicited mss, synopses and ideas for books welcome.

Royalties paid twice yearly. *Overseas sister company* **Kluwer Inc.**, Boston.

Granville Publishing

102 Islington High Street, London N1 8EG ☎ 01–226 2904

Managing Director *John Murray-Brown*

Approximate Annual Turnover 'very small'

FOUNDED 1983. Part of a bookshop. *Publishes* literature reprints.

TITLES *The Future in America* H. G. Wells; *The American Scene* Henry James. Do not welcome unsolicited material.

Gresham Books

PO Box 61, Henley-on-Thames, Oxon RG9 3LQ ☎ 073522 3789

Managing Director *Mary V. Green*   **Approximate Annual Turnover** £80,000

Bought by Mary Green in 1980 from **Martins Publishing Group**. A small specialist one-woman publishing house. *Publishes* Hymn and service books for schools; *The Headmasters' Conference Hymnbook*. No unsolicited material or ideas. Only deals with schools and music publishers.

Grevatt & Grevatt

9 Rectory Drive, Newcastle-upon-Tyne NE3 1XT

Chairman *Dr S. Y. Killingley*

Part time business started in 1981 as an alternative publisher of works not normally commercially viable. Authors waive royalties on the first 500 copies. Three books have appeared with financial backing from professional bodies. *Publishes* Academic books, especially on language, linguistics and religious studies. Some poetry.

Editorial Head *Dr S. Y. Killingley* No unsolicited mss. Synopses and ideas should be accompanied by an s.a.e.
Royalties annually after the initial 500 copies.

Authors' Rating Since print runs rarely exceed 500 copies, the prospect of making money is far outweighed by the probability of spending it.

Grosvenor Books

54 Lyford Road, Wandsworth, London SW18 3JJ ☎ 01–870 2124

Managing Director *J. H. V. Nowell*

FOUNDED 1967. Part of **The Good Road Ltd**. Publishers for Moral Rearmament. *Publishes* books on contemporary issues, biographies, religious, educational and children's books. 10 titles in 1986.

TITLES *Listen for a Change*; *Making Marriage Work* Annejet Campbell; *For the Love of Tomorrow* Jacqueline Piguet; *A Different Accent* Michael Henderson; *The Return of the Indian Spirit* Phyllis Johnson. Do not welcome unsolicited mss but will consider synopses.

Royalties paid twice yearly. *Overseas associates* in Australia, New Zealand, USA, Canada.

Grotius Publications

PO Box 115, Cambridge CB3 9BP ☎0223 311032

Managing Director *C. J. Daly*

FOUNDED 1979 for the publication of the International Law Report and other related titles in the international law sphere. Approximately 20 titles in 1986.

Editorial Director *S. R. Pirrie* TITLES *The International Law Reports* E. Lauterpacht QC (editor); *International Law* Dr Shaw; *The International Wildlife Law* Simon Lyster. Welcome unsolicited mss and synopses/ideas for books if within the specialist framework.
Royalties paid annually.

Guinness Superlatives Ltd

33 London Road, Enfield, Middlesex EN2 6DJ ☎01–367 4567 Telex 23573

Chairman *Shaun Dowling* **Managing Director** *David F. Hoy*
Approximate Annual Turnover £4 million

FOUNDED 1954 to publish *The Guinness Book of Records*, now the highest selling copyright book in the world, published in 26 languages. In the late 1960s, the company set about expanding its list with a wider range of titles, mostly linked to records and record breaking. 30 titles in 1986.

Editorial Director *Michael Stephenson* TITLES *The Guinness Book of Records*; *British Hit Singles*; *Trivial Pursuit* (the book). Welcome ideas and synopses for books if they come within their publishing field.
Royalties paid quarterly.

Authors' Rating Any idea must seem inferior to the first book – in itself a record breaker. However the company does want to broaden its base and it has the resources to achieve its aim.

Peter Haddock Ltd

Pinfold Lane, Bridlington, E. Yorkshire YO9 5BT ☎0262 678121

Managing Director *Peter Haddock*

FOUNDED 1952. *Publishes* Children's picture story books, activity books. Published 120 series in 1986. Welcomes ideas for picture books.
Royalty payments vary according to contract.

Authors' Rating Cheap end of the market. Authors need to work very fast to make a living.

Robert Hale Ltd

Clerkenwell House, 45–47 Clerkenwell Green, London EC1R 0HT ☎01–251 2661

Chairman and Managing Director *John Hale*

FOUNDED 1936, and still a family company. *Publishes* most types of adult fiction; every kind of adult non-fiction, excluding specialist areas (such as educational/legal/medical and scientific). 405 titles in 1986.

Editorial Director *Carmel Elwell* TITLES Non-fiction: *Elvis in Private*, Peter Haining; *The People in Britain*, Roy Kerridge; *Psychic Animals*, Dennis Bardens. Fiction: *A Demon Close Behind*, Leslie Halliwell; *Nothing Larger Than Life*, David Holbrook; *Never Laugh at Love*, Barbara Cartland; *Personal Relations*, Pamela Street. Unsolicited mss, synopses and ideas for books welcome.
Royalties paid twice yearly.

Authors' Rating A publisher which believes in good communications and generally takes trouble with its authors. But tough in negotiations on advances.

The Hambledon Press

102 Gloucester Avenue, London NW1 8HX ☎01–586 0817

Chairman/Managing Director *Martin Sheppard*
Approximate Annual Turnover £120,000

FOUNDED 1980 when cricket books were top of the list. These have now been dropped. *Publishes* Academic history, some academic literature; history – English and European post classical to modern. 10–15 titles annually.

Editorial Head *Martin Sheppard* TITLES *Studies in Medieval Thought from Abelard to Wycliff* Beryl Smalley. No unsolicited mss. Preliminary letter. Synopses and ideas for books welcome.
Royalties paid annually. *Overseas associates* The Hambledon Press (USA), West Virginia.

Hamilton House

17 Staveley Way, Brixworth Industrial Estate, Northampton NN6 9EL ☎0604 881889

Chairman and Managing Director *Tony Attwood*
Approximate Annual Turnover £400,000

FOUNDED 1979 BOOK PACKAGER. Often works in collaboration with inexperienced authors, repackaging material, clearing copyright, etc., before selling the infant product on. *Publishes* business, employment, careers. Also book packagers for educational (secondary school), TV and radio tie-ins, directory and diary titles. 10 titles in 1986.

DIVISIONS
Careerscope *Tony Attwood* TITLES *Careers in Radio*. **Lifescope** *Tony Attwood*

TITLES *Into Business*. Letter first. Mss should enclose s.a.e., return postage. Synopses and ideas for books also considered if accompanied by s.a.e.
Royalties paid annually.

Hamish Hamilton Ltd
27 Wright's Lane, London W8 5TZ   ☎01–928 3388   Telex 917181

Managing Director *Christopher Sinclair-Stevenson*
Approximate Annual Turnover £6.5 million

FOUNDED 1931, subsequently bought by the Thomson Organisation and taken over by Penguin in 1985. *Publishes* fiction, biography, history, politics, travel, language and literature, Africana and natural history, current affairs, children's books. 253 titles in 1986.

DIVISIONS
Elm Tree *Penny Hoare*   AUTHORS Philip Norman, Les Dawson, Val Doonican, Roger Phillips.   **Hamish Hamilton** *Penny Hoare*   AUTHORS Peter Ackroyd, William Boyd, Paul Theroux, Brigid Brophy, Jennifer Johnston, Ed McBain.   **Hamish Hamilton Children's** *Jane Nissen*   AUTHORS Raymond Briggs, Eric Carle, Joan Lingard, Mollie Hunter.

IMPRINTS
Hamish Hamilton Trade Paperbacks *Penny Hoare*   AUTHORS Harold Acton, Nancy Mitford, Kenneth Clark, Sir Peter Hall, Marina Warner. Unsolicited mss and synopses/ideas for books welcome.
Royalties paid twice yearly. *Overseas associates* as **Penguin**.

Authors' Rating One of the best of the general publishers and they know it. With many highly marketable names among its authors, editors can afford to pick and choose from the newcomers. Do not expect a quick response to correspondence. Exciting children's list.

The Hamlyn Publishing Group
Bridge House, 69 London Road, Twickenham, Middx TW1 3SB
☎01–891 6261/6271   Telex Plesbk 256 50

Chairman *Paul Hamlyn*   **Managing Director** *David Blunt*
Approximate Annual Turnover £20 million

Founded by Paul Hamlyn 1984, and is today part of the **Octopus Publishing Group**. As a major illustrated popular reference and information publisher, Hamlyn have a worldwide reputation for quality and value. The current list includes more than 840 titles. *Publishes* Children's, reference, general interest, atlases, gardening, aviation & military history, sport, natural history, cookery. 200 titles in 1986.

DIVISIONS
Children's *Derek Hall*   TITLES *All-Colour Animal Encyclopedia; Treasury of Literature for Children; Giant World Atlas; Richard Scarry Books; Tell Me Why Series;*

My Biggest Bedtime Book Ever; Little Bear Series; Enid Blyton titles; *Pop-up Books.* **General Interest/Atlas & Reference** *Andrew Branson* TITLES *Country Life Book of Castles & Houses; Michelin Motoring Atlas of France; Ordnance Survey Motoring Atlas; The Concorde Story; Country Life Guides; Marilyn Monroe; The Official James Bond Movie Book; Scottish Clans & Tartans; Encyclopedia of Golf; The Cambridge Atlas of Astronomy; The Amateur Photographer's Handbook; Practical Astrologer; You and the Law.* **Home Interest** *Frances Naldrett* TITLES *Hamlyn All Colour Cookbook; The Seafish Cookbook; The Complete Book of Microwave Cookery; Women's London; Woman; Knitted Toys; Modern Art of Flower Arranging; The Organic Garden.*

PAPERBACK IMPRINTS
Collingridge   Country Life   Dean & Son   Temple Press No unsolicited mss but welcome unsolicited synopses and ideas for books.
Royalties paid twice yearly.

Authors' Rating Scc Octopus.

Harcourt Brace Jovanovich Ltd
24–28 Oval Road, London NW1 7DX   ☎01–267 4466
Managing Director *Joan Fujimoto*

Harcourt Brace Jovanovich Inc., New York, owns **Academic Press** (see separate listing). *Publishes* academic, accountancy and taxation, archaeology, biology/ zoology, business and industry, chemistry, children's, cinema and video, computer science and business software, economics, educational and textbooks, EFL, fiction fine art, geography and geology, history, antiquarian, languages and linguistics, law, literature and criticism, mathematics and statistics, medical, music, philosophy, physics, poetry, politics, psychology, religious, sociology and anthropology, theatre and drama, training and careers, women's studies. Sixty-eight titles in 1985.

Editorial Director *Peter Brown* Unsolicited mss welcome.
Royalties paid twice yearly.

Harper & Row Ltd
28 Tavistock Street, London WC2E 7PN   ☎01–836 4635/379 3237
Managing Director *Paul R. Chapman*

Publishes non-fiction, academic, religious, professional, medical and nursing books. Five hundred titles in 1986 (450 of these American). Unsolicited mss and synopses welcome in academic and nursing subjects only.
Royalties paid twice yearly.

Harrap Ltd

19–23 Ludgate Hill, London EC4M 7PD ☎01–248 6444   Telex 28673 CONSOL G

Chairman *N. W. Berry*   **Managing Director** *Eric R. Dobby*

Part of the **Harrap Columbus Group**. *Publishes* Biography & autobiography, cinema & video, cookery, wines & spirits, crime, costume, fine art & art history, guide books, history & antiquarian, humour, illustrated and fine editions, magic & the occult, military & war, photography, political & world affairs, reference books & dictionaries, sports & games, theatre & drama, travel & topography. 145 titles in 1986.

DIVISIONS

Columbus Books *Gill Rowley* (see separate entry)   **Harrap** *Derek Johns*   TITLES Biography & Memoirs: *Rosa Luxemburg* Elzbieta Ettinger; Astronomy: *TV Astronomer* Patrick Moore; The Occult: *The Encyclopedia of Unsolved Mysteries* Colin Wilson; Photography: *Perspectives* Don McCullin; General: *Backstage* Judith Cook; Dictionaries: *Harrap's Paperback French–English Dictionary*.   **Impact Books** *Jean Luc Barbanneau*   TITLES *Wiltshire Village* Heather and Robin Tanner; *College On a Shoestring* Eve Luddington; *It's Never Too Late . . .* Joan Perkin.   **Threshold Books Ltd**   TITLES *Priceless* Virginia Leng; *Long Distance Riding* Marion Eason; *Pick Your Own Cookbook* Ann Nicol. Unsolicited mss and synopses welcome.
Royalties paid twice yearly.

Authors' Rating Strong on language teaching and reference books but otherwise has an old-fashioned feel.

The Harvester Press Ltd

16 Ship Street, Brighton, East Sussex BN1 1AD   ☎0273 723031   Telex 877101

Chairman/Managing Director *John Spiers*

Approximate Annual Turnover £3 million

FOUNDED 1970, and since then have published nearly 1300 titles and 12 million pages of microform. The majority of their titles are co-published with American publishers. Best sellers have included J. L. Carr's *A Month In the Country* – short-listed for the Booker Prize, and Hofstadter's Pulitzer prize-winning *Godel, Escher, Bach: The Eternal Golden Braid*. Current major projects include the *Key Women Writers* series. The company has no shareholders (externally at least) and the group is still owned by its founder, John Spiers. **Harvester** *publishes* quality fiction, philosophy, psychology, literature, women's studies, and reference in these subjects. **Wheatsheaf** *publishes* economics, politics, defence & strategic studies, Soviet studies, women's studies & reference books in these subjects. **Harvester microform** *publishes* rare printed sources and archival collections. 110 titles in 1986.

IMPRINTS

Harvester Press *John Spiers*   TITLES *Philosophers in Context: Aristotle; New Readings: George Eliot; Descartes' Dream: the world according to Mathematics;* Fiction: *Sense and Sensuality* by Rosalind Brackenbury.   **Microform** *William Pidduck*

TITLES *Music Manuscripts from Great English Collections*; *Modern America: Key Archival Collections for Teaching and Research*; *The Condition of England 1800–1900*; *Eighteenth Century: English Provincial Newspapers*. **Wheatsheaf Books** *John Spiers* TITLES *Capitalism, Competition, and Economic Crisis*; *Mesoeconomics: A Micro–Macro Analysis*; *The Making of Modern Society*; *The Economics of Business Enterprise*; *How Democracies Perish*; *Women in Western Political Philosophy*; *The New Right: The Counter-Revolution in Political Economic and Social Thought*. Unsolicited mss will be considered if include return postage; letters of enquiry with synopses are preferred.
Royalties paid twice yearly.

Authors' Rating Success story of a small publisher growing up. Started with reprints for academic libraries in the days when education budgets were flush. Reputation for tough contracts.

Haynes Publishing Group
Sparkford, nr Yeovil, Somerset BA22 7JJ ☎ 0963 40635   Telex 46212 HAYNES G

Chairman *John H. Haynes*   **Managing Director** *Jim Scott*
Approximate Annual Turnover £8.5 million

FOUNDED 1960 by John H. Haynes. In the mid-sixties produced the first *Owners' Workshop Manual*, now the mainstay of the programme. A family run business which does its own typesetting and printing on the premises. *Publishes* DIY Workshop Manuals for cars and motorbikes. Now branching out into wider areas but keeping a strong bias towards motoring and transport. 104 titles in 1986.

IMPRINTS
G. T. Foulis & Co. Ltd *R. Grainger* Cars and motoring-related books.   **J. H. Haynes & Co. Ltd** *J. R. Clew and P. Ward*   **Oxford Illustrated Press** *Jane Marshall* General titles: photography; sports & games; gardening; travel and guide books.   **Oxford Publishing Company** *R. Grainger* Railway titles. Welcome unsolicited mss if they come within the subject areas covered.
Royalties paid annually. *Overseas associates* Haynes Publications Inc., California, USA.

Headline Publishing Ltd
Headline House, 79 Great Titchfield Street, London W1P 7FN   ☎ 01–631 1687
Telex 268326 HEADLN G

Managing Director Tim Hely-Hutchinson

Set up in July 1986 by Tim Hely-Hutchinson, Sue Fletcher and Sian Thomas, and specialising in commercial fiction. *Publishes* fiction and non-fiction (hardback and paperback).

Editorial Director *Sue Fletcher* TITLES *The Hermit of Eyton Forest*, Ellis Peters; *Regrets Only*, Sally Quinn. Welcome unsolicited mss and synopses.
Royalties paid twice yearly.

Authors' Rating One of three major newcomers to the UK publishing scene – and the only one to embrace both hardcovers and paperbacks. Started well with authors by accepting Minimum Terms Agreement. Hope to publish some 20 titles in 1987, and 50 titles in 1988.

Heinemann Educational Books Ltd

22 Bedford Square, London WC1B 3HH ☎01–637 3311 Telex 261888 Hebldn G

Chairman *Nicolas Thompson*   **Managing Director** *David Fothergill*

Parent Company **The Heinemann Publishing Group Ltd**, owned by **The Octopus Publishing Group plc**. Founded 25 years ago having broken away from **William Heinemann Ltd**. *Publishes* Atlases & maps, computer software (educational), educational & textbooks, English as a foreign language, African writers series, Caribbean writers series. 250 titles in 1986.

DIVISIONS
English Language Teaching *Mike Esplen*   **Schools Publishing** *Bob Osborne*   **Science & Maths** *Stephen Ashton*   **English** *Jill Evans*   **Humanities** *Janice Brown*   **African & Caribbean** *Vicky Unwin*   **Medical** *Richard Barling*

TITLES *The Windmill School Library, Scottish Primary Maths, Sunshine, Encounters and Exchanges, Snap.* Unsolicited mss welcome and synopses/ideas for books.
Royalties paid twice yearly. *Overseas associates* same as for **William Heinemann**.

Authors' Rating See Octopus.

William Heinemann Ltd

10 Upper Grosvenor Street, London W1X 9PA*   ☎01–493 4141
Telex 8954961 Whl   Fax 01–629 0067

Chairman *Nicolas Thompson*   **Managing Director** *Brian Perman*

FOUNDED 1890 by William Heinemann, whose policy of publishing a broad range of literary and popular fiction, non-fiction, children's, illustrated and information books has, despite many changes and the development of specialised divisions of the list, remained the characteristic publishing style. In 1985 the Heinemann Group became part of the **Octopus Publishing Group**. *Publishes* Adult fiction and general non-fiction, children's, self-tuitional, business, management and professional, sport and leisure, popular psychology, inspirational. 155 titles in 1986.

DIVISIONS
Fiction & General *Fanny Blake*   TITLES *Rage* Wilbur Smith, *The Parson's Daughter* Catherine Cookson, *Hollywood Husbands* Jackie Collins, *Secret Service* Christopher Andrew, *Pocket Money* Gordon Burn.   **Children's Books** *Ingrid Selberg*   TITLES *The Jolly Postman, Where's The Spot?*   **The Kingswood Press** *Derek Wyatt*   TITLES *Cricket XXXX Cricket, Kitty Godfree, Eamonn McCabe: Photographer.*   **Business & Professional** *Kathryn Grant*   TITLES *The Frontiers of Management, Escoffier's Guide Culinaire.*   **Heinemann/Newnes (Technical)** *Peter Dixon*   TITLES *Newnes Elec-*

tronics Pocket Book. **Vocational Books** *Anne Martin* TITLES *The Complete Computer Servicing Book.* **Technical, Textbooks and Reference** *Bridget Buckley* TITLES *Communications Satellites and Higher Electrical Technology.*

PAPERBACK IMPRINTS

Cedar Books *Margot Richardson* TITLES *How To Win Friends and Influence People, The Power of Positive Thinking, How To Succeed in Selling.* **Made Simple** *Doug Fox* TITLES *Education Made Simple, Music Made Simple, Politics Made Simple.* Unsolicited mss, if preceded by a preliminary enquiry, and synopses and ideas for books welcome.

Royalties paid twice yearly. *Overseas subsidiaries* **Heinemann Books Australia (Pty)**, 85 Abinger Street, Richmond 3121, Victoria, Australia; **Heinemann Publishers (NZ) Ltd**, PO Box 36064, Auckland 9, New Zealand; **Heinemann Publishers Southern Africa (Pty)**, PO Box 61581, Marshalltown 2107, Johannesburg, RSA.

Authors' Rating See Octopus.

The Herbert Press Ltd

46 Northchurch Road, London N1 4EJ ☎01–254 4379　Telex 8952022

Managing Director *David Herbert*

Publishes archaeology, architecture and design, biography and autobiography, crafts and hobbies, fashion and costume, fine art and art history, natural history, photography, travel and topography. Nine titles in 1986.

Editorial Director *David Herbert* Unsolicited mss welcome.
Royalties paid twice yearly.

G. W. & A. Hesketh

PO Box 8, Ormskirk, Lancs L39 5HH ☎0695 422227

Chairman *Gordon Hesketh*　　　**Approximate Annual Turnover** £90,000

Founded to publish history, social science and humanities titles, the company expanded in 1986 to include a new division (**Cronos**) and in-house typesetting facilities. *Publishes* History, social science, geography and general interest. 7 titles in 1987.

DIVISIONS

G. W. & A. Hesketh *Dr Gordon Hesketh* TITLES *Politics of Class; Pioneers of Pre-History; Hypnosis – The Entrancing Art.* **Cronos Software** *Dr Gordon Hesketh* TITLES *Maths Trek; Sigma; Accounting Part 1; Weather Station.* Unsolicited mss, synopses and ideas for books welcome.
Royalties paid annually. *Editorial office overseas* California.

---

* New address for both **Heinemann & Octopus** from early 1988 will be Michelin House, 81 Fulham Road, London SW3.

Hobsons Ltd

Bateman Street, Cambridge, CB2 1LZ ☎0223 354551 Telex 81546 HOBCAM

Managing Director *A. A. Bridgewater*

Approximate Annual Turnover £3.7 million

Founded by Adrian Bridgewater in 1973, went public in 1986. *Publishes* textbooks, career guides, computer software; particularly successful in the directories market, with advertisements giving job information to school children/leavers. Financially supported by its consultancy work for employers and the government. 49 titles in 1986.

Editorial Head *Julie Horne*

Authors' Rating After modest beginnings, **Hobsons'** recent success is based on a shrewd analysis of the education and business markets.

Hodder & Stoughton Ltd

47 Bedford Square, London WC1B 3DP (editorial office) ☎01–636 9851
Telex 885887

Chairman/Managing Director *Philip Attenborough*

Approximate Annual Turnover £53 million

FOUNDED 1868. An independent company which engages in a diverse range of publishing. *Publishes* fiction, non-fiction, children's books, religious, academic, medical. Also paperbacks – see imprints list below. 800 titles in 1986.

Publishing Director *Michael Attenborough*

DIVISIONS
Children's *David Grant* AUTHORS R. Goscinny/A. Uderzo (Asterix), Eric Carle. **Educational** Now fully merged with Edward Arnold – see below. **General** *Eric Major/Ion Trewin* AUTHORS John le Carré, Jeffrey Archer, James Clavell, Thomas Keneally, Morris West, Mary Stewart. **New English Library** *Clare Bristow* AUTHORS Stephen King, Harold Robbins. **Religious** *David Wavre* AUTHORS Catherine Marshall, John Wimber, Michael Green (also publish the NIV Bible).

IMPRINTS
Coronet Books **Edward Arnold** *Anthony Hamilton* (Managing Director) Brian Steven (ed. school books) *John Wallace* (ed. tertiary publishing). *Publishes* secondary education, further education, Teach Yourself Series, colleges of education books, medical, ELT. **Knight Books** *Elizabeth Roy* AUTHORS as for Children's list. **Sceptre** *Ian Chapman* AUTHORS as for General/New English Library lists. Hodder & Stoughton actively discourage the submission of unsolicited mss, though 'the company is very willing to assess synopses and sample chapters'.
Royalties paid twice yearly. *Overseas associates* Australia, New Zealand and a widespread network of other overseas companies and agencies.

Authors' Rating A paternalistic reputation but renowned for loyalty to authors.

There is a heartening story of Philip Attenborough's shocked surprise and angry rejection of a suggestion by a fellow publisher that if booksellers are late in paying, authors should wait for their royalties.

Holmes McDougall Ltd

Allander House, 137–141 Leith Walk, Edinburgh EH6 8NS   ☎031–554 9444

Telex 727508 Holmes G

Managing Director *F. J. Baillie*   **Approximate Annual Turnover** £1.5 million

FOUNDED 1962. *Publishes* educational and textbooks (primary & secondary). Twenty-five titles in 1986.

Editorial Director *E. Ketley*   **Senior Commissioning Editor** *M. G. Watson* TITLES *Schools Council History; Link-Up Reading Scheme.* Welcome unsolicited manuscripts and synopses.
Royalties paid twice yearly.

Holt Rinehart & Winston

24–28 Oval Road, London NW1 7DX   ☎01–267 4466

Owned by **CBS Inc.**, USA, until bought by **Academic Press** in 1987. *Publishes* academic, accountancy and taxation, biology and zoology, business and industry, chemistry, computer science, computer software (business and educational), economic, educational and textbooks, engineering, languages and linguistics, mathematics and statistics, physics, reference books and dictionaries, scientific and technical, sociology and anthropology.

Holt Saunders Ltd (formerly of Eastbourne)

Recently bought by **Academic Press** and moved to Oval Road. Editorial future unclear at the time of going to press.

C. Hurst & Co

38 King Street, London WC2E 8JT   ☎01–240 2666

Chairman/Managing Director *Christopher Hurst*

FOUNDED 1967. Independent, and active in the **Publishers' Association**. Aims to cultivate a small publisher's concern for literacy, detail and the visual aspects of the product. *Publishes* Contemporary History, Political Science, Religion, Autobiography. 12 titles published in 1986.

Editorial Head *Christopher Hurst* with *Michael Dwyer*   TITLES *German Imperialism in Africa; Muslims in the Soviet Empire; The Spanish Economy; Venezuela: A Century of Change; Political Parties and Elections in West Germany* (also in paper). No unsolicited mss but unsolicited synopses and ideas for books welcome.
Royalties paid twice yearly twice after publication and annually thereafter.

Authors' Rating Sound knowledge of marketing achieves worthy sales for minority interest titles.

Michael Joseph Ltd

27 Wright's Lane, London W8 5TZ ☎01–937 7255   Telex 917181/2

Managing Director *Alan Brooke*   **Editorial Director** *Susan Watt*

FOUNDED 1936. Parent company **Penguin Books Ltd.** *Publishes* Belles-lettres, biography & memoirs, current affairs, fiction, general, history, humour. 150 titles in 1986.

MERMAID BOOKS Paperback imprint. *Publishes* non-fiction colour illustrated. *Overseas associates* Penguin Overseas.

Unsolicited manuscripts welcome.
Royalties paid twice yearly.

Authors' Rating See Penguin.

The Journeyman Press Ltd

97 Ferme Park Road, Crouch End, London N8 9SA ☎01–348 9261
Telex 265871 MONREF G

Chairman *R. Weinstein*   **Managing Director** *P. Sinclair*
Approximate Annual Turnover Less than £100,000

FOUNDED 1974 to publish fiction and historical reprints, and run part-time until 1983. Recently restructured, 15–20 titles are scheduled for 1987, with the emphasis on fiction, art and history. Journeyman is now a literary political publisher with a feminist/socialist identity. *Publishes* general, art and graphics, poetry, feminist and socialist fiction, social history, politics.

No unsolicited mss. Synopses and ideas for books welcome.
Royalties paid twice yearly.

Authors' Rating Thumbs up for sticking to MTA despite being a tiny company.

Kahn & Averill

9 Harrington Road, London SW7 ☎01–743 3278

Managing Director *M. Kahn*

FOUNDED 1967. Originally published juvenile titles but gradually changed to music titles. A small independent publishing house. *Publishes* mainly music titles with some general non-fiction. Six titles in 1986. Do not welcome unsolicited mss but will consider synopses and ideas for books.
Royalties paid twice yearly.

The Kensal Press

Kensal House, Abbotsbrook, Bourne End, Bucks SL8 5RE ☏06285 28744

Telex 849462 Telfac G

Managing Director *Mrs Betty Millan*

FOUNDED 1982. *Publishes* Historical biographies, biographies. 12 titles in 1986.

General Manager *Miss Georgina Shomroni* TITLES *David Bowie, Theatre of Music* Robert Matthew Walker; *Farmer George's Black Sheep – The Lives and Loves of George III's Siblings* Charles Neilson Gatty. Prefer to see a synopsis rather than completed mss.

Royalties paid twice yearly for the first year and annually thereafter.

William Kimber Ltd

100 Jermyn Street, London SW1Y 6EE ☏01–930 0446

Chairman & Managing Director *William Kimber*

FOUNDED 1950. *Publishes* Biography & memoirs, current affairs, fiction, general history, travel, sport, naval, military and aviation. 45 titles in 1986.

TITLES *Nigel Mansell, The Makings of a Champion* Christopher Hilton; *The Fighting Tenth, The History of the Tenth Submarine Flotilla* John Wingate; *Stratagem* Harman Grisewood; *The Way It Changed* James McMillan; *The Escape From Singapore* Richard Gough; *Dracula's Children* R. Chetwynd-Hayes. No unsolicited mss. Prefer preliminary letter and synopsis.

Royalties paid twice yearly. *Overseas associates* in Australia, Canada, Ireland, Isle of Man, New Zealand, Scandinavia & Western Europe, South Africa.

Kingfisher Books Ltd

Elsley Court, 20–22 Great Titchfield Street, London W1P 7AD ☏01–631 0878

Telex 27725 Gridem G

Managing Director *Daniel Grisewood*

Part of **Grisewood and Dempsey**. *Publishes* Children's books, cookery, wine & spirits, gardening, guide books, history & antiquarian, natural history, reference books and dictionaries, travel and topography. 57 titles in 1986.

Editorial Head *Jane Olliver* TITLES Children's reference: *Picture Encyclopedia of Our World; Astronomy Today; The Age of Dinosaurs;* Kingpin Superbooks/Factbooks. Science & Nature: *Exploring the Countryside; Dictionary of Animals; National Trust Book of the Armada.* Poetry/Fiction: *A Spider Bought a Bicycle; The Odyssey.* ADULT TITLES *Coastline: Britain's Threatened Heritage; Historical Atlas of Britain;* Guides to Birds/Mushrooms/Herbs; Field Guides to the Wildlife/Plantlife/Birds of Britain and Europe. Welcome unsolicited mss.

Royalties paid twice yearly.

Kluwer Publishing Ltd

1 Harlequin Avenue, Great West Road, Brentford, Middlesex TW8 9EW

☎01–568 6441

Managing Director *Colin B. Ancliffe*

Parent company Kluwer, Deventer, a Dutch company founded in 1900. *Publishes* Books for the professional and business markets, science and technology, legal and fiscal, educational, literary and reference works.

DIVISIONS

Professional *Colin B. Ancliffe*   **Law** *Elizabeth A. O. Bramwell* 99% of the work is commissioned and therefore synopses and outlines are preferred to complete mss. *Royalties* paid twice yearly.

Authors' Rating A highly respected company noted for its skilful marketing of English language business and learned books.

Kogan Page Ltd

120 Pentonville Road, London N1 9JN   ☎01–278 0433   Telex 263088 KOGAN G

Managing Director *Philip Kogan*   **Approximate Annual Turnover** £2.5 million

ESTABLISHED 1967 by Philip Kogan, the company originally published one title only: *The Industrial Training Yearbook*. Now *Publishes* science and technology, business and management, personnel, training and industrial relations, transport, marketing, small business, personal finance, education and careers, plus three journals. Continuing to expand, particularly in the professional and technical areas. 120 titles in 1986.

DIVISIONS

Kogan Page *Pauline Goodwin*   TITLES *Advances In Artificial Intelligence; Fundamentals of Robot Technology; Employment and Safety in the Offshore Oil Industry; Electronic Publishing; The Business Fact Finder; Essential Management Checklists; Assessing Students – How Shall We Know Them?* and the *Kogan Page Working For Yourself* series.   **North Oxford Academic Publishers** *Publishes* computer science, geology, electrical, electronic engineering, physics, maths and economics. Unsolicited mss, synopses and ideas for books welcome. *Royalties* paid twice yearly.

Authors' Rating One of the more energetic of the smaller publishers whose success is based on a close knowledge of the commercial and industrial scene.

Ladybird Books Ltd

Beeches Road, Loughborough, Leics. LE11 2NQ   ☎0509 268021   Telex 341347

Chairman *T. J. Rix*   **Managing Director** *M. P. Kelley*

Approximate Annual Turnover £12 million

FOUNDED 1860s. Part of the **Longman Group**. The **Ladybird** name and format was established as a result of the development of a children's list during World War I. In the early 1960s the printing side of the operation was abandoned in favour of publishing and in 1971 the company was bought by the **Pearson Longman Group**. *Publishes* children's trade titles only. 80 titles in 1987.

Editorial Head *M. H. Gabb*   TITLES *Well Loved Tales; Puddle Lane* series; Activity Books, *Big and Little; Counting; Learning to Read; Thomas the Tank Engine; Barbie; She-Ra Princess of Power;* Classics; Friezes. Very rarely able to make use of unsolicited mss as material is generally commissioned once publication programme has been determined.
Overseas associates Ladybird Books Lewiston, Maine, USA.

Authors' Rating Good, simple stuff for kiddies of a sentimental turn of mind. Criticised for perpetuating the image of female subservience. But popular in the bookshops. One of few imprints everybody has heard of.

Lawrence & Wishart Ltd

39 Museum Street, London WC1A 1LQ   ☎01–405 0103

Chairman *R. Simon*   **Managing Director** *Jeff Skelley*

Established in its present form in 1936. *Publishes* politics, cultural politics, economics, sociology history. 13–20 titles a year.

Editorial Head *Stephen Heyward*   TITLES *Shattering Illusions: West Indians in British Politics; The Signal was Spain: The Aid Spain Movement in Britain 1936–39; Deadly Parallels: Film and the Left in Britain; Rethinking Italian Fascism; The Cutting Edge: Women and the Pit Strike.* Unsolicited mss welcome if in keeping with the character of the list. Synopses preferred to complete mss. Ideas welcome.
Royalties paid annually, unless by arrangement.

Authors' Rating One of the few genuine left wing publishers. Authors should expect to surrender profits to principles.

Leicester University Press

Fielding Johnson Building, University of Leicester, University Road, Leicester, LE1 7RH   ☎0533 523333   Telex 341198

Secretary to the Press *P. L. Boulton*

Part of the university of Leicester. *Publishes* academic and senior school books in history, archaeology, politics and international relations, defence studies, literature. 15 titles in 1986.

Unsolicited mss considered if in appropriate subjects. Synopses and ideas for books welcome.
Royalties paid annually.

Authors' Rating Strong academic list but delays in responding to mss and to ideas suggests heavy committee work.

Line One Publishing
Unit 2, Mead Park, Mead Road, Cheltenham, Glos GL53 7EF   ☎0242 584407

Managing Director *Malcolm Cook*

Publishes aviation, biography and autobiography, military and war, nautical, transport. Ten titles in 1986.

Editorial Director *Malcolm Cook* (editor to be appointed). Unsolicited mss not welcome.
Royalties paid twice yearly.

Lion Publishing plc
Icknield Way, Tring, Herts. HP23 4LE   ☎0442 82 5151   Telex 825850 LION G

Chairman *David S. Alexander*   **Managing Director** *David R. Vesey*
Approximate Annual Turnover £5 million

FOUNDED 1971; went public 1975. A Christian book publisher strong on illustrated books for a popular readership. International market, with rights sold in 41 languages worldwide. Set up US subsidiary in 1984. *Publishes* diverse list with Christian viewpoint the common denominator. All ages, from board books for children to multi-contributor adult reference. Children's fiction and non-fiction, educational, paperbacks, and colour co-edition. 60 titles in 1986.

Contacts Unsolicited adult mss: *Mrs Pat Alexander* (Editorial director); unsolicited children's mss *Ms Sue Box.* Unsolicited mss welcome providing they have a positive Christian viewpoint intended for a wide general and international readership. No books on academic theology, or books intended expressly for the church. Unsolicited synopses and ideas for books also welcome.
Royalties paid twice yearly. *Overseas associates* Lion Publishing Corp., USA.

Liverpool University Press
PO Box 147, Liverpool, L69 3BX   ☎051–709 6022   Telex 627095

Managing Director *Mr Robin Bloxsidge* (Acting)

FOUNDED 1899 as the publishing arm of the university, LUP has made its mark in the social sciences and humanities. Recently, the list has expanded to take in medicine and veterinary science. *Publishes* academic and scholarly, hardback and paperback books in the fields of: archaeology, architecture, geography, ancient & modern history, English literature, commerce, business studies, economics, education, philo-

sophy, politics, psychology, sociology, town planning, veterinary science & medicine. 12 titles in 1986.

Acting Publisher/Editorial Head *Robin Bloxsidge* TITLES *Hill Forts of the Iron
Age; Memory & Writing from Wordsworth to Lawrence; Stendhal et L'Angleterre;
Democracy & Sectarianism – a Political & Social History of Liverpool; The Analysis of
Tides; The Earth Sciences and Planning in the Third World.* Unsolicited mss, synopses
and ideas for books welcome.
Royalties paid annually.

Longman Group UK Ltd
Longman House, Burnt Mill, Harlow, Essex CM20 2JE

☎0279 26721   Telex 81259

Chairman *Tim Rix*   **Approximate Annual Turnover** £71 million

FOUNDED 1724 by Thomas Longman. Now the largest educational publishing house in
the English-speaking world (outside the United States). Part of **Pearson plc**.
Publishes educational, professional, reference, medical books and journals. Over
1000 titles in 1986 (excluding **Pitman** and **Ladybird**). All unsolicited mss should go
to Mr David Lea, Contracts & Copyright Manager.

DIVISIONS
Academic Scientific and Technical *Andrew McLennan*   **Africa & Caribbean** *Jeff
Andrew*   **Arab World** *Colin Hayes*   **Churchill Livingstone** *Andrew Stevenson*
English Language Teaching *Michael Johnson*   **Professional & Business** *Laurence
Herbert*   **Professional Reference and Information** *Mark Todd*   **UK Schools**
Roger Watson.

IMPRINTS
Longman African Classics *Jeff Andrew*   **Longman Caribbean Writers** *Jeff
Andrew*   **Oliver & Boyd** *Alex Paulin* Textbooks in all subjects from infants to A
Level. Unsolicited mss welcome.
Royalties paid yearly (generally). *Overseas associates* in 23 countries around the
world.

Authors' Rating It is one of the curiosities of UK publishing that authors have so
little to say about Longmans. Maybe this is because the output is so predictable and
the lines of organisation so cut and dried. But it is difficult to believe there is no sense
of excitement or adventure left over from the sixties and early seventies. Are the
accountants that much in control?

Lund Humphries Publishers Ltd
16 Pembridge Road, London W11 3HL   ☎01–229 1825
                                                Telex Lundhump 8952387

Chairman *Lionel Leventhal*   **Managing Director** *Clive Bingley*

Part of **Book Publishing Development plc** (same address). Founded to publish fine
art books, the first Lund Humphries title appeared in 1895. The company became
Percy, Lund Humphries in the 1930s and achieved its present identity in 1969.
Publishes graphics, design, art and architecture, plus language guides. 20 titles in
1986. Plans are in progress to expand the graphic arts and design list in the years to
come. Unsolicited mss welcome, although an advance letter is preferred. Synopses
and ideas for books considered.
Royalties paid twice yearly.

Lutterworth Press
7 All Saints' Passage, Cambridge CB2 3LS   ☎0223 350865

Managing Director *Adrian Brink*

Lutterworth Press dates back to the eighteenth century when it was founded by the
Religious Tract Society. In the nineteenth century it was best known for its
children's books, both religious and secular, including *The Boys' Own Paper*. Bought
by the Cambridge publishing house, **James Clarke & Co. Ltd**, in 1984 and absorbed
Patrick Hardy Books. An early integration of the Lutterworth Press and Patrick
Hardy lists is planned. *Publishes* general non-fiction: antiques & collecting, architecture & design, children's books, crafts & hobbies, educational & textbooks, fine
art & art history, gardening, natural history, religion & theology, sports & games,
theatre & drama. 25 titles in 1986.

Senior Editor *Linda Yeatman*   TITLES *All Things Bright and Beautiful* Pauline
Baynes; *Shots* Nigel Gray; *The Cult of Information* Theodore Roszak. Unsolicited mss
and synopses are welcome.
Royalties paid both quarterly and bi-annually.

Authors' Rating Emerging from the doldrums. Still closely tied to evangelical publishing but good children's list.

Macdonald & Co. Ltd
3rd Floor, Greater London House, Hampstead Road, London NW1 7QX
                                    ☎01–377 4600   Telex 885233

Managing Directors *Ken Pickett and Charles Merullo*
                      Approximate Annual Turnover in excess of £30 million

Founded in the 1930s. Part of **BPCC** since the 1960s. *Publishes* architecture & design,
auto/biography, children's books, cinema, cookery, wines & spirits, crafts &
hobbies, DIY, educational/textbooks, fiction, gardening, geography/geology, guide
books, history, humour, illustrated editions, medical, natural history, nautical, pho-

tography, poetry, reference, sports/games, theatre & drama, travel & topography. 801 titles in 1986.

DIVISIONS

Children's *Mary Tappissier* Many titles, from board books for the very young to the new Junior Fiction series. **Fiction** TITLES *A Long Road Winding* Margaret P. Kirk; *Shadows on the Snow* Madge Swindells; *The Eyes of the Dragon* Stephen King; *Patience of a Saint* Andrew M. Greeley. **Non-Fiction** TITLES *World War I in Photographs*; *Travelling With Children*; *The Psychology of Cancer*; *Francoise Bernard's French Cooking*; *Les Routiers Guide to France 1987*; *How To Draw and Sketch/Paint Nature, etc.*; *Creative Knitting*.

IMPRINTS

Macdonald Futura *Richard Evans* TITLES *Eavesdropper* John Francombe & James MacGregor; *Down Our Street* Lena Kennedy; *Children First and Always* Derek & Gillian Mercer; *Joyful Voices* Doris Stokes. **Macdonald Orbis** *Sarah Snape* Illustrated books. **Optima** *Philippa Stewart* Alternative publishing. **Queen Anne Press** *Alan Samson* TITLES *Joan Sutherland* Norma Major; *The Complete British Motorist* Lord Montagu of Beaulieu; *You'll Never Walk Alone* Stephen Kelly; *Middle Stump* Graham Thompson; *Playfair Racing Annual*; *The Good Golf Guide*; *Glassfibre Boat Manual*. Welcome unsolicited mss.
Royalties paid twice yearly.

Authors' Rating A company propelled forward on a sharp kick from Robert Maxwell. Cosiness is out, efficiency is in. Can be a bit unnerving for authors who are used to kid-glove treatment.

Macmillan Publishers Ltd
4 Little Essex Street, London WC2R 3LF ☎01–836 6633 Telex 262024

Chairman *The Earl of Stockton* **Managing Director** *N. G. Byam Shaw*
Approximate Annual Turnover £130 million

DIVISIONS

Parent Company of **Macmillan Children's Books Ltd, Macmillan Educational Ltd, Macmillan London Ltd, The Macmillan Press Ltd, Macmillan Magazines Ltd, Sidgwick & Jackson Ltd** (p. 111), **Pan Books Ltd** (p. 99) (See individual entries.

Overseas associates Gill & Macmillan (Eire), Macmillan India Ltd, The Macmillan Co. of Australia Ltd, Macmillan Shuppan KK Ltd (Japan), Macmillan South-East Asia Pty Ltd, Macmillan Publishers Overseas Ltd, Peninsula Publishers Ltd (Hong Kong), Macmillan Kenya (Publishers) Ltd, The Macmillan Co. of New Zealand Ltd, Macmillan Boleswa Publishers Ltd, Macmillan Nigeria Ltd, St Martin's Press (New York), The College Press Ltd (Zimbabwe), Editorial Macmillan de Mexico SA de CV, Macmillan China Ltd, Macmillan Publishers (Malaysia), Grove's Dictionary of Music Inc. (New York), Stockton Press Inc. (New York).

The Macmillan Press Ltd
4 Little Essex Street, London WC2R 3LF ☎01–836 6633   Telex 262024

Chairman *A. Soar*   **Managing Director** *C. J. Paterson*

Publishes academic & scholarly; accountancy & taxation; agriculture; animal care & breeding; archaeology; architecture & design; bibliography & library service; biography & autobiography; biology & zoology; business & industry; chemistry; cinema & video; computer science; economics; engineering; art history; geography & geology; guide books; history & antiquarian; languages & linguistics; law; literature & criticism; mathematics & statistics; medical; military & war; music; natural history; philosophy; physics; politics & world affairs; psychology; dictionaries; religion & theology; scientific & technical; sociology & anthropology; theatre & drama; transport; travel & topography; business reference and directories; biotechnical reference; telecommunications; vocational training & careers; women's studies. 400 titles in 1986.

Divisions
Medical & Scientific Books & Journals *H. Holt* **Postgraduate & Scholarly** *T. M. Farmiloe* **Reference & Professional** *J. F. K. Ashby* **Music** *S. Littlewood* Unsolicited mss welcome.
Royalties paid annually.

Macmillan Children's Books Ltd
4 Little Essex Street, London WC2R 3LF ☎01–836 6633   Telex 262024

Publishing Director *Michael Wace*

Publishes Children's fiction and non-fiction. Mss & synopses welcome.
Royalties paid twice yearly.

Macmillan Education Ltd
Houndmills, Basingstoke, Hants RG21 2XS ☎0256 29242   Telex 858493

Chairman *A. Soar*   **Managing Director** *J. E. Jackman*

Publishes Biology & zoology; business & industry; chemistry; computer science; computer software (educational); economics; educational & textbooks; engineering; geography & geology; history & antiquarian; languages & linguistics; law; literature & criticism; mathematics & statistics; medical; music; natural history; philosophy; physics; politics & world affairs; psychology; reference books & dictionaries; religion & theology; scientific & technical; sociology & anthropology; theatre & drama; vocational training & careers; women's studies.

Publishing Director (primary & secondary) *R. S. Balkwill* **Publishing Director** (college) *P. I. Murby* TITLES *New Way Reading Scheme*; *Macmillan Master Series*; *Macmillan Work Out Study Aids*. Unsolicited mss welcome.
Royalties paid annually.

Macmillan London Ltd

4 Little Essex Street, London WC2R 3LF ☎ 01–836 6633 Telex 262024

Chairman *Nicholas Byam Shaw* **Managing Director** *Philippa Harrison*

Publishes Biography & autobiography; computer science; cookery; wines & spirits; crime; fashion & costume; fiction; fine art & art history; gardening; guide books; health & beauty; history & antiquarian; humour; literature & criticism; music; natural history; photography; poetry; politics & world affairs; psychology; sports & games; theatre & drama.

Crime *Hilary Hale* AUTHORS Colin Deeks, Paula Gosling, Julia Symonds, Loren D. Estleman **Fiction** *James Hale* AUTHORS Barbara Pym, Anne Schlee, Derek Robinson, Iain Banks, Mary Wesley, E. V. Thomson **Non-Fiction** *Adam Sisman* AUTHORS Geoffrey Boycott, Alistair Horne, Anton Mosiman, Hugo Young **Papermac** *Kyle Cathie* AUTHORS Victoria Glendinning, Anthony Howard, Marcella Hazan, Lyn Macdonald. Unsolicited mss & synopses welcome. *Royalties* paid twice yearly.

Authors' Rating Despite its size (estimated turnover £130 million) **Macmillan** is a shadowy company. Though the second Earl of Stockton is a well-known figure in the book world, he does not represent a particular style of publishing, while those who exercise real power keep a low profile and seldom get involved in publishing politics outside their own patch. Consequently it is difficult to know what **Macmillan** are likely to do next.

The huge number of books appearing under the **Macmillan** imprint range from education (recently restored as the strong right arm of the company) to music reference (the biggest single money spinner is *Grove's Dictionary of Music*). But achievement stops short of blockbusters. The recent purchase of **Sidgwick & Jackson** may remedy this but there remains the suspicion that **Macmillan** are unwilling to chance the necessary resources on high risk general publishing.

The corollary is that **Macmillan** can boast some of the sharpest financial brains in the business. No writer, however eminent, should look for easy gains though few complain of unfair treatment and many praise the superior overseas network which promises an export bonus – if the product is thought to be worth the effort.

Mainstream Publishing Co Ltd

7 Albany Street, Edinburgh EH1 3UG ☎ 031–557 2959 Telex 265871

Directors *Peter MacKenzie, Bill Campbell*

Publishes biography, autobiography, fiction, health and beauty, illustrated and fine editions, literature and criticism, military and war, politics and world affairs, reference books and dictionaries, sports and games. Forty titles in 1986.

Editorial Director *Bill Campbell* Unsolicited mss welcome. *Royalties* paid twice yearly.

Manchester University Press

Oxford Road, Manchester M13 9PL   ☎061–273 5539   Telex 668932 MCHRUL

Chief Executive *J. M. N. Spencer*   **Approximate Annual Turnover** £1 million

A department of Manchester University founded early this century. The list remained largely history based until after the war, when it took up anthropology with great success. It remained very small until J. M. N. Spencer took over as publisher in 1973, since when MUP has increased five-fold and is now Britain's third largest university press. *Publishes* academic and educational in the areas of literature, modern languages, history, law (especially international), biomedical science and non-linear dynamics, politics and sociology. 80 titles in 1986.

DIVISIONS
Humanities *John Banks*   **Science** *Alec McAulay*   Unsolicited mss welcome.
Royalties paid annually.

Authors' Rating Like all the university presses, MUP can give the impression it is doing its authors a favour by publishing their books. As with many University Presses, advances are low.

George Mann Books

PO Box 22, Maidstone, Kent ME14 1AH   ☎0622 59591

Chairman & Managing Director *John Arne*
                    Approximate Annual Turnover £50–75,000

FOUNDED 1972 originally as library reprint publishers but with the collapse of the library market moved on to other things. *Publishes* selected reprints with some original non-fiction, prophecy, and the occult. No new fiction. Plan to publish selected reprints in magazine book form to compete with paperbacks for the impulse buyer retailing at £1.50–£1.95. 4 titles in 1986.

TITLES *Connecting The Fragments* Harry Holmes; *Humanism* Harry Holmes. Prefer synopsis with preliminary letter.
Royalties paid twice yearly.

Marshall Morgan & Scott Publications Ltd

3 Beggarwood Lane, Basingstoke, Hants RG23 7LP ☎0256 59211   Telex 858669

Managing Director *John T. Hunt*

Part of **Zondervan Corporation**, USA. One of the biggest Christian paperback publishers. *Publishes* academic and scholarly, biography and autobiography, children's, fiction, music, poetry, reference books and dictionaries, religion and theology. 107 titles in 1986.

Editorial Director *Deborah Thorpe*

IMPRINTS
Contemporary Christian Studies   Lakeland Paperbacks   Marshall Pickering   Marshalls Paperbacks   Marshalls Theological Library   New Century Bible Commentaries   Oliphants   Samuel Bagster & Sons Ltd   Unsolicited mss welcome.
Royalties paid twice yearly.

McGraw-Hill Book Co. (UK) Ltd

McGraw-Hill House, Shoppenhangers Road, Maidenhead, Berks. SL6 2QL
☎ 0628 23432   Telex 848484

Managing Director *Stephen White*

Parent Company McGraw Hill Book Co. Inc., New York.

FOUNDED 1899 in London and moved to Maidenhead in 1963. The British publishing programme started in 1965. *Publishes* high level textbooks, academic books in the fields of sciences and chemistry; educational and reference books for the professions and management. Forty titles in 1986.

DIVISIONS
Market Focus Groups: Professional *Roland Elgey*   **University & college** *Jeremy Dicks*   TITLES *Begg Economics*.   **Vocational** *John Watson*. Unsolicited mss, synopses and ideas for books welcome.
Royalties paid twice yearly.

Authors' Rating Nowadays, tends to keep a low profile, but works on a solid foundation of academic and high level textbooks. No way-out ideas. Not to be confused with the aggressive American parent company.

Merlin Press Ltd

3 Manchester Road, London E14 9BD   ☎ 01–987 7959

Managing Director *Martin Eve*   **Approximate Annual Turnover £100,000**

FOUNDED 1956 by Martin Eve. *Publishes* Leftwing politics, history, economics and philosophy. 10 titles in 1986.

Editorial Head *Martin Eve*   AUTHORS Georg Lukacs, Ernest Mandel, Istvan Meszaros, Ralph Miliband, E. P. Thompson. No unsolicited mss; letter essential before sending either finished mss or synopses.
Royalties paid twice yearly.

Merrill Publishing Company

Finsbury Business Centre, 40 Bowling Green Lane, London EC1R 0NE
☎ 01–278 0333   Telex 267427

Manager *Michael Brightmore*

Part of **Bell & Howell Inc.**, USA. *Publishes* academic & scholarly, business and industry, computer science, educational and textbooks, engineering, geography and geology, psychology, scientific and technical. 80 titles in 1986. Editorial office is in America (sales and marketing function only in UK) but all mss and queries should go through Michael Brightmore in London. Unsolicited mss will be passed on to **Merrill Publishing Co.**, 1300 Alum Creek Road, Columbus, Ohio 43216, USA.

Methuen & Co. Ltd
11 New Fetter Lane, London EC4P 4EE   ☎01–583 9855   Telex 263398

Chairman *John Naylor*

Part of **Associated Book Publishers UK Ltd.** *Publishes* academic & scholarly. 163 titles in 1986.

Editorial Head *Janice Price* Welcome unsolicited mss, synopses and ideas for books. *Royalties* paid twice yearly.

Authors' Rating See **Associated Book Publishers**.

Methuen Children's Books Ltd
11 New Fetter Lane, London EC4P 4EE   ·   ☎01–583 9855   Telex 263398

Chairman *Christopher Falkus*

Part of **Associated Book Publishers UK Ltd.** *Publishes* children's fiction and non-fiction for the very young to mid-teens, including *Winnie The Pooh* (in English and Latin versions) and *Wind in the Willows*.

Editorial head *Janetta Otterbarry*

IMPRINT
Magnet paperbacks Welcome unsolicited mss, synopses and ideas for books. *Royalties* paid twice yearly.

Authors' Rating See **Associated Book Publishers**.

Methuen Educational Limited
11 New Fetter Lane, London EC4P 4EE   ☎01–583 9855   Telex 263398

Chairman *John Naylor*

Part of **Associated Book Publishers UK Ltd.** *Publishes* school books, both primary and secondary.

Editorial head *Geoffrey Strachan* Welcome unsolicited mss, synopses and ideas for books.
Royalties paid twice yearly.

Authors' Rating See **Associated Book Publishers**.

Methuen London Ltd
11 New Fetter Lane, London EC4P 4EE   ☎01–583 9855   Telex 263398

Chairman *Christopher Falkus*

Part of **Associated Book Publishers UK Ltd**. *Publishes* general (adult fiction and non-fiction).

Editorial head *Geoffrey Strachan*   TITLES *Tin Toys*, Ursula Holden; *Kabul*, M. E. Hirsch; *A Bit of a Do*, David Nobbs; *The Imperial Way*, James Melville; *Gor Saga*, Maureen Duffy; *Coffin Scarcely Used*, Colin Watson. Welcome unsolicited mss, synopses and ideas for books.
Royalties paid twice yearly.

Authors' Rating See **Associated Book Publishers**.

Mildmay Books
Glen House, 200–8 Tottenham Court Road, London W1P 9LA   ☎01–323 4770

Managing Director *Grahame Griffiths*

Founded by three ex-employees of Century Hutchinson, Mildmay published its first title in 1986. *Publishes* general trade hard and paperbacks, predominantly non-fiction. 9 titles in 1987, but set on an expansionist course, with an anticipated turnover of over £1 million by 1990.

Editor *Pauline Bayne*   TITLES the autobiography of *Arthur English*; a *Sports Year-book* for the Budweiser League; and the first of a series of travel books, *Burgundy on a Budget*. Unsolicited mss, synopses and ideas for books welcome.
Royalties paid twice yearly.

Milestone Publications
62 Murray Road, Horndean, Hants PO8 9JL   ☎0705 597440

Managing and Editorial Director *Nicholas J. Pine*

Part of **Goss & Crested China Ltd**. *Publishes* antiques and collecting, business, economics, guide books, local history, military and war, reference books, sport, theatre, transport. 15 titles in 1986. Unsolicited mss not welcome. Approach in writing in first instance.
Royalties paid twice yearly.

Mills & Boon Ltd
Eaton House, 18–24 Paradise Road, Richmond, Surrey TW9 1SR   ☎01–948 0444
Telex 24420 Milbon G

Chairman *John T. Boon*   **Managing Director** *R. J. Williams*

FOUNDED 1909. *Publishes* fiction only. 300 titles in 1986.

Editorial Director *H. Bausch*

IMPRINTS
Doctor Nurse & Masquerade *Judith Murdoch* Established in the 1950s, and still going, Doctor Nurse romances are love stories set in a realistic medical world. **Masquerade** are historical romances, slightly longer than usual. **Harlequin** *Linda Fildew* Longer still, and aim to be 'sophisticated, unpredictable and well-written'. **Harlequin Love Affair** aim to be very contemporary in feel and are set in the USA. **Mills & Boon Romances** The traditional formula, with happy endings assured. **Mills & Boon Temptation** *Linda Fildew* Modern storylines aimed at younger readers; temptation and choices with satisfying resolutions. **Silhouette** *Linda Fildew* Stories where 'there is more to love than mere romance'. **Silhouette Desire** are provocative and highly sensual. Mills & Boon also publish **Gold Eagle** – big macho adventure stories, and are currently developing their **Harlequin Audio Publishing** range: not only fiction but business/finance, health/fitness, personal development. Unsolicited mss very welcome.
Royalties paid twice yearly.

Authors' Rating A publishing industry in its own right. So overwhelmed are they by writers 'dreaming of becoming romantic novelists', Mills & Boon have produced a 40 minute cassette tape, *And Then He Kissed Her*, which gives advice on how to construct a novel for this highly specialist market. (£2.99 from PO Box 236, Croydon, Surrey.) Writing for Mills & Boon is nowhere near as easy as it looks. But for those who can work the formula, the rewards are great.

Mitchell Beazley Ltd
Artist's House, 14/15 Manette Street, London W1V 5LB ☎01–439 7211
Telex 24892 MbbookG

Chairman *Mrs Janice Mitchell* **Managing Director** *Duncan Baird*
Approximate Annual Turnover £78 million

FOUNDED 1969 by James Mitchell and John Beazley. Bought by **Octopus**, May 1987 for £4.85 million. *Publishes* illustrated non-fiction only, in general and leisure subjects: antiques, archaeology, cinema, cookery, wines, crafts, fine art, gardening, geography/geology, guide books, health/beauty, history, humour, medical, music, natural history, photography, reference books/dictionaries, religion/theology, travel & topography. 35 titles in 1986.

DIVISIONS
Mitchell Beazley Encyclopaedias *Frank Wallis* TITLES *The Joy of Knowledge*. **Wine** *Chris Foulkes* TITLES *World Atlas of Wine*. **Gardening** *Bob Saxton* TITLES *R. H. S. Gardening Guides*. **Travel** *Chris Foulkes* TITLES *American Express Travel Series*. **House & Interiors** *Bob Saxton* TITLES *The House Book*. **General Reference** *James Hughes* TITLES *World Atlas of Archaeology; Atlas of the Universe*. **Photography** *Bob Saxton* TITLES *Kodak Encyclopaedia of Creative Photography*.

IMPRINTS
Miller's Publishing *Judith Miller* TITLES *Miller's Antiques Price Guide Yearbook*.

Artist's House *Kelly Flynn*   TITLES *Men of the Stars* Patrick Moore. **Emblem** Trade paperbacks. Welcome unsolicited mss, synopses and ideas for books within their subject areas listed.
Royalties paid twice yearly.

Authors' Rating Started off as a book packager and much of the publishing output is still in this tradition. Should fit well into the **Octopus** set-up with benefit to authors whose work lends itself to mass marketing.

The MIT Press Ltd

126 Buckingham Palace Road, London SW1W 9SD   ☎01–730 9208   Telex 23993

Chairman *F. Urbanowski*   **Managing Director** *N. C. Gosling*

Part of **MIT Press**, USA. *Publishes* academic, architecture and design, bibliography, biography and autobiography, biology and zoology, business and industry, chemistry, cinema and video, computer science, economics, educational and textbooks, engineering, fine art and art history, geography and geology, history and antiquarian, languages and linguistics, law, mathematics and statistics, medical, music, natural history, philosophy, photography, physics, politics and world affairs, psychology, reference, scientific and technical, sociology and anthropology, transport, travel and topography. 150 titles in 1986.

All mss should go to the American office: 55 Hayward Street, Cambridge, Mass. 02142.

Moorland Publishing Co. Ltd

Moorfarm Road, Airfield Estate, Ashbourne, Derbyshire DE6 1HD
                                         ☎0335 44486   Telex 377106 Chacom G MPC

Managing Director *Dr J. Robey*   **Approximate Annual Turnover** £500,000

FOUNDED 1971. Represented by **David & Charles** since 1986. *Publishes* travel guides, history of transport, collecting, and countryside guides. 16 titles in 1986.

Editorial Head *Dr J. Robey*   Unsolicited mss will be considered, but synopses accompanied by letters of introduction preferred.
Royalties paid annually.

H. R. Mowbray

Saint Thomas House, Becket Street, Oxford OX1 1SJ   ☎0865 242507

Chief Executive *Dennis Edwards* **Managing Director** (Publishing Division) *Kenneth Baker*   **Approximate Annual Turnover** £400,000

FOUNDED 1858. Member of the **Publishers' Association** since 1899, Mowbray has since opened retail shops in London, Cambridge and Birmingham. *Publishes* theology, Christian paperbacks, handbooks for clergy and laity. 43 titles in 1986.

Editorial Head *Robert Williams* Unsolicited mss welcome if accompanied by postage. Synopses/ideas for books considered.
Royalties paid twice yearly (unless under £10 is due).

MTP Press Ltd

Falcon House, Queen Square, Lancaster LA1 1RN 0524 68765/6/7 Telex 65212

Managing Director (Joint) *Mr C. K. Timms, Dr F. W. B. van Eysinga*
Approximate Annual Turnover £1.5 million

MTP Press is a specialist medical and scientific publishing house, with its head office in Lancaster, and additional marketing centres in Boston, USA, and Dordrecht, Holland. The company was founded in 1967. *Publishes* research monographs, post-graduate textbooks, colour atlases, and primary medicine texts for family physicians. Its authorship is distinguished and international and the current list includes many important reviews of major new advances in medicine. A member of Kluwer Academic Group of Publishers, MTP is especially strong in the field of gastroenterology, pathology, cardiology, immunology and primary medicine. 63 titles in 1986.

Publishing Director *Dr P. L. Clarke* TITLES *AIDS, The Second Edition* Dr V. H. Daniels; *Management of Common Diseases* J. Fry (series ed.); *Current Histopathology* E. Gresham (series ed.); *Clinical Cardiology* Prof. J. Shillingford (series ed.). Welcome unsolicited mss, synopses and ideas for books.
Royalties paid annually.

John Murray (Publishers) Ltd

50 Albermarle Street, London W1X 4BD 01–493 4351 Telex 21312 Murray G

Chairman *John R. Murray* **Managing Director** *Nicholas Perren*

FOUNDED 1768 and continuously independent since then with its own distribution operation. Original publishers of Lord Byron, Jane Austen, Charles Darwin, Thackeray, the Brownings and Sir Arthur Conan Doyle. Remain the custodian of Lord Byron's ring. *Publishes* General trade books, educational (secondary school and college textbooks), success studybooks. 64 titles in 1986.

DIVISIONS
General Books *Grant McIntyre* TITLES *Between the Woods and the Water* Patrick Leigh Fermor; *Three Continents* Ruth Prawer Jhabvala. **Educational Books** *Keith Nettle* **Success Studybooks** *Bob Davenport* Do not welcome unsolicited mss or synopses.
Royalties paid twice yearly.

Authors' Rating Rather staid on the literary side; more exciting on education, particularly science.

Thomas Nelson & Sons Ltd

Nelson House, Mayfield Road, Walton-on-Thames, Surrey KT12 5PL

☎0932 246133   Telex 929365 Nelson G

Managing Director *Michael Thompson*

Approximate Annual Turnover £10 million

FOUNDED 1798. Part of the **International Thomson Organisation**. *Publishes* Educational (infant, primary, secondary); school atlases & dictionaries, English language teaching world-wide, educational books for Africa, Caribbean & SE Asia.

Editorial Director *Graham Taylor*   TITLES *Breakaway; Deutsche Heute; Peak Maths*. Unsolicited mss and synopses are welcome.
Royalties paid twice yearly.

Authors' Rating Never really found its way since the Nelson family sold out in the early sixties. There have been recent cut-backs on staff and publishing programme.

NFER-Nelson Publishing Co. Ltd

Darville House, 2 Oxford Road East, Windsor, Berks. SL4 1DF   ☎0753 858961

Telex 937400

Managing Director *Michael Jackson*

FOUNDED 1983. Part of the **Nelson Group**. *Publishes* educational and psychological books and journals. 25 titles in 1986.

Editorial Head *Tim Cornford* All books are commissioned and linked to the **National Foundation for Educational Research**, and so do not welcome unsolicited material.
Royalty payments vary according to contract.

Octopus Books Ltd

59 Grosvenor Street, London W1X 9DA*   ☎01–493 5841 Telex 27278 Octobk G

Chairman *Paul Hamlyn*   **Managing Director** *David Blunt*

FORMED in 1971. Launched its first list in 1972 with 55 titles. Went public in 1983. The **Octopus Group** acquired **Bookwise Service Ltd** in 1984, and the **Heinemann Group** merged with Octopus in September 1985. Acquired **Hamlyn Publishing Group** in March 1986 and half of the Collins share of **Pan Books** in September 1986. Acquired **Mitchell Beazley** in May 1987. Now owned by **Reed International**. *Publishes* antiques & collecting, cookery, wine & spirits, crafts & hobbies, DIY, fiction, gardening, health & beauty, humour, photography, sports & games, transport. 300 titles in 1986.

---

*New address for both **Heinemann & Octopus** from early 1988 will be Michelin House, 81 Fulham Road, London SW3.

DIVISIONS
Fiction/Children's *Theresa Carlson*   TITLES Fiction: *Treasury of World Master-pieces: Charles Dickens; H. G. Wells* (Omnibus editions).   AUTHORS Jeffrey Archer, Robert Ludlum, Dick Francis, Wilbur Smith, Frank Herbert, Catherine Cookson. Children's Titles *Roland Rat; Postman Pat; Thomas the Tank Engine; Adventure Stories for Girls/Boys; War Stories; Ghost Stories.* **Non-Fiction** *Isabel Moore*   TITLES *Lean Cuisine; 1000 Freezer Recipes; The World of the Horse; The Illustrated Book of Birds; Container Gardening; The MGM Story; Cadillac Poster Book; Great Marques: BMW; Origami in Colour; Vogue Entertaining; Colour by Quant; Pocket Book on Food Processors.*   **Marks & Spencer Books** *Margaret McLean* No unsolicited mss but welcome unsolicited synopses and ideas.
Royalties paid both once and twice yearly.

Authors' Rating Paul Hamlyn is one of the great buccaneers of publishing, who never ceases to amaze. Having started with **Hamlyn Publishing** in 1950, he sold out fifteen years later to IPC which after divesting itself of the **Mirror Group** to Robert Maxwell, reverted to the name of its printing base, **Reed International**. Hamlyn, meanwhile, went off to found **Octopus** to exploit opportunities for mass marketing of books with multiples like **Marks and Spencer** and **British Home Stores**. Having made his fortune a second time, Paul Hamlyn went on a shopping spree to buy **Heinemann** (with its share of **Pan**), and in 1986, **Hamlyn Publishing**, a company **Reed International** was only too happy to sell back to its founder. Now, just one year later, the whole **Octopus** shooting match has been bought by − yes, that's it, − **Reed International,** for an impressive £540 million.

What all this means to authors is almost impossible to assess. Distress at **Heine-mann** at being thrown into the same pool as **Octopus** (the analogy hardly needs elaboration) cannot have been alleviated by news of the takeover by **Reed**. Yet it is difficult to resist the thought that **Heinemann** badly needed a shakeup. Paul Hamlyn predicts that the latest changes will put his publishing empire into the 'international super league'. Some of his authors may wonder if they are up to the challenge.

Omnibus Press
8/9 Frith Street, London W1V 5TZ   ☎01−434 0066   Telex 21892

Managing Director *Robert Wise*

FOUNDED 1971 by Robert Wise and remains independent. Produces books, song sheets, songbooks, educational tutors, cassettes, videos and software. *Publishes* Music books and rock & pop biographies. 45 titles in 1986.

Editorial Head *Chris Charlesworth*

IMPRINTS
Omnibus, Bobcat, Amsco, Wise, Oak, Proteus. Welcome unsolicited mss and synopses/ideas for books.
Royalties paid twice yearly. *Overseas subsidiaries* Music Sales Corporation, New York; Music Sales Pty, Sydney.

Open Books Publishing Ltd
Beaumont House, Wells, Somerset BA5 2LD   ☎ 0749 77276

Managing Director *Patrick Taylor*

FOUNDED 1974. *Publishes* academic and general. 6 titles in 1986. All books are commissioned and therefore do not welcome unsolicited mss and synopses.
Royalties paid twice yearly. *Overseas associates* Cambridge University Press Australia, Century Hutchinson South Africa.

Peter Owen Ltd
73 Kenway Road, London SW5 0RE   ☎ 01–373 5628/370 6093

Chairman *Peter Owen*   **Managing Director** *Michael Levien*

ESTABLISHED 1951. Known for its fiction, both English and translated. Authors include Shusako Endo, Paul Bowles, Anaïs Nin, Jane Bowles, Anna Kavan, Peter Vansittart. *Publishes* General books, literary fiction, biography, sociology. No romance, thrillers, or children's books. 18 titles in 1986. Unsolicited synopses welcome; mss should be preceded by a descriptive letter with s.a.e.
Royalties paid annually. *Overseas associates* 'Represented throughout the world'.

Authors' Rating A small publisher with a high profile. Very good on translations.

Oxford University Press
Walton Street, Oxford OX2 6DP   ☎ 0865 56767   Telex 837330

Chief Executive *G. B. Richardson*   **Approximate Annual Turnover** £85 million

A department of the university for several hundred years, which grew out of the university's printing works and developed into a major publishing business in the 19th century, concentrating on bibles and education. *Publishes* academic books in all categories, student texts, scholarly journals, schoolbooks, ELT material, dictionaries, reference books, music, bibles, imported titles from the USA and beyond, as well as paperbacks, general non-fiction and children's books. Approximately 1000 titles in 1986.

DIVISIONS
Academic *R. D. P. Charkin* TITLES include the *Concise Oxford Dictionary*. **Education** *P. R. Mothersole* GCSE titles. **ELT** *G. P. Lewis* Streamline ELT course.

IMPRINTS
Clarendon Press *R. D. P. Charkin* Monographs in sciences, humanities, and social sciences. OUP welcomes first class academic material in the form of proposals or accepted theses.
Royalties paid once/twice yearly. *Overseas subsidiaries* branches in Australia, India, Canada, Singapore, Hong Kong, Japan, East Africa, South Africa, New Zealand, plus sister company in New York.

Authors' Rating Inhibited for many years by its ties with the university and by the fanciful notion that academics know all there is to know about publishing, OUP has lately streamlined its administration and editorial services for a belated leap into the second half of the twentieth century. Can safely claim one of the finest academic lists in the world. Authors who still complain of production delays and unanswered correspondence agree that OUP are at least good payers.

Pan Books Ltd
18–21 Cavaye Place, London SW10 9PG   ☎01–373 6070   Telex 917466

Managing Director *Successor to Simon Master to be appointed*

Mass market paperback house. FOUNDED 1944. Published its first list in 1947. In 1961 had its first million-selling title, *The Dam Busters*. In 1961 published *Dr No* which went on to sell over 2 million copies. In 1962 instituted the Golden Pan Award for authors whose titles sold a million. The first winner was Alan Sillitoe for *Saturday Night, Sunday Morning*. **Piccolo**, the children's imprint was set up in 1971. **Picador**, international modern fiction and non-fiction, started in 1972. First Pan book shop opened in the Fulham Road in 1975. **Pavanne** set up in 1984. **Macmillan** took over warehousing and distribution in 1981. Now jointly owned by **Macmillan** and **Octopus**. The third founding partner, **Collins**, sold out to the other two in 1986. *Publishes* archaeology, architecture & design, atlases & maps, biography & autobiography, business & industry, children's, cinema & video, cookery, wines & spirits, crafts & hobbies, economics, fiction, gardening, guide books, history & antiquarian, humour, languages & linguistics, literature & criticism, medical, military & war, natural history, philosophy, photography, politics & world affairs, psychology, reference books & dictionaries, sports & games, theatre & drama, travel & topography. Approximately 300 titles in 1986.

IMPRINTS
Picador *Geoff Mulligan*   TITLES *Travels in Hyper-Reality* Umberto Eco; *The Joy of Stress* Peter Hansom.   **Piccolo** *Marion Lloyd*   TITLES *An Insular Profession* Timothy Mo; *The Travellers' Quiz Book* Deborah Manley.   **Pavanne** *Caroline Upcher* (fiction), *Hilary Davies* (non-fiction)   TITLES *The Power of the Sword* Wilbur Smith. Welcome unsolicited mss and synopses/ideas for books.
Royalties paid twice yearly. *Overseas associates* Pan Books Australia (Pty) Ltd.

Authors' Rating One of the best of the paperback houses turning out a huge range of titles all of which benefit from skilful presentation and marketing. Has enthusiasm for new ideas and willingness to back commercial judgement with hard cash, but the future is unclear. The recent departure of Sonny Mehta who ran **Picador**, the quality side of **Pan**, for fourteen years was sad news for his authors, as too was the elevation of Simon Master, former MD of Pan, to become Chief Executive of **CVBC**. Then again, the buyout of the **Collins** share by the other two owners, **Macmillan** and **Octopus**, raises the question of how far **Pan** can progress without a supply of titles from another major hardback house. Since both Master and Mehta have gone to **Random House** (the latter to head **Knopf**), an obvious solution does suggest itself.

Pavilion Books Ltd
196 Shaftesbury Avenue, London WC2H 8JL ☎01–836 1306 Telex 268369

Managing Director *Colin Webb* **Editorial Director** *Vivien Bowler*

Publishes children's, cinema & video, cookery, wines & spirits, fashion, humour, sports and games. 40 titles in 1986. Unsolicited mss not welcome. Synopses and ideas considered.
Royalties paid twice yearly.

Authors' Rating Strong on multi-media deals. A publisher with a sense of style, open to ideas for potential bestsellers.

PBI Publications
Britannica House, High Street, Waltham Cross, Hertfordshire EN8 7DY
☎0992 23691 Telex 23957

Chairman & Managing Director *Dr D. G. Hessayon*

Part of the **Tennant Group.** Paperback publisher of gardening and agriculture books by Dr D. G. Hessayon. 2 titles in 1986.

TITLES *The Armchair Book of the Garden*; *The Garden Expert* D. G. Hessayon. Do not consider unsolicited material.

Pelham Books Ltd
27 Wright's Lane, London W8 5TZ ☎01–937 7255 Telex 917181/2

Chairman *Alan Brooke* **Publisher** *Roger Houghton*

FOUNDED 1960 specifically to publish *Pears Cyclopedia* when the rights were bought from Lever Bros. The general imprint of **Michael Joseph**; parent company, **Penguin Books Ltd.** *Publishes* sport and some leisure, crafts, cookery, DIY, sports biographies, handbooks. 50 titles in 1986.

Editorial Director *Muriel Gascoin* TITLES *Pears Cyclopedia*; *Benson & Hedges Cricket Year*; *Benson & Hedges Snooker Year*; *Born Lucky* John Francome; *Cross Country Riding* Lucinda Green. Welcome unsolicited mss, synopses and ideas for books. *Royalties* paid twice yearly. *Overseas associates* Penguin Overseas.

Authors' Rating Roger Houghton has just taken over. It will be interesting to see where this imaginative publisher takes a company which is ripe for expansion.

Penguin Books Ltd
27 Wrights Lane, London W8 5TZ ☎01–938 2200

Chairman *Peter Mayer* **Managing Director** *Trevor Glover*
Approximate Annual Turnover £133.3 million (1986)

Publishes general and academic books of all kinds; atlases & maps, auto/biography, children's, business, EFL, guide books, fiction, science fiction, literature and criticism, poetry, reference books and dictionaries, scientific and technical, sports, women's studies. 748 titles in 1986. (See also **Michael Joseph**, **Hamish Hamilton**, **Rainbird**, **Sphere**.)

Publishing Director *Peter Carson* Responsible for the general **Penguin** list (not children's books, not **Viking**, not **Frederick Warne**).

IMPRINTS
Frederick Warne (see separate listing).   **Pelican** *Peter Carson* High quality paperback fiction.   **Puffin** *Elizabeth Attenborough* Children's books.   **Viking Kestrel** (see separate listing **Viking**).   **Viking** (see separate listing). Unsolicited mss generally welcome. (Preliminary letter essential in the case of **Frederick Warne**.)
Royalties paid twice yearly. *Overseas associates* in Australia, Canada, New Zealand, and USA. Associate companies throughout the world.

Authors' Rating Once the star turn of British publishing, **Penguin** slid into deep trouble in the seventies when one author after another fell victim to ferocious internal politics. Then Peter Mayer came in from America with bright ideas for broadening the list (which was beginning to look like a *Who's Who* of the thirties) and for beefing up the marketing department. Sighs of relief and satisfaction all round. With recovery well underway, **Penguin** embarked on a series of acquisitions – all good names like **Michael Joseph** and **Hamish Hamilton** which nonetheless were able to benefit from the Mayer touch. One of the cleverest purchases was **Frederick Warne**, who had been underplaying the Beatrix Potter backlist. **Viking**, the new hardback list from **Penguin**, is a wonderful revelation for those who remember the last Penguin attempt (**Allen Lane Press**) to straddle the two sides of publishing. Generally authors feel themselves lucky to be with Penguin. The name is still one of the most easily recognisable in publishing. When it is backed by efficient marketing it can do wonders for authors who might not otherwise expect a big return on their efforts. The only notes of dissent are to be heard from those who fear a shift of control from London to New York. Peter Mayer recently moved back across the Atlantic where **Penguin** have just added **New American Library** to their collection of trophies. This latest development should lead to opportunities for British writers to break into the lucrative American mass market. But does it also mean that all important editorial decisions will be taken in Manhattan?

Pergamon Press
Headington Hill Hall, Oxford OX3 0BW   ☎ 0865 64881   Telex 83177 Pergap P

Joint Managing Directors *W. A. Snyder and A. J. Steel*

FOUNDED 1948. *Publishes* academic & scholarly, agriculture, atlases & maps, bibliography & library service, biology & zoology, business & industry, chemistry, computer science, economics, educational & textbooks, engineering, geography & geology, languages & linguistics, mathematics & statistics, medical, philosophy, physics, politics & world affairs, psychology, reference books & dictionaries, scientific & technical, sociology & anthropology, vocational training & careers, women's studies. 300 titles in 1986. Also publish journals in all the same subjects as their book list. **Chief Executive** (for Pergamon Journals) *Kevin Maxwell.* **Deputy Chief Executive** (for Pergamon Journals) *G. F. Richard.* **Associate Publisher** (for Pergamon Journals) *Dr Ivan Klimes.*

Deputy Director for academic books, *Barbara Barrett.* **Deputy Director** for major reference works, *Colin Drayton.* Welcome unsolicited mss and synopses if within specialist range.
Royalties paid annually. *Overseas associates* in USA, Australia, Japan, China, Germany and France.

Authors' Rating Factory publishing true to the ideals of Robert Maxwell. Impersonal but efficient as long as the author is prepared to do his own editing.

Phaidon Press Ltd
Littlegate House, St Ebbe's Street, Oxford OX1 1SQ ☎0865 246681   Telex 83308

Chairman *George J. Riches*   **Managing Director** *D. M. Phillips*

Publishes academic & scholarly, antiques & collecting, archaeology, architecture & design, crafts & hobbies, fine art & art history, guide books, photography, theatre & drama. 60 titles in 1986.

Editorial Head *Simon Haviland*   TITLES *Art Expo '87; Berthe Morisot; Manet; Designing with Computers;* Phaidon Cultural Guides; Colour Library Series; *The Anglo-Saxons; The Book of the Violin; The Chinese Potter; Discover Unexpected London; The Complete Guide to Calligraphy; When Advertising Tried Harder; Produce: A Fruit and Vegetable Lovers' Guide.* Welcome unsolicited mss although 'only approximately one per cent of unsolicited material gets published'.
Royalties paid quarterly.

Authors' Rating One of the two leading art publishers (the other is **Thames and Hudson**). Beautiful books on esoteric subjects.

Piccadilly Press
15 Golders Green Crescent, London NW11 8LA   ☎01–209 1326   Telex 295441

Chairman *Brenda Gardner*   **Approximate Annual Turnover** £400,000

FOUNDED 1983 by Brenda Gardner. First titles published February 1984. Piccadilly plans to stay small, publishing between 20 and 25 titles per year. A total staff of 4. *Publishes* children's hardbacks, picture and story books, some teenage non-fiction. Just moving into teenage fiction. Unsolicited synopses and ideas for books welcome. *Royalties* paid twice yearly.

Authors' Rating Small company with exciting ideas inspired by the former children's editor of W. H. Allen.

Pitman Publishing

128 Long Acre, London WC2E 9AN ☎01–379 7383   Telex 261367 Pitman G

Chairman *Robert Duncan*   **Managing Director** *Ian Pringle*
Approximate Annual Turnover £6.5 million

Part of the Longman Group. FOUNDED 1837 as the publisher of the Pitman Shorthand System ('150 years of innovation in business education.') Pitman has now joined Longman as its specialist Business Education and Information Technology publishing house. *Publishes* textbooks, reference and dictionaries in business education, including secretarial, business studies, management and professional studies. Professional and textbook publishers in all areas of information technology, including computers, microelectronics and telecommunications. 164 titles in 1986.

DIVISIONS
Secretarial Studies *K. C. Roberts*   TITLES Universal typing   **Business Education** *K. C. Roberts*   TITLES *Business A/Cs 1 & 2* Frank Wood   **Business Management** *Simon Lake*   TITLES *English Law; Accounting Theory and Practice*   **Professional Studies** *Helen Beltran*   TITLES *M & E Handbooks*   **Information Technology** *John Cushion*   TITLES *Research Notes in Artificial Intelligence; Systems Design with Advanced Microprocessors.*

IMPRINTS
M & E *Helen Beltran*   TITLES *M & E Handbook*   **Pitman** *Ian Pringle*   **Polytech Publishers** *Ian Pringle*   TITLES *Finance* Frank Wood. Unsolicited mss, synopses and ideas for books welcome.
Royalties paid annually.

Authors' Rating Formerly a medical publisher of note, some authors were unhappy when they were hived off to other parts of the Longman empire. But Pitman are reasserting themselves with a growing reputation for good quality business books.

Plenum Publishing Ltd

88–90 Middlesex Street, London E1 7EZ   ☎01–377 0686

Chairman *Martin E. Tash (USA)*   **Managing Director** *Dr Ken Derham*

FOUNDED 1940. Part of Plenum Publishing Corporation, New York. The London office is the editorial and marketing base for the UK and Europe. *Publishes* postgraduate, professional and research level scientific, technical and medical monographs, conference proceedings, reference books. 325 titles (worldwide) in 1986.

Editorial Head *Dr Ken Derham (UK and Europe)*

IMPRINTS
Consultants Bureau, IFI Plenum Data Company, Plenum Medical Company, Plenum Press. Synopses preferred to finished mss.
Royalties paid annually.

Plexus Publishing Ltd

30 Craven Street, London WC2N 5NT   ☎01–839 1315/6   Telex 947157

Chairman *T. C. Porter*   **Managing Director** *S. M. Wake*

FOUNDED 1973. *Publishes* high quality illustrated books, specialising in international co-editions with an emphasis on biography, popular music, rock'n'roll, popular culture, art and cinema. 8 titles in 1986.

Senior Editor *Sandra Wake*   Unsolicited mss, synopses and ideas welcome. *Royalties* paid twice yearly.

Pluto Press Ltd

11–21 Northdown Street, London N1 9BN   ☎01–837 3322

Bought by **Zwan Publishers** in 1987. At the time of writing, editorial future uncertain. *Publishes* (prior to takeover) academic and scholarly, atlases and maps, biography and autobiography, cinema and video, crime, economics, fiction, fine arts, health, history, law, literature and criticism, philosophy, photography, poetry, politics and world affairs, psychology, reference books, sociology and anthropology, theatre and drama, women's studies. 54 titles in 1986.

Prism Press Book Publishers Ltd

2 South Street, Bridport, Dorset DT6 3NQ   ☎0308 27022
Telex 265871 MONREF G 84 MNU 247

Managing Director *Julian King*   **Approximate Annual Turnover** £250,000

FOUNDED 1974 by Julian King and Colin Spooner. *Publishes* alternative medicine, occult, mysticism, wholefood cookery, health, architecture, building, farming, conservation, the environment, feminism, politics, philosophy, and law. 12 titles in 1986.

PRISM EXPRESS LTD is a new sister company. *Publishes* advanced research, primarily in social and political science, Asian and Middle Eastern studies and the third world. 6 titles initially.

Unsolicited mss and unsolicited synopses/ideas welcome.
Royalties paid twice yearly. *Overseas associates* Prism Press USA.

Quartet Books

27–29 Goodge Street, London W1P 1FD   ☎01 636 3992   Telex 919034

Chairman *Naim Attalah*   **Approximate Annual Turnover** £1 million

FOUNDED in 1972 by four ex-Granada employees, the company was acquired by Naim Attalah in 1976. Part of the **Namara Group**, which also includes **The Women's Press** (1977) and **Robin Clark Ltd** (bought in 1980). *Publishes* fiction, popular non-fiction, Middle Eastern politics, jazz, and Sloane Ranger books. 64 titles in 1986.

DIVISIONS
Quartet Crime *Tim Binyon* TITLES *Counterfeit of Murder* **Quartet Encounters** *Stephen Pickles* TITLES *The Sleepwalkers*. Welcome unsolicited mss and synopses/ideas for books.
Royalties paid twice yearly.

Authors' Rating A high profile company riding on the flamboyant reputation of its owner, Naim Attalah, a wealthy Palestinian-born entrepreneur whose other publishing interests include the best of the book journals, *The Literary Review*. The potential rewards are great for quality fiction and non-fiction.

Quiller Press

50 Albermarle Street, London W1X 4BD   ☎01–499 6529   Telex 21100

Managing Director *Jeremy Greenwood*

Quiller specialise in sponsored books and publications sold through non-book trade channels. But not vanity publishing. *Publishes* business and industry, children's, cookery, wine and spirits, crafts and hobbies, DIY, gardening, guide books, humour, reference, sports and games, travel and topography. 15 titles in 1986.

Editorial director *Jeremy Greenwood*   Unsolicited mss not welcome, as ideas nearly always originate in house.
Royalties twice yearly.

Authors' Rating Quality publisher with sound ideas.

Rainbird Publishing Group Ltd

27 Wrights Lane, London W8 5TZ   ☎01–938 2200   Telex 917181

Managing Director *Valerie Reuben*

Part of the **Penguin Group**. *Publishes* archaeology, auto/biography, cookery, wines & spirits, crafts and hobbies, fashion, gardening, illustrated, magic and the occult, military and war, natural history, reference books and dictionaries, travel and topography. 10 titles in 1986.

Editorial Director *Diana Levinson* (Commissioning)   Unsolicited mss welcome.
Royalties paid twice yearly.

Authors' Rating See **Penguin**.

The Ramsay Head Press

15 Gloucester Place, Edinburgh EH3 6EE   ☎031–225 5646

Joint Managing Directors *Mrs Christine Wilson & Conrad Wilson*

A small independent family publisher founded in 1968 by Norman Wilson OBE. *Publishes* Scottish fiction and non-fiction, biographies, cookery. Approximately 6 titles in 1986.

TITLES *White Stone Country; Reminiscences of Growing Up in Buchan* David Ogston; *Murder, Murder, Polis* Maureen Sinclair; *A Handy Guide to Scots* William Graham; *The Autobiography of a Poet* Duncan Glen. Welcome synopses and ideas for books if they come within their range (Scottish).
Royalties paid twice yearly.

Robinson Publishing
11 Shepherd House, Shepherd Street, London W1Y 7LD ☎01–493 1064
Telex 28905 Ref 778

Managing Director *Nick Robinson*

FOUNDED 1983. *Publishes* general fiction and non-fiction trade paperbacks, some hardbacks. Specialist areas include science fiction, fantasy, crime and country matters. 12 titles in 1986. 20 titles in 1987.

Editorial Head *Nick Robinson* No unsolicited mss. Synopses and ideas for books welcome.
Royalties paid twice yearly.

Robson Books Ltd
Bolsover House, 5–6 Clipstone Street, London W1P 7EP ☎01–637 5937

Managing Director *Jeremy Robson*

FOUNDED in 1984 by Jeremy Robson. *Publishes* fiction and general non-fiction including biography & autobiography, cinema & video, cookery, wine & spirits, gardening, guide books, health & beauty, humour, science fiction, sports & games, theatre & drama, travel & topography. 60 titles in 1986.

Editorial Head *Susan Rea* TITLES *Something to Fall Back On* Maureen Lipman; *Anneka Rice Adventure Series: Ski-ing With Anneka; Sailing With Anneka; Scuba Diving With Anneka; Bernard Haitink: A Working Life.* Unsolicited mss, synopses and ideas for books welcome.
Royalties paid twice yearly.

Authors' Rating A pleasant company to deal with, but it can take some time to get a response.

Routledge & Kegan Paul
11 New Fetter Lane, London EC4P 4EE ☎01–583 9855 Telex 263398

Chairman *Norman Franklin* **Managing Director** *John Naylor*
Approximate Annual Turnover £6 million

Bought by **Associated Book Publishers** (who were themselves taken over by **International Thomson Organisation** in 1987) in 1985. George Routledge set up business as a bookseller in 1836 and published his first book in that year. In 1911 Routledge took over the management of **Kegan Paul, Trench, Trübner**, which was a soundly based academic company. It became **Routledge & Kegan Paul** in 1977. At the beginning of the war it published a mixture of trade books, political books and an increasing academic list. 1979 published their first best seller since *Uncle Tom's Cabin*, Stephen Pile's *Book Of Heroic Failures*. **Ark** paperbacks launched in 1982 as a low-priced mass market venture. 1983 launched **Pandora Press**, an imprint for women. **Arkana**, a Mind, Body & Spirit list launched in 1984. 280 titles in 1986.

Editor *John Naylor*   *Publishes* academic and scholarly; archaeology; architecture and design; biography and autobiography; business and industry; cinema and video; crafts and hobbies; economics; general science; geography and geology; guide books; history and antiquarian; humour; languages and linguistics; literature and criticism; magic and the occult; mathematics and statistics; military and war; nautical; philosophy; politics and world affairs; psychology; reference books and dictionaries; religion and theology; sociology and anthropology; theatre and drama; transport; travel and topography; women's studies.

IMPRINTS
Ark *Norman Franklin* TITLE *The Rosicrucian Enlightenment*. **Arkana** *Eileen Campbell* TITLE *A Course In Miracles*. **Pandora Press** *Phillipa Brewster* TITLE *Women Talking* Mary Stott (ed.). Prefer to see synopses and ideas rather than complete mss.
Royalties paid yearly and half-yearly.

Authors' Rating See **Associated Book Publishers**.

Robert Royce Ltd
93 Bedwardine Road, London SE19 3AY   ☎01–771 2496
                                                    Telex 858846 T BOOKS G

Chairman *Sir Emmanuel Kaye CBE*   **Managing Director** *Robert Royce*
                                    Approximate Annual Turnover £100,000

FOUNDED 1984. Editorial commitment to careful attention to authors, as 'every title is important to a small company'. No publishing divisions; prospective titles are considered by the firm as a whole. *Publishes* fiction, historical, and some educational. 6 titles in 1986.

Editorial Head *Robert Royce* TITLES *Harry* (fiction); *The History of the Royal Academy*; *Teaching Shakespeare*. Unsolicited mss, synopses and ideas welcome.
Royalties paid twice yearly. *Overseas associates* agents in Australia, New Zealand and the Far East.

Authors' Rating Good reports. Independent company set up on the basis of solid experience in the industry.

Sage Publications Ltd
28 Banner Street, London EC1Y 8QE   ☎01–253 1516   Telex 296207 SAGE

Managing Director *David Brooks*

Founded in 1967 in California. The London office has been going for ten years. *Publishes* academic and scholarly. 35 titles in 1986.

Editorial Director *David Hill* TITLES *Robert Colquhoun* Raymond Arron. Welcome unsolicited mss and synopses.
Royalties paid quarterly.

Sangam Books Ltd
57 Fruit Exchange, Brushfield Street, London E1 6EP ☎01–377 6399

Chairman/Managing Director *Anthony de Souza*

Publishes mainly non-fiction, including sociology, school textbooks, medical with some fiction. TITLES *The Mahabharata* Shanta Rameshwar, *In Worship of Shiva* Shanta Rameshwar. Unsolicited mss and synopses welcome.

W. B. Saunders Co.
Now part of **Academic Press** (same address)

Publishes academic and scholarly, animal care and breeding, biology and zoology, medical, veterinary, nursing. 120 titles in 1985.

Scholastic Publications Ltd
Marlborough House, Holly Walk, Leamington Spa, Warwickshire CV32 4LS
☎092681 3910   Telex 312138 SPLS G

Chairman *M. Robinson*   **Managing Director** *J. E. Cox*
Approximate Annual Turnover £7.5 million

Founded in 1964 as part of Scholastic Inc. of New York, Scholastic is the largest school-based book club operator in the UK, publishing teachers' magazines including *Child Education*, as well as general children's titles. The Hippo children's paperback imprint was launched in 1980, and educational books were added to the list in 1984. A major expansion of the educational book publishing programme is planned for the near future. *Publishes* children's paperbacks, professional reference books for primary school teachers, primary school pupil materials, plus magazines for primary school teachers. 85 titles in 1986.

DIVISIONS
Hippo Children's paperbacks *Dorothy Wood* TITLES *Postman Pat; Cheerleaders; 101 Dalmations* and other Disney Classics; *Roland Rat Living Legend; Conrad's War*. **Scholastic Educational Books** *Priscilla Chambers* TITLES *Bright Ideas* series; teacher handbooks. Unsolicited mss, synopses and ideas for books welcome. *Royalties* paid twice yearly.

Authors' Rating An excellent marketing operation selling directly to schools and to school book clubs. Can be highly profitable for authors.

Scorpion Publishing Ltd

Victoria House, Victoria Road, Buckhurst Hill, Essex IG9 5ES   ☎01–506 0606
Telex 896988 SCOOPS G

Managing Director *Leonard Harrow*

FOUNDED 1976. Part of the Scorpion Group. *Publishes* Islamic art, history and culture plus a socialist list. 6 titles in 1986.

Editorial Director *Leonard Harrow*   Welcome unsolicited mss and synopses if they come within their subject areas.
Royalty payments vary according to contract.

Scottish Academic Press

33 Montgomery Street, Edinburgh EH7 5JX   ☎031–556 2796

Managing Director *Dr Douglas Grant*

FOUNDED 1969. *Publishes* academic (architecture, education, geology, history, journals, literature, social sciences, theology). Work in conjunction with **Handsel Press** (theology). Distribute titles for **Sussex University Press**. 30 titles in 1986.   TITLES *The Novels of Neil Gunn: A Critical Study* Margery McCulloch, *An Excursion Guide to the Geology of the Lothians* D. McAdam and E. Clarkson. Most of the books are commissioned, but will consider unsolicited mss and synopses.
Royalties paid annually.

SCM Press Ltd

26–30 Tottenham Road, London N1 4BZ   ☎01–249 7262/5

Managing Director Rev. Dr John Bowden

Publishes mainly religion and theology with some ethics and philosophy. 50 titles in 1986. Will consider unsolicited mss and synopses.
Royalties paid annually.

Authors' Rating Leading publisher of religious ideas with reputation for open mindedness dating back to the *Honest To God* controversy of the 1960s.

Search Press Ltd/Burns & Oates

Wellwood, North Farm Road, Tunbridge Wells, Kent TN2 3DR   ☎0892 44037/8
Telex 957258

Chairman/Managing Director *Countess de la Bedoyere*

Burns & Oates were founded in 1847 and were publishers to the Holy See. **Search Press** publishes full colour arts & craft books and cookery books. *Publishes* art, craft, cookery, needlecrafts, philosophy, social sciences, theology, literary criticism, history, spirituality, educational and Third World. 12 titles in 1986.

Craft etc *Pamela Dawson* (**Search Press**)   Academic *John Bright-Holmes* Unsolicited mss, snyopses and ideas for books welcome.
Royalties paid annually.

Authors' Rating A conservative Catholic publisher which has never quite come to terms with Vatican liberalisation.

Secker & Warburg Ltd
54 Poland Street, London W1V 3AF   ☎01–437 2075   Telex 267613 Secker G

Chairman *Nicolas Thompson*   **Publishing Director** *David Godwin*

Part of the **Heinemann & Octopus Publishing Group**. Founded by Fred Warburg in 1936 when he bought out Martin Secker. *Publishes* academic & scholarly; architecture & design; autobiography & biography; cinema; crime; fiction; fine art & art history; history; humour; illustrated & fine editions; literature & criticism; photography; poetry; politics & world affairs; theatre & drama. 120 titles in 1986.

Editorial Director *John Blackwell*   TITLES *Porterhouse Blue* Tom Sharpe; *Legacy* James A. Michener; *The Collected Stories of Angus Wilson*.

IMPRINT
The Alison Press   TITLE *More Die Of Heartbreak* Saul Bellow. Welcome unsolicited mss and synopses.
Royalties paid twice yearly. *Overseas associates* Same as **Heinemann**.

Authors' Rating After the departure of Tom Rosenthal to **Deutsch, Secker & Warburg** seemed to opt for a lower profile. While respecting the list some authors thought the publisher was in danger of losing its identity. But recently there have been signs of a comeback starting with a new look to the poetry list.

Severn House Publishers
2nd Floor, 40–42 William IV Street, London WC2N 4DF   ☎01–240 9683
Telex 295041 SEVERN G

Chairman *Edwin Buckhalter*

FOUNDED 1974, a leader in library fiction publishing. Several bestsellers both in the UK and overseas. *Publishes* mainly hardcover fiction, with a growing paperback non-fiction list plus some mass market titles. 135 titles in 1986.

DIVISIONS
Fiction *Stephanie Townsend*   **Non-Fiction** *Lucy Lloyd*. NB All unsolicited mss should be sent to *Hilary Gibb*. Welcome unsolicited mss. Synopses/proposals only through bona fide literary agents.
Royalties paid twice yearly. *Overseas associates* Severn House Publishers Inc, New York.

Shire Publications Ltd

Cromwell House, Church Street, Princes Risborough, Aylesbury, Buckinghamshire
HP17 9AJ   ☎08444 4301

Managing Director *John Rotheroe*

FOUNDED 1967. *Publishes* Original non-fiction paperbacks. 60 titles in 1986. No unsolicited material. Prefer introductory letter with detailed outline of idea.
Royalties paid annually.

Sidgwick & Jackson Ltd

1 Tavistock Chambers, Bloomsbury Way, London WC1A 3AA   ☎01–242 6081
                                                      Telex 8952953 SIDJAK G

Chairman *Sir William Rees-Mogg*   **Managing Director** *William Armstrong*
                            Approximate Annual Turnover £3.75 million

FOUNDED 1908, the company was controlled by Lord Forte from the early 1960s until
its sale to **Macmillan** in 1986. Sir William Rees-Mogg took over from Lord Longford
as Chairman in 1986. *Publishes* biography, autobiography, military history, women's
fiction, sport, humour, management and business, pop/rock, cookery, craft, current
affairs, illustrated gift books, astronomy, religion, illustrated classics, cinema and
theatre. 100 titles in 1986.

Editorial Director *Robert Smith*   **Deputy Editorial Director** *Susan Hill*   **Editor**
Carey Smith. Bestselling titles have included *Superwoman* and *Lace* Shirley Conran;
The Third World War General Sir John Hackett; Lee Iacocca's autobiography; *Is That
It?* Bob Geldof. Unsolicited mss are always welcome but rarely published. Prefer to
see a synopsis and sample chapter. Most of the titles published are as a result of
commissioned ideas (such as the Geldof autobiography), submissions from agents, or
from staff contacts.
Royalties paid twice yearly.

Authors' Rating Once renowned for stealing a march on bigger publishers by its
imaginative promotion of best selling titles, the company has got more cautious of
late with its range of middle brow culture. The first result of the Macmillan connection is a new fiction department, with a specialist fiction editor and assistant, who
will commission about 24 books a year.

Simon & Schuster Ltd

West Garden Place, Kendal Street, London W2 2AQ   ☎01–724 7577   Telex
21702

Chairman *Clyde Hunter*   **Managing Director** *Clyde Hunter*

A new publisher on the British scene. *Publishes* general books (no academic or
technical), specialising in trade books – sport, travel and children's particularly.
Only one fiction title thus far – the *Blue Murder* series of classic US crime. As the
company has only been in Britain since August 1986, it started out with a mainly
American list, which has now been reduced to a 50/50 balance between US and

British titles. Planning to do more fiction in the future. Around 50 titles by the end of 1987.

EDITORIAL DIRECTORS

Fiction *Robyn Sisman*   **Non-Fiction** *Nicholas Brearley*   **Children's books** *Denise Johnstone-Burt*

Unsolicited mss welcome.
Royalties paid twice yearly.

Authors' Rating A breath of fresh air on the UK publishing scene. Eager for product and open to new ideas. Healthy advances.

Charles Skilton Ltd

2 Caversham Street, London SW3 and Whittingehame House, Haddington, Scotland
☎01-351 4995/03685 345

Managing Director *Charles Skilton*

FOUNDED in 1944, Charles Skilton now have offices in London and the West Country, as well as in Haddington. *Publishes* biography, art, architecture, local history, fiction, poetry, limited editions. 50 titles in 1986.

Editorial Head *Leonard Holdsworth*

IMPRINTS

Albyn Press *Leonard Holdsworth* Titles of Scottish interest   **Fudge & Co** *Leonard Holdsworth*   **Luxor Press** *Leonard Holdsworth*   **Mitre Press** *Leonard Holdsworth*. Poetry, biography   **Tallis Press** *Leonard Holdsworth*. Unsolicited mss, synopses and ideas for books welcome.
Royalties paid twice yearly.

Authors' Rating Strong leaning towards vanity publishing. The usual warnings apply.

Society for Promoting Christian Knowledge (SPCK)

Holy Trinity Church, Marylebone Road, London NW1 4DU   ☎01–387 5282

Chairman *Rt Rev David Young*, Bishop of Ripon   **Gen Secretary** *Mr P. N. G. Gilbert*   **Approximate Annual Turnover** £1.5 million

FOUNDED 1698, SPCK is the oldest religious publisher in England. *Publishes* theological works and self-help of a serious-minded pastoral nature. 80 titles in 1986.

DIVISIONS

SPCK *Judith Longman*   TITLES *Dictionary of Pastoral Care*.

IMPRINTS

Triangle (paperback) *Myrtle Powley*   TITLES *Agenda for Biblical People*   **Sheldon Press** *Darley Anderson*   TITLES *Overcoming Common Problems* Unsolicited synopses/ideas for books welcome.
Royalties paid annually.

Authors' Rating Anglican publisher in the conservative mould.

Souvenir Press Ltd
43 Great Russell Street, London WC1B 3PA ☎ 01–580 9307
Telex 24710 SOUVNR G

Chairman/Managing Director *Ernest Hecht*

Publishes academic and scholarly, animal care/breeding, antiques and collecting, archaeology, auto/biography, business and industry, children's, cookery, crime, crafts and hobbies, educational, fiction, gardening, health and beauty, history/antiquarian, humour, illustrated and fine editions, magic and the occult, medical, military, music, natural history, philosophy, psychology, religious, sociology, sports, theatre, veterinary and women's studies. 46 titles in 1986.

Senior editor *Tessa Harrow*

IMPRINTS
Condor, Human Horizons, Souvenir Press Ltd Unsolicited mss welcome. *Royalties* paid twice yearly.

Authors' Rating One of the best independent publishers in London. Ernest Hecht takes all important decisions which can make life difficult if he happens to be away. But he does have a wonderful ability for judging public taste two years in advance. Authors feel comfortable with him.

Spellmount Ltd
12 Dene Way, Speldhurst, nr Tunbridge Wells, Kent TN3 0NX ☎ 089 286 2860

Chairman *Brian Austin*   **Managing Director** *Ian Morley-Clarke*
Approximate Annual Turnover £175,000

FOUNDED 1983. Jointly owned by Ian & Kathleen Morley-Clarke and Vale Packaging Ltd, of Tonbridge. *Publishes* Non-fiction hardback titles; biographies of composers, popular musicians, jazz, cricketers, county anthologies, militaria, companion guides to music and the arts. 11 titles in 1986.

DIVISIONS
Companion Guides *Peter Gammond* **County Anthologies** *John Bright-Holmes* **Cricket biographies** *John Bright-Holmes* **Jazz biographies** *Bruce Crowther* **Militaria** *Kathleen Morley-Clarke*. No unsolicited mss. Synopses/ideas for books in Spellmount's specialist fields only.
Royalties paid annually.

Sphere Books Ltd
27 Wrights Lane, London W8 5TZ ☎ 01–937 8070   Telex 917181

Managing Director *Nicholas Webb*
Approximate Annual Turnover £10 million

FOUNDED 1967. A medium sized paperback house, formerly belonging to **Thomson International**, now part of the **Penguin Group**. Remaining chiefly mass market, it has also successfully diversified into Management and Reference publishing. The trade paperback imprint, **Abacus**, is covered by the Sphere umbrella.

Publishes paperback fiction and non-fiction of all kinds, except children's books. Particularly strong on literary/popular fiction, reference and management titles. 230 titles in 1986.

DIVISIONS
Abacus *Mike Petty* TITLES *Hawksmoor* Peter Ackroyd **Sphere** *Barbara Boote* TITLES *Secrets* Danielle Steel **Sphere Reference** *James Tindall* TITLES *Manager's Handbook*. Unsolicited mss are tolerated, despite being time-consuming and rarely bringing to light a commercially appealing book. A qualified welcome for synopses. These should be accompanied by a sample chapter: 'execution is all'. Similarly, authors of ideas must show some evidence of their ability to deliver a publishable finished book.
Royalties paid twice yearly.

Authors' Rating More the pop side of Penguin, though the overlap is such it is sometimes difficult to understand why a book should be **Sphere** (or **Abacus**) and not **Penguin**. Room for rationalisation?

Springwood Books Ltd
Springwood House, The Avenue, Ascot, Berkshire SL5 7LY ☎ 0990 24053
Telex 8813271 GECOMS G

Chairman & Managing Director *Christopher K. Foster*

FOUNDED 1977. *Publishes* General non-fiction: sports, astrology, children's books, company histories, autobiographies. 10 titles in 1986.

Publishing Director *Mrs Lesley Morris* TITLES *Schweppes, The First Two Hundred Years*; *The Open Championship Annual*; *A Story of Hand Knitting*. No unsolicited mss. Will consider synopses/ideas for books.
Royalties vary from contract to contract.

Squirrel Publications Ltd
210 Carlton Road, Romford, Essex RM2 5BA ☎ 0708 20343

Managing Director *L. W. H. Pepall*

FOUNDED 1984. First title was *The Book of Arguments*. A very young company still finding their feet but hoping to branch out into wider fields in due course. *Publishes* fiction, humour, children's books. 5 titles in 1986.

Editorial Head *L. W. H. Pepall*. TITLES *The Wags* series (4 titles); *The Lolobal Book*. Do not welcome unsolicited mss. Prefer to see synopsis or outline first.
Royalties paid annually.

Stainer & Bell Ltd
PO Box 110, 82 High Road, London N2 9PW ☎01–444 9135

Chairman *Allen Dain Percival* **Managing Director** *Bernard Arthur Braley*
Approximate Annual Turnover £437,000

FOUNDED 1907 to publish sheet music. Now *Publishes* music and religious subjects.
2 titles in 1986.

Editorial Director *A. D. Percival* Mss welcome only if preceded by letter enclosing
brief precis. Unsolicited synopses/ideas for books welcome.
Royalties paid annually.

Studio Publications (Ipswich) Ltd
The Drift, Nacton Road, Ipswich, Suffolk IP3 9Q3 ☎0473 270880
Telex 98551 STUDIO G

Chairman *Mr M. Kelley* **Managing Director** *Mr B. J. Henderson*
Approximate Annual Turnover up to £1 million

FOUNDED 1973. Part of **Ladybird Books** (which is part of the Longman Group).
Initially published sports books, but soon branched out into children's titles.
Acquired by Ladybird in 1986. Studio Publications intend to broaden their range of
titles to cater for older children, but will remain mass market publishers. *Publishes*
picture story books, board books, early educational, novelty and activity books; age
range 0–10 years. Also television character series, and short stories. 50 titles in 1986.

Editorial Head *H. V. Jones*

IMPRINTS
Badger Books TITLES Wacky Races series. **Bunny Books** TITLES Cobweb
series. Unsolicited mss welcome if illustrated; otherwise submit synopses/ideas only.
Royalties paid twice yearly.

Surrey University Press
Bishopbriggs, Glasgow G64 2NZ ☎041–772 2311 Telex 777283 BLACKI G

Chairman & Managing Director *R. Michael Miller*

An imprint of **Blackie & Sons Ltd**. *Publishes* Academic, scientific and technical.
3 titles in 1986.

Editorial Head *A. Graeme Mackintosh* TITLES *Handbook of Engineering Geomor-
phology; Management Accounting for Hotels and Restaurants, Second Edition*. Prefer
synopses rather than complete mss.
Royalties paid annually and twice yearly.

Alan Sutton Publishing Ltd
30 Brunswick Road, Gloucester GL1 1JJ   ☎0452 419575   Telex 43690

Managing Director *Alan Sutton*

FOUNDED 1979. *Publishes* archaeology, countryside, history, letters and diaries, topography, biography. 100 titles in 1986.

Editorial Director *Peter Clifford*

PAPERBACK IMPRINT
Pocket Classics Prefer to see synopses rather than complete mss.
Royalties paid twice yearly.

Sweet & Maxwell Ltd
11 New Fetter Lane, London EC4P 4EE   ☎01–583 9855   Telex 263398

Chairman *C. D. O. Evans*   **Managing Director** *A. Prideaux*

Part of **Associated Book Publishers Ltd (ABP)**. *Publishes* law books. 120 titles in 1986.

Editorial Directors *Robert McKay, Jane Belford, Hugh Jones.*   TITLES (For the practitioner) *Company Accounts; Encyclopedia of Professional Partnerships; Planning Decisions Digest.* (For the student) *Litigation for the Law Society Finals; Administrative Law; ILEX: Introduction to Law.* Although mss will be considered it is unlikely they will be published due to the highly specialised nature of the list. Synopses and outlines welcome.
Royalty payments vary according to contract.

Tavistock Publications Ltd
11 New Fetter Lane, London EC4P 4EE   ☎01–583 9855   Telex 47214

Managing Director *Gill Davies*

Part of **Associated Book Publishers Ltd (ABP)**. *Publishes* non-fiction: academic/scholarly, bibliography/library, educational and textbook, medical, philosophy, psychology, sociology, anthropology, women's studies. 56 titles in 1986.

Editorial Head *Gill Davies*   TITLES *Jane Austen and the State, Hinduism in Great Britain, Gender, Images of Art Therapy, International Bibliography of the Social Sciences.* Prefer to see a proposal and outline rather than complete manuscript.
Royalties paid twice yearly.

Thames & Hudson Ltd
30–34 Bloomsbury Street, London WC1B 3QP   ☎01–636 5488   Telex 25992

Managing Director *Thomas Neurath*

Publishes art books. Also academic & scholarly, archaeology, architecture & design, children's books, crafts & hobbies, history & antiquarian, illustrated & fine editions, literature & criticism, medical, music, philosophy, psychology, sociology & anthropology, theatre & drama, travel & topography. 120 titles in 1986.

Editorial Head *Jamie Camplin*.   TITLES *World of Art series*; *The Triumph of Light and Nature*; *The International Design Yearbook*; *Fashion Illustration Today*; *Henri Cartier-Bresson in India*; *Exploring the World of the Pharaohs*; *Basic Perspective*; Thames & Hudson Literary Lives; *Beethoven*; *The Ancient Science of Geomancy*; *Photography as Fine Art*; *Silversmithing*; *Exploring Cornwall 100 Years Ago*. No unsolicited mss. Prefer to see preliminary letter and outline.
Royalties paid twice yearly.

Authors' Rating One of the two leading art publishers (the other is Phaidon). High quality books which make you proud to be an author.

Thornhill Press
24 Moorend Road, Cheltenham, Gloucestershire GL53 0EU   ☎0242 519137

Managing Director *Desmond Badham-Thornhill*
                                        Approximate Annual Turnover £50,000

FOUNDED 1972. *Publishes* mainly walking and touring guides, sport, plus some general titles (no fiction or poetry). 5 titles in 1986.

Editorial Head *Desmond Badham-Thornhill*. Unsolicited mss, synopses and ideas for books welcome.
Royalties paid quarterly.

Thorsons Publishing Group Ltd
Denington Estate, Wellingborough, Northants NN8 2RQ   ☎0933 76031
                                        Telex 311072 THOPUB G

Chairman *Mr J. A. Young*   **Managing Director** *Mr David Young*
                                        Approximate Annual Turnover £10 million

FOUNDED 1930, acquired the **Aquarian Press** in 1955, and added **Patrick Stephens** to the group in 1984. The **Crucible** imprint was launched in 1986, and the **Equation** imprint in May 1987. 215 titles in 1986.

DIVISIONS
Thorsons *John Hardaker*   Health, Self Improvement, Cookery, Medical, Alternative Medical, Self-help cassettes; Crafts & Hobbies; Children's non-fiction.   TITLES *The Vitamin Fact Finder*; *The Joy of Touch*; *Vegetarian Pasta Dishes*; *Hypnothink*; *Soft tissue Manipulation*; *The Changing Image of Woman*.

IMPRINTS
The Aquarian Press *Michael Cox*   Healing/Yoga; Occultism; Divination, paranormal; Tarot; Astrology; Self development; Freemasonry   TITLES *Highways of the Mind*; *The Alternative I Ching*; *Yeats' Golden Dawn*; *You & Your Aura*; *Practical Celtic Magic*.   **Crucible** *Michael Cox*   History of Religion; of Occultism; Women's Studies; Literature/Supernatural Fiction; Biography; Dance.   TITLES *Ghosts & Scholars*; *Isadora: Portrait of the Artist as a Woman*; *The Illustrated J. S. Le Fanu*; *The*

Rosicrucians. **Equation** *Michael Cox.* The new general interest imprint. TITLES *I Remember Jazz; Country Music USA; The Home-Made Xmas; Dining in Grand Styles; Naughty Dots Around the World.* **Patrick Stephens Ltd** *Darryl Reach* Aviation, Railways, Maritime, Commercial Vehicles, Motoring, Astronomy. TITLES *Classic Fighter Aircraft; Wreck & Recovery; Famous Ocean Liners; Planetary Exploration.*

Authors' Rating Under David Young, who is also the new chairman of the **Book Marketing Council, Thorsons** is coming up fast as a publisher of popular non-fiction. Open to new ideas and prepared to back them with imaginative promotion.

Times Books Ltd

16 Golden Square, London W1R 4BN ☎01–434 3767 Telex 897284 ARPUB G

Managing Director *Barry Winkleman*

Part of **News International** *Publishes* mainly atlases with some reference and non-fiction. 8 titles in 1986.

Editorial Head *Paul Middleton* Unsolicited mss should be preceded by letter with outline.
Royalties paid twice yearly.

Titan Books

58 St Giles High Street, London WC2H 8LW ☎01–836 4056

Managing Director *Nick Landau*

FORMED 1981 by Nick Landau and has grown 'incredibly' in the last six years to become the largest publisher of graphic novels and graphic albums in the UK. Moving into mass market paperbacks with a range of Star Trek novels. *Publishes* film and television fantasy, comic strip. 25 titles in 1986.

Managing Editor *Bernie Jaye* TITLES *Batman, Dark Night Returns* Frank Miller; *The Ballad of Halo* Jones Alan Moore; *Judge Dread, No. 12* Wagner Grant and R. Smith. Although they do not originate a lot of new material unsolicited ideas will be considered.
Royalties paid twice yearly.

Transworld Publishers Ltd

61–3 Uxbridge Road, London W5 5SA ☎01–579 2652 Telex 267974

Managing Director *Paul Scherer*

FOUNDED 1953. Part of Bantam Books New York until the early 1980s when the company was taken over by Bertlesmann, the West German publishers who also own **Doubleday**. *Publishes* general fiction and non-fiction, children's books, sports and leisure. 420 titles in 1986.

IMPRINTS

Bantam *Anthony Mott* TITLES Young adult titles *Bantam Sweet Dreams: The Summer Jenny Fell in Love, Bantam Sweet Valley High, Bantam Couples: Changing*

Partners. Adult fiction   *The Two Mrs Grenvilles, The Alchemist*. Non-fiction *The Iacocca Management Technique, Creative Visualisation*.   **Bantam Press** *Mark Barty-King*   TITLES Hardcover fiction *The Markoff Women* June Flaum Singer, *The Class* Erich Segal, *Destiny* Sally Beauman, *The Sicilian* Mario Puzo, *Redback* Howard Jacobson, *I'll Take Manhattan* Judith Krantz. Non-fiction *What Do You Really Want For Your Children?, Dancing in the Light* Shirley Maclaine; *Hello Campers* Sue Read.   **Black Swan** *Patrick Janson Smith* TITLES Paperback fiction: authors Joseph Heller, John Irving, Mary Wesley, Florence King, Isabel Allende, James Baldwin.   **Corgi Books** *Patrick Janson-Smith* TITLES Fiction: *The Fourth Protocol* Frederick Forsyth, *Sophie's Choice* William Styron, *The Haj* Leon Uris.   **Young Corgi** *Philippa Dickinson* TITLES *My First Joke Book, A Dragon in Class 4, Transformers – Peril from the Stars*.   **Partridge Press** *Christopher Forster* Hardcover nonfiction   TITLES *Francome in Pictures, Running – The Power and the Glory, Cricket 1986*. Mss welcome only if preceded by preliminary letter or phone call.
Royalties paid twice yearly. *Overseas associates* Transworld Australia/New Zealand/South Africa book distributors.

Authors' Rating Bantam take first prize for publisher's hype with the extravagant launch of the Sally Beaumann saga, *Destiny*. And, in terms of advances, £4 million for 10 books by Catherine Cookson takes a lot of beating. But much of the output is unpretentious middle of the road stuff which does well on the station bookstalls. Fun children's books. Authors mostly impressed by efficiency and happy with rewards.

University of California Press
15A Epsom Road, Guildford, Surrey GU1 3JT   ☎0483 68364

Director (in the USA) *James Clark*

Became part of **The University Presses** of Columbia & Princeton in June 1987. *Publishes* scholarly, academic, art, Asian studies. 200 titles in 1986. Editorial work carried out in the USA. It is very rare for unsolicited works to be published since most of the list is derived from the University of California.

University of Chicago Press Ltd
126 Buckingham Palace Road, London SW1W 9SA   ☎01–730 9208   Telex 23933

Chairman *N. C. Gosling*   **Approximate Annual Turnover** £2 million

An outpost of the American based company, University of Chicago Press, London acts as a distribution and marketing office by and large, servicing not only the UK, but Europe, the Middle East, Africa and Asia. With the exception of MIT Press, all the editorial decision-making machinery is in the USA. If a potential title does not have a market in the States it has no chance of even being considered. *Publishes* scholarly books in the arts, social sciences, humanities and sciences (Chicago/Harvard); Engineering and computers (MIT). 550 titles in 1986.

DIVISIONS
Chicago Press *Mrs P. Kaiserlian* (Chicago office) Chicago Press, 5801 Ellis Avenue, Chicago, Illinois 60637, USA. All enquiries to Harvard University, Cambridge MA

02138, USA. **MIT Press** *Robert Bolick*, Executive Editor, 30 Linkside Avenue, Oxford OX2 8JB. The only part of Chicago Press which has an active mss procurement programme in this country. *Publishes* psychology, economics, computer science. No unsolicited mss. Synopses/ideas for books considered.
Royalties on application (MIT only).

University of Exeter Publications
Publications Office, Reed Hall, Streatham Drive, Exeter EX4 4QR ☎0392 263061
Telex 42894

Publications Officer *Mrs B. V. Mennell*

FORMED in 1956 as a publisher of scholarly books for members of staff and research students. *Publishes* academic books. 17 titles in 1986. Do not welcome unsolicited material as the University only publishes works by members of staff and present or former research students.
No royalties paid.

University of Wales Press
6 Gwennyth Street, Cathays, Cardiff CF2 4YD ☎0222 31919

Managing Director *John Rhys* **Approximate Annual Turnover £250,000**

Set up as an extension of the university in 1922. *Publishes* academic and scholarly books, mainly within the humanities and social sciences. Also works of Celtic scholarship. Occasionally publishes on behalf of learned bodies, such as the National Museum of Wales. 36 titles in 1986.

DIVISIONS
GPC Books *John Rhys. They Sank the Red Dragon* Captain Bernard Edwards. **University of Wales Press** *John Rhys* TITLES *The Modern Italian Lyric* F. J. Jones. *Gwasg Prifysgol Cymru* John Rhys. *Drych Yr Oesoedd Canol* Nesta Lloyd & Morfydd Owen. Unsolicited mss welcome.
Royalties paid once yearly; more frequently by negotiation.

Unwin Hyman Ltd
37/39 Queen Elizabeth Street, London SE1 2QB ☎01–407 0709
Telex 886245

Managing Director *Robin Hyman*

Allen & Unwin and **Bell & Hyman** merged in 1986, and in their first full year have published over 70 trade hardbacks and over 100 paperbacks. The combined lists of the two companies amount to over 3000 titles, with Tolkien and Pepys the most prominent names on the reprint list. To the new company Hyman brings a strong craft and leisure markets list, and Unwin brings academic titles. Sport, science fiction/fantasy and general interest non-fiction are also important elements of the new look set-up. Future plans include the phasing out of some imprints, and the introduction of more quality titles for the serious general reader. Humour will probably disappear altogether.

Publishing Director *Mary Butler* TITLES *Victoria* Stanley Weintraub; *Hot Money and the Politics of Debt* R. T. Naylor; *Kinnock* Michael Leapman; *The Family Handbook*. Welcome unsolicited mss, synopses and ideas for books.
Royalty payments vary according to contract.

Authors' Rating Should have a big future but editorial tensions have been created by the merger and integration is taking longer than expected. The time for a firmer judgement will be if and when Robin Hyman takes over the reins.

Usbourne Publishing Ltd
20 Garrick Street, London WC2E 9BJ ☎01–379 3535 Telex 8953598 USPUB G

Managing Director *T. Peter Usbourne*

Approximate Annual Turnover £4.5 million

FOUNDED 1975. *Publishes* visual information books for children and young adults. 50–60 books in 1986.

Editorial Directors *Heather Amery, Jenny Tyler, Judy Tatchell*. TITLES Parents' Guides series: *Entertaining and Educating Young Children*. The Practical Guides series: *Fashion*; *Design*; *Ski-ing*; *Lettering & Typography*. Stephen Cartwright 'Duck' books: *Duck on Holiday*; *Duck in Trouble*.

DIVISIONS
Usbourne Books at Home, Mayfield House, 256 Banbury Road, Oxford OX2 7DQ. Books are written in-house to a specific format and therefore do not welcome unsolicited mss. Will consider ideas which may then be developed in-house. Always very keen to hear from new illustrators and designers.
Royalties paid twice yearly.

Van Nostrand Reinhold (UK)
Molly Millars Lane, Wokingham, Berkshire RG11 2PY ☎0734 789456
Telex 848268 VNR UK G

Managing Director *Mr P. A. Gardner*

VNR (UK) has been owned by **International Thomson Organisation** since 1981. *Publishes* academic, professional and reference titles, and is responsible for the distribution of all Thomson books into the UK, Europe, the Middle East and Africa. It has worldwide agreements/agencies, mainly in the States, Canada, Australia and the Far East. 40 titles in 1986.

Publishing Director *Dr D. Recaldin*

DIVISIONS
Professional & Reference *L. Browne* **University & College** *S. Wellings* **Vocational & Technical** *R. Horton*

IMPRINTS
Brooks Cole *P. McKay* **Boyd & Fraser** *P. Gardner* **Gee** *Dr D. Recaldin* **Delmar** *R. Horton* **Jones & Bartlett** *P. Gardner* **PWS Kent** *P.*

Gardner   **VNR (US)** *P. Gardner*   **Wadsworth** *P. McKay*   Unsolicited mss welcome in Van Nostrand's subject areas. Unsolicited synopses and ideas for books considered.
Royalties paid twice yearly.

Authors' Rating Highly regarded in technical and scientific publishing.

Viking
27 Wrights Lane, London W8 5TZ   ☎01–938 2200

Part of **Penguin**. Founded as the 'quality hardback imprint' of **Penguin Books** in 1983, **Viking** has grown and grown, developing a distinct identity in the course of those 5 years. In 1987 published more hardcover titles than **Hamish Hamilton** and **Michael Joseph**, 130 in all (adult titles). Authors include John Mortimer, V. S. Naipaul, Dirk Bogarde. *Publishes* upmarket and commercial fiction, highly illustrated art books, thrillers, biography, history and gardening, as well as children's books under the **Viking Kestrel** imprint.

Editorial Director *Tony Lacey*   **Viking Kestrel** *Elizabeth Attenborough* Children's books.

Authors' Rating (See **Penguin**).

Virago Press Ltd
41 William IV Street, London WC2N 4DB   ☎01–379 6977   Telex 299080

Chairman *Carmen Callil*   **Managing Directors Joint** *Ursula Owen and Harriet Spicer*   **Approximate Annual Turnover** £1.6 million

Escaped from the **Cape, Virago, Bodley Head and Chatto** group just before the latter was taken over by **Random House**. Founded in 1972 by Carmen Callil, with the aim of publishing a wide range of books – history, literature, fiction, health and education – which illuminate and celebrate all aspects of women's lives. Nearly all titles are published in paperback; a distinguished reprint list makes up two-thirds of these, with one-third original titles commissioned across a wide area of interest. These areas currently include: fiction and non-fiction, educational, reference, biography, history, philosophy, politics, women's studies, health, poetry, young adults. 83 titles in 1986.

Editorial Director *Ursula Owen*   TITLES Fiction *Union Street* Pat Barker; Education & Health *Make It Happy* Jane Cousins; *The Art of Starvation* Sheila Macleod; Politics *Wigan Pier Revisited* Bea Campbell; Virago Travellers – including Mary Kingsley and Isabelle Bird; Diaries *The Diary of Beatrice Webb*. Unsolicited mss welcome. Prefer to see a synopsis and a few sample chapters in the first instance in the case of non-fiction; for fiction prefer to see whole mss.
Royalties paid twice yearly *Overseas associates* Australasian Publishing Company, Australia Book Reps, New Zealand.

Authors' Rating One of the new generation of exciting and inventive publishers who satisfy specialist but powerful sectors of the market. Having recovered its independent status authors can look forward to a revival of energy and style which seemed to fade when Virago was part of a publishing conglomerate. Can be tough in advances and subsidiary rights.

Walker Books

Second Floor, 184–192 Drummond Street, London NW1 3HP   ☎01–387 2000
Telex 8955572

Managing Director *David Ford*

FOUNDED 1979. *Publishes* illustrated children's books and teenage fiction. 100 titles in 1986.

Editor *Wendy Boase*   TITLES *Five Minutes' Peace* Jill Murphy, *Fun to Read series*, *The Tough Princess* Martin Waddell and Patrick Benson. Welcome unsolicited mss and synopses.
Royalties paid twice yearly.

Authors' Rating An extraordinary success story based on sound marketing. Walker Books publish more original children's books than any other British firm. One third of total sales goes through Sainsbury's supermarkets. Good terms for authors who can achieve the necessary standard.

Ward Lock Ltd

8 Clifford Street, Mayfair, London W1X 1RB   ☎01–439 3100
Telex 262364 WARLOK G

Chairman *Robin H. D. Wood*   **Managing Director** *Chris Weller*
Approximate Annual Turnover £3 million

FOUNDED 1854. Part of **Egmont UK Ltd**. The original list consisted of popular information and general education, supplemented by Mrs Beeton. A magazine interest was also developed late last century. The now defunct list was founded on Conan Doyle, Edgar Wallace and Leslie Charteris, with children's information books, most notably the Wonder Books, coming later. *Publishes* general non-fiction, including cookery, gardening, crafts, decorating & design, leisure pursuits. 70 titles in 1986.

Editorial Head *David Holmes*

IMPRINTS
Ward Lock *David Holmes*   TITLES *In Stitches* Una Stubbs; *Beautiful Backyards* Roddy Llewellyn.   **Warwick Press** *David Holmes*   TITLES *Bible Stories*; *Creative Cooking*. Unsolicited mss, ideas and synopses welcome.
Royalties paid twice yearly.

Authors' Rating A publisher which has suffered some terrible ups and downs over the years with changes of ownership leading to financial troubles. Now seems to be on an even keel but complaints about publication delays rumble on.

Frederick Warne
Penguin Books Ltd, 27 Wrights Lane, London W8 5TZ   ☎01–938 2200
Telex 917181

See **Penguin**. **Frederick Warne** publishes children's books including *Beatrix Potter* – children's list is dominated by classics and reprints; also Beatrix Potter non-fiction books for adults; general books, including walking guides, natural history and wildlife (the **Observer** books) and history. Around 50 titles in 1986.

Editorial Director *Sally Sloyer* No unsolicited mss. Letter essential – many books are commissioned.
Royalties paid twice yearly.

Franklin Watts Ltd
12A Golden Square, London W1R 4BA   ☎01–437 0713   Telex 262655 GROLUK G

Managing Director *David Howgrave-Graham*

Part of the Franklin Watts Group, New York. *Publishes* general non-fiction, information and picture books for children. 180 titles in 1986.

DIVISIONS
Franklin Watts *Chester Fisher* TITLES *Making Pencils* Ruth Thomson. **Julia MacRae Books** *Julia MacRae* TITLES *Piggybooks* Anthony Browne. **Orchard Books** *Judith Elliott* TITLES *Little Monsters* Jan Pieńkowski. Unsolicited mss, synopses and ideas for books welcome.
Royalties paid twice yearly. *Overseas associates* in India, Caribbean, Scandinavia, Germany, France, Japan, South Korea, N. Ireland, Eire, S. Africa, Australia and New Zealand, US and Canada.

Wayland (Publishers) Ltd
61 Western Road, Hove, East Sussex, BN3 1JD   ☎0273 722561
Telex 878170 Waylan G

Managing Director *John Lewis*   **Approximate Annual Turnover** £5 million

Part of the **Wolters Samson Group**, Zwolle. FOUNDED 1969. Specialised in history in those days. Now publish a broad range of subjects – in approximately 23 subject areas – illustrated almost entirely in colour. *Publishes* illustrated non-fiction for children of 7 years and upwards. 200 titles in 1986.

Editorial Director *Paul Humphrey*   Do not welcome unsolicited mss or synopses as all books are commissioned.
Royalties paid annually. *Overseas associates* Bookright Press Inc., USA.

Webb & Bower (Publishers) Ltd

9 Colleton Crescent, Exeter, Devon EX2 4BY ☎0392 35362
Telex WEBBOW 42544

Managing Director *Richard-Webb*

Publishes High quality general interest illustrated books for the UK, US and international markets. 25 titles in 1986.

Editorial Head *Delian Bower* TITLES *AA Visitors' Guide*; *Country Diary Crafts*; *V & A Colour Books*; *Countryside Commission*; *National Parks series*. Unsolicited mss, synopses and ideas for books welcome so long as they conform to type. *Royalties* paid twice yearly.

Authors' Rating Small publisher devoted to a high standard of book production.

Weidenfeld & Nicolson Ltd

91 Clapham High Street, London SW4 7TA ☎01–622 9933 Telex 918066

Chairman *Lord Weidenfeld* **Managing Director** *Mark Collins*

Founded by George W. and Nigel N. in 1949, the original list revolved around history, biography, memoirs, quality fiction and politics. Ten years later the sports/leisure publisher **Arthur Barker** was acquired; art and illustrated books followed, and the company developed the 'Great' series – houses, gardens, rivers and so on. Today the reputation of the company rests in part on superbly produced and illustrated volumes on art, architecture, history and nature. Also *publishes* academic, archaeology, atlases & maps, auto/biography, business, cinema, health and beauty, humour, law, literature & criticism, philosophy, politics and sports. 205 titles in 1986.

DIVISIONS

Academic *Juliet Gardiner*   TITLES *Introduction to Positive Economics*; *Law in Context*; *Voltaire*; *Social History of Rural England*; *Beginning Psychology*; *Economics of the Welfare State*.   **General Non-fiction** *Juliet Gardiner*   TITLES *The Wallis & Edward Letters*; *Royal Sunset*; *Vivien Leigh*; *Harold Wilson Memoirs*; *Kissinger Memoirs*; *Olivier Memoirs*; *Marcus Sieff Memoirs*. **Humour/Sport/Business** *David Roberts*   TITLES *Bunbury Series*; *Great Disasters*; *Geoff Boycott*; *Mick Channon*; *Steve Davis*; *Alan Border*; *Lloyd's*; *Saatchi & Saatchi Story*. **Art/Illustrated** *Michael Dover*   TITLES *Royal Academy Catalogues*; *National Trust titles*; *Westminster Abbey*; *Gardens*; *Britain/London/Italy From the Air*; *Liberty Style*; *Laura Ashley titles*. **Fiction** *Victoria Petrie-Hay*   TITLES *Jemima Shore stories* Antonia Fraser; *The Radiant Way* Margaret Drabble; *Time* Charlotte Vale Allen; Claire Rayner titles; Neville Steed thrillers. Unsolicited mss welcome if legible: 'most publications come from selected authors' however. Synopses and ideas for books welcome.
Royalties paid twice yearly for the first two years, annually thereafter. *Overseas associates* Weidenfeld & Nicolson, New York.

Authors' Rating Recently made secure by Getty money. A publishing house dominated by a single, charismatic personality. This can work fine for authors who are favoured by Lord Weidenfeld. Signs of embarking on an expansionist course.

John Wiley & Sons Ltd

Baffins Lane, Chichester, Sussex PO19 1UD   ☎0243 779777   Telex 86290

Chairman *Mr W. Bradford Wiley* (USA)   **Managing Director** *Michael Foyle*

Part of **John Wiley & Sons**, New York, which dates from 1807. The London office was opened in 1960. *Publishes* scientific, technical, medical, professional, reference and text books. 234 titles in 1986 (includes USA).

DIVISIONS
BIO Medical Group *Dr John Jarvis*   **Chemistry and Earth Sciences** *Dr Peter Shepherd*   **Maths and Engineering** *Ian McIntosh*. Unsolicited mss welcome, as are synopses and ideas for books.
Royalties paid annually.

Authors' Rating Do well by the specialist writer who can be sure of excellent standards of production.

The Women's Press

34 Great Sutton Street, London EC1V 0DX   ☎01–251 3007
                                                  Telex 919034 NAMARA G

Managing Director *Ros De Lanerolle*
                              Approximate Annual Turnover £1 million

Part of the Namara Group (who also own **Quartet**). First titles appeared in 1978; expanded to 60 titles in 1987. **The Women's Press** also publish a Women Artists Diary annually and feminist postcards. *Publishes* feminist fiction and non-fiction. Fiction usually has a female protagonist and a woman-centred theme. International writers and subject matter encouraged; some novels appear in translation and considerable emphasis is placed on the work of third world and black women. Non-fiction: general subjects of interest to feminists, both practical and theoretical, and to women generally; art books, literary criticism, feminist theory, health and psychology. 38 titles in 1986.

DIVISIONS
Women's Press Crime *Jen Green*   **Women's Press Science Fiction** *Sarah Lefanu/Jen Green*.

IMPRINTS
Livewire *Carole Spedding/Christina Dunhill*   Fiction and non-fiction for the teenage market. Unsolicited mss, synopses and ideas for books welcome.
Royalties paid twice yearly, in September and March.

Authors' Rating Energetic devotion to the feminist cause. Politics come before literary excellence.

Yale University Press (London)
13 Bedford Square, London WC1B 3JF

☎01–580 2693
Telex 896075 WUPLDN G

Managing Director *John Nicoll*

The UK company of Yale University Press, New Haven, Connecticut, USA. FOUNDED 1961. *Publishes* academic and humanities. 160 titles (jointly with the US company) in 1986.

Editorial Director *John Nicoll*   TITLES *Monet, Nature Into Art* John House; *The Count Duke of Olivares* J. H. Elliott. Unsolicited mss and synopses welcome if within specialised subject areas.
Royalties paid annually.

Critics and Writers – an uneasy relationship

Any writer who seeks the attention of the critics should first write a play. It is amazing how much coverage the press gives to the theatre. And not simply to West End shows. A new play of remote literary significance presented on an improvised stage in the back room of a draughty pub will bring at least half a dozen well-known critics hurrying along to deliver their verdict. The writer may not like what he/she reads a day or two later, but at least he has been noticed.

How is it that theatre enjoys such attention? It is, after all, a minority taste. The explanation is partly historical – theatre critics have been around as long as book reviewers – but there is also the feeling among editors that theatre adds tone to their publications. One of the first signals of a paper going up-market is when it gives generous space to theatrical criticism.

Cinema also does well (for the first time since the war there are now fewer cinemas than theatres in Britain). But because films are director dominated, screenwriters seldom get the recognition they think they deserve.

With television, any new programme in the top fifty ratings is certain to attract critical interest. Likewise any programme which has a topical connection. Then there are the programmes which have a special interest for hardly anybody except the critics. Earlier in the year a sub-standard adaptation of Evelyn Waugh's Fleet Street satire, *Scoop*, achieved acres of space because it was about journalism. As Patrick Stoddart of the *Sunday Times* admitted, 'not half as much would have been written if its hero had been a plumber.'

As for the rest, it's pot luck. A vast amount of television, much of it high quality (television for young people, for example) passes almost entirely without notice. It is lonelier still for those in radio. Not for critical attention (nor money for that matter) do writers enjoy working for radio. More important are the possibilities for breaking through the limitations of the visual media and for working with superb acting talent. Still, bearing in mind that radio drama can attract an average audience of 50,000–100,000 in the evening, and up to 750,000 in the afternoon, it is curious that it does not attract more notice.

But it is authors who complain loudest of their treatment by the critics. Why are so few books reviewed, and why does it take so long for reviews to appear? The quick answer is that the sheer quantity of new titles – at least 50,000 a year in the UK alone, is about 49,500 more than any literary editor can reasonably accommodate. Even allowing for the vast number of books which, in any circumstances, are not likely to be noticed outside the pages of a technical or professional journal, interesting titles fail to get exposure because there is no space for them.

This begs another question, at least from those authors who have suffered neglect. Why are some books chosen and others not? A title with a famous name attached to it is an obvious candidate for review but more important is the suitability of the subject matter for what is, in effect, a short feature article. Romances and thrillers are largely ignored because there is little a critic can say about them except that they are good, bad or indifferent. Conversely, political biographies achieve wide coverage because they are susceptible to interpretation and debate.

But surely there is a case for shifting the balance from books which are easy to write about, to books which are more likely to interest readers. Political biographies are a case in point. Notoriously bad sellers, they take up a disproportionate amount of space in papers which are already overendowed with political comment. The quality press has a powerful urge to deal with the esoteric. It is almost as if the literary editors are trying to live up to their own intellectual pretensions. A book page in the *Sunday Times*, picked at random, encompassed *American Newness (Culture and Politics in the Age of Emerson)*, Elizabeth Longford's biography, *Love Unknown* by A. N. Wilson, the collected writings of Pierre Boulez, and *The Piano Players* by Anthony Burgess. With one possible exception this is hardly the stuff *Sunday Times* readers are likely to take on holiday. About the most interesting item on the page was an ad for **Blackwells**.

So many of the literary pages have a dull look which may come from too much inbreeding. Martin Amis on Frederick Raphael next to Frederick Raphael on Martin Amis. Same names, same subjects, same narrow preoccupations. It takes a talent like Auberon Waugh, who has made *Literary Review* a joy to read, to show what can be achieved when a lively mind is joined with a sense of fun.

But the comfort for authors is the general niceness of their critics. Savage reviewers are a rarity. There is always the feeling that book critics are looking hard for something pleasant to say. Not so theatre critics who give every impression of training for their craft in the boxing ring. And when they do get nasty, they are quite capable of delivering a knock-out blow. Without favourable quotations a play will close.

Television and film critics are also sacred in the school of hard knocks (giving rather than receiving them) but their victims can survive the most horrendous attacks and even come back for more. Authors too, are capable of overcoming critical hostility or, more frequently, indifference. A new Barbara Cartland book, for example, will pass unnoticed in the review pages yet her four hundred or so novels have each sold about one million copies.

It is a frequent lament of authors that they are so seldom invited on radio or television. Yet they do much better than other writers. When did you last hear a screenwriter or even a less than famous dramatist discussing his work? Authors, on the other hand, are always popping up on chat shows and arts programmes. Maybe the real complaint is that this sort of exposure does not necessarily sell books. An appearance on *Wogan* may be a high point in an otherwise placid career but the millions who look in are not foremost in the book market. A smaller, more select audience for, say, *Start the Week* on Radio 4 can have a much bigger impact on sales. Likewise, *Bookshelf,* though low down the ratings, by definition attracts a high proportion of bookbuyers.

There is always regret that British television has not been able to replicate the French book programme, *Apostrophe*. Going out at prime time on a Friday evening, *Apostrophe* attracts a mass audience who easily identify with the presenter, Bernard Pivot, a gentle, humorous man who never talks down to viewers. The nearest comparison in the UK is the late lamented *Read All About It*, fronted by Melvyn Bragg, which was axed in 1978. The only television book programme is Channel 4's five-minute review slot, *Book Choice*.

But while opportunities for frontal promotion of books are rare on radio and television, the power of broadcasting can work in authors' favour in more devious ways. When Sue Townsend happily contemplates the five million sale of the Adrian Mole saga, no doubt she registers a note of gratitude to Radio 4. It was the serialisation of the first Mole book which started the bandwagon rolling. After that, whatever the critics said was irrelevant. Maybe there is a lesson here. If a writer is after sales, he should seek promotion more than praise, and let the product speak for itself.

Public Lending Right – Making the Most From the Libraries

The Public Lending Right (PLR) allows for payments to authors (writers, translators and illustrators) whose books are lent out from public libraries. The amount each author receives is proportionate to the number of times his/her books were lent out during the previous year.

PLR is calculated on a representative sample based on all loans from twenty public libraries. This is then multiplied in proportion to total library lending to produce, for each book, an estimate of its total annual loans throughout the country. To participate in PLR, an author must register his titles and dates of publication.

The sample represents only public libraries (no academic private or commercial ones) and only loans made over the counter (not consultations of books on library premises). The reference sections of public libraries are not included in PLR. Sample loans are about one per cent of the national total. In order to counteract sampling error, libraries in the sample change every two to four years.

When registration closed for the fourth year (30 June, 1986) the number of books registered was 113,473 for 12,990 authors. The number of authors increased by 1725 (15%) during the year. The increase in applications (there was a 20% jump in 1985) is partly due to recent amendments in PLR eligibility rulings. These allow:

- Books under 24/32 pages
- Books written by foreign citizens living in the United Kingdom
- Applications where a co-author is dead or cannot be traced
- 30% shares to translators
- Shares (20% or more) for editing or compiling in certain conditions
- Applications from authors living in West Germany
- Simpler application procedures

For 1986/7 the PLR Fund stood at £2.75 million. After deducting administrative costs the rate per loan was set at 1.20 pence. Last year's rate per loan was 1.27 pence. But there are upper and lower limits on payments. If the registered interest in a book scores so few loans that it would earn less than £1 in a year, no payment is due. No author can earn more than £5000 in PLR in any one year. The bottom limit operates for each edition of a book, the top limit per author.

Under PLR, the author of a book is the writer, illustrator, translator compiler, editor or reviser, provided that his name is on the book's title page. He is eligible for PLR as an author even if he does not own the copyright. PLR and copyright are different. Illustrators include photographers, provided that the photographer is 'the person who, at the time when the photograph is taken, is the owner of the material on which it is taken.'

The sole writer of a book may not be its sole author because, for PLR, all the eligible contributors named on the title page are its co-authors. Writers and illustrators must apply for registration jointly. At least one of them must be eligible and they must jointly specify the share of PLR each will take.

Translators may apply, without reference to other authors, for a 30% fixed share (to be divided equally between joint translators).

An editor or compiler who is named on the title page, may apply to register a 20% share provided he has written 10% of the book or at least 10 pages of text. This should be substantiated by photocopies of the title and contents pages. The shares of joint editors/compilers is 20% in total to be divided equally. An application from an editor or compiler to register a greater percentage share must be accompanied by supporting documentary evidence of actual contribution. A special form is available from the PLR Office.

Where it is impossible to include a co-author on the form because that person is dead or untraceable, the surviving co-author must provide supporting evidence as to why he alone is making application. The living co-author will then be able to register a share in the book which will be 20% for the illustrator and the residual percentage for the writer.

Writers or illustrators may apply for a different percentage apportionment, and the Registrar will register different percentage shares if it is reasonable in relation to the authors' contribution to the particular book. Detailed advice and forms are available from the PLR Office.

The PLR Office keeps a file of missing authors (mostly illustrators) to help applicants locate co-authors. Help is also available from publishers, the writers' organisations, and the **Association of Illustrators,** 1 Colville Place, London W1P 1HN.

Authors and books can be registered for PLR only when the authors apply during
their lifetime. However, once an author's books have been registered, the PLR in
those books continues until 50 years after the author's death. Registered authors can
assign the PLR in each or all of their registered books to other people and they can
bequeath it by will.

To be eligible for PLR an author must be resident in the United Kingdom or the
Federal Republic of Germany. For PLR, the United Kingdom does not include the
Channel Islands or the Isle of Man.

Each separate edition of a book is registered and treated as a separate book. A book
is eligible for PLR registration provided that:

1 it has an eligible author (or co-author) named on its title page.
2 it is printed and bound (paperbacks counting as bound).
3 copies of it have been put on sale (i.e. it is not a free handout and it has already
   been published).
4 it is not a newspaper, magazine, journal or periodical.
5 it does not have more than three writers or illustrators named on the title page.
6 the authorship is personal (i.e. not a company or an association) and the book is not
   Crown copyright.
7 it is not wholly or mainly a musical score.

Every registered author receives an annual statement of estimated loans for each
book and the PLR due.

In the four years in which PLR has operated in the UK, authors' criticism has
focused on the level of funding. At 1.27 pence, the current rate per loan is consider-
ably less than the figure suggested by the first campaigners for PLR thirty years ago.
If Britain was to match the PLR outlay of countries like Germany, Sweden, the
Netherlands and Australia, a budget of £10 million would be in order. As it is, a clear
majority of PLR authors fail to break the £100 barrier and close to 90 per cent make
less than £500.

One of the problems in arguing the case for PLR is that most of the larger payments
go to popular lowbrow authors who are already doing very nicely from bookshop
sales. At a time when public expenditure is under tight scrutiny, writers of the order
of Barbara Cartland and Jeffrey Archer are unlikely to figure as priorities for government handouts.

John Sumsion, the PLR Registrar, hastens to point out that 'serious novelists of
high literary standing' figure prominently in the list of those getting £1000 or more.
Authors of the quality of Iris Murdoch and Kingsley Amis are cited as examples. But
conspicuous by their absence from the list of beneficiaries are young and experimental writers of acknowledged talent who are also likeliest to be hard up. Should
PLR be used to help the needy as it is in Germany and Scandinavia?

There may be a case for subsidies for literature but the prevailing view is that PLR
is an inappropriate instrument for managing them. Brigid Brophy, a leading cam-

paigner for PLR, whose own payment from the fund is less than £250, argues the justice of paying authors in proportion to the use made of their books by the public libraries. 'I may not like the judgement of the reading public but it is not for me to say that it is wrong.' John Sumsion agrees, 'You should not confuse books with literature.'

But there is evidence to suggest that PLR is something more than a windfall for the wealthy. Making a start on analysing the mass of information on public reading habits accumulated by PLR, John Sumsion has identified a group of writers whose main sale is to the libraries. According to Brigid Brophy, many of these are now making more from PLR than from hardback royalties.

PLR is also a boon to those writers whose work has long been out of print but, possibly to the surprise of their publishers, is still widely sought by the library borrowers.

Everyone agrees there is room for improvement in the way PLR is operated. Brigid Brophy wants to persuade the Government to agree a sum per loan rather than an overall figure for distribution. Then the amount handed out would depend entirely on public demand. The Arts Minister may see this as too much of a hostage to fortune. At the same time, he is under great pressure to find extra cash for PLR. With the increase in the number of authors signing on, failure to do so may turn a brave experiment into a bad joke.

PLR Application forms and details can be obtained from The Registrar, **PLR Office**, Bayheath House, Prince Regent Street, Stockton-on-Tees, Cleveland TS18 1DF ☎0642 604699. The Minister's Annual Report to Parliament and the statutory accounts may be obtained from this address or from HMSO.

Poetry Back in Fashion

Publishing is full of surprises. One of the latest is the revival of interest in poetry, previously thought to be as dead as mutton and about half as interesting. You have to be very young indeed not to remember when the only sure seller in the poetry list (apart from school texts) was a collection of John Betjeman as a Christmas present for Aunt Edna. Throughout the book trade, T. S. Eliot's dictum held true:

> 'The most important difference between poetry and the other department of publishing is that, whereas with most categories of books you are aiming to make as much money as possible, with poetry you are aiming to lose as little as possible.'

Then along came Desmond Clarke, formerly of the **Book Marketing Council**, to beef up the sales department at **Faber**. With the best part of the **Faber** backlist embracing poets of the stature of Auden, Plath, Eliot, Durrell, Pound, Hughes, Lowell, MacNeice and Heaney, the new director of marketing saw his opportunity to strike for gold. Clarke devoted a large part of his considerable energies and **Faber's** promotion budget to propagating the idea that poetry was more than a hobby for eggheads. Before long, his enthusiasm was reflected in increased sales. Other publishers jumped on the bandwaggon with the result that this year was the first *Poetry Live*, hyped as the 'largest, most exciting book campaign ever in Britain.' Cleverly staged newsworthy events included readings over the Tannoy at Waterloo Station. As an exercise in bringing poetry to the people it could hardly have been bettered.

Poetry sales continue to show an upward trend. **Faber** and **Penguin** report a 60 per cent increase over five years. **Grafton** has brought out a list of contemporary British poets, **Penguin** has revived its list of international poets, **Secker** is about to launch a new list and **OUP**, **Chatto** and **Hutchinson** are pitching strongly. Among less familiar names **Anvil**, **Bloodaxe** and **Carcanet** have emerged as important poetry imprints.

Meanwhile, Desmond Clarke has founded the **Poetry Catalogue**, a book club to rival the **Poetry Book Society** which formerly had the discount market to itself. The market booms.

But hold. The success story does need to be put into context. Overall, poetry is small business, worth maybe less than £10 million a year with a third of this spent by schools and colleges. Even established poets are lucky to have print runs of more than 4000, and the average is under 1000. Then again, by far the greater proportion of new poetry is brought out not by the leading houses but by small, even minute, publishers (see **Association of Little Presses**) and by the journals. Some of these like **Anvil Press**, who have a proud record of discovering new talent, feel that the national promotions somehow pass them by. The much acclaimed resurgence of interest in poetry may only affect the top names who already enjoy public recognition and shelf space in the book stores.

Aspiring poets have a wide choice of journals on which to try their work (see listing at the end of this article) but the backlog of submissions can be formidable. The **Poetry Society** alone receives up to 2000 unsolicited manuscripts a year.

As in every other area of writing a close study of the market is essential. Aside from reading the journals, help is on hand from the poetry groups and workshops which are active throughout the country. Most of these groups meet specifically to discuss the work of members and to advise on how to achieve publication. For addresses check with your nearest **Regional arts association** (see list on page 419).

Many colleges of further education run poetry courses but these vary enormously in quality. The only sensible advice is to shop around. The best residential courses are provided by the **Arvon Foundation** at Lumb Bank, Hebden Bridge, West Yorkshire and Totleigh Barton, Sheepwash, near Beauworthy, North Devon. Arvon is a charity supported by the **Regional Arts Associations** which accounts for its modest fees – currently £100 per person for a five day course.

The **Poetry Society** (see *Professional Associations*) offers advice to aspiring poets, administers competitions, organises readings and publishes *Poetry Review*.

Poetry Magazines

Acumen **Editor** *Patricia Oxley*, 6 The Mount, Higher Furzeham, Brixham, South Devon TQ5 8QY

Agenda **Editor** *William Cookson, Peter Dale*, 5 Cranbourne Court, Albert Bridge Road, London SW11 4PE

Ambit **Editor** *Martin Bax*, 17 Priory Gardens, London N6 5QY

The Anglo-Welsh Review **Editor** *Greg Hill*, College of Further Education, Llanbadarn, Fawr, Aberystwyth, Dyfed

Aquarius **Editor** *Eddie S. Linden* (Annual publication), Flat 3, 116 Sutherland Avenue, London W9

Argo **Editor** *Hilary Davies*, Old Fire Station, 40 George Street, Oxford OX1 2AQ

Aynd **Editor** *Duncan Glen, Tom Hubbards*, 25 Johns Road, Radcliffe-on-Trent, Nottingham NG12 2GW

Chapman **Editor** *Joy Hendry*, 35 East Claremont Street, Edinburgh EH7 4HT

The Echo Room **Editor** *Brendan Cleary*, c/o 45 Bewick Court, Princess Square, Newcastle-upon-Tyne

Envoi **Editor** *Anne Lewis-Smith*, Pen Ffordd, Newport, Dyfed, Wales SA42 0QT

The Frogmore Papers **Editor** *A. J. Evans, Jeremy Page*, 10 Marten Road, Folkestone, Kent

Giant Steps **Editor** *Graham Mort*, The Beeches, Riverside, Clapham nr. Lancaster LA2 8DT

Grand Piano **Editor** *John Gohorry, Roger Burford Mason*, 17 Bedford Road, Letchworth, Herts

The Honest Ulsterman **Editor** *Frank Ormsby*, 70 Eglantine Avenue, Belfast BT9 6DY

Iron **Editor** *Peter Mortimer*, 5 Marden Terrace, Cullercoats, North Shields, Tyne & Wear NE30 4PD

Label **Editor** *Paul Beasley*, 57 Effingham Road, Lee Green, London SE12 8NT

Lines Review **Editor** *Trevor Royle*, Macdonald Publishers, Edgefield Road, Loanhead, Midlothian EH20 9SY

Litmus **Editor** *Laurie Smith*, The City Lit, Stukeley Street, Drury Lane, London WC2B 5LJ

London Magazine **Editor** *Alan Ross*, 30 Thurloe Place, London SW7 2HQ

Margin **Editor** *Richard Burns, Robin Magowan, Walter Perrie*, 20 Brook Green, London W6 7BL *or* 51a Argyle Street, Cambridge CB1 3LS

New Departures **Editor** *Michael Horovitz* (Annual publication), Piedmont, Bisley, nr Stroud, Glos GL6 7BU

Ninth Decade **Editor** *Tony Frazer, Ian Robinson, Robert Vas Dias*, 52 Cascade Avenue, London N10

Numbers **Editor** *John Alexander, Alison Rimmer, Peter Robinson, Clive Wilmer*, 6 Kingston Street, Cambridge CB1 2NU

The Old Police Station 'Tops' **Editor** *Anthony Cooney*, The Old Police Station, 80 Lark Lane, Liverpool L17 8XH

Orbis **Editor** *Mike Shields*, 199 The Long Shoot, Nuneaton, Warwickshire CV11 6JQ

Outposts **Founder Editor** *Howard Sergeant MBE* **Editor** *Roland John*, 2b Cedar Road, Sutton, Surrey SM2 5DA

Oxford Poetry **Editor** *Nicholas Jenkins, Bernard O'Donoghue, Elise Paschen*, Magdalen College Oxford OX1 4AU

P N Review **Editor** *Michael Schidt, Michael Freeman*, 208–212 Corn Exchange Buildings, Manchester M4 3BG

Pennine Platform Editor *Brian Merrikin Hill*, Ingmanthorpe Hall Farm Cottage, Wetherby, West Yorkshire LS22 5EQ

Poetry Durham Editor *Michael O'Neill, Gareth Reeves*, Dept. of English, University of Durham, Elvet Riverside, New Elvet, Durham DH1 3JT

Poetry Ireland Editor *Terence Brown*, 35 Nth Great Georges Street, Dublin 1

Poetry Nottingham Editor *Stanley Cook*, 600 Barnsley Road, Sheffield S5 6UA

Poetry Now Editor *Rian Cooney, Ravi Mirchandani*, Scotswood South Park, Sevenoaks, Kent TN13 1EL

Poetry Review Editor *Peter Forbes*, The Poetry Society, 21 Earls Court Square, London SW5 9DE

Poetry Wales Editor *Cary Archard*, 56 Parcau Avenue, Bridgend, Mid-Glamorgan, Wales CF31 4SZ

The Poet's Voice Editor *Fred Beake*, 12 Dartmouth Avenue, Bath BA2 1AT

Prospice Editor *J. C. R. Green, Roger Elkin*, Johnston Green Publishing (UK) Ltd, PO Box 418, Leek, Staffordshire ST13 8UX

Rialto Editor *Michael Mackmin, Jenny Roberts, John Wakeman*, 32 Grosvenor Road, Norwich NR2 2PZ

School's Poetry Review Editor *David Orme*, Twyford School, Winchester, Hants SO21 1NW

Sheaf Editor *Anne Cluysenaar*, Sheffield Polytechnic, Sheffield, South Yorkshire

Slightly Soiled Editor *David Crystal, Tim Cumming*, 4 Crawford Gardens, London N13 5TD

Slow Dancer Editor *John Harvey*, 19 Devonshire Promenade, Lenton, Nottingham NG7 2DS

Smoke Editor *Dave Ward*, The Windows Project, 22 Roseheath Drive, Halewood, Liverpool L26 9UH

Stand Magazine Editor *Jon Silkin, Lorna Tracey, Michael Blackburn*, 179 Wingrove Road, Newcastle-upon-Tyne NE4 9DA

Staple Editor *D. C. Measham, R. O. Windsor*, c/o School of Humanities, Derbyshire College of Higher Education, Matlock DE4 3FW

Stride Editor *Rupert Loydell*, 80 Lord Street, Crewe, Cheshire CW2 7DL

Temenos, 47 Paulton's Square, London SW3 5DT

Two Plus Two Editor *Ion Caraion, Jaems Gill, Dedwydd Jones, Jamie Lehrer*, Mylabris Press, 1018 Lausanne, Switzerland

Verse Editor *Robert Crawford, Henry Hart, David Kinloch*, Robert Crawford, St Hugh's College, Oxford OX2 6LE

Westwords 15 Trelawney Road, Peverell, Plymouth PL3 4JS

Weyfarers Editor *Margaret Pain, Peggy George, John Emuss, Susan James* (in rotation), Guildford Poets Press, 9 White Rose Lane, Woking, Surrey GU22 7JA

The Wide Skirt, 8 Melberk Court, Chapeltown, Sheffield, South Yorkshire S30 4YQ

Writing Women Editor *Eileen Aird, Linda Anderson, Cynthia Fuller, Sheila Whitaker*, 59 Holly Avenue, Newcastle-upon-Tyne NE2 2PX

Literary Agents: Books, Features, Radio, TV and Film Scripts

The Writers' Friend – Choosing an Agent

Ten per cent of earnings is a small price to pay for a good agent. The question is, can you find one?

There is a popular illusion among writers that a large part of an agent's day is spent by the telephone, hand poised over the receiver, awaiting the summons to do battle on behalf of a new client. But unless he/she is fresh to the business – and thus untried – the agent who gives value for money already has a substantial portfolio of writers. If it were otherwise he would not be in business. Before taking on another responsibility, he needs to be persuaded that it is worth his while.

Think of it in economic terms. Giles Gordon, a leading agent with **Anthony Sheil Associates**, calculates that it costs an average, adequately staffed agency from one to two thousand pounds a year in overheads to have an author on its books. These overheads include, but are not limited to, rent, rates, salaries, secretarial expenses, postage, telephone, printing, stationery, photocopying, entertaining publishers and, just as frequently, entertaining clients. This means that on standard terms, a writer must earn between ten and twenty thousand pounds a year before his agent even begins to see a profit.

Most writers are not in this league, though quite a few more might get there and well beyond, with the right sort of help. They are the clients an agent is looking for, the ones who show promise of literary achievement and of a decent return on his investment of time and effort.

The best approach to an agent is to send an example of work in hand with a background letter and a bit of whatever you have had published or performed. When submitting a completed manuscript state openly if any publishers have already turned it down. Make sure you direct your sales pitch at an agent who covers your area of interest. Some agencies do not deal directly with plays or television scripts, for example, though they may well have outside associates who handle this side of the business.

Most agents do not charge reading fees but a writer who sends a stamped addressed envelope with his material will be off to a good start. It has been argued, by writers as well as agents, that a reading fee is a guarantee of serious intent; that if an agent is paid to assess the value of a manuscript, he is bound to give it professional attention. Sadly, this is not necessarily the case. While there are respectable agents who deserve a reading fee they are outnumbered by the charlatans who take the money and run. Do not be disappointed if an agent, or even several agents, turn you down. All writing is in the realm of value judgements. Where one agent fails to see talent, another may be more perceptive. So, keep trying.

When you do strike lucky, the first priority is to arrive at a clear understanding as to the scope of your mutual commitment. Do you want your agent to handle all your freelance work including, for example, journalism, personal appearances on radio and television, and lecturing – or just plays and scripts – or just books?

Are you prepared to let the agent take a percentage of all your earnings including those which he does not negotiate? This is a touchy subject. Some writers think of their agency as an employment exchange. Any work they find themselves should not be subject to commission. But this is to assume a clear dividing line between what the agent does and what the writer achieves on his own account. In reality the distinction is not always apparent. A good agent is also a good salesman.

Understanding the market, what subjects are needed, by whom, in what form and in which media is all part of his job. Once he knows what you can do, he is able to promote your talents to the people most likely to want to buy. Eventually, when your reputation is established, offers will come out of the blue – an invitation to write for a newspaper, say, or an editing job or a chance to present a television programme. It is at this point that the writer is tempted to bypass his agent. 'Why should I pay him, he didn't get me the work?' But the chances are he did, by making you into a sellable property in the first place.

An agent negotiates contracts, often a fiddly and worrying business if handled without professional advice, and secures the best possible financial terms. Writers are generally inhibited when it comes to arguing money. It is a brave man who can say 'This is the figure I want because this is what I believe I am worth'. But an agent who has the full range of market rates at his fingertips, can more easily assert the incomparable talents of his client and press for a reward that is commensurate with his ability. Moreover, when it is time for money to be paid to the writer, the agent is usually in the best position to put the squeeze on recalcitrant company accountants.

The other big area of responsibility for an agent is the sale of subsidiary rights. For an author, these may include first serial rights, TV, film and radio adaptations, US and other overseas rights outside the publisher's declared market and translation rights.

Agency commission on overseas sales can go as high as twenty per cent to allow for their associates abroad who naturally expect their cut for acting on the author's behalf. When an author does not have an agent, the sale of subsidiary rights remains the prerogative of the publisher.

Earlier, I said that an agent must be a good salesman. But if he was asked to provide his own job definition, an agent would probably call himself a professional adviser. (Not, he would hasten to add, a teacher. An agent does not expect to tell anyone *how* to write.)

Yet another way of describing an agent is to think of him as a partner. The relationship between writer and agent, assuming they get on well together, invariably lasts longer than any connection with individual editors, publishers, producers or directors. To a fast changing world, the agent can bring a welcome note of stability.

A. & B. Personal Management Ltd

5th Floor, Plaza Suite, 114 Jermyn Street, London SW1Y 6HJ ☎01–839 4433
Telex 21901 JWPPLG

Contact *Bill Ellis*

FOUNDED 1982. Interested in anything that has the potential to become a film or play. TV/radio and theatre scripts. No books. No unsolicited mss. Prefer preliminary letter with synopsis, with s.a.e. No reading fee.
Commission Home $12\frac{1}{2}\%$; US 15%; Translation either $12\frac{1}{2}\%$ or 15%.

Aitken & Stone Ltd

29 Fernshaw Road, London SW10 0TG ☎01–351 7561 Telex 298391

Contact *Gillon Aitken, Brian Stone, Antony Harwood.*

Gillon Aitken joined with **Hughes Massie** in 1986. Fiction and non-fiction. No plays or scripts unless by existing clients. Require a preliminary letter, synopsis and return postage in the first instance. No reading fee. CLIENTS include Germaine Greer, Paul Theroux, Agatha Christie.
Commission Home 10%; US 15%; Translation 20%. *Overseas office* **Wylie, Aitken & Stone Inc.**, 250 West 57th Street, New York, NY 10107, USA.

Jacintha Alexander Associates

47 Emperor's Gate, London SW7 4HJ ☎01–373 9258

Contact *Jacintha Alexander, Julian Alexander*

FOUNDED 1981. Jacintha Alexander previously with **Curtis Brown**. Fiction and non-fiction of all kinds, e.g. *Killing for Company* Brian Masters; *Beautiful Backyards* Roddy Llewellyn; *Banana Cat* Christopher Hood; *Sons of War* Beverley Hughesdon. Scripts handled for established clients only. No romantic fiction, science fiction, academic books. Mss should be preceded by a letter. No reading fee. CLIENTS include Ann Barr, Michelle Berriedale Johnson, Brian Masters, Roddy Llewellyn.
Commission Home 15%; US 20%; Translation 20%.

AZA Artists Ltd

652 Finchley Road, London NW11 7NT ☎01–458 7288

Contact *Morris Aza*

FOUNDED 1972. Television scripts, sketches, comedy material and film scripts only. No books. No reading fee.

Badcock & Rozycki

12 Flitcroft Street, London WC2H 8DJ   ☎01–836 0782   Telex 923995

Contact *June Badcock, Barbara Rozycki*

Not literary agents in the usual sense. **Badcock & Rozycki** are scouts representing nine European publishers. They seek out suitable books for translation, and deal with other agents and publishers only. Do not send mss of any kind to them direct.

Blake Friedmann Literary Agency Ltd

37–41 Gower Street, London WC1E 6HH   ☎01–631 4331   Telex 27950

Contact *Carole Blake* (books); *Julian Friedmann* (film/TV); *Conrad Williams* (radio); *Marisa Lesser* (short stories/journalism)

FOUNDED 1977. All kinds of fiction, from genre to literary; a varied range of specialised and general non-fiction; some juvenile titles, plus scripts. No poetry. *Special interests* thrillers, commercial women's fiction. Unsolicited mss welcome, but preferably preceded by a letter with a synopsis and the first 2 chapters. Letters should contain as much information as possible on previous writing experience, aims for the future, etc. No reading fee. CLIENTS include Ted Allbeury, John Trehaile, Barbara Erskine, Pamela van dyke Price.
Commission Home 15%; US 20%; Translation 20% (books); Radio/TV/film 15%. Journalism/short stories 25%. *Overseas associates* throughout Europe and USA.

David Bolt Associates

12 Heath Drive, Send, Surrey GU23 7EP   ☎04862 21118

Contact *David Bolt*

FOUNDED 1983. Ex-**David Higham**. Fiction, general non-fiction. No books for small children, or verse (except in special circumstances). No scripts. *Special interests* fiction, military, history, theology, African writers, biography. Preliminary letter with s.a.e. essential. £25 reading fee. CLIENTS include Colin Wilson, Professor Arthur Jacobs, Eilis Dillon, Chinua Schebe.
Commission Home 10%; US 19%; Translation 19%.

Curtis Brown Ltd

162–168 Regent Street, London W1R 5TB   ☎01–437 9700
                                           Telex 261536 BRNSPK G

Contact No one person. Material should be addressed to the company and is dealt with by a clearing house.

Long established literary agency. First sales were made in 1899. Wide range of subjects including fiction, general non-fiction, children's, academic, professional and specialist, scripts for TV/radio and television. 'Being a large agency we will consider anything.' Prefer to see a synopsis with covering letter and c.v. rather than complete mss. No reading fee.

Commission Home 10%; US 15%; Translation 20%. *Overseas offices* Curtis Brown (Australia) Pty Ltd; Curtis Brown Associates Ltd, New York; Curtis Brown, Toronto, Canada.

Peter Bryant
51 Allerton Road, London N16 5UF   ☎01–802 0798

Contact *Peter Bryant*

FOUNDED 1980. Mostly fiction, but also handle scripts of all kinds, with drama the agency's special interest. Unsolicited mss welcome, and no one should write unless they also send 'something to read'. No reading fee. CLIENTS include Gerald Frow, Owen Holder, Gwen Cherrell.
Commission Home 10%; US 10%. *Overseas associates* **James Brookes & Associates**, New South Wales, Australia.

Diane Burston Literary Agency
46 Cromwell Avenue, Highgate, London N6 5HL   ☎01–340 6130

Contact *Diane Burston*

FOUNDED 1984. Fiction, non-fiction and short stories. No scripts. Particularly interested in short stories suitable for women's magazines, middle of the road fiction, and adventure non-fiction. Unsolicited mss usually considered, but preliminary letter or phone call preferred.
Commission Home 10%; US 15%; Translation 20%.

Campbell, Thomson & McLaughlin Ltd
31 Newington Green, London N16 9PU   ☎01–249 2971

Contact *John McLaughlin, Timothy Webb, John Richard Parker, Charlotte Bruton, Hal Cheetham*

FOUNDED 1972. All mss except plays, film scripts, articles or poetry. Short stories from existing clients only. No reading fee. Steady income provided by Nicholas Monserrat estate. *Overseas associates* Fox Chase Agency and Raines & Raines (both New York).

Carnell Literary Agency
Danes Croft, Goose Lane, Little Hallingbury, Herts CM22 7RG   ☎0279 723626

Contact *Pamela Buckmaster*

FOUNDED 1951. Fiction and general non-fiction but mainly specialises in science fiction and fantasy books. No poetry and no scripts unless by published authors. No unsolicited mss. S.a.e. and preliminary letter essential. No reading fee. Works in conjunction with agencies worldwide.
Commission Home 10%; US and Translation 19%.

Chappell Plays Ltd (formerly English Theatre Guild)
129 Park Street, London W1Y 3FA   ☎01–629 7600   Telex 268403

Contact *Adline Finlay*

Chappell are both agents and publishers of scripts for the theatre. No unsolicited mss – introductory letter essential. No reading fee. CLIENTS include Arthur Miller, John Steinbeck, Ray Cooney.
Commission Home 10%; US 20%. *Overseas* represented in USA, Canada, Australia, New Zealand, South Africa and Zimbabwe.

Serafina Clarke
98 Tunis Road, London W12 7EY   ☎01–749 6979

Contact *Serafina Clarke; Jan Ward* (children's)

FOUNDED 1980. Fiction: romance, horror, thrillers, literary. Non-fiction: travel, humour, cookery, gardening, biography. No science fiction. Only deal in scripts by authors already on the books. *Special interests* gardening, history, country pursuits. Unsolicited mss welcome, though introductory letter with synopsis (and return postage) preferred. No reading fee. CLIENTS include Elizabeth Walker, Christopher Fowler, Avryl Johnson, Leonid Borodin.
Commission Home 10%; US 20%; Translation 20%.

Jonathan Clowes Ltd
22 Prince Albert Road, London NW1 7ST   ☎01–722 7674   Telex 23973

Contact *Jonathan Clowes; Ann Evans; Lydia Ludlow; Brie Burkeman*

FOUNDED 1960. Pronounced Clewes. Now one of the biggest fish in the pond, and not really for the untried unless they are true high-flyers. Fiction and non-fiction, plus scripts. No text books or children's. *Special interests* situation comedy, film and television rights. No unsolicited mss; authors come by recommendation or by successful follow-ups to preliminary letters. CLIENTS include Doris Lessing, Kingsley Amis, Len Deighton, David Bellamy, Carla Lane.
Commission Home 10%; US 15%; Translation 19%. *Overseas associates* Andrew Nurnberg Associates, London; Lennart Sane Agency, Sweden; Tuttle Mori Agency, Japan; Agenzia Letteraria Internazionale, Italy.

Elspeth Cochrane Agency
11–13 Orlando Road, London SW4 0LE   ☎01–622 0314

Contact *Elspeth Cochrane; Donald Baker*

FOUNDED 1960. Fiction, biography and autobiography, children's books, picture books. Books are usually a spinoff from show business deals, books on Lord Olivier, Leonard Rossiter, Sir Ralph Richardson, Shakespeare, Sir John Gielgud, Dame Peggy Ashcroft. Also handle scripts for all media. *Special interest* drama. No unsolicited mss. Preliminary letter with a description of the work, a brief outline, plus s.a.e. No reading fee. CLIENTS include David Pinner, Michael Dibdin, John Charters, Robert Tanitch.

Commission Home 10%; US 10%; Translation 10% ('but this can change – the % is negotiable, as is the sum paid to the writer').

Dianne Coles Literary Agent

The Old Malthouse, St John's Road, Banbury, Oxon. OX16 8HX   ☎0295 50731
Telex 83556 LUXUS G

Contact *Jim Reynolds* (Managing Director)

FOUNDED 1980. Dianne Coles also has a successful bookshop in Banbury. She deals with non-fiction and Jim Reynolds with fiction. Biography, history (social, political, military), investigative journalism and quality fiction. No scripts, category fiction (i.e. romances, detective stories, science fiction). No unsolicited mss; send outline of plot or non-fiction project, with 10–15 pages of text. No reading fee. CLIENTS include General Farrar-Hockley, Philip Warner, Keith Kyle, Peter Flanders, Graham Leach, John Lloyd, Judy Lomas, Dora Bryan.
Commission Home 10%; US 19%; Translation 19%. *Overseas associates* in USA, Germany, Italy, France, Spain, Japan, Scandinavia, Holland.

Rosica Colin Ltd

1 Clareville Grove Mews, London SW7 5AH   ☎01–370 1080

Contact *Joanna Marston*
FOUNDED 1949. At its heyday in the 1950s a superb reputation for foreign rights/American deals. All full length mss handled, plus theatre, film, television and sound broadcasting. Preliminary letter with return postage essential; writers should outline where their mss have previously been submitted. Takes 3 to 4 months to consider full mss; would prefer to see synopsis. No reading fee.
Commission Home 10%; US 15%; Translation 20%.

Vernon Conway Ltd

19 London Street, Paddington, London W2 1HL   ☎01–262 5506

Contact *Vernon Conway*

FOUNDED 1977. *Special interests* novels, biography, plays. No textbooks or academic. Welcomes unsolicited mss, preceded by an introductory letter, plus return postage. No reading fee. CLIENTS include Ian Grimble, Elspeth Sandys, Clive Barker.
Commission 10% on all sales.

Jane Conway-Gordon

213 Westbourne Grove, London W11 2SE   ☎01–229 4451

Contact *Jane Conway-Gordon*

FOUNDED 1982. Fiction and Self Help books; e.g. *Conversations with Lord Byron* (Cape); *Talleyman* (Gollancz); *The Working Mother's Survival Guide* (Simon & Schus-

ter); *Women Who Love Too Much* (Arrow). Occasionally handle scripts for TV/radio/theatre. No poetry or science fiction. Unsolicited mss welcome; preliminary letter and return postage preferred. No reading fee. CLIENTS include Amanda Prantera, John James, Dr Brian Roet, Juliet Dymoke.
Commission Home 10%; US 20%; Translation 20%. *Overseas associates* **McIntosh & Otis Inc.**, New York; plus agencies throughout Europe and Japan.

Rupert Crew Ltd
King's Mews, London WC1N 2JA   ☎01–242 8586

Contact *Mrs D. Montgomery, Miss S. Russell*

FOUNDED 1927. Fiction and non-fiction. No plays, scripts or poetry. No unsolicited mss. Preliminary letter essential. No reading fee.
Commission 10–20% by arrangement.

Harriet Cruickshank
97 Old South Lambeth Road, London SW8 1XU   ☎01–735 2933

Contact *Harriet Cruickshank*

FOUNDED 1983. Fiction, general non-fiction, scripts for TV/radio/film. No unsolicited mss. Preliminary letter with synopsis and s.a.e. essential. Works with foreign agents abroad.
Commission Home 10%; US and Translation varies according to contract.

Judy Daish Associates
83 Eastbourne Mews, London W2 6LG   ☎01–262 1101

Contact *Judy Daish*

FOUNDED 1977. Theatrical literary agent only. Scripts for film/TV/theatre/radio. No books. Preliminary letter essential. No unsolicited mss.
Commission negotiable.

Reg Davis-Poynter
118 St Pancras, Chichester, West Sussex PO19 4LH and 11 Bolt Court, Fleet Street, London EC4A 3DQ   ☎0243 779047/01–353 9365

Contact *R. G. Davis-Poynter*

Books and scripts (TV, radio, theatre, film). *Special interests* sociology, politics, history, biography, autobiography, theatre. No children's or religious. Unsolicited mss welcome if accompanied by letter, synopsis, sample chapter and return postage. Prefer that writers approach with preliminary letter and return postage, than send complete mss. No reading fee.
Commission Home 15%; US 20%; Translation 15%; Theatre, films, Television and radio 10%. *Overseas associates* in Germany, Scandinavia, Japan, Italy, France and USA.

Felix de Wolfe

1 Robert Street, London WC2N 6BH   ☎01–930 7514/7

Contact *Felix de Wolfe*

FOUNDED 1938. Handle quality fiction and scripts only. No non-fiction or children's. No unsolicited mss – write a letter in the first instance. No reading fee. CLIENTS include Jennifer Johnston, John Kershaw, Bill Magilwraith, Julian Slade, S. Campbell-Jones.
Commission Home $12\frac{1}{2}\%$; US 20%.

John Dorman

The Old Parsonage, Lower Brailes, Banbury, Oxon OX15 5HT   ☎0608 85584
                                                Telex 418253

Contact *John Dorman*

FOUNDED 1983. Sport – autobiography and instructional, and sports-related subjects, leisure activities. Autobiographies of John Francome, Geoff Boycott. No scripts, no fiction, no children's. *Special interests* cricket, horse racing, rugby union, soccer. No unsolicited mss – initial letter and typed synopses essential. No reading fee. CLIENTS include Matthew Engel (*Guardian* cricket correspondent), Peter Scudamore (National Hunt jockey), Clive Norling (rugby referee) and Graham Gooch.
Commission Home 10%; US 15%; Translation 15%.

Toby Eady Associates Ltd

7 Gledhow Gardens, London SW5 0BL   ☎01–370 6292

Contact *Toby Eady*

FOUNDED 1969. All subjects considered ('except the sadistic'). Scripts not generally handled. Renowned as a wheeler dealer, Toby Eady now lives in NY, but he is the contact name supplied by the agency. Has been known to charge hefty reading fees. *Special interests* Africa, politics, fishing, Middle East. Authors should send an intelligent letter, giving the background and describing the mss with details of how the author came to write it. CLIENTS include Tim Jeal, Bernard Cornwell, David Taylor, Susan Lewis, Julia Hamilton.
Commission Home 10%; US 20%; Translation 20%. *Overseas offices* Toby Eady NY; Mohr Books; La Nouvelle Agence; Lennart Sane.

Fact & Fiction Agency Ltd

16 Greenway Close, London NW9 3FA   ☎01–205 5716

Contact *Roy E. Lomax*

Television and radio scripts. Currently not taking on new writers. No unsolicited mss.
Commission Home 10%; Overseas 15%.

John Farquharson

162–168 Regent Street, London W1R 5TB   ☎01–437 9700   Telex 261536

Contact *Vivienne Schuster, Vanessa Holt, Andrew Lownie, Rachel Calder*

FOUNDED 1919. Sister company to Curtis Brown. 'We pride ourselves on being a general agency'. Commercial and literary fiction, and general non-fiction. *Special interests* bestseller fiction, top crime novels. No academic, no technical, no scripts. Detailed brochure available giving full guidelines and listing clients. Unsolicited mss welcome.
Commission Home 10%; US 20%; Translation 20%.

Film Link Literary Agency

31 Oakdene Drive, Tolworth, Surrey KT5 9NH   ☎01–330 3182

Contact *Yvonne Heather*

FOUNDED 1979. Fiction, general non-fiction and TV scripts. No poetry, short stories. No unsolicited mss. Send synopsis, sample pages and introductory letter, together with s.a.e. No reading fee. CLIENTS include Peter May and Michael Elder (writers for *Take The High Road*).
Commission Home 10%; 15–20% Overseas.

Film Rights Ltd

4 New Burlington Place, Regent Street, London W1X 2AS   ☎01–437 7151

Contact *Laurence Fitch*

FOUNDED 1932. Only handle film/TV theatre scripts. Do not consider unsolicited mss or synopses. Preliminary letter giving full details, including cv of the writer, essential. No reading fee.
Commission Home and Abroad 10%.

Laurence Fitch Ltd

4 New Burlington Place, London W1X 2AS   ☎01–437 7151

Contact *Laurence Fitch, Judy Quinn*

FOUNDED 1954. Scripts only, for all media. Particularly interested in plays for the stage, especially comedies. Ambivalent about unsolicited scripts; writers should send a preliminary letter. Can take up to 6 months to consider mss. CLIENTS include Dodie Smith, John Chapman and Ray Cooney.
Commission Home 10%; US 15%; Translation 20% 'sometimes'.

Jill Foster Ltd

35 Brompton Road, London SW3 1DE   ☎01–581 0084

Contact *Jill Foster, Alison Finch, Ann Foster, Malcolm Hamer*

FOUNDED 1976. Non-fiction and scripts only (mainly TV, drama and comedy). No fiction, short stories or poetry. *Special interests* sports subjects. No unsolicited mss;

approach by letter in the first instance. No reading fee. CLIENTS include Colin Bostock-Smith, Chris Bryant, Julia Jones, Michael Palin, Chris Ralling.
Commission Home 10%; US 15%; Translation 15%. *Overseas associates* Candace Lake, Los Angeles, USA.

Fraser & Dunlop Scripts Ltd
91 Regent Street, London W1R 8RU   ☎01–734 7311   Telex 28965

Contact *Kenneth Ewing* (theatre); *Tim Corrie* (film); *Richard Wakeley* (television); *Mark Lucas* (books)

FOUNDED 1959. Scripts of all kinds, but also fiction, non-fiction (especially humorous) books. Vastly experienced as a show business agency, and good for radio and television writing. Book side coming on with Mark Lucas (ex Futura). No unsolicited mss; synopsis/treatment (sample chapter optional) with accompanying letter essential. No reading fee. CLIENTS include Tom Stoppard, Charles Wood, David Butler, Gerald Scarfe, Jane Asher and Bernice Rubens.
Commission Home 10%; US 20%; Translation 20%. *Overseas offices* New York and Los Angeles.

French's
26 Binney Street, London W1   ☎01–629 4159

Contact *John French*

FOUNDED 1973. Novels and factual material; also scripts for all media. No religious or medical books. No unsolicited mss. 'For unpublished authors we offer a reading service at £70 per ms, inclusive of VAT and postage'. Interested authors should write a letter in the first instance. CLIENTS include Barry Heath, James Duke, Hal Middleton, Shaun Prendergast.
Commission Home 10%.

Pamela Gillis Management
46 Sheldon Avenue, London N6 4JR   ☎01–340 7868

Contact *Pamela Gillis*

FOUNDED 1975. TV scripts and radio material. No books. Prefer preliminary letter of introduction. No reading fee.
Commission 10% Home and Abroad.

Eric Glass Ltd
28 Berkeley Square, London W1X 6HD   ☎01–629 7162   Telex 296759 KALLIN G

Contact *Eric Glass; Janet Crowley; Nicola Richards*

FOUNDED 1934. Fiction and non-fiction; e.g. *Gioconda* Wolf Mankowitz; *The Prime Ministers* ed. William Douglas-Home; *Somerset And All The Maughams* Robin Maugham; *The Unforgiving Minute* Beverley Nichols. No poetry, biographies and

autobiographies of unknown people. Handle scripts both for publication and production in all media. Not the best agency for new writers. Resumés and sample chapters in the first instance (complete mss by request) with return postage. No reading fee. CLIENTS include Philip King, estates of Jean Cocteau and Jean-Paul Sartre, Wolf Mankowitz, William Douglas-Home.
Commission Home 10%; US 15%; Translation 20% (minimum rates). *Overseas associates* in USA, Germany, Scandinavia, France, Italy, Spain, Rumania, Czechoslovakia, Holland.

Goodwin Associates
12 Rabbit Row, Kensington Church Street, London W8 4DX   ☎01–229 8805

Contact *Ms Phil Kelvin*

FOUNDED 1977. Scripts for film/TV/theatre/radio only. No prose or poetry. Welcome unsolicited mss with return postage. No reading fee. CLIENTS include Susan Boyd, Jim Hill, Stephen Lowe, Louise Page, Christina Reid, Fay Weldon.
Commission 10% on all sales.

Christine Green Ltd
8 Albany Mews, Albany Road, London SE5 0DQ   ☎01–703 9285

Contact *Christine Green*

FOUNDED 1984. Fiction – general and literary; general non-fiction. No scripts, poetry, or children's. Unsolicited mss welcome if include return postage. Initial letter and synopsis preferred. No reading fee. CLIENTS include Maeve Binchy, Claire Francis.
Commission Home 10%; US 15%; Translation 20%.

Elaine Greene Ltd
31 Newington Green, Islington, London N16 9PU   ☎01–249 2971

Contacts *Elaine Greene, Ilsa Yardley*

A small, choosy agency that likes to really involve itself with its chosen. Novels and quality non-fiction, journalists' books. No academic, no original scripts for theatre, film or television. *Special interests* crime writing. CLIENTS include P. D. James, Colin Forbes, William Shawcross, Connor Cruise O'Brien. No unsolicited mss without preliminary letter.
Commission Home 10%; US 15%; Translation 20%.

Jane Gregory Agency
4 Westwick Gardens, London W14 0BU   ☎01–603 9998/1669   Telex 268141

Contact *Jane Gregory, Felicia Dykstra*

FOUNDED 1982. Fiction and non-fiction. No plays, poetry, academic or children's. No unsolicited mss; preliminary letter essential. No reading fee. Represent three American companies, including **Simon & Schuster**.
Commission Home 10%; US 20%; Translation 20%.

Gregory & Radice Author's Agents

4 Westwick Gardens, London W14 0BU ☎01–603 5168 Telex 268141

Contact *Jane Gregory, Lisanne Radice*

FOUNDED 1986. Crime and thrillers only; a single-minded approach makes them specialists in the field. No scripts. No unsolicited mss; preliminary letter with synopsis and couple of sample chapters (plus return postage) essential. No reading fee. *Commission* Home 10%; US 20%; Translation 20%.

David Grossman Literary Agency Ltd

110–114 Clerkenwell Road, London EC1M 5SA ☎01–251 5046
Telex 263404 Bk Biz G

Contact *David Grossman*

FOUNDED 1976. Full-length fiction and general non-fiction. No verse or technical books for students. No original screenplays or teleplays but sell performance rights in works existing in volume form. *Special interests* suspense and thriller writers, historical novelists, sagas, biographies, political affairs, health, contemporary history, travel, film. Prefer a preliminary letter giving full description of the work. No unsolicited mss. No reading fee. *Overseas associates* throughout Europe, Japan, Brazil, and USA.
Commission rates vary for different markets.

June Hall Literary Agency

19 College Cross, London N1 1PT ☎01–609 5991

Contacts *June Hall, Clare Loessler, Shan Morley-Jones*

FOUNDED 1979. Fiction and general non-fiction. No scripts. No unsolicited material. Preliminary letter and s.a.e. essential. No reading fee. Nov 1981 sponsored 'Woman of the '80's' book award with Hodder & Stoughton. *Overseas associates* Brazil, France, German-speaking countries, Israel, Italy, Japan, Netherlands, Scandinavia, Spanish-speaking countries, Turkey.
Commission on application.

Roger Hancock Ltd

8 Waterloo Place, Pall Mall, London SW1Y 4AW ☎01–839 6753

Contact *'The company'*

FOUNDED 1961. *Special interest* drama and light entertainment. Scripts only. No books. Unsolicited mss not welcome. Initial phone call required. No reading fee. *Commission* 10% throughout.

Alec Harrison & Associates
International Press Centre, Shoe Lane, London EC4A 3JB ☎04022 24523

FOUNDED 1954. Mostly non-fiction, with particular emphasis on biography and auto-biography, which are frequently ghosted, and usually commissioned. Preliminary letter and synopses preferred to unsolicited mss. No reading fee.
Commission Home 10%; Overseas 19%.

Sally Harrison Management
100 Albert Palace Mansions, Lurline Gardens, London SW11 3DH ☎01–720 9203

Contact *Sally Harrison*

FOUNDED 1979. Film/TV/theatre/radio scripts. No books. Preliminary letter preferred. No reading fee.
Commission Home and Abroad 10%.

Hatton & Baker Ltd
18 Jermyn Street, London SW1Y 4AW ☎01–439 2971

Contacts *Terence Baker, Richard Hatton*

FOUNDED 1980. Scripts and screenplays only. No books. Unsolicited mss welcome with s.a.e. No reading fee. *Overseas associates* worldwide.
Commission Home 10%; US 15%; Translation 15%.

Headline Enterprises Ltd
35 Brompton Road, London SW3 1DE ☎01–584 8568

Contact *Malcolm Hamer, Jill Foster, Alison Finch*

FOUNDED 1971. Non-fiction only especially sporting/leisure, show business auto-biography, guide books, food and wine. No fiction or poetry. No unsolicited mss; writers should send a letter in the first instance. No reading fee. CLIENTS include Gareth Edwards, Cliff Temple, David Lemmon, Tony Pawson.
Commission Home 10/15%; US 20%.

A. M. Heath & Co. Ltd
79 St Martin's Lane, London WC2N 4AA ☎01–836 4271

Contact *Mark Hamilton, William Hamilton, Michael Thomas*

FOUNDED 1919. Fiction and general non-fiction. No scripts or poetry. Preliminary letter and synopsis essential. No reading fee. CLIENTS include Anita Brookner, Saul Bellow and Jean Plaidy. *Overseas associates* in USA.
Commission Home 10%; US 15%; Translation 20%.

Duncan Heath Associates Ltd

Paramount House, 162–170 Wardour Street, London W1R 4HA ☎01–439 1471

FOUNDED 1973. Film/TV/theatre scripts. No books. No unsolicited mss. Preliminary letter essential. No reading fee. *Overseas associates* ICM New York and Los Angeles. *Commission* 10% throughout.

David Higham Associates Ltd

5–8 Lower John Street, Golden Square, London W1R 4HA ☎01–437 7888
Telex 28910 HIGHAM G

Contact *Bruce Hunter, Jacqueline Korn*; scripts *John Rush, Elizabeth Cree*

FOUNDED 1935. Ex-Laurence Pollinger. Fiction, general non-fiction; biography, history, current affairs, art, music etc. Good for romantic fiction bestsellers. CLIENTS include Richard Adams, James Herriot and the estate of John Wyndham. Also scripts. No educational, highly specialised books or children's story books. Unsolicited mss welcome, provided they are preceded by introductory letter and accompanied by return postage. No reading fee.
Commission Home 10%; US 15%; Translation 19%.

Valerie Hoskins (in association with Jeremy Conway Ltd)

Eagle House, 109 Jermyn Street, London SW1Y 6HB ☎01–839 2121

Contact *Valerie Hoskins*

FOUNDED 1983. Script agent dealing in film, theatre, television and radio. *Special interests* feature films. No unsolicited scripts; preliminary letter of introduction essential. No reading fee. CLIENTS include Tony Craze, Robin Miller, Gillian Richmond, Gardner McKay, Peter Berry, Arthur Ellis, Jeremy Newson.
Commission Home 10%; US 20% (max).

Theresa Howard Associates

78 Killyon Road, Clapham, London SW8 2XT ☎01–627 3084

Contact *Theresa Howard*

FOUNDED 1985. Script agent only (in association with **Laurence Pollinger Ltd**). Not currently in the market for new writers.
Commission Home 10%; US 10%; Translation 12.5%.

Tanja Howarth

19 New Row, London WC2N 4LA ☎01 240 5553   Telex 27370

Contact *Tanja Howarth*

FOUNDED 1970. Specialise in translations from the German, e.g. *Perfume – The Story of a Murder* Patrick Suskind; also interested in taking on both fiction and non-fiction English writers. Tanja Howarth is also 'constantly on the look-out for suitable plays for Germany', as she represents the theatre department of S. Fischer, Frankfurt.

Reputation for smooth efficiency. No children's books. All subjects other than this considered, providing the treatment is intelligent. Unsolicited mss welcome, preliminary letter preferred. No reading fee.
Commission Home 10%; Translation 15%.

Hughes Massie Ltd

(now *Aitken & Stone Ltd*)

Michael Imison Playwrights Ltd

28 Almeida Street, Islington, London N1 1TD   ☎01–354 3174
Telex 934999 TX Link G

Contact *Michael Imison, Alan Brodie*

FOUNDED 1944. Michael Imison is the brother of Richard Imison, deputy head of radio drama (BBC). Plays, plus books based on scripts, e.g. *Yes Minister*. TV, radio and theatre. Specialise in theatre writing. No fiction or general books. *Specially interested in* writers who are primarily motivated by writing for the theatre; translators, particularly from the Russian and Italian. Unsolicited mss not welcome. Initial letter with recommendation from a known theatre professional essential. S.a.e. No reading fee. CLIENTS include David Edgar, Dario Fo, John Godber, Doug Lucie, the Noel Coward estate.
Commission Home 10%; US 12.5%; Translation 12.5%. *Overseas associates* Judy Ferris at Stagewise, Sydney, Australia. Abbe Levin, New York.

International Copyright Bureau Ltd

Suite 8, 26 Charing Cross Road, London WC2H 0DG   ☎01–836 5912

Contact *Joy Westendarp*

FOUNDED 1905. Handles exclusively scripts for TV/theatre/film. No books. Preliminary letter essential. No synopses or mss. Agents in New York and most foreign countries.
Commission Home 10%; US 19%; Translation 19%.

International Scripts

1 Norland Square, Holland Park, London W11 4UE   ☎01–229 0736

Contact *Bob Tanner, Mrs J. Lawson, Sheelagh Thomas*

FOUNDED 1980. All types of books handled, as well as scripts for all media. No poetry. Unsolicited mss welcome, though preliminary letter preferred. No reading fee. CLIENTS include Robert A. Heinlein, Peter Haining, Richard Laymon, Shaun Hutson.
Commission Home 10–15%; US 20%; Translation 20%. *Overseas associates* Raphy Vicinanza, Spectrum, New York.

Mary Irvine
11 Uplands Park Road, Oxford OX2 7RU ☎0865 513570

Contact *Mary Irvine*

FOUNDED 1974. Mainly fiction with a little non-fiction and children's books. *Special interest* in women's fiction and saga fiction. Mary Irvine was fiction editor of a women's magazine prior to becoming an agent. No scripts. Require a preliminary letter in the first instance. No reading fee. CLIENTS include Marie Joseph (1987 RNA Award winner), Elvi Rhodes, Katharine Gordon, Susan Sallis, Isobel Lambot, David Serafin, Margaret Hinxman. *Overseas associates* in France, Italy, Scandinavia, Germany, USA and Japan.
Commission Home 10%; US 15%; Translation 20%.

John Johnson Ltd
Clerkenwell House, 45–47 Clerkenwell Green, London EC1R 0HT ☎01–251 0125

Contact *Andrew Hewson, Margaret Hewson*

FOUNDED 1956. Once noted for their close working relationship with publishers **Robert Hale**. Very conscientious and sympathetic to new writers. Full length and short mss; dramatic works for radio and television. No unsolicited mss; preliminary letter with synopsis and s.a.e. essential. No reading fee. CLIENTS include Dick Francis, D. M. Thomas and David Pownall.
Commission Home 10%; US 10% (20% with sub-agent); Translation 20%. *Overseas* works in conjunction with agents in the US and many European countries.

Lemon & Durbridge Ltd
24–32 Pottery Lane, London W11 4LZ ☎01–727 1346 Telex 27618 Author G

Contact *Rowena Skelton-Wallace*

Theatrical literary agency (see also **Unna & Durbridge Ltd**, same address) which came out of the merging of Stephen Durbridge Ltd with Sheila Lemon Ltd in February 1986. Theatre, TV, film and radio scripts. No books. No unsolicited mss; preliminary letter and outline essential. No reading fee. *Overseas associates* worldwide.
Commission Home 10%; US and Translation varies.

L'Epine Smith & Carney Associates
10 Wyndham Place, London W1H 1AS ☎01–724 0739

Contact *Eric L'Epine Smith*

FOUNDED 1957. Interested in good material of all categories: fiction, general non-fiction, scripts. Welcome unsolicited mss preceded by introductory letter or phone call. CLIENTS include Barry Bliss, Terence Dudley, Stuart Cameron, Michael Sawyer.
Commission Home 10% (No US or translation work at present).

Christopher Little

49 Queen Victoria Street, London EC4N 4SA   ☎01–236 5881   Telex 883968

Contact *C. J. Little, R. R. Overnell, B. Godfrey*

FOUNDED 1979. Full length fiction, non-fiction, film scripts. TV scripts. *Special interests* crime, thrillers, historical fiction. Unsolicited mss welcome. No reading fee. CLIENTS include Erin Pizzey, A. J. Quinnell, Carolyn Terry, and W. Wright (alias David Graham).
Commission Home 20%; US 20%; Translation 20%.

Lloyd-George & Coward

12 Fairfax Place, Dartmouth, Devon TQ6 9AE   ☎08043 2448

Contact *Bruce Coward*

FOUNDED 1959. Biography, travel, natural history, general fiction and nautical. No scripts, poetry, educational, academic or translations. *Special interests* Nautical. No unsolicited mss; send introductory letter with synopsis and s.a.e. No reading fee. CLIENTS include Jane Gillespie, Tom Jaine, Jeremy Purseglove, Wallace Breem.
Commission Home 10%; US 15%. *Overseas associates* Lyle Steele & Co., New York.

London Independent Books Ltd

1a Montague Mews North, London W1H 1AJ   ☎01–935 8090

Contact *Mrs C. Whitaker*

FOUNDED 1971. A self-styled 'small and idiosyncratic' agency, which handles fiction and non-fiction reflecting the tastes of the proprietors. All subjects considered (except computer books) providing the treatment is strong and saleable. Scripts handled only if by a writer already on the books. *Special interests* boats, travel, travelogues, commercial fiction. No unsolicited mss – letter, synopsis and first two chapters with return postage the best approach. No reading fee. CLIENTS 'none are household names, yet!'
Commission Home 15%; US 20%; Translation 20%.

London Management

235–241 Regent Street, London W1A 2JT   ☎01–493 1610   Telex 27498

Contact *Heather Jeeves, Tony Peake* (general), *Marc Berlin* (TV/film/theatre), *Nigel Britten* (radio/TV/film).

FOUNDED 1959. Part of the Grade organisation, the biggest show-biz agency in the country. Recent build up on the book side. Sympathetic to new talent. Full length fiction and general non-fiction, including illustrated books, craft, health, music, theatre, film, the arts, graphic design, humour/cartoon, military. No science fiction/fantasy, educational, short stories, category romance or children's. *Special interests* South African fiction and non-fiction. Writers should approach by tele-

phone in the first instance, followed by letter with synopsis/sample chapters, and s.a.e. No unsolicited mss. No reading fee.
Commission Home 10%; US 19%; Translation 19%. *Overseas* The Lantz Office, New York, plus full coverage by foreign rights agents.

Maclean Dubois (Writers & Agents)
10 Rutland Square, Edinburgh EH1 2AS   ☎031–229 6185

Contact *Charles Maclean, Geraldine Coates* (UK), *Patrick Deedes-Vincke* (Paris)

FOUNDED 1977. General fiction and non-fiction, children's, biography, history, photography. No poetry or plays (unless, occasionally, for own authors). *Special interests* literary fiction, Scottish history and topography, food and wine, historical fiction. Unsolicited mss welcome. Reading fee for supply of detailed report on mss offered. Writers should approach the agency by phone or in writing for explanation of terms. CLIENTS include Colin Mackay (literary fiction); Ken Begg (thrillers); David Williams (photos); Helen Mackenzie (children's) Seamus Carney (Scottish history).
Commission Home 10%; US 15%; Translation varies. *Overseas associates* Patrick Deedes-Vincke, 11 Rue de Turenne, Le Marais, 75004 Paris.

Andrew Mann Ltd
1 Old Compton Street, London W1V 5PH   ☎01–734 4751

Contacts *Anne Dewe, Tina Betts*

FOUNDED 1975. Fiction and general non-fiction. Film/TV/theatre/radio scripts. No unsolicited mss. Preliminary letter, synopsis and s.a.e. essential. No reading fee. Associate agencies overseas.
Commission Home 10%; US 15%; Translation 20%.

Marjacq Scripts Ltd
32 Cumberland Mansions, Nutford Place, London W1H 5ZB   ☎01–724 0565

Contact *Jacqui Lyons*

FOUNDED 1974. Fiction and non-fiction, plus radio and television scripts. No children's or religious. Unsolicited mss welcome with s.a.e. but telephone conversation first preferred. No reading fee.
Commission Home 10%; US 10%; Translation 20%.

Marlu Literary Agency
26 Stratford Road, London W8   ☎01–937 5161   Telex 268141

Contact *Mary Hall Mayer*

All subjects except children's and poetry. *Special interests* general fiction, non-fiction, computer and visual books.
Commission Home 10%; US 20%.

Marsh & Sheil Ltd

43 Doughty Street, London WC1A 2LF   ☎01–405 7473   Telex 946240

Contact *Paul Marsh*

FOUNDED 1985. Marsh & Sheil deals in translation rights only, on behalf of selected British and American agents. CLIENTS include **Anthony Sheil Associates, Wallace & Sheil Agency, Don Congdon Associates, Barrie & Jenkins Ltd**. No unsolicited mss, ideas or synopses.
Translation commission 10%.

Blanche Marvin

21a St John's Wood High Street, London NW8 7NG   ☎01–722 2313

Contact *Blanche Marvin*

FOUNDED 1968. Fiction, general non-fiction and play scripts. No poetry. Welcomes synopses if accompanied by introductory letter, giving author's c.v. and outline of the work. No reading fee.
Commission $12\frac{1}{2}$% throughout.

MBA Literary Agents Ltd

45 Fitzroy Street, London W1P 5HR   ☎01–387 2076/4785
Contact *Diana Tyler, John Richard Parker, Meg Davis*

FOUNDED 1971. All types of fiction and non-fiction. A large proportion of their business lies in scripts for all media. No poetry, short stories (unless by established authors). Unsolicited mss only after preliminary letter with s.a.e. Letter should describe book in full, and give author's credits and background. No reading fee. *Special interests* science fiction, crime, thrillers, sagas, 'mainstream' fiction.
Commission Home 10%; US 20%; Translation 20%.

Bill McLean Personal Management

23b Deodar Road, Putney, London SW15 2NP   ☎01–789 8191

Contact *Bill McLean*

FOUNDED 1972. Scripts only, for all media. No books, no unsolicited mss. Phone call or introductory letter essential. No reading fee. CLIENTS Jeffrey Segal, Bill Lyons, Peter Batt, John Maynard, Dwynwen Berry.
Commission Home 10%.

Richard Milne Ltd

28 Makepeace Avenue, London N6 6EJ   ☎01–340 7007

Contact *R. M. Sharples, K. N. Sharples*

FOUNDED 1956. Specialises in drama and comedy scripts for radio and television, but are not presently in the market for new clients – they are 'fully committed in handling work by authors we already represent'. No unsolicited mss.
Commission Home 10%; US 15%; Translation 25%.

William Morris Agency UK Ltd

31/32 Soho Square, London W1V 5DG   ☎01–434 2191   Telex 27928

Contact *Lavinia Trevor*

FOUNDED 1967. Fiction and general non-fiction. No scripts, academic, technical, poetry, children's. Welcome unsolicited mss but must be preceded by a preliminary letter with s.a.e.
Commission Home 10%; US 20%; Translation 20%.

Michael Motley Ltd

78 Gloucester Terrace, London W2 3HH   ☎01–723 2973

Contact *Michael Motley*

FOUNDED 1973. All subjects except short mss (e.g. freelance journalism), poetry, original dramatic material. No scripts. *Special interests* crime novels and thrillers. Unsolicited mss will be considered but must be preceded by a preliminary letter. No reading fee. CLIENTS include Simon Brett, K. M. Peyton, Barry Turner.
Commission Home 10%; US 15%; Translation 20%. *Overseas associates* in all publishing centres.

Jolie Mulvany Literary Agency

85c Linden Gardens, London W2 4EU   ☎01–229 8042
Telex 291829 TLX G Attn: IBIS

Contact *Jolie Mulvany*

FOUNDED 1979. Literary fiction: *Bearn* Lorenzo Villalonge; Thrillers: *Domino Man* Domini Wiles; Sagas: *Genesis* D. Highsmith; Non-fiction: *GCHQ – The Failures and the Cover-up* Jock Kane (banned by the government), *You and Your Handwriting* Peter West. Also Cookery and Health (*The Wholefood Cookbook*); Crime; Science Fantasy; Art/Art History; Auto/biography; Humour; Feminist titles, both fiction and non-fiction. No category romances, science fiction, poetry, history, medical or academic. *Special interests* cookery, astrology and related subjects. No unsolicited mss. Preliminary letter (with s.a.e.) giving information about the author, previous credits, and with synopsis. No reading fee. CLIENTS include Jock Kane, Peter West, Ian Crichton, Domini Wiles, Loren D. Estleman, Sean Flannery.
Commission Home 10%; US 20%; Translation 20%.

The Maggie Noach Literary Agency

21 Redan Street, London W14 0AB   ☎01–602 2451

Contact *Maggie Noach*

FOUNDED 1982. Ex-**A. P. Watt**. Noach (pronounced to rhyme with 'spoke'). Handles a wide range of books, including literary fiction, general non-fiction, and some children's. Scripts considered in association with **Linda Seifert Associates** (see entry). No scientific, academic or specialist non-fiction, romantic fiction, poetry, or books for the very young. Recommended for promising young writers but slow on

correspondence. Unsolicited mss not welcome. Approach by letter giving a brief description of the book and enclosing a few sample pages. Return postage essential. £2 reading fee.
Commission Home 10%; US 20%; Translation 20%.

Andrew Nurnberg Associates Ltd
Clerkenwell House, 45–47 Clerkenwell Green, London EC1R 0HT ☎01–251 0321
Telex 23353

Contact *Andrew Nurnberg*

FOUNDED mid 1970s. *Specialises* in foreign rights for UK and USA publishers and agents. (Andrew Nurnberg is a Russian speaker). Now considering taking on a very few of their own authors.
Commission on application.

Deborah Owen Ltd
78 Narrow Street, Limehouse, London E14 8BP ☎01–987 5119/5441

Contact *Deborah Owen, Judith Dooling*

FOUNDED 1971. Wife of a well-known politician. 'Not for old ladies who write knitting books'. Very high-powered. International fiction and non-fiction (books which can be translated into a number of languages). No scripts, poetry, science fiction, children's books, short stories. No unsolicited mss. Not taking on new authors ('haven't done so for some time'). CLIENTS include Jeffrey Archer, Delia Smith, Ellis Peters, Wendy Savage.
Commission Home 10%; US 15%; Translation 15%.

Mark Paterson & Associates
10 Brook Street, Wivenhoe, Colchester, Essex CO7 9DS ☎0206–225433/4

Contact *Mark Paterson*

FOUNDED 1961. *Special interest* Psychiatric books, psychoanalytical, psychotherapy. No song or play scripts. No articles. No unsolicited mss. Prefer preliminary phone call. May possibly charge reading fee. CLIENTS include Peter Moss, Hugh Brogan, Hugh Schonfield, Vivian Cook. Represent the estate of Sigmund Freud.
Commission 20% throughout.

John Pawsey
Hollybrae, Hill Brow Road, Liss, Hants GU33 7PS ☎0730 893065

Contact *John Pawsey*

FOUNDED 1981. Non-fiction and fiction, e.g. Showbusiness (the Meryl Streep biography); Gardening (*The Window Box Book*); DIY; Travel; Sport (Lester Piggott biography); Cookery; Humour (*How To Survive School*); Crafts. Also thrillers, crime, historical, war, women's and fantasy fiction. Experience in the publishing business has helped to attract some top names but the agency is a long way from any centre of

publishing. No scripts, poetry, science fiction, academic and educational. *Special interests* sport, political, current affairs, and popular fiction. Preliminary letter with s.a.e. essential. No reading fee.
Commission Home 10%; US 19%; Translation 19%.

Norman Payne TV Scripts (Abermarle Scripts)
109 Ullswater Crescent, London SW15 3RE   ☎01–546 9747

Contact *Norman Payne*

FOUNDED 1947. Television and radio scripts, but mostly television. Particularly interested in comedy sitcom and sketch material. Prospective writers should write a letter in the first instance.
No reading fee. *Overseas associates* West Germany (Cologne).

Penman Literary Agency
175 Pall Mall, Leigh-on-Sea, Essex SS9 1RE   ☎0702 74438

Contact *Leonard G. Stubbs FRSA*

FOUNDED 1950. Mainly fiction. Small amount of non-fiction (biography and autobiography). Occasional scripts. No Westerns. No unsolicited mss. Prefer preliminary letter with synopsis. No reading fee.
Commission Home 10%; Overseas 15%.

Peterborough Literary Agency
135 Fleet Street, London EC4P 4BL (until Oct/Nov 1987, then)
         ☎01–353 4242 ext 3681/3683
181 Marsh Wall, London E14 9SR   ☎01-538 5000

Contact *Ewan MacNaughton*

FOUNDED 1973. General non-fiction only. No unsolicited mss. Preliminary letter essential. No reading fee.
Commission Home 10%; US 20%; Translation 20%.

A. D. Peters & Co Ltd
10 Buckingham Street, London WC2N 6BN   ☎01–839 2556

Contact *Michael Sissons* (books); *Anthony Jones* (Film/TV); *Pat Kavanagh* (books and serials); *Norman North* (TV drama/fiction); *Caroline Dawnay* (books); *Sara Drake* (TV documentary/non-fiction).

FOUNDED 1924. All sorts of books, plus scripts. No third-rate DIY. *Special interests* 'Building careers for writers of talent'. Michael Sissons, Pat Kavanagh and Anthony Jones are one of the most high-powered teams in London. Not really for beginners. Pat Kavanagh, married to Julian Barnes, was recently fêted for the astounding deal she came to on behalf of Sally 'Destiny' Beauman. Agency handles Evelyn Waugh estate. No unsolicited mss. Prospective clients should write 'a full and honest letter, with a clear account of what he/she has done and wants to do'. No reading fee.

CLIENTS include John Mortimer, Margaret Drabble, Ruth Rendell, Sally Beauman, Anthony Sampson, Douglas Reeman, Clive James, Robert McCrum.
Commission Home 10%; US 20%; Translation 20%.

Laurence Pollinger Ltd
18 Maddox Street, Mayfair, London W1R 0EU   ☎01–629 9761

Contact *Gerald J. Pollinger, Margaret Pepper, Romany van Bosch* **Negotiating Editor** *Juliet Burton* **Children's Books** *Lesley Hadcroft*

FOUNDED 1958. A breakaway from **Pearn, Pollinger & Higham**. All types of books handled, except pure science, academic, technological. Scripts occasionally. Made comfortable by lead client Graham Greene and by literary estates of H. E. Bates, Scott Fitzgerald and other notables. Good for romantic fiction but Rosemary Gould who handled this section has now retired. Where are the younger agents? Unsolicited mss welcome if preceded by letter (not phone). Charge £5 'contribution towards editorial costs'!
Commission Home 15%; US 15%; Translation 20%.

Murray Pollinger
4 Garrick Street, London WC2E 9BH   ☎01–836 6781

Contact *Murray Pollinger, Gina Pollinger*

FOUNDED 1969. Part of the Pollinger dynasty (Murray is the younger brother of Gerald) with a particularly strong name for new writers. Securely based on Roald Dahl and one or two big selling romantic authors. All types of general fiction and non-fiction, except poetry, plays and travel. No scripts of any kind. No unsolicited mss; writers should send a letter with synopsis and names of other agents and publishers previously approached. CLIENTS include Roald Dahl, Lyall Watson, Molly Keane, J. M. Coetzee, Penelope Lively, John Gribbin.
Commission Home 10%; US 15%; Translation 20% *Overseas associates* in all major cultural countries.

Shelley Power Literary Agency Ltd
48 Kings Road, Long Ditton, Surrey KT6 5JF   ☎01–398 7723/8723 Telex 265871
(postal address) PO Box 149a, Surbiton, Surrey KT6 5JH

Contacts *Shelley Power, Christine Bridge*

FOUNDED 1976. General commercial fiction, quality fiction, self-help, film and entertainment, investigative exposés, black writers from South Africa. No scripts, children's, poetry. Preliminary letter essential describing briefly the project offered, and enclosing s.a.e. No reading fee. CLIENTS include Madge Swindells, Lewis Nkosi, Peter Lambley, Penny Vincenzi, Helen Joseph.
Commission Home 10%; US 15–19%; Translation 19%.

PVA Management Ltd
Alpha Tower, Paradise Circus, Birmingham B1 1TT ☎021–643 4011

Contact *Ruth Scriven*

FOUNDED 1978. Mainly non-fiction with some fiction. Scripts. *Overseas office* **Paul Vaughan Associates**, Los Angeles. Prefer preliminary letter with synopsis and return postage.
Commission 15% Home and Abroad.

Radala & Associates
17 Avenue Mansions, Finchley Road, London NW3 7AX ☎01–794 4495
Telex 295441

Contact *Richard Gollner, Istvan Siklos* (East European expert), *Prince Radala* (East European)

The philosophy of the agency is oriented towards representing authors rather than specialising in particular areas of publishing. Radala 'invented' the popular computing book, and handled over 1000 titles in the early 1980s. Now targeting itself towards the audio tapes market. 'We handle anything that our clients can produce, including TV, radio and theatre'. Not interested in 'books that authors have written in lieu of going to a psychotherapist . . . we wish to hear from people who can write (at least a letter, to start with)'. They avoid on principle mss entitled 'Battle of the River Plate', 'Battle of the Bulge', 'My Battle', or anything else including 'My' in the title. Prospective clients should approach the agency with a shortish letter plus synopsis and sample chapter (double spaced) in the first instance.
Commission Home 10%; Abroad 15–20%; Translation 20%. *Overseas associates* Writers House (Al Zuckermann), New York, plus agents throughout Europe.

Douglas Rae Ltd
28 Charing Cross Road, London WC2H 0DB ☎01–836 3903

Contact *Douglas Rae, Jenne Casarotto*

FOUNDED 1975. Novels, biographies, screenplays, theatre and TV plays. No short stories or poetry. Good reputation for both film and television rights, the main work of the company. Not so happy with books. *Special interests* novels with film and television potential. Unsolicited mss not welcome. Write, enclosing s.a.e. However, 'Not taking on new clients at present.' No reading fee. CLIENTS include John Briley, Derek Marlowe, David Yallop.
Commission Home 10%; US 15%; Translation 20%.

Margaret Ramsay Ltd
14a Godwins Court, St Martins Lane, London WC2N 4LL
☎01–240 0691/01–836 7403

Contact *Margaret Ramsay; Tom Erhardt* (foreign rights), *Stephanie Tanner* (television)

Established in the 1960s. The grand dame of the agency business Margaret (Peggy) Ramsay has been immortalised in book, play and film as Joe Orton's business brain. In the spring of 1987, the following plays on in London or touring had come out of the Margaret Ramsey agency: *Les Liaisons Dangereuses; Coming in to Land; Woman in Mind; A Piece of my Mind; A Chorus of Disapproval*. Also handles scripts for TV, radio and film. Writers should approach by letter or phone in the first instance. No reading fee. CLIENTS include David Wood, Samuel Beckett.
Commission Home 10%; US 10% Translation 10%. *Overseas associates* South America, France, Germany, Holland, Israel, Italy, Japan and Scandinavia.

Deborah Rogers Ltd
49 Blenheim Crescent, London W11 2EF   ☎01–221 3717   Telex 25930 Debrog G

Contact *Deborah Rogers*

FOUNDED 1969. CLIENTS then included Cyril Connolly, Eva Figes, Joseph Heller, Philip Roth. The fashionable literary agent of the 1970s. Fiction and non-fiction. No poetry, plays, technical books.

Commission Home 10%; US 15%. *Overseas associate* International Creative Management, New York.

Herta Ryder
c/o Toby Eady Associates Ltd, 7 Gledhow Gardens, London SW5 0BL
☎01–948 1010/370 6292

Contact *Herta Ryder*

FOUNDED 1984. Fiction; non-fiction (except technical/text books); children's (particularly for older children); popular music (i.e. 'Lives' rather than specialist); military history; German books of quality. No scripts, poetry, individual short stories/articles. Reliable and conscientious. *Special interests* children's and books from Canada (London agent for Macmillan of Canada and McClelland & Stewart, Toronto). Unsolicited mss considered but explanatory letter first preferred. CLIENTS include Gwyneth Jones (Ann Halam), Jean Morris, Farley Mowat, Judy Blume.
Commission Home 10%; US 15%; Translation 20%. *Overseas associates* **Harold Ober Associates**, New York, plus associates in most other countries.

Sheri Safran Literary Agency
8 Pembridge Studios, 27a Pembridge Villas, London W11 3EP

☎01–221 3355   Telex 262284

Contact *Sheri Safran*

FOUNDED 1976. Health books for, by, and about women only. No scripts, no other subjects. No unsolicited mss. Letter essential in first instance. CLIENTS include Janet Horwood (*Comfort*); Shere Hite (*Hite Report*); Julie Orbach (*Understanding Women*). Commission Home 15%; US 20% Translation 20%.

Tessa Sayle Agency
11 Jubilee Place, London SW3 3TE   ☎01–352 4311 (books); 01–352 2182 (drama)

Contact *Tessa Sayle* (books), *Penny Tackaberry* (drama)

FOUNDED 1976 (under present ownership; previously traded as *Hope, Leresche & Sayle*). Fiction: literary, upmarket novels, rather than category fiction. Non-fiction: current affairs, social issues, biographies, historical. Also scripts handled for all media. No children's, poetry or textbooks. Quick to catch on to new talent. No unsolicited mss. Preliminary letter essential, including a brief biographical note and a synopsis. No reading fee. CLIENTS include Thomas Keneally, David Pallister, William Styron, Phillip Knightley (books); Shelagh Delaney, Robert David McDonald, Geoff McQueen (film/TV plays).
Commission Home 10%; US 20%; Translation 20%. *Overseas associates* in USA, Japan and throughout Europe.

Richard Scott Simon Ltd
32 College Cross, London N1 1PR   ☎01–607 8533

Contact *Vivien Green, Richard Simon*

FOUNDED 1971. General non-fiction and fiction, biography, travel cookery, humour. Recent examples include *Bolts from the Blue* Rabbi Lionel Blue; *Pocket Money* Gordon Burn; *The Character of Cricket* Tim Heald; *Cordon Vert* Colin Spencer; *The Sadness of Witches* Janice Elliott, and *Mrs Caliban* Rachel Ingalls. No scripts, romantic novels, poetry, academic, scientific, educational or children's. Prior letter with s.a.e. essential. CLIENTS include Susan Hill, Melvyn Bragg, Wendy Perriam, Barry Humphries. *Commission* Home 10%; US 15%; Translation 20%. *Overseas associates* Georges Borchardt Inc., 136 East 57th Street, New York, NY 10022.

Linda Seifert Associates
18 Ladbroke Terrace, London W11 3PG   ☎01–229 5163/221 0692

Telex Linda London 21879 G

Contact *Linda Seifert, Elizabeth Dench, Nicky Hart*

FOUNDED 1972. Scripts for television, radio and film only. Unsolicited mss will be read, but a letter with sample of work and c.v. (plus s.a.e.) is better. CLIENTS include Stephen Volk *Gothic*; Michael Hirst *The Deceivers*; Michael Radford *White Mischief*.

Commission Home 10% *Overseas associates* Leading Artists, Triad (both Los Angeles).

James Sharkey Associates Ltd

3rd Floor, 15 Golden Square, London W1R 3AG ☎01–434 3801
Telex 295251 Jsalon G

Contact *Sebastian Born*

FOUNDED 1983. Actors' and literary agency. *Special interest* all dramatic scripts: film/TV/theatre/radio. Some books. Preliminary letter preferred. No reading fee. *Commission* 10% across the board.

Vincent Shaw Associates

20 Jays Mews, Kensington Gore, London SW7 2EP ☎01–581 8215

Contact *Vincent Shaw, Cherry Palfrey*

FOUNDED 1954. TV, radio and theatre scripts only. Unsolicited mss welcome; approach in writing (no phone calls) enclosing s.a.e. No reading fee. *Commission* Home 10%; US and Translation by negotiation. *Overseas associates* Herman Chessid, New York.

Anthony Sheil Associates Ltd

43 Doughty Street, London WC1N 2LF ☎01–405 9351 Telex 946420

Contact *Anthony Sheil, Giles Gordon, Gill Coleridge, Mic Cheetham* (books), *Janet Fillingham* (film)

FOUNDED 1962. Full length fiction and non-fiction mss. Theatre, film and radio scripts. Clients include Catherine Cookson and John Fowles. Also handles some royal books. Was the leading agency in the 1970s, with a wide range of clients and good foreign contacts. Unsolicited mss welcome. Preliminary letter with outline of work and autobiographical note on writer preferred. No reading fee. *Commission* Home 10%; US 20%; Translation 20%. *Overseas offices* Wallace & Sheil Inc., 177 East 70th Street, New York, NY 10021, USA.

Caroline Sheldon Literary Agency

23 Cumberland Street, London SW1V 4LS ☎01–821 8051

Contact *Caroline Sheldon*

FOUNDED 1985. Adult fiction, and in particular women's, both commercial sagas and literary novels. Full length children's fiction. No scripts unless the writer also does books. Unsolicited mss welcome, but preliminary letter, with all relevant details of ambitions and 4 chapters of proposed book (and large s.a.e.) preferred. No reading fee. *Commission* Home 10%; US 20%; Translation 20% (Translation handled by Jennifer Luithlen, The Rowans, 88 Holmfield Road, Leicester).

Jeffrey Simmons
10 Lowndes Square, London SW1X 9HA ☎01–235 8852

Contact *Jeffrey Simmons*

FOUNDED 1978. Biography and autobiography; cinema and theatre; fiction (both quality and commercial); history; law and crime; politics and world affairs; parapsychology; sports and travel (but not exclusively). No children's books, cookery, crafts and hobbies, gardening. Scripts handled only if by book writing clients. *Special interests* personality books of all sorts and fiction from young writers (i.e. under 40) with a future. Writers become clients by personal introduction or by letter, enclosing a synopsis if possible, a brief biography of the author, a note of any previously published books, plus a list of any publishers/agents who have already seen the ms. CLIENTS include Michael Bentine, Fenton Bresler, Doris Collins, Daniel Easterman, Sir David Mapley, Tony Parsons, Rosie Swale. *Commission* Home 10–15%; US 15–20%; Translation 20%.

Carol Smith Literary Agency
25 Hornton Court, Kensington High Street, London W8 7RT ☎01–937 4874

Contact *Carol Smith*

FOUNDED 1976. Ex-**A. P. Watt.** Fiction and general non-fiction. Scripts for TV/film only rarely. Absolutely no children's or technical. Good for prolific crime novelists but not strong on literary works. Reputed to be good on encouraging talented young novelists. Unsolicited mss welcome with return postage. Introductory letter preferred. No reading fee. CLIENTS include Sarah Harrison, Madhur Jaffrey, Mike Wilks, Alexander Frater. *Commission* Home 10%; US 15%; Translation 20%.

Solo Syndication & Literary Agency Ltd
8 Bouverie Street, London EC4Y 8BB ☎01–583 9372 Telex 858623

Contact *Dawn Mills* (agent), *Pamela McLoughlin* (accounts)

FOUNDED 1978. Non-fiction: beauty, health, etc; celebrity autobiographies; fiction only from established writers. Also handles freelance articles for newspapers and magazines, plus photos and strip cartoons, on 50/50 terms. No scripts. No unsolicited mss, preliminary letter essential. No reading fee. CLIENTS include Sir James Mancham, Britt Ekland, Val Doonican and Mike Gatting. *Commission* Home 15%; US 20%; Translation 20–30%; 50% on the placing of articles.

Abner Stein
10 Roland Gardens, London SW7 3PH ☎01–373 0456

Contact *Abner Stein*

FOUNDED 1971. Abner Stein quickly earned a reputation for finding serious young writers. Full-length fiction and non-fiction. General non-fiction only; no scientific,

technical etc. No scripts. Letter and outline preferred to unsolicited mss.
Commission Home 10%; US 15%; Translation 20%.

Peter Tauber Press Agency
94 East End Road, London N3 2SX   ☎01–346 4165

Contact *Peter Tauber, Robert Tauber* (directors)
FOUNDED 1950. Celebrity biographies/autobiographies; popular medical (by experts
only), quality full-length fiction, literature, and well researched historical fiction.
No poetry, short stories, scripts, plays or children's. Preliminary letter with syn-
opsis, author's c.v. and s.a.e. essential. No reading fee.
Commission Home 20%; US 20%; Translation 20%.

J. M. Thurley
213 Linen Hall, 156–170 Regent Street, London W1R 5TA   ☎01–437 9545/6

Contact *Jon Thurley, Mary Alderman*

FOUNDED 1976. All types of fiction, non-fiction, coffee table books, etc. Also scripts
for TV/radio/theatre. No short stories or children's illustrated books. No unsolicited
mss; approach by letter in first instance. No reading fee. CLIENTS Roger Marshall (film
and TV drama), Richard Narine (TV comedy); Donald Zeo (biographer and novelist).
Commission Home 10%; US 15%; Translation 15%.

Harvey Unna & Stephen Durbridge Ltd
24–32 Pottery Lane, London W11 4LZ   ☎01–727 1346   Telex 27618 Author G

Contact *Rene Timmins*

Theatrical literary agency, specialising in theatre/TV/film/radio scripts. No books.
No unsolicited mss; preliminary letter and outline essential. No reading fee. *Overseas
associates* worldwide.
Commission Home 10%; US and Translation varies.

Ed Victor Ltd
162 Wardour Street, London W1V 3AT   ☎01–734 4795   Telex 263361

Contact *Ed Victor, Maggie Phillips*

FOUNDED 1976. A broad range, from Iris Murdoch to Irving Wallace, Paula Yates to
Stephen Spender, tending towards the more commercial ends of the fiction and non-
fiction spectrums. No scripts, or heavily academic. Preliminary letter essential, setting out very concisely and clearly what the book aims to do. No unsolicited mss.
'Not looking for new writers at present'. After trying book publishing and literary
magazines, Ed Victor, an ebullient American, found his true vocation. Now he is the
leading contender for the 'Trendiest Agent in London' title. Strong opinions, very
pushy and works hard for those whose intelligence he respects. Loves nothing more
than a good title auction. CLIENTS include Iris Murdoch, Erich Segal, Irving Wallace,
Douglas Adams, Stephen Spender.
Commission Home 15%; US 15%; Translation 20%.

S. Walker Literary Agency
96 Church Lane, Goldington, Bedford, MK41 0AS ☎0234 216229

Contacts *A. Oldfield, C.-L. Oldfield, E. K. Walker*

FOUNDED 1939. Full-length fiction, some non-fiction, children's stories. No poetry, short topical articles. No unsolicited mss. Preliminary letter enclosing synopsis and return postage required. *Overseas associates* works in conjunction with agencies in most European countries and also negotiates directly with foreign publishers. *Commission* Home 10%; US 20%; Translation 20%.

Cecily Ware Literary Agency
19c John Spencer Square, Canonbury, London N1 2LZ ☎01-359 3787

Contact *Cecily Ware* (film/television); *Gilly Schuster* (film/television); *Elizabeth Comstock-Smith* (books, theatre, radio)

FOUNDED 1972. Primarily a script agency, with particular interest in television material. But also handles film and TV tie-ins (*Rockliffe's Babies, Howard's Way*); children's books (Stanley Bagshaw books by Bob Wilson) and fiction, both popular and literary. Also non-fiction which relates to film, theatre etc. No poetry, auto-biography, sport, joke books or technical. Books that have a strong potential as television series, single plays or even films, with a strong storyline and good characterisation, are particularly sought after. No unsolicited mss, or phone calls, and no synopses; approach in writing only. No reading fee. CLIENTS include Charles Humphries, Gerry Huxham (*Eastenders*), Bob Wilson, Helen Wykham, James Andrew Hall (who did the adaptation of *David Copperfield* for the BBC), Jenny McDade (script writer for *Supergran*). *Commission* Home 10%; US 10%; Translation 10%.

Watson Little Ltd
Suite 8, 26 Charing Cross Road, London WC2H 0DG ☎01-836 5880

Contact *Sheila Watson, Amanda Little*

Very catholic range of subjects. *Specialist interests* military and business books. No scripts. Would not be interested in an author who wishes purely to be an academic writer. Always write a preliminary ('intelligent') letter rather than send unsolicited synopsis. £5.75 reading fee. *Commission* Home 10%; US 19%; Translation 19%. *Overseas associates*: MacIntosh & Otis, New York; Mohrbooks, Zurich; La Nouvelle Agence, Paris; Agenzia Lettaria Internazionale, Milan; Rombach & Partners, Netherlands; Suzanne Palme, Scandinavia; Carmen Balcells Spanish & Portuguese (world-wide); Tuttle Mori, Japan.

A. P. Watt Ltd

26–28 Bedford Row, London WC1R 4HL ☎01–405 6774

Telex 297903 APWATT G

Contact *Hilary Rubinstein, Caradoc King, Linda Shaughnessy, Lisa Eveleigh* (unsolicited material)

FOUNDED 1875. Oldest established literary agency in the country, but can be rather impersonal. All full-length typescripts, including children's books, screenplays for film and TV, and plays. No poetry, academic or specialist works. Unsolicited mss welcome if include postage and preceded by introductory letter. Synopsis and/or specimen chapter preferred; an outline at the very least to solicit interest. No reading fee. CLIENTS include Alison Lurie, Nadine Gordimer, Michael Holroyd, Lucy Irvine, Jan Morris, Bill Tidy, Frank Muir, Yeats and Kipling estates.

Commission Home 10%; US 20%; Translation 20%. *Overseas associates* Georges Borchardt Inc. (US).

David Wilkinson Associates

Greener House, 66–68 Haymarket, London SW1Y 4AW ☎01–839 6753

Telex 265871 RESRHL 001

Contacts *David Wilkinson, Abigail Concannon*

General fiction and non-fiction and scripts. No unsolicited material. Prefer initial phone call or introductory letter. No reading fee.

Commission varies according to contract.

National Newspapers

The Pain and Pleasure of Freelancing

Time was when the typical freelance journalist dealt in news, hard news. In popular mythology he wore a trilby hat, had nicotine stained fingers, a capacity for hard liquor and a tendency to march in on the editor shouting 'Hold the front page!' The modern freelance is more likely to work with features than with news, on a lead time days or weeks ahead. He/she rarely appears in the office except when called for a meeting or to collect his expenses. Often, he has specialist knowledge which entitles him to declare his value judgements.

The switch from news to features is partly the result of a change in newspaper format. The space allocated to features has increased enormously in recent years. Think of the boom in colour magazines or the rash of supplements aimed at business people, teachers, computer buffs and other special interest groups. Then again, features are a prominent part of the huge range of periodicals which crowd the newsagents' shelves. Journals come and go, sometimes with startling rapidity, but the overall market has remained on an expansionist course.

The economics of publishing have also helped to promote the freelance feature writer. It makes sense for editors to keep a news team on the payroll, but no sense at all to take on board occasional contributors who can just as easily work from home. Quite a few of the top freelances are journalists who previously held full-time jobs. Though income is variable and the demands heavy, none of them would willingly go back to regular employment.

For the newcomer, the way into the market is simply to have a go. *The Writer's Handbook* listings offer guidance on where to try your luck and how best to make an approach but there is no substitute for a careful study of the paper or journal in which you hope to see your byline. The aim of the freelance who wants to make all or a regular part of his income from writing should be to move quickly from speculative work – where it is up to the editor to accept or reject whatever is sent in – to commissioned articles where the journalist can claim certain rights. Wherever possible, before accepting a commission, extract some sort of agreement in writing. True, a verbal commitment is binding, but if disaster strikes like a paper folding or the editor changes is job, it is often difficult to prove that the commission was ever made.

The other advantage of a written agreement is that it compels both sides to think carefully of what is involved. What level of expenses is required? Do you want part of the fee up front? (The answer here must always be 'Yes'.) What happens if the material submitted does not fulfil the terms of the commission or is suitable but not published for other reasons? In the first case, a reject fee, not less than half the original figure, should be paid. In the second case, the full fee should be paid.

Beware of talking too freely about great ideas for articles before you have a piece of paper acknowledging that you are the writer who will transform them into copy. In the chaos of the typical newspaper or magazine office, it is common for ideas to be purloined, accidentally, of course.

A freelance who contributes regularly to a single publication has the right to ask for a contract, renewable say every year or six months. One of the many virtues of a contract is that it offers an element of security in an otherwise highly insecure business. At the very least, it can be waved at the bank manager when asking for an extension of the overdraft.

Both the **National Union of Journalists** and the **Institute of Journalists** have freelance sections which offer constructive advice to members and give welcome backing in disputes where a journalist who speaks for himself is liable to be shouted down. Two years ago, the NUJ adopted a code of practice for the treatment of freelances. It decrees that conditions and rates of pay should be established clearly when work is accepted or commissioned, that freelances should be paid for providing background information and research material, and that work commissioned or accepted should be paid for at a date agreed which should normally be no more than a month after delivery. Other clauses relate to expenses (to be paid on the same basis as for permanent staff), copyright (to remain with the freelance unless there is a signed agreement to transfer) and the responsibility of staff journalists to watch over the interests of their freelance colleagues.

The rewards of freelancing vary wildly and though where possible we have shown the minimum rates on offer from papers and journals it must be emphasised that all publications are prepared to pay over the odds for contributors and articles they really want. As a general guide there are the comprehensive freelance agreements negotiated by the NUJ with leading publishers. For magazines, the highest band is £250 per thousand words for features and £25 a hundred words for news. This applies to magazines like *Reader's Digest, Woman's Own* and *Radio Times*. On the lowest band (*Film Review, India Times, Everywoman*) rates fall to £80 per thousand words for features and £8 per hundred words for news. Many journals, including some of the most prestigious, pay below these rates. When it is clear that a publication is run on a shoestring, you may feel justified in giving it support by contributing on derisory terms. But as a principle, writers should not expect, or be expected, to provide a charity service for their readers. On the national press, news reports start at £15–£20 for up to a hundred words, features at £175 per thousand words (£188 for Sundays) and colour supplement features £250 per thousand words.

The regional and local press is more of a gamble. The NUJ minimum for weekly papers is £6.80 up to one hundred words and £6.40 a hundred thereafter. The rate for dailies is a straight £8.74 per hundred words. But if our research shows anything it is that in the provinces, all deals are possible. Newspaper editors who plead poverty are seldom to be taken seriously.

Daily Express
121 Fleet Street, London EC4P 4JT   ☎01–353 8000   Telex 21841

Owner *Express Newspapers plc*   **Editor** *Nicholas Lloyd*   **Circulation** 1.85 million

Politics Populist right. Unsolicited mss generally welcome, though the weekly total is 'too numerous to count'. The general rule of thumb is to approach in writing with an idea; all departments are prepared to look at mss without commitment. *Payment* depends on the nature of the article accepted.

News Editor *Michael Parry*

Diary Editor *Ross Benson*   **Features Editor** *Christopher Williams*   **Literary Editor** *Peter Grosvenor*   **Sports Editor** *David Emery*   **Woman's Page** *Katharine Hadley*

Daily Mail
Northcliffe House, Tudor Street, London EC4Y 0JA ☎01–353 6000   Telex 28301

Owner *Lord Rothermere*   **Editor** *Sir David English*   **Circulation** 1,732,413

In house feature writers and regular columnists provide much of the material for this Tory middle-class popular daily. Photo-stories and crusading features often appear; it's essential to hit the right note to be a successful Mail writer, so close scrutiny of the paper is strongly advised. Not a good bet for the unseasoned.

News Editor *Ron Birch*

Diary Editor *Nigel Dempster*   **Features Editor** *Gerald Rudge*   **Literary Editor** *Gordon McKenzie*   **Showbiz** *Baz Bamigboye*   **Sports Editor** *Arthur Firth*   **Woman's Page (Femail)** *Diana Hutchinson*

Daily Mirror
Holborn Circus, London EC1P 1DQ   ☎01–353 0246   Telex 27286

Owner *Robert Maxwell*   **Editor** *Richard Stott*   **Circulation** 3,139,079

No freelance opportunities for the inexperienced. Strong writers who understand what the tabloid market demands are, however, always needed.

News Editor *Tom Hendry*

Diary Editor *Garth Gibbs*   **Features Editor** *John Penrose*   **Literary Editor** *George Thaw*   **Sports Editor** *Ted Graham*   **Women's Page** *Christena Appleyard*

The Daily Telegraph
South Quay Plaza, Marsh Wall, Isle of Dogs, London E14 8NX   ☎01–353 4242
Telex 22874 Telenews London

Owner *Daily Telegraph plc*   **Editor** *Max Hastings*   **Circulation** 1.2 million

Politics Right. Unsolicited mss not generally welcome – 'all are carefully read and considered, but only about one in a thousand is accepted for publication'. As they receive about 20 weekly, this means about one a year. Contenders should approach the paper in writing making clear their authority for writing on that subject. No fiction.

News Editor *James Allan* Tip-offs or news reports from *bona fide* journalists. Must phone the news desk in first instance. *Words* initial 200. *Payment* minimum £10 (tip)

Arts Editor *Miriam Gross*　**Business Editor** *Roland Gribben*　**Diary Editor** *Peter Birkett* Diary pieces always interesting, contact *Peterborough*.　**Features Editor** *Veronica Wadley* By commission from established contributors. However, new writers are tried out by arrangement with the features editor. Approach in writing. *Words* 1500. *Payment* Between £60–£450 and by special arrangement.　**Literary Editor** *David Holloway*　**Sports Editor** *Radford Barrett* Occasional opportunities for specialised items.

Financial Times

Bracken House, 10 Cannon Street, London EC4P 4☏ 01–248 8000　Telex 8954871

Owner *Pearson plc*　**Editor** *Geoffrey Owen*　　　　　　　**Circulation** 280,000

FOUNDED 1888. Business and Finance oriented certainly, but by no means as 'Featureless' as some suppose. All feature ideas must be discussed with the department's editor in advance, but the FT isn't presently snowed under with unsolicited contributions, – they get only about one a week, the lowest of any national newspaper. Approach in writing in the first instance.

News Editor *David Walker*

Arts Editor *J. D. F. Jones*　**City/Financial Editor** *Barry Riley*　**Features Editor** *Ian Hargreaves*　**Literary Editor** *Anthony Curtis*　**Sports Editor** *Michael Thompson-Noel*　**Woman's Page** *Lucia van der Post*

The Guardian

119 Farringdon Road, London EC1R 3ER　　　☏ 01–278 2332　Telex 8811746

Owner *Guardian Trust*　**Editor** *Peter Preston*　　　　　**Circulation** 524,264

Left of centre quality daily. Probably the greatest opportunities for freelance writers of all the nationals, if only because it has the greatest number of specialised pages which use freelance work. But mss should be directed at a specific slot.

News Editor *Melanie Phillips* No opportunities except in those regions where there is presently no local contact for news stories.

'Computer Guardian' Editor *Jack Schofield* A major part of Thursday's paper, almost all written by freelances. Expertise essential – but not a trade page, written for 'the interested man in the street', and from the user's point of view. Prefer delivery of mss by disk or electronic mail.　**Diary** *Stephen Cook*　**Education Editor** *John Fairhall* Expert pieces on modern education (covers many pages of Tuesday's paper).　**Features Editor** *Richard Gott* Receive up to 30 unsolicited mss a day; these are passed on to relevant page editors. **'Grassroots' Editor** *John Course* Manchester based 'forum' page dealing with a wide variety of subjects: 'the only rule of thumb is, nothing to do with London', and ordinarily not by London writers. However, the page is heavily oversubscribed; probably only 1% of contributions are successful. **Media Editor** *Peter Fiddick* 4 pieces a week plus diary, of which 3 are open to outside contributions. All aspects of modern media, advertising, PR, consumer trends in arts/entertainments. Background insight important. Best approach: note followed by phone call. **People** *Stuart Wavell* Contributions should be 'offbeat, humorous, topical'. Phone first. **'Society Tomorrow'** **Editor** *Ann Shearer* Social welfare, psychology and theology, both academic and popular. Experts who write well rather than journalists. Forward looking, offbeat. Maximum of 12 pieces weekly. **Women** *Brenda Polan* What was 'Guardian Women' has now diversified into 'Monday Women', 'Open Space', 'First Person' and 'Guardian Style'. Unsolicited mss used if they show an appreciation of the page in question.

The Independent

40 City Road, London EC1Y 2DB ☎01–253 1222 Telex 9419611

Owner *Newspaper Publishing plc* **Editor** *Andreas Whittam Smith*
Circulation 300,000

Politics Self-styled independent; generally liberal. Founded October 1986, the first new quality national in over 130 years, and the first newspaper to be very precisely targeted and researched before its launch. Aimed at a professional/office working readership, better educated and more affluent than their parents, the label 'the first yuppie newspaper' is not without justification. The content is geared towards those who only have time to dip into a paper at odd times during the day. Particularly strong on its arts/media coverage. The paper has a high proportion of feature material, and theoretically opportunities for freelances are good. However, unsolicited mss are not welcome; most pieces originate in-house or from known and trusted outsiders. Ideas should be submitted in writing.

News Editor *Jonathan Fenby*

Arts Editor *Thomas Sutcliffe* **Business Editor** *Sarah Hogg* **Diary Editor** *Francis Wheen* **Features Editor** *John Morrison* **Literary Editor** *Sebastian Faulks* **Sports Editor** *Charles Burgess*

The Mail on Sunday

Northcliffe House, Tudor Street, London EC4Y 0JA ☎01 353 6000 Telex 28372

Owner *Lord Rothermere* **Editor** *Stewart Steven* Circulation 1,601,038

Pro-right Sunday paper with a high proportion of newsy features and articles (see also Magazines for *You Magazine*, the liveliest of the colour supplements). Experience and judgement required to break into its band of regular feature writers.

News Editor *John Ryan*

Arts Editor *John Butterworth*   **Diary** *Nigel Dempster*   **Features Editor** *Sue Reid*   **Literary Editor** *Paula Johnson*   **Sports Editor** *Ken Haskell*

Morning Star
75 Farringdon Road, London EC1M 3JX   ☎01–405 9242   Telex 28749

Editor *Tony Chater*   Circulation 28,749

Not to be confused with the *Star* (formerly the Daily Star), the Morning Star is our farthest left national daily. Those with a penchant for a Marxist reading of events and ideas can try their luck, though feature space is as competitive here as in the other nationals.

News Editor *Roger Bagley*

Arts Editor *John Blevin*   **Features Editor** *John Blevin*   **Literary Editor** *Helen Bennett*   **Sports Editor** *Tony Braisby*   **Woman's Page** *Helen Bennett*

The News of the World
1 Virginia Street, London E1 9XR
                                              ☎01–481 4100   Telex 262136

Owner *Rupert Murdoch – News International*   **Editor** *David Montgomery*
                                              Circulation 4,954,416

Highest circulation paper. Thrives on the public's insatiable demand for scandal, tragedy and sex.

News Editor *Robert Warren*

Diary *Paul Connew*   **Entertainments** *Ivan Waterman*   **Features Editor** *Paul Connew*   **Literary Editor** *Roy Stockdill*   **Sports Editor** *Bill Bateson*   **Woman's Page** *Unity Hall*.

See also *Sunday* in magazines section.

The News on Sunday
31 Corsham Street, London N1 6DR   ☎01–253 7876   Telex ????

Editor *Bill Nuttings*

1987's new Sunday newspaper, beset by teething troubles in the first months of its life. Aiming to be a lively left of centre hard news Sunday read, it came up looking just plain downmarket and dull. At time of writing, future uncertain.

News Editor *Malcolm Evans*

Features Editor *Jim Reid*

The Observer

8 St Andrews Hill, London EC4V 5JA   ☎01–236 0202   Telex 888963

Owner *Lonhro plc*   **Editor** *Donald Trelford*   **Circulation** 769,000

FOUNDED 1791. WEEKLY. Occupies the middle ground of Sunday newspaper politics. Unsolicited mss are not generally welcome, 'except from distinguished, established writers'. Receive too many unsolicited offerings. No news, fiction, or 'special pages' opportunities. However, Features concede that 'occasional opportunities' arise.

News Editor *Angela Gordon*

Arts/Features Editor *Nicholas Wapshott*   **Business Editor** *Melvyn Marckus* **Diary Editor** *Peter Hillmore*   **Literary Editor** *Blake Morrison*   **Sports Editor** *Peter Corrigan*   **Woman's Page** *Anne Barr*

The People

Orbit House, New Fetter Lane, London EC4A 1AR   ☎01–353 0246   Telex 888963

Owner *Robert Maxwell*   **Editor** *Ernest Burrington*   **Circulation** 2,982,781

Slightly up-market version of The News of the World. Keen on exposés and big name gossip.

News Editor *P. J. Wilson*

Arts Editor *Maurice Krais*   **Diary** *Frank Jeffery*   **Features Editor** *John Smith* **Sports Editor** *N. Holtham*   **Woman's Page** *John Smith*

The Star

121 Fleet Street, London EC4P 4JT   ☎01–353 8000   Telex 21841

Owner Express Newspapers Ltd   **Editor** *Lloyd Turner*   **Circulation** 1,278,058

Tabloid in competition with *The Sun* for 'most flesh and least hard news' title. Freelance opportunities almost non existent. Few features and both these and news coverage supplied in house or from regular outsiders.

News Editor *David Mertens*

Diary *Peter Tory*   **Entertainments** *Patt Codd*   **Features Editor** *Jill Guyte*   **Sports Editor** *J. Pyke*   **Woman's Page** *Alix Palmer*

The Sun

1 Pennington Street, London E1 9BD   ☎01–481 4100   Telex 267827

Owner *News International – Rupert Murdoch*   **Editor** *Kelvin Mackenzie*
                                               Circulation 4,049,991

Highest circulation daily newspaper. Right wing populist outlook; very keen on gossip, pop stars, tv soap, scandals and exposés of all kinds. Not much room for feature writers; 'investigative journalism' of a certain hue is always in demand, however.

News Editor *Tom Petrie*

Entertainments *Nick Ferrari*   **Features Editor** *Gerry Holmberg*   **Sports Editor** *David Balmforth*   **Woman's Page** *Martin Dunn*

Sunday Express
121 Fleet Street, London EC4P 4JT   ☎01–353 8000   Telex 21841

Owner *Express Newspapers plc*   **Editor** *Robin Esser*   **Circulation** 2,200,000

FOUNDED 1918. *Politics* Popular Conservative. Unsolicited mss are generally welcome. Prefer to be approached in writing with an idea. One of that rare breed, a newspaper which still uses fiction. *Payment* by arrangement.

News Editor *Henry Macrory*. Occasional news features by experienced journalists only. All submissions must be preceded by ideas. *Words* 750.

Diary Editor *Lady Olga Maitland*   **Features Editor** *Max Davidson* General features *words* 1000. Profiles of personalities *words* 900. Showbiz features *words* 1000–1500.   **Fiction Editor** *Max Davidson* Short stories of around 1800 words.   **Literary Editor** *Graham Lord*   **Woman's Page** *Veronica Papworth*

Sunday Mirror
Mirror Group Newspapers, 33 Holborn, London EC1P 1DQ

                                             ☎01–353 0246
                                               Telex 27286

Owner *Robert Maxwell*   **Editor** *Michael Molloy*   **Circulation** + 3 million

Politics Maxwellian; Labour right. The *Sunday Mirror* receives anything up to 90 unsolicited mss weekly. In general terms, these are welcome, though the paper patiently points out it has 'more time for contributors who have taken the trouble to study the market'. Initial contact in writing preferred, unless 'a live news situation'. No fiction.

News Editor *Wensley Clarkson* The news desk is very much in the market for tip-offs and inside information. Contributors would be expected to work with staff writers on news stories.

Arts Editor *Madeleine Harmsworth*   **Features Editor** *Robert Wilson* 'Anyone who has obviously studied the market will be dealt with constructively and courteously.' Cherishes its record as a breeding ground for new talent.   **Literary and Diary Editor** *Peter Miller*   **Sports Editor** *Anthony Smith*   **Woman's Page** *Frankie McGowan*

Sunday Sport
50 Eagle Wharf Road, London N1 7ED   ☎01–251 2544   Telex 269277 SSPORTG

Owner *David Sullivan BSc (Econ)*   **Editor** *John Bull*   **Circulation** 400,000

FOUNDED 1986. Newish Sunday tabloid catering for a particular sector of the male 18–35 readership. As concerned with 'glamour' (for which, read page 3) as with human interest news features and sport. Unsolicited mss are welcome; they apparently receive about 90 a week. Approach should be made by phone in the case of news and sports items, by letter for features. No fiction. *Payment* is negotiable, agreed in advance and made on publication.

News Editor *Rab Anderson* Offbeat news, human interest, preferably with photographs.

Features Editor *Sue Blackhall* Regular items: 'Glamour', Showbiz and television, as well as general interest. **Sports Editor** *Tony Flood* Hardhitting sports stories on major soccer clubs and their personalities, and leading clubs and people in other sports. Strong quotations to back up the news angle essential.

Sunday Telegraph

135 Fleet Street, London EC4P 4BL ☎01–353 4242

Owner *Conrad Black*   **Editor** *Peregrine Worsthorne*   Circulation 686,163

Right of centre quality Sunday paper (meaning it has the least tendency to bend its ear to the scandals of the hour). Traditionally starchy and correct, it is in the process of trying to pep up its image and attract a younger readership.

News Editor *Graham Paterson*

Arts Editor *Derwent May* **Diary** *Kenneth Rose* **Features Editor** *Denis Pilgrim* **Literary Editor** *Derwent May* **Sports Editor** *David Grice*.

See also *Telegraph Sunday Magazine* in magazines section.

The Sunday Times

1 Pennington Street, Wapping, London E1 9BD ☎01–481 4100   Telex 262139

Owner *News International – Rupert Murdoch*   **Editor** *Andrew Neil*

Circulation 1.3 million

FOUNDED 1820. Generally right of centre with a strong crusading, investigative tradition. Unsolicited mss are always welcome, especially on the features pages, which are, by virtue of the sheer size of the newspaper, more extensive than other papers. Approach the relevant editor with an idea in writing. Close scrutiny of the style of each section of the paper is strongly advised before sending mss. No fiction. All fees by negotiation.

News Editor *Andrew Hogg* Opportunities are very rare.

Arts Editor *John Whitley* **Business Editor** *Roger Eglin* **Diary Editor** tba **Entertainments Editor** *Patrick Stoddart*   **Features Editor** *Robin Morgan* Submissions are always welcome, but the paper commissions its own, uses staff writers or works with literary agents, by and large. The features sections where most opportunities exist are 'Screen', 'Look', 'Leisure' and 'Spectrum'. **Literary Editor** *Penny Perrick* **Look Editor** (includes Women's/Beauty/Fashion) *Liz Jobey* **Review Editor** *David Sinclair*.

The Times
1 Pennington Street, London E1 9BD   ☎ 01–481 4100   Telex 262141

Owner *News International – Rupert Murdoch*   **Editor** *Charles Wilson*

Circulation 470,000

Politics Generally right (though columns/features can range in tone from the SDP to the libertarian). *The Times* receives a great many unsolicited offerings. Writers with feature ideas should approach by letter in the first instance. No fiction.

Arts Editor *John Higgins*   **Business Editor** *Kenneth Fleet*   **Diary Editor** *Rosemary Unsworth*   **Features Editor** *Nicholas Brett*   **Home News Editor** *John Jinks* Approach by phone   **Literary Editor** *Philip Howard*   **Sports Editor** *Tom Clarke.*

Today
Allen House, 70 Vauxhall Bridge Road, Pimlico, London SW1V 2RP

☎ 01–630 1300   Telex 919925

Owner *News UK Ltd*   **Editor** *David Montgomery*   **Circulation** 307,150

The first of the new technology papers. Originally middle-of-the-road but now under Rupert Murdoch, turning sharply to the right. Feature opportunities look to be declining fast.

News Editor *Colin Myler*

Business Editor *Jonathan Hunt*   **Entertainments Editor** *Paul Donovan*   **Features Editor** *Sue Ryan* **Sports Editor** *Colin Mafham* **Weekend Editor** *Bill Hagerty*   **Woman's Page** *Sue Ryan*

Regional Newspapers

Evening Express (Aberdeen)
PO Box 43, Lang Stracht, Mastrick, Aberdeen AB9 8AF ☎0224 690222

Owner *Thomson Regional Newspapers*   **Editor** *R. J. Williams*   **Circulation** 80,000

Unsolicited mss welcome 'but if possible on a controlled basis'. Receive up to four a week.

News Editor *David Smith* Freelance news contributors welcome.

Features Editor *Moreen Simpson* Women, Fashion, Showbiz, Health, Hobbies, Property – anything will be considered on its merits. *Payment* £30–40.

The Press & Journal (Aberdeen)
Lang Stracht, Mastrick, Aberdeen AB9 8AF   ☎0224 690222   Telex 73133

Owner *Thomson Regional Newspapers*   **Editor** *Harry Roulston*

Circulation 110,000

A well-established regional daily (approaching its 240th year) which receives more unsolicited mss a week than the *Sunday Mirror* – about 120 on average. Unsolicited mss are nevertheless welcome; approach should be made in writing. No fiction.

News Editor *Eric Stevenson* Wide variety of hard or off beat news items, relating to 'the northern half of Scotland'. *Words* 500. *Payment* by arrangement.

Features Editor *Norman Harper* Tightly written topical pieces, preferably with a Scottish flavour. *Words* 1000. *Payment* by arrangement.

Evening Echo (Basildon)
Newspaper House, Chester Hall Lane, Basildon Essex SS1 3BL   ☎0268 22792

Owner *Westminster Press*   **Editor** *J. J. Worsdale*   **Circulation** 60,000

Rely almost entirely on staff/regular writers' contributions, but will consider material sent on spec. Approach the editor in writing.

Belfast Telegraph
Royal Avenue, Belfast BT1 1EB   ☎0232 221242

Owner *Thomson Regional Newspapers*   **Editor** *Roy Lilley*   **Circulation** 150,000

News Editor *Norman Jenkinson*

Features Editor *Tom Carson*   **Woman's Page** *Lindy McDowell*. Plus colour supplement 4 times yearly.

News Letter
Donegall Street, Belfast BT1 2GB   ☎0232 244441

Owner *Century Newspapers Ltd*   **Editor** *Sam Butler*   **Circulation** 44,483

News Editor *Harry Robinson*

Arts Editor *Theo Snoddy*   **Features Editor** *Harry Robinson*   **Woman's Page** *Niki Hill*. Also 6 issues a year of supplement *Accent*.

Birmingham Daily News
78 Francis Road, Edgbaston, Birmingham B16 8SP   ☎021–454 8800

Owner *Reed International*   **Editor** *Malcolm Ward*   **Circulation** 341,000

Unsolicited mss generally welcome. Approach the editor in writing in the first instance.

News Editor *Claire Wolfe*.

Birmingham Post & Mail Ltd
PO Box 18, 28 Colmore Circus, Queensway, Birmingham B4 6AX ☎021–236 3366

Editor *Keith Whetstone*   **Features Editor** *Peter B. Ricketts*

One of the leading regional newspapers. Freelance contributions are welcome for both the Post and Evening Mail. Particularly welcome are topics of interest to the West Midlands and Women's Page pieces offering original and lively comment.

Sunday Mercury
Colmore Circus, Birmingham B4 6AZ   ☎021–236 3366

Editor *John Bradbury*   **Circulation** 168,024

News Editor *Bob Haywood*

Features Editor *Peter Whitehouse*

Bolton Evening News
Newspaper House, Churchgate, Bolton, Greater Manchester BL1 1HU
                                                       ☎0204 22345

Owner *Northern Counties Newspapers*   **Editor** *Leslie Gent*   **Circulation** 54,578

News Editor *Melvyn Horrocks*

Features Editor *Derrick Grocock*   **Woman's Page** *Angela Kelly*.

Evening Echo (Bournemouth)
Richmond Hill, Bournemouth BH2 6HH   ☎0202 24601

Owner *Southern Newspapers plc*   **Editor** *W. M. Hill*   **Circulation** 58,000

FOUNDED 1900. DAILY. Unsolicited mss welcome, but the needs of the paper are specialised and the rejection rate is high. Receive and use a large number of features from established agencies. Ideas in writing, rather than by phone. Prefer to see finished copy, or well thought out suggestions backed up by evidence of writing ability.

News Editor *Ray Horsfield* Few opportunities.

Features Editor *Allan Bannister*   **Fiction** Opportunities rare; fiction may be considered if topical.

Telegraph & Argus (Bradford)
Hall Ings, Bradford BD1 1JR   ☎0274 729511

Owner *Westminster Press*   **Editor** *Terry Quinn*   **Circulation** 83,000

Unsolicited mss not welcome. Approach in writing with samples of work. No fiction.

News Editor/Features Editor *Neil Benson* Local features and general interest. Showbiz pieces. *Words* 600–1000, max 1500. *Payment* NUJ rates for members; negotiable for others.

Evening Argus (Brighton)
89 North Road, Brighton, Sussex BN1 4AU   ☎0273 606799

Owner *Westminster Press*   **Editor** *Terry Page*   **Circulation** 99,275

News Editor *Chris Oswick*

Deputy Editor (features) *Chris Fowler*.

Bristol Evening Post
Bristol United Press, Temple Way, Old Market, Bristol BS99 7HD   ☎0272 20080

Owner *Bristol United Press*   **Editor** *Brian Jones*   **Circulation** 113,304

Unsolicited mss welcome; they get around a dozen a week. Approach in writing with ideas.

Western Daily Press
Temple Way, Bristol, BS99 7HD   ☎0272 20080

Owner *Bristol United Press*   **Editor** *Ian Beales*   **Circulation** 70,000

News Editor *Peter Gibbs*

Features Editor *Nic Petkovik*

Burton Mail
65–68 High Street, Burton upon Trent, Staffs DE14 1LE   ☎0283 43311

Editor *Brian Vertigen*   **Circulation** 22,000

News Editor *Gordon Smith*

Cambridge Evening News
51 Newmarket Road, Cambridge CB5 8EJ   ☎0223 358877

Owner *Cambridge Newspapers Ltd*   **Editor** *Robert Satchwell*   **Circulation** 47,003

News Editor *Peter Wells*

Features Editor *Rodney Tibbs.*

Western Mail
Thomson House, Cardiff CF1 1WR   ☎0222 33022

Owner *Thomson Regional Newspapers*   **Editor** *J. S. Rees*   **Circulation** 78,500

Mss welcome if of a topical nature, and preferably of Welsh interest. No short stories
or travel. Approach in writing to the features editor, who receives between 5 and 10
mss daily.

News Editor *Denis Gane*

Features Editor *Gareth Jenkins* 'Usual subjects already well covered, e.g. motoring,
travel, books, gardening. We look for the unusual.' Maximum 1000 words. *Payment*
dependent on quality and importance. Also opportunities on **Femail** women's page,
and **That's Entertainment** television previews and interviews.

Evening News & Star
Newspaper House, Dalston Road, Carlisle CA2 5UA   ☎0228 23488

Owner *Cumbrian Newspapers Group Ltd*   **Editor** *J. Vernon Addison*

News Editor *Steve Johnston*

Features Editor *Keith Richardson*

Evening Gazette (Colchester)
43–44 North Hill, Colchester, Essex CO1 1TZ   ☎0206 761212

Owner *Essex County Newspapers*   **Editor** *Ken Runicles*   **Circulation** 32,500

Unsolicited mss not generally used, as 'we rely on regular contributors' and don't receive very many.

News and Features Editor *Kelvin Brown.*

Coventry Evening Telegraph
Corporation Street, Coventry CV1 1FP   ☎0203 25588

Owner *Coventry Newspapers Ltd*   **Editor** *Geoffrey Elliott*   **Circulation** 95,000

Unsolicited mss are read, but few are published. Approach in writing with an idea. No fiction. **Features** maximum 600 words. *Payment* £25–30. All unsolicited material should be addressed to the editor.

Derby Evening Telegraph
Northcliffe House, Derby, DE1 2DW   ☎0332 42400

Owner *Northcliffe Newspapers*   **Editor** *Alex Leys*

News Editor *Stan Szecowka*

Features Editor *Chris Ward*

Herald Express (Devon)
Harmsworth House, Barton Hill Road, Torquay TQ2 8JN   ☎0803 213213

Owner *Western Times Co Ltd*   **Editor** *J. C. Mitchell*   **Circulation** 30,000

Unsolicited mss generally not welcome. Receive about 2 dozen a year. Approach the editor in writing.

Doncaster Star
40 Duke Street, Doncaster DN1 3EA   ☎0302 344001

Editor *John Clarke*

Dorset Evening Echo
57 St Thomas Street, Weymouth, Dorset DT4 8EQ   ☎0305 784804

Owner *Southern Newspapers plc*   **Editor** *Michael Woods*   **Circulation** 23,459

News Editor *Paul Thomas*

Dundee Courier and Advertiser

7 Bank Street, Dundee DD1 9HU ☎0382 23131

Editor *Iain Stewart* **Features Editor** *Eddy McLaren* **News Editor** *Irene Rowe* **Woman's Page** *Sandra Young*

Welcome features on a wide variety of subjects, not only of local/Scottish interest. Two pages devoted to features each weekend, supplied by freelances and in-house. Also Women's Page/Thursday Pop Page. Only rule of thumb: keep it short. *Words* 500 max. Very occasionally publish fiction.

Evening Telegraph & Post (Dundee)

Bank Street, Dundee DD1 9HU ☎0382 23131

Editor *Harold Pirie* Circulation 48,395

News Editor *Alan Proctor.* All material should be addressed to the editor.

East Anglian Daily Times

30 Lower Brook Street, Ipswich, Suffolk 1P4 1AN ☎0473 56777

Owner *Eastern Counties Newspapers* **Editor** *Ken R. Rice*

Circulation 50,000

FOUNDED 1874. DAILY. Unsolicited mss generally unwelcome; 3 or 4 received a week, almost none are used. Prefer to be approached in writing in the first instance. No fiction.

News Editor *David Henshall* Hard news stories involving East Anglia (Suffolk, Essex particularly) or individuals resident in the area are always of interest. *Words* vary. *Payment* NUJ rates. **Features Editor** *John Tomlinson* Mostly in-house, but will occasionally buy in when the subject is of strong Suffolk/East Anglian interest. Photo-features preferred (extra payment). *Words* 1000. *Payment* £15. **Special features pages** *Carmen Moyes* Special advertisement features are regularly run, in for instance 'Home Improvements', 'Holidays', 'Properties of Distinction'. Arranged in liaison with Carmen Moyes. *Words* 1000. *Payment* £20.

Eastern Daily Press

Prospect House, Rouen Road, Norwich ☎0603 628311 Telex 975276

Owner *Eastern Counties Newspapers* **Editor** *L. Sear* Circulation 92,000

Unsolicited mss welcome. Approach in writing. News if relevant to Norfolk. Features up to 900 words. Other pieces by commission. Submissions and suggestions to the editor.

Eastern Evening News

Prospect House, Rouen Road, Norwich, Norfolk NR1 1RE ☏0603 628311

Owner *Eastern Counties Newspapers* **Editor** *Peter Ware* **Circulation** 51,857

News Editor *Paul Durrant*

Features Editor *Marjorie Brutnell*

Evening News (Edinburgh)

North Bridge, Edinburgh EH1 1YT ☏031–225 2468 Telex 72255/727600

Owner *Thomson Regional Newspapers* **Editor** *Ian A. Nimmo*

Circulation 123,000

FOUNDED 1873. DAILY. Unsolicited feature material welcome. Approach by telephone call to appropriate department head.

News Editor *Douglas Middleton* NUJ only.

Features Editor *Bill Clapperton* Features for 'Weekender' magazine supplement of broad general interest/historical interest. Occasionally run 'Platform' pieces (i.e. sounding off, topical or opinion pieces) *words* 1000. *Payment* NUJ/House rates.

The Scotsman

20 North Bridge, Edinburgh EH1 1YT ☏031–225 2468

Editor *Chris Baur* **Circulation** 98,863

Despite its smallish circulation, a national Scottish newspaper of quality. Conservative in outlook, it vies with the Glasgow Herald for the top dog position in the Scottish press. Many unsolicited mss come in, and stand a good chance of being read, although a small army of regulars supply much of the feature material not written in-house.

News Editor *James Seaton*

Senior Assistant Editor (features) *Ruth Wishart* The features page carries a great variety of articles. The 6 page *Weekend* section ditto, including book reviews and travel articles. **Lifestyle Editor** *Melanie Reid* Lifestyle replaces the Woman's Page. Once weekly (features welcome).

Express & Echo (Exeter)

160 Sidwell Street, Exeter, Devon EX4 6SB ☏0392 73051

Editor *John Budsworth* **Circulation** 36,210

News Editor *Mike Byrne*

Daily Record
Anderston Quay, Glasgow G3 8DA ☎041–248 7000

Owner *Mirror Group Newspapers*   **Editor** *Bernard Vickers*   **Circulation** 763,866

Mass Market Scottish tabloid.

News Editor *M. B. Speed*

Features Editor *J. Cassidy*   **Woman's Page** *Fidelma Cook*.

Evening Times (Glasgow)
195 Albion Street, Glasgow G1 1PQ ☎041–552 6255

Owner *George Outram & Co Ltd*   **Editor** *George McKechnie*   **Circulation** 191,910

News Editor *Robert Sutter*

Arts Editor *John Fowler*   **Features Editor** *Raymond Gardner*   **Woman's Page** *Anne Simpson*

Glasgow Herald
195 Albion Street, Glasgow G1 1GP ☎041–552 6255

Owner *George Outram & Co Ltd*   **Editor** *Arnold Kemp*   **Circulation** 127,636

Lively quality Scottish daily whose readership spreads beyond the city of Glasgow.

Arts Editor *John Fowler* **Business Editor** *R. E. Dundas* **Diary** *T. Shields* **Features Editor** *Raymond Gardner* **Sports** *E. Rodger* **Woman's Page** *Anne Simpson*

Sunday Mail
Anderston Quay, Glasgow G3 8DA ☎041–248 7000

Owner *Scottish Daily Record*   **Editor** *Endell J. Laird*   **Circulation** 839,166

Downmarket Scottish Sunday paper.

Features Editor *Archibald McKay*

Sunday Post
144 Port Dundas Road, Glasgow G4 0HZ ☎041–332 9933

Owner *D. C. Thomson & Co Ltd*   **Editor** *William Anderson* **Circulation** 1,481,640

All material should be sent to the editor.

Features Editor Brian Wilson

The Citizen (Gloucester)
St John's Lane, Gloucester GL1 2AT ☎0452 424442

Owner *Northcliffe Newspapers* **Editor** *Colin Walker* **Circulation** 39,685

News Editor *R. Gardiner*

Gloucestershire Echo
1 Clarence Parade, Cheltenham, Glos. GL50 3NY ☎0242 526261

Owner *Cheltenham Newspaper Co. Ltd* **Editor** *Sean Dooley* **Circulation** 29,512

News Editor *Tony Shaw*

Greenock Telegraph
2 Crawford Street, Greenock, PA15 1LH ☎0475 26511

Owner *United Provincial Newspapers* **Editor** *Kenneth Thomson*

Circulation 22,500

Unsolicited mss are considered 'if they relate to the newspaper's general interests'. Don't receive too many. Approach by letter. No fiction.

News Editor *David Carnduff* Regional material only. *Words* 600. *Payment* lineage: 12p per line.

Features Editor *James Hunter* Locally slanted material wanted. *Words* 1500. *Payment* lineage: 12p per line.

Grimsby Evening Telegraph
80 Cleethorpe Road, Grimsby, South Humberside ☎0472 59232

Owner *Northcliffe Newspapers* **Editor** *Peter Moore* **Circulation** 75,000*
*Combined with sister paper, *Scunthorpe Evening Telegraph*

In general the Telegraph welcomes unsolicited mss. Receive 'not too many'. Approach in writing. No fiction.

News Editor *Vince McDonash* Hard news stories welcome. Approach in haste by telephone. No fiction.

Features Editor *Patrick Otter*

Guernsey Evening Press & Star
Braye Road, Vale, Guernsey CI ☎0481 45866

Editor *Dave Prigent* **Circulation** 16,160

Arts Editor *Peter Witterick* **Features Editor** *Peter Witterick* **Woman's Page** *Jill Chadwick*

Evening Courier (Halifax)
PO Box 19, Halifax, West Yorkshire HX1 2SF   ☎0422 65711

Editor *Dennis Taylor*   Circulation 37,873

News Editor *David Hanson*

Features Editor *William Marshall*

Hartlepool Mail
Clarence Road, Hartlepool, County Cleveland TS24 8BX   ☎0429 274441

Owner *Portsmouth & Sunderland Newspapers Ltd*   **Editor** *Andrew C. Smith*
                                                        Circulation 29,365

Huddersfield Daily Examiner
Ramsden Street, Huddersfield, West Yorkshire HD1 2TD   ☎0484 537444

Editor *Ivan M. Lee*   Circulation 44,118

News Editor *P. D. Hinchcliffe*

Features Editor *Malcolm Cruise*

Daily Mail (Hull)
PO Box 34, 84 Jameson Street, Hull HU1 3LF   ☎0482 27111

Owner *Northcliffe Newspaper Group*   **Editor** *Michael Wood*   **Circulation** 107,113

News Editor *Keith Perch*

Features Editor *Roy Woodcock*   **Woman's Page** *Heather Dixon*

Evening Star (Ipswich)
30 Lower Brook Street, Ipswich, Suffolk IP4 1AN   ☎0473 56777

Owner *East Anglian Daily Times Co Ltd*   **Editor** *Rodney Kiddell*
                                                        Circulation 36,664

News Editor *David Henshall*

Features Editor *Carol Carver*   **Woman's Page** *Judy Rimmer*

The Irish News
Donegall Street, Belfast BT1 2GE   ☎0232 242614

Editor *Jim Fitzpatrick*   Circulation 42,439

News Editor *Noel Russell*

Features Editor *Dave Culbert*   **Woman's Page** *Anne Donegan*

Jersey Evening Post
Five Oaks, St Saviour, Jersey CI ☎0534 73333

Editor *M. Rumfitt* Circulation 24,128

News Editor *Chris Bright*

Features Editor *P. Stuckey* **Woman's Page** *Elaine Hanning*

Kent Evening Post
395 High Street, Chatham, Kent ME4 4PG ☎0634 48354

Owner *South Eastern Newspapers Ltd* **Editor** *David Jones* Circulation 26,936

News Editor *John Hammond*

Features Editor *John Nurden*

Lancashire Evening Post
127 Fishergate, Preston, Lancs PR1 2DN ☎0772 54841

Owner *United Newspapers* **Editor** *Steve Kendall* Circulation 70,000

Generally unsolicited mss are not welcome. Receive anything up to 100 a year. All ideas in writing to the editor.

Lancashire Evening Telegraph
New Telegraph House, High Street, Blackburn, Lancs BB1 1HT ☎0254 63588

Owner *Thomson Regional Newspapers* **Editor** *Peter R. Butterfield*

Circulation 54,951

Both news stories and feature material with an East Lancashire flavour welcome. Approach in writing with an idea in the first instance. No fiction.

News Editor *David Allin*

Features Editor *Neil Preston* Either a local angle or written by a local person.

Leamington & District Morning News
Heart of England Newspaper Group, PO Box 45, Tachbrook Road, Leamington Spa
CV31 3EP ☎0926 21122

Editor *Bruce Harrison* Circulation 10,950

News Editor *Helen Penrice*

Leicester Mercury
St Georges Street, Leicester LE1 9FQ ☎0533 512512

Owner *Northcliffe Newspaper Group* **Editor** *Neville Stack* Circulation 150,000

News Editor *Roger De Bank*

Lincolnshire Echo
Brayford Wharf East, Lincoln LN5 7AY   ☎0522 25252

Owner *Northcliffe Newspaper Group*   **Editor** *Neil Fowler*   **Circulation** 34,513

News Editor *Alan Whitt*

Daily Post (Liverpool)
PO Box 48, Old Hall Street, Liverpool L69 3EB   ☎051–227 2000   Telex 629396

Owner *Trinity International Holdings*   **Editor** *John Griffith*   **Circulation** 75,000

Unsolicited mss welcome. Receive about six a day. Approach in writing with an idea.
No fiction.

News Editor *Neil Maxwell*

Features Editor *Keith Ely* Local national and international news, current affairs,
profiles – with pictures. *Words* 800–1000. *Payment* £30–50.

Liverpool Echo
PO Box 48, Old Hall Street, Liverpool L69 3EB   ☎051–227 2000   Telex 629396

Owner *Trinity International Holdings*   **Editor** *Chris Oakley*   **Circulation** 207,489

One of the major regional dailies. Unsolicited mss welcome; they receive on average
20 a week. Prefer to be approached in writing first.

News Editor *Joe Holmes*

Features Editor *Carolyn Taylor*. *Words* 1000.

London Evening Standard
PO Box 136, 118 Fleet Street, London EC4P 4DD   ☎01–353 8000   Telex 21909

Editor *John Leese*   **Circulation** 504,388

Long established and staunchly conservative evening paper serving Londoners with
news and feature material (owned by the Mail-Express-Standard group). Genuine
opportunities for both general but particularly London based features, which
abound particularly at the weekend.

News Editor *Philip Evans*

Arts Editor *Michael Owen*   **Literary Editor** *Christopher Hudson*   **London Life**
Maggie Alderson   **Londoner's Diary** *Richard Addis*   **Metro** (Thursday, Arts)
Victoria Keir   **Sports Editor** *Douglas Jackson*   **Weekend** *Maggie Alderson*

Manchester Evening News
164 Deansgate, Manchester M60 2RD   ☎061–832 7200   Telex 668920

Owner *The Scott Trust*   **Editor** *Michael Unger*   **Circulation** 313,000

One of the major regional dailies. Unsolicited mss are welcome. Initial approach in writing preferred. No news or fiction opportunities.

Features Editor *Ken Wood* Personality pieces and showbiz profiles particularly welcome. *Words* 1000. *Payment* by negotiation.

Evening Gazette (Middlesbrough)
Borough Road, Middlesbrough, Cleveland TS1 3AZ   ☎0642 245401

Owner *Thomson Regional Newspapers*   **Editor** *David James*   **Circulation** 78,733

News Editor *Graham Marples*

Features Editor *David Whinyates*   **Woman's Page** *Jennifer McQuillen*

Evening Chronicle (Newcastle upon Tyne)
Thomson House, Groat Market, Newcastle upon Tyne, Tyne and Wear
☎091–232 7500

Owner *Thomson Regional Newspapers*   **Editor** *Graeme Stanton*

Circulation 142,479

The Evening Chronicle receive 'an awful lot' of unsolicited material, much of which they can't use. Approach initially in writing.

News Editor *John Ritson*

Features Editor *Ian Wilson* Limited opportunities due to full time feature staff. maximum 1000 words.   **Sports Editor** *John Gibson*

The Journal
Thomson House, Groat Market, Newcastle upon Tyne, NE1 1ED   ☎0632 327500

Owner *Thomson Regional Newspapers*   **Editor** *Phillip Crawley*

Circulation 66,106

News Editor *Neville Rigby*

Features Editor *John Griffith*   **Woman's Page** *Avril Deane*

Sunday Sun
Thomson House, Groat Market, Newcastle upon Tyne, NE1 1ED ☎091–232 7500

Owner *Thomson Regional Newspapers*   **Editor** *Jim Buglass*   **Circulation** 125,058

News Editor *Alistair Baker* All material should be sent to him.

Northcliffe Newspapers Group Ltd
Editorial Department, 31–32 John Street, London WC1N 2QB   ☎01–242 7070

Editor *Bill Sneyd*

Central editorial office of the regional papers belonging to the group: *The Citizen* (Gloucester); *Daily Mail* (Hull); *Derby Evening Telegraph*; *Evening Herald* (Plymouth); *Evening Sentinel* (Stoke); *Express & Echo* (Exeter); *Glos. Echo* (Cheltenham); *Grimsby Evening Telegraph*; *Devon Herald Express*; *Leicester Mercury*; *Lincolnshire Echo*; *Scunthorpe Evening Telegraph* and *South Wales Evening Post*. See separate listings for details.

Chronicle and Echo (Northampton)
Upper Mounts, Northampton, NN1 3HR ☎ 0604 21122

Owner *United Newspapers plc*   **Editor** *Philip Green*   **Circulation** 42,000

Unsolicited mss are 'not necessarily unwelcome but opportunities to use them are rare'. Some 3 or 4 arrive weekly. Approach in writing with an idea. No fiction.

News Editor *Mrs J. Oldfield*

Features Editor *Chris Hilsden*

Northamptonshire Evening Telegraph
Northfield Avenue, Kettering, Northants NN16 9JN ☎ 0536 81111

Owner *EMAP*   **Editor** *Paul Deal*   **Circulation** 42,804

News Editor *Ian Donaldson*

Arts Editor *Anne Bratley*   **Features Editor** *Lester Cowling*   **Woman's Page** *Sara Smith-Petersen*

The Northern Echo
Priestgate, Darlington, Co. Durham DL1 1NF ☎ 0325 381313

Owner *Westminster Press Ltd*   **Editor** *Allan Prosser*   **Circulation** 90,000

FOUNDED 1870. DAILY. Freelance pieces welcome if arranged by telephone first.

News Editor *Brian Lavery* Reports involving the North East or North Yorkshire. Preferably phoned in. *Words* and *payment* by negotiation.

Celebrity interviews *S. Pratt*   **Features Editor** *Terry Ramsey* Background pieces to topical news stories relevant to the area. Must be arranged with the features editor before submission of any material. *Words* and *payment* by negotiation.   **Fiction** *Serialisation of best-sellers only.*   **Holiday Pages/Supplements** *D. Kelly*   **Local industrial reports** *P. Eastham*   **Special Pages** *Words* and *payment* by arrangement.   **Sports features** *J. Todhunter*

Nottingham Evening Post
Forman Street, Nottingham NG1 4AB ☎0602 475521 Telex 377884

Editor *Barrie Williams* **Circulation** 136,000

Unsolicited mss welcome. Send ideas in writing. **Features Editor** *Tony Moss* Good local interest only. Maximum 800 words. No fiction. **Special pages** *Tony Moss*

Evening Tribune (Nuneaton)
Watling House, Whitacre Road, Nuneaton, Warwicks CV11 6BJ ☎0203 382251

Owner *Watling Publications Ltd* **Editor** *Roger Jeffrey* **Circulation** 13,500

All material to be addressed to the editor.

Oldham Evening Chronicle
172 Union Street, Oldham, Lancs OL1 1EQ ☎061–633 2121

Owner *Hirst Kidd & Rennie Ltd* **Editor** *Gordon Maxwell* **Circulation** 42,000

'We welcome the good but not the bad'. Receive two or three weekly.

News Editor *Jim Williams*

Features Editor *Robert Morton* Humour, travel, local history and the unusual. Maximum 1500 words. *Payment* £15–20.

Evening Leader (Oswestry)
Caxton Press, Oswald Road, Oswestry, Salop SY11 1RB ☎0691 655321

Owner *North Wales Newspapers* **Editor** *Reg Herbert*

News Editor *Steven Rogers*

Arts Editor *Steve Brauner* **Features Editor** *Jeremy Smith* **Woman's Page** *Sandy Mewies*

Oxford Mail
Osney Mead, Oxford OX2 0EJ ☎0865 244988

Owner *Westminster Press Ltd* **Editor** *Edward Duller* **Circulation** 39,970

Unsolicited mss are considered; a great many unsuitable offerings are received. Approach in writing with an idea rather than phoning. No fiction. All fees negotiable.

News Editor *J. Chipperfield* Phone first.

Features Editor *B. Conolly* Any features of topical or historical significance. *Words* maximum 800. **Special Pages** *B. Conolly* Woman's, Art, Music, Motoring, Leisure. *Words* maximum 800.

Paisley Daily Express
14 New Street, Paisley, Scotland PA1 1YA   ☎041–887 7911

Owner *Scottish & Universal Newspapers*   **Editor** *Murray Stevenson*

Circulation 13,000

Unsolicited mss welcome only if of genuine Paisley interest. The paper does not commission work, and will consider submitted material: 'we are more in the business of encouraging amateur writers on local topics than professionals. The budget does not extend to "scale" fees.' *Words* 1000–1500. *Payment* maximum £25. All submissions to the editor.

Peterborough Evening Telegraph
Telegraph House, 57 Priestgate, Peterborough PE1 1JW   ☎0733 555111

Owner *EMAP*   **Editor** *Barrie Holden*   **Circulation** 33,500

Unsolicited mss not welcome. Approaches should be made in writing.

Sunday Independent
Burrington Way, Plymouth, PL5 3LN   ☎0752 777151

Owner *West of England Newspapers Ltd*   **Editor** *John Noble.*

Western Evening Herald (Plymouth)
Leicester Harmsworth House, 65 New George Street, Plymouth, Devon PL1 1RE

☎0752 266626

Owner *Western Morning News Co Ltd*   **Editor** *Alan Goode*   **Circulation** 60,413

News Editor *Roger Clift*

All material to be addressed to the editor or news editor.

The News (Portsmouth)
The News Centre, Hilsea, Portsmouth PO2 9SX   ☎0705 664488   Telex 86316

Owner *Portsmouth & Sunderland Newspapers*   **Editor** *R. C. C. Poulton*

Circulation 100,000

Unsolicited mss not generally welcome. Approach by letter.

News Editor *Chris Owen*

Features Editor *Keith Ridley*   General subjects of SE Hants interest. Maximum 600 words. No fiction. **Sports Editor** *Chris Erskine* Sports background features. Maximum 600 words.

Evening Post (Reading)
8 Tessa Road, Reading, Berks. RG1 8NS ☎0734 55833

Owner *Thomson Regional Newspapers*   **Editor** *Trevor Wade*   **Circulation** 36,000

Unsolicited mss welcome. They get one or two every day, plus mountains of PR material. Finished copy only – no phone calls or written ideas. Fiction very rarely used.

News Editor *Bert May*

Business Post (weekly) Topical – especially hi-tech pieces. *Country Matters* (bi-monthly) Non-technical and topical.   **Features Editor** *Brian Ransome* Topical subjects, particularly of Thames valley interest. *Words* 800–1000.

Scarborough Evening News
17/23 Aberdeen Walk, Scarborough Yorks YO11 1BB ☎0723 363636

Editor *John Bird* **Circulation** 18,585

News Editor *Iain Meekley*

Arts Editor *Jeannie Swales*   **Woman's Page** *Elizabeth Johnson*

Scunthorpe Evening Telegraph
Doncaster Road, Scunthorpe DN15 7RG ☎0724 843421

Owner *Northcliffe Newspaper Group*   **Editor** *P. L. Moore*   **Circulation** 74,000

News Editor *Mick Robins*

All correspondence should go to the news editor.

The Star (Sheffield)
York Street, Sheffield S1 1PU ☎0742 767676

Owner *United Newspapers plc*   **Editor** *Michael Corner*   **Circulation** 150,000

Unsolicited mss not welcome unless topical and local.

News Editor *Martin Ross* Do accept contributions from freelance news reporters if relate to the area.

Features Editor *Stuart Machin* Very rarely require outside features, unless on specialised subjects. *Payment* negotiable.

Shropshire Star
Ketley, Telford, Shropshire TF1 4HU ☎0952 44377

Owner *Midland News Association* **Editor** *Robert Jones* **Circulation** 93,000

Unsolicited mss not welcome. Essential to approach the editor in writing in the first instance with ideas. No news, no fiction.

Features: Limited opportunities here; mostly use in-house or syndicated material. *Words* maximum 1200.

Shields Gazette and Shipping Telegraph
Chapter Row, South Shields, Tyne & Wear NE33 1BL ☎091–455 4661

Owner *Northern Press* **Editor** *Kie Miskelly* **Circulation** 28,091

Features Editor *Margaret Nicholls* **Woman's Page** *Janis Blower*

South Wales Argus
Cardiff Road, Maesglas, Newport, Gwent NP9 1QW ☎0633 62241

Editor *Ken Griffin* **Circulation** 42,385

News Editor *Tom Ellis*

Features Editor *Josephine Type* **Woman's Page** *Josephine Type*

South Wales Echo
Thomson House, Cardiff CF1 1WR

☎0222 33022

Owner *Thomson Regional Newspapers* **Editor** *Geoffrey Rich*

Circulation 100,704

News Editor *Stuart Minton*

Features Editor *Alan Gathergood* **Woman's Page** *Jenny Longhurst*

South Wales Evening Post
Adelaide Street, Swansea, Glamorgan SA1 1QT ☎0792 50841

Owner *Northcliffe Newspaper Group* **Editor** *Iorwerth Lewis* **Circulation** 66,445

News Editor *Frank Gold*

Arts Editor *Frank Gold* **Features Editor** *George Edwards* **Woman's page** *Betty Hughes*

Southern Evening Echo
45 Above Bar, Southampton, Hants SO9 7BA ☎0703 634134

Owner *Southern Newspapers* **Editor** *Duncan Jeffery* **Circulation** 90,000

Unsolicited mss are 'tolerated'. Few are received. Approach in writing with strong ideas; realistically, staff supply almost all the material. All correspondence should be addressed to the editor.

Evening Sentinel (Stoke on Trent)

Sentinel House, Etruria, Stoke on Trent, Staffs ST1 5SS   ☎0782 289800

Owner *Northcliffe Newspaper Group*   **Editor** *R. A. Randall*   **Circulation** 111,676

News Editor *Michael Wood*

All material should be sent to the news editor.

Sunderland Echo

Pennywell Industrial Estate, Pennywell, Sunderland, Tyne & Wear SR4 9ER

☎091–534 3011

Owner *Portsmouth and Sunderland Newspapers*   **Editor** *Andrew Hughes*

Circulation 66,815

News Editor *David Anderson*

Evening Advertiser (Swindon)

100 Victoria Road, Swindon, Wilts SN1 3BE   ☎0793 28144

Owner *Wiltshire Newspapers*   **Editor** *John Mayhew*   **Circulation** 37,000

Unsolicited mss welcome, and many are received. Finished copy much preferred to ideas. 'All need to be strongly related to or relevant to the town of Swindon, the Borough of Thamesdown, or the county of Wiltshire, in that order of interest.' Little scope for non-staff work. Fees by the editor's valuation if by non-NUJ members.

News Editor *Alan Johnson*

Features Editor *Pauline Leighton*   **Fiction** *Pauline Leighton.* Seldom used. Absolutely no poetry.   **Special Pages:** numerous and various.

Thomson Regional Newspapers Ltd

3rd Floor, Pemberton House, East Harding Street, London EC4A 3AS

☎01–353 9131

Editor *Alastair Stuart*

London office of the group which owns the following regional daily papers: *Belfast Telegraph; Edinburgh Evening News; Evening Chronicle* (Newcastle); *Evening Express* (Aberdeen); *Evening Gazette* (Middlesbrough); *Evening Post* (Reading); *The Journal* (Newcastle); *Lancashire Evening Telegraph; Press & Journal* (Aberdeen); *South Wales Echo* (Cardiff); *Sunday Sun* (Newcastle); *Western Mail* (Cardiff). See separate listings for details.

West Lancashire Evening Gazette
PO Box 20, Victoria Street, Blackpool, Lancs. FY1 4RG   ☎0253 25231

Owner *United Newspapers*   **Editor** *Brian Hargreaves*   **Circulation** 53,500

In theory unsolicited mss are welcome. Approach the editor in writing with an idea.

Express & Star (Wolverhampton)
Queen Street, Wolverhampton, West Midlands WV1 3BU   ☎0902 313131

Owner *Midlands News Association*   **Editor** *Keith Parker*   **Circulation** 245,872

News Editor *Derek Tucker*

Arts Editor *Barry Cox*   **Features Editor** *Barry Cox*   **Woman's Page** *Sandra Parsons*

Evening News (Worcester)
Berrows House, Worcester WR2 5JX   ☎0905 423434

Editor *David Griffin*   **Circulation** 29,256

News Editor *Stephen Grocott*

Arts Editor *David Ford*   **Features Editor** *Chris Lloyd*   **Woman's Page** *Mary Johns*

Yorkshire Evening Post
Wellington Street, Leeds, West Yorkshire LS1 1RF   ☎0532 432701

Owner *United Newspapers plc*   **Editor** *M. G. Barker*   **Circulation** 150,000

News Editor *Fred Willis*

Diary *Derek Naylor*   **Features Editor** *Howard Corry*   **Woman's Page** *Anne Patch*

Evening sister of the *Yorkshire Post*.

Yorkshire Evening Press
York & County Press, 15 Coney Street, York YO1 1YN   ☎0904 53051

Owner *York & County Press*   **Editor** *Richard Wooldridge*   **Circulation** 55,000

Unsolicited mss not generally welcome, unless submitted by journalists of proven ability. Receive about six a week. Approach in writing only – 'phone calls always come at the wrong time, and we'd have to see the written work anyway'. No fiction.

News Editor *Richard Wooldridge* Accredited journalists only.

Features Editor *Terry Watson* Exceptional pieces of local relevance considered. *Words* 1000. *Payment* negotiable.

Yorkshire Post

Wellington Street, Leeds, West Yorkshire LS1 1RF 📞0532 432701 Telex 55245

Owner *United Newspapers plc* **Editor** *John Edwards* **Circulation** 92,000

A serious minded, quality regional daily with a generally conservative outlook. 3 or 4 unsolicited mss arrive a day; all will be considered. Initial approach in writing preferred. All submissions should be addressed to the editor. No fiction. **Features:** open to suggestions in all fields (though ordinarily commission from specialist writers).

Addendum

Bath & West Evening Chronicle

33 Westgate Street, Bath, Avon BA1 1EZ 📞0225 63051

Owner *Wessex Newspapers* **Editor** *David Flintham* **Circulation** 27,188

News Editor *Simon Whitby*

Diary Editor *Simon Toft* **Features Editor** *David Hamlett* **Woman's Page** *Tina Currie*

National Magazines

Accountancy

40 Bernard Street, London WC1N 1LD   ☎01–628 7060

Owner *Institute of Chartered Accountants of England and Wales*   **Editor** *Brian O'Kane*   **Circulation** 68,000

FOUNDED 1889. MONTHLY. Written ideas welcome. Approach by phone with news items.

Features *Gillian Bird*   Accounting/tax/business-related articles of high technical content aimed at professional/managerial reader. Maximum 800–3000 words. *Payment* £82 per printed page.   **Main features** *Brian O'Kane*   Major feature articles comprising part or all of cover story. Features list available. Material planned and commissioned at least six months in advance. Maximum 800–5000 words. *Payment* £82 per printed page or by negotiation.   **News** *Julia Irvine*   News items – investigative reports related to City, EEC, industry, accounting and international accountancy in business context, maximum 500 words; Commentary – opinionated piece on any similar subject; Accounting ideas – technical based; Economic trends – up-to-date reviews or predictions. Maximum 1200 words. *Payment* by arrangement.

Accountancy Age

32–34 Broadwick Street, London W1A 2HG ☎01–439 4242   Telex 23918 VNUG

Owner *VNU*   **Editor** *Robert Bruce*   **Circulation** 85,000

FOUNDED 1969. WEEKLY. Unsolicited mss welcome, and ideas may be suggested in writing or by telephone provided they are clearly thought out.

Features Topics right across the accountancy/business/financial world. Maximum 1500 words. *Payment* at NUJ rates.

The Accountant's Magazine

27 Queen Street, Edinburgh EH2 1LA   ☎031–225 5673   Telex 727530

Owner *The Accountant's Publishing Co.*   **Editor** *Winifred Elliott*   **Circulation** 13,500

FOUNDED 1897. MONTHLY. New contributors are welcome, but should approach in writing in the first instance.

Features Articles welcome on topics of interest to the accountancy profession; finance, economics, business, management etc. Must be authoritative. Maximum length 3000 words (1000–2000 preferred). *Payment* by negotiation.

Adviser

Williams Savory Ltd, 1 Winckley Street, Preston PR1 2AA ☎0772 201536

Owner *British Dietetic Association* **Editor** *Neil Donnelly* Circulation 3000

FOUNDED 1981. QUARTERLY. Unsolicited manuscripts are welcomed from dietitians, nutritionists and 'food and health' journalists. Make initial approach in writing. All pieces should be appropriate to dietitians. Maximum 1200 words. *Payment* £40–50.

African Affairs

Dept. of Politics, University of Bristol, 12 Priory Road, Bristol BS9 4DZ
☎0272 303200

Owner *Royal African Society* **Editor** *Richard Hodder-Williams/Peter Woodward*
Circulation 2500

FOUNDED 1901. QUARTERLY learned journal publishing articles on contemporary developments on the African continent. Unsolicited mss welcome.

Features Should be well-researched and written in a style that is immediately accessible to the intelligent lay reader. Maximum 8000 words. *Payment* for non-academics £40 per 1000 words. No payment for academics.

A La Carte

King's Reach Tower, Stamford Street, London SE1 9LS ☎01–261 5000
Telex 915748 MAGDIV G

Owner *IPC Magazines Ltd* **Editor** *Jeanette Arnold* Circulation 50,000

FOUNDED 1984. TEN ISSUES PER YEAR. Specialised food, drink and gourmet travel magazine. Unsolicited contributions welcomed from food and/or wine writers of experience and authority. All mss should be sent to the Editor. At present, about ten unsolicited manuscripts are received each week. Most of these are inappropriate for the magazine.

Amateur Film Maker

33 Gassiot Way, Sutton, Surrey SM1 3AZ ☎01–644 0839

Owner *Film Maker Publications* **Editor** *Tony Pattison* Circulation 3000

FOUNDED 1930. BI-MONTHLY of the **Institute of Amateur Cinematographers**. Reports news and views of the Institute. Unsolicited mss welcome, but all contributions are unpaid.

Amateur Gardening

Westover House, West Quay Road, Poole, Dorset BH15 1JG ☎0202 680586

Owner *IPC Magazines*   **Editor** *Graham Clarke*   **Circulation** 84,825

FOUNDED 1884. WEEKLY. New contributions are welcome provided that they have a professional approach. Of the twenty unsolicited manuscripts received each week, 90% are returned as unsuitable.

Features Topical gardening articles – to be agreed with Editor before submission. Maximum length 1100 words.   **News** Gardening news items are compiled and edited in-house. Maximum 200 words.   ALSO One-off gardening features – to be agreed with Editor before submission. Maximum length 1100 words. *Payment* at IPC/NUJ rates.

Amateur Photographer

Prospect House, 9–13 Ewell Road, Cheam, Surrey SM1 4QQ ☎01–661 4300

Owner *Business Press International*   **Editor** *Barry Monk*   **Circulation** 90,550

For the competent amateur with a technical interest. Freelances are used, but writers should be aware that there is ordinarily no use for words without pictures.

Amateur Stage

1 Hawthorndene Road, Hayes, Bromley, Kent BR2 7DZ ☎01–462 6461

Owner *TEAM Publishing Ltd*   **Editor** *Charles Vance*

Ambit

17 Priory Gardens, Highgate, London N6 5QY ☎01–340 3566

Owner *Dr Martin Bax*   **Editor** *Dr Martin Bax*   **Circulation** 2000

FOUNDED 1959. QUARTERLY literary magazine. Publishes short stories, experimental fiction and poetry, but no features. A large number of unsolicited manuscripts received. But these are welcomed if accompanied by an s.a.e. All approaches should be made in writing; never by phone.

American Express Gazette,
Exchange Travel News, Pickfords Travel News

1 Munro Terrace, London SW10 and 3rd Floor, Foundation House, Perseverance Works, 38 Kingsland Road, London E2 ☎01–351 3643

Owner *Robert MacBeth-Seath* (Travelscope Travel Publications)   **Editor** *Roger Edwards*   **Joint Circulation** 360,000–800,000

FOUNDED 1972. QUARTERLY travel magazines, which all welcome unsolicited manuscripts. Prospective contributors can make initial approach either by telephone or in writing. If an idea is considered suitable for publication, the editor would brief the writer as to style and emphasis.

Angling Times

Bretton Court, Bretton, Peterborough PE3 8DZ   ☎0733 266222

Owner *EMAP*   **Editor** *Neil Pope*   **Circulation** 126,155

Do not send your fishing stories here: this weekly is more concerned with angling news than feature material, most of which is provided by their large staff. Occasional features from outsiders. **Features Editor** *Kevin Wilmott*. *Payment* NUJ rates.

Animal World

Causeway, Horsham, West Sussex RH12 1HG   ☎0403 64181   Telex 878484

Owner *RSPCA*   **Editor** *Elizabeth Winson*   **Circulation** 35,000

BI-MONTHLY RSPCA magazine. Most technical articles (pet care etc.) are written in-house. Unsolicited mss welcome.

Features and fiction Articles and stories should not contradict RSPCA policy. Illustrative photographs welcome. Maximum 1000 words. *Payment* £18 (more for illustrated articles).

Annabel

80 Kingsway East, Dundee, Scotland DD1 9QJ   ☎0382 44276

Owner *D. C. Thomson & Co Ltd*   **Editor** *David McColl*   **Circulation** 152,754

Apart from the domestic content of the magazine, material is mainly supplied by freelance writers (this is typical of a DC Thomson publication). Currently trying to change its image, and going for a younger, Daily Mail reading audience. Need general women's interest features, interviews and topical articles. Also fiction – it doesn't have to be about marriage: 'we've also published Fay Weldon'. A maximum of 3000 words. A good bet for freelances; although 'the slush pile' does not generally yield much in the way of ready made features, it can provide new writers for the future. Fees negotiable. **Features Editor** *David McColl*.

The Antique Collector

National Magazine House, 72 Broadwick Street, London W1V 2BP

  ☎01-439 7144   Telex 263879 NATMAG G

Owner *National Magazine Co. Ltd*   **Editor** *David Coombs*   **Circulation** 16,500

FOUNDED 1930. MONTHLY. Opportunities for freelance features. It is best to submit ideas in writing. Feature articles have a set format; maximum length 2000 words with eight illustrations in colour and/or black and white. Their acceptance depends primarily on how authoritative and informative they are. *Payment* by negotiation.

The Antique Dealer and Collectors' Guide
Kings Reach Tower, Stamford Street, London SE1 9LS ☎ 01–261 6894
Telex 915748 MAGDIV G

Owner *IPC Magazines Ltd* **Editor** *Philip Bartlam* Circulation 14,139

FOUNDED 1946. MONTHLY covering all aspects of the antiques and fine art world. Unsolicited mss are welcomed.

Features Maximum length 1500 words. Practical but readable articles welcomed on the history, design, authenticity, restoration and market aspects of antiques and fine art. **News** *Philip Bartlam* Maximum length 150 words. Items welcomed on events, sales, museums, exhibitions, antiques fairs and markets. *Payment* £68 per 1000 words.

Apollo
4 Davies Street, London W1Y 1LH ☎ 01–629 4331

Owner *A. Cluff and N. Attallah* **Editor** *Anna Somers Cocks*
Circulation *c.*15,000

MONTHLY. A magazine for art collectors, art historians and dealers. Articles are either art historical or critical and almost always written by experts in their fields. Unsolicited mss not welcome.

Arabia
Crown House, Crown Lane, East Burnham, Bucks SL2 3SG ☎ 02814 5177

Telex 847031 ARABIA G

Owner *Islamic Press Agency* **Editor** *Dr Fathi Osman* Circulation 30,000

FOUNDED 1981. MONTHLY Islamic world review. Unsolicited mss welcome.

Features Lives and affairs of Muslims around the world. Pictures an advantage. Maximum length 1200 words. *Payment* by negotiation. **News** Maximum length 200 words. *Payment* by negotiation.

The Architect
66 Portland Place, London W1N 4AD ☎ 01–580 5533

Owner *RIBA Magazines Ltd* **Editor** *Jose Manser* Circulation 27,500

MONTHLY journal of Royal Institute of British Architects.

Features Specialist articles on architecture and matters of practice. Maximum 1200 words. *Payment* £100 per 1000 words.

The Architectural Review
9 Queen Anne's Gate, London SW1H 9BY ☎ 01–222 4333   Telex 8953505

Owner *The Architectural Press*   **Editor** *Peter Davey*

MONTHLY. Unsolicited mss welcome, but no news stories only features.

Arena
The Old Laundry, Ossington Buildings, London W1M 3HY ☎ 01–935 8232

Owner *Wagadon Ltd*   **Editor** *Nick Logan*

New style and general interest magazine for the young and trendy man about town.
Male fashion, intelligent feature articles (sports articles are more likely to be about
cycling or rock-climbing than bar billiards); no reviews or arts coverage; no fiction –
but interested in developing this area. Good literary short stories welcome. *Payment*
'competitive'.

Art Monthly
36 Great Russell Street, London WC1B 3PP ☎ 01–580 4168

Owner *Britannia Art Publications*   **Editor** *Peter Townsend, Jack Wendrer*

Circulation 4000

FOUNDED 1976. MONTHLY. News and features of relevance to those interested in
modern art. Unsolicited manuscripts, of which approximately two per month are
received, are welcomed.

Features Alongside exhibition reviews, which are usually 600–1000 words long and
are almost invariably commissioned, articles are published on art theory (e.g. modernism, post-modernism), individual artists, art history (of the modern period) and
issues affecting the arts (e.g. funding and arts education). These articles can be up to
3000 words in length. Book reviews are usually 600–1000 words but occasionally go
up to 3000 words. Payments in all cases are negotiable, and all contributions should
be addressed to the editors.   **News** Brief reports on conferences, public art etc.
(250–300 words).

The Artist (Inc. Art & Artists)
102 High Street, Tenterden, Kent TN30 6HT ☎ 05806 3673

Owner *Irene Briers*   **Editor** *Sally Bulgin*

Circulation 18,000

FOUNDED 1931. MONTHLY.

Features *Sally Bulgin*   Art journalists, artists, art tutors and writers with a good
knowledge of art materials are invited to write to the editor with ideas for practical,
discursive and informative features about art, materials and artists.

Arts Express

25–31 Tavistock Place, London WC1H 9SF ☎01–388 9521

Editor *Rick Rogers* **Circulation** 5000

Theoretical and practical journal of arts and education published ten times yearly. No reviews of arts events please. Interested in theoretical articles, reports on projects, and series on, for example, education policies in the public sector. Contact the editor with ideas. *Payment* £60 per 1000 words.

Arts Review

69 Faroe Road, London W14 0EL ☎01–603 7530

Editor *Graham Hughes*

A vehicle for both London and regional reviews of arts events. Opportunities for reviewers exist, depending on your specialisation, and the region you represent. They do have a large number of such people already. *Payment* currently (1987) £30 per 1000 words, but this is under review.

Artscribe International

41 North Road, London N7 9DP ☎01–609 4565 Telex 24453 OMNIBUG

Editor *Matthew Collings* **Circulation** 13,000

FOUNDED 1975. BI-MONTHLY. Unsolicited mss welcome, but freelance opportunities are limited.

Features *Matthew Collings* Most pieces commissioned. Unlikely that freelance pieces will be used unless by established art critics. Length and payment varies. **News** *Matthew Collings/Ian Brunskill* Most news stories are written by staff, but pieces on major events in the art world considered. Contact editor in first instance. **Reviews** *Ian Brunskill* Opportunities are greatest here: reviews of exhibitions more likely to be used than feature articles. Maximum 500 words. *Payment* negotiable.

Athletics Weekly

342 High Street, Rochester, Kent HE1 1ED ☎0634 409269

Editor *Barry Trowbridge* **Circulation** 24,827

FOUNDED 1945. WEEKLY. Features news and articles on track and field athletics, road running and cross-country. Interviews, profiles, historical articles and exclusive news. Length and payment of all articles by arrangement. Unsolicited mss welcome.

The Author

84 Drayton Gardens, London SW10 9SB ☎01–373 6642

Owner *Society of Authors* **Editor** *Derek Parker* **Circulation** 5000

FOUNDED 1890. QUARTERLY. Unsolicited mss not welcome.

Autocar

38–42 Hampton Road, Teddington, Middlesex TW11 0JE   ☎01–977 8787
Telex 8952440 (HAYMRT G)

Owner *Haymarket Publishing*   **Editor** *Matthew Carter*   **Circulation** 56,307

FOUNDED 1895. WEEKLY. Uses only commissioned material, but ideas may be sent in writing to the relevant editor.

Features *Mark Gillies*   No unsolicited articles accepted.   **News** *Ian Adcock*.   Tip-offs, hard industry and product news. *Payment* £90 per 1000 words.

Baby – The Magazine

21 Cross Street, Islington, London N1 2BH   ☎01–359 3575

Owner *Harrington Kilbridge & Partners*   **Editor** *Mrs J. Harrington*

QUARTERLY for young mothers with small babies. Always interested in new writers who should contact Kim Sheaf for further details.

The Banker

102–108 Clerkenwell Road, London EC1M 5SA   ☎01–251 9321
Telex 23700 FINBI G

Owner *Financial Times*   **Editor** *Colin Jones*   **Circulation** 13,000

FOUNDED 1926. MONTHLY. New contributors are welcome and may approach either by telephone or in writing. News and features only on banking and finance world-wide.

Basketball Monthly

'The Hollies', Hoton, Leics LE12 5SF   ☎0509 880208

Owner *English Basketball Association*   **Editor** *Richard Taylor* **Circulation** 10,000

FOUNDED 1961. MONTHLY featuring technical, specialist, foreign and personality pieces for basketball enthusiasts. Unsolicited mss welcome.

BBC Wildlife Magazine

Broadcasting House, Whiteladies Road, Bristol BS8 2LR   ☎0272 732211
Telex 265781 BSA

Owner *BBC Enterprises Ltd* and *Wildlife Publications Ltd*   **Editor** *Rosamund Kidman Cox*

FOUNDED 1983. MONTHLY. Unsolicited mss not welcome.

Competition The magazine runs an annual competition for professional and amateur writers with a first prize of £800.   **Features** Most features commissioned from amateur writers with expert knowledge on wildlife or conservation subjects. Unsolicited mss are usually rejected. Maximum 2000 words. *Payment* £120.   **News** Most news stories commissioned from known freelances. Maximum 800 words. *Payment* £40.

The Beat

1 Lower James Street, London W1R 3PN ☎01–734 9201

Owner *Beat Productions*   **Editor** *Johnny Black*   **Circulation** 250,000

FOUNDED 1984. MONTHLY (except January and August). Best approach is with idea in writing, enclosing samples of published work. Unsolicited mss are not welcome.

Features Feature articles (subjects and market as below). Maximum 2000 words. *Payment* £65 per 1000 words.   **News** Items of interest to people 16–30. Music, film, TV and general interest. Maximum 500 words. *Payment* £65 per 1000 words.   **Reviews** Some opportunities for freelance album reviewers – 100 words. *Payment* as News and Features.

Bee World

18 North Road, Cardiff CF1 3DY   ☎0222 372409   Telex 23152 monref G 8390

Owner *International Bee Research Association*   **Editor** *Dr M. E. Adey*
                                                              Circulation 2000

FOUNDED 1919. MONTHLY high-quality factual journal with international readership. Features on apicultural science and technology. Unsolicited mss welcome.

Bicycle

Northern and Shell Building, PO Box 381, Mill Harbour, London E14 9TW
                                        ☎01–987 5090   Telex 24676

Owner *Cover Publications Ltd*   **Editor** *Nick Rearden*   **Circulation** 16,000

FOUNDED 1981. MONTHLY for cyclists and cycling enthusiasts. Unsolicited mss welcome.

Features Maximum 3000 words.   **Fiction** Maximum 800 words (plus illustration ideas).

Birds

The Lodge, Sandy, Beds SG19 2DL ☎0767 80551

Owner *RSPB*   **Editor** *Annette Preece*   **Circulation** 351,000

QUARTERLY magazine which covers not only wild birds, but wildlife and conservation topics as well. No interest in features on pet birds. Usually commission, but mss or ideas welcome.

Blitz

1 Lower James Street, London W1R 3PN ☎01–734 8311

Owner *Jigsaw Publications*   **Editor** *Tim Hulse*   **Circulation** 60,000

Magazine covering style and media related subjects for a young and trendy market: music, film, fashion, art, politics and style. Aimed at an intelligent 18–30 audience. Always interested in seeing unsolicited mss. *Payment* £70 per 1000 words.

Blue Jeans

D.C. Thomson & Co Ltd, Albert Square, Dundee DD1 9QJ   ☎ 0382 23131
Telex 298937

Owner *D.C. Thomson*   **Editor** *Gayle Anderson*   **Circulation** 120,727

FOUNDED 1977. WEEKLY. Unsolicited mss welcome, but about 100 are received each week. All approaches should be made in writing.

Features *Alison Kuker*   Features on popular trivia: information on jeans, hair, romance, etc. A lot of light-hearted information and interesting facts. Maximum 1500 words. *Payment* £40.   **Fiction** *Jane Rattray*   Very keen for good-quality short stories – bearing in mind that they are for the teenage girl market. Maximum 1500 words. *Payment* £40. **Pop** *Lesley Ross*   Interviews (mainly question and answer type) with chart bands who have a teenage appeal. Gossipy style: nothing too technical. Maximum 1500 words. *Payment* £40.

Bookdealer

Suite 34, 26 Charing Cross Road, London WC2H 0DH   ☎ 01–240 5890

Editor *Barry Shaw*

Weekly trade paper which acts almost exclusively as a platform for people wishing to buy or sell rare or out of print books. Very little editorial; occasional articles and regular book reviews done by regular freelance writers.

Books

43 Museum Street, London WC1A 1LY   ☎ 01–404 0304

Editor *Carolyn Hart*   **Circulation** 100,000

Formerly known as **Books and Bookmen**. A consumer rather than trade magazine, dealing chiefly with features on authors, reviews of books, and general aspects of the publishing business. *Payment* negotiable.

The Bookseller

12 Dyott Street, London WC1A 1DF   ☎ 01–836 8911

Owner *J. Whitaker & Sons Ltd*   **Editor** *Louis Baum*

Trade journal of the publishing and book trade. Trade news and features, including special features, company news, trends in publishing etc., are ordinarily done in-house or by commissions offered to experts within the business. Unsolicited mss rarely used. Approach in writing.

News Editor *Penny Mountain*

Features Editor *Helen Paddock*

Brides and Setting Up Home

Vogue House, Hanover Square, London W1R 0AD ☎01–499 9080

Telex 27338 VOLON G

Owner *Condé Nast Publications*   **Editor** *Sandra Boler*   **Circulation** 56,000

BI-MONTHLY. Freelance contributions are considered provided they are relevant. Much of the magazine is produced 'in house', but a good feature on cakes, jewellery, music, flowers etc. is always welcome. Prospective contributors should telephone with an idea. Maximum length (features) 1000 words. *Payment* £115.

British Airways High Life

47 Whitcomb Street, London WC2H 7DX ☎01–930 8691

Owner *Headway Publications*   **Editor** *William Davis*   **Circulation** 215,000

MONTHLY GLOSSY. Almost all the content of this magazine is commissioned, so there are few opportunities for freelances and unsolicited manuscripts are not welcome. Approach with ideas in writing only.

British Birds

Fountains, Park Lane, Blunham, Bedford MK44 3NJ ☎0767 40340

Owner *British Birds Ltd*   **Editor** *Dr J. T. R. Sharrock*   **Circulation** 10,000

FOUNDED 1907. MONTHLY ornithological magazine. Unsolicited mss welcome, but from ornithologists only.

Features Well-researched, original material relating to West Palearctic birds. Maximum 6000 words.   **News** *Mike Everett/Robin Prytherch*   News items ranging from conservation to humorous notes. Maximum 200 words. *Payment* All contributions are unpaid.

British Judo

16 Upper Woburn Place, London WC1H 0QH ☎01–387 9304

Telex 27830 SPORTCG

Owner *British Judo Association*   **Editor** *Tony Reay*   **Circulation** 38,000

FOUNDED 1978. QUARTERLY. Issued free to all British Judo Association members and licence holders. Unsolicited mss are welcome but all ideas must be presented to Management Committee in writing.

Features Profiles of star competitors; features, e.g. sports injuries, sponsorship. Maximum 2000–3000 words. Humorous anecdotes 250–500 words.   **Fiction** Anything relevant to the sport. Maximum 2000–3000 words.   **News** Reports and results of judo competitions. Maximum length 500–1,000 words; other sports 2,000 words. *Payment* At standard rates.

British Medical Journal

BMA House, Tavistock Square, London WC1H 9JR ☎01–387 4499

Owner *British Medical Association* **Editor** *Dr Stephen Lock*

No market for freelance writers.

Broadcast

100 Avenue Road, Swiss Cottage, London NW3 3TP ☎01–935 6611
Telex 299973 ITP LNG

Owner *International Thomson* **Editor** *Peter Monteith* **Circulation** 8000

FOUNDED 1960. WEEKLY. Very few opportunities for freelance contributions, but write in the first instance to the relevant editor.

Features *Roma Felstein* Features on broadcasting issues. Maximum length 1500 words. *Payment* £100 per 1000 words. **News** *Marta Wohrle* News stories on broadcasting. Maximum length 400 words. *Payment* £90 per 1000 words.

The Brownie

17–19 Buckingham Palace Road, London SW1W 0PT ☎01–834 6242

Owner *Girl Guides Association* **Editor** *Mrs J. V. Rush*

FOUNDED 1962. WEEKLY. Aimed at Brownies aged 7–10 years.

Articles On crafts and simple make-it-yourself items using inexpensive or scrap materials. **Features** General interest. Maximum 350–400 words. *Payment* £26 per 1000 words pro rata. **Fiction** Brownie content an advantage. No adventures involving children in dangerous situations – day or night – unaccompanied. Maximum 350–400 words. *Payment* £26 per 1000 words pro rata.

Building

Builder House, 1/3 Pemberton Row, Fleet Street, London EC4P 4HL

☎01–353 2300 Telex BUILDAG 25212

Owner *Builder Group Ltd* **Editor** *Graham Rimmer* **Circulation** 21,000

FOUNDED 1842. WEEKLY. Features articles on aspects of the modern building industry. Unsolicited mss not welcome, but freelances with specialist knowledge of the industry are often used.

Features Focussing on the modern industry, no building history required. Maximum 1500 words. *Payment* by arrangement. **News** Maximum 500 words. *Payment* by arrangement.

The Burlington Magazine
6 Bloomsbury Square, London WC1A 2LP   ☎01–430 0481   Telex 291072

Owner *The Burlington Magazine Publications Ltd*   **Editor** *Caroline Elam*
Circulation not disclosed

FOUNDED 1903. MONTHLY. Unsolicited contributions are welcome provided that they are on the subject of art history and are previously unpublished. All preliminary approaches should be made in writing.

Exhibition Reviews Usually commissioned, but occasionally unsolicited reviews are published if appropriate. Maximum length 1000 words. *Payment* £15 (average). **Main Articles** Maximum length 4500 words. *Payment* £40 (average). **Shorter Notices** Maximum length 2000 words. *Payment* £25 (average).

Business
234 Kings Road, London SW3 5UA   ☎01–351 7351   Telex 914549 INTMAG G

Owner *Business People Publications*   **Editor** *Stephen Fay*   **Circulation** 45,000

FOUNDED 1986. MONTHLY. Some opportunities for freelance feature writers, but unsolicited manuscripts are not welcomed. Prospective contributors are best advised to write in the first instance with feature ideas. Maximum length 2500 words. *Payment* £200 per 1000 words.

Business and Professional Women
10 St John's Road, Farnham, Surrey GU9 8NT   ☎0252 712367

Owner *BPW Federation*   **Editor** *Linda Findlay*   **Circulation** 10,000

FOUNDED 1930s. QUARTERLY magazine of the Business and Professional Women's Federation. Unsolicited mss not welcome and features on Federation members only are required.

Camera Weekly
38–42 Hampton Road, Teddington, Middlesex TW11 0JE   ☎01–977 8787
Telex 895 2440 HAYMART G

Owner *Haymarket Publishing*   **Editor** *George Hughes*   **Circulation** 61,227

FOUNDED 1976. WEEKLY. Considerable opportunities for freelance contributors, but up to 100 unsolicited mss are received each week. There is a market here for features which detail exciting, exotic experiences within photography – plus pictures. Features should have lots of 'how-to-do-it' or factual information. No travelogues. Approach with an idea by telephone or in writing. Maximum length for articles, 1000 words. *Payment* negotiable.

Campaign

22 Lancaster Gate, London W2 3LY ☎01–402 4200

Owner *Marketing Publications* **Editor** *Christine Barker* **Circulation** 23,008

FOUNDED 1968. WEEKLY. Lively magazine serving the advertising and related industries. Freelance contributors are advised to write in the first instance.

Features Articles of up to 1500–2000 words. *Payment* £100 per 1000 words. **News** *Jan Hawkins* Relevant news tips of up to 300 words. *Payment* between £35 and £50. Also *City Diary, Close-up* and *Media* sections.

Camping and Caravanning

11 Lower Grosvenor Place, London SW1W 0EY ☎01–828 1012

Owner *Camping and Caravanning Club* **Editor** *Peter Frost* **Circulation** 88,000

FOUNDED 1901. MONTHLY. Unsolicited, relevant mss are welcomed. Out of London journalists are often commissioned to cover events. Local journalists with camping and caravanning knowledge should write if they wish to be on magazine's contact lists. **News/Features** Items and pieces, up to a maximum of 800 words, are always welcomed, especially if illustrated.

Canal and Riverboat

Stanley House, 9 West Street, Epsom, Surrey KT18 7RL ☎03727 41411
Telex 291561 VIA SOS G (AEM)

Owner *A. E. Morgan Publications Ltd* **Editor** *Norman Alborough*
Circulation 13,500

Unsolicited mss are welcomed and prospective contributors are advised to make initial approach in writing.

Features *Norman Alborough* Maximum length 2000 words on all aspects of waterways and narrow boats and motor cruisers, including cruising reports, practical advice etc. Unusual ideas and personal comments are particularly welcome. *Payment* approx. £50. **Fiction** Only considered when subject matter is relevant. Maximum length 1500 words. *Payment* around £35. **News** *Paul Roome* Items up to 300 words on Inland Waterways System, plus photographs if possible. *Payment* £10.

Car

FF Publishing, 97 Earls Court Road, London W8 6QH ☎01–370 0333

Owner *FF Publishing Ltd* **Editor** *Steve Cropley* **Circulation** 128,000

FOUNDED 1962. MONTHLY. Unsolicited manuscripts of at least 1500 words are welcomed.

Features are usually commissioned from staff and known writers, but other material on new and old cars, special events and travel experiences, is considered. Maximum length 3000 words. **Fiction** Short stories and satire (up to 3000 words) considered.

Payment £100–200 per 1000 words (negotiable).   **News** Items (up to 250 words) and photographs are always welcome, especially on new car models. *Payment* £50 (negotiable).

Cars and Car Conversions Magazine

Link House, Dingwall Avenue, Croydon, Surrey CR9 2TA   ☎01–686 2599

Telex 947709 LINK HOG

Owner *Link House Magazines Ltd*   **Editor** *Russell Bulgin*   **Circulation** 80,000

FOUNDED 1965. MONTHLY. Unsolicited mss are welcomed, but preferably after previous contact. Prospective contributors are advised to make initial contact by telephone.   **Features** *Russell Bulgin*   Articles of up to 2000 words on current motorsport and unusual sport-oriented roadcars are welcomed. *Fee* by negotiation.

Catholic Herald

Lamb's Passage, Bunhill Row, London EC1Y 8TQ   ☎01–588 3101

Editor *Terence Sheehy*   **Circulation** 30,000

Feature material from freelances is used. Interested in not only straight Catholic issues, but general humanitarian matters, Third World etc. No demand for freelance news writers, 'unless they happen to be on the spot'. *Payment* 'very little, £20 uppermost'.

Celebrity

80 East Kingsway, Dundee DD4 8SL   ☎0382 44276   Telex 76380

Owner *D. C. Thomson & Co. Ltd*   **Editor** *David Burness*   **Circulation** 150,000

WEEKLY. Opportunities for freelance contributors, but twenty or so unsolicited manuscripts are received every week. There are no hard news pages as such, but *Celebrity* carries regular crime, royal and medical articles written in the style of 'tabloid' newspapers. There is a six-week lead time, so forward planning is essential and features should, if possible, have a topical theme, coinciding with a new TV series, film releases etc. There is always scope for human interest articles and any offbeat or unusual stories, but no fiction.

Features Maximum length is 1000–1500 words. *Payment* £75 per 1000 words or by arrangement.   **Photo-features** (transparencies or black and white prints) on almost any subject will also be considered. Photos should be captioned or accompanied by a short article. *Payment* by arrangement.

Certified Accountant

8A Hythe Street, Dartford, Kent, DA1 1BX   ☎0322 28584   Telex 896747

Editor *Richard Garlick*   **Circulation** 37,000

MONTHLY. Specialist, professional readership; unsolicited mss not welcome. About 100 are received each year and prospective contributors are advised to make initial contact in writing. No news or fiction.   **Features** Maximum length 3000 words. All features tend to be commissioned, professional articles and accountancy analyses. *Payment* £150.

Chacom
1A East Cliff, Preston PR1 3JE ☎0772 50246

Owner *Winckley Publishing*   **Editor** *Debbie Worsnop*   **Circulation** 3000

FOUNDED 1984. MONTHLY for commerce and industry. Unsolicited mss welcome.

Features Various topical areas of business, exports, Chamber of Commerce business, etc.   **News** *Joyce Searle*   Items on commerce and industry. Maximum 500 words. *Payment* minimal.

Challenge
Revenue Buildings, Chapel Road, Worthing, W. Sussex BN11 1BQ ☎0903 200775

Owner *Challenge Literature Fellowship*   **Editor** *Donald Banks*

Circulation 10,000

FOUNDED 1958. MONTHLY Christian magazine which welcomes unsolicited mss. Prospective contributors should send for sample copy and writers' guidelines.

Features Commissioned only.   **Fiction** Short children's stories – maximum 600 words.   **News** Items up to 500 words 'showing God at work'. *Fees* negotiable.

Channel Hopper
3 New Burlington Street, London W1X 1FE ☎01–439 2431

Owner *Centurion Press*   **Editor** *Lyn Thompson*   **Circulation** 100,000

FOUNDED 1985. QUARTERLY. A travel information magazine, covering France and Belgium. Unsolicited mss are not welcome: prefer to discuss material with the writer before it is submitted.

Features On places of interest to a traveller. Maximum length 1000 words.   **News** Should be brief. *Payment* £80.

Channel TV Times
The TV Centre, St Helier, Jersey, Channel Islands ☎0534 73999

Owner *Channel Islands Communications (Television) Ltd*   **Editor** *Stuart C. Guilliard*

Circulation 9595

FOUNDED 1962. WEEKLY. Mainly about the Channel Islands. Very few unsolicited mss are received and are not welcomed, but feature ideas on island subjects considered.   **Features** Maximum of 2000 words on topics of interest to Channel Islanders. *Payment* £30 per 1000 words.

Chat

195 Knightsbridge, London SW7 1RE   ☎01–589 8877

Owner *ITP*   **Editor** *Peter Genower*   **Circulation** 600,000

FOUNDED 1985. WEEKLY WOMEN'S TABLOID. No unsolicited contributions; the magazine receives far too many of these. The Features Editor may be approached by phone with an idea.

Features Editor *Nora McGrath* Maximum length of features 700 words.   **News Editor** *Peter Genower* Items usually around 400–500 words.

Chic

36 Skylines, Lime Harbour, Docklands, London E14 9TS   ☎01–538 1151/4

Owner *Rate Press Ltd*   **Editor** *Mary Fitzpatrick*   **Circulation** 35,000

FOUNDED 1984. MONTHLY glossy magazine aimed at a young black readership. Unsolicited manuscripts are welcome, but prospective contributors are advised to write in the first instance with idea.

Fiction *Carmen Harris* Keen to publish stories that relate directly to black people. Maximum 3000 words. *Payment* NUJ rates.

Chief Executive

30 Calderwood Street, London SE18 6QH   ☎01–855 7777

Owner *Morgan-Grampian*   **Editor** *Garrod Whatley*   **Circulation** 21,500

FOUNDED 1968 (as *Business Administration*). MONTHLY. Unsolicited mss not welcome.

Features Limited opportunities for freelances as much of the magazine is written in-house or by known specialists with backgrounds in management journalism. Maximum 2000 words. *Payment* by negotiation.

Choice

12 Bedford Row, London WC1R 4DU   ☎01–404 4320

Owner *EMAP*   **Editor** *Annette Brown*   **Circulation** 100,000

MONTHLY magazine for the fun of pre-retirement planning. Aimed at 'better-off' people approaching retiring age, (i.e. 50–60). Unsolicited manuscripts are not welcome; approach in writing only.

Features *Alison Davies* Features on items, hobbies and adventure affecting 50–60 year olds considered. Maximum length usually 800 words (occasionally 1500 words). *Payment* £80–100 (occasionally £150). **Fiction** Three-part fiction considered. **Finance** *Annette Brown* Features on finance/property/legal matters affecting the magazine's readership. **News** *James Pringle* All items affecting the magazine's readership. Maximum length 100 words. *Payment* £25.

Christian Herald

96 Dominion Road, Worthing, West Sussex BN14 8JP ☎0903 212171

Owner *Herald House Ltd*   **Editor** *Colin Reeves*   **Circulation** 33,000

FOUNDED 1866. WEEKLY. Conservative evangelical Christian magazine aimed at adults with families. Most theological and spiritual articles are commissioned.

Family round up Short articles on wide range of subjects, some religious, some non-religious. Articles should appeal to whole family, especially women. Maximum 200–500 words. *Payment* at Herald House rates.   **Fiction** Moral, non-religious short stories, light and entertaining. Avoid Christian conversion stories. Maximum 1600 words. *Payment* £20.   **General interest** Various non-religious subjects. Historical subjects need light, enthusiastic touch and crisp, clear illustrations (no slides). Maximum 900–1000 words. *Payment* £20–30.

Christian Science Monitor

Eggington House, 25–28 Buckingham Gate, London SW1E 6LD ☎01–630 8666

Owner *Christian Science Publishing Society*. **Contact** *British Isles Correspondent*

The London office is not an editorial one, and all unsolicited material is passed on to head office in the United States for consideration. WEEKLY in Britain, the *Monitor* has a huge circulation in America, where it is a DAILY paper. Always on the look out for general interest feature material which appeals to an international audience.

Church of England Newspaper

Livingstone House, 11 Carteret Street, London SW1H 9DJ ☎01–222 3464

Owner *Christian Weekly Newspapers Ltd*   **Editor** *Rev. Wallace Boulton*
Circulation 13,500

FOUNDED 1892. WEEKLY. Almost all material is commissioned, but unsolicited mss considered.

Features *Polly Hudson*   Unless commissioned, preliminary enquiry in writing is essential. 1700 words maximum. *Payment* NUJ/IOJ rates.   **News** *Rev. Wallace Boulton*   News items must be sent promptly and have a church/Christian relevance. 250 words maximum. *Payment* NUJ/IOJ rates.

Church News

College Gate House, Bury St Edmunds, Suffolk IP33 1NN ☎0284 3530

Owner *Home Words & Canon Cecil Rhodes*   **Editor** *Canon Cecil Rhodes*
Circulation 95,000

FOUNDED 1946. MONTHLY small magazine featuring news and information on events, persons and religious subjects and debates. Unsolicited mss welcome. Maximum for articles 600 words. *Payment* by agreement.

Church Times

7 Portugal Street, London WC2A 2HP ☎01–405 0844 Telex 892542

Owner *G. J. Palmer & Sons Ltd* **Editor** *Bernard H. Palmer* **Circulation** 44,721

FOUNDED 1863. MONTHLY. Unsolicited mss welcome.

Features *Bernard Palmer* Articles on religious or social topics. Length 700–1500 words. *Payment* £25 per 1000 words. **News** *Susan Young* Occasional reports on out of London events, but only when commissioned. Length by arrangement. *Payment* £2.50 per 100 words.

Classical Music

241 Shaftesbury Avenue, London WC2H 8EH ☎01–836 2383
Telex 264675 GILDED G

Owner *Rhinegold Publishing Ltd* **Editor** *Graeme Kay* **Circulation** Unaudited

FOUNDED 1976. FORTNIGHTLY. A specialist magazine using precisely targeted news and feature articles, so unsolicited manuscripts are not welcome. Prospective contributors may approach in writing with an idea, but should familiarise themselves beforehand with the style and market of the magazine. *Payment* £50 per 1000 words.

Climber

Ravenseft House, 302–304 St Vincent Street, Glasgow G2 5NL ☎041–221 7000

Owner *Holmes McDougal Ltd* **Editor** *Cameron McNeish* **Circulation** 20,000

FOUNDED 1962. MONTHLY. Unsolicited mss welcome (they receive about 10 a day). Finished features only – no ideas. No fiction.

Features Freelance features (maximum 2000 words) are accepted on climbing, mountaineering and hill-walking in UK and abroad. The standard of writing must be extremely high. **News** No freelance opportunities – all in-house. *Payment* negotiable.

Coarse Fisherman/Big Fish

61 Main Street, Long Lawford, Rugby, Warwickshire, CV23 4AZ ☎0788 73963

Owner *W. M. Print Ltd* **Editor** *Dave Phillips* **Circulation** 22,500

Coarse Fisherman – MONTHLY. *Big Fish* – QUARTERLY. Unsolicited mss welcomed but prospective contributors should first study magazines for content and style. Up to 20 mss arrive each month.

Features Material 'must be top rate to be accepted'. **Fiction** Fiction on the subject of angling is welcome – but it must be *funny* and satire should not be clichéd. Maximum length 1500 words. **News** Particularly keen to hear from writers with an understanding of angling who can relate it to environmental and current affairs. Maximum length 2000 words. *Payment* negotiable.

Coarse Fishing Handbook

Bretton Court, Bretton, Peterborough PE3 8DZ ☎0733 264666 Telex 32157

Owner *EMAP* **Editor** *Mike George* Circulation 23,109

FOUNDED 1983. BI-MONTHLY. Unsolicited material on all coarse fishing subjects is very welcome and prospective contributors are advised to make initial contact by telephone. As the magazine is aimed at experienced anglers, submissions should be in-depth studies.

Features Maximum length 2500 words. All articles should be illustrated either with black and white photos or colour transparencies. **Fiction** There is usually one piece per issue and humorous submissions are preferred. All fees by arrangement.

Company

National Magazine House, 72 Broadwick Street, London W1V 2BP 01–439 7144

Editor *Maggie Goodman* Circulation 317,281

Women's MONTHLY magazine, founded, as the name suggests, to appeal to the young working woman. Consider themselves a good market for freelances: 'we've got more space for them, as we have fewer staff feature writers'. Occasionally use fiction. Around 2000 words.

Features Editor *Gill Hudson* More likely to use established magazine writers, as there is little time to bring people on. Mss rather than ideas essential for unknowns; 'with inexperienced writers, we need to see something in black and white'. *Payment* negotiable.

Computer Weekly

Quadrant House, The Quadrant, Sutton, Surrey SM2 5AS ☎01–661 3122

Owner *Reed Business Publishing* **Editor** *David Craver* Circulation 113,000

FOUNDED 1966. Unsolicited material generally not welcome unless an outline has been discussed and agreed. Unsolicited items (up to 700 words) are welcomed for the 'Platform' section, but there is no fee. No fiction.

Features *David Barrett* Always looking for new, good writers with specialised industry knowledge. Maximum length 1500 words. Special Show Features for industry events (e.g. Previews) up to 1200 words welcomed. **News** *Rob Parry* Maximum length 300 words. Some possibilities for regional or foreign news items only. *Payment* £100 per 1000 words.

Computing

32–34 Broadwick Street, London W1A 2HG ☎01–439 4242 Telex 23918 VNU G

Owner *VNU* **Editor** *Graham Cunningham* Circulation 115,000

WEEKLY. New contributors are welcome, and are advised to write in the first instance with ideas.

Connections
Sea Containers House, 20 Upper Ground, London SE1 9PF

Editor *Alison Booth*   **Circulation** over 2 million

The thrice yearly magazine of Sealink Ferries, distributed to those travelling with the company. Carry around 3 articles per issue, mostly connected with places en route. Unsolicited material not generally welcome, nor ideas; happy with their current contributors, and commission when necessary.

Contemporary Review
61 Carey Street, London WC2A 2JG   ☎ 0252 713883

Owner *Contemporary Review Co. Ltd*   **Editor** *Rosalind Wade*, OBE

FOUNDED 1866. MONTHLY. One of the first periodicals to devote considerable space to the arts. Today it remains liberal without any specific political affiliations. A wide spectrum of interests includes home affairs and politics, literature and the arts, history, travel and religion. There is also a monthly book section, quarterly fiction and film reviews. Unsolicited mss welcome: maximum 3000 words. No fiction.

Cosmopolitan
National Magazine House, 72 Broadwick Street, London W1V 2BP ☎ 01–439 7144

Editor *Linda Kelsey*   **Circulation** 404,234

Popular mix of articles, emotional advice and strong fiction designed to appeal to a late-teen/early twenties modern minded female. Known to have a policy of not considering unsolicited mss, but does nevertheless sometimes look at those it receives. This is because it is always on the look out for new writers. 'The thing to do is to ring the features desk with an idea; if they are interested they will ask to see something.'   **Features Editor** (and long standing humour writer for the magazine) *Marcelle D'Argy Smith*.

Country
361A Upper Richmond Road West, London SW14 8QN   ☎ 01–392 1499

Owner *Country Gentlemen's Association*   **Editor** *Jeanne Griffiths*
                                              Circulation 33,000

FOUNDED 1903. MONTHLY magazine of the Country Gentlemen's Association. Unsolicited mss are welcomed and prospective contributors are advised to make initial contact in writing. No fiction.

Features Country subjects of national interest, preferably accompanied by good photos, are welcomed. Historical articles are also considered. No stories about my cat/dog/budgie. Very few travel story opportunities. *Payment* £60–80 per 1000 words.   **News** Short items (up to 300 words) on country matters. *Payment* £60 per 1000 words.

Country Homes and Interiors
Carlton House, 25 Newman Street, London W1P 3HA ☎ 01–631 3939

Owner *Carlton Magazines Ltd* **Editor** *Vanessa Berridge*   **Circulation** 88,130

FOUNDED 1986. MONTHLY. The best approach for prospective contributors is with an idea in writing as unsolicited manuscripts not welcomed.

Features *Vanessa Berridge*   There are two main features per month, one a personality interview, the other an examination of a topic of interest to an intelligent, affluent readership (both women and men) aged 25–44. Maximum length 1500–2000 words. *Payment* negotiable.   **Travel** *Orlando Murrin*   Pieces of 1200 words. Also hotel reviews, leisure pursuits, weekending pieces in England & abroad – 750 words. *Payment* negotiable.

Country Life
King's Reach Tower, Stamford Street, London SE1 9LS ☎ 01–261 7070

Owner *IPC Magazines* **Editor** *Jenny Greene*   **Circulation** 48,900

Part of the social fabric of English rural life, the magazine has recently come under the wing of a new editor determined to widen the readership and generally blow the dust off. Features which relate to the countryside, wildlife, rural events, sports and pursuits welcome. Strong, informed material, rather than amateur enthusiasm. *Payment* £100 per 1000 words.

Country Living
National Magazine House, 72 Broadwick Street, London W1V 2BP ☎ 01–439 7144

Editor *Deirdre McSharry*   **Circulation** 118,000

Regards itself as a women's magazine, but has a strong male readership as well. Upmarket, takes living in the country seriously (generally in a soft-focus middle-class way) and tends to be people oriented. Welcomes features on people, conservation, wildlife, houses, gardens, animals, country businesses etc. Suggestions welcome. Pays good fees as very keen to be literate and well researched; often uses 'name writers'. Articles are mostly commissioned; writers new to the magazine should send a synopsis and examples of published work. *Payment* negotiable, but never less than £150 per 1000 words, often more.

The Countryman
Sheep Street, Burford OX8 4LH ☎ 099 382 2258

Owner *The Countryman Ltd* **Editor** *Christopher Hall*   **Circulation** 81,000

FOUNDED 1927. QUARTERLY. Unsolicited mss are welcome; about 75 are received each week. Prospective contributors are advised to make initial approach in writing having read a few issues of the magazine to understand its policies.

Creative Camera

Battersea Arts Centre, Old Town Hall, Lavender Hill, London SW11 5TF

☎ 01–924 3017

Owner *Registered Charity*   **Editor** *Peter Turner*   **Circulation** *c*.6000

FOUNDED 1968. MONTHLY. Most of the magazine's content is commissioned, but new contributors are welcome and are best advised to approach in writing.

Features Reviews of photographic books and exhibitions. Maximum length 750 words. *Payment* £50.

Creative Review

50 Poland Street, London W1V 4AX

☎ 01–439 4222

Editor *Bernard Barnett*

The trade magazine of advertising and related industries, including film, design, and illustration. Expert contributors only. Send in samples of work, whether published or not; feature needs are organised on a commission basis, and writers of talent may be taken up.

The Creditor

162 Lord Street, Southport PR9 0QA

☎ 0704 44433

Owner *Goldfinch Publications*   **Editor** *Julian Desser*   **Circulation** 20,000

FOUNDED 1986. MONTHLY magazine of the National Association of Unsecured Creditors. Deals mainly with insolvency and liquidation practices, but there is scope for high-quality features on finance and business topics. Unsolicited mss from specialist writers welcome. Maximum 2000 words. *Payment* £120 per 1000 words.

The Cricketer International

29 Cavendish Road, Redhill, Surrey RH1 4AH

☎ 0737 72221

Owner *Ben G. Brocklehurst*   **Editor** *Christopher Martin-Jenkins*

Circulation 41,000

FOUNDED 1921. MONTHLY. Unsolicited mss welcome.

Cue World

Cavalier House, 202 Hagley Road, Edgbaston, Birmingham B16 9PQ

☎ 021–455 6230

Owner *Snooker Publications Ltd*   **Editor** *John Dee*   **Circulation** 24,000

FOUNDED 1976. MONTHLY for snooker enthusiasts. Unsolicited mss not welcome. All approaches should be made in writing.

Dance Theatre Journal

Laban Centre for Movement and Dance, Laurie Grove, London SE14 6NW

☎01–692 4070 ext 38

Owner *Laban Centre*   **Editor** *Chris de Marigny*

FOUNDED 1983. QUARTERLY. Interested in features on every aspect of the contemporary dance scene. Unsolicited mss welcome. Specially interested in articles concerning issues such as the funding policy for dance as well as critical assessments of choreographers' work and latest developments in various schools of contemporary dance. Maximum 3700 words. *Payment* £15 per 1000 words.

The Dancing Times

Clerkenwell House, 45–47 Clerkenwell Green, London EC1R 0BE   ☎01–250 3006

Owner *Private company*   **Editor** *Mary Clarke*   **Circulation** 12,000

FOUNDED 1910. MONTHLY. Approaches in writing should be made by specialist dance writers only.

Darts World

2 Park Lane, Croydon, Surrey CR9 1HA   ☎01–681 2837

Owner *World Magazines Ltd*   **Editor** *A. J. Wood*   **Circulation** 24,500

Unsolicited mss welcome; approximately 100 are received each year.

Features Single articles or series on technique and instruction welcomed. Maximum length 1200 words.   **Fiction** Short stories with darts theme of no more than 1000 words.   **News** Maximum length 800 words. Tournament reports, general and personality news required. *Payment* negotiable.

David Hall's Coarse Fishing

51/53 Albert Street, Rugby, Warks CB21 2SG   ☎0788 535218

Owner *Chris Reel Ltd*   **Editor** *David Hall*   **Circulation** 20,000

FOUNDED 1985. MONTHLY for coarse fishing enthusiasts. News and features on pollution, fishing matches, events and general fishing topics. Unsolicited mss welcome. Maximum 2000 words. *Payment* £40.

Decanter

St John's Chambers, 2–10 St John's Road, London SW11 1PN   ☎01–350 1551

Editor *Paul Dymond*   **Circulation** 25,000

FOUNDED 1975. Glossy wines and spirits magazine. Unsolicited material welcomed. No fiction.

News and **Features** All items and articles should concern wines and spirits and related subjects.

Departures
6 Haymarket, London SW1Y 4BS ☎01–930 4411   Telex 8950931

Owner *American Express*   **Editor** *Lucretia Stewart*   **Circulation** 300,000

FOUNDED 1984. BI-MONTHLY. A literary travel magazine, specialising in high-quality travel writing and glossy colour photography. Prospective contributors are best advised to approach with an idea in writing only.

Descent
Wych Cottage, Langport Road, Somerton, Somerset TA11 6HX   ☎0458 73238

Owner *Ambit Publications*   **Editor** *Bruce Bedford*

FOUNDED 1969. BI-MONTHLY for cavers. Plenty of opportunities for freelance contributors who can write accurately and knowledgeably on aspects of caving.

Features Maximum 3000 words. *Payment* varies.

Design
28 Haymarket, London SW1Y 4SU   ☎01–839 8000

Owner *Design Council*   **Editor** *Stephen Braidwood*   **Circulation** 15,000

FOUNDED 1948. MONTHLY. Unsolicited mss not welcome; approach by phone or in writing.

Book Reviews Maximum length 500 words. *Payment* £100 per 1000 words. **Features** On most design-related areas, particularly product and consumer goods design. Interviews with designers, managers and consultancies. Maximum length 1500 words. *Payment* £100–140 per 1000 words.

Director
10 Belgrave Square, London SW1X 8PH   ☎01–235 9122

Editor *George Bickerstaffe*   **Circulation** 36,000

Published by the Institute of Directors for its members. Wide range of features from design to employment to general interest articles; plus book reviews, technology, health. Use regulars, but unsolicited mss will be considered. *Payment* negotiable.

Dog and Country
Corry's Farm, Roestock Lane, Colney Heath, St Albans, Herts AL4 0QW
☎0727 22614

Owner *Gilbertson & Page Limited*   **Editor** *Edward Askwith*

MONTHLY magazine regularly featuring gundog training, veterinary, countryside matters and gardening. Unsolicited mss welcome.

Features Articles, maximum 1200 words, based on actual experience or expert knowledge, of household, gun and working dogs, natural history, game, coarse and sea angling, and conservation are particularly welcomed. *Payment* £7.50 per A5 page.

Drama

British Theatre Association, Regent's College, Inner Circle, Regent's Park, London NW1 4NW ☎01–935 2571

Owner *British Theatre Association* **Editor** *Christopher Edwards*

Circulation 7000

FOUNDED 1919. QUARTERLY theatre review. Unsolicited manuscripts are rarely used, due to a shortage of space, but prospective contributors are advised to approach by phone or in writing (with samples of their work). All enquiries should be directed to the **Assistant Editor** *Jane Yettran* Feature articles on current theatrical scene (bearing in mind that *Drama* is a quarterly), interviews and profiles. Maximum length *c*.3000 words. *Payment* £30–40 per printed page. Also book reviews; maximum length *c*.1500 words. *Payment* £15–30.

Early Days

16 Trinity Churchyard, Guildford, Surrey GU1 3RR ☎0483 57533

Owner *Bond Clarkson Russell* **Editor** *Fiona Macpherson* **Circulation** 400,000

FOUNDED 1984. Three issues a year dealing with all aspects of the first few months of a baby's life. Unsolicited mss not welcome as all features are commissioned. Readers' letters on relevant issues and experiences are considered for publication. No fees.

The Economist

25 St James's Street, London SW1A 1HG ☎01–839 7000 Telex 24344

Owner *50% Financial Times 50% individual shareholders*
Editor *Rupert Pennant-Rea* **Circulation** 290,000

FOUNDED 1843. WEEKLY. Prospective contributors should approach the editor in writing. Unsolicited contributions are not welcomed.

Edinburgh Review

48 Pleasance, Edinburgh EH8 9TJ ☎031–558 1117/8

Owner *Polygon Books* **Editor** *Peter Kravitz* **Circulation** 1500

FOUNDED 1969. QUARTERLY. Articles and fiction on Scottish and international literary, cultural and philosophical themes. Unsolicited contributions are welcomed (1600 received each year) but prospective contributors are strongly advised to study the magazine first. Maximum length for fiction should be 6000 words, and translations from little known world writers are particularly welcomed. Feature articles do not have to be tied in to a recent anniversary, and interest will be shown in accessible articles on philosophy and its relationship to literature. In addition, each issue now contains an Encyclopaedia Supplement, consisting of approximately twenty pages of short items on matters of cultural and political importance which aims to show knowledge and ideas to be 'the collective property of humankind'. Entries for this supplement may vary from a few words to a maximum of 1000 words.

Education
21–27 Lamb's Conduit Street, London WC1N 3NJ ☎01–242 2548

Owner *Longman Group*   **Editor** *George Low*   **Circulation** 10,000

WEEKLY journal read by educational administrators and professionals; articles which appeal to these groups only. Practical administration, and 'how schools are run', plus comment on the state of administration at the present time. Freelances tend to be a regular network of writers. *Payment* NUJ rates.

Education and Training
62 Toller Lane, Bradford, West Yorkshire, BD8 9BY ☎0274 499821

Telex 51317 MCBUNI G

Owner *MCB University Press Ltd*   **Editor** *Derek Bradley*   **Circulation** 3000

FOUNDED 1959. BI-MONTHLY. Unsolicited mss are welcomed provided they are practically orientated and not purely academic. No fees are paid for contributions.

Elle
Rex House, 4–12 Lower Regent Street, London SW1Y 4PE ☎01–930 9050

Owner *News International/Hachette Ltd*   **Editor** *Sally Brampton*

Circulation 222,000

FOUNDED 1985. MONTHLY GLOSSY. Unsolicited contributions, of which 20 are received each week, are welcomed only if written specifically for *Elle*. Prospective contributors are best advised to approach the relevant editor in writing.

Features *Louise Chunn, Tim Rostron* Maximum length 2000 words. **News** (Insight) *Lisa Armstrong* Short articles on current/cultural events with emphasis on national and not just London based readership. Maximum length 500 words. *Payment* for all pieces £150 per 1000 words.

Embroidery
PO Box 42B, East Molesey, Surrey KT8 9BB ☎01–943 1229

Owner *Embroiders Guild*   **Editor** *Christine Bloxham*   **Circulation** 12,100

FOUNDED 1933. QUARTERLY. Features articles on embroidery techniques with illustrations. Unsolicited mss welcome. Maximum 2000 words. *Payment* £25–100.

Encounter

44 Great Windmill Street, London W1V 7PA ☎01–434 3063

Owner *Encounter Ltd* **Editors** *Melvin J. Lasky, Richard Mayne*

Circulation 20,000

FOUNDED 1953. 10 ISSUES P.A. Publishes reportage and articles of a political and philosophical interest together with one short story per issue and a maximum of six poems. Intending contributors are strongly advised to study the magazine in advance. Unsolicited manuscripts generally welcomed but thousands are received each year and, due to lack of space, very few accepted. Short stories should be 5000 words maximum, *Payment* £10 per 1000 words, and should be sent to the Literary Editor. The fee for poetry varies. An s.a.e. is essential if unsuitable work is to be returned.

The Engineer

30 Calderwood Street, London SE18 6QH ☎01–855 7777

Telex 896238 MORGAN G

Owner *Morgan-Grampian* **Editor** *John Pullin* **Circulation** 40,000

FOUNDED 1856. WEEKLY specialist magazine for engineers.

Features *Martin Ince* Most outside contributions are specially commissioned, but good ideas are always welcome. Maximum 2000 words. *Payment* by arrangement. **News** *Peter Eustace* Some scope for specialist regional freelances and for tip-offs. Maximum 500 words. *Payment* by arrangement. **Techscan** *Colin MacIlwain* Technology news. Freelance opportunities as for **News**. Maximum 500 words. *Payment* by arrangement.

Engineering

28 Haymarket, London SW1Y 4SU ☎01–839 8000

Owner *Design Council* **Editor** *Graham Cooper* **Circulation** 22,000

FOUNDED 1866. MONTHLY. Unsolicited manuscripts not welcome, but prospective contributors may approach by telephone with an idea, which should be followed up with a written synopsis.

Features *Graham Cooper, R. Wood* Developments in technology, product design, marketing and trade. Maximum 1800 words. *Payment* £200. **News** *Graham Cooper* Little opportunity for freelances here, but 'outstanding new developments in technology' always considered. Maximum 350 words. *Payment* £40. Also, applications of advanced plastic composite materials are of great interest – good stories in this area always required. Maximum 1800 words. *Payment* £200.

Everywoman

34a Islington Green, London N1 8DU ☎01–359 5496

Editor *Barbara Rogers* **Circulation** 15,000

Magazine which aims to provide general news and features angled towards women's interest, rather than being a traditional 'for women' glossy. Interested in general interest features, and particularly keen on current affairs (from a woman's angle); also regular slots on health, style, etc. Some areas are not open to freelance contributions, including Arts – no reviewers please. Keen on getting more humour in the magazine, and to get away from a London bias.

Executive Post

2–4 Fitzwilliam Gate, Sheffield S1 4JH ☎0742 704602

Editor *Sue Davis* **Circulation** 130,000

Mailed to jobseekers registered with the PER agency. Will consider any aspect of executive level employment or jobhunting as a feature. No news opportunities. *Payment* NUJ rates to NUJ members.

Executive Travel

242 Vauxhall Bridge Road, London SW1V 1AU ☎01–821 1155
Telex 924015 TRANEW G

Editor *Mike Toynbee* **Circulation** 49,738

FOUNDED 1979. MONTHLY for business travellers. Unsolicited mss welcome.

The Expatriate

25 Brighton Road, South Croydon, Surrey CR2 6EA ☎01–681 5545
Telex 295112 NHG G

Owner *Expatriate Publications Ltd* **Editor** *Jack Walder* **Circulation** *c.*500

FOUNDED 1977. MONTHLY serving the British expatriate community. Unsolicited mss are welcome.

Features Special features on working in particular countries. Psychological problems for spouses, education difficulties, investment and taxation features. Maximum 1200 words. **News** Information on facilities for expatriates, e.g. mail-order presents, financial services, relocation agents, etc. Maximum 1000 words. *Payment* negotiable.

Expatxtra!

PO Box 3000, Jersey, Channel Islands   ☎0534 36241

Owner *Expatxtra Ltd*   **Editor** *Harry Brown*   Circulation 20,000

FOUNDED 1982. MONTHLY aimed at working or retired UK expatriates. The magazine is dominated by the laid-back style of Harry Brown; it is therefore important to look at a copy before sending mss. No news or fiction.

Features *Vikki Clair*   Up to a maximum of 1500 words on Travel, Fashion, Education, etc. *Articles on all financial matters* are popular, e.g. taxation, investment, banking, life assurance, etc. *Payment* £100 per 1000 words.

Exploring the Supernatural

89 East Hill, Colchester, Essex CO1 2QN   ☎0206 861130

Owner *Aceville Ltd*   **Editor** *Greg Payne*

MONTHLY publication on all aspects of the paranormal. Freelance contributors are welcomed. 'No guarantee is offered for the safety or return of manuscripts.' Articles are paid for on publication. *Payment* £14 per 1000 words.

Expression

143–144 Drury Lane, London WC2B 5TF   ☎01–836 2441

Editor *Jeffrey Aquiline-Ross*   Circulation 570,000

Upmarket glossy mailed to American Express Cardholders. Upmarket glossy features always welcome, on travel, food, wine, and general consumer matters – anything of genuine interest to the discerning with a disposable income. Some features are produced in house, others by regular freelances, but they occasionally find unsolicited articles which hit the right note. *Payment* £150 a printed page (generally between 800 and 1000 words).

Extra Special

63 Shrewsbury Lane, Shooters Hill, London SE18 3JJ   ☎01–854 7309

Owner *Impex Fashions Ltd*   **Consultant Editor** *Dennis Winston*

Circulation 50,000 +

FOUNDED 1986. BI-MONTHLY colour magazine for the larger woman (size 16 +) of all ages.

Features Upbeat articles on fashion, psychology, medicine, beauty, business, show business success stories about larger people, fitness, humour. No pieces on how to lose weight or diet required. Contributors must show appreciation of everyday and long-term problems of the fit larger woman and her need for understanding and practical support. Most articles are commissioned from known writers, but approaches should be made in writing. Maximum 1500 words. *Payment* by negotiation.

The Face
The Old Laundry, Ossington Buildings, London W1   ☎ 01–935 8232

Owner *Wagadon Ltd*   **Editor** *Nick Logan*   **Circulation** 95,000

FOUNDED 1980. Perhaps the ultimate magazine of the Style Generation, concerned with who's what and what's cool. Profiles, interviews and stories. No fiction. Acquaintance with the 'voice' of *The Face* is essential before sending mss on spec.

Features 3000 words. *Payment* £80 per 1000 words. New contributors are welcome, but should telephone with their ideas and speak to Kimberley Leston and Elissa Van Poznak, features editors. Also *Intro* (diary) pages, with photo-based short pieces (350 words). *Payment* as for **Features**.   **Diary editor** *Kate Flett*   No news stories.

Family Circle
38 Hans Crescent, London SW1X 0LZ   ☎ 01–589 2000   Telex 21746

Owner *International Thomson Publishing Ltd*   **Editor** *Jill Churchill*
Circulation 565,978

FOUNDED 1964. 13 issues per year. Most of the magazine's material is produced in-house, and there is very little scope for freelances. Unsolicited material is never used, although 15 such manuscripts are received each week. Prospective contributors are best advised to send written ideas to the relevant editor.

Beauty *Helen Speed*   **Cookery** *Gilly Cubitt*   **Fashion** *Caroline Sullivan*   **Features** *Jill Churchill*   Very little outside work commissioned. Maximum length for features 2500–3000 words.   **Fiction** *Jill Churchill*   Maximum length for serial fiction 6000 words.   **Home** *Lindsey Stock*   **News** ('Inner Circle') *Margaret Rignell*. *Payment* for all contributions £100 per 1000 words.

Farmers Weekly
Carew House, Railway Approach, Wallington, Surrey SM6 0DX   ☎ 01–661 4867

Owner *Reed Business Publishing*   **Editor** *Gary Noble*   **Circulation** 120,593

Wide ranging feature material relating to practising farmers' problems and interests, plus news stories. Farm life, whether practical or general interest, also specific sections on arable, livestock farming, etc. Unsolicited mss considered. *Payment* negotiable.

Farming News
Morgan Grampian House, 30 Calderwood Street, London SE18 6QH
     ☎ 01–855 7777

Owner *Morgan Grampian Ltd*   **Editor** *Marcus Oliver*   **Circulation** 105,773

Occasionally use freelance writers.

Fast Lane

Prospect House, 9–13 Ewell Road, Cheam, Surrey SM1 4QQ   ☎ 01–661 4384

Telex 892084 BISPRS G

Owner *Prospect Magazines*   **Editor** *Peter Dron*   **Circulation** 55,400

FOUNDED 1984. Monthly car magazine. Many unsolicited mss are received but they are rarely used. Prospective contributors are advised to make initial approach in writing.

Fiction Magazine

12–13 Clerkenwell Green, London EC1R 0DP   ☎ 01–250 1504

Editor *Judy Cooke*

Short stories are published of between a few hundred words and 8000, though 3000–5000 is the more usual length. As they receive around 250 stories a month, be prepared for delay on a decision. All genres of fiction welcome, though as a general rule successful stories tend to be literary rather than, say, emotional–romantic in the women's magazine style. Reviews are commissioned, and occasional poetry is initiated by the editor, not usually from unsolicited contributions. *Payment* at time of going to press £40–60; this may have improved by 1988.

The Field

Carmelite House, Carmelite Street, London EC4Y 0JA   ☎ 01–353 6000

Owner *Mail Newspapers Ltd*   **Editor** *S. P. Courtauld*   **Circulation** 27,000

FOUNDED 1853. MONTHLY magazine for those serious about the British countryside and its pleasures. Unsolicited mss welcome; preliminary approach should be made in writing.

Features On any subject concerning the countryside. Maximum 1200 words. *Payment* £100.

Financial Weekly

14 Greville Street, London EC1N 8SB   ☎ 01–405 2622

Owner *Staff and other investors*   **Editor** *Tom Lloyd*

Circulation 15,000

FOUNDED 1979. WEEKLY. There are few opportunities for freelances here, as most of the stories and features are produced in-house. Unsolicited manuscripts not encouraged.

Features *Jane Wynn* An occasional 'perspective' feature, well written, well researched and accompanied by appropriate artwork might be bought. Maximum length

1500 words.   **News** *Maurice Anslow*   An exclusive news story, supported by evidence and analysis, may be bought very occasionally. Maximum length 800 words. *Payment* £80–100 per 1000 words.

First Down

Spendlove Centre, Charlbury, Oxon OX7 3PQ   ☎0608 811266

Telex 837883 SPEND G

Owner *Mediawatch*   **Editor** *Alan Lees*   **Circulation** 45,000

FOUNDED 1986. Unsolicited mss welcome.

Features *Alan Lees*   Ideas for commission are welcome.   **News** *Peter Rowe*   Tip-offs and news items, maximum 300 words, relating to American Football in the UK are welcome. *Payment* by negotiation.

Fitness

Northern & Shell Building, PO Box 381, Mill Harbour, London E14 9TU

☎01–987 5090   Telex 24676

Owner *Richard Desmond*   **Editor** *Claire Gillman*   **Circulation** 70,000

FOUNDED 1983. MONTHLY. Freelance contributions are welcome; it is advisable to write with ideas in the first instance.

Folk Roots

PO Box 73, Farnham, Surrey GU9 7UN   ☎0252 724638

Owner *Southern Rag Ltd*   **Editor** *Ian A. Anderson*   **Circulation** 12,000

FOUNDED 1979. MONTHLY. Unsolicited mss welcome, but a large number are received and an initial phone call is preferred.

Features Features on folk and roots music and musicians. Maximum 3000 words. *Payment* c.£15 per 1000 words.

Footloose

26 Commercial Buildings, Dunsten, Tyne & Wear NE11 9AA   ☎091–460 9958

Owner *Footloose Ltd*   **Editor** *Chris Townsend*

FOUNDED 1982. MONTHLY magazine of outdoor pursuits. Features only. Between four and six illustrated features per month on hill walking, backpacking, ski touring, non-technical mountaineering and other related subjects. Article length is 2500 words. *Payment* negotiable, but not less than £12 per published page. Unsolicited contributions are welcomed, but it is advisable to telephone first with ideas.

Garden Answers

Bushfield House, Orton Centre, Peterborough, PE2 0UW ☎0733 237111

Telex 32157

Owner *EMAP* **Editor** *Adam Pasco* Circulation 64,205

FOUNDED 1982. MONTHLY. 'It is unlikely that unsolicited manuscripts will be used, as writers rarely consider the style and format of the magazine before writing'. Prospective contributors should approach the editor in writing.

Garden News

Bushfield House, Orton Centre, Peterborough PE2 0UW ☎0733 237111

Telex 32157

Owner *East Midland Allied Press* **Editor** *Pam Deschamps* Circulation 129,716

FOUNDED 1958. WEEKLY news and features on gardening topics. Most material is written in-house, but there are opportunities for news items or offbeat articles. All approaches should be made in writing.

Gay Times inc. Gay News

283 Camden High Street, London NW1 7BX ☎01–482 2576

Owner *Millivres Ltd* **Editor** *John Marshall*

Publish a wide range of feature articles on all aspects of gay life, and general interest likely to appeal to the gay community. Includes arts reviews and news section. Use regular freelance writers and also consider unsolicited contributions. Also publish fiction.

Features Editor *Peter Burton*. *Payment* negotiable.

Girl

Commonwealth House, 1–19 New Oxford Street, London WC1A 1NG

☎01–404 0700

Owner *IPC Magazines* **Editor** *June Smith* Circulation 134,244

Teen magazine for girls. Photostories only (i.e. strips done in storyboard-with-words fashion). Always on the look out for new writers with strong photostory plotlines. Send ideas to the editor.

Giroscope

c/o Girobank plc, Bootle, Merseyside G1R 0AA

Editor *Ned Halley*

The National Girobank magazine, published four times yearly, carries around four features in each issue. Articles are welcome on housing, personal finance, holidays and leisure, and similar consumer interest topics.

Gloss

Baltic Chambers, 50 Wellington Street, Glasgow G2 6HJ

☎ 041–248 7799/041–221 2658

Owner *Lorraine Chassels*   **Editor** *Lorraine Chassels*   **Circulation** 50,000

FOUNDED JULY 1985. MONTHLY Glasgow/Edinburgh women's glossy. Unsolicited mss welcome; any approach in writing should include a telephone number.

Features *Kirsty Morrison*   Maximum 3000 words. *Payment* £15–50.

Golf World

Advance House, 37 Mill Harbour, Isle of Dogs, London E14 9TX   ☎ 01–538 1031

Owner *New York Times*   **Editor** *Peter Haslam*   **Circulation** 80,000

FOUNDED 1962. MONTHLY. Unsolicited mss not welcome, but prospective contributors should approach with ideas in writing.

Good Food Retailing

161–165 Greenwich High Road, London SE10 8JA   ☎ 01–853 5444

Owner *Dewberry Publications*   **Editor** *Nicola Graimes*

Circulation 10,203 (controlled)

FOUNDED 1980. MONTHLY. Serves the food retailing industry. Unsolicited mss are welcome.

Good Health

13 Park House, 140 Battersea Park Road, London SW11 4NB   ☎ 01–720 2108

Owner *Hawker Publications*   **Editor** *D. Hawkins*   **Circulation** 30,000

FOUNDED 1986. BI-MONTHLY. Freelance material welcome; approach in writing in first instance.

Features Health-related topics. Maximum length 700 words. *Payment* £100 per 1000 words.

Good Housekeeping

National Magazine House, 72 Broadwick Street, London W1V 2BP

☎ 01–439 7144   Telex 263879

Owner *National Magazine Co. Ltd*   **Editor** *Charlotte Lessing*

Circulation 346,000

FOUNDED 1922. MONTHLY GLOSSY. Freelance contributors are advised to write in the first instance to the appropriate editor. Unsolicited manuscripts are always read, but are not encouraged.

Features *Gillian Fairchild*   Most features are specially commissioned, but there is room for freelance contributions of approximately 900 words to the 'Comment' page.

Payment £120.   **Fiction** *Shirley Heron*   Most fiction is received from agents or publishers, though unsolicited manuscripts will be read.   **News** *Noelle Walsh* 'Newslines', four pages of short news stories on subjects from food and travel to film stars and money. Maximum 350 words. *Payment* £120 per 1000. New ideas for writing about food are always welcome.

Good Living
141–143 Drury Lane, London WC2B 5TS ☎01–836 4433

Owner *GAT Publishing*   **Editor (acting)** *Ruth Wallace*   **Circulation** 2,200,000

FOUNDED 1985. MONTHLY. Features news and articles on home, children, food, etc. Unsolicited mss welcome, especially local stories from Scotland and N.E. England. *Payment* £25 per 250 words.

Good Ski Guide
1/2 Dawes Court, 93 High Street, Esher, Surrey KT10 9QD ☎0372 69799
Telex 8951417

Owner *John Hill*   **Editor** *John Hill*   **Circulation** 150,000

FOUNDED 1976. Four issues a year. Unsolicited mss are welcomed from writers with a knowledge of skiing and ski resorts. Up to 2000 manuscripts are solicited through the magazine. Prospective contributors should make contact in writing only as ideas and work need to be seen before any discussion can take place. *Payment* 'better than NUJ'.

Gramophone
177–179 Kenton Road, Harrow, HA3 0HA ☎01–907 4476

Editor *Christopher Pollard*   **Circulation** 64,682

Classical music magazine which is 95% reviews. At any one time they are using around 50 regular freelance writers, who provide classical music reviews, and on occasion, features or interviews. Reviewing is the starting place on the magazine, however. Submit samples or work, whether published or not, to the editor.

Granta
Bill Buford, 44a Hobson Street, Cambridge, CB1 1NL ☎0223 315290

Editor *Bull Buford*

Magazine of literature and politics published in book form in association with **Penguin**. Highbrow, diverse, contemporary, it works in a thematic way. Presently quarterly, this may increase to six times yearly in 1988. Do consider unsolicited mss and fiction, and do a lot of commissioning. Important to read the magazine first to appreciate its very particular fusion of cultural and political interests. No reviews. *Payment* depends on length, but not less than £100 per 1000 words.

The Great Outdoors

Ravenseft House, 302–304 St Vincent Street, Glasgow G2 5NL   ☎041–221 7000

Owner *Holmes McDougall Ltd*   **Editor** *Roger Smith*   **Circulation** 27,000

FOUNDED 1970. MONTHLY. Deals with walking, backpacking and countryside topics. Unsolicited mss are welcome.

Features *Roger Smith*   Well-written and illustrated items on relevant topics. Maximum 2000 words. Payment £60–80.   **News** *Peter Evans*   Short topical items or photographs. Maximum 300 words. *Payment* £10–20.

Green Cuisine

30 Station Approach, West Byfleet, Surrey KT14 6NF   ☎09323 49123

Owner *Argus Health Publications*   **Editor** *Helen Vintner*   **Circulation** 40,000

FOUNDED 1986. QUARTERLY. Unsolicited mss are welcomed on anything relevant to conservation, animal cruelty and relating to vegetarians and vegans, including recipes. Prospective contributors are advised to make initial approach in writing.

Hairflair

141–143 Drury Lane, London WC2B 5DF   ☎01–836 2441

Owner *Redwood Publishing*   **Editor** *Karen McCartney*   **Circulation** 50,000

FOUNDED 1982. MONTHLY featuring original, interesting hair-related ideas written in a young, lively style to appeal to readership aged 16–24 years. Unsolicited mss not welcome, but ideas in writing are considered.

Features Maximum 2000 words. *Payment* £75 per 1000 words.

Handgunner

39 High Street, Brightlingsea, Essex CO7 0AQ   ☎0206 305204

Owner *J. A. Stevenson*   **Editor** *J. A. Stevenson*   **Circulation** 28,000

FOUNDED 1980. BI-MONTHLY. Unsolicited mss are welcome, but material should be incisive and in-depth. Make initial contact by telephone.

Features Really top quality material can be used, related to firearms in economic, political, industrial, police, military and technical fields. Length is dictated by subject matter. *Payment* about £20 per page.

Harpers & Queen

72 Broadwick Street, London W1V 2BP   ☎01–439 7144

Owner *National Magazines*   **Editor** *Nicholas Coleridge*   **Circulation** 100,000

MONTHLY. Up market glossy that combines the Sloaney and the streetwise. Receive 1000 unsolicited mss a year and publish 4 or 5 of these. Approach in writing (not phone) with ideas.

Features *Meredith Smith* Ideas only in the first instance. **Fiction** *Selina Hastings* Fiction welcome. Maximum 6000 words. **News** *Nicholas Coleridge* Snippets welcome if very original. *Payment* negotiable.

Health Express
30 Station Approach, West Byfleet, Surrey KT14 6NF ☎09323 49123

Owner *Argus Health Publications* **Editor** *Lesley Keen* **Circulation** 500,000

Free health magazine distributed at Holland & Barrett healthfood shops. Do use freelance writers occasionally, usually for specific projects, but also 'names' like vegetarian cookery writer Rose Elliott. Features on health and health related topics, including products sold at the stores, and alternative medicine. Write with ideas. *Payment* negotiable.

Health Now
Seymour House, South Street, Godalming, Surrey ☎04868 20863 Telex 859511

Owner *J. E. Peet* **Editor** *Alice Peet* **Circulation** 325,000

FOUNDED 1877. BI-MONTHLY. Unsolicited manuscripts welcome only if related to the specialised interests of the magazine. Prospective contributors are advised to make their first approach in writing.

Healthy Living
16 Ennismore Avenue, London W4 1SF ☎01–994 1314

Owner *Askin Publishers Ltd* **Editor** *Helene Hodge* **Circulation** 80,000

FOUNDED 1966. MONTHLY. Unsolicited mss welcome.

Features *Lindsay Roberts* Stimulating and relevant focus on health. **News** *Helene Hodge*.

Here's Health
30 Station Approach, West Byfleet, Surrey KT14 0NX ☎09323 49123

Owner *Argus Health Publications* **Editor** *Sarah Bounds* **Circulation** 65,000

FOUNDED 1956. MONTHLY dealing with health and related subjects. Unsolicited mss welcome.

Features Maximum 1500 words. *Payment* £100 per 1000 words.

Hi-Fi News and Record Review
Link House, Dingwall Avenue, Croydon CR9 2TA ☎01–686 2599

Owner *Link House* **Editor** *Steve Harris* **Circulation** 39,000

FOUNDED 1956. MONTHLY. Write in the first instance with suggestions based on knowledge of the magazine's style and subject. All articles must be written from an informed technical or enthusiast viewpoint.

Him (formerly known as National Gay)
283 Camden High Street, London NW1 7BX   ☎01–482 2576

Owner *Out Publications Ltd*   **Editor** *Bryan Derbyshire*

MONTHLY gay magazine concentrating more on entertainment, gay pubs and clubs, etc., than general features. No features editor, no news.

Holiday Which?
14 Buckingham Street, London WC2N 6DS   ☎01–839 1222

Owner *Consumer Association*   **Editor** *Jonathan Shepherd*   **Circulation** 170,000

QUARTERLY. All research and writing is by permanent staff or by occasional special commission. No real opportunities for freelancers. Unsolicited mss not considered.

Home and Country
39 Eccleston Street, Victoria, London SW1W 9NT   ☎01–730 0307

Owner *National Federation of Women's Institutes*   **Editor** *Penny Kitchen*
Circulation 101,200

FOUNDED 1919. MONTHLY official journal of the Federation of Women's Institutes. General interest articles of interest to women considered. Unsolicited mss welcome. *Payment* by arrangement.

Home & Freezer Digest
Glenthorne House, Hammersmith Grove, London W6 0LG   ☎01–846 9922
Telex 919001

Owner *British European Associated Publishers*   **Editor** *Maggie Rowlands*
Circulation 200,000

FOUNDED 1974. MONTHLY for freezer owners. Unsolicited mss welcome, but most features are commissioned so freelance opportunities are scarce.

Homebrew Today
30 Station Approach, West Byfleet, Surrey KT15 6NF   ☎09323 49123

Owner *Argus Publications*   **Editor** *Evelyn Barrett*   **Circulation** 250,000

FOUNDED 1986. QUARTERLY featuring articles on all aspects of home brewing and the use of homemade wine in cooking, etc. Unsolicited mss welcome.

Home Farm
Broad Leys Publishing Co., Widdington, Saffron Walden, Essex CB11 3SP
☎0799 40922

Owners *D. & K. Thear*   **Editor** *Katie Thear*   **Circulation** 14,000

FOUNDED 1975. BI-MONTHLY journal of the Small Farmers' Association. Unsolicited mss welcome, and around 30 are received every week. Articles should be detailed and practical, based on first-hand knowledge, about aspects of small farming and country living. 'We do not welcome twee urban nostalgia about the countryside.' 'Poetry Corner' publishes verse which 'reflects some aspect of country living today'.

Homes and Gardens

King's Reach Tower, Stamford Street, London SE1 9LS 　　　　☎ 01–261 5000

Telex 915748 MAGD**1**V G

Owner *IPC Magazines/Reed Publishing*　**Editor** *Amanda Evans*

Circulation 200,000 +

FOUNDED 1919. MONTHLY. Almost all published articles have been specially commissioned. No fiction or poetry. Best to approach in writing with an idea.

Homes Overseas

387 City Road, London EC1V 1NA 　　　　☎ 01–278 9232

Owner *Cablecoin Ltd*　**Editor** *Michael Furnell*　　**Circulation** 17,000

FOUNDED 1965. MONTHLY of interest to those buying or owning property overseas. Unsolicited mss welcome.

Features Well-researched articles on residential towns and districts in the south of Spain, Algarve, France, Italy, Cyprus and Malta. Maximum 1500 words. *Payment* £30 approximately.　**News** Up-to-date information on private housing developments in southern European countries. Maximum 1000 words. *Payment* £30 approximately.

Horse and Hound

Kings Reach Tower, Stamford Street, London SE1 9LS 　　　☎ 01–261 6315

Owner *IPC Magazines*　**Editor** *Michael Clayton*　　**Circulation** 72,000

The oldest and most conservative of equestrian magazines. More hunting and show oriented than most, and with no interest in general horse-care or riding features typical of other horse publications in the market. News and show reports always needed. A regular stable of contributors, but interesting new writers will be tried out.

Horse & Pony

Bretton Court, Bretton, Peterborough, PE3 8DZ 　　　☎ 0733 264666

Owner *EMAP*　**Editor** *Lesley Eccles*　　**Circulation** 47,637

Magazine for owners and addicts of the horse, generally aged between 12 and 16. Features include horse-care articles, pony club news, celebrities in the horse world. Not really interested in freelances: most feature material is produced in house by staff writers.

Horse and Rider

104 Ash Road, Sutton, Surrey SM3 9LD ☎01–641 4911

Owner *D. J. Murphy (Publishers) Ltd*   **Editor** *Kate O'Sullivan*

Circulation 30,000

FOUNDED 1949. MONTHLY. Unsolicited mss welcome, and should be addressed to the editor. Adult readership, largely horse-owning. Fiction especially welcome. General interest features welcome. News and instructional features, which make up the bulk of the magazine, are almost all commissioned. Approach in writing with ideas.

House & Garden

Vogue House, Hanover Square, London W1R 0AD ☎01–499 9080

Owner *Condé Nast*   **Editor** *Robert Harling*   Circulation 123,652

Much of their feature material is produced in house, but do use a small proportion of freelances, particularly in the wine and food sections. These are mostly commissioned or from known writers, but ideas and mss will be considered.

House Buyer

137 George Lane, South Woodford, London E18 1AJ ☎01–530 7555

Owner *Brittain Publications*   **Editor** *Editor Con Crowley*   Circulation 25,000

MONTHLY magazine with features and articles for house buyers. Unsolicited mss welcome.

Ice Hockey World and Skating Review

9 Victoria Road, Mundesley-on-Sea, Norfolk NR11 8JG ☎0263 720038

Editor *Phil Drackett*   Circulation 5000

FOUNDED 1935. MONTHLY during the season. Submissions welcome if preceded by letter/phone. All mss to be addressed to the editor.

Features always welcome. Maximum 1000 words. *Payment* maximum £20.   **Fiction** rarely, but interested in occasional good short story. Maximum 1000 words. *Payment* by negotiation.   **News** from local stringers – occasional vacancies.

I D Magazine

27–29 Macklin Street, London WC2E 5LX ☎01–430 0871

Editor *Caryn Franklin*   Circulation 50,000

Fashion and style magazine for both sexes ages 16–24. Very hip. 'We have opportunities for freelance writers but can't offer fees for non-commissioned work.' Tend to use known writers. A different theme each issue – past themes included the green politics issue, taste, and film – mean it is advisable to discuss feature ideas in the first instance.

Ideal Home

King's Reach Tower, Stamford Street, London SE1 9LS ☎01–261 6505

Owner *IPC Magazines* **Editor** *Terence Whelan* Circulation 197,572

FOUNDED 1920. MONTHLY GLOSSY. Unsolicited feature articles are welcomed when appropriate to the magazine (one or two are received each week). Prospective contributors wishing to submit ideas should do so in writing only.

Features editors *David Spittles, Linda Gray* Home interest features, length of article and payment negotiable. Features should be on furnishings and decoration of houses, kitchens or bathrooms; interior design, soft furnishings; furniture; home improvements, etc. No fiction. **News editor** *Linda Gray* Suggestions/press releases etc.

The Illustrated London News

20 Upper Ground, London SE1 9PF ☎01–928 6969 Telex 8955803

Owner *James Sherwood* **Editor** *Henry Porter* Circulation 53,000

FOUNDED 1842. MONTHLY. There are few opportunities for freelances but all unsolicited manuscripts are read – on average, ten a week. The best approach is with an idea in writing.

In Britain

Thames Tower, Black's Road, London W6 9EL ☎01–846 9000

Owner *BTA* **Editor** *Bryn Frank* Circulation 100,000

Magazine of the British Tourist Authority, about things to do and places to visit. Unsolicited mss not encouraged.

Interior Design

Audit House, Field End Road, Eastcote, Ruislip, Middx HA4 9LT ☎01–868 4499

Owner *AGB Business Publications Ltd* **Editor** *Katherine Tickle*

Circulation 10,000

The trade magazine of the commercial interior design industry (no domestic interior design interest). Freelance opportunities are limited, as much of the material is produced in house or by commission. Informed contributions, case studies etc. are always considered. (Also do *Lighting Design* supplement, for which informed contributions are welcome.) *Payment* £100 per 1000 words.

Interzone

124 Osborne Road, Brighton BN1 6LU   ☎0273 504710

Owners *Simon Ounsley, David Pringle*   **Editors** *Simon Ounsley, David Pringle*
Circulation 3000

FOUNDED 1982. QUARTERLY magazine of science fiction and fantasy fiction. Unsolicited manuscripts are welcome from writers who have a knowledge of the magazine and its contents.

Features Science Fiction and fantasy book reviews, film reviews, interviews with writers and occasional short articles. Length and payment by arrangement. **Fiction** Science fiction and fantasy stories. Maximum length 8000 words. *Payment* £30 per 1000 words.

Investors Chronicle

Greystoke Place, Fetter Lane, London EC4A 1ND   ☎01–405 6969
Telex 883694 IC LON G

Owner *Financial Times*   **Associate Editor** *David Webster*   **Circulation** 53,000

FOUNDED 1861. MONTHLY. Opportunities for freelance contributors in the survey section only. All approaches should be made in writing. About thirty surveys are published each year on a wide variety of subjects mainly with a financial, business or investment emphasis. Copies of survey list and synopses of individual surveys are obtainable from the Associate Editor. Maximum length 1000 words. *Payment* from £100.

Jackie

D. C. Thomson, Albert Square, Dundee DD1 9QJ   ☎0382 23131

Owner *D. C. Thomson & Co. Ltd*   **Editor** *Maggie Dun*   **Circulation** 250,000

FOUNDED 1964. WEEKLY. Scope for freelance contributors; write in the first instance to the relevant editor.

Features *Sheena Miller*   Emotional/fun features dealing with boys, school, friends, parents and growing up. Maximum length 1500 words.   **Fiction** *Ria Leggat, Steve le Comber*   Romantic/humorous text stories and serials. Also photo stories. Maximum length 1500 words. *Payment* for all contributions £45 + .

Jazz Journal International

35 Great Russell Street, London WC1B 3PP   ☎01–580 6976

Owner *Jazz Journal Ltd*   **Editor-in-Chief** *Eddie Cook*   **Circulation** 12,000

FOUNDED 1948. MONTHLY. A specialised jazz magazine using only expert contributors whose work is known to the editor. Unsolicited mss not welcome, with the exception of news material (for which no payment is made).

Jewish Chronicle

25 Furnival Street, London EC4A 1JT ☎01–405 9252

Owner *Kessler Foundation* **Editor** *Geoffrey D. Paul* Circulation 50,000

Unsolicited mss welcome if 'the specific interests of our readership are borne in mind by writers'. Approach in writing unless it's urgent current news. No fiction. In all cases, maximum 2000 words. *Payment* negotiable. This also applies to the *Jewish Chronicle Colour Magazine*.

News Editor (home) *Hyam Corney*; (foreign) *J. Finklestone*

Colour Magazine/Supplements *Gerald Jacobs* **Features Editor** *Meir Persoff* **Women's Page** *Jan Shure*

The Journalist

NUJ, Acorn House, 314–320 Grays Inn Road, London WC1K 8DP ☎01–278 7916
Telex 892384

Owner *NUJ* **Editor** *Bernie Corbett* Circulation 35,000

MONTHLY journal of the NUJ. Pieces of interest to journalists or relevant to the industry welcome, though most material is produced in house and outside contributions are not usually paid for.

Just Seventeen

52–55 Carnaby Street, London W1V 1PF ☎01–437 8050

Owner *EMAP Metro* **Editor** *Bev Hillier* Circulation 268,370

FOUNDED 1983. WEEKLY. News, articles and fiction of interest to girls aged 12–20. Ideas are sought in all areas. Prospective contributors should send ideas to the relevant editorial department, then follow up with phone call.

Beauty *Fiona Gibson* **Features** *Jenny Tucker* **Fiction** *Jacqui Deevoi* No more than 2000 words **News Editor** *Tim Nicholson*. *Payment* £90 per 1000 words.

Keep Fit Magazine

7th Floor, Albany House, Hurst Street, Birmingham B5 4BD ☎021–622 2899

Owner *Second City Advertising & Publishing* **Editor** *Mrs Rajinder Lawley*
Circulation 75,000

FOUNDED 1985. MONTHLY for keep-fit enthusiasts. Length of articles and fees by negotiation. Unsolicited mss welcome.

Kennel Gazette

Kennel Club, Clarges Street, Piccadilly, London W1Y 8AB ☎01–493 6651

Owner *Kennel Club* **Editor** *Charles Colborn* Circulation 9000

FOUNDED 1873. MONTHLY concerning dogs and their breeding. Unsolicited mss welcome.

Features Maximum 2500 words. **Fiction** Maximum 1500 words. **News** Maximum 500 words. *Payment* £30 per 1000 words.

Keyboard Player

18 Tileyard Road, Off York Way, London N7 9AN   ☎01–609 5781/2

Owner *Mr S. Miller & Mr I. Seymour*   **Editor** *S. Miller*   **Circulation** 14,000

FOUNDED 1979. Unsolicited mss welcome. Prospective contributors should make initial contact in writing to the Editor who is particularly interested in hearing from writers with a technical/playing knowledge of any keyboard instrument.

Knit and Stitch

PO Box 553, Iver, Bucks SL0 0PD   ☎0753 656221   Telex 847505 PINEWD G

Owner *Ingrid Publishing Ltd*   **Editor** *Sheila Berriff*   **Circulation** 30,000

FOUNDED 1985. MONTHLY. Mostly patterns, with occasional features. Unsolicited mss not welcome; approach in writing only.

The Lady

39–40 Bedford Street, Strand, London WC2E 9ER   ☎01–836 8705

Owner *T. G. A. Bowles*   **Editor** *Joan L. Grahame*   **Circulation** 64,332

FOUNDED 1885. WEEKLY. Unsolicited manuscripts are welcome: they get about 5000 every year. Nothing is accepted on politics, religion or medicine, nor on topics covered by staff writers, i.e. fashion and beauty, household, gardening, finance and shopping.

Features Pieces on British and Foreign travel are particularly welcomed, and on all other topics except those already mentioned. Maximum length 1500 words. All material to the editor. *Payment* £38 per 1000 words.

Le Weekend Express

Newspaper House, 22 Vineyard Road, Wellington, Shropshire TF1 1DJ

    ☎0952 51100

Owner *Leisure Newspapers Ltd*   **Editor** *Ron Newell Evans*   **Circulation** 100,000

MONTHLY magazine which welcomes unsolicited manuscripts. Prospective contributors may make initial contact either in writing or by telephone.

Lean Living

2nd Floor, 67–73 Worship Street, London EC2A 2DU ☎01–377 5082

Owner *Reginald Taylor* **Editors** *Lisa Pritchard and Tessa Thomas*

Circulation 20,000

BI-MONTHLY for 'the meat-free lifestyle'. Unsolicited mss welcome.

Features Articles with a positive approach to subjects such as sex, medical, travel, food, etc. Light-hearted and easy to read style. Maximum 3500 words. *Payment* £35 per 1000 words. **News** Short snippets of news on people and places: gossip, eating out, etc. Maximum 450 words. *Payment* £35 per 1000 words.

The Legion

Maidstone Press Centre, Bank Street, Maidstone, Kent ME14 1P2 ☎0622 674177

Owner *The Royal British Legion* **Editor** *David Bosley* **Circulation** 25,000

BI-MONTHLY magazine of the Royal British Legion.

Features *Debbie Eales* Articles of interest to the ex-service community, the elderly or disabled are welcomed, as well as those relating to Royal British Legion activities. Maximum length 1200 words. *Payment* negotiable.

Leisure Express

Newspaper House, 22 Vineyard Road, Wellington, Shropshire TF1 1DJ

☎0952 51100

Owner *Leisure Newspapers Ltd* **Editor** *Ron Newell Evans* **Circulation** 400,000

MONTHLY railway magazine (British Rail) which welcomes unsolicited manuscripts. Prospective contributors may make initial contact either in writing or by telephone.

Liberal News

1 Whitehall Place, London SW1A 2HE ☎01–839 1533

Telex 89565511 LIB HQ G

Owner *Liberal Party* **Editor** *Paul Sample* **Circulation** 10,000

FOUNDED 1946. WEEKLY. Public and political issues of interests to Liberal Party members. Unsolicited mss welcome.

Features Articles of interest to Party members and supporters. Maximum 1000 words. **News** Items concerning the Party and its membership. Maximum 350 words. *Payment* All contributions are unpaid.

The Listener
35 Marylebone High Street, London W1M 4AA ☎01–927 4457

Owner *BBC Publications*   **Acting Editor** *Michael Perle*   **Circulation** 40,000

The literate, critical magazine of radio and television programmes. 98% (at least) is commissioned, and new writers are advised to submit an outline of their idea to **Senior Editor** *Michael Poole*   His Guide Section is the 'nursery' where new writers are tried out, by invitation.

Literary Review
51 Beak Street, London W1R 3LF ☎01–437 9392   Telex 919034

Owner *Namara Group*   **Editor** *Auberon Waugh*   **Circulation** 11,000

FOUNDED 1979. MONTHLY. Publishes book reviews (commissioned), features and articles on literary subjects, plus short fiction. Prospective contributors are best advised to contact the editor in writing. Unsolicited manuscripts not welcomed (over 500 a month are currently received). *Payment* Book reviews: £25 for 800 words. Literary features: £25–40. Maximum length 1000 words. Short stories: £50 for stories up to 1500 words.

Living
38 Hans Crescent, London SW1X 0LZ ☎01–589 2000

Owner *International Thomson*   **Editor** *Dena Vane*   **Circulation** 354,423

Women's and family interest magazine sold at supermarket check-outs. One feature writer on the staff only, so a great proportion of material comes from outsiders.

Features Editor *Barbara Baker* is very keen to encourage new talent; ring or write with ideas in the first instance rather than sending in unsolicited mss. Wide ranging feature needs include family, education, medical issues, 'successful women in small businesses' type one-offs, and major issues (divorce, drugs etc.).

London Review of Books
Tavistock House South, Tavistock Square, London WC1H 9JZ ☎01–388 6751

Owner *LRB Ltd*   **Editor** *Karl Miller*   **Circulation** 15,000

FOUNDED 1980. FORTNIGHTLY. Fiction, news, poems and short stories plus reviews, essays and articles on political, literary, cultural and scientific subjects. Unsolicited contributions welcomed (approximately 35 received each week) and it is best to contact the editor in writing. There is one editorial department covering all aspects of the magazine.

Look-In

195 Knightsbridge, London SW7 1RS ☎01–589 8877 Telex 27813

Owner *ITV Publications Ltd* **Editor** *Colin Shelbourn* **Circulation** 196,000

FOUNDED 1971. WEEKLY children's TV magazine featuring ITV programmes and personalities. Unsolicited mss not generally welcome; prospective contributors are advised to make initial approach in writing.

Features TV, pop, sport, general interest, quizzes, etc – all aimed at children aged 7–12. *Payment* by negotiation.

Look Now

25 Newman Street, London W1P 3HA ☎01–631 3939

Owner *Carlton Magazines* **Editor** *Deborah Bibby* **Circulation** 101,283

FOUNDED 1972. MONTHLY. Freelance contributions are welcomed, but five are received a day and many are unsuitable for the magazine. Prospective contributors are advised to read the magazine thoroughly to pick up on its style. It is best to send ideas in writing to the relevant editor.

Features *Doretta Sarris* **Fiction** *Dee Pilgrim* **News** *Dee Pilgrim*

Material should be suitable for the 18–24 age range and can be short fiction, serious topical features or lighthearted 'fun' pieces. Maximum length for contributions 1000–2500 words. *Payment* £150 per 1000 words.

Looks

42 Great Portland Street, London W1N 5AH ☎01–637 9181

Owner *EMAP* **Editor** *Ramune Burns* **Circulation** 137,017

Teen magazine for girls which concentrates on beauty, fashion and hair matters. Also general teen interest features, including occasional celebrity interviews; freelance writers are used for these. No fiction. Contact the editor with ideas. *Payment* varies.

Loving

Commonwealth House, 1–19 New Oxford Street, London WC1A 1NG ☎01–829 7902

Owner *IPC Magazines* **Editor** *Ms Gerry Fallon* **Circulation** 80,000

Downmarket romantic weekly. About 50–75 unsolicited manuscripts are received each week, but many are unsuitable for the magazine. No features.

Fiction *Lorna Read* New writers are encouraged but are best advised to send an s.a.e. for 'Authors Guidelines' and to read at least three copies of the magazine before attempting to write their stories. All must be in the first person in a young, breezy, slangy style and conversational tone. 'Plots and characters should be rooted in everyday working-class experience and situations; stories which sound middle-class, with well-educated characters, are automatically rejected.'

Management Today
30 Lancaster Gate, London W2 3LP   ☎01–402 4200

Editor *Lance Knobel*   Circulation 77,024

General business topics and features: 'anything which appears in the *Financial Times* could appear in our publication'. A brief synopsis to the editor. *Payment* negotiable.

Marketing Week
St Giles House, 50 Poland Street, London W1V 4AX   ☎01–439 4222

Editor *Howard Sharman*   Circulation 37,095

Trade magazine of the marketing industry. Features on all aspects of the business written in a newsy and up to the minute style from expert commentators always welcome. Ideas first, to **Features Editor** *Stuart Smith   Payment* negotiable.

Match
Stirling House, Bretton Court, Bretton, Peterborough PE3 8DJ   ☎0733 260333
Telex 32157

Owner *EMAP*   **Editor** *Melvyn Bagnall*   Circulation 89,230

FOUNDED 1979. WEEKLY football magazine aimed at 10–18 year olds. Consult the editor or the news editor before making any submission. Contact may be made either by telephone or in writing. Most material is generated in-house by a strong news and features team.

Features/News *Paul Stratton*   Good and original material is always welcome. Maximum length: 600 words.   **Gossip column** Humorous, off-beat snippets for this regular column. Quality Scottish material will also be considered. *Payment* negotiable.

Maternity and Mothercraft
Greater London House (ground floor), Hampstead Road, London NW1 2QP   ☎01–388 3171

Editor *Catherine Fleischmann*   Circulation 130,000

FOUNDED 1965. BI-MONTHLY. Unsolicited mss are not welcomed but any prospective contributor should make initial contact by telephone.

Features There is a features list and there are occasional opportunities for writers with relevant experience. (Being a mother of young children is an added advantage.) Maximum length: 600 words. *Payment* around £100 per 1000 words.

Matrix
114 Guildhall Street, Folkestone, Kent CT20 1ES ☎0303 52939 (evenings)

Owner *British Science Fiction Association* **Editor** *Maureen Porter*

Circulation 1000

FOUNDED 1965. BI-MONTHLY newsletter of the BSFA giving all Science Fiction oriented news, gossip, pre-publication details of new SF books, details of SF societies, magazines, media, etc. Initial approach in writing preferred. No fiction. No literary criticism or author interviews. No fees.

Melody Maker
1st floor, Berkshire House, 168–173 High Holborn, London WC1V 7AA

☎01–379 3581

Owner *IPC Magazines* **Editor** *Allan Jones* **Circulation** 69,313

Freelance contributors are used on this tabloid magazine competitor to *NME* and *Sounds*, but opportunities exist in reviewing rather than features. Send in sample reviews, whether published or not, on pop, rock, soul, funk, etc. to **Reviews Editor** *Ted Mico* **Features Editor** *Steve Sutherland* A large inhouse team plus around six regulars produce the feature material. *Payment* NUJ rates in all cases.

Mensa Magazine
British Mensa Ltd, Bond House, St John's Square, Wolverhampton WV2 4AH

☎0902 772771/2/3

Owner *British Mensa Ltd* **Editor** *Simon Clark* **Circulation** 18,000

MONTHLY. Unsolicited mss welcome (about ten per month are received). Priority is given to members of the Society, but contributions from non-members are also considered.

Features *Simon Clark* Any general interest topic (e.g. science, travel, education, astrology, etc.) maximum 2500 words. Pieces should be entertaining, informative and concise. Other short articles (500–1200 words) are welcome which offer the writer's own opinions on controversial issues.

Mind Your Own Business
106 Church Road, London SE19 2UB ☎01–771 3614 Telex 97991

Owner *B. Gledhill/M. Brown* **Editor** *Bill Gledhill* **Circulation** 61,000

FOUNDED 1978. MONTHLY. Unsolicited material with management appeal is welcomed. About 12 articles are received each week, of which one or two may be of interest.

Features *Bill Gledhill* Should appeal to management. **Fiction** *Sarah Pritchard* Light-hearted, humorous articles with a moral to the story and management oriented.

Mizz

Commonwealth House, 1–19 New Oxford Street, London W1A 1NG

☎01–404 0700

Owner *IPC Magazines*   **Editor** *Maureen Rice*   **Circulation** 104,472

Fortnightly magazine for the 15–19 year old girl: 'a useful rule of thumb is to write for a 16 year old'. A wide range of freelance articles welcome, from emotional issues to careers to beauty features. Also fiction – short stories published every issue. Send samples with a letter, or an idea with synopsis in the case of features; the finished mss in the case of fiction, to Maureen Rice.

Moneycare

Clareville House, 47 Whitcomb Street, London WC2H 7DX   ☎01–930 8953

Telex 922488 Bureau G

Owner *Headway Publications*   **Editor** *Alison James*   **Circulation** 1,000,000

FOUNDED 1983. BI-MONTHLY on money management. Most articles are commissioned so unsolicited mss are rarely used.

Money Week

Scriptor Court, 155 Farringdon Road, London EC1R 3AD   ☎01–430 1200

Owner *EMAP*   **Editor** *Jenny Harris*   **Circulation** 50,000

Enthusiastic about freelance writers and use them in all areas of this personal finance magazine. As **Money Week** is aimed at the personal finance industry itself, writers tend to be specialised, or experienced financial journalists. Major part of the magazine is given to features of around 800 words on all aspects of the business.

Features Editor *Chris Vecchi*

The Mortgage Magazine

12 Sutton Row, London W1V 5FH   ☎01–434 2579

Owner *Brass Tacks Publishing*   **Editor** *Stephen Quirke*   **Circulation** 30,000

FOUNDED 1986. MONTHLY magazine covering finance and property. Unsolicited mss welcome. Make initial approach by telephone to discuss idea, and follow up in writing.

Features Ideas concerning finance and building are always welcome. More peripheral subjects such as interior design, legal matters and housing politics will also be considered. *Payment* £100 per 1000 words.

Mother

12–18 Paul Street, London EC2A 4JS   ☎01–247 8233   Telex 8951167

Owner *Argus Consumer Publications Ltd*   **Editor** *Tessa Hilton*

Circulation 73,029

FOUNDED 1936. MONTHLY. New contributors are welcome, but should study the specific style of the magazine in advance. The best approach is in writing with an idea.

Features Bright, lively features on being a mother and on aspects of babies and children. No fiction. Maximum length 1500 words. *Payment* varies.   **News** Very little opportunity for freelances, as there is just one page of news per issue. Maximum length 200 words. *Payment* varies.

Mother and Baby

12–18 Paul Street, London EC2A 4JS   ☎01–247 8233

Owner *Argus Consumer Publications*   **Editor** *Chris McLaughlin*

Circulation 100,000

FOUNDED 1956. MONTHLY. No unsolicited mss, except personal 'birth stories' and 'Viewpoint' pieces. Approaches may be made by telephone or in writing.

Motor Boat and Yachting

Quadrant House, The Quadrant, Sutton, Surrey SM2 5AS   ☎01–661 3500

Telex 892084 BISPRS G

Owner *Reed Business Publishing*   **Editor** *Tom Willis*   **Circulation** 36,000

FOUNDED 1904. MONTHLY for those interested in motor cruising.

Features *Alan Harper*   Cruising features, practical features especially welcome. Illustrations (mostly colour) as important as the text. Maximum 3000 words. *Payment* £70 per 1000 words or by arrangement.   **News** *Alan Harper*   Factual pieces only, without comment. Maximum 200 words. *Payment* up to £25 per item.

Motor Cycle News

PO Box 11, Huxloe Place, High Street, Kettering, NN16 8SS   ☎0536 81651

Owner *EMAP*   **Editor** *Malcolm Gough*   **Circulation** 143,364

Use freelances, but mostly an established network of contributors. As a weekly, the magazine is news oriented: particularly keen on motor racing, rallying and events reportage. Feature material is mostly produced in house. Ideas to **Deputy Editor** *Simon Arron*.

Motorway Express

Newspaper House, 22 Vineyard Road, Wellington, Shropshire TF1 1DJ

☎0952 51100

Owner *Leisure Newspapers Ltd*   **Editor** *Ron Newell Evans*   **Circulation** 250,000

MONTHLY magazine which welcomes unsolicited manuscripts. Prospective contributors may make initial contact either in writing or by telephone.

The Musical Times

8 Lower James Street, London W1R 4DN   ☎01–734 8080   Telex 27937

Owner *Novello & Co. Ltd*   **Editors** *Andrew Clements and Alison Latham*

Serious minded journal with a scholarly approach to its subject. Information on their use of freelance material not readily available at the time of going to press.

My Guy

Commonwealth House, 1–19 New Oxford Street, London WC1   ☎01–829 7770

Owner *IPC*   **Editor** *Lesley Robb*

FOUNDED 1977. WEEKLY teen magazine for girls. Unsolicited mss welcomed, provided they suit the magazine's style. Best approach by telephone with idea.

Fiction *Lesley Robb* One 1000-word story published each week.

My Story

PO Box 94, London W4 2ER   ☎01–995 0590

Owner *Atlantic Publishing Co.*   **Editor** *Geoff Brown*   **Circulation** 34,000

FOUNDED 1956. Downbeat romantic story monthly. Fiction only, provided it is in keeping with the usual style publishing. Best to study previous issues before sending anything in. *My Story* receives around 250 mss a week.

My Weekly

80 East Kingsway, Dundee DD4 8SL   ☎0382 44276

Owner *D. C. Thomson & Co. Ltd*   **Editor** *S. D. Brown*   **Circulation** 696,279

A traditional women's weekly which, like others in the **D. C. Thomson** stable, is currently trying to attract a younger readership, and compete for the young working woman's attention in the marketplace (while not alienating its traditional, loyal readership). Particularly interested in humour and human interest pieces which by their very nature appeal to all age groups, 1000–2500 words; and fiction. Three stories a week range from the emotional to the offbeat and unexpected: 2000–4000 words. Also serials. **D. C. Thomson** has long had a philosophy of consultation and help for writers of promise. *Payment* negotiable.

Nature
4 Little Essex Street, London WC2R 3LF ☎01–836 6633

Owner *Macmillan Magazines Ltd* **Editor** *John Maddox* Circulation 33,530

Covers all fields of science. Very little use for freelance writers or unsolicited mss; approach specialists when appropriate. No features – articles and news on science policy only.

Netball
Francis House, Francis Street, London SW1P 1DF ☎01–828 2176

Owner *All England Netball Association Ltd* **Editor** *Sylvia Eastley*
Circulation 5000

FOUNDED 1940. QUARTERLY. No freelance or unsolicited mss are accepted.

New Democrat
9 Poland Street, London W1V 3DG ☎01–434 1059

Owner *Letterhurst Ltd* **Editor** *Harry Cowie* Circulation 8000

FOUNDED 1982, published five times a year. Unsolicited mss welcome. Submissions should be in writing.

Features Profiles, or features on policies and events of interest to Alliance (Liberal/SDP) supporters. Maximum length 1500 words. No payment.

New Home Economics
Forbes Publications Ltd, 120 Bayswater Road, Queensway, London W2 3JH
☎01–229 9322

Owner *Joan Forbes* **Editor** *Sue Barnard* Circulation 5100

Ten issues a year. Contributors should bear in mind that all readers are fully qualified home economists or students of the subject.

Features *Sue Barnard* Articles up to 1200 words welcomed on the topics listed below. **News** *Sue Barnard* Items welcomed on food and nutrition, textile studies, childcare and development, health education, money topics and consumerism. Maximum length 500 words.

New Humanist
88 Islington High Street, London N1 8EW ☎01–226 7251

Owner *Rationalist Press Association* **Editor** *Jim Herrick* Circulation 3000

FOUNDED 1885. QUARTERLY. Unsolicited mss welcome.

Features Articles with a humanist perspective are welcomed in the following fields: religion (critical), humanism, human rights, philosophy, current events, literature, history and science. Usual length 2000–4000 words. *Payment* negotiable, but 'minimal'. No fiction. **Book reviews** by arrangement with the editor. Usually between 750 and 1000 words.

New Internationalist
42 Hyth Bridge Street, Oxford OX1 2EP   ☎ 0865 728181

Editor *Chris Brazier*   Circulation 60,000 worldwide

Concerned with world poverty and global issues of peace and politics, with the emphasis on the Third World: radical, and broadly leftist in approach, though unaligned. Difficult to use unsolicited material, as they work to a theme each month, and the editor commissions features on that basis. The way in is to send examples of published or unpublished work; writers of interest are taken up.

New Left Review
6 Meard Street, London W1V 3HR   ☎ 01–734 8839

Editor *Robin Blackburn*   Circulation 35,000

Magazine of theoretical politics, history and related issues, plus (to a lesser degree) a Marxist reading of the arts and humanities. Generally provided by academics and expert commentators in the field rather than journalists. No payment.

New Musical Express
4th Floor, Commonwealth House, 1–19 New Oxford Street, London WC1A 1NJ
☎ 01–404 0700

Owner *IPC Magazines Ltd*   **Editor** *Ian Pye*   Circulation 125,646

NME does use freelances, but always for reviews in the first instance. Specialisation in areas of music (or in film, which is also covered) is a help. Review editors: **Live** *Alan Jackson*   **Film** *Sean Cosgrove*   **Books** *Sean O'Hagan*   **LPs** *Alan Jackson* Send in examples of work, whether published or specially written samples.

New Socialist
150 Walworth Road, London SE17 1JT   ☎ 01–703 0833

Owner *Labour Party*   **Editor** *Stuart Weir*   Circulation 16,000

FOUNDED 1981. MONTHLY. Unsolicited mss (with s.a.e.) welcome.

Features Articles on socialist themes. Maximum 2000–3000 words. **News** Frontline section – short news items. 500 words. **Reviews** *Stephen Pope* Short reviews of film, theatre, music, television, books, etc. 500 words. *Payments* variable.

New Society

42/43 Lower Marsh, London SE1 7RQ ☎01–620 0025

Owner *New Society Ltd*   **Editor** *David Lipsey* **Circulation** 25,000

FOUNDED 1962. WEEKLY. Freelance contributions welcomed, but 50 are received each week.

Book reviews *Tony Gould* Maximum length 1000 words **Features** *Sean French* A wide range of features considered. Best to submit ideas in writing in the first instance. Maximum length 3000 words. **News** *Steve Platt* Occasional social policy news stories used. Maximum length 400–500 words. No fiction. *Payment* varies by arrangement.

New Statesman

Foundation House, Perseverance Works, Kingsland Road, London E2 8DQ
☎01–739 3211   Telex 28449 NSTAT

Owner *NSPC*   **Editor** *John Lloyd* **Circulation** 28,000

FOUNDED 1913. WEEKLY magazine of the political left. New contributors are best advised to contact the editor in writing. Unsolicited contributions welcomed, but it should be noted that over 50 are received every week.

Newsweek

25 Upper Brook Street, London W1Y 1PD ☎01–629 8361

Editor *Tony Clifton*, Bureau Chief, London office

No freelance material.

19 (incorporating Honey)

Kings Reach Tower, Stamford Street, London SE1 9LS ☎01–261 6360

Editor *Deirdre Vine* **Circulation** 145,000

MONTHLY magazine aimed at the 17–20 year old girl. A little different to the usual teen magazine mix: *19* are now aiming for a 50/50 balance between the fashion/lifestyle aspects and meatier, newsier material on *Young Guardian* lines, e.g. articles on women in prison, and life in East Berlin. Also *Speak for Yourself*, a platform page for ordinary readers rather than professional journalists to speak out on any subject. 40% of the magazine's feature material is commissioned, ordinarily from established freelances. 'But we're always keen to see original bold vigorous writing from people just starting out...' Letter with ideas first, to **Deputy Editor** *Jane Dowdeswell*.

Nursing Times

4 Little Essex Street, London WC2R 3LF ☎01–836 1776

Owner *Macmillan Journals Ltd* **Editor** *Niall Dickson*

A large proportion of **Nursing Times'** feature content is from unsolicited contributions sent on spec, although they also commission articles. Pieces on all aspects of nursing, both practical and theoretical, welcome; written in a lively and contemporary way. *Payment* varies; NUJ rates of £100 per 1000 words for commissioned work.

Observer Colour Magazine

8 St Andrew's Hill, London EC4V 5JA ☎01–236 0202

Editor *Jo Foley*

Freelance writers used extensively, but an experienced and competitive pool of writers; only very strong ideas and demonstrable talent will succeed here. Contact Angela Mason with ideas (if you can get through).

Office Secretary

Streatfeild House, Carterton, Oxford OX8 3XZ ☎0993 845484

Owner *Trade Media Ltd* **Editor** *Penny Comerford* **Circulation** 160,000

FOUNDED 1986. QUARTERLY. Features articles of interest to female office staff aged 23–50. Unsolicited mss welcome.

Features Chatty but informative pieces on current affairs, health, office-related topics. Maximum 2500 words. *Payment* £100 per 1000 words or by negotiation.

On Skis

4 Granada House, Lower Stone Street, Maidstone, Kent ME15 6JP ☎0622 690606

Owner *Fastrax Ltd* **Editor** *Caroline Hardie* **Circulation** 25,000

FOUNDED 1986. Six issues a year. Unsolicited mss are welcomed, especially informative articles on skiing (maximum 2500 words). Prospective contributors are advised to make initial approach in writing. *Payment* £30 per 1000 words.

On The Move

South Bank Business Centre, 13 Park House, 140 Battersea Park Road, London SW11 4NB ☎01–622 4185

Owner *Transit Publications* **Editor** *Clive Lewis* **Circulation** 12,000

FOUNDED 1985. BI-MONTHLY. Specialist magazine on travel and transport-related subjects. Unsolicited mss welcome. Prospective contributors are advised to make initial contact by telephone.

Features *Anne Rummey* Maximum 1500 words. Specialised, in-depth studies specifically commissioned. Views and opinions on travel and public transport (up to a maximum of 1000 words) are welcomed. News *Clive Lewis* All pieces are specially commissioned. Maximum 600 words. *Payment* negotiable.

Opera

1A Mountgrove Road, London N5 2LU 01–359 1037

Owner *Harold Rosenthal* **Editor** *Rodney Milnes* Circulation 15,500

FOUNDED 1950. MONTHLY review of the current opera scene. Almost all articles are commissioned and unsolicited mss are not welcome. All approaches should be made in writing.

Options

25 Newman Street, London W1P 3HA 01–631 3939

Owner *Carlton Magazines Ltd* **Editor** *Penny Vincenzi* Circulation 226,380

Penny Vincenzi, one of the most successful freelance feature writers in the country, recently became the new editor of this most balanced of women's magazines. Options aims to entertain the modern renaissance woman, worker, mother and wife; more for the woman who has arrived than the Cosmo emotional/sexual issues market. Almost all written by freelances, these tend to be a regular bunch, but new writers are encouraged, and 'commissioned non-commissioned pieces' are requested from new feature writers of promise. The full page *Speak Out* column is a platform for even the most amateur writer with something to say.

Out Of Town

Standard House, Epworth Street, London EC2A 4DL 01–628 4741

Owner *Narod Press Ltd* **Editor** *Richard Cavendish* Circulation 15,000

FOUNDED 1983. MONTHLY. Unsolicited mss are welcomed and prospective contributors are advised to make initial contact in writing.

Features up to a maximum of 2000 words on heritage, countryside matters and places to visit are welcome. *Payment* from £50 per 1000 words.

Over 21 Magazine

Greater London House, Hampstead Road, London NW1 7QZ 01–837 6611

Owner *United Magazines Ltd* **Editor** *Pat Roberts* (Managing Editor)
Circulation 91,000

FOUNDED 1972. MONTHLY. When a writer is new to them, they prefer ideas in writing, together with examples of the writer's published work, details of experience etc. They do not accept unsolicited manuscripts, of which they receive approximately 30 per week (features and fiction), but mss accompanied by an s.a.e. will be returned.

Features Feature ideas appropriate to the magazine should be submitted in writing. Not generally interested in 'round robin' lists of ideas circulated to other publications. **Fiction** For the past two years *Over 21* has been running an extremely successful Short Story Competition and publishing the winners and runners-up. A third competition is planned for 1987. They are therefore not currently in the market for fiction.   News The 'News and Views' pages at the beginning of the magazine occasionally use freelance contributors who should contact *Guy Pierce*, editor of the 'Now' Section.

Paperback Inferno

1 The Flaxyard, Woodfall Lane, Little Neston, South Wirral L64 4BT

☎051–336 3355

Owner *British Science Fiction Association*   **Editor** *Andy Sawyer*

Circulation 1000

FOUNDED 1977. BI-MONTHLY. Publishes reviews of Science Fiction paperbacks and professional SF magazines. Unsolicited material not welcome as all reviews are commissioned.

Parents

Victory House, Leicester Place, London WC2H 7NB   ☎01–437 9011

Telex 266400

Owner *Gemini Magazines Ltd*   **Editor** *Jackie Highe*   **Circulation** 92,500

FOUNDED1976. MONTHLY. Specialist writers only are requested to write with suggestions for consideration.

Patches

Albert Square, Dundee, DD6 8JB   ☎0382 23131

Owner *D. C. Thomson & Co. Ltd*   **Editor** *Sandra Monks*

Magazine for the 12–16 year old girl. A mixture of photostories, short stories and features, which should be teen-oriented and deal with the emotional and practical issues affecting girls of this age. Unsolicited pieces sent in on spec. will be considered. *Payment* for features starts at around £40.

People's Friend

80 Kingsway East, Dundee DD4 8SL   ☎0382 44276

Owner *D. C. Thomson & Co. Ltd*   **Editor** *Douglas Neilson*   **Circulation** 625,000

Traditional weekly magazine whose readership is mostly northern female and middle aged, and which caters for a family audience. Mostly fiction: short stories should be suitable for family reading: 'the normal problems of the normal family next door'. Any length from 1000–4000 words. Not much of a market for non-fiction, but short filler articles of 500–2000 words are welcome. *Payment* negotiable.

Personnel Management

1 Hills Place, London W1R 1AG   ☎01–734 1773   Telex 51714 PRINTN G

Owner *Personnel Publications Ltd*   **Editor** *Susanne Lawrence*   **Circulation** 36,000

FOUNDED 1969. MONTHLY specialist magazine for personnel managers. Unsolicited mss welcome, from personnel managers only.

Features *Susanne Lawrence*   Only interested in material written by specialists in their field. Occasional scope for articles by those with experience or knowledge of employment, industrial relations, training, pay areas. Maximum 3000 words. *Payment* NUJ rates.   **News** *David Turner*   Sometimes interested in reports of events where staff member was not present. Length varies. *Payment* NUJ rates.

Plays and Players

145–147 North End, Croydon, Surrey CR0 1TN   ☎01–681 7817

Owner *Brevet Publications*   **Editor** *Robert Gore-Langton*   **Circulation** 8000

Theatre monthly, which publishes a mixture of reviews, features on aspects of the theatre, festival reports etc. Rarely use unsolicited material, but writers of talent are taken up. Almost all material is commissioned. *Payment* under review, but small.

Plays International

55 Hatton Garden, London EC1N 8HP   ☎01–720 1950

Owner *Chancery Publications*   **Editor** *Peter Roberts*

Freelance writers are used, but are a well established team of regulars, and unsolicited material cannot be considered. **Plays International** is a mixture of interviews, reviews and a complete play text every month. One-off pieces are only rarely commissioned.

Poetry Review

21 Earls Court Square, London SW5 9DE   ☎01–373 7861

Owner *The Poetry Society*   **Editor** *Peter Forbes*   **Circulation** 3500

FOUNDED 1909. QUARTERLY poetry magazine. Approximately 5000 unsolicited manuscripts received each year (mostly poetry) and these are welcome, but the odds should be taken into account by prospective contributors. Almost all prose is commissioned. A preliminary letter is advisable before submitting reviews or features.

Powerboating International

The Poplars, New Road, Armitage, Staffs WS15 4BJ   ☎0543 4981818

Telex 335628

Owner *Pat Ainge*   **Editor** *Pat Ainge*   **Circulation** 8000–10,000

FOUNDED 1983. MONTHLY. This is a specialised magazine whose policy is to welcome outside contributions. The length of any given article, and the fee paid, is subject to individual discussion. At present only one or two unsolicited contributions are received a month.

Practical Computing
Reed Business Publishing Ltd, Quadrant House, The Quadrant, Sutton, Surrey SM2 5AS   01–661 3633   Telex 892084 BISPRS G

Owner *Reed Publishing Ltd*   **Editor** *Glyn Moody*   **Circulation** 37,000

FOUNDED 1977. MONTHLY. Unsolicited mss not welcome; prospective contributors must send an outline in writing before sending mss. *Payment* negotiable.

Practical Gardening
Bushfield House, Orton Centre, Peterborough, Cambs PE2 0UW
                                                      0733 237111   Telex 32157

Owner *EMAP*   **Editor** *Mike Wyatt*   **Circulation** 84,825

FOUNDED 1960. MONTHLY. Unsolicited mss welcome, but there are few acceptances out of 150 offered each year. Submit ideas in writing.

Features Occasionally features/photos on gardens (*not* famous gardens or stately homes) are required if they suit the *Practical Gardening* style. Maximum length 1200 words. *Payment* from £45 per 1000 words.

Practical Photography
Bushfield House, Orton Centre, Peterborough, Cambs PE2 0UW   0733 237111
                                                                Telex 32157

Owner *EMAP*   **Editor** *Dominic Boland*   **Circulation** 100,000

MONTHLY. Unsolicited mss welcome if relevant to the magazine and its readers. Preliminary approach may be made by telephone. Always interested in new ideas.

Features Anything relevant to the readership – but not 'the sort of feature produced by staff writers'. Bear in mind that there is a three-month lead-in time. Maximum 2000 words. *Payment* varies. **News** Only 'hot' news applicable to a monthly magazine. Maximum 800 words. *Payment* varies.

Prediction
Link House, Dingwall Avenue, Croydon, CR9 2TA   01–686 2599
                                                    Telex 947709 LINKHO G

Owner *Link House Magazines*   **Editor** *Jo Logan*   **Circulation** 35,000

FOUNDED 1936. MONTHLY. The magazine covers astrology and topics with an occult slant and unsolicited material in these areas are welcomed. 200–300 mss are received every year.

Astrology Pieces ranging from 800–2000 words should be practical as well as of general interest. Charts and astro data should accompany them, especially if profiles.

Payment £25–75. **Features** *Jo Logan* Articles on earth mysteries, alternative medicine and psychical/occult experiences and phenomena are considered. Maximum length 2000 words. **News** *Jackie Brock* News items of interest to readership welcomed. Maximum length 300 words. No fee.

Prima

Portland House, Stag Place, London SW1E 5AU ☎ 01–245 8700

Owner *G&J* **Editor** *Iris Burton* **Circulation** 1,000,000

FOUNDED 1986. The new, hit, German import women's magazine.

Features *Donna Riche* Features are mostly practical and written by specialists or commissioned from known freelances. Unsolicited mss not welcome.

Private Eye

6 Carlisle Street, London W1V 5RG ☎ 01–437 4017

Editor *Ian Hislop* **Circulation** 240,000

FOUNDED 1961. FORTNIGHTLY humour and satire magazine. A great number of unsolicited contributions are received and these are welcomed if they are stories or cartoons, but no jokes are required. Prospective contributors are best advised to approach the editor in writing. News stories and feature ideas are always welcomed. *Payment* in all cases is 'not great', and length of piece varies as appropriate.

Property International

Regent Arcade House, 19 Argyll Street, London W1V 1AA ☎ 01–734 1655
Telex 916752 FALCON G

Owner *Falcon Publishing Europe* **Editor** *Kenneth MacTaggart*
Circulation 30,000

FOUNDED 1984. BI-MONTHLY. Unsolicited mss are welcome, particularly from journalists with a knowledge of property who travel regularly abroad.

Features International property, real estate and related topics such as mortgages, legal advice, house market trends, investment prospects, etc. Emphasis on residential rather than commercial or industrial property. Also, property personalities and some travel. Maximum 1500 words. *Payment* varies. **News** International property stories. Maximum 500 words.

Property Mail

90–92 King Street, Maidstone, Kent ME14 1BH ☎ 0622 670246

Owner *Property Mail Ltd* **Editor** *Allan Bishop* **Circulation** 347,000

FOUNDED 1983. WEEKLY. Unsolicited manuscripts are welcome, but it is advisable for a prospective contributor to make a preliminary approach in writing.

Psychic News

20 Earlham Street, London WC2H 9LW ☎01-240 3032

Editor *Tony Ortzen*

Weekly tabloid of the psychic subculture. Never use unsolicited material (although receive enormous amounts).

Punch

23–27 Tudor Street, London EC4Y 0HR ☎01–583 9199 Telex LDN 265863

Owner *United Newspapers* **Editor** *Alan Coren* **Circulation** 65,000

FOUNDED 1841. WEEKLY humorous magazine. Unsolicited contributions 'are tolerated', but prospective contributors should note that *Punch* receives 50 to 60 unsolicited manuscripts per week. Only finished pieces are accepted and these should be around 1200 words, typed and accompanied by an s.a.e.

Q

42 Great Portland Street, London W1N 5AH ☎01–637 9181

Owner *EMAP Metro* **Editor** *Mark Ellen* **Circulation** 50,000 (est.)

FOUNDED 1986. MONTHLY. Very few opportunities for freelance writers, and unsolicited mss are strongly discouraged. Prospective contributors should approach in writing only.

RA

Friends of the Royal Academy of Arts, Royal Academy of Arts, Burlington House, Piccadilly, London W1V 0DS ☎01–734 9052 ext. 52

Owner *Friends of the Royal Academy* **Editor** *Nick Tite* **Circulation** 40,000

FOUNDED 1983. QUARTERLY magazine with a controlled circulation. Articles relating to or about the Royal Academy, its members and exhibitions. Unsolicited mss considered but no unsolicited material has yet been published. Important to make initial contact in writing. Features should be no longer than 1500 words. *Payment* £100.

The Racing Pigeon

19 Doughty Street, London WC1N 2PT ☎01–242 0565

Owner *Racing Pigeon Publishing Co. Ltd* **Editor** *Colin Osman*

Circulation 33,000

FOUNDED 1898. WEEKLY news magazine for racing pigeon enthusiasts. Only specialist writers considered. Maximum 1000 words. Unsolicited mss welcome.

Radio Times

35 Marylebone High Street, London W1M 4AA   ☎01–580 5577

Owner *BBC Publications*   **Editor** *Brian Gearing*   **Circulation** 3,224,038

Detailed BBC television and radio listings in this weekly magazine are accompanied by interviews and feature material relevant to the week's output. 95% of this is provided by freelance writers, but, obviously, the topicality of the pieces needed means close consultation with editors. Unlikely to use the unsolicited material they receive, but do take up writers of interest to work on future projects.

Features Editor *John Davies*

Rambler

1/5 Wandsworth Road, London SW8 2XX   ☎01–586 6826

Owner *Ramblers' Association*   **Editors** *Frances Rowe/Alan Mattingly*
     Circulation 53,500

BI-MONTHLY. Unsolicited material welcome.

Features Freelance features are invited on walking in Britain and abroad, the natural world and conservation. Transparencies should accompany when possible and pieces should be 1500–2000 words long. *Payment* around £50 per 1000 words.

Readers Digest

25 Berkeley Square, London W1X 6AB   ☎01–629 8144

Editor *Russell Twisk*   **Circulation** 1.5 million

In theory, a good market for general interest features of around 2500 words. However, 'a tiny proportion' comes from freelance writers. Opportunities are strongest in the 'short paragraphs' pages *Life's Like That* and *Humour in Uniform*, for which the fee is £100.

Record Collector

43 St Mary's Road, Ealing, London W5 5RQ   ☎01–579 1082

Owner *Johnny Dean*   **Editor** *Peter Doggett*

FOUNDED 1979. MONTHLY. Features detailed, well-researched articles on any aspect of record collecting or any collectable artiste in the field of popular music (1950s–1980s) with complete discographies where appropriate. Unsolicited mss welcome. *Payment* by negotiation.

Record Mirror (RM)

Greater London House, Hampstead Road, London NW1 7QZ

☎01–387 6611   Telex 299485 MUSIC G

Owner *Spotlight Publications*   **Editor** *Betty Page*   **Circulation** 52,000

FOUNDED 1954. WEEKLY. Unsolicited manuscripts are not welcome except as examples of a writer's work not intended for publication. Prospective contributors are advised to make initial contact by telephone.

Features *Eleanor Levy*   Opportunities for young, new writers with specific feature ideas.   **News** *Robin Smith*   News tips used occasionally.   **Review Pages (Lives)** *Stuart Bailie*   Opportunities for young writers nationwide wanting to review young new bands. *Payment* at current NUJ rates.

Resident Abroad

108 Clerkenwell Road, London EC1M 5SA   ☎01–251 9321

Owner *Financial Times*   **Editor** *William Essex*   **Circulation** 17,199

FOUNDED 1979. MONTHLY magazine aimed at British expatriates. Unsolicited mss welcome.

Features of up to 2000 words on finance, employment opportunities and other topics likely to appeal to readership such as living conditions in 'likely countries'. **Fiction** rarely published, but exceptional, relevant stories (no longer than 2000 words) might be considered. *Payment* on acceptance £100 per 1000 words.

RIBA Interiors

66 Portland Place, London W1N 4AD   ☎01–580 5533

Owner *RIBA Magazines Ltd*   **Editor** *Richard Wilcock*   **Circulation** 21,000

BI-MONTHLY sister journal to **The Architect**.

Features Interiors by architects and other relevant subjects treated in specialist manner. Maximum 1200 words. *Payment* £100 per 1000 words.

Riding

8 Stamford Hill, London N16 6XZ   ☎01–806 3221

Owner *Scott Publications Ltd*   **Editor** *Elwyn Hartley Edwards*

Circulation 36,918

Most of the writers on *Riding* are freelances. It's aimed at a mostly adult, horse-owning audience: the 'serious leisure rider'. Feature opportunities are limited, as regular columnists take up much of the magazine. However, new and authoritative writers always welcome. *Payment* negotiable.

Running Magazine
57–61 Mortimer Street, London W1N 7TD ☎01–637 4383

Owner *Stonehart Magazines Ltd* **Editor** *David Calderwood* **Circulation** 60,331

Freelances are used, but are mostly a team of regular contributors. Specialist knowledge is needed to have features accepted – 'we would never take a feature from someone new'. However, they do accept and publish personal accounts from readers – personal experience running stories are welcome.

RYA News
Victoria Way, Woking, Surrey, GU21 1EQ ☎04862 5022 Telex 859554 Boating

Owner *Royal Yachting Association* **Editor** *Vicki Davies* **Circulation** 65,000

FOUNDED 1975. QUARTERLY. Unsolicited mss welcome if they concern general cruising matters with a RYA slant. Prospective contributors are advised to make their first approach in writing.

Features Maximum length 1500 words. *Payment* negotiable but small.

Sailplane and Gliding
281 Queen Edith's Way, Cambridge CB1 4WH ☎0223 247725

Owner *British Gliding Association* **Editor** *Gillian Bryce-Smith* **Circulation** 7000

FOUNDED 1930. BI-MONTHLY for gliding enthusiasts. A specialised magazine with very few opportunities for freelances. *Payment* No fees for contributions.

Sales and Marketing Management
ISE Publications Ltd, 13 Vaughan Road, Harpenden, Herts AL5 4HU

☎05827 62038

Owner *David Waler* **Editor** *Jayne Bridges* **Circulation** 18,682

Eleven issues a year. A great many unsolicited mss are received. These are welcome if on topics relevant to sales and marketing management. Prospective contributors are advised to make initial contact in writing and to present other published work where possible.

Features up to 2000 words dealing with Sales Techniques, Motivation, Modern Management Practice, etc, are welcomed. No fiction. *Payment* negotiable.

Sales Direction
2 St John's Place, London EC1M 4DE ☎01–253 2427

Editor *Nick De Cent* **Circulation** 40,000

FOUNDED 1986. MONTHLY. Unsolicited mss are welcomed as long as they are relevant to sales management/business readership. It is strongly advised that initial contact (either by telephone or in writing) is made with an idea before full submission is made.

Features Lifestyle features up to 1000 words and interesting sports pursuits relevant to business people.   **Interviews** with top sales directors and business people in the public eye. Prior discussion essential. Between 1500 and 2000 words.   **News** No longer than 300 words. *Payment* £100 per 1000 words.

Sanity
22–24 Underwood Street, London N1 7JG ☎01–250 4010

Owner *CND Publications Ltd*   **Editor** *Caroline Williamson*   **Circulation** 40,000

FOUNDED 1961. MONTHLY CND magazine. Unsolicited mss are welcomed. About 100 mss come in each month, most not suitable for publication.

Features Mostly written by people involved in the peace movement or with specialist political/scientific knowledge. Maximum length 3000 words.   **News** Most news is commissioned on arms race, international and domestic news. Maximum length 500 words. *Payment* NUJ rates.

Scenefit
Clareville House, 47 Whitcomb Street, London WC2H 7DX ☎01–930 8953
Telex 922488

Owner *Headway Publications*   **Editor** *Sandra Hewett*   **Circulation** 65,000

FOUNDED 1985. BI-MONTHLY sports and fitness magazine. Unsolicited mss not welcome; would-be contributors should approach by telephone.

Features about specialists in sports medicine, profiles of sports players and stories related to health and fitness, maximum 1000 words. No fiction.   **News** Research stories, relevant humorous stories and personality pieces up to a maximum of 250 words. *Payment* £100 per 1000 words.

Screen
29 Old Compton Street, London W1V 5PL ☎01–734 3211

Owner *Society for Education in Film & Television*   **Editor** *Mandy Merck*
Circulation 2,500

QUARTERLY academic journal of film and television studies for a readership ranging from undergraduates to media professionals. There are no specific departments but articles – based on a knowledge of the magazine and its markets – are welcomed from freelances. The best approach is with an idea in writing.

Screen International
6–7 Great Chapel Street, London W1V 4BR ☎01–734 9452

Editor *Terry Ilott*

Trade paper of the film, video and television industries. No unsolicited mss, though expert freelance writers are occasionally used in all areas.

Sea Breezes

202 Cotton Exchange Building, Old Hall Street, Liverpool L3 9LA

☎051–236 3935

Owner *Jocast Ltd*   **Editor** *Mr C. H. Milsom*   **Circulation** 18,500

FOUNDED 1919. MONTHLY. The magazine covers virtually everything relating to ships and shipping of a non-technical nature. Unsolicited mss welcome; they should be thoroughly researched and accompanied by relevant photographs. *Articles* about nautical history, shipping company histories, epic voyages etc. should be up to 5000 words. *Payment* £5 per 1000 words.

She Magazine

National Magazine House, 72 Broadwick Street, London W1V 2BP☎01–439 7144

Editor *Joyce Hopkirk*   **Circulation** 232,000

Women's glossy with less gloss and much more general interest reading than comparable monthlies. Feature material can include social issues, health, spiritual matters, unusual subjects of any kind, as well as traditionally 'female' concerns. Articles should be of around 1200 words. Fiction is used from time to time: again, general rather than 'women's' reading. Regular freelances used, but open to new talent. *Payment* NUJ rates.

Shoot Magazine

Kings Reach Tower, Stamford Street, London SE1 9LS

☎01–261 5280   Telex 915748

Owner *IPC Magazines*   **Editor** *Peter Stewart*   **Circulation** 158,000

FOUNDED 1969. WEEKLY football magazine. Present ideas for news, features or colour photo-features to the editor in writing. No unsolicited mss.

Features Hard-hitting, topical and offbeat. 450–1500 words. **News** items welcome, especially exclusive gossip and transfer speculation. Maximum length 150 words. *Payment* £36–75.

Shooting and Conservation

Marford Mill, Rossett, Wrexham, Clwyd LL11 0HL

☎0244 570881

Owner *BASC*   **Editor** *James McKay*   **Circulation** 69,202

QUARTERLY. Unsolicited mss are welcomed. In both **Features** and **Fiction** sections, good articles, stories on shooting, conservation and related areas, up to 2000 words, are always sought. *Payment* negotiable.

Shooting News

Unit 21, Plymouth Road Ind. Est, Tavistock, Devon, PL19 9QN ☎0822 66460

Owner *V. Gardner* **Editor** *C. Binmore* Circulation 11,500

FOUNDED 1982. WEEKLY. Unsolicited material is welcome, six or seven submissions are received each week, and a list of special editions and subjects covered by the magazine is available on request.

Features Should be on any fieldsport topic and no longer than 1500 words. **News** Items considered. No fiction.

Shooting Times & Country

10 Sheet Street, Windsor, Berks SL4 1BG ☎0753 856061

Owner *Burlington Publishing Co. Ltd* **Editor** *Jonathan Young*

Circulation 44,000

FOUNDED 1882. WEEKLY. Articles on field sports, natural history and the countryside. Unsolicited mss welcome. Maximum 1000 words. *Payment* £50.

The Sign

St Thomas House, Becket Street, Oxford OX1 1SJ ☎0865 242507

Owner *Mowbray Publishing* **Editor** *Dr A. L. Moore* Circulation 256,000

FOUNDED 1907. MONTHLY inset for Church of England parish magazines. Unsolicited mss welcome.

News, Features and Fiction all considered. Maximum 400 words. *Payment* negotiable.

Signature

3rd Floor, 364–366 Kensington High Street, London W14 8PE ☎01–602 9811

Owner *Diners Club International* **Editor** *Erica Brown* Circulation 50,000

RELAUNCHED 1986. Ten issues a year. Unsolicited mss rarely used, but written suggestions welcome.

Features Most of the main features are commissioned from regular writers. Most articles are based on travel or food. Maximum 2000 words. *Payment* negotiable.
Special One special section each month on subjects such as health, sport, gardening and fashion. Maximum 1000 words. *Payment* negotiable.

Singles Magazine

23 Abingdon Road, London W8 6AH ☎01–938 1011

Owner *John Patterson* **Editor** *Lorraine Furneaux* Circulation 23,000

FOUNDED 1976. MONTHLY magazine for single people. Unsolicited mss welcome; ideas in writing only.

Features Anything of interest to, or directly concerning, single people. Maximum 2500 words. *Payment* from £35/45 per 1000 words.   **News** All news items required at least six weeks ahead. Maximum length 2500 words. *Payment* from £35/45 per 1000 words.

Ski Survey

118 Eaton Square, London SW1W 9AF ☎01–245 1033

Owner *Ski Club of Great Britain*   **Editor** *Elisabeth Hussey*   **Circulation** 20,000

FOUNDED 1903. Five issues a year. All articles are commissioned.

The Skier

1 Grimsdells Corner, Sycamore Road, Amersham, Bucks HP6 5EL ☎02403 28967
Telex 838791 JMC

Owner *Charles Hallifax*   **Editor** *Charles Hallifax*   **Circulation** 25,000

MONTHLY from September to January. Unsolicited manuscripts welcome. Approximately 15 are received each season.

Features of 1000–3000 words on any topic involving 'action' such as skiing, climbing, white-water rafting, etc. Articles of 1000–3000 words, written in a light, humorous style are particularly welcome.   **News** Items of varying length are always welcome. *Payment* negotiable.

Skiing UK Ltd

22 King Street, Glasgow G1 5QP ☎041–552 4067

Owner *Skiing UK Ltd*   **Editor** *Ian McMillan*   **Circulation** 12,500

FOUNDED 1985. Five issues a year. Unsolicited mss are welcome on all skiing topics. Approach either in writing or by telephone. No fiction.

Features Should be no longer than 1200 words. *Payment* £60 per 1000 words. **News** Items should be no longer than 300 words. *Payment* £50 per 100 words.

Slimmer

Tolland, Lydgard St Lawrence, Taunton, Somerset TA4 3PS ☎0984 56676

Owner *Slimmer Publications Ltd*   **Editor** *Judith Wills*   **Circulation** 130,000

FOUNDED 1976. BI-MONTHLY. Freelance contributors should write with synopsis and c.v., or with cuttings of previously published work. Ideas for features are preferred to completed manuscripts.

Features First person slimming stories and features on nutrition, research etc. Must be in a chatty style. Maximum length 1500 words. *Payment* £10 per 100 words.   **News** Titbits – serious or amusing – on slimming and fitness. Payment on publication. Maximum length 200 words. *Payment* £10 per 100 words.

Slimming

Victory House, Leicester Place, London WC2H 7NB   ☎01–437 9011

Owner *Argus Press*   **Editor** *Patience Bulkeley*   **Circulation** 250,000

FOUNDED 1969. BI-MONTHLY. Basically a scientific magazine with most of its material written by staff, so the opportunities for freelance contributors are very few indeed. There is some scope for first person experiences of weight control loss, but only a small number of those received prove suitable. It is best to approach with an idea in writing.

Smash Hits

52–55 Carnaby Street, London W1V 1PF   ☎01–437 8050

Owner *EMAP Metro*   **Editor** *Barry McIlhengy*   **Circulation** 515,000

FOUNDED 1979. FORTNIGHTLY. Unsolicited manuscripts are not accepted, but prospective contributors may approach in writing.

Snooker Scene

Cavalier House, 202 Hagley Road, Edgbaston, Birmingham B16 9PQ

    ☎021–454 2931

Owner *Everton's News Agency*   **Editor** *Clive Everton*   **Circulation** 18,000

FOUNDED 1971. MONTHLY. Unsolicited material is not welcome; any approach should be in writing with an idea.

The Social Democrat

4 Cowley Street, London SW1P 3NB   ☎01–222 7999

Owner *Social Democratic Party*   **Editor** *Val Taylor*   **Circulation** 11,000

FOUNDED 1982. FORTNIGHTLY of political and social topics of interest to Social Democratic Party members and supporters. Unsolicited mss welcome.

Features Maximum 800 words. *Payment* NUJ rates.

Sounds

Greater London House, Hampstead Road, London NW1 7QZ   ☎01–387 6611

Owner *Spotlight Publications Ltd*   **Editor** *Tony Stewart*   **Circulation** 89,600

Popular music weekly tabloid. 99% of their material is provided by freelances. Send trial reviews in to be considered for work; reviews writers of talent can go on to feature-writing.

Reviews Editor *Robbi Millar*   **Features Editor** *Tony Stewart*.

South Magazine

New Zealand House, 13th Floor, Haymarket, London SW1Y 4TS ☎01–930 8411
Telex 8814201

Owner *Humayun Iauhar*   **Editor** *Andrew Graham-Yooll*   **Circulation** 86,000

FOUNDED 1980. MONTHLY magazine of the Third World. Unsolicited mss considered, but it's better to make initial contact in writing so that editors can consider the subject and discuss it with writer. Many articles are received from all over the world.

Features *Raana Gauhar* and *Judith Vidal Hall*. Any Third World topic is considered, as long as it carries a strong business and financial interest. Also **Arts & Leisure** of interest to the Third World.   **Fiction** Rarely published.   **News** *Melvyn Westlake*. **Science and Technology** *Maria Elena Hurtado*   Innovations in the field – all pieces must consider the problems of the Third World.

The Spectator

56 Doughty Street, London WC1N 2LL   ☎01–405 1706   Telex 25455

Owner *John Fairfax & Sons Ltd*   **Editor** *Charles Moore*   **Circulation** 34,000

FOUNDED 1828. WEEKLY political and literary magazine. Maximum length for all contributions is 1500 words, and prospective contributors should write in the first instance to the relevant editor. Unsolicited manuscripts welcomed, but over 20 received every week.

Arts *Jenny Naipaul* **Books** *Mark Amory* **Features** *Charles Moore, Andrew Gimson* **News** *Charles Moore. Payment* in all cases is 'small'.

The Sporting Life

Alexander House, 81–89 Farringdon Road, London EC1M 3LH   ☎01–831 2102

Owner *Odhams Newspapers Ltd*   **Editor** *Monty Court*   **Circulation** 79,291

DAILY magazine-newspaper of the horse-racing world. Always on the look out for specialised racing writers – not necessarily established sports writers, but certainly well-informed. No unsolicited mss – phone or write with an idea. The talented will be taken up and used again. *Contact* The **Features Editor**.

Sporting Life Weekender

Alexander House, 81–89 Farringdon Road, London EC1M 3HJ   ☎01–831 1808
Telex 263403

Owner *Odhams Newspapers Ltd*   **Editor** *Neil Cook*
Circulation 40,000

FOUNDED 1983. WEEKLY. Prospective contributors should write with ideas in first instance as no articles are published before discussion.

Sportswoman International (1), Sportsworld International (2)
25 Prentis Road, London SW16 1QB   ☎01–769 0753/01–749 0262

Owner *Lyn Guest de Swarte*   **Editor** *Lyn Guest de Swarte*
Circulation (1) 20,000   (2) 30,000

Many unsolicited mss are received, and are welcome. A crisp, non-sexist style is preferred. No fiction.

Features *Lyn Guest de Swarte*   Particularly human interest and 'inside' sports stories as well as articles on health-related topics. Maximum length 1500 words.   **News** *Cathy Gibb*   Interesting snippets up to a maximum of 300 words needed. *Payment* NUJ fees.

Squash Player International
Stanley House, 9 West Street, Epsom, Surrey KT18 7RL   ☎03727 41411

Owner *AE Morgan Publications Ltd*   **Editor** *I. R. Mackenzie*   **Circulation** 10,000

MONTHLY. Mss welcome; sample material and synopsis preferred.

Features Instructive, club and commercial news.   **News** Tournament reports.

Squash World
Chiltern House, 184 High Street, Berkhamsted, Hertfordshire HP4 3AP
☎04426 74947

Owner *Dennis Fairey Publishing Ltd*   **Editor** *Larry Halpin*   **Circulation** 10,000

FOUNDED 1986. MONTHLY. Unsolicited mss welcome; approach by telephone with ideas. Resident experts generally cover topics of Health, Diet, Fitness and Coaching, but material of 1200–1500 words from other experts would be considered.

Features *Larry Halpin*. Phone with ideas for articles of 1200–1500 words.   **News** *Larry Halpin*. Stories of a maximum of 500 words on tournaments, new clubs, sponsorship, etc., always welcome. *Payment* by negotiation.

The Stage and Television Today
47 Bermondsey Street, London SE1 3XT   ☎01–403 1818

Owner *Carson and Comerford Ltd*   **Editor** *Peter Hepple*   **Circulation** 42,750

FOUNDED 1810. WEEKLY. Unsolicited manuscripts are not welcome; prospective contributors should write with ideas in the first instance.

Features Occasional feature suggestions are considered. Preference is given to material with a business or financial orientation rather than personal pieces or interviews. Maximum length 1200 words. *Payment* £100 per 1000 words.   **News** News stories from outside London are always welcome. Maximum length 300 words. *Payment* £10 + .

The Strad

8 Lower James Street, London W1R 4DB ☎01–734 8080 Telex 27937

Owner *Novello & Co.* **Editor** *Eric Wen* Circulation 10,000

FOUNDED 1889. MONTHLY for classical string musicians and enthusiasts. Unsolicited mss welcome.

Features Profiles of string players and musical instruments. Maximum 3000 words. Payment £150.

Sunday

18 Ogle Street, London W1P 7LG ☎01–636 5010

Owner *News International* **Editor** *Wendy Henry* Circulation 5,000,000

FOUNDED 1981. WEEKLY colour supplement magazine published with the *News of the World*. There are very few opportunities for freelance writers, but prospective contributors should submit ideas in writing together with samples of published work. No unsolicited manuscripts; fiction is of the 'Best seller' variety and usually acquired via an agent or publisher.

Features *Sally Morris* Length and payment subject to negotiation.

Sunday Express Magazine

Newspaper House, 8–16 Great New Street, London EC4A 3AJ ☎01–353 8000
Telex 21841

Owner *Lord Stevens of Ludgate* **Editor** *Dee Nolan* Circulation 2,206,494

WEEKLY. Unsolicited mss are not welcome or considered, as features on all topics are commissioned from freelance writers. Any ideas, however, should be offered in writing.

The Sunday Times Magazine

200 Gray's Inn Road, London WC1X 8EZ ☎01–837 1234

Owner *News International* **Editor** *Philip Clarke* Circulation 1,300,000

FOUNDED 1962. WEEKLY colour supplement distributed with *The Sunday Times*. Almost all features are specially commissioned, prospective contributors should write in the first instance with ideas. No unsolicited mss are accepted.

Supercar Classics

FF Publishing, 97 Earls Court Road, London W8 6QH ☎01–370 0333

Owner *FF Publishing Ltd* **Editor** *Steve Cropley* Circulation 40,000

FOUNDED 1983. MONTHLY. Unsolicited mss of at least 1500 words are welcomed: make initial contact either by phone or in writing.

Features are usually commissioned from staff and known writers, but other reports of classic older cars, no longer in production, would be welcomed. Maximum length 3000 words. **Fiction** Short stories and satire (up to 3000 words) are considered. *Payment* £100–200 per 1000 words (negotiable).

Survival Weaponry & Techniques
89 East Hill, Colchester, Essex CO1 2QN   ☎0206 861130

Owner *Aceville Ltd*   **Editor** *Greg Payne*

MONTHLY publication on outdoor survival techniques. The only unsolicited material welcomed are specialist articles from experienced survival writers. Articles are paid for on publication. *Payment* £14 per 1000 words.

Swimming Times
Harold Fern House, Derby Square, Loughborough LE11 0AL   ☎0509 234433

Owner *Amateur Swimming Association*   **Editor** *R. H. Brown*

Circulation 15,600

FOUNDED 1923. MONTHLY about competitive swimming and associated subjects. Unsolicited mss welcome.

Features Technical articles on swimming, diving or synchronised swimming. Length and fees negotiable.

The Tablet
48 Great Peter Street, London SW1P 2HB   ☎01–222 7462

Owner *The Tablet Publishing Co. Ltd*   **Editor** *John Wilkins*   **Circulation** 12,394

FOUNDED 1840. WEEKLY (50 p.a.). Quality magazine featuring articles of interest to Roman Catholic laity and clergy. On average, five unsolicited manuscripts are received daily, but these are only accepted when relevant. The usual article length is 1500 words. *Payment* is approximately £30. All approaches should be made in writing.

Taste
58 Old Compton Street, London W1V 5PA   ☎01–846 9922

Editor *Marie-Pierre Moine*

A small staff means articles are mostly by freelance writers, and usually commissioned. Always on the look out for 'new regulars' though. Food, travel, cookery, wine/drink, kitchen, and general interest features with a foodie angle, e.g. the growth of Nouvelle Cuisine. Glossy and upmarket, 'but not as upmarket as *A La Carte*'. New writers should approach the editor with ideas and samples of written work, whether published or not.

The Tatler
Vogue House, Hanover Square, London W1R 0ED ☎01–499 9080

Owner *Condé Nast*   **Editor** *Mark Boxer*   Circulation 49,124

Upmarket glossy from the *Vogue* stable. New writers should send in copies of either published work or unpublished material; writers of promise will be taken up. The magazine works largely on a commission basis: they are unlikely to publish unsolicited features, but will ask writers to work to specific projects.

Features Editor *Alexandra Shulman.*

Telegraph Sunday Magazine
75 Farringdon Street, London EC4P 4BL ☎01–353 4242

Editor *Felicity Lawrence*   Circulation 700,000

WEEKLY magazine supplement to the *Sunday Telegraph*. Well-written articles on subjects of national interest with a human angle. Must have very good picture potential. Interested contributors should write in first instance. *Payment* negotiable. Maximum length 1500 words.

Tennis World
Chiltern House, 184 High Street, Berkhamsted, Herts HP4 3AP ☎04427 74947/8

Owner *Dennis Fairey Publishing Ltd*   **Editor** *Henry Wancke*   Circulation 16,000

FOUNDED 1969. MONTHLY. Unsolicited mss welcome.

Features Any ideas on tennis features or tennis personalities are welcome. Maximum 1000 words. *Payment* £75.

This England
PO Box 52, Cheltenham, Glos GL50 1YQ ☎0242 577775

Owner *Pickwick Press Ltd*   **Editor** *Roy Faiers*   Circulation 175,000

Published four times yearly, and with a strong foreign readership. Celebration of England and all things English: famous people, natural beauty, towns and villages, history, traditions, customs and legends, crafts etc. Generally a rural basis. The 'Forgetmenots' section publishes readers' recollections and nostalgia. They receive up to 100 unsolicited pieces a week. 250–2000 word articles will be considered. *Payment* negotiable.

Time

Time & Life Building, New Bond Street, London W1Y 0AA   ☎01–499 4080
Telex 22557

Owner *Time Inc.*   **Editor** *Christopher Ogden* (London Bureau Chief)
Circulation 509,000,000 (worldwide)

FOUNDED 1923. WEEKLY current affairs and news magazine. There are no opportunities for freelances on *Time* as almost all the magazine's content is written by staff members from the various bureaux around the world. Unsolicited manuscripts are not read.

Time and Tide

20 New Bond Street, London W1Y 9HF   ☎01–409 0081   Telex 24378

Owner *Trust House Forte plc*   **Editor** *David Jones*   **Circulation** 110,000

FOUNDED 1921. MONTHLY. Some opportunities for freelances of appropriate standard. Best approach is with idea in writing, together with copies of previously published work.

Features *Roger Baker.* Social issues, business enterprise, travel, 'lifestyle', arts, music, health, motoring etc. Maximum length – 2000 words. *Payment* £300 (maximum). Also food, wine and theatre pieces up to 1000 words. *Payment* £150 (maximum).

Times Educational Supplement

Priory House, St John's Lane, London EC1M 4BX   ☎01–253 3000
Telex 24460 TTSUPP

Owner *News International*   **Editor** *Stuart MacLure CBE*   **Circulation** 109,000

FOUNDED 1910. WEEKLY. New contributors are welcome, and should phone with ideas for news or features, write for reviews.

Arts and Books *Michael Church*   Unsolicited reviews are not accepted. Anyone wanting to review should write, sending examples of their work and full details of their academic and professional background to either the Literary Editor or the Media and Resources Editor. Maximum length 1200 words. **Media and Resources Editor** *Gillie Macdonald* **Features** *Bob Doe*   *Platform*: A weekly slot for a well-informed, cogently argued viewpoint – maximum length 1500 words; *Second Opinion*: A shorter comment on an issue of the day by somebody well placed to write on the subject – maximum length 570 words; *Features*: These are longer articles on contemporary practical subjects of general interest to the *TES* reader. Longer or multi-part features are rarely accepted – maximum length 1000–1500 words. *Payment* varies. **Extra** *Pamela Cooley*   Subjects covered include: science, travel, music, modern languages, home economics, school visits, primary education, history, geography, mathematics, health, life skills, environmental education, CDT, special needs. Articles should relate to current educational practice. Age range covered is primary to sixth form. Maximum length 1000–1300 words. *Payment* £65 per 1000 words.

Times Educational Supplement Scotland
56 Hanover Street, Edinburgh EH2 2DZ ☏031–225 6393

Owner *Times Newspapers Ltd* **Editor** *Willis Pickard* Circulation 6500

FOUNDED 1965. WEEKLY. Unsolicited mss welcome, but many more are received than can be used.

Features Articles on education in Scotland. Maximum 1500 words. *Payment* NUJ rates for NUJ members. **News** News items on education in Scotland. Maximum 600 words.

The Times Literary Supplement
Priory House, St John's Lane, London EC1M 4BX ☏01–253 3000
Telex 24460 Answerback TTSUPP

Owner *News International* **Editor** *Jeremy Treglowan* Circulation 30,000

FOUNDED 1902. WEEKLY review of literature. Contributors should approach in writing, and be familiar with the general level of writing in the *TLS*.

Libraries Articles considered on libraries and archives, both famous and out of the way, in which the author has spent some time engaged on a particular subject. Potential contributors are advised to consult back issues, and write briefly to the Editor proposing their subject. **News** *Andrew Hislop* News stories and general articles concerned with literature, publishing and new intellectual developments anywhere in the world. Length by agreement. *Payment* at NUJ rates.

Titbits
Northcliffe House, London EC4Y 0JA ☏01–583 0350

Owner *Mail Newspapers plc* **Editor** *Brian Lee* Circulation 160,000

FOUNDED 1881. MONTHLY. There are opportunities for freelance contributors with features on show business, television, pop music, medical topics, women's interests, animals and pets, royalty and the supernatural. Unsolicited manuscripts are welcomed, but ten are received every day so write with ideas in first instance.

Features Maximum length 1500 words. *Payment* £80–120. No news stories or fiction required, but there is a call for 100-word 'fillers'. *Payment* for these is £8.

Today's Guide
17–19 Buckingham Palace Road, London SW1W 0PT ☎01–834 6242

Owner *Girl Guides Association* **Editor** *Mrs J. V. Rush* Circulation 25,000

FOUNDED 1962. MONTHLY aimed at Girl Guides aged 10–14 years. Unsolicited mss welcome.

Features and Fiction General interest with a Guiding background. Maximum 750–1000 words. *Payment* £26 per 1000 words pro rata.

Tracks
5 Pemberton Row, London EC4 3BA ☎01–353 0369 Fax 01-583 1415

Owner *Trevor Wells* **Editor** *Deanne Pearson* Circulation 500,000

FOUNDED 1985. MONTHLY aimed at singles and albums buyers, mainly of chart music but also country, retro and film soundtracks. The magazine also covers films, video and books. Unsolicited manuscripts are not welcome: telephone with idea in the first instance and follow up with brief synopsis in writing.

Features Should be tied in with monthly albums/singles releases. Also major film/video releases, books and compact discs. There is also a new band section focusing predominantly on signed bands. Freelance suggestions welcome in this area, particularly exclusive access to big name artists. Maximum length 2000 words. *Payment* £70 per 1000 words.   **News** Not much opportunity for freelance contributions, but inside information, not available from usual PR sources, is welcome. Maximum length 200 words. *Payment* £70 per 1000 words (£10 minimum). **Reviews** Subjects as for **Features**. 350 words maximum. *Payment* £70 per 1000 words (£10 minimum).

Traditional Homes
Schweppes House, Grosvenor Road, St Albans, Herts, AL1 3TN ☎0727 59166

Owner *Benn Consumer Publications* Circulation 25,000

FOUNDED 1984. MONTHLY magazine covering conservation, architecture, antiques and interior design. Unsolicited mss are welcome. *Payment* £100 per 1000 words.

Traditional Interior Decoration
BCP Schweppes House, Grosvenor Road, St Albans, Herts, AL1 3TN
☎0727 59166

Owner *Benn Consumer Publications* **Editor** *Jo Newson* Circulation 40,000

FOUNDED 1986. BI-MONTHLY from Autumn 1987. Unsolicited mss welcome but it's preferable to submit a full proposal in writing. They receive around four per issue.

Features of up to 3000 words considered on houses with impressive interiors, decoration, furnishing and collections.   **News** Under 'Carousel' section, short write-ups of a maximum of 500 words are welcomed on conservation, interiors, events, exhibitions in art and antiques world. Other sections include 'Bazaar' which covers new products and companies including crafts and design; and 'Under the Hammer' which reviews and previews auctions. Maximum length 2500 words. *Payment* varies.

Trailfinder Magazine
42–48 Earls Court Road, London W8 6EJ ☎01–937 9631 Telex 919670

Owner *Trailfinders Ltd* **Editor** *Linda Nightingale/Richard Greenhill*

Circulation 175,000

FOUNDED 1971. Three issues a year (March, July & December) of this travel magazine. Unsolicited mss are welcome and prospective contributors should make initial contact in writing. No fiction. **Features** *Linda Nightingale* Lightweight, anecdotal travel features, specialising in Asia, Australasia, Far East, North and South America and Africa are welcomed. Maximum length 1000 words. *Payment* £50 (plus £15 for accompanying colour transparency & £10 B & W).

The Traveller
45 Brompton Road, London SW3 1DE ☎01–581 4130 Telex 297155 WEXAS G

Owner *Dr I. M. Wilson/Wexas* **Editor** *Melissa Shales* **Circulation** 31,000

FOUNDED 1970. Three issues a year. Unsolicited mss welcome, but a preliminary letter is preferred.

Features Four colour features per issue – authors should supply pictures. Contributors' guidelines available with s.a.e., but all articles should be off-beat, independent, travel-based. Maximum 2000 words. *Payment* £50 per 1000 words.

Travelling on Business
St George's House, 44 Hatton Garden, London EC1N 8ER ☎01–242 7744

Owner *Ravenshead Press Ltd* **Editor** *Peter D. Smith* **Circulation** 21,000

FOUNDED 1982. QUARTERLY. Most articles, which are about business travel and of general management interest, are commissioned. Any approach should be in writing.

Features Maximum length 1500 words. *Payment* negotiable.

Tribune
308 Gray's Inn Road, London WC1X 8DY ☎01–278 0911

Editor *Phil Kelly* **Circulation** 10,000

'We have plenty of opportunities for freelances, though unfortunately we can't pay them anything.' Opportunities in features – current affairs with the emphasis on left politics; reviewing, and newswriting. Either send mss in on spec or ring to discuss an idea.

Features Editor *Paul Anderson*

Trout Fisherman
Bretton Court, Bretton, Peterborough PE3 8DZ ☎0733 264666

Owner *EMAP Pursuit Publications* **Editor** *Chris Dawn* Circulation 36,000

FOUNDED 1977. MONTHLY instructive magazine on trout fishing. Most of the articles are commissioned, but unsolicited mss welcome.

Features *Steve Windsor* Maximum 1500 words. *Payment* varies.

True Romances
12–18 Paul Street, London EC2A 4JS ☎01–247 8233 Telex 8951167

Owner *Argus Consumer Publications* **Editor** *Isobel Irvine* Circulation 90,000

FOUNDED 1934. MONTHLY. Confessional romantic fiction aimed at the teen and twenties market.

Fiction Editor *Gill Pilcher* Occasionally use unsolicited mss, though receive 'too many'. Subjects: teenage/young love/young marrieds, written in first person. More offbeat than others in this market. 'Lovemaking takes place only within long-term faithful relationships'. *Words* 1000–6000. *Payment* negotiable on acceptance. **News/Features** all written in-house.

TV Times
247 Tottenham Court Road, London W1P 0AU ☎01–323 3222 Telex 24643

Owner *ITP Ltd* **Editor** *Anthony Peagam* Circulation 3,003,017

FOUNDED 1968. WEEKLY magazine of listings and features serving the viewers of Independent Television. Almost no freelance contributions used, except where the writer is known and trusted by the magazine. No unsolicited contributions.

The Universe
33–39 Bowling Green Lane, London EC1R 0AB ☎01–278 7321

Editor *Kevin Rafferty* Circulation 160,902

Occasional use of new writers, though a substantial network of regular contributors exists. Interested in a very wide range of material, all subjects which might bear on Christian life, from politics to occasional fiction. *Payment* negotiable.

Vector
23 Oakfield Road, Croydon, Surrey CR0 2UD ☎01–688 6081

Owner *British Science Fiction Association* **Editor** *David V. Barrett*
Circulation 1300

FOUNDED 1957. BI-MONTHLY. The critical journal of the BSFA, containing articles mainly about science fiction and its writers. Unsolicited mss welcome, especially if authoritative and well-written, but most contributors are either professional science fiction authors or BSFA members. No fiction.

Book Reviews *Paul Kincaid.* Most are submitted by BSFA members. Should be no longer than 500 words. **Features** Articles up to 4000 words are welcome. **Interviews** with SF authors, editors, publishers etc. are welcome. Maximum length 4000 words. No payment.

The Vegan
33/35 George Street, Oxford OX1 2AY ☎0865 722166

Owner *Vegan Society* **Editor** *Colin Howlett* **Circulation** 10,000

FOUNDED 1944. QUARTERLY. Features articles on the ethical, dietary, ecological or other aspects of veganism. Unsolicited mss welcome. Maximum 1500 words. *Payment* low but negotiable.

The Vegetarian
Parkdale, Dunham Road, Altrincham, Cheshire WA14 4OG ☎061–928 0793

Owner *Vegetarian Society UK Ltd* **Editor** *Bronwen Humphreys*

Circulation 20,000

FOUNDED 1848. BI-MONTHLY. Unsolicited mss welcome, but no cookery or herb growing, please.

Consumer News *Rosie Billings* All products must be vegetarian. **Features** Animal rights issues, world food problem with vegetarian angle, vegetarian sports people or celebrities, plus anything vegetarian with an unusual slant, organic gardening etc. Maximum 1000 words plus photo or illustration. **Young vegetarians** *Jean Anderson* Special pages for young people. *Payment* negotiable (small).

Video – The Magazine
8 Dorset Square, London NW1 6PU ☎01–723 8823

Owner *Alan Walsh* **Editor** *Martin Coxhead* **Circulation** 24,000

FOUNDED 1983. MONTHLY. Few opportunities for freelances, but ideas for original topics within the video field may be considered if submitted in writing.

Vogue
Vogue House, Hanover Square, London W1R 0AD ☎01–499 9080

Owner *Condé Nast* **Editor** *Anna Wintour* **Circulation** 166,639

The arrival of Anna Wintour from America is still causing ripples of change in the look and style of the magazine. Features are upmarket general interest rather than 'women's', with a good proportion of highbrow art and literary articles, as well as travel features, gardens, food, home interest, reviews. Typically of Condé Nast magazines, tend to use known writers and commission what's needed, rather than using unsolicited mss. Contacts are useful. No fiction.

Features Editor *Emma Soames*

Waterways World

Kottingham House, Dale Street, Burton-on-Trent, Staffs DE14 3TD ☎0283 42721
Telex 342260 Zilec G

Owner *Waterway Productions Ltd* **Editor** *Hugh Potter* **Circulation** 18,129

FOUNDED 1972. MONTHLY magazine for inland waterway enthusiasts. Unsolicited mss welcome, provided the writer has a good knowledge of the subject. No fiction.

Features *Hugh Potter* Articles (preferably illustrated) are published on all aspects of inland waterways in Britain and abroad including recreational and commercial boating on rivers and canals. **News** *Euan Corrie* Maximum length 500 words. *Payment* £20 per 1000 words.

Wedding and Home

Greater London House, Hampstead Road, London NW1 7SD ☎01–388 3171

Owner *Home and Law* **Editor** *Maggi Taylor* **Circulation** 40,000

BI-MONTHLY for newlyweds setting up home. Most features are written in-house or commissioned from known freelances. Unsolicited mss are not welcome, but approaches may be made in writing.

Weekend

New Carmelite House, Carmelite Street, London EC4Y 0JA ☎01–353 6000

Owner *Mail Newspapers plc* **Editor** *Graham Love* **Circulation** 280,000

FOUNDED 1953. WEEKLY. Freelance contributions are welcomed, should be 800 words maximum, and sent to the Features Editor. Preferred subjects are showbiz features, especially British and American 'soaps', royalty, fashion and beauty, general human interest and true life dramas.

Features *Grant Lockhart* *Payment* £100 for 800 words.

Weekly News

Albert Square, Dundee DD1 9QJ ☎0382 23131

Owner *D. C. Thomson & Co. Ltd* **Editor** *W. Kelly* **Circulation** 786,096

Newsy, family oriented and quaintly old fashioned magazine designed to appeal to the busy housewife. 'We get a lot of unsolicited stuff and there is great loss of life among them'. Usually commission, but writers of promise will be taken up. Series include Showbiz, Royals, Television. No fiction. *Payment* negotiable.

Weight Watchers Magazine

141–143 Drury Lane, London WC2B 5TS ☎01–836 4433

Owner *GAT Publishing* **Editor** *Gilly Love* **Circulation** 107,000

Bi-MONTHLY. For slimmers and the health-conscious. Unsolicited mss not normally accepted, but approaches may be made in writing.

Features *Joanna Briscoe* Features are usually commissioned by editor or features editor – length and rates vary depending on subject.

What Car
38–42 Hampton Road, Teddington, Middlesex TW11 0JE ☎01–977 8787

Owner *Haymarket Publishing Ltd* **Editor** *Sam Brown* **Circulation** 115,053

Reports on cars, and consumer based articles to do with motoring generally. Freelances are used for both, but testing is only offered to the few, and general articles on aspects of driving must be by writers known and trusted by the magazine, as some of the conclusions they come to can be controversial, and need to be scrupulously researched. Not interested in receiving unsolicited mss. *Payment* NUJ rates.

What Investment
Consort House, 26 Queensway, London W2 3RX ☎01–229 3488 Telex 23260

Owner *Publishing Holdings* **Editor** *Stephen Ellis* **Circulation** 30,000

FOUNDED 1983. MONTHLY. Features articles on a variety of savings and investment matters. Unsolicited mss not welcome. All approaches should be made in writing.

Features Maximum 2000 words (usually less). *Payment* NUJ rates.

What Mortgage
26 Queensway, London W2 3RX ☎01–229 3488

Owner *Publishing Holdings* **Editor** *Valerie Bayes* **Circulation** 20,000

FOUNDED 1983. MONTHLY magazine on property purchase, choice and finance. Unsolicited mss welcome; prospective contributors may make initial contact either by telephone or in writing.

Features Up to 1500 words on related topics are considered. Particularly welcome are new angles, new ideas or specialities. *Payment* £100 per 1000 words.

What's New in Building
Morgan-Grampian House, Calderwood Street, Woolwich, London SE18 6QH
☎01–855 7777 Telex 896238

Owner *Morgan-Grampian* **Editor** *Derrick Jolley* **Circulation** 35,500

MONTHLY. Specialist magazine covering new products for building; unsolicited manuscripts not generally welcome. The only freelance work is rewriting press release material. This is offered on a monthly basis of 25–50 items of about 150 words each. *Payment* £4.25 per item.

What's New in Farming

Morgan-Grampian plc, 30 Calderwood Street, Woolwich, London SE18 6QH
☎01–855 7777 (ext. 420)   Telex 896238

Owner *United Newspapers*   **Editor** *Stephen Mitchell*   **Circulation** 77,000

FOUNDED 1977. MONTHLY. The magazine is primarily a guide to new agricultural products, with little feature space. Most copy is written in-house, and unsolicited mss are not welcome.

Features *Stephen Mitchell/Jonathan Theobald*   Articles on relevant agricultural topics. Maximum length 2000 words. *Payment* negotiable.

What's New in Interiors

Morgan Grampian House, 30 Calderwood Street, London SE18 6QH
☎01–885 7777   Telex 896238 Morgan G

Owner *Morgan-Grampian Ltd*   **Editor** *Anthea Bain*   **Circulation** 13,519

FOUNDED 1981. Ten issues a year aimed at interior designers, architects and specifiers. Unsolicited manuscripts welcome if they are exclusive, well-researched and aimed at readership. Make initial contact in writing.

Features Good, technical journalists who know the market are always sought. Maximum length: 1500 words. Opportunity for writers of interiors application stories and specialised profiles.   **News** rarely published. *Payment* £100 per 1000 words.

Windsurfers Magazine

4 Granada House, Lower Stone Street, Maidstone, Kent ME15 6JP ☎0622 690606

Owner *Pacificon Limited*   **Editor** *Tym Manley*   **Circulation** 25,000

FOUNDED 1984. Nine issues a year. Unsolicited manuscripts are welcomed, if informative articles on windsurfing (maximum 2500 words). Prospective contributors are advised to make initial approach in writing. *Payment* £30 per 1000 words.

Wine

55 Heath Road, Twickenham, Middlesex TW1 4AW   ☎01–891 6070

Owner *The Euro Publishing Co.*   **Editor** *Joanna Simon*   **Circulation** 40,000

FOUNDED 1983. MONTHLY. Unsolicited mss not welcome.

News and Features Wine, food and travel stories. Prospective contributors should approach in writing.

Wisden Cricket Monthly
6 Beech Lane, Guildford, Surrey GU2 5ES ☎0483 32573

Owner *Wisden Cricket Magazines Ltd*   **Editor** *David Frith*   **Circulation** *c*.42,000

FOUNDED 1979. MONTHLY. Very few uncommissioned articles are used, but would-be contributors are 'not discouraged': approach in writing.

Woman and Home
King's Reach Tower, Stamford Street, London SE1 9LS
☎01–261 5423   Telex 915748 MAGDIV G

Owner *IPC Magazines*   **Editor** *Sue Dobson*   **Circulation** 557,604

FOUNDED 1926. MONTHLY. Unsolicited contributions – of which 200 are received each month – are not welcome; prospective contributors are advised to write with ideas, plus photocopies of other published work or details of magazines to which they have contributed. Most freelance work is specially commissioned.

Features *Jean Williams*   **Fiction** *Kati Nichol*   Short stories are usually submitted by agents, serials are always submitted by agents or publishers.

OTHER DEPARTMENTS

Fashion, home, knitting, beauty, cookery and travel, all covered by staff writers and specially commissioned freelances. No poetry is published. An s.a.e. is required for return of mss. *Payment c*.£90 per 1000 words.

Woman's Journal
IPC Magazines, King's Reach Tower, Stamford Street, London SE1 9LS
☎01–261 6220   Telex 915748 MAGDIV G

Owner *IPC Magazines*   **Editor** *Laurie Purden*

MONTHLY. Unsolicited non-fiction mss welcome.

Features *Victor Olliver*   Maximum length 2500 words. Major features are generally commissioned but new ideas on all subjects welcome.   **Fiction** *Christie Hickman* Maximum length 4000 words. Unsolicited material is not accepted; stories are mainly bought from agents and publishers direct. Also **Food** *Katie Stewart*   **Fashion** *Alex Parnell* **Beauty** *Vicci Bentley* **Design and Homes** *Jane Graining*. *Payment* negotiable.

Woman's Own
King's Reach Tower, Stamford Street, London SE1 9LS ☎01–261 5474

Owner *IPC Magazines*   **Editor** *Bridget Rowe*   **Circulation** 1,065,367

WEEKLY. Prospective contributors should contact the features editor in writing in the first instance before making a submission.

Features *Caro Thompson*   **Fiction** *Susan Oudot*   Unsolicited fiction manuscripts are not accepted, but there is an annual short story competition, for which the first prize in 1986 was £5000 of Prudential Unit Trusts. Maximum length for fiction is 3000 words.

Woman's Realm

King's Reach Tower, Stamford Street, London SE1 9LS ☎01–261 5708

Owner *IPC Magazines Ltd* **Editor** *Judith Hall* **Circulation** 608,034

FOUNDED 1958. WEEKLY. Scope here for freelances who should write in the first instance to the appropriate editor.

Features *Sarah Touquet* Interested in one page human interest pieces or emotional features. 1200–2000 words. *Payment* at NUJ rates. Best vehicle for new freelances is the half-page humorous slot, described as 'wry looks at family life', *c.*700 words. *Payment* £100. **Fiction** *Sally Bowden* One short story and a serial instalment used every week. Aimed at an intelligent, family-minded woman aged 23 upwards. Very wide range; not much romance. A high standard of writing is essential. Serials are usually bought from agents or publishers but ideas for serials (with sample chapter) welcomed. 1000–4000 words. *Payment* £150 and upwards.

Woman's Story

12–18 Paul Street, London EC2A 4JS ☎01–247 8233

Owner *Argus Consumer Publications* **Editor** *Gillian Pilcher* **Circulation** 58,000

MONTHLY sister magazine to *True Story* and *True Romances*.

Fiction welcome: finished manuscripts, not ideas, should be addressed to the editor. No serials. Receive 80–100 mss weekly. Subjects: romantic, domestic crises, marriage and job problems. An older market than its sister magazines. No explicit sex. Written in 1st or 3rd person, possibly from a man's viewpoint. Twists of plot, uncertain endings are frequent features. 1500–5000 words. *Payment* on acceptance.

Woman's Weekly

King's Reach Tower, Stamford Street, London SE1 9LS ☎01–261 6131

Owner *IPC Magazines* **Editor** *Brenda McDougall* **Circulation** 1,338,553

Mass market women's weekly, now competing with *Woman* and *Woman's Own*, and like them concerned with strong human interest, film and television personalities, as well as a more traditional, homemaking angle. Occasionally use freelances, but at this level tend to be experienced magazine journalists. **Fiction Editor** *Linda O'Byrne*. Short stories 2500–4500 words; serials of 45–55,000 words. Their guidelines for fiction writers – 'a strong romantic emotional sensual theme . . . with a conflict not resolved until the end' (serials); short stories are more varied. They get around 500 unsolicited stories a month.

Woman's World
25 Newman Street, London W1   ☏ 01–631 3939

Owner *Carlton Publishing*   **Editor** *Kerry Mackenzie*   **Circulation** 208,000

FOUNDED 1977. MONTHLY. There are opportunities for freelances but it is best advised
to write with ideas and samples of published work in the first instance. Approximately 150 unsolicited mss are received every week.

Women's Review
Unit 1, Second Floor, 1–4 Christina Street, London EC2A 4PA   ☏ 01–739 4906

Owner *Women's Review Ltd*   **Editors** *Helen Carr, Nicci Gerrard*
                                                         Circulation 16,000

FOUNDED 1985. MONTHLY. Arts based magazine. Freelance contributors are used for
features on the arts. Each issue carries about ten features. Feature length articles are
usually 750–1000 words or 1500–2000 words long. One short story (2000 words) is
published per issue. Also reviews of books, music, visual arts, theatre, television and
film. Ten pages of reviews per issue. Prospective contributors are asked to supply
samples of previous work, and contact in writing with the editors is preferable to
sending unsolicited mss. *Payment* All contributors are paid at the rate of £45 per 1000
words.

Workbox
40 Silver Street, Wiveliscombe, Somerset TA4 2NY   ☏ 0984 24033

Owner *Audrey Babington*   **Editor** *Audrey Babington*   **Circulation** 30,000

FOUNDED 1984. Two issues a year. Articles are commissioned; no unsolicited manuscripts. The magazine caters for the enthusiast and professional in all branches of
needlecrafts.

Features cover a *very* wide range of needlecrafts and should *not* be 'how to make'
items.   **News** Any items welcomed especially about new products.

Work-out Magazine
City House, 72–80 Leather Lane, London EC1N 7TR   ☏ 01–831 6219

Owner *W. V. Publications Ltd*   **Acting Editor** *Julie Milton*   **Circulation** 42,000

Title bought in 1985. MONTHLY. Health and exercise magazine. Unsolicited mss
welcome; however a number of freelance contributors are regularly used.

Features on topics covered by magazine, often with human interest involvement.
Maximum length 1000 words.   **News** In-house only. *Payment* approximately
£50–60.

World of Knitting

1–2 East Market Street, Newport, Gwent NP9 2AY   ☎ 0633 58216

Owner *Sandra Williams*   **Editor** *Sandra Williams*   Circulation 29,114

FOUNDED 1983. Unsolicited mss welcome on knitting and related crafts. Prospective contributors are advised to make initial contact in writing, outlining proposal and accompanied by illustration where appropriate. No fiction.

Features up to 1000 words on yarns, knitwear fashions as well as 'how-to-make' pieces. Special features, e.g. picture knitting, Fair Isle patterns, etc., are particularly sought after.   **News** Reports up to 1000 words on knitting-related subjects. *Payment* around £50 per 1000 words.

Yachting Monthly

Room 2209, King's Reach Tower, Stamford Street, London SE1 9LS

☎ 01–261 6040   Telex 915748 MAGDIV G

Owner *IPC Magazines*   **Editor** *Andrew Bray*   Circulation 41,656

FOUNDED 1906. MONTHLY magazine for yachting enthusiasts. Unsolicited mss are welcome, but between 40 and 50 are received each month. Prospective contributors should make initial contact in writing.

Features *Miles Clark* A wide range of features concerned with maritime subjects & cruising under sail; well researched and innovative material always welcome, especially if accompanied by photographs. Maximum length 2250 words. *Payment* maximum £72 per 1000 words.   **News** *Andrew Bray*   News items (up to a maximum of 500 words) are received from a series of correspondents 'Round the Coast'. *Payment* £4.75 per 100 words.

You Magazine (Mail on Sunday)

New Carmelite House, Carmelite Street, London EC4Y 0JA   ☎ 01–353 6000

Editor *Eve Pollard*

Lively, substantial colour supplement whose many feature articles are supplied entirely by freelance writers. These tend to be established magazine journalists: 'as far as we know there hasn't yet been a single case of an unsolicited feature ending in publication'. In such a competitive market there is a glut of talent anyway. On the other hand, always hoping to find new writers who understand their needs. Articles, whether general interest or issue based, are always people oriented, and interview based. This is the only general guideline in writing for the magazine; otherwise, it's a strong idea that counts. Send these to the **Commissioning Editor** *John Koski*. Other contacts on the Commissioning Desk are *Laurie Sharples*, *Tim Willis*, *Hugh St Clair*, and *Gordon McKenzie*.

Young Mother

24/25 Cowcross Street, London EC1M 6DQ ☎01–253 1691

Owner *Family Publications Ltd* **Editorial Director** *David Peck*

Circulation 100,000

FOUNDED 1986. BI-MONTHLY. Features information and articles of interest to those caring for young children aged 2–5 years. Unsolicited mss welcome, but ideas in writing are preferred.

Features Maximum 2500 words. *Payment* by negotiation.

Your Horse

Bretton Court, Bretton, Peterborough, Cambs PE3 8DZ ☎0733 264666

Owner *EMAP* **Editor** *Liz Benwell* Circulation 37,783

A magazine for all ages which deals with practical horsecare: the skills and problems involved in keeping or riding horses. They get a lot of unsolicited offerings from knowledgeable readers, some of which are used. But it's best to send ideas in the first instance, to the editor.

Yours Newspaper

12 Bedford Row, London WC1R 4DU ☎01–404 4320 Telex 32157 EMAPPB G

Owner *Help the Aged* **Editor** *Andrew Blackford* Circulation 131,300

FOUNDED 1973. MONTHLY. Readership is in the age group of 55 plus and unsolicited mss are welcome.

Features Maximum length 1000 words, and genuinely appealing to readership, would be considered. **Fiction** – as for features. **News** Short newsy items (300 to 500 words) of interest to readership are welcomed. *Payment* negotiable.

Sound and Screen

Broadcasting is the writers' honeypot. Anyone who flicks through the *Radio* or *TV Times* can spot the goodies. Plays, features, documentaries – the opportunities are apparently limitless. But hold on. Nothing in writing is ever that easy.

Remember, first, that all the broadcasting organisations are generously staffed with producers, directors, researchers and reporters who, in varying degrees, believe themselves to be capable of writing their own material.

Then there is the huge input of the regular freelancers and independents to accommodate. Notwithstanding the ever inflating schedules, whole areas of broadcasting are overendowed with programme material. This is why, for example, the chances of breaking into TV or radio documentaries depends on the good fortune of catching the right producer with the right idea at the right time. It also helps to boast either a household name or one that inspires respect within an area of relevant expertise. David Hockney on modern art is more than likely to attract interest; Fred Nugget on the same subject, less so.

Next, bear in mind that there are closely confined limits to what is regarded by the career broadcasters as acceptable viewing or listening. Bound by convention to seek a balanced presentation of topical issues, the effect is to avoid promoting one main line political or social argument at the expense of any other main line political or social argument, and to relegate all controversial minority opinions to the sidelines.

The tendency towards conservatism has been reinforced by worries that a Tory government might push harder for a deregulation of the broadcasting authorities if they too obviously step out of line. The BBC is the prime target for ministerial criticism – over staffed, over paid and over powerful – but the independent network is nervous that its turn will come. The signal all round is not to take risks by offending the power brokers.

Another guideline in trying to judge what is likely to find favour is the character of the broadcasters themselves. Mostly they tend towards the Oxbridge liberal tradition. This does not mean that they necessarily attended Oxford or Cambridge (though a very high proportion do spring directly from those universities into the BBC or ITV). It does mean that they lean towards certain attitudes associated with the higher education best favoured by the intellectual middle class. These embrace a higher regard for British institutions (including those responsible for making TV and radio programmes), a suspicion of the offbeat, a devotion to worthy causes, and a respect for money contrasted with a tepid interest in the processes of wealth creation. When there is a choice, culture comes before commerce.

It is within this context that writers should assess the market. Idealists who want to change the world, or even a small part of the world, are best advised to write books, articles or fringe plays. The time to take to the airwaves is when they have worked off their excess radicalism in another medium. Broadcasters will deny the criticism, pointing to their bold patronage of such diverse and innovative talents as Dylan Thomas, Joe Orton and Dennis Potter. But the days of living dangerously are long ago and far away. It is doubtful if any of these writers would have made their breakthrough in today's setting.

An overwhelming proportion of broadcasting output is bland and inoffensive. Though possibly good of its sort, it will not set the world on fire or be remembered in twenty years.

Thus disabused of false optimism, where should fledgling writers try their luck? If money is not the prime consideration, local radio is a good place to start.

Talks and contributions to magazine programmes are welcomed if they are limited to subjects close to home and delivered in a style which grabs attention. What that style might be is a value judgement reserved by the producer. But do not be inhibited by an unconventional accent. Nowadays, as Derek Jameson will tell you, there is no such thing as a 'current' radio accent.

Plays are a rarity on local radio. The stations simply do not have the resources. The way might be made easier if direct sponsorship of plays by advertisers was allowed but this is against the rules. A few of the more enterprising stations, like **Radio Clyde**, skirt the problem by cooperating with public service groups to produce drama documentaries.

Radio

To jump to the other end of the scale, national radio (another way of saying the BBC) is the biggest single market for freelancers in the country. Quite apart from special reports, story readings and talks, Radios 3 and 4 transmit some five hundred new plays every year – about fifty times more than the **National Theatre** and the **Royal Shakespeare Company** put together. One unit alone, *The Afternoon Play*, is responsible for three productions a week. But competition is stiff. Richard Imison, chief script editor and deputy head of radio drama, receives anything up to ten thousand scripts a year and about half that number again of synopses. He says his department is 'almost overwhelmed with material', adding, 'the general standard of what is submitted is remarkably competent'.

It is easy to understand why radio drama attracts so many talented writers. Even with the restraints on subject matter, there is the chance on radio to let the imagination fly in a way that would be impossible in live theatre or on screen. Then there is the comforting knowledge that the words will be spoken by masters of their craft. Many a modest radio play has been lifted above its station by the quality of the actors. The best of them work on radio and, like writers, tolerate the miserable fees because they enjoy the freedom to play against physical type and age. It also helps that they do not have to put on costumes or learn lines.

The writer who is making his first assault on radio drama, and is not best buddy of an influential producer, should send his script to the Script Editor (Drama) at Broadcasting House (see listing for full address). The professional will include a brief description of the play, a list of characters and the approximate running time. His name and address will appear on the first page.

To be readable a script needs, above all, plenty of spacing. There is no need to embellish the text with detailed studio instructions – they are bound to be changed anyway – as long as it is clear who is speaking to whom and in what circumstances.

A synopsis with specimen dialogue may well lead to encouraging words. But unless the writer is established, ideas alone rarely lead to a direct commission. Newcomers are expected to turn in the complete product before hearing their verdict. This makes an interesting contrast to book publishing where even the beginner can expect some cash up front to help him finish the manuscript. It is all a question of supply and demand. Publishers have to try harder for quality material.

By all accounts, BBC readers are conscientious in evaluating everything that is sent to them. But for this reason, nobody should expect a quick response. A two or three months wait is common even for a straight rejection. A further wait suggests that the writer has become part of the BBC's internal politics. Somebody for some reason is nervous of saying 'yes' but reluctant to say 'no'. Early in his career when Alan Bennett sent a play to the BBC (television in this case) they took so long to think about it that when an acceptance did come through the play had been on in the West End for six months.

To move on from radio plays to talks and features, here again there is an excess of material. The story goes that when Michael Green took over as controller of Radio 4 he inherited over four hundred features commissioned and produced but never transmitted.

For the contributor, the frustration is in finding the right person to talk to and then, having sold an idea, to make sure it is written and broadcast before his patron changes jobs, or otherwise loses interest.

Though the freelance slots are less obvious than in drama, long running programmes like *Woman's Hour* or *You and Yours*, which also have their quota of specials, are worth cultivating. A feature sent to a head of department responsible for several programmes is likely to start a marathon from one producer's desk to another. Unless the writer strikes lucky, the process can last for ever.

Comedy programmes like *Week Ending* and *The News Huddlines* are in the market for short sketches. Success here can be an entrée to the world of comedy series where, for once, there is a dearth of good material. But if demand is high so is the failure rate. Perhaps the broadcasters are their own worst enemies in calling for more and yet more situation comedies – a patch of humour which has been so heavily cultivated as to be close to exhaustion. Iconoclastic humour in the tradition of The Goons and Monty Python is now a rarity though when it is tried, as in the marvellous *Radio Active* series, the BBC achieves its declared objective of reaching a younger audience.

Morning Story is a great radio institution which relies exclusively on outside contributors. With a quarter hour slot, anything of more than two and a half thousand words is overwritten. A strong plot stands a better chance with the editor than impressive writing. Steer clear of controversial topics.

Specialist journalists who are not career broadcasters can often find themselves a comfortable niche within the BBC, in sports, say, or current affairs where they are not so much reporters as professional interviewers. The call for expertise also attracts certain voluble academics.

Educational broadcasting is thick with specialists but is ever hungry for more. Despite having to stick with a narrow curriculum and to work on pathetic budgets, programmes for school and college are a good training ground for those who want to talk and write.

Television

All that has been said of radio carries over to television – but with double emphasis. The competition between the BBC and ITV increases the value of the writer but the complexity of the system can make it difficult for even the most talented newcomer to find a suitable point of entry.

The market for single plays has contracted over the years under pressure from series and serials. These have the advantage of building up audience loyalty to a point where viewers switch on as a matter of routine. The temptation is to try to break into a series by offering a sample episode. But this is nearly always a waste of time either because the programmes will have been stockpiled before transmission or because one or more writers will have been hired at an early stage to cover the entire run.

An easier way forward is to contact the various departments or individual producers to ask what is coming in the future. There is a chance then of getting in on the ground floor. The prospects of success are improved enormously if the writer is in an alliance with a good expert who specialises in film and TV (see *Agents* listing). But agents who stay in business are very choosy about their clients. Not one of them will move a step on behalf of a dubious or untried talent.

A writer who is prepared to try his luck by sending in material to one or other of the script units (see listing for addresses) should first study the advice and information leaflets put out by the BBC. Here, for example, are the guiding principles for writing situation comedy:

'The laughs should arise naturally and logically from the interactions of character and plot, not from a string of gags and funny lines fired off into the blue. Where so many beginners go wrong is that they provide no situation: the characters are not at grips with each other over some matter that is important to them, in which something crucial is at stake. Famous comedy series like *Dad's Army, The Good Life, Porridge* and *Sorry* were very different, but they all had one thing in common: fundamentally they were about the serious matter of sheer survival in the teeth of perilous circumstances. This is what made them funny. Do not be seduced into following in the steps of somebody like, say, Roy Clarke since it needs great experience and tremendous skill to pull off something like *The Last of the Summer Wine*.'

There is no need to write an entire series to prove the attractions of an idea – one pilot episode with a few brief storylines is the most that is needed.

Schools television programmes and children's programmes are open to ideas for drama series and single plays. A telephone call to these departments at the BBC or at any of the independent companies will indicate the latest range of opportunities.

In the next few years the television market for writers is likely to expand and to diversify. Part of the reason is the development of satellite TV. A recent deal between **British Telecom International** and the Luxembourg-based **Astra** satellite company will soon allow British households to tune in to eight additional channels. And more are on the way. But while investment in technology increases apace, little thought seems to have been given to programme making. When the realisation finally sinks in that viewers are not prepared to tolerate endless repeats of old movies, the demand for new writing will show an encouraging growth.

Diversification will come about with the greater contribution of the independent production companies to the output of the BBC and ITV. Their role was established with the birth of Channel 4 in 1980 but since then the Peacock Committee on broadcasting has recommended that 40 per cent of BBC and ITV programmes should be supplied by independent producers. A first move in this direction was taken recently by the BBC who have set aside twenty million pounds over the next three years to commission four hundred network and one hundred regional programme hours from the independents. ITV is set to follow.

Corporate Television

Contacts with independent producers (see listings) might bring other dividends in the shape of offers to write for corporate television. This latest piece of jargon refers to videos and films made for commercial, industrial and government organisations. They can range from training programmes and the video equivalent of house magazines to prestige propaganda and advertising features. The market is difficult to assess but estimates go as high as an annual expenditure of three hundred million pounds which translates into at least six thousand productions.

The problems for writers involved in corporate television is the absence of any guidelines on payment. No doubt the **Writers' Guild** and other professional associations will soon have something to say about this. Meanwhile, the writer must fend for himself. Since he is working to a tight brief, usually with material supplied by the client, he is expected to surrender copyright. There is therefore no question of repeat fees or royalties. But if the production company is honest and the client is sensible enough to want a professional writer, the rewards can be up to the level of network television and far beyond that of radio.

A guess at standard rate would be two thousand pounds plus for an hour long programme. Some writers prefer to value their time on a daily rate and this too is generally acceptable.

If a writer and production company have not previously worked together it is as well to ask for an advance on payment to show goodwill. Some production companies with respectable client lists are nonetheless run on a shoestring. They are not above telling their accounts departments that when it comes to payments, writers are last in the pecking order. Whereas, of course, if there was any justice in the world, they would be first.

Basic Pay – Radio, Television and Film

The **Writers' Guild, The Society of Authors** and the **National Union of Journalists** have led the way in negotiating minimum fees for writers of radio and television scripts. Full details of their agreement with the broadcasting authorities can be obtained from these bodies (see *Professional Associations* listings for addresses) but the following is a guideline to the offers that writers might expect from the BBC and ITV.

Radio

- A beginner in radio drama should receive at least £915 for a sixty minute script. For an established writer – one who has three or more plays to his credit – the minimum rate goes up to £1386.
- Fees for dramatisations range from 60 to 85 per cent of the full drama rate depending on the degree of original material and dialogue.
- An attendance payment of £23.10 per production is paid to established writers.
- For talks, the level of fees starts at £9.15 per minute for script only and £12.45 per minute for script and read.
- Features and documentaries begin at £16.50 per minute with a minimum fee of £115.50.
- Higher fees are limited to writers' experience and to 'the particular circumstances of the engagement'.
- Fees for short stories start at a beginner's rate of £82.00 for 15 minutes rising to £107.50 for writers who have contributed six or more stories.
- Repeat fees are nearly always part of an agreement but terms vary according to the type of production.
- Basic rates for news reporting are covered by an NUJ agreement with the BBC and the Association of Independent Radio Contractors.
- For the BBC, news reports start at £25.10 for up to two minutes plus £5.68 for each extra minute on network radio. Local radio is £12.85 for up to two minutes plus £4.62 for each extra minute.
- In the commercial sector news reports make £13.50 for the first two minutes and £4.50 a minute thereafter.
- There are special day rates and separately negotiated fees for specialist reporting such as sports coverage.

Television

The following are examples of minimum rates negotiated by the **Writers' Guild** with the BBC and ITV.

- For a sixty minute teleplay the BBC will pay an established writer at least £4212 and a beginner £2673. The corresponding figures for ITV are £5189 for the

established writer, £3688 for a writer new to television, but with a solid reputation in books, film, radio or theatre, and £3535 for other writers.

● The day rates for attendance at read-throughs and rehearsals is £35 for the BBC
and £37.25 for ITV.

● The NUJ agreement on news reporting guarantees a BBC rate to freelances of
£30.94 for up to two minutes and £7.68 for each extra minute. The ITV rate is tied
to a minimum of £32.61.

Feature Films

An agreement between the **Writers' Guild, The British Film and Television
Producers' Association** and **The Independent Programme Producers' Association** allows for a minimum writer's fee of £20,000 on a high budget feature film (in
excess of £1½ million) and £12,000 on a lower budget movie. Writers can also expect
additional TV fees to cover transmission at home and abroad.

Television

London

BBC Breakfast Time
Lime Grove, London W12 7RJ   ☎01–576 7502

Editor *David Stanford*   **Contact** *Forward Planning*

BBC Television
Television Centre, Wood Lane, London W12 7RJ   ☎01–743 8000

Editor, Television News *Ron Neil* **Head of Current Affairs** *Peter Pagnamenta* **Head of Drama** *Jonathan Powell* **Features & Documentaries** *Will Wyatt* **Light Entertainment** *Jane Moir* **Comedy** *Gareth Gwenlan* **Music & Arts** *Alan Yentob* **Religious Programmes** *John Whale* **Children's Programmes** *Anna Home* **Series & Serials** *Colin Rogers* **Community Programmes** *Tony Laryea*

BBC TV Documentary Features
Kensington House, Richmond Way, London W14 0AX   ☎01–743 1272

Contact *Angela Holdsworth*

Channel 4
60 Charlotte Street, London W1P 2AX   ☎01–631 4444

Launched in November 1982, Channel 4 broadcasts 80 hours of programmes a week, all of them made by independent producers or other independent television companies. Channel 4 does not make any of its great diversity of programmes, except for the weekly *Right to Reply*. The role of its commissioning editors is to sift through proposals for programmes and see interesting projects through to broadcast.

Controller of Programmes *Paul Bonner* **Commissioning Editors: Entertainment** *Mike Bollard* **Fiction** *David Rose* **Education** *Naomi Sargeant* **Drama Series** *David Benedictus* **Young People** *John Cummins* **Multi Cultural** *Farrukh Dhondy* **Single Documentaries** *Nick Hart-Williams* **Arts** *Michael Kustow* **Current Affairs** *David Lloyd* **Documentary Series** *John Ranelagh*.

London Weekend Television

South Bank Television Centre, Kent House, Upper Ground, London SE1 9LT

☎01–261 3434

Makers of weekend entertainment viewing: *Blind Date, Cannon & Ball, Me & My Girl*; drama series like *A Fine Romance, To Have and to Hold, Mapp & Lucia*; also *The South Bank Show, Weekend World, The Late Clive James*. LWT provides a large proportion of the network's drama and light entertainment, and is a major supplier to Channel 4.

Head of Light Entertainment *Marcus Plantin* **Controller of Drama and Arts** *Nick Elliot* **Head of Arts** *Melvyn Bragg* **Deputy Controller of Drama** *Linda Agran* **Head of Features** *Jane Hewland* **Head of Current Affairs** *David Cox*.

Thames Television

306 Euston Road, London NW1 3RB ☎01–387 9494

Controller Drama *Lloyd Shirley* **Controller Features** *Catherine Freeman* **Head of Comedy** *James Gilbert* **Head of Documentaries** *Ian Martin* **Children's and Education** *Allan Horrox* **Controller Light Entertainment** *Philip Jones* **Head of News and Current Affairs** *Barrie Sales*. Perhaps the strongest of drama production departments: *Minder, Lytton's Diary, Paradise Postponed, Rumpole of the Bailey, The Secret Diary of Adrian Mole*. Light entertainment output includes *The Benny Hill Show, Give us a Clue, Fresh Fields* and *Executive Stress*. Documentaries have included *A People's War* and *Broken Hearts*. Children's programmes: *Rainbow, Sooty, Danger-mouse, Wind in the Willows*.

Midlands

BBC TV Midlands

Broadcasting Centre, Pebble Mill Road, Birmingham B5 7QQ ☎021–472 5353

Home of the Pebble Mill studio.

Head of Drama *Robin Midgley* One off plays, e.g. for the BBC 2 Summer Season series: *Rachel and the Roarettes, Boogie Outlaws, Lizzie's Pictures*, the 5 part thriller *Murder of a Moderate Man*, and Howard Brenton's *Dead Head*.

News and Current Affairs *Richard Thompson*

Also makers of one-offs like *Cool It* with Phil Cool, *Ebony*, the black magazine series, *Top Gear*, and *Farming*. *Farming*'s editor John Kenyon will seriously consider un-solicited material if well researched.

BBC TV Nottingham (BBC Midlands)

Wilson House, Derby Road, Nottingham N91 5HX ☎0602 472395

An opt-out station from BBC TV Midlands Birmingham office, and served by the programmes made in Birmingham. Nottingham makes local news only.

Central Independent Television

East Midlands Television Centre, Lenton Lane, Nottingham NG7 2NA
☎0602 863322 Telex 377696

Contact *Christopher Walker* (Head of Scripts)

'Although some television companies ask to see a synopsis first, the Script Unit always prefers to read scripts from new writers. However, it is rare for a finished script to be purchased – writers are normally assessed for possible future commissions.' A few single plays are made by the company, but the bulk of the Drama output takes the form of series and serials. The Light Entertainment department makes situation comedy series, and other shows which need sketches and one liners. Young People's Programmes include single plays for the 'Dramarama' slot, serials and light entertainment. The Script Unit welcomes scripts and tries to read everything which comes in. 'However, this process does take time, so writers should not expect an instant response'.

North-East

BBC TV Newcastle upon Tyne (North East)

Broadcasting House, 54 New Bridge Street, Newcastle upon Tyne, NE1 8AA
☎091–232 1313

Although Leeds is now the headquarters of the North East region, Newcastle continues to make its own programmes.

Features Editor *John Mapplebeck* Features, documentaries and drama come under this department. Very little drama is made, but there is a strong feature-making unit, particularly for programmes of direct local relevance. Recent programmes have included *Northwards*, and *Townscapes*. They make forty thirty-minute programmes a year, some of which are nationally broadcast. **News and Current Affairs** *John Bird*.

BBC TV North East

Broadcasting Centre, Woodhouse Lane, Leeds LS2 9PX ☎0532 441181

Since the reorganisation of the BBC television regions in 1987, Leeds is now the head of the North East region. Though presently its major production is the nightly news magazine programme *Look North*, there are plans to expand the repertoire.

Features Editor *Mark Roland* ·*Paper Kisses*, about love letters found from a soldier in the back of a cabinet. **Drama** none. **News Editor** *John Lingham*.

Tyne Tees

City Road, Newcastle upon Tyne, NE1 2AL ☎091–261 0181

Light Entertainment *Royston Mayoh* **Arts** *Heather Ging* **Current Affairs and Documentaries** *Michael Parthington* **Young People's Programmes** *Malcolm Gerrie* **News and Sport** *Clive Page* **Religious Programmes** *Maxwell Deas*.

Makers of *Supergran, Redbrick, Sayonara Pet*, and *Is Democracy Working?* among its most recent production credits. Also *The Tube, How Dare You* and *Get Fresh* in the light entertainment department. Under the aegis of Arts come programmes like *The Fancy*, about the devotion of man for pigeon, as well as more traditional arts subjects.

Yorkshire Television
TV Centre, Leeds LS3 1JS ☎0532 438283   Telex 557232

Editor *Richard Gregory*

Drama *Carol Williams*   Drama series, film productions, studio plays, and long-running series like *Emmerdale Farm*. Always looking for strong writing in these areas, and make great use of agents to find it. Around 20 unsolicited mss received weekly. Unknowns should submit at least the first act, ideally the first episode if submitting a series, and synopsis. **Documentaries** *John Willis*   Opportunities are rare here, as scripts are usually provided by producers. However, adaptations of published work put to the department as a documentary subject are considered. **Light Entertainment** *Vernon Lawrence*   Comedy series like *Rising Damp, Only When I Laugh*. Opportunities for writers of series/episodes in theory, but in reality there is a well-established circle of professionals in this area which it is difficult to infiltrate. Best approach is through a good agent. **Regional Features** *David Lowen*   Documentaries and special features. No scripts, ideas only. Recent output has included *Yorkshire Childhoods*.

North-West
BBC TV North West
New Broadcasting House, Oxford Road, Manchester M60 1SJ   ☎061–236 8444

Network production in Manchester breaks down into 4 departments: features, children's, sports, and entertainments.

Features *(General Programmes) Brass Tacks* **Editor** *Colin Cameron. Open Air* **Editor** *Peter Weil*   **Children's Editor** *Edward Pugh*   No children's drama – light entertainment for kids, like *It's Wicked*, and *The Saturday Picture Show*.   **Sports Editor** *Ian Edwards   A Question of Sport.   Entertainments* 'in a fragmented state at the moment'. *No Limits* and *Fax* current programmes.   **Executive Producer, Independent Productions** *Peter Ridsdale Scott*   Deals with proposals from independent producers (which the BBC is increasingly using), though not direct from writers alone.

Border Television
Television Centre, Durranhill, Carlisle, Cumbria CA1 3NT   ☎0228 25101
Telex 64122

Contact *Paul Corley* (Programme Controller)

News Editor *Lis Howell*   **Features** *Ken Stephinson*   **Drama/Light Entertainment** *Ken Stephinson*   **Documentaries etc** *Ken Stephinson, Paul Corley*   Most scripts are provided in-house but are occasionally commissioned. Writers should not submit written work apart from notes before their ideas have been fully discussed. In the last couple of years, Border has greatly increased its programme production, including children's television – light entertainment rather than drama. Also contributes programmes to Channel 4: *Land of the Eastern Borders, Sheepman of Ennerdale* and *The Gnostic Gospels*.

South
Television South
Television Centre, Southampton SO9 5HZ   ☎0703 34211

Controller Entertainment *John Kaye Cooper* **Head of Features** *John Miller* **Children's Programmes** *Nigel Pickard* **Head of Religious Programmes** *Andrew Baur* **Local Documentaries** *Anthony Howard* **Science and Industry** *Philip Geddes* **Youth Programming** *John Dale* **Head of News and Sport** *Mark Sharman*.

Recent output has included *CATS Eyes, The Boys of 66, The Human Factor; Hello Campers*. For Channel 4: *Murrow, Greece: the Hidden War*, and *After the Dream*.

Anglia Television
Anglia House, Norwich, Norfolk NR1 3JG   ☎0603 615151

Head of Drama *John Rosenberg* Anglia has a strong tradition of drama production. Recently, *A Killing on the Exchange, Cause Celebres,* P. D. James' *A Taste of Death*, as well as *Tales of the Unexpected*. The **Natural History Unit**, headed by *Aubrey Buxton*, makes eight *Survival* programmes a year. **Features, Documentaries and Children's** come under the aegis of *Colin Ewing*, assistant programme controller. Regional programmes include *Frontiers*, the science and technology series, *Livewire*, a series on business ventures. Light entertainment tends to be regional only, and of the talent show/quiz kind. **Head of News** *Jim Wilson* **Political Editor/Head of Current Affairs** *Michael Allsop* Occasionally make current affairs documentaries for the network.

South-East
BBC TV Norwich (South & East)
St Catherine's Close, All Saints Green, Norwich NR1 3ND   ☎0603 28841

The second centre (after Elstree) of the BBC TV South and East region. They occasionally make network programmes; Norwich is more than a regional opt-out station simply making its own local news programmes. Very locally oriented scripts should be sent to their small features unit. **Television Features** *Dick Meadows* and *Mike Purton*.

BBC South and East

BBC Elstree Centre, Clarendon Road, Borehamwood, Herts WD6 1JF

☎01–953 6100

Home of the history and archaeology unit, Global Report and the general programmes unit which makes leisure and one-off programmes. No drama production. **History & Archaeology** *Bruce Norman* *Timewatch* and *The Great Journeys* series. **Global Report** Barry Dixon Documentary programmes on, for example, Third World issues. Usually devised and made in-house. **General Programmes Unit** *Mastermind, Masterteam*, chess and bridge programmes, and *Lifeline*.

South West

BBC TV Plymouth (South West)

Broadcasting House, Seymour Road, Plymouth PL3 5BD   ☎0752 229201

Programmes for the South West region are made in the regional network centre in Bristol. Plymouth makes one 'opt-out' programme for its own region a week. Direct mss to the Bristol office.

BBC TV South West

Broadcasting House, Whiteladies Road, Clifton, Bristol BS8 2LR   ☎0272 732211

Bristol no longer has a drama department, but does have a strong features department, and houses the BBC's much praised natural history unit.

Features *John Shearer* Output has included *Antiques Roadshow, Scott Free, Whicker's World, Probation, Under Sail, Mountain Men* and *The Healing Arts*. **Natural History** *Dr John Sparks* Programmes have included *Kingdom of the Ice Bear, The Living Planet, The Living Isles*, and *Wildlife on One*. Specialist writers only.

BBC TV Southampton (South West)

South Western House, Canute Road, Southampton SO9 1PF   ☎0703 26201

Programmes for the South West region are made in Bristol, to whom all mss and programme ideas should be sent. Southampton makes one weekly local opt-out programme only.

HTV West

Television Centre, Bath Road, Bristol BS4 3HG   ☎0272 778366

Head of News and Current Affairs *Steve Matthews*

There are no heads of departments as such (unlike its sister company HTV Wales). For **Drama**, contact *Patrick Drongoole*, Senior Producer. *Ron Evans*, **Director of Programmes**, and **Programme Controller** *Derek Clarke* make programme-planning decisions in other areas. Strong local programme making in all departments has included feature programmes like *Along the Cotswold Way* and *The Royal Forest of Dean*.

Television South West
Derry's Cross, Plymouth PL1 2SP   ☎0752 663322   Telex 45566

News and Current Affairs *David Atkins*   **Features/Drama/Light Entertainment** *Paul Stewart Laing*

Programmes made for the network have included *The Search for Wealth, Horse Sense*, and *More than Meets the Eye*. TSW also makes arts programmes, particularly documentaries, and young people's programmes, *Treasures of the Mindlord, Look and See*.

Ireland
BBC Northern Ireland
Broadcasting House, 25–27 Ormeau Avenue, Belfast BT2 8HQ   ☎0232 244400

Current Affairs *Keith Baker*   *The Boys are Dead* (for *Everyman*).   **Drama** *Danny Boyle We'll Support You Evermore*, Douglas Livingstone; *Reservations*, Tony Marchant. Local programmes include *Gallery* (an arts series) and *Lifetimes* contemporary profiles series. These come under **General Programmes** *Ultan Guilfoyle* **Religious Programmes** *Father Jim Skelly* **Series** *Spotlight*, Editor *Andrew Colnan* **Children's** *Tony McAuley* **Sport** *Joy Williams*.

Ulster Television
Havelock House, Ormeau Road, Belfast BT7 1EB   ☎0232 22812

News Editor *Colm Williams*

Other than news, there are no heads of departments as such – general programme planning comes under the office of **Assistant Controllers** *Michael Beattie* and *Andrew Crockart*. *Michael Beattie* is particularly responsible for current affairs; *Andrew Crockart* for documentary features. Drama, light entertainment, children's and religious programme ideas can be addressed to either. Recent credits include a local adult education programme, *A Heritage from Stone*, and a children's programme, *Life After School*. Channel 4 took their *How Does Your Garden Grow, Rejoice*, and from their drama department, *Last of a Dyin' Race* by local writer Christina Reid for the new writers' series.

Scotland
BBC Scotland
Broadcasting House, Queen Margaret Drive, Glasgow G12 8DG   ☎041 330 2345

Head of Drama *Bill Bryden*   'A strong commitment to drama production'. Productions have included *The Holy City, Blood Hunt*, and Ronald Frame's *Winter Journey*. Recently, *Tutti Frutti*. **Head of Features** *David Martin*   Encompasses the old Light Entertainment department, plus documentaries. *Animal Roadshow, Secret*

Society, the schools quiz show *First Class*.   **Special Projects** *Desmond Wilcox The Visit, The Marriage*. No children's programmes except those made in the Gaelic department.   **Head of Gaelic** *Neil Fraser*.

BBC Scotland (Aberdeen)

Beechgrove Terrace, Aberdeen, Scotland AB9 2ZT   ☎0224 635233   Telex 739622

Editor *Dennis Dick*   **Contact** *Dennis Dick*

No real market. BBC Aberdeen make features, but these are nearly always commissioned.

BBC Scotland (Dundee)

12/13 Dock Street, Dundee DD1 4BT   ☎0382 25025

News only.

BBC Scotland (Edinburgh)

Broadcasting House, 5 Queen Street, Edinburgh EH2 1JF   ☎031–225 3131

All programmes made in Glasgow.

Grampian Television

Queen's Cross, Aberdeen AB9 2XJ   ☎0224 646464

Grampian Television serves an area stretching from Fife to Shetland.   **Head of Documentaries** *Edward Brocklebank*   Both regional and networked – *The Last of the Hunters* for Channel 4, and *Oil*, an eight-part documentary also for Channel 4.   **Head of News and Current Affairs** *Alistair Gracie*   Other areas of production, light entertainment, schools, children's and religious programmes come under **Head of Production** *John Hughes*. These tend to be for regional broadcast only. Light entertainment is usually of the chat show/quiz show sort, and children's programmes are both light entertainment and educational.

Scottish Television

Cowcaddens, Glasgow G2 3PR   ☎041–332 9999

Controller of News and Current Affairs *David Scott*   **Sport and Features** *Russell Galbraith*   **Controller Drama** *Robert Love*   **Controller Entertainment** *Sandy Ross*

'Encouragingly, an increasing number of STV programmes are networked, and seen nationally'. Recently the detective series *Taggart, The Horse* (seen on Channel 4), the popular series *Take the High Road*, and a documentary about Gaelic poet *Sorley Maclean*.

Wales
BBC Wales (Bangor)
Broadcasting House, Meirion Road, Bangor LL57 2BY   ☎0248 362214

News only.

BBC Wales
Broadcasting House, Llantrisant Road, Llandaff, Cardiff CF5 2YQ ☎0222 564888

News and Current Affairs *David Morris Jones*

Drama *John Hefin*   *Shadowlands* (made for *Everyman*); *Penyberth*, Kingsley Amis' series *That Uncertain Feeling*; *The Mimosa Boys*.   **General Programmes** *Huw Brian Williams*   *Ms Rhymney Valley 1984; The Treble* (about Aled Jones). Also health education programmes like *Don't Break Your Heart*, and *Juice*. **Producer** *Barry Lynch* **Children's Programmes** *Dyfed Glynn Jones* BBC Wales also make programmes for S4C in Welsh.

HTV Wales
TV Centre, Cardiff CF5 6XJ   ☎0222 590590

Productions sought with an authentic Welsh dimension. **News** *Bob Symonds* **Features** *Cenwyn Edwards* **Drama/Fiction** *Graham Jones* **Light Entertainment** *Peter Elias-Jones* **Documentaries** *Huw Davies* Recent productions include the documentary *There Was a Crooked Man*, the *Ageless Ageing* health series, and comedy series *Very Small Business*.

Sianel Pedwar Cymru (Welsh 4th Channel)
Clos Sophia, Cardiff CF1 9XY   ☎0222 43421   Telex 497146 PEDWAR G

Editor *Emlyn Davies*   **Contact** *Emlyn Davies*

S4C commissions some 4½ hours of programmes from independent producers each week, to be produced in the Welsh language. There is a demand for drama scripts, comedy and documentary programmes.

National Radio

BBC Radio News and Current Affairs
Room 3106, Broadcasting House, London W1A 1AA ☎01–580 4468

Editor *John Wilson* **News Editor** *John Williams*

Radio 4 Editors *Going Places* Irene Mallis; *Kaleidoscope* Anne Winder; *Radio Active* Andrew Wilson (producer); *Today* Jenny Abramsky; *Week Ending* Harry Thompson (producer); *Woman's Hour* Sandra Chalmers; *The World at One/PM* Derek Lewis; *The World This Weekend* Derek Lewis; *The World Tonight* Blair Thomson; *You and Yours* Amanda Metcalfe (producer). See also **BBC Radio 4** (fiction and drama opportunities).

Radio 3 Talks and Documentaries department welcomes either finished mss or written ideas for twenty- or forty-minute talks and documentaries for broadcast on the BBC's 'classical music station'. These should be sent to George Fischer at Room 8053, Broadcasting House.

Radio 2 has no general opportunities for original work, but welcomes and uses contributions from outside writers to existing series. These, naturally, change with the seasons, but presently include *The News Huddlines*, producer Mark Robson; *Hinge and Brackett* and the *Frankie Howerd Show*.

BBC Radio 4 (fiction and drama opportunities)
Broadcasting House, London W1A 1AA ☎01–580 4468

Contributions to *Morning Story* (see introductory article) should be sent to Mitch Raper or Sheila Fox, Producers, Morning Story, Room 7074, at the above address.

There are three evening dramas at Radio 4. The first, *Classic Serial*, is for obvious reasons not a good bet for new writing. What Radio 4 call their *Non Classic Serial* is theoretically open to new plays (it's put out for three months every year, usually beginning in November) but for the moment unsolicited scripts cannot be considered (or even read). *Saturday Night Theatre* is open to new writing of either seventy-five or ninety minutes length. Scripts should be sent to Enyd Williams at Room 6087. Tel 01–580 4468, extension 2168.

Probably the best bet for new plays on Radio 4 is *Afternoon Theatre*. Its producers are too numerous to list here; scripts should be sent to John Tideman, Head of Drama,

BBC Radio at the above address. The deputy head of radio drama is Richard Imison, to whom scripts can also be submitted.

BBC External Services

Central Talks and Features Department, Bush House, Strand, London WC2B 4PH
☎ 01–240 3456

Contact *Alan Jones*

Provide scripts in English for translation and broadcast by the thirty-six foreign language services that make up the BBC External Services. Cover the following areas: (a) analysis of international current affairs; (b) cultural, social and economic affairs in Britain; (c) science, technology and export promotion. Contributors should bear in mind that the target audience cannot be taken to have a ready familiarity with life in this country or with British institutions. Translation skills are not necessary, as this is done exclusively by their own professionals.

BBC Radio Scotland

Queen Margaret Drive, Glasgow G12 8DG *and* 5 Queen Street, Edinburgh EH2 1JF
☎ 041–330 2345 (G); 031–225 3131 (E)

News Editor *Jack Regan* (G)　**Features Editor** *John Arnott* (E)　**Fiction/Drama Producer** *Stewart Conn* (E)　**Comedy** *Colin Gilbert* (G)　**Talks and Features** *John Arnott* (E)

Produces a full range of news and current affairs programmes; drama, comedy, talks and features, short stories, documentaries. The emphasis is on speech-based programmes (rather than music etc.) and programmes reflecting Scottish culture.

Scottish BBC Radio has two aspects: a national radio service contributed to by programme-making in Glasgow, Edinburgh, Aberdeen and Dundee (this listing); and the local community stations, which take the national programmes and splice this with local material. These stations, BBC **Highland, nan Gaidheal, Orkney, Shetland, Solway** and **Tweed** are listed under *Local Radio*.

BBC Scotland (Aberdeen)

Beechgrove Terrace, Aberdeen, Scotland AB9 2ZT　☎ 0224 635233　Telex 739622

Editor *Chris Lovell*　**Contact** *Brian Hall*

No real market. Only involved in features (don't make any drama) and these are virtually all commissioned. News, local only.

BBC Radio Scotland (Dundee)

12/13 Dock Street, Dundee DD1 4BT　☎ 0382 25025

Small office producing news coverage only. No openings.

BBC Radio Wales

Broadcasting House, Llantrisant Road, Llandaff, Cardiff CF5 2YQ   ☎0222 564888

Contact *Bob Atkins, editor Radio Wales* (room 2038)

As with BBC Radio Scotland, there are two aspects to the working of the Welsh network. There are three centres of programme-making, in Cardiff, Bangor and Swansea (this listing), for the national Welsh BBC network, but in addition two community stations which provide local material for local audiences. These, **Radio Clwyd** and **Gwent**, are listed under *Local Radio*.

BBC Radio Wales (Bangor)

Broadcasting House, Meirion Road, Bangor LL57 2BY   ☎0248 362214

Contact *Elwyn Jones, senior producer*

BBC Radio Wales (Swansea)

32 Alexandra Road, Swansea SA1 5DZ   ☎0792 54986

Contact *Lyn Jones (Mr), programme controller*

BBC Northern Ireland

Broadcasting House, 25–27 Ormeau Avenue, Belfast BT2 8HQ   ☎0232 244400

Contact *Arwel Ellis Owen, programme controller*

For BBC Northern Ireland radio see also **Radio Foyle** (*Local Radio*).

Independent Radio News

Communications House, Gough Square, London EC4P 4LP   ☎01–353 1010

Editor *Dave Wilsworth*   **News Editor** *Bob Francomb*

IRN supplies national and international news coverage to all independent local radio stations throughout Britain.

Local Radio

Radio Aire
PO Box 362, Leeds LS3 1LR
☎0532 452299

Contact *Christa Ackroyd*

Beacon Radio
PO Box 303, Wolverhampton WV6 0DQ
☎0902 757211

Contact *Pete Wagstaff (programme controller)*

BBC Radio Bedfordshire
PO Box 476, Hastings Street, Luton, Beds. LU1 5BA
☎0582 459111
Telex 825979 RADBED G

Editor *Mike Gibbons*   Contact *Jim Latham*

No news opportunities, and few in drama and light entertainment. Locally written contributions about Bedfordshire, north and west Hertfordshire and north Buckinghamshire are encouraged. Particularly interested in historical topics (five minutes maximum). Also encourage freelance contributions from the community across a wide range of radio output, including interview and feature material.

BRMB
PO Box 555, Birmingham B6 4BX
☎021–359 4481   Telex 339707

Programme Controller *Mike Owen*   **Contact** *Brian Savin*

Occasionally use drama; hold an annual short story competition; have some demand for comedy material; and there are opportunities for writers in the various feature series the station puts out.

Light Entertainment *Brian Valk*   **News** *Brian Sheppard*

Radio Broadland
47/49 St Georges Plain, Colgate, Norwich NR3 1DD
☎0603–630621

Contact *Mike Stuart, programme controller*

BBC Radio Cambridgeshire

104 Hills Road, Cambridge, CB2 1LD   ☎0223 315970

Contact *Margaret Hyde (station manager), Mike Robinson (programme organiser)*

Capital Radio

PO Box 958, Euston Tower, London NW1 3DR   ☎01–388 1288

Contact *Matthew Bannister*

Matthew Bannister covers news, talks, current affairs and features. Opportunities exist on the daily (weekdays) 7 pm programme *The Way It Is*. Also opportunities for comedy writing.

Chiltern Radio

Chiltern Road, Dunstable, Beds. MK43 0TY   ☎0582 666001   Telex 825175

Radio scripts contact *Phil Fothergill*   **News Editor** *Katrina Balmforth*

Opportunities existing for radio drama only, and these are rare. However, if a script of exceptional local interest is offered, Radio Chiltern will consider it.

Radio City (Sound of Merseyside)

PO Box 194, Liverpool L69 1TD   ☎051–227 5100   Telex 628277

Contact *Brian Cook*

Opportunities for writers are very few and far between.

BBC Radio Cleveland

Broadcasting House, PO Box 1548, Middlesbrough, Cleveland TS1 5DG

       ☎0642 225211

Editor and Contact *Mick Wormald*

Material used is almost exclusively local to Cleveland, County Durham, and North Yorkshire, or written by local writers.

BBC Radio Clwyd

The Old School House, Glanrafon Road, Mold CH7 1PA   ☎0352 59111

Contact *John Shone (senior producer)*

Radio Clyde

Clydebank Business Park, Clydebank, G81 2RX Scotland

      ☎041–941 1111
      Telex 779537

Contacts *Hamish Wilson (drama), Alex Dickson (other)*

Radio Clyde has few opportunties for outside writers, as programmes usually originate in-house or by commission. Good local news items always considered. Feature openings rare. Few opportunities for dramatists, beyond the work of Scottish writers. 'A set-in-Glasgow very funny comedy script/series is always considered'. All documentary material is made in-house.

BBC Radio Cornwall

Phoenix Wharf, Truro, Cornwall TR1 1UA ☎ 0872 75421

Contact *Malcolm Brannar, programme organiser*

County Sound

The Friary, Guildford, Surrey GU1 4YX ☎ 0483 505566

Contact *Paul Owens, deputy programme controller*

BBC Radio Cumbria

Hilltop Heights, London Road, Carlisle CA1 2NA ☎ 0228 31661

Contact *Eric Smith, programme organiser*

BBC Radio Derby

PO Box 269, Derby DE1 3HL ☎ 0332 361111

Contact *Bryan Harris, station manager*

BBC Radio Devon

PO Box 100, Exeter EX4 4DB ☎ 0392 21561   Telex 42440

Manager *Ray Corlett*   **Contact** *John Lilley*

Special projects mounted annually have included a short story competition (1985) and a play writing competition (1986).

Devonair Radio

St David's Hill, Exeter, EX4 4DA ☎ 0392 30703

No opportunities for freelance writers.

Essex Radio

Radio House, Cliftown Road, Southend on Sea, Essex SS1 1SX *and* Radio House, 53 Duke Street, Chelmsford CM1 1SX ☎ 0702 33371 *and* 0245 51141

Telex 995480 (Southend)

Editor *Bob Smith*   **Contact** *Keith Rogers*

No real opportunities for writers' work as such, but will often interview local authors of published books.

Radio Forth

Forth House, Forth Street, Edinburgh EH1 3LF   ☎ 031–556 9255   Telex 727374

Editor *Tom Steele*   **Contact** *Tom Steele*

Features *Colin Somerville*   Opportunities in the two-minute feature series *The story of...*   **Light Entertainment** *Tom Steele*   Sixty-minute *Radio Cartoons*.   **News** *David Johnston*   News stories welcome from freelances.

BBC Radio Foyle

PO Box 927, Londonderry BT48 7NE   ☎ 0504 262244/5/6

Contact *Joe Mahon*

Radio Foyle broadcasts both its own programmes and those made in Belfast for national transmission. Occasionally programmes made by Radio Foyle will be taken up by the national network.

BBC Radio Furness

Hartington Street, Barrow-in-Furness, Cumbria LA14 5FH   ☎ 0229 36767

Contact *Keith Daniels, senior producer*

A Radio Cumbria community sub-station.

BBC Radio Gwent

Powys House, Cwmbran, Gwent NP44 1YF   ☎ 06333 72727

Contact *Adrian Hearn (senior producer)*

GWR Radio

PO Box 2000, Swindon, SN4 7EX/PO Box 2000, Watershed, Cannon's Road, Bristol BS99 75N   ☎ 0793 853222/0272 279900   Telex 44450 (Swindon)

Contact *Simon Cooper, programme organiser*

Very few opportunities. Almost all material originates in-house.

Radio Hallam

PO Box 194, Hartshead, Sheffield S1 1GP   ☎ 0742 766766

Contact *Dean Pepall, presentation co-ordinator*

Hereward Radio

PO Box 225, Peterborough PE1 1XJ   ☎ 0733 46225   Telex 32738

Editor *Andy Gillies*   **Contact** *Andy Gillies*

Not usually any openings offered to writers as all material is compiled and presented by in-house staff.

BBC Highland

Broadcasting House, 7 Culduthel Road, Inverness IV2 4AD ☎0463 22171

Contact *Allan Campbell, station manager*

BBC Highland radio is a community station.

BBC Radio Humberside

63 Jameson Street, Hull, North Humberside HU1 3NU ☎0482 23232
Telex 597031

Programme Organiser *Barry Stockdale*   **Contact** *Margaret Garbett*

Broadcast a daily short story each afternoon at 2.35 pm. 75% of the material is provided by local writers.

Invicta Radio

15 Station Road East, Canterbury, Kent CT1 2RB ☎0227 67661

Contact *Roger Day, programme manager*

BBC Radio Kent

Sun Pier, Chatham, Kent ME4 4EZ ☎0634 46284   Telex 965011

Manager and Contact *Michael Marsh*

Opportunities exist for writers on the afternoon magazine programme plus the specialist arts programme *Scene and Heard*. Features need to be of strong local interest, as does drama/fiction, for which there are few openings. Occasional commissions are made for local interest documentaries and other one-off programmes.

LBC

Communications House, Gough Square, London EC4P 4LP ☎01–353 1010

Contact *Philip Thornton, programme controller*

BBC Radio Lancashire

King Street, Blackburn BB2 2EA ☎0254 62411

Manager *Michael Chapman*   **Contact** *Programme Organiser*

Not very many opportunities for writers. Some use of local features about Lancashire life, past and present. Generally no interest in material from outside the county. Radio plays not used unless invited to enter the North West BBC stations playwriting competition (next one not yet announced).

BBC Radio Leeds

Broadcasting House, Woodhouse Lane, Leeds LS2 9PN ☎0532 442131

Contact *Stuart Campbell, programme organiser*

BBC Radio Leicester
Epic House, Charles Street, Leicester LE1 3SH   ☎0533 27113

Contact *Roger Eames, programme organiser*

Leicester Sound
Granville House, Granville Road, Leicester LE1 7RW   ☎0533 551616

Contact *Chris Hughes, programme controller*

BBC Radio Lincolnshire
PO Box 219, Newport, Lincoln LN1 3XY   ☎0522 40011   Telex 56186

Manager *David Wilkinson*   **Contact** *Chris Olney*

Unsolicited material only considered if locally relevant. Maximum 1000 words straight narrative preferred, ideally with a topical content.

BBC Radio London
PO Box 4LG, 35a Marylebone High Street, London W1A 4LG   ☎01–486 7611

Contact *Vin Bootle, programme organiser*

Radio Luxembourg (London) Ltd
38 Hertford Street, London W1Y 8BA   ☎01–493 5961   Telex 263912

Editor and Contact *Rodney Collins*

Some freelance opportunities in news only. Contact the editor.

BBC Radio Manchester
New Broadcasting House, Oxford Road, PO Box 90, M60 1SJ   ☎061–228 3434

Programme Organiser *Tony Inchley*   **Contact** *John McManus*

Very few opportunities, apart from a planned playwriting competition for local writers.

Features *Dave Holme, senior producer*

Marcher Sound
The Studios, Mold Road, Gwersyllt, Wrexham LL11 4AF   ☎0978 752202

Contact *Paul Mewies, programme controller*

Mercia Sound
Hertford Place, Coventry, West Midlands CN1 3TT   ☎0203 28451   Telex 31413

News Editor *Mark Foster*   **Contact** *Stuart Linnell*

Radio Mercury

PO Box 1, Crawley, West Sussex RH11 9TT   ☎0293 519161   Telex 87503

Programme Controller *J. Wellington*

No fiction or features opportunities. The newsroom occasionally take freelance news stories, though most of these come from established contacts.

Radio Merseyside

55 Paradise Street, Liverpool L1 3BP   ☎051–708 5500

Contact *The Producer, First Heard*   **News Editor** *Ken Murray*

No opportunities in news. Very rarely in light entertainment, drama or fiction. However, *First Heard* broadcasts previously unpublished work by local writers, gives information about workshops and competitions, and features interviews with successful authors. *First Heard* goes out fortnightly, with every fourth edition devoted to poetry and poets.

Metro Radio

Newcastle upon Tyne, NE99 1BB   ☎091–488 3131   Telex 537428

Features Editor *Steve Martin*   **Contact** *Steve Martin*

Very few opportunities for writers.

Moray Firth Radio

PO Box 271, Scourgurie Place, Inverness IV6 3SF   ☎0463 224433

Contact *Brian Anderson, programme controller*

BBC Radio Newcastle

Broadcasting Centre, PO Box Newcastle upon Tyne NE99 1RN   ☎091–281 4243

Manager *Bob Wrack*

Opportunities for freelance writers are extremely rare.

BBC Radio Norfolk

Norfolk Tower, Surrey Street, Norwich NR1 3PA   ☎0603 617411   Telex 975515

Contact *Keith Salmon, station manager*

Features/Documentaries *Keith Salmon*   Good local material welcome, but must relate directly to Norfolk/North Suffolk.   **News Editor** *Jill Bennett*   'Minimal' opportunities.

BBC Radio Northampton
PO Box 1107, Abingdon Street, Northampton NN1 2BE   ☎0604 20621

Contact *Denzil Dudley*

Features rarely used; judged on merit plus local relevance. No drama or fiction, no news opportunities.   **Light Entertainment** rarely used, perhaps one series a year.

NorthSound
45 King's Gate, Aberdeen AB2 6BL   ☎0224 632234

Contact *Edith Stark, senior producer*

BBC Radio Nottingham
York House, Mansfield Road, Nottingham NG1 3JB   ☎0602 415161

Contact *Nick Brunger, programme organiser*

Ocean Sound Ltd
Whittle Avenue, Segensworth West, Fareham, Hants. PO15 5PA   ☎04895 89911
Telex 47474

Programme Controller *Michael Betton*   **Contact** *Michael Betton*

For economic reasons, Ocean Sound rarely considers commissioning an external writer to produce drama/short stories for the station. All submissions are, however, considered, but only those with a special local connection are likely to be taken further.

News *Chris Rider*

Radio Orwell
Electric House, Lloyds Avenue, Ipswich, Suffolk IP1 3HZ
☎0473 216971   Telex 98548

Editor *Simon Cornes*   **Contact** *Simon Cornes*

Features Editor *Sally Gordon*   Few openings here; 'even fewer' in drama and light entertainment.

BBC Radio Oxford
242–254 Banbury Road, Oxford OX2 7DW   ☎0865 53411

Contact *David Freeman*

Limited opportunities: short stories are used from time to time.

Pennine Radio
PO Box 235, Pennine House, Forster Square, Bradford BD1 5NP   ☎0274 731521

Contact *Colin Slade, programme controller*

Piccadilly Radio

PO Box 261, Manchester M1 4AW ☎061–236 9913

Editor and Contact *Michael Briscoe*

Documentaries submit draft plans for discussion. **Drama** if of a 'pop' nature, especially short comedies or soaps. No light entertainment. **Features** only if local interest. **News** qualified journalists only.

Plymouth Sound

Earl's Acre, Alma Road, Plymouth PL3 4HX ☎0752 227272

Contact *Louise Churchill, head of programmes*

Red Dragon Radio

Radio House, West Canal Wharf, Cardiff CF1 5XJ ☎0222 384041

Contact *Mike Henfield, programme controller* (also head of programmes at **Red Rose Radio** and based in Preston).

Red Rose Radio

PO Box 301, St Paul's Square, Preston, Lancs PR1 1YE ☎0772 556301

Contact *Mike Henfield, head of programmes* (see also **Red Dragon Radio**).

Saxon Radio

Long Brackland, Bury St Edmunds, Suffolk IP33 1JY ☎0284 701511

Contact *Sally Gordon, programme controller*

Severn Sound

PO Box 388, 67 Southgate Street, Gloucester GL1 2DQ ☎0452 423791

Contact *Eddie Vickers, programme controller*

BBC Radio Sheffield

60 Westbourne Road, Sheffield S10 2QU ☎0742 686185

Programme Organiser *Frank Mansfield* **Contact** *Frank Mansfield*

'Radio Sheffield is keen to develop local writing talent through the radio station. We broadcast short stories from local writers on merit in our *Afternoon Edition* programme and occasionally plays.' Also involved, with Sheffield City Libraries, in a scheme called 'Write Back', and hope to broadcast material coming out of this in the near future.

BBC Radio Shropshire

PO Box 397, Shrewsbury, Shropshire SY1 3TT   ☎0743 248484   Telex 35187

Editor *Lawrie Bloomfield*   **Contact** *Diane Kemp*

Opportunities exist in the afternoon programme (2–3.30 pm) for Shropshire writers. Stories or prose pieces of around 1000 words, or poetry 'if it is easily understood'. Because the programme is not an arts slot as such, the work should be of general interest. Aims to be an outlet for local creative talent. *Payment* not usually.

Signal Radio

Studio 257, Stoke Road, Shelton, Stoke on Trent ST4 2SR   ☎0782 417111

Contact *John Evington, head of presentations*

BBC Radio Solent

South Western House, Canute Road, Southampton SO9 4PJ   ☎0703 631311
                                                                                                        Telex 47420

Editor and Contact *Steve Panton*

Occasional short story competitions.

Radio Solway Dumfries

Lovers Walk, Dumfries DG1 1NZ   ☎0387 68008

Editor *Iain McConnell*

Southern Sound

Radio House, Franklin Road, Portslade, Brighton, Sussex BN4 2SS ☎0273 422288

Contact *Andy Ivy (features), Vince Geddes (programme controller)*

Radio Stoke

Cheapside, Hanley, Stoke on Trent, ST1 1JJ   ☎0782 208080   Telex 36104

Programme Organiser *Mervyn Gamage*   **Contact** *Arthur Wood*

The station has long had a policy of encouraging material suitable for a Radio Stoke audience, whether this be short or longer essays, short stories, original research and writing on local history, or other subjects of local interest. The station is particularly keen on receiving these from locally based authors. Very occasionally use scripts of great local relevance. (All scripts lacking local links are rejected.)

BBC Radio Sussex

Marlborough Place, Brighton, Sussex BN1 1TU   ☎0273 680231

Contact *George Pixley, programme organiser*

Swansea Sound

Victoria Road, Gowerton, Swansea SA4 3AB ☎0792 893751 Telex 48594

Programme Controller and Contact *David Thomas*

Features, drama/fiction and light entertainment *David Thomas* **News** *Hugh Turnbull.*

Radio Tay

PO Box 123, Dundee DD1 9UF ☎0382 200800

Contact *Tom Steele, programme controller* (also of **Radio Forth**)

Radio Tees

74 Dovecot Street, Stockton on Tees, TS18 1HB ☎0642 615111

Programme Controller *Brian Lister* **Features** *Andy Hollins*

Limited opportunities at present – 'however, we are always willing to consider new ideas'.

Radio Trent

29–31 Castlegate, Nottingham NG1 7AP ☎0602 581731
Telex Rad Trent Nottm 37463

Editor *Chris Hughes* **Contact** *Chris Hughes*

Few opportunities, although a short story series is run from time to time. **Documentaries** 'perhaps if locally orientated and discussed up front'. **Features** *John Shaw* Rarely used. **Light Entertainment** Christmas material only.

BBC Radio Tweed

Municipal Buildings, High Street, Selkirk TD7 4BU ☎0750 21884

Contact *Steve Haigh, senior producer*

Two Counties Radio

5 Southcote Road, Bournemouth BH1 3LR ☎0202 294881 Telex 418362

Contact *Rosemary Mundy*

Documentaries *Stan Horobin* **Features, drama/fiction and light entertainment** *Rosemary Mundy.*

Radio 210

PO Box 210, Reading RG3 5RZ ☎0734 413131

Contact *Terry Mann, programme controller*

Viking Radio
Commercial Road, Hull HU1 2SG ☎ 0482 25141   Telex 597572

Editor *Colin Palmer*   **Contact** *Steve Palmer*

Features *Steve King*   **News** *Colin Palmer*

BBC Radio WM
PO Box 206, Birmingham B5 7SD ☎ 021–472 5141

Editor and Contact *John Pickles*

Interested in short stories, plays, documentaries, preferably but not necessarily local interest.

West Sound
Radio House, 54 Holmston Road, Ayr KA7 3BE ☎ 0292 283662

Contact *John McCauley, programme controller*

Radio Wyvern
PO Box 22, 5–6 Barbourne Terrace, Worcester WR1 3JZ ☎ 0905 612212

Contact *Norman Bilton, managing director*

One of the smallest of the regional radio stations; has little money for contributors. Very occasionally, a local writer may be commissioned to produce something of interest to the Wyvern audience.

BBC Radio York
20 Bootham Row, York YO3 7BR ☎ 0904 641351   Telex 57444

Editor *John Jefferson*   **Contact** *Tony Fish*

'A limited outlet for short stories and features provided they are either set locally or have some other local relevance.'

Addendum

BBC Essex
198 New London Road, Chelmsford CM2 9XB ☎ 0245 262393

Editor *Richard Lucas*   **Contact** *Martin Ward*

News Editor *Simon Ellis*   **Features/Drama/Fiction/Documentaries** *Keith Roberts*

Film, Television & Video Producers

A & M Sound Pictures

136 New Kings Road, London SW6 4LZ   ☎ 01–736 3311

Contact *Steven Lavers*

Not currently acting as producers; commission other production companies when required.

Abbey Video Ltd

Five Lamps Studio, West Avenue, Derby DE1 3HR   ☎ 0332 40693

Contact *Richard Faulkner*

Makers of corporate video for a variety of industrial clients.

Acme Arts Ltd

12 Vauxhall Grove, London SW8 1SY   ☎ 01–735 9099

Contact *Jim Field*

Horticultural and educational films for television and video.

Acorn Pictures Ltd

49 Old Bond Street, London W1X 3AF   ☎ 01–493 1420   Telex 21737 ACORN G

Contact *Robert Peake*

Produce films for the discerning cinema going public. OUTPUT *Educating Rita; Not Quite Jerusalem.* Unsolicited mss from recognised agents/producers only. 'If it's good, we're avid for it'.

Action Time

22 Woodstock Street, London W1R 1HF   ☎ 01–409 3421

Contact *Jeremy Fox*

Makers of television programmes: 'format shows' like *Game For A Laugh, Odd One Out* and *The Krypton Factor*, both for the UK and America.

Advent Video Productions

Ely House, 37 Dover Street, London W1X 4AH   ☎01-409 1343

Contact *Dominic Roncoroni*

Documentary, educational and corporate video; also commercials.

After Image Ltd

32 Acre Lane, London SW2 5SP   ☎☎01–733 1782

Contact *Jane Thorburn*

Makers of television for all ages, with a particular interest in the arts and unusual people and events. OUTPUT *Alter Image*, the alternative arts magazine, with no presenter; *Pookiesnackenburger*, musical series; *Map of Dreams*, arts video, dance and effects. Though *After Image* has concentrated on the visual aspects of television in the past, it is interested to read new writing, and to work with authors, perhaps towards new pieces for *Alter Image*.

Agender Films

5 Gower Street, London WC1 6HA   ☎01–637 7920

Contact *Sarah Boston*

Documentaries. *Just Sex* (which they made as **51% Productions**); *Merely Mortal*, Channel 4. No unsolicited mss, as all writing is at present done in-house by Sarah Boston.

Britt Allcroft Ltd

11 Blenheim Avenue, Southampton, Hants SO2 1DW   ☎0703 585844

Contact *Britt Allcroft*

Television programmes in the fields of documentary, light entertainment, music and arts. Family and children's programmes particularly, including *Thomas the Tank Engine*.

Allied Stars

Cannon Elstree Studios, Borehamwood, Herts WD6 1JG
          ☎01–953 1600   Telex 922436 E Films G

Contact *Bob Kellett*

Feature films. OUTPUT *Chariots of Fire*; *Breaking Glass*; *F/X Murder by Illusion*; and recently *Government Issue*; *Rocket*; *Burn Out*. Unsolicited mss welcome: 'we read everything'.

Alligator Productions Ltd

68–70 Wardour Street, London W1V 4JA   ☎01–734 0101

Contact *Catherine Skinner*

A collection of freelance directors and other professionals who make commercials and promo films for video and television, and also act as a useful bridge between scripts and potential directors.

Amber Films

5 side (rear), Newcastle upon Tyne, NE1 3JE   ☎0632 322000

Contact *Peter Roberts*

Television programmes, cinema and animation. OUTPUT has included *Keeping Time* and *Byker*.

Antelope Films

3 Fitzroy Square, London W1P 5AH   ☎01–387 4454

Contact *Jane Wellesley*

Makers of television documentaries. OUTPUT has included *The Triple Crown: the Paradox of the Papacy*; *The Spirit of the Alcazar: 50 Years of Change in a Spanish City*; *Vidal in Venice* and *Heart of the Dragon*, twelve part documentary on China for **Channel 4** television.

Antonine Productions

6 Queen Margaret Road, Glasgow G20 6DP   ☎041–945 1717

Contact *Paddy Higson, Alan J. Wands*

Also **Black Cat Studios**, 830 Springfield Road, Glasgow G31, Tel. 041–554 4667. Films for television, feature films (particularly thrillers and road movies). OUTPUT *The Girl in the Picture*, 1985. Scripts accepted from both writers and agents: 'delighted to see new work'.

Arbor Productions Ltd

13 Carlisle Road, London NW6 6TL   ☎01 968 6542

Contact *Maggie Williams*

Makers of television programmes, cinema, corporate and educational video. Specialise in music, arts, documentary and drama. OUTPUT has included *Body Style* for **Channel 4**; a series for the **Design Council** and a **Channel 13** film (New York) about the composer Steve Reich.

Aspect Film Productions Ltd
36 Percy Street, London W1P 9FG ☎ 01–636 5303

Contact *Marian Lacey*

Drama, documentary and corporate television. OUTPUT has included *On the Piste*, a documentary about skiing and *Stirring Stuff*, about tea drinking.

Aspen Television Ltd
Aspen House, 1 Gayford Road, London W12 9BY ☎ 01–743 8618

Contact *Mike Raggett*

Commercials and corporate film and video production for company and product promotion. OUTPUT has included training films for **Marks and Spencer** and commercials for the **Post Office**.

Associated Video Productions
29a Eccleston Road, London W13 0RA ☎ 01–840 4222

Contact *Jon Sinigaglia*

Corporate production for big name commercial clients; also documentary, drama, music and arts for television.

Astramead Ltd
38 Gloucester Mews, London W2 3HE

Contact *Mark Shivas*

Television programmes, cinema and drama on film and video. OUTPUT has included the television series *Telford's Change, Can You Hear Me at the Back?* and *The Price* for **Channel 4**; *Late Starter* for the **BBC**.

AVC Group
Walters Farm Road, Tonbridge, Kent TN9 1QT ☎ 0732 365107

Contact *Steven Fowler*

Makers of sales training films on video for major clients, also corporate and educational products for commercial and industrial use.

AVL
1 Rectory Road, Wokingham, Berks RG11 5AS ☎ 0734 790500

Contact *Gerry Clarke*

Video production and corporate communications for commercial and industrial clients; documentary, current affairs and training films.

Michael Barratt Ltd
108 Cromwell Road, London SW7 4ES   ☎01–370 4391

Contact *Michael Barratt*

Corporate and educational video, also television programmes – but these are exclusively about the Royal Family, for Australian television.

Peter Batty Productions
Claremont House, Renfrew Road, Kingston, Surrey KT2 7NT   ☎01–942 6304

Contact *Peter Batty*

Television programmes and commercials. Primarily broadcast documentaries. OUTPUT has included *The Divided Union* on the American Civil War; *The Perfect Partnership* about Nureyev and Fontaine, a one-off for **Channel 4**.

Beat Productions
Studio 13, 10–11 Archer Street, London W1V 7HG   ☎01–734 4588

Contact *Michael Jackson*

Also **The Media Show Ltd** (same address). Documentary series/features. OUTPUT *The Sixties*, for RSO; *Open the Box*, for **Channel 4**; *The Media Show* also for **Channel 4**. Material is produced in-house, or by commission direct to writers. Rarely use agents. Happy to consider new documentary ideas: write in the first instance with outline. Of **The Media Show Ltd**, intended expansion means 'there should be more opportunities for writers here'.

Bentorm Ltd
26B Thorney Crescent, London SW11 3TR   ☎01–585 1592

Contact *David Deutsch*

Television and cinema producers, particularly in drama and arts fields. OUTPUT has included *Shakespeare Lives* and *Reflections*, both for **Channel 4**; and the feature film *The Chain* (script by Jack Rosenthal).

Paul Berriff Productions
Chestnuts, Woodfield Lane, Hassle, North Humberside HU13 0EW

☎0482 641158

Contact *Jane Dillon-Guy*

Television, current affairs, documentary and children's programmes, plus corporate video. OUTPUT has included *Lakeland Rock* for **Channel 4**; *Lifeboat* series for **BBC 2**; *No Limits* also for **BBC 2**; and *Motorway* for **ITV**.

Bevanfield Films
15 Napier Place, London W14 8LG   ☎01–603 5137

Contact *Mary Swindale*

Television programmes, cinema and animation, including an animation series for
Channel 4, and *Bill the Minder* for **Central**.

Black Cat Studios
See **Antonine Productions**.

Blackrod Ltd
Threeways House, 40–44 Clipstone Street, London W1P 7EA   ☎01–637 9376

Contact *Clive Moffatt*

Television film and video services to commercial and industrial clients. One of the
biggest corporate video makers, they have won a fistful of awards for excellence in
the field.

Blackwell Videotec Ltd
7 John Street, London WC1N 2ES   ☎01–430 0044

Contact *Jo-Anne Winston*

Subsidiary of **Blackwell Scientific Publications** (see *Publishers*). Educational, medical, scientific, corporate and promotional programmes. OUTPUT has included *Risk*,
looking at the risks in medical practice which won the gold award in the 1985 New
York film and television festival.

Braham Hill Ltd
14 King Street, Covent Garden, London WC2E 8HN   ☎01–240 6941

Contact *Michael Braham, Liz Beaumont*

Factual/current affairs/business programmes and corporate video. TELEVISION *The
Business Programme*. CORPORATE WORK training, customer care, safety at work, and
financial matters such as pensions. 'All material has a tendency towards the financial
sector, where most of our clients come from'. No unsolicited mss.

Britannic Film & TV Ltd
Pinewood Studios, Iver, Bucks SL0 0NH   ☎0753 651700   Telex 847505

Contact *Peter R. E. Snell* (Chief Executive)

Film production. OUTPUT *Turtle Diary*; *Lady Jane*; *A Prayer for the Dying*. No unsolicited mss.

Broadside Ltd

74 Moss Lane, Pinner, Middlesex HA5 3AU   ☎01–866 5271

Contact *Angela Spindler-Brown*

An all woman independent production company. OUTPUT has included a current affairs series for **Channel 4**; *Thinking About Conflict, Female Focus* and *Five Women Photographers*, also for **Channel 4**.

Brook Productions

2 Newburgh Street, London W1V 1LH   ☎01–439 9871

Contact *Anne Lapping*

Makers of documentary, music, arts and current affairs television. OUTPUT has included *A Week in Politics* for **Channel 4**; *Shape of the World, Voices, The Writing on the Wall* and *David Low*.

Burrill Productions

51 Lansdowne Road, London W11 2LG   ☎01–727 1442

Contact *Fiona Procter*

Feature film production company. OUTPUT *Alpha Beta* for BBC; *Tess* Roman Polanski; *Pirates of Penzance*; *Supergirl*; *The Fourth Protocol*. No unsolicited mss. Policy of encouragement for new screenwriters.

The Callender Company

4th floor, 82 Wardour Street, London W1V 3LF
                    ☎01–240 8644   Telex 25166 CALLCO G

Contact *Andi Wright*

Major drama series and feature films. OUTPUT *The Belly of an Architect* by Peter Greenaway; *The Bretts*, co-produced with **Central TV** for Mobil Masterpiece Theatre. Mss are considered only if they come by way of established literary agents.

Camden Productions Ltd

20 Jeffreys Street, London NW1 9PR   ☎01–482 0527

Contact *Theresa Fitzgerald, Philip Kemp*

Camden Productions consists of two writers and develops their work exclusively, so there is no market here for other hopefuls. No unsolicited mss.

Celador Productions
39 Long Acre, London WC2E 9JT   ☎01–240 8101

Contact *Frank Hayes*

Documentary, light entertainment, music and arts television for both British and international markets. OUTPUT has included *Get Fresh* for **Tyne Tees**; *Masterword*, co-produced with **Ulster TV**; and the documentary *Sotheby's*.

Chameleon Film & Video
The Magistretti Building, 1 Harcourt Place, West Street, Leeds LS1 4RB
                                                 ☎0532 438536

Contact *Chris Lister*

Television has included documentaries for **Channel 4**, a natural history series, and PR videos for corporate clients.

Charisma Films
Russell Chambers, Covent Garden, London WC2E 8AA   ☎01–379 4267

Contact *David Gideon Thomson*

Contrary to popular belief, don't make music promos (the company grew out of **Charisma records**). Theatrical and drama television producers. OUTPUT has included *The Best of British* – a compilation of old **Rank** film clips for the **BBC** and *Sir Henry of Rawlinson End*, a feature film broadcast on **Channel 4** in 1987.

Chatsworth Television Ltd
97–99 Dean Street, London W1V 5RA   ☎01–934 4302   Telex 28604

Contact *Malcolm Heyworth*

Drama and Light Entertainment television makers of 15 years experience.

Cheerleader Productions
36–44 Brewer Street, London W1R 3FW   ☎01–439 9955

Contact *Derek Brandon*

Sports programme makers. Have produced American football, tennis and golf programmes for **Channel 4**. Also corporate video makers.

Colchester Filmmakers
74 High Street, Colchester CO1 1UE   ☎0206 560255

Contact *Carol Comley*

Promotion and documentary work for the voluntary and arts sectors. New writing welcome.

Collier Marsland Films

44 Berwick Street, London W1V 3RE   ☎01–437 6684

Contact *Kevin Marsland*

Documentary, light entertainment, children's television programmes, but the main emphasis recently has been corporate video for architects (Lloyds building, Hong Kong Bank etc.). Work proceeding on a documentary for television, and *Ali Bongo* for video sale.

Colstar Communications Entertainment Ltd

1 Wardour Mews, D'Arblay Street, London W1V 3FF   ☎01–437 5725

Contact *Robert Angell*

Make sponsored, corporate, training and promotion films, plus documentary films for an international market. OUTPUT has included *The Poacher, The Hunter, The Gamekeeper* and *Roots of Tomorrow*.

Columbia Pictures Corporation

19/23 Wells Street, London W1P 3HP   ☎01–580 2090   Telex 263392

Contact *Colin Vaines* (Director of Literary Affairs, UK)

London office of the American film company now headed by David Puttnam. Recent OUTPUT: *84 Charing Cross Road; Stand By Me; Ghostbusters*. Film projects range from small British subjects to large-scale Hollywood blockbusters. Unsolicited mss welcome, providing they come from an agent, or are accompanied by a lawyer's letter. Interested in good scripts which can be made into films suitable for an international market – 'If they come from new writers we'd be very pleased, but we can only encourage along material we feel has a good chance of getting off the ground.'

Compact Television

13 Imperial Studios, 7 Imperial Road, Fulham, London SW6 2AG

☎01–731 6151   Telex 895525 Flyin G

Contact *Kent Walwin*

Drama and light entertainment for television and cinema.

Compass Film Productions Ltd

Third floor, 18–19 Warwick Street, London W1R 5RB   ☎01–439 6456

Contact *Simon Heaven*

Specialists since 1974 in documentary, educational and promotional programmes for television and corporate clients. Recent credits include *Another Way of Life*, on mental handicap for **Channel 4**; *Music of the Outsiders* for **Channel 4**, and *The Green Line*, a two-part documentary on Cyprus also for **Channel 4**.

Consolidated Productions Ltd
5 Jubilee Place, London SW3 3TD ☎01–376 5151   Telex 946449

Contact *Annette Kieley*

World-wide television. OUTPUT *Deceptions*, mini-series co-produced with Columbia and BBC; *Gathering of Old Men*, 2 hour feature film; *Where Do I Come From?*, animated cartoon. No unsolicited mss.

Cosmos Productions
42–44 Hanway Street, London W1P 9DE ☎01–631 3041

Contact *Ronis Varlaam*

Television makers. OUTPUT includes *Enthusiasts*, six half hour documentaries for **Channel 4**; plus *Well You Didn't Expect Us To Sit Around Doing Nothing Did You?*, on unemployment, also for **Channel 4**.

David Cox Associates
Hadrian House, Higham Place, Newcastle upon Tyne, NE1 8AF ☎0632 616881

Contact *David Cox*

Film and video production company with many commercial clients.

Cristo Films and Television
New Tythe Street, Long Eaton, Nottingham NG10 2DC ☎0602 727160

Contact *D. Barton*

Documentary, light entertainment, children's and current affairs television.

CTR Productions
31 Lismore Crescent, Broadfield, Crawley, West Sussex RH11 9DA ☎0293 548475

Contact *Ian Cunningham*

Corporate, educational, documentary, music and arts video producers. Specialise in promotional work/documentaries for churches, schools, education authorities and voluntary organisations. OUTPUT includes *Sex Matters* for **Channel 4** and *Christians and Trade Unions*.

Cwmni'r Castell Cyf
1 Rhiw Road, Colwyn Bay, Clwyd, LL29 7TE ☎0492 33148

Contact *Elwyn Vaughan Williams*

Television programmes. OUTPUT has included *The Scouts Holiday*, a light entertainment series for the Welsh 4th channel, **S4C**.

Dareks Production House

58 Wickham Road, Beckenham, Kent BR3 2RQ ☎01–658 2012

Contact *David Crossman*

Independent producers of broadcast television. Situation comedies, children's factual and fictional programmes for **ITV** and **Channel 4**. OUTPUT *The Cannon & Ball Show*; *Metal Mickey*; *The Pocket Money Programme*. Unsolicited mss welcome: 'we are looking for original minds, and have an interest in tragic situations in modern contexts.'

DBA Television

21 Ormeau Avenue, Belfast, BT2 8HD ☎0232 231197

Contact *David Barker*

Makers of documentary, news and current affairs television and also corporate video. OUTPUT includes *McCrea Goes to Nashville* and *Someone's Always Leaving*; also contributed to **Channel 4's** *Irish Angle*, its *Poets* series, plus *The Other Emerald Isle*.

Deptford Beach Productions Ltd

79 Wardour Street, London W1V 3TH ☎01–734 8508

Contact *Tony Kirkhope*

FOUNDED 1985 to make independent productions for **Channel 4**. OUTPUT includes documentary about Jean-Luc Godard, directed and written by him. Unsolicited mss welcome.

Dibgate Productions Ltd

Studio 4, Parkstead Lodge, 31 Upper Park Road, London NW3 2UL ☎01–722 5634

Contact *Nicholas Parsons*

Make documentary and travel films for television, and, increasingly in recent years, shorts for cinema audiences. OUTPUT has included *A Fair Way to Play*, *Mad Dogs and Cricketers*, *Relatively Greek* and *Viva Menorca*.

Diverse Productions Ltd

6 Gorleston Street, London W14 8XS ☎01–603 4567

Contact *Graham Walker*

News and current affairs programmes for **Channel 4**, all produced in-house. OUTPUT has included *Diverse Reports*, *The Aids Brief* and *Election Brief*; plus films for **NUPE** and the **TGWU**.

Dumbarton Films

Dumbarton House, 68 Oxford Street, London W1N 9LA   ☏ 01–631 4926

Contact *Jane Lighting*

Makers of television, cinema, educational and home videos. Specialises in developing and producing feature films. OUTPUT has included *No Surrender*, Alan Bleasdale; *Loyalties*, Sharon Riis; and *Birdsville*, a Carl Schultz film.

Kenneth Earle London Management

235–241 Regent Street, London W1A 2JT   ☏ 01–439 1610   Telex 27498

Contact *Kenneth Earle*

Light entertainment, comedy, television and radio. OUTPUT *Huddlines*; *Mooney's Monday Magazine*; *Blankety Blank*. Unsolicited mss are encouraged: 'good comedy writers are hard to find'.

The Elstree (Production) Co. Ltd

Cannon Elstree Studios, Shenley Road, Borehamwood, Herts WD6 1JG

☏ 01–953 1600   Telex 922436 E FILMS G

Contact *Lynne Donovan, Development Executive*

Produces feature films and television drama/situation comedy. OUTPUT *Prospects* for **Euston Films/Channel 4**; *Rude Health* for **Channel 4**. Two feature films currently in development with Australian partners, and another twelve projects on the boil: 'we are actively looking for more, across the whole range of television and films'. Unsolicited mss welcome. Elstree has a positive policy towards new writers, and is proud to have brought some of them on to the point of having their material produced.

Emitel

65 Beak Street, Soho, London W1R 3LF   ☏ 01–439 9882

Contact *Malcolm Craddock*

Shorts for the cinema, corporate video, training and educational films, sponsored films. Multi award winning company.

Enigma Productions Ltd

11 Queens Gate Place Mews, London SW7 5BG   ☏ 01–581 8248

As David Puttnam has gone to Columbia Pictures in Hollywood, **Enigma** has closed down for at least the next 2 years, and is functioning simply as his private London office meanwhile.

Equal Time

Heath Lodge, Heathside, London NW3 1BL ☎01–431 1927

Contact *Martin Minns*

Documentaries on music, the arts and current affairs. No opportunities as all material is produced in-house.

Eurofilm Productions Ltd

47 Ossington Street, London W2 4LY ☎01–243 1613

Contact *Andrzej Swoboda*

OUTPUT includes *Modern Polish Composers* for **Channel 4** and *King Size*, a short science fiction comedy feature.

Euston Films

365 Euston Road, London NW1 3AR ☎01–387 0911

Contact *Johnny Goodman*

Television programmes and films for cinema. **Euston** is the film making arm of **Thames Television**: their most recent credit is the mini-series *The Fear*. OUTPUT also includes *A Month in the Country* and *Bellman & True*; and the feature film *Consuming Passions*, for release in 1988.

Fairwater Films

Unit 2, Fairwater Workshops, Norbury Road, Fairwater, Cardiff CF5 3BG
☎0222 552555

Contact *Naomi Jones*

Makers of animated films for **BBC Wales**, **HTV Wales**, and other outlets. OUTPUT includes a cartoon series for **S4C**, *Hanner Dwsin*.

Filmfair Ltd

Jacobs Well Mews, London W1H 5PD ☎01–935 1596

Contact *Barrie Edwards*

FOUNDED 1966. Makers of children's and educational television, cable, video. OUTPUT *The Wombles*; *Paddington Bear*; *Portland Bill*. 'If unsolicited mss come in, they are read.'

Flamingo Pictures

47 Lonsdale Square, London N1 1EW ☎01–607 9958

Contact *Christine Oestreicher*

Television programmes and cinema films. Mostly cinema and mostly fiction. OUTPUT has included *Every Picture Tells a Story* for **Channel 4**; *Loser Takes All*, Graham Greene, for cinema release in 1988; and *Dibs*, also for cinema release.

Flickers Productions
Dumbarton House, 68 Oxford Street, London W1N 9LA   ☎01–580 0044

Contacts *Neil Zeiger, Baz Taylor*

Intelligent feature films and comedies. OUTPUT *Lamb*, Bernard MacLaverty. Developing nine screenplays at present. Very interested in young writers with strong scripts. Writers for Flickers have included Howard Brenton, P. G. Duggan, Anthony Garner, Ron Hutchinson.

Forever Films
82D Warwick Avenue, London W9 2PU   ☎01–286 1948

Contact *Clare Downs*

Describe their intended audience as 'art house to crossover feature film audience'. OUTPUT *The Dress*, short romantic fantasy (BAFTA award winner); *High Season*, serious comedy feature; *Buster's Bedroom*, absurdist drama. No unsolicited mss. Very interested in new writing which has energy and wit, with a serious undertone.

Mark Forstater Productions Ltd
42a Devonshire Close, London W1N 1LL   ☎01–631 0611   Telex 8954664

Contact *Nicola Lund*

Active in the selection, development and production of material for film, television and theatre. OUTPUT *Monty Python and the Holy Grail*; *The Odd Job*; *The Grass is Singing*; *Xtro*; *Forbidden*; *The Fantasist*. Unsolicited mss considered, but prefer writers to send synopses in the first instance.

Freeway Films
31 Albany Street, Edinburgh EH1 3QN   ☎031–557 0882

Contact *John McGrath*

Film outlet for John McGrath's work. OUTPUT has included *Blood Red Roses* and *There is a Happy Land* for **Channel 4**. New project – *The Dressmaker*, from the novel by Beryl Bainbridge, scripted by John McGrath.

Frontroom Productions Ltd
79 Wardour Street, London W1   ☎01–734 4603

Contact *Angela Topping*

Television and cinema, both shorts and full length features. OUTPUT has included *Acceptable Levels*, *Ursula Glenys* and *Intimate Strangers*.

John Gau Productions

2a Greyhound Road, Hammersmith, London W6 8NX ☎01–385 1229

Contact *John Gau*

Documentaries and series for television, plus corporate video. OUTPUT has included *Assignment Adventure, Money Spinners* and *The Faiths Next Door* for **Channel 4** and the *Soldiers* series for **BBC 1**.

Malone Gill Productions Ltd

16 Newham Passage, London W1P 3PE ☎01–580 6594   Telex 8951182

Contact *Georgina Denison*

Mainly documentary, but also some drama productions. OUTPUT *Treasure Houses of Britain; Pride of Place: Building the American Dream; Space Craft; Matisse in Nice; The Ghost Writer* (from Philip Roth's novel). Prefer an outline proposal with letter in the first instance: 'always interested in seeing new writing of quality'.

Bob Godfrey Films

55 Neal Street, London WC2 ☎01–240 1793/1889

Contact *Mike Hayes, Lisa Leoni*

Animated films, children's TV series, adult political work, plus shorts for cinema and television. Unsolicited mss welcome provided they are suitable for animation. Bob Godfrey is one of the judges in the **Ryman's Short Story/Essay Writing Competition** for children.

Goldcrest Films and Television Ltd

Waverly House, 7–12 Noel Street, London W1V 3PB ☎01–437 8696
Telex 267458 Goldcr

Contact *Greg Dinner*

Goldcrest are no longer developing material for feature films or television, and now operate solely as a distribution company. No unsolicited mss.

Grasshopper Productions Ltd

20 Brunswick Gardens, London W8 4AJ ☎01-229 1181

Contact *Joy Whitby*

Children's programmes and adult drama. FOUNDED 1970 by Joy Whitby, who has no use for outside writing as this is her own area of expertise. No unsolicited mss.

Greenpark Productions Ltd
St Wilfrids, 101 Honor Oak Park, London SE23 3LB ☎01–699 7234
Telex 25247 GPK

Contact *David Morphet*

Makers of specialised and business sponsored films, television (general) who welcome unsolicited mss.

Greenpoint Films
5a Noel Street, London W1V 3RB ☎01–437 6492

Contact *Ann Scott*

A small company whose members act as individual producers and directors. No facilities for reading or using unsolicited mss.

Colin Gregg Films Ltd
Floor 2, 1–6 Falconberg Court, London W1V 5SG ☎01–439 0257

Contact *Colin Gregg*

Feature films for **Channel 4** and **BBC 2**. OUTPUT *Remembrance*; *To The Lighthouse*; *Lamb*; *Hard Travelling*. Unsolicited mss are welcome. Original scripts are preferred to adapted material.

Griffin Productions Ltd
3 Fitzroy Square, London W1P 5AH ☎01–388 5811

Contact *Adam Clapham*

Drama, documentary, arts and current affairs television. OUTPUT has included *Painting With Light* with Tom Keating for **Channel 4**; *The Bombay Hotel* for *Forty Minutes*, **BBC 2**; *Odyssey*, the monthly magazine for **Channel 4**; and *Maharajas* for **BBC 2**.

Handmade Films
26 Cadogan Square, London SW1X 0JP ☎01–581 1265   Telex 8951338 EURODO

Contact *Margot Gavan Duffy*

OUTPUT *Mona Lisa*; *Shanghai Surprise*; *A Private Function*; *Water*; *Privates on Parade*; *The Missionary*; *Time Bandits*. Company policy is not to accept unsolicited mss direct from writers, though they do consider submissions from literary agents, publishers and producers.

Holmes Associates
10–16 Rathbone Street, London W1P 1AH ☎01–637 8251

Contact *Andrew Holmes*

Prolific originators, producers and packagers of documentary, comedy, children's and music television. OUTPUT includes *Who Dares Wins* and the *Well Being* series for

Channel 4; *Video and Chips* for **HTV**; *Chish and Fips* for **Central**; and the drama *Mohegans* for **Channel 4**.

ICM International
ICM House, 53–55 Frith Street, London W1V 5TE ☎01–434 0929

Contact *Linda Lucas*

Prominent makers of corporate video for major commercial and industrial clients.

ICP Films Ltd
Studio Centre, Ackhurst Road, Chorley, Lancs PR7 1ND ☎02572 66411/4

Contact *Michael Mulvihill*

Corporate video makers for a great variety of clients.

Illuminations
16 Newman Passage, London W1P 3PE ☎01–580 7877 Telex 23152 Monret G

Contact *John Wyver, Linda Zuck*

Primarily a documentary production company, making cultural programmes for a **Channel 4** audience. OUTPUT *State of the Art*, six-part documentary series; *Ghosts in the Machine*, six-part video compilation series, plus other documentaries about art and television. No unsolicited mss.

Imagicians
5 Newburgh Street, London W1V 1LH ☎01–439 2244

Contact *Alan Scales*

Diverse productions, from television documentary features to in-flight videos. OUTPUT includes *The Great Palace – the Story of Parliament*.

Independent Film Production Associates
87 Dean Street, London W1V 5AA ☎01–734 3847 Telex 265871

Contact *Aileen McCracken*

Makers of documentary and entertainment television, plus corporate video. Unsolicited mss are 'sometimes welcome . . . if it's good we go with it.'

Infovision Ltd
Bradley Close, White Lion Street, London N1 9PN ☎01–837 0012

Contact *Angela Brook*

Corporate video makers in the areas of training, marketing, and internal communications. Household name clients.

Insight Productions Ltd
37 Soho Square, London W1V 5DG   ☎01–434 3655

Contact *Brian Skilton*

Television and cinema producers. OUTPUT for **Channel 4** in the year 1986/7 includes
Streets Ahead, What a Way to Run a Revolution, Asian Arts, Dartmoor and *Barra*.
Also **Film on Four** presentation *Playing Away*.

Paul Joyce Productions
5 Townley Road, Dulwich, London SE22   ☎01–693 6006

Contact *Paul Joyce*

Development and production of drama, documentary, music, arts, adventure and
current affairs television and cinema. OUTPUT has included *Nothing As it Seems* (the
films of Nicholas Roeg); *The Man Who Left His Soul on Film*; *Summer Lightning* for
Film on Four; and *Out of the Blue and Into the Black*, about Dennis Hopper.

Knaves Acre Productions
The Crest, Hoe Lane, Abinger Hammer, Dorking, Surrey RH5 6RL ☎0306 731007

Contact *Bryan Izzard*

Makers of broadcast television principally for **Channel 4** and **ITV**. Unusual biographies of unusual composers, comedy (particularly sit-com), popular drama (live
soaps). OUTPUT *The Middle of the Road*, with **HTV**, 1987; *The Garden of Evelyn*,
Channel 4, 1987; *Video Alice*, 90 minute special for **Channel 4**, 1986. Unsolicited mss
welcome.

Landseer Film and Television Productions
100 St Martin's Lane, London WC2N 4AZ   ☎01–240 3161
Contact *Lin Brown*

Drama, documentary, music, arts, children's, adventure and current affairs television. Principally arts documentaries (and videos of performances), but also television
drama. OUTPUT has included *Mr Pye* with Derek Jacoby; *A Penny for Your Dreams*, a
co-production with **BBC Wales** and **S4C**.

Limehouse Productions
Limehouse Studios, Canary Wharf, West India Docks, London E14 9SJ
                                                 ☎01–987 2090

Contacts *Janet Walker, Terence Pritchard*

Dramatic adaptations made for television and video (mostly video). OUTPUT *What if
it's Raining; Rocket to the Moon; To Have and To Hold*. 'Not besieged' by unsolicited
scripts, which are welcome direct from writers.

Little Bird Films Ltd
8 West Street, London WC2H 9NG   ☎01–836 2112

Contact *James Mitchell*

Makers of television programmes. Recent credits include *The Irish RM.*

London Film Productions Ltd
44a Floral Street, London WC2E 9DA   ☎01–379 3366   Telex 896805

Contact *Rose Baring*

Makers of a wide range of international television and film. OUTPUT *The Scarlet Pimpernel; Kim; Country Girls; Poldark; I Claudius.* No unsolicited mss; a brief synopsis/outline is essential. Work by new writers is considered, and a strong speculatively written script would be taken up; however, the commissioning of a new writer to complete a script is a rare event.

Magic Hour Productions Ltd
143 Chatsworth Road, Willesden Green, London NW2 5QT   ☎01–459 3074

Contact *Ms D. J. Robinson*

Makers of television and films for a serious adult audience. Television and feature films, drama series, serials, documentaries, shorts. Unsolicited mss welcome, provided an s.a.e. is provided for their return.

MediaLab Ltd
Chelsea Wharf, 15 Lots Road, London SW10 0QH   ☎01–351 5814
                                                         Telex 297606 POLYIS G

Contact *John Gaydon (Chairman)*

FOUNDED 1982. Film and video production. Pop promos, TV documentaries, video, and a feature film with Godley & Creme. Interested in ideas for pop promos and investigative journalistic documentaries.

The Media Show Ltd
See **Beat Productions**.

Meditel Productions Ltd
Bedford Chambers, The Piazza, Covent Garden, London WC2 8HA
                                         ☎01–836 9216/9364   Telex 262284

Contact *Joan Shenton, Jad Adams*

Intelligent documentaries, afternoon programmes factually based but with an element of fun, evening programmes with hard story lines (no fun required). OUTPUT *Who Cares*, series of 4 health care documentaries; *Kill or Cure?* on the international drugs industry; *10 Million*, consumer series for the over 60s. No unsolicited mss;

writers should submit programme ideas on factual subjects including drama-documentary ideas with strong story lines. Either previous experience is essential, or new writers will work closely with a producer appointed by the company.

Bill Melendez Productions Ltd
32–34 Great Marlborough Street, London W1V 1HA ☎01–439 4411/01–734 0691

Contact *Steven Melendez, Graeme Spurway*

Animated films aimed mainly at a family audience, produced largely for the American market, and prime time network broadcasting. Also develops and produces feature films (six thus far). OUTPUT *Peanuts* half hour TV specials; *The Lion, the Witch and the Wardrobe*; *Babar the Elephant*, TV specials; *Dick Deadeye or Duty Done*, a rock musical based on Gilbert & Sullivan operettas. Generally produces own projects or work in collaboration with other producers/TV companies; 'however, three of the above walked in through the door'. Always interested in seeing new scripts and ideas.

Merchant Ivory Productions
34 South Molton Street, London W1

Contact *Ismail Merchant, James Ivory*

Makers of quality, literate cinema for an international market. Credits include *Shakespeare Wallah, Heat and Dust, The Bostonians, Quartet, Room With A View* and *Maurice*. A tradition of adaptation rather than original work seems by 1987 to have become entrenched.

Mersey Television Ltd
18 Rodney Street, Liverpool, L1 2TQ ☎051–259 1602

Contact *Paul Kerr*

Makers of television programmes – drama and fiction serials for popular consumption only. Credits include *Brookside* and *What Now?* for **Channel 4**.

Metropolis Pictures Ltd
Farringdon House, 105/107 Farringdon Road, London EC1R 3BT ☎01–278 7879

Contact *Elizabeth Taylor-Mead, Nicholas Dubrule*

A small independent film production company producing commissioned work for television. Its twelve year track record has been in quality documentaries/drama documentaries, though there are plans to produce low budget fictional projects in the future. OUTPUT *Before Hindsight*, documentary feature on 1930s newsreels; *Of Muppets And Men*, documentary for Henson Associates; *10 Years In An Open Necked Shirt*, featuring John Cooper Clarke; *The Rupert Bear Story* directed by Terry Jones. Very interested in working with new writers; but are presently too small a company to cope with unsolicited mss.

Midnight Films Ltd
26 Soho Square, London W1V 5FJ   ☎01–434 0011   Telex 268157 OJK G

Contact *Fiona Dent*

Recently the emphasis has been on pop promos, in which the directors usually bring in their own writers. On the TV/Cinema side, there are several scripts in development. OUTPUT *White City* (Pete Townshend); *Come Dancing* Kinks promo.

Mirus Productions
1–4 Argyll Street, London W1V 1AD   ☎01–437 7015

Contact *Mike Wallington*

Documentary, music and arts television. OUTPUT has included *Deep Roots Music* for **Channel 4**; *Black Hollywood, Songs of Freedom* and *Rockers Roadshow*.

Moving Picture Company
25 Noel Street, London W1V 3RD   ☎01–434 3100

Contact *David Jeffers*

Drama and documentary for television, corporate video and commercials. Credits include *In the Shadow of Fujisan* for the **BBC**; *Heinz Superchamps*, children's programme for **Channel 4**; *The Stars*, sequel to *The Planets*, plus the feature film *The Assam Garden*.

Ocean Pictures Ltd
39 Great Windmill Street, London W1V 7PA   ☎01–434 2495/2713

Contact *Roger Brown, Lucinda Sturgis*

From docu-drama through comedy to horror. Most interested in contemporary commercial scripts that have wide audience appeal for feature films and TV drama series.

Orion Picture Corporation
31–32 Soho Square, London W1V 3FF

London office of an American giant.

Oxford Film & Video Makers
The Stables, North Place, Headington, Oxford OX3 9HY   ☎0865 60074

Contact *Anne Marie Sweeney*

Makers of film and video for community, educational, trade union audiences. OUTPUT *Aids: Myth and Reality*; *Road or Reservation*. Unsolicited mss not welcome; 'we have enough work on already'. Though all their productions involve new writing, most of it is done in-house on a low budget.

Oxford Scientific Films
Long Hanborough, Oxford OX7 2LD   ☎0933 881881

Contact *Ian Moar*

Commercials, corporate and documentary film production.

Pacesetter Productions Ltd
New Barn House, Leith Hill Lane, Ockley, Surrey RH5 5PH   ☎0306 70 433

Contact *Adele Spencer*

Television, corporate and educational material. No unsolicited mss; all material is produced in-house.

Palace Productions
16–17 Wardour Mews, London W1V 3FF   ☎01–734 7060

Contact *Stephen Wooley, Nik Powell*

Company of Wolves; *Letter to Brezhnev*; *Absolute Beginners*; *Mona Lisa*. Unsolicited mss not welcome. As a small company, they aim to encourage new writing but can only do so 'on a limited basis'.

Parallax Pictures Ltd
7 Denmark Street, London WC2H 8LS   ☎01–836 1478

Contact *Sally Hibben*

Feature films, documentary and drama. An 'industrial co-operative' servicing **Channel 4** projects.

Paramount Pictures (UK) Ltd
162–170 Wardour Street, London W1V 4AB   ☎01–437 7700
Telex 263361 PARAUK G

'It is **Paramount's** policy not to accept unsolicited scripts'.

Pelicula Films
7 Queens Margaret Road, Glasgow G20 6DP   ☎041–945 3333

Contact *Mike Alexander*

Television producers. Makers of drama documentaries for **Channel 4**, including *Gramsci*, *Down Home* and *Scapa Flow – 1919*.

Picture Palace Productions Ltd

1 Beak Street Studios, 65–69 Beak Street, London W1R 3LF

☎01–439 9882   Telex 268048

Contact *Malcolm Craddock, Tim O'Mara*

Television and cinema film and drama. OUTPUT *Tandoori Nights* series; *Ping Pong*, for Film Four International; *Four Minutes* for **Channel 4**. Unsolicited mss welcome for feature length films and TV drama, and also for *Four Minutes*, which uses only writers new to television. 'Always interested in new writers'.

Picture Partnership Productions Ltd

73 Newman Street, London W1R 3LS   ☎01–637 8056

Contact *Brian Eastman*

FOUNDED 1978. **Picture Partnership** makes feature films and popular entertainment television, with the emphasis on comedy. OUTPUT *Father's Day*, **Channel 4**; *Blott on the Landscape*, **BBC**; *Whoops Apocalypse* and *Porterhouse Blue*. Unsolicited mss welcome if relevant to their particular field. In general terms encourage new writing.

Polygram Movies

45 Berkeley Square, London W1X 5DB   ☎01–493 8800

Contact *Michael Kuhn*

Music related visual programming, suspense/thriller movies with psychological depth and integrated commercial musical score.

Portman Productions

Tennyson House, 159–165 Great Portland Street, London W1N 6NR

☎01–637 4041

Contact *Victor Glynn*

The production arm of **Global Television** sales company. Feature films and mini-series for television. OUTPUT *Praying Mantis*; *Letters to an Unknown Lover*; *Tusitala*; *A Woman of Substance*; *Hold the Dream* (Bradford–Portman co-production). They receive a great many unsolicited scripts, all of them thus far unsuitable for production. Letters with treatments/outlines are read in hope: send these before submitting a finished script.

Poseidon Productions Ltd

113–117 Wardour Street, London W1V 3TD   ☎01–734 4441/5140
Telex 22347 POSFILM

Contact *Frixos Constantine*

Television and film makers/distributors, for an adult, educated art-loving film audience. OUTPUT *Pavlova* (drama); television series for **Channel 4** on the Greek philosophers. No unsolicited mss.

Quanta Ltd
44 Newman Street, London W1P 3PA   ☎(temporary) 01–580 7222

Contact *Nicholas Jones*

Documentary makers, with science programming a speciality. Also produces corporate video. OUTPUT *Horizon*, **BBC 2**; *Equinox*, **Channel 4**. A relatively young company (FOUNDED 1982), *Quanta* currently write all their own material in-house. No unsolicited mss.

Ragdoll Productions
34 Harborne Road, Edgbaston, Birmingham B15 3AA   ☎021–454 5453

Contact *Anne Wood*

Makers of children's television programmes. OUTPUT has included *Pob's Programme* and *Pob's Playtime* for **Channel 4**.

Red Rooster Films
11–13 Macklin Street, London WC2B 5NH ☎01–405 8147   Telex 291829 TLX G

Contact *Roxana Knight, Linda James*

A small independent film and television production company, whose productions range from drama series and feature films to documentaries, all destined for international distribution. A speciality in the past has been quality drama for older children. OUTPUT *Joni Jones*, five-part drama series about a 1940s Welsh childhood; *The Flea and the Giants*, three-part documentary series on the technological revolution; *Coming Up Roses*, full length feature film for **S4C**. Although unsolicited mss are not encouraged, treatments or outlines are welcome, and much more likely to receive a prompt response.

Riverfront Pictures Ltd
G4 Warehouse, New Crane Wharf, Garnet Street, Wapping, London E1 9QT
                                                    ☎01–481 2939

Contact *Jeff Perks*

Drama, documentary, music, arts, science, young people's programmes and comedy for television. OUTPUT has included *Our Lives, A Wee Bit Cheeky, Everyone a Special Kind of Artist* and *Breaking Through*, all for **Channel 4**.

Sandfire Productions
Pinewood Studios, Iver, Bucks SL10 0NH   ☎0753 651700
                                            Telex 847505 PINEWD G

Contact *Anthony Williams*

Feature films. Unsolicited mss welcome; 'interested to see new stories or completed screenplays but unlikely to commission'.

Schonfield Productions International

BCM Summer, London WC1N 3XX   ☎01–435 1007

Contact *Victor Schonfield*

Arts, natural history, current affairs documentary programmes for television. OUTPUT has included *Shattered Dreams* for **Central**; *The Animals Film* and *Like Other Children, to Live in the Same World*; plus contributions to **Channel 4**'s *Years Ahead* and *The Friday Alternative*.

Scimitar Films Ltd

6–8 Sackville Street, London W1X 1DD   ☎01–734 8385

Contact *Michael Winner, Chairman*

Feature films for the international market. OUTPUT *The Sentinel*; *The Big Sleep* (1977); *Death Wish I, II & III*; *The Wicked Lady*; *Appointment with Death*. No unsolicited mss. **Scimitar** has employed many first time scriptwriters in the past, however, including Dick Clement and Ian La Frenais, Peter Draper, Gerald Wilson and Michael Hastings.

Scope Films

38 Canfield Gardens, London NW6 3LA   ☎01–624 5571

Contact *Maggie Coates*

Drama and documentary television. OUTPUT has included *Common Interest, Politics of Health, People of the Islands* and *Backstage at the Kirov*.

Siren Film & Video Co-op

Customs House, St Hildas, Middlesbrough, Cleveland TS2 1EA   ☎0642 221298

Contact *Sally Constant*

Local distribution to community groups, etc; plus work for **Channel 4**.

Siriol Animation Ltd

3 Mount Stuart Square, Butetown, Cardiff CF1 6RW   ☎0222 488400
                                                        Telex 497244

Contact *Robin Lyons*

Animated films aimed at a family audience. OUTPUT TV specials *A Winter Story*; *Space Baby*; serials *SuperTed*; *Wil Cwac Cwac*; also *The Easter Egg*; *The Princess and The Goblin*. Ideas and scripts for animated programmes are welcome (though no un-solicited ms has thus far been produced). Shorts and full length films. Presently most of the writing is done by Robin Lyons, but new blood will be needed in the future.

Skyline Productions Ltd
1st floor, 24 Scala Street, London W1P 1LU ☎01–631 4649

Contact *Julia Cornelius*

also at 4 Picardy Place, Edinburgh EH1 3JT ☎031–557 4580

Contact *Trevor Davies*

A major supplier of programmes to **Channel 4**, **Skyline** also make health, educ-ational and corporate films. OUTPUT includes *Years Ahead, Radicals, 98 Not Out, Roy and Bob* and *International Volleyball*, all for **Channel 4**.

Tom Steel Productions
56 Sutherland Square, London SE17 3EL ☎01–701 6695

Contact *Tom or Jackie Steel*

Documentary television. The company write and develop their own material (though not necessarily always). OUTPUT has included *Touch and Go – the Battle for Crete* and *Scotland's Story* (twenty-four half hour episodes for **Channel 4**).

The Television Co-Operative
7 Strath Terrace, London SW11 1RF ☎01–223 4591

Contact *John Underwood*

A production co-operative specialising in the media, arts, politics, making documen-tary television. OUTPUT has included *Ireland the Silent Voices* for **Channel 4**; *A Beauty Awakes* for the **National Trust**; *Between Object and Image* for the **British Council**.

Third Eye Productions Ltd
Phillip House, 20 Chancellors Street, Hammersmith, London W6 9RL

☎01–741 0631

Contact *Margaret Young*

Makers of television programmes. *Talking Shop* for **Channel 4**; *All in a Day's Life* and *Bert Hardy's World*, also for **Channel 4**. Although a major supplier of documentary programmes to **Channel 4**, this exclusivity isn't by design.

Twentieth Century Fox Productions Ltd
Twentieth Century House, 31–32 Soho Square, London W1V 6AP

☎01–437 7766   Telex 27869

Contact *Company Secretary*

London office of the American giant. Unsolicited mss will be considered.

Tyburn Productions

Pinewood Studios, Iver Heath, Bucks SL0 0NH ☎0753 651700

Contact *Kevin Francis*

Television producers, specialising in popular drama. OUTPUT has included TV movies *The Masks of Death*, *Murder Elite*, *Courier* and *The Abbot's Cry*.

Ty Gwyn Films Ltd

Y Ty Gwyn, Llanllyfni, Caernarfon, Gwynned LL54 6DG ☎0286 881235

Contact *Gareth Wynn Jones*

Situation comedy, contemporary gritty Welsh subjects, spy thrillers (spies are the current vogue). Bilingual productions. New writing welcome, in English as well as Welsh. Their primary role is to provide output for the Welsh fourth channel, **S4C**.

UBA (Developments) plc (United British Artists)

Russell Chambers, Covent Garden, London WC2E 8AR

☎01–240 9891   Telex 269141 STRAT G

Contact *Lael McCall*

Quality feature films for an international market. OUTPUT *Turtle Diary*; *Castaway*; in development: *Batavia*; *The Lonely Passion of Judith Hearne*; *Rebel Magic*; *One Last Glimpse*; *Happy Feet*; *Kerry Babies*. Unsolicited mss welcome. Prepared to commission new writing, whether from an original idea based on a short outline/treatment, or adapted from some other medium. Concerned with the quality of the script (*Turtle Diary* was done by Harold Pinter) and the breadth of appeal; they do not welcome 'exploitation material'.

Umbrella Films

31 Percy Street, London W1P 9FG ☎01–631 0625   Telex 296538

Contact *Marc Samuelson*

British feature films: *Nineteen Eighty Four*; *Another Time Another Place*; *Loose Connections*; *Hotel du Paradis*; *White Mischief*. No scripts, treatments only.

Verronmead Ltd

257 Liverpool Road, London N1 1LX ☎01–607 8405

Contact *Maureen Harter, David Wood*

Children's programmes, dramas, women's programmes and documentaries mostly for **Channel 4**. Unsolicited mss and new writing welcome.

Video Arts Television
Dumbarton House, 68 Oxford Street, London W1N 9LA   ☎01–636 9421

Contact *Jane Lighting*

A division of **Dumbarton Films** which specialises in the production of major series for an international market. OUTPUT has included *Fairly Secret Army* for **Channel 4**; *From the Face of the Earth, Free to Choose, The Search for Alexander the Great* and *Start Here – Adventures into Science*.

Videotel Productions & Living Tape Productions
Ramillies House, 1–2 Ramillies Street, London W1V 1DF
                                    ☎01–439 6301   Telex 298596

Contact *Nick Freethy*

Education and training films, plus broadcast drama/documentaries and education series. OUTPUT *Catering Hygiene*; *Educating Deaf Children*; *Anything We Can Do*; *Home & Dry*; *Look What it Can Do*. Unsolicited mss if they are relevant to education/training areas only. Particularly keen to hear from good technical writers, 'who are in short supply'.

Virgin Films and Video
328 Kensal Road, London NW10 5XJ   ☎01–968 8888

Contact *Mike Watts*

Television programmes, cinema, educational and animated films. In 1987, made Ken Russell's *Gothic*. Also made *Absolute Beginners* (co-producers) and *Captive*. No television at present, but will be exploring this avenue in the future.

Vulgar Productions
20 Aden Grove, London N16   ☎01–254 7338

Contact *Sue Hayes*

Makers of television programmes. Recent credits include *Arthur and Phil Go Off* for **Channel 4**.

Brent Walker Film and Theatre Division
Knightsbridge House, 197 Knightsbridge, London SW7 1RB   ☎01–225 1941

Contact *Tony Murphy*

Currently making very little: in 1987, *American Gossip*, a feature film; the previous production was *Mountbatten*, made for video in 1985.

Warner Sisters
21 Russell Street, London WC2B 5HP   ☎01–836 0134

Contacts *Lavinia Warner, Terry Hughes*

Television and film drama, documentaries. OUTPUT *Tenko*; *Lizzie – An Amazon Adventure*; *GI Brides*. Now expanding in other directions. Several series are in development, plus a feature film based on the Hitler Diaries scandal. New scripts will always be considered.

Wildacre Productions
10 Parsonage Lane, Windsor, Berks SL4 5EN   ☎0753 864114

Contact *Hugh David*

Drama, documentary, light entertainment, arts, children's religious television, plus corporate production. OUTPUT has included *Apocalypse* for **Channel 4**; *David Watson – a Tribute*, and *Alisa*, both also for **Channel 4**; and *Troeon Treftadaeth* for **S4C**.

Maurice Winnick Associates Ltd/Philip Hindin Ltd
30 Albert Street, London NW1 7LU

Contact *Vera Marsh, Philip Hindin*

Makers of TV Panel and Quiz Game Shows and light entertainment. No unsolicited mss (not appropriate).

Working Title
35 Little Russell Street, London WC1   ☎01–323 2741

Contact *Tim Bevan*

Television programmes and cinema, drama and documentary subjects. OUTPUT has included *The Man Who Shot Christmas* (short), *My Beautiful Laundrette*, *Caravaggio* and *Personal Services*.

Zenith Productions Ltd
8 Great Titchfield Street, London W1P 7AA   ☎01–637 7941   Telex 23348

Contact *Scott Meek (Head of Development)*

Feature films and television. (The feature film arm of **Central TV**.) OUTPUT *The Hit*, *Insignificance*, *Wetherby*, *Personal Services*, *Prick Up Your Ears*, *Slam Dance*, *Wish You Were Here*; television: *Heart of the Country*, *Finnegan Begin Again*, *Fields of Fire*. Unsolicited mss are acceptable.

Zooid Pictures

52 Crouch Hill, London N4 4AA ☎ 01–272 9115

Contact *Richard Philpott, Jasmine Nicholas*

Zooid aim to combine their experimental, multi-media interests with commercial viability. OUTPUT *Road Movie, The Spirit of Albion*, both for **Channel 4**. Writing has been entirely in-house so far, but if mss which understand their work are submitted they will always be considered.

Theatre Producers

Up in Lights – Writing a Play

Live drama is more of a gamble than any other form of writing. Not surprisingly, because instability is endemic to this business. Producers come and go, sometimes very quickly indeed and bad debts are a way of life.

According to Peter Nichols, one of our best playwrights, whose experience of the West End has left him with an uncharitable view of human nature,

'a living author will hear only twice from the producer's office after his play has opened; first to ask him to waive his fee; secondly to tell him the play is coming off.'

Still, the rewards of creative a marketable play can be enormous. Even a modest success, say a production which runs in a mainstream London theatre for six months, can bring a healthy return on time and talent. Fees can vary from 4% to as high as 10% of the box office receipts (the big subsidised companies pay the best rates). This means that a production at, say, the **Lyttelton Theatre** at the **National** which is playing to 70 per cent capacity at an average ticket price of £8 (all conservative estimates) should bring the author something of the order of £500 a night.

Then there is a good chance of repeat productions around the country, the sale of subsidiary rights and royalties from the published text. This last is a fast expanding source of income as publishers like **Methuen** and **Faber** make strong efforts to promote their drama lists. Last year John Osborne's *Look Back in Anger*, first produced in 1956, sold 20,000 copies, a figure matched by Tom Stoppard's *Rosencrantz and Guildenstern Are Dead* (1967) and closely approached by Harold Pinter's *Caretaker* (1960). One of the more encouraging marketing initiatives of recent years has been the sale of combined text/programmes. Around a quarter of the playgoers to the **Royal Court** buy the text of the play they have booked to see. But to achieve big money in the theatre, the writer needs to start with a high level of commitment. Commissions are rare and advances for all but the biggest names are modest even by publishing standards.

One encouraging pointer to the future is the willingness of the **National Theatre**, the **Royal Shakespeare Company** and the **Royal Court** to come to terms with the **Writers' Guild** and the **Theatre Writers' Union** on rates for the job. For example, for a commissioned play, the **National** and **RSC** now pay a minimum advance of £3500 with £1750 up front. The corresponding figures for main theatre at the **Royal Court** are £3250 and £1500 while at the **Theatre Upstairs**, the Royal Court's own fringe venue, the advance is £1200 with £600 up front. Other parts of the agreements range from West End and overseas options to payment for attendance at rehearsals.

The fringe too is falling into line with agreements, in principle, to guarantee payment to writers equal to an actor's salary for twenty-six weeks (the **Equity** minimum is £137.50) for a non-commercial play and thirteen weeks plus a negotiated fee for a commissioned play. The **Theatre Writers' Union** is also fighting hard for the right of consultation on casting and the appointment of directors and designers.

The theatre is hungry for product as a glance at our list of production companies will quickly indicate. In fact, we have not taken account of every known producer. This is because there are so many of them, we could probably fill this book with their names and addresses alone. What we have tried to do is to choose those who are sufficiently well known to figure on any writer's hit list and those who at least have a sympathy for new writing.

By the same token, we have not listed all regional theatres. While many repertory companies profess an interest in new plays this rarely translates into practical offers. Shortage of funds is one reason; the tendency to play safe with an audience schooled in Agatha Christie and *Bless The Bride* is another. That said, your own local theatre may be an exception. But to save time, before submitting material, write or phone first to check their policy on new writing.

Throughout Britain there are only some fifteen theatres which actively seek new plays by new writers (as distinct from new plays by established writers). Leading the pack is the **Royal Court** which employs no less than three literary managers and eighteen readers to deal with an average yearly intake of five hundred unsolicited scripts. A new play which is judged to be at all interesting is seen by at least three readers before it enters what is known as *The Grid*. This means it is available to be read by directors, designers and anyone else working within the theatre who might have a point of view. Luck enters here in a big way because much depends on the play attracting the interest of a particular director who might then act as patron, encouraging the writer to make necessary changes while at the same time promoting his cause to influential colleagues.

While this sort of break is rare (it is said that the odds on it happening to an untried writer are about five thousand to one) the submission of a new play which is judged to be less than brilliant need not be a waste of time. The **Royal Court** is scrupulous in its efforts to offer constructive criticism. Moreover, writers who are ready to look for ways to improve their skills are very often those who end up being asked to submit work. As Colin Chambers at the **RSC** points out, 'A good percentage of the writers we're commissioning now at one time or another sent a play to us unsolicited.'

Among the smaller theatres dedicated to new writing, pride of place goes to the **Soho Poly**, which broke with tradition just recently by actually staging a revival. All writers of promise who send in scripts to the **Soho Poly** are invited to a Workshop session in which they get together with actors and directors to discover how best to develop their work.

One of the most exciting schemes of this kind is run by the **National** as its **Studio Theatre**. Plays selected by the National's literary department are given the chance of a reading by professional actors. A similar project is run by the **Riverside Studios** where promising scripts advance from a private to a public reading.

Other schemes up and down the country which aim to help new writers are mentioned in our listing of production companies. But for full information on opportunities in your area, contact the nearest regional arts association (list on p. 419).

The next step up is to be associated with a particular theatre. This can be achieved by special grants such as the **Thames Television** bursaries (worth £5000 a year) which aim to give young playwrights the chance to develop their skills within a sympathetic and stimulating environment. Among those who have benefited from Thames bursaries are Alan Bleasdale, Mike Stott and Mary O'Malley. One of the great virtues of the bursary scheme is that it teaches the budding playwright that the theatre is a collaborative enterprise. But this is not to everyone's style or taste. Writers who are averse to having their words changed about, often so dramatically that the end product is unrecognisable against the original conception, are not likely to be happy in the theatre. For them, the best advice is: stick to books.

Aba Daba Ltd
30 Upper Park Road, London NW3   ☎ 01–722 5395

Plays and satirical pantomimes performed at venues like the Water Rats and the Canal Café in London. The company write all their material themselves: they would be happy to consider some of the great piles of unsolicited mss they receive, were it not for the fact that there is absolutely no money available for outsiders.

Actors Touring Company
Alford House, Aveline Street, London SE11 5DQ   ☎ 01–753 8311

Contact *Mark Brickman* (Artistic Director)

ATC are well known for producing lively new versions of classic works. They take plays by Shakespeare, Molière, Ibsen, Vanburgh, and others, and work with writers in adapting them for **ATC** use. Unsolicited mss with classic/epic features or intentions are welcome. Intend to work more with writers in the future.

Akela Ltd
14 Talbot House, 98 St Martin's Lane, London WC2N 4AX   ☎ 01–379 0123

Contact *Colin Brough*

A new company which aims to continue the policy and West End profile of Colin Brough's former outfit, the Lupton Theatre Company. As Lupton, produced *Rose*, Andrew Davis; *When the Wind Blows*, Raymond Briggs; *Big in Brazil*, Bamber Gascoigne; *Phedra*, adapted from Racine by Robert David Macdonald, among other West End and touring shows. Akela hope to produce a high proportion of new work. No unsolicited mss – they aren't read. Scripts preferred through agents; if approaching direct, write in the first instance.

Albermarle of London

13 Liverpool Street, London W1N 7DF ☏ 01–631 0135

Pantomimes only, and Albemarle write their own scripts for these.

Aldersgate Productions

12 Palace Street, London SW1E 5JF ☏ 01–828 6591

Contact *Ronald Mann* (Artistic Director)

Produce plays of a broadly Christian nature, for children, family groups and church groups. Productions have included *Ride Ride*, a musical about John Wesley; *Sentenced to Life*, a play about euthanasia; *Song of the Lion*, a one man show about C. S. Lewis. Unsolicited mss welcome. Almost all their scripts are original, and many by new writers.

Alternative Theatre Company

Bush Theatre, Shepherds Bush Green, London W12 8QD ☏ 01–602 3703

Contact *Timothy O'Grady*

FOUNDED 1972. They produce six shows (principally new plays from Britain and abroad) a year, plus two visiting company productions of new work: 'we are a writer's theatre'. The benefits of dealing with a writer's theatre include: a well-organised script reading set-up (around 3 months from arrival to final decision); 'recommissions' – fees to complete further drafts of promising plays; and a guaranteed fee against royalties, which protects the writer from small houses. New plays at the Bush have included *The Fosdyke Saga*, Bill Tidy and Alan Plater; *City Sugar*, Stephen Poliakoff; *Duet for One*, Tom Kempinski; *Commitments*, Dusty Hughes (written during a residency at the Bush).

Yvonne Arnaud Theatre

Millbrook, Guildford, Surrey GU1 3UX ☏ 0483 64571

Contact *Val May* (Artistic Director)

New work always considered. Credits include *Melon*, Simon Gray; *Mr & Mrs Nobody*, Keith Waterhouse; *Breaking the Code*, Hugh Whitemore; *Holiday Snaps*, Michael Pertwee and John Chapman; *Cuckoo*, Emlyn Williams.

Tom Arnold Associates Ltd

33 Museum Street, London WC1A 1LD ☏ 01–631 4596

Contact *Gaynor Ramsey*

Musicals of the *The King and I* sort (1979) and light entertainment musical shows like *Dancing* (1983) for the West End, though haven't produced anything since then. But keen to see strong musical play scripts or receive good ideas for future consideration.

Arts Management

Redroofs, Littlewick Green, Maidenhead, Berks.   ☎0628 822982

Contact *June Rose* (Artistic Director)

Only interested in full-scale children's musicals based on classic titles, and potted versions of Shakespeare for schools. Mss are welcome if they meet these exact requirements. Recent productions have included *Charlie and the Chocolate Factory*; *The Lion, the Witch and the Wardrobe* (musical); and *Once Upon a Time*.

Belgrade Theatre, Coventry

Belgrade Square, Coventry CV1 1GS   ☎0203 56431

Contact *Bob Hamlyn* (Artistic Director)

Both the main house and the studio theatre are keen to put on new work, but the studio does most. In the past year the studio has had 2 world premières – *Boys From Hibernia* by Mark Power, and Bob Mason's *Sad Arthur's Trip*. 'Our main house also has a better track record on new work than most . . .' recently producing *Johnny Bull*, Kathleen Betsko, and Julian Garner's *Guardian Angels*. Bob Hamlyn with a team of readers try to give time to everything submitted, and also make commissions where appropriate.

Birmingham Repertory Theatre

Broad Street, Birmingham B1 2EP   ☎021–236 6771

Contact *John Adams* (Artistic Director)

John Adams took over from longstanding Artistic Director Clive Perry in 1987. Future policy on new writing looks likely to change only in respect of a greater concentration on fewer playwrights. There had been criticism of Clive Perry's 'open door' policy, and the feeling that plays had not been nurtured sufficiently because too many were accepted. The theatre has long had a policy of encouragement of new work, and one of Clive Perry's main achievements was to get new plays out of the **Studio Theatre** and into the main house. In the 1986/87 season, five out of nine productions there were new, including *Heavenly Bodies*, Stuart Parker; *Outside Broadcast*, Peter Woodward; *Mouthful of Birds*, Caryl Churchill and David Lamb. Mss or synopses to John Adams (the founder of *Paines Plough*).

Borderline Theatre Company

Darlington New Church, North Harbour Street, Ayr KA8 8AA   ☎0292 281010

Contact *Morag Fullerton* (Artistic Director)

FOUNDED 1974. A touring company taking shows to main house theatres in city centres and small venues in outlying districts, plus the Edinburgh Festival, Mayfest and, occasionally, London. Mainly new and contemporary work, plus revivals: *Trumpets and Raspberries*, Dario Fo; *Threepenny Opera*, Bertolt Brecht; *Writers Cramp*, John Byrne; *A Night in the Ukraine*, Voxburgh & Laxarus; *Four in a Million*,

Les Blair; *Shanghied*, Liz Lochhead; plus pantomime and children's plays. Synopsis with cast size preferred in the first instance. **Borderline** try to include one new work every season: 'once we commission a writer we would want him to work very closely with the company . . . we want the work to be enlightening and have some relevance to our audience'.

Bristol Express Theatre Company

20 Mocatta House, Brady Street, London E1 5DL   ☎01–247 4156

Contact *Eileen Quinn*

Regularly hold 'research and development workshops' and playreadings which aim to bring on and encourage promising new playwrights. The material for these comes both from people known to them and from interesting unsolicited scripts. The other element of their work is the touring of plays – which can come from their own workshops. It's unusual for a play sent to the company to be accepted for production as it stands; Bristol Express thrives on a spirit of co-operation.

Bristol Old Vic

Theatre Royal, King Street, Bristol BS1 4ED   ☎0272 277466

Contact *Rodney West*

A producing theatre which receives around 10 unsolicited scripts a week – synopses and letters preferred in first instance. New work is produced both in the main house – recently Alan Plater's *Foot On the Earth* – and in the studio (the New Vic) where more experimental writing has a foothold.

Bush Theatre

See **Alternative Theatre Company**.

Cambridge Theatre Company

8 Market Passage, Cambridge CB2 3PE   ☎0223 357134

Contact *Bill Pryde* (Artistic Director)

Cambridge Theatre Company have no script reading facilities, and rarely produce new work. They admit that unsolicited mss are seldom read, though letters and synopses are welcome.

Cameron Mackintosh

40 Museum Street, London WC1A 1LY   ☎01–242 8808

Producer of *Cats, Les Miserables, Abracadabra*, Cameron Mackintosh is one of the most important producers in London's West End. Unsolicited scripts are read and considered (there is no literary manager however) but chances of success are slim. This is because they only produce musicals, and produce no more than one musical a year – which is more likely to come by way of contacts. Fixed up for the whole of 1988 by June 1987, and there is a strong possibility that his production of new musicals will cease at the end of the year.

Caricature Theatre Ltd
Perch Buildings, 9 Mt Stuart Square, Cardiff CF1 6EE   ☎0222 497918

Contact *Jane Phillips* (Artistic Director)

Formerly a specialist children's theatre company working with masks and puppets, **Caricature** no longer functions as a company, as its Arts Council grant has been withdrawn after 19 years.

Channel Theatre Trust Ltd
Granville Theatre, Victoria Parade, Ramsgate, Kent CT11 8DG   ☎0843 888280

Contact *Philip Dart*

Based at the Granville Theatre, the company divides its productions between a commercial summer season there and Arts Council tours to smaller venues, arts centres etc. Productions have included *The Normal Heart*, the play about AIDS; *Dracula: A Pain in the Neck*; *Adrian Mole*, and *Bedroom Farce*. Not interested in new writing uless a small-scale work of quality, although averse to kitchen sink dramas and 'pretend Ayckbourn'. Of the hundreds of unsolicited mss received, none has yet come to anything – 'but that's only because we haven't had a good script thus far'. Letters and brief synopses much preferred to finished mss.

Jean Charles Productions
4A Jointon Road, Folkestone, Kent CT29 2RF   ☎0303 52413

Contact *Jean Charles*

Jean Charles produces variety, panto and summer shows, much of which is scripted elsewhere. However, she is always on the look out for good new comedy material – sketches and jokes particularly. Write a letter first.

Churchill Theatre
High Street, Bromley BR1 1HA   ☎01–464 7131

Contact *Nick Salmon*

Almost all plays produced by the theatre are revivals. Recent productions have included *Corpse*, Gerald Moon; *The Prisoner of Zenda*, adapted by Warren Graves; *Charlie's Aunt* and several Agatha Christies. Though a great many unsolicited scripts are received, they are generally not suitable for Churchill audiences.

City Theatre Productions
11A Friern Mount Drive, London N20 9DP   ☎01–445 7961

Contact *Jon Rumney*

The company is currently dormant, but if a good script came along, would awake to produce it. Enjoyed great success at the Edinburgh Festival in the past, with international plays and new work. 'We're after topical interest, humour, a small cast and strong actors' parts . . .'

Alan Clements Productions
Mill House, St Ives Cross, Sutton St James, South Lincs ☎ 094 585 466

Contact *Alan Clements*

Small-scale operation, producing pantomimes and only one or two plays a year. Of these, very little is new – *Sweeney Todd* being a recent exception. There is generally little hope for new writers here: 'because we're a commercial, non-subsidised company, everything we do has to be a fairly safe bet'.

Ron Coburn International
Vaudevilla, Elliot Road, Dundee DD2 1SY ☎ 0382 69025

Contact *Ron Coburn*

Ron Coburn writes and produces internationally touring musical variety shows like *A Breath of Scotland* and *The Waggle o' the Kilt*. Venues range from Carnegie Hall to Mablethorpe and Skegness. As the material needs to travel to North America and is usually of a topical nature, it's not feasible to use outside writers.

Michael Codron Ltd
Aldwych Theatre offices, Aldwych, London WC2B 4DF ☎ 01–240 8291

Contact *Joe Scott Parkinson* (General Manager)

Michael Codron Ltd manage the Aldwych and Adelphi theatres, and own the Vaudeville Theatre in London's West End. The plays they produce don't necessarily go into these theatres, but always tend to be big-time West End fare like *Woman in Mind* with Julia Mackenzie. There is no particular rule of thumb on subject matter or treatment, the acid test being 'whether something appeals to Michael'. 'The reason we haven't done much in the last six months is that nothing has appealed sufficiently.' Straight plays rather than musicals. Generally enthusiastic about new work, and resolve to read everything which is submitted.

The Coliseum
Fairbottom Street, Oldham, OL1 3SW ☎ 061–624 1731

Contact *John Retallack*

Considered a good bet for new playwrights, The Coliseum is besieged by more scripts than it can read. However, they do put on new work: 'we like to do new writing that's popular and relevant to our audience . . . it's got to be popular'. Letters and synopses much preferred to finished scripts. Recent plays have included *A Night on the Tiles*, Frank Pickering; *Girlfriends*, Howard Goodall. Often plays come by way of contacts or commissions, but good unsolicited scripts still stand a chance. Just don't expect a swift decision . . . .

Comedy Hall Productions

1 Maplesbury Court, Shoot-Up-Hill, London NW2 3PU   ☎01–452 2590

Contact *Tony Worgan*

Established in 1985, Comedy Hall is 'not producing at the moment' (July 1987). Their only production so far has been the successful *Laugh? I Nearly Went To Miami*, Miles Tredinnick, published by Samuel French. Although the company exists to produce comedies and farces, they are not interested in receiving unsolicited scripts – 'we get so many, and there's no time to read them'. New plays come to them by way of personal contacts, or 'we go out and find something if we want it'. No mss, letters or synopses.

Compass Theatre Company

13 Shorts Gardens, London WC2H 9AT   ☎01–379 7501

Contact *Julian Forrester* (General Manager)

Sir Anthony Quayle founded this company three years ago to produce revivals and large-cast classics. Productions have included *King Lear, Dandy Dick, The Tempest, St Joan, The Clandestine Marriage* and *After The Ball is Over*. To date, not much demand for new writing, but there is change in the air, in the form of Don Taylor, who has recently joined the company and is very keen to tackle new plays.

Mervyn Conn Organisation

MC House, 14 Orange Street, London WC2H 7ED   ☎01–930 7502

The *Annie* tour is the first theatre Mervyn Conn have produced (ordinarily they present one-offs like the Silk Cut Country & Western Festival) and though more plays will probably follow in 1988, these will certainly be revivals. No facilities for reading mss, and no interest in new work.

Contact Theatre Company

Oxford Road, Manchester M15 6JA   ☎061 274 3434

Contact *Anthony Clark* (Artistic Director)

FOUNDED 1966. Play predominantly to a young audience (15–35) with a particular interest in new work, especially from the North West. Up to 5 plays a year are commissioned. In 1986 productions included *The Snowman*, Raymond Briggs; *The Wheel Tricycle*, John Chambers; *Firestone*, Peter Fieldson. **Contact** is also involved closely in the North West Playwrights Workshops organised by the **Theatre Writers' Union**.

Crosskeys Productions Ltd

6 Wharfedale Street, London SW10 9AL   ☎01–370 2618

No longer acting as producers.

Croydon Warehouse

Warehouse Theatre, Dingwall Road, Croydon CR0 2NF ☏ 01–680 4060

Contact *Steve Gooch* (Literary Manager)

A new writing theatre on a small scale, seating around 120, producing six new plays a year. Recent new plays have included *Beached*, Kevin Hood; and *Screamers*, Anthony Davison. Hold a playwriting festival every September, and aim in general to be the new writing theatre of South London. Receive between two and five unsolicited scripts a day. It can take a long time for promising mss to come to anything because the theatre is committed so far in advance – nine months, in some cases.

Crucible Theatre

Norfolk Street, Sheffield, S1 1DA ☏ 0742 760621

Contact *Mike Kay* and *Steven Pimlott* (Associate Directors)

Under the artistic direction of Clare Venables, the Crucible has developed a strong policy on new writing, and tries to do one new main house show a year, with plenty of others appearing in the Studio. These are often commissioned from established writers or from new writers of promise: unsolicited scripts are rarely used as they stand, but can lead to higher things in a set-up keen to grab new talent. Recent new plays have included *A Passion in 6 Days*, Howard Barker; *It's A Bit Lively Outside*, Joyce Holliday; *Here We Go*, Andy de la Tour. The Crucible was, incidentally, the producer to commission Chris Martin's *Who Killed Hilda Murrell?* Finished scripts are always preferred to synopses or ideas.

Leslie Parker Davies Productions

Chequers, Barton Road, Farndon, Chester CH3 6NL ☏ 0829 270467

Not for the moment acting as theatrical producer.

Bernard Delfont Organisation Ltd

Prince of Wales Theatre, Coventry Street, London SW1 ☏ 01–930 9901

No longer acting as theatre producers.

Charles Dickens Theatre Company

Sunrise House, Gibraltar Road, Otley, Ipswich IP6 9LL ☏ 047385 672

Contact *Charles Peter Mugleston*

A new company which will consider plays of all kinds. New writing considered; s.a.e. in all cases.

Dramatis Personae

122 Kennington Road, London SE11 6RE ☎01–735 0831

Contact *Nathan Silver*

Run by Nathan Silver and Maria Aitken, the company turns its hand to a great variety of projects (and is presently co-producing for the BBC on documentary subjects). Interested to read new plays, which most often come by way of contacts in the business, but can occasionally be taken up from unknowns who send scripts on spec. Good plays are put into provincial rep, and brought in to London if successful. Letters and synopses preferred in first instance.

E & B Productions Ltd

Suite 1, Waldorf Chambers, Aldwych, London WC2B 4DA ☎01–836 2795

Contact *Paul Elliott, Brian Hewitt-Jones*

Theoretically at least, interested in seeing new scripts, although the schedule for the last half of 1987 was taken up with touring shows like *Run for Your Wife* and *Double Double*, plus the preparation of 14 pantomimes for the winter. In 1986 productions included *Crown Matrimonial, Gaslight* and *Crystal Clear*, as well as the new play *The Secret Life of Cartoons* by Clive Barker.

Field Day Theatre Company

22 Waterloo Place, Derry BT48 6BU, Northern Ireland ☎0504 260196

Contact *Julie Barber* (Administrator)

A touring company which usually commissions its plays from Irish writers. Past productions have included *Carthaginians*, Frank McGuinness; *Pentecost*, Stewart Parker. No scripts or ideas as all work is commissioned.

Foco Novo

1–2 Alfred Place, London WC1 ☎01–580 4722

Contact *Tunde Ikoli* (resident dramatist)

Foco Novo is a new writing company, existing to commission and produce new work. They were the first company to do *The Elephant Man*; other productions have included *Death Watch*, Jean Genet; *Needles of Light*, James Pettifer; and Tunde Ikoli's *Banged Up*. Unsolicited mss are welcome; synopses and letters especially so. Two touring productions a year, in spring and autumn.

Vanessa Ford Productions Ltd

62 Overdale Road, London SW10 0SS ☎01–352 1948

Contact *Vanessa Ford*

Recent work has included *Winnie the Pooh*, touring and West End, and a London classical season, including *The Lion, The Witch and The Wardrobe*. Often do their own writing and adaptation in-house but also keen to see new plays of all kinds, whether finished scripts, ideas or synopses.

Clare Fox & Brian Kirk Ltd
Suite 3c, 26 Charing Cross Road, London WC2H 0DG   ☎01-379 4985

Contact *Clare Fox*

Producers for the commercial West End. Past productions include *Bent*, Martin Sherman; *Mr & Mrs Nobody*; *Breaking the Code*, Hugh Whitemore; *Of Mice and Men*, John Steinbeck; *The Amen Corner*, James Baldwin. Unsolicited mss are welcome, 'but they take a long time to process'. Very interested in new writing.

Robert Fox Ltd
6 Beauchamp Place, London SW3 1NG   ☎01-584 6855

Contact *Robert Fox*

In 1987, co-producers of *Chess* in London's West End, and about to co-produce Peter Shaffer's *Lettice and Lovage*, with Robert Harwood's new play *J. J. Farr* to follow. Scripts, while usually by established playwrights, are always read. Bear in mind that the company is usually concerned with work suitable for West End production, however.

Freeshooter Productions Ltd
10 Clorane Gardens, London NW3 7PR   ☎01-794 0414

Contact *Andrew Empson*

Past productions have included: *The Petition*, Wyndhams Theatre; *Siegfried Sassoon*, Apollo Theatre; *Kipling*, Mermaid Theatre; *St Mark's Gospel*, on tour; and *March of the Falsettos*, Manchester and the Albery Theatre, London. Unsolicited scripts welcome.

Mark Furness Ltd
10 Garrick Street, London WC2E 9BH   ☎01-836 7373

Contact *Mark Furness*

In 1987 their summer seasons included tours of *Run for Your Wife* and *The Mating Game*, *'Allo 'Allo* in the West End, and a new play by Donald Churchill, *Mixed Feelings*. Unsolicited mss welcome, but bear in mind that they need to be suitable for touring. Not necessarily comedy – also produce thrillers such as *A Murder is Announced*.

John Gale
Strand Theatre, Aldwych, London WC2B 5LD ☎ 01–240 1656

Contact *John Gale*

John Gale is also director of Chichester Festival Theatre (scripts can also be sent to him there: Festival Theatre Productions Co. Ltd, Oaklands Park, Chichester, Sussex, Tel. 0243 784437). In London, *No Sex Please We're British* has run and run; other recent plays have included *Jane Eyre* and *Miranda* with Penelope Keith. The general pattern is, typically, classic revivals in the main house, new plays in the studio (unless very saleable). But both London and Chichester are interested in seeing new work of quality.

Gallery Productions Ltd
The Old Fire Station, South Road, Merstham, Surrey RH1 3EE ☎ 073 744833

Contact *Robert Kennedy*

A touring company founded in 1985, with seven productions planned for 1987, and increasingly interested in new work. Past productions have included *Widow's Weeds*, Anthony Shaffer; *Rough Crossing*, Tom Stoppard; *The Haunting*, Shirley Jackson. No 'avant garde' work, prefer contemporary subjects traditionally written. Synopses in the first instance; scripts by invitation.

Glasgow Citizens Theatre
Gorbals, Glasgow, G5 9DS ☎ 041–429 5561

Contact *Paul Bassett*

The Cits has no formal policy on new writing; although interested in seeing new work, in practice they haven't produced any in the last couple of years. Productions tend to be classic revivals, or else adaptations/translations done by the resident dramaturge Robert David MacDonald. There isn't generally the money to put on new plays which may not be popular.

Globe Players Theatre Company
36 St James Avenue, Hampton Hill, Middlesex TW12 1HN ☎ 01–979 5497

Shakespeare and fairy stories only, for touring to schools in the London area. All fairy stories originate in house, for financial reasons. Not interested in receiving mss or synopses.

Derek Glynne Pty Ltd
25 Haymarket, London SW1 ☎ 01–930 1981

Contact *Mrs Tarkhurst*

Derek Glynne (who also trades at the same address as **The London Company Ltd**) is in partnership with American and Australian producers. There are two aspects of the company's work – taking companies like the **RSC** abroad and producing plays largely for Australian and American audiences. Most of these originate abroad, so in general there is little hope for playwrights here. However, they are about to do a new play which was commissioned by them, and unsolicited mss/ideas of promise are passed on for consideration. In addition, they are often consulted or asked to co-produce.

Great Eastern Stage

Lincolnshire & Humberside Arts, Steinkirk Block, Dunkirk Road, Lincoln LN1 3UJ
☎ 0522 34924

Contact *Ian McKeand* (Artistic Director)

Active in local (and some national) touring. Welcome plays with a local theme particularly; planning to do more locally based plays in the near future.

Greenwich Theatre

13 Nevada Street, London SE10 8ES   ☎ 01–858 4447

Contact *Alan Strachan* (Artistic Director)

A repertory company which usually hosts other people's productions but has a policy of reading all submitted scripts ('eventually') and perhaps passing on those with promise. For example, *Scout's Honour* which went on to success at the Lyric Theatre Hammersmith. A big backlog of scripts to read; approach with ideas in first instance.

Raymond Gubbay Ltd

125 Tottenham Court Road, London W1P 9HN   ☎ 01–387 4206

Although Raymond Gubbay does from time to time act as a theatrical producer, these are mostly one-offs and rarely straight plays. For the moment, he is concentrating on music and acting solely as a concert promoter.

Half Moon Theatre

213 Mile End Road, London E1 4AA   ☎ 01–791 1141

Contact *Chris Bond* (Artistic Director)

The Half Moon produce six shows a year, and are very interested in new writing, but 'we're not a writers' theatre for the sake of it, and aren't prepared to produce new work unless it's of a high standard'. A third to a half of their output meets these exacting requirements. Occasionally commissions to complete further drafts of promising work will be offered. Productions have included *Moll Flanders*, Clare Luckham; *Sink the Belgrano*, Steven Berkoff; *Elizabeth*, Dario Fo (first English translation); and the first English production of the Jamaican pantomime *Trash*, by Barbara Gloudon.

Hampstead Theatre
Swiss Cottage Centre, London NW3 3EX   ☎01–722 9224

Contact *Alan Drury*

A new writing theatre, with 85 per cent of plays produced new to Britain. Looking for a distinctive quality in the writing rather than a worthy attempt at a responsible subject. Past productions have included *Particular Friendships*, Martin Allen; *The Gambler*, Mel Smith, Bob Goody and Peter Brewis; *Observe the Sons of Ulster Marching Towards the Somme*, Frank McGuiness; *Ask for the Moon*, Shirley Gee; *Selling the Sizzle*, Peter Gibbs; *This Story of Yours*, John Hopkins. Starting a workshop scheme jointly with the **Tricycle Theatre**.

Hazemead Ltd
4th floor, 235–241 Regent Street, London W1R 5DD   ☎01–629 4817

Contact *Anne Chudleigh*

Producers of summer seasons and pantomimes all over the country. Interested in plays, sitcoms and sketches. New writers and scripts come to them principally through recommendation, but unsolicited mss and letters are always welcome.

Al Heath
Harmony House, Sussex Lane, Spencer's Wood, Berks RG7 1BY   ☎0734 884773

Contact *Al Heath*

Acts solely as an agent for international light entertainment/cabaret. No straight plays, no interest in mss or synopses.

Hiss & Boo Ltd
24 West Grove, Walton on Thames, Surrey KT12 5NX   ☎0932 248931

Contact *Ian Liston*

1978. Productions have included *Novello, Benefactors, Cluedo, Mr Men Musical, The Rivals*. Keen to see and read as much new work as possible, providing a synopsis and introductory letter is offered in the first instance. Unsolicited mss not welcome.

Horseshoe Theatre Company Ltd
The Shrubbery, Cliddesden Road, Basingstoke, Hants RG21 3ER   ☎0256 55844

Contact *Ian Mullins* (Artistic Director)

Productions last season included *And A Nightingale Sang*, C. P. Taylor; *The Beaux' Stratagem*, George Farquhar; *Passion Play*, Peter Nichols and their own adaptation of *Jane Eyre*. New work appearing in the **Studio** included *Red Saturday*, Martin Allen; and *The Children's Room*, Juliet Ackroyd, the world première of a specially commissioned play. New plays are more likely to be commissioned than taken up from unsolicited scripts, and the theatre can't afford to do as much new work as it would like. In 1988 new work will include a new musical, *Castaway* (which was an unsolicited script) and a commissioned straight play, *Plucked in a Far Off Land* by Paul Dowst.

Thomas Howard

10 Garrick Street, London WC2E 9BH ☎ 01–836 0600

No longer acting as a theatre producer.

Hull Truck Theatre Company

Spring Street, Hull HU2 8RW ☎ 0482 224800

Contact *Barry Nettleton* (Administrator)

John Godber, the Artistic Director of this high profile northern company since 1984, dominates the scene with his own successful plays. However, a change of direction is in the offing. Although the company will be doing at least one of John's plays a year, there is a new emphasis on outside writers. (Already this has produced plays like Phil Woods' *The Dock* and Jane Thornton's *Cut and Dried*.) Most of the new plays have been commissioned, and the company admits it doesn't always get around to reading unsolicited mss. Synopses and letters are preferred. Bear in mind the artistic policy of Hull Truck, which is 'accessibility and popularity'. In general they are not interested in musicals, or in plays with many more than 5 characters.

Richard Jackson

59 Knightsbridge, London SW1 ☎ 01–235 3671

Independent minded producer who does 'strong plays which appeal to me'. Besieged by mss, and tends to go out for what he wants (particularly European material). Currently working in smaller scale London fringe theatre, like the Offstage Downstairs, where he can take risks the West End can no longer afford. Credits include the discovery of *Quentin Crisp; A Day in Hollywood, a Night in the Ukraine* (1979); *The Singular Life of Albert Nobbs*. More recently *Latin*, Stephen Fry (1983); *Swimming Pools at War*, Yves Navarre; *Matthew, Mark, Luke and Charlie*, Robert Gillespie (1986).

Stephen Joseph Theatre

Valley Bridge Parade, Scarborough YO11 2PL ☎ 0723 370540

Contact *Alan Ayckbourn* (Artistic Director)

A small theatre in the round seating 307 people, with positive policy on new work. For obvious reasons, Alan Ayckbourn's work is featured heavily in the repertoire, but plays from other sources are encouraged. Recently, productions of *Touch Wood and Whistle*, Steven Mallatratt, and *Calling*, Paul Copley. Produce at least two new plays in every season.

Bill Kenwright Productions

55–59 Shaftesbury Avenue, London W1V 7AA   ☎ 01–439 4466

Contact *Bill Kenwright*

Both revivals and new shows for West End and touring theatres. New work tends to be by established playwrights: *The Business of Murder*, Richard Harris; *A Fighting Chance*, Norman Crisp; *Up On The Roof*, Jane Prowse and Simon Moore. For children, *James And The Giant Peach*, Herbert Chappell (adapted from Roald Dahl). 'We have no particular system established for the reading of unsolicited mss': send a letter with synopsis and a few sample pages in the first instance.

King's Head Theatre Club

115 Upper Street, London N1   ☎ 01–226 8561

Contact *Dan Crawford* (The Administrator)

New scripts are welcome and are farmed out to consultants for reading and evaluation. An unpretentious little café theatre, the **King's Head** nevertheless produces some strong work, notably in 1987 *Diary of a Somebody* by John Lahr, about the life and death of Joe Orton. Other productions have included *Heyday* by Herbert Appleman and *The Secret Garden* adapted by Diana Morgan.

David Kirk Productions

12 Panmuir Road, London SW20 0PZ   ☎ 01–947 0130

Contact *David Kirk*

Commercial management touring post-London revivals and some new plays to provincial and suburban theatres. Productions usually have two or three TV names in them, but David Kirk very interested in scripts strong enough not to need these. Not interested in verse plays, rock musicals, or 'scripts more suited to the fringe'. No unsolicited mss without preliminary letter and return postage. Productions have included Roger Hall's *Middle Age Spread*; David Pownall's *Master Class*; and of the new plays, *Murder Sails at Midnight*, Ngaio Marsh; *The Gold Umbrella*, William Douglas Home.

Knightsbridge Theatrical Productions

2 Goodwin's Court, London WC2N 4LL   ☎ 01–836 7517

Contact *John Wallbank* (General Manager)

Straight plays suitable for production in the West End only. No musicals. Occasionally plays are then taken on tour. New writing is welcome; unsolicited mss will always be considered.

Leeds Playhouse

Calverley Street, Leeds LS2 3AJ   ☎0532 442141

Contact *John Harrison, Artistic Director*

'Always on the look out for new plays, but good ones are hard to find.' Of 10 or 11 plays a season, at least one is likely to be a première. Recently, *Torpedoes in the Jacuzzi*, Phil Young, which came out of improvisation, and Barry Hillman's *The Amazing Dancing Bear*. Also do 'regional premières' – i.e. plays new to Leeds though not new as such.

Leicester Haymarket Theatre

Belgrave Gate, Leicester LE1 3YQ   ☎0533 530021

Contact *Keith Boak*

Peter Lichtenfels, the new artistic director of the theatre since mid-1987, brings from his old job at the **Traverse Theatre** in Edinburgh a desire to put on more new work in Leicester, both in the studio and main house. He plans to do at least six new plays a year. Scripts preferred to outlines or ideas.

Liverpool Playhouse

Williamson Square, Liverpool L1 1EL   ☎051–709 8478

Contact *Kate Rowland* (Associate Director)

Regional theatre very active in promoting new writing, with a particularly impressive record on first plays: *Watching*, Jim Hitchmough, which transferred to the Bush Theatre in London; *Shamrocks And Crocodiles*, Heidi Thomas; and Anne Devlin's *Ourselves Alone*, were all first plays premiered at the Liverpool Playhouse. Finished scripts preferred to synopses and ideas: 'it's the quality of the writing that counts'.

Logan Theatres Ltd

112 Hamilton Avenue, Pollokshields, Glasgow G41 4EX   ☎041–427 6743

Contact *Jimmy Logan*

Productions vary, but mostly star Jimmy Logan. Laughter and comedy appealing to a genuine family audience. Past productions include *Run for Your Wife, A Bedful of Foreigners, Not Now Darling* and *Lauder*. Prepared to consider new writing if it is funny, and doesn't rely on extraneous four letter words for laughs.

The Lyric Theatre, Hammersmith

King Street, London W6 0QL   ☎01–741 0824

Contact *Peter James* (Artistic Director)

Theatre with a long tradition of putting on new work, and always keen to receive scripts, which are read by a permanent team of 3. Currently the main house is concentrating on modern European drama, rather than new plays by British playwrights, but the studio is always on the look out for good new scripts. Productions have included *Scout's Honour*, Christopher Douglas; *Massage*, Michael Wilcox; *Your Obedient Servant*, Kay Eldridge, and Kenneth Branagh's *Public Enemy*. Finished scripts only – they take at least 6 weeks to process, but a report is made on every ms received.

Marcellus Productions Ltd
3 Bristol Gardens, London SW15 3TG ☎ 01–788 5663

Contact *Jimmy Thompson*

Jimmy Thompson acts more as a director than producer, but is always on the look-out for new plays. Recent productions have included *Don't Misunderstand Me* (Patrick Cargill); and *The Quiz Kid* which was written by the Thompsons. At the time of going to press they are planning a revue for the West End, *The Englishman Amused*. Not interested in avant garde or social issue plays, but popular pantomime/revue/farce/romantic comedy.

Barry McDonald
7 Ilfracombe Flats, London SE1 1EW ☎ 01–407 5866

Not presently operating as a theatre producer.

Marianne McNaghten
c/o 8 Redwoods, Alton Road, London SW15 4NL ☎ 02657 31215

Contact *Marianne McNaghten*

One of the army of freelance directors who also act as producers. Consulted by other producers so often able to pass on good ideas. Handles many revivals/classic works, but also interested in new writing: 'I don't see nearly enough', whether straight plays, musicals or good children's plays. Both scripts or synopses are welcome.

Lee Menzies Ltd
20 Rupert Street, London W1V 7FN ☎ 01–437 0127

Contact *Lee Menzies*

'Ideally I'd like something which is going to run for 5 years and earn me a lot of money...' Interested in strong new plays (though not musicals or children's), finished scripts preferred to ideas. Currently producing Jeffrey Archer's *Beyond Reasonable Doubt*, and the touring production of *Daisy Pulls It Off*.

Mermaid Theatre
Puddle Dock, Blackfriars, London EC4V 3DB ☎ 01–236 9521

Occupied by the **Royal Shakespeare Company**; this will probably continue throughout 1988.

Merseyside Everyman Theatre Company
5–9 Hope Street, Liverpool L1 9BH ☎ 051–708 0338

Contact *The Artistic Director*

Of 5 shows a year, two to three are usually new plays. The theatre tend to produce new versions of old classics, idiosyncratic Shakespeares, Willy Russell, Brecht, rock and roll panto – a very catholic repertoire. The common ingredient is an upfront bold style; productions are designed to appeal to non traditional audiences. But no working class angst plays please: 'if you spend all day in a tower block, you don't want to go out and see a play about it.' Contributors should be aware that mss can take ages to read and process, but constructive comments will usually result.

Midlands Arts Centre
Cannon Hill Park, Birmingham B12 9QH ☎ 021–440 4221

Contact *Robert Petty*

Produce puppet theatre, music theatre, youth theatre and the work of the Young People's Opera Company. Unsolicited mss particularly welcome if by young writers, about young people, and designed for performance by young people. A writer-in-residence has been at the Centre since April 1987, and workshops for playwrights will hopefully follow.

Barry J. Mishon Associates
159 Great Portland Street, London W1N 5FD ☎ 01–637 7548

Contact *Barry Mishon*

Not in the market for straight plays by either new or established writers. Devise and produce one-offs, events such as *The Night of 100 Stars*.

Kenneth More Theatre
Oakfield Road, Ilford, Essex IG1 1BT ☎ 01–553 4464

Contact *Vivyan Ellacott*

Productions range from rock musicals to grand opera, gay theatre to Shakespeare, for an audience of both local senior citizens and young upwardly mobile East-Enders. Unsolicited mss are not welcome, as there aren't the resources to cope with them; studio plays around 30 minutes long are welcome, however, as there is great demand for these.

Norman Murray & Anne Chudleigh Ltd
1st floor, 235/241 Regent Street, London W1 ☎ 01–629 4871

Contact *Anne Chudleigh*

Present pantomimes, but in general act more as agents than producers, handling light entertainment performers as well as comedy writers. 'We are always looking for new ideas in respect of comedy.'

The National Theatre

South Bank, London SE1 9PX   ☎01–928 2033   Telex 297306

Contact *Nicholas Wright*

Unsolicited mss are read, but the majority of the National's new plays come about as a result of a direct commission. There is no quota for new work, though so far more than a third of plays presented have been the work of living playwrights. Writers new to the theatre would need to be of extraordinary talent to be successful with a script here, though the **NT Studio** acts as a bridge between the theatre and a limited number of playwrights through readings, workshops and discussion. In some cases a new play is presented as a Studio Night in the **Cottesloe Theatre**. **NT Platforms**, 45-minute plays with the minimum of décor, are a further outlet for original work.

Newgate Theatre Company

13 Dafford Street, Larkhall, Bath, Avon BS1 6BW   ☎0225 318335

Contact *Jo Anderson*

'We need more than a script, we need a concept.' Newgate might be termed 'theatre packagers'; formed as a loose ensemble of actors and directors, they both write their own material and respond to specific projects (often on a commission basis) for festivals, the BBC, and fringe theatres such as the **Bush**, **Half Moon** and **Theatre Royal Stratford East**. In 1987 Jo Anderson's play *Solstice* was co-produced with *Bristol Express*. Other productions have included *The Oldest Profession*, a compilation by Coward and Anderson for the Bankside Festival at the Globe Theatre. New concepts always welcome.

Newpalm Productions

26 Cavendish Avenue, Finchley, London N3 3QN   ☎01–349 0802

Contact *Phil Compton*

Don't often produce new plays: *As Is* by William M. Hoffman, which came from Broadway to the **Half Moon Theatre** in August 1986 is a recent exception to this. National tours of *Noises Off, Seven Brides for Seven Brothers* and *Rebecca* at regional repertory theatres are examples of their more usual shows. However, unsolicited mss, whether plays or musicals, are welcome; scripts are always preferable to synopses.

North Bank Productions

103B Victoria Road, London NW6 6TD   ☎01 328 8563

Contacts *John Bromwich, Chris Hayes*

An established production company interested in both revivals and new plays. New writing often comes to them through writers they know and have used in the past, like Colin Bennett, who did *Hancock's Finest Hour* for them at the Boulevard Theatre, London. Other productions have included *The Anastasia File*, Royce Ryton (now published by French), and the nationally touring *Supergran*. Anything which comes in will be read – scripts are preferred to synopses.

Northcott Theatre
Stocker Road, Exeter, Devon EX4 4QB   ☎0392 56182

Contact *George Roman*

A self producing regional theatre keen to present new writing of quality. However, much of the material which comes in is uninspiring, and the theatre often find they need to go out and find new work. Commissions and contacts are generally the order of the day, and in 1988 two new plays will be produced which they got by these means. Productions have included a new musical, *Katerina; Peter's Passion*, by Martin Harvey; and *The Cape Orchard* by Michael Picardie (a co-production with **Foco Novo**).

Norwich Puppet Theatre
St James, Whitefriars, Norwich, Norfolk NR3 1TN   ☎0603 615564

Contact *Denise Coates*

Mostly a very young audience (ages 4–16), although on occasions shows are put on for an adult audience interested in puppetry. Christmas and summer season shows, plus schools tours. Unsolicited mss welcome if relevant. Puppeteer-writers are available to help those interested in writing for puppet theatre.

Nottingham Playhouse
Nottingham Theatre Trust, Wellington Circus, Nottingham NG1 5AF
☎0602 474361

Contact *Les Smith* (Director of New Writing)

They expect to do around two new plays a season, though no quota exists. Plays must, however, have popular appeal – they have to fill a 700 seat main house. No formal studio space exists, though a small room which can seat forty people is used for rehearsed readings (including the Writing '87 Festival, which presented four plays chosen from a submitted 130). Les Smith gets around 300 scripts a year, and tries to constructively criticise all of these, though only 5% or so show genuine promise. Past productions include *Y'Shunta Joined*, Barry Heath; *Queer Folk*, Rosie Logan; *Too Good for This World*, John Ward and *A Tossed Coin*, Will Coburn. Unsolicited mss welcome.

Nuffield Theatre
University Road, Southampton, SO9 5NH   ☎0703 585633

Contact *Justin Greene* (Artistic Director)

Well known as a good bet for new playwrights, the Nuffield get an awful lot of scripts. They tend to do a couple of new plays every season, often by established playwrights, though not as a matter of policy. Recent productions have included *The Hired Man*, Goodall and Bragg; *A Month of Sundays*, Bob Larby; *A Piece of My Mind*, Peter Nichols, and *The Sit Up* by John Constable. They are open minded about subject and style, and produce musicals as well as straight plays. Scripts preferred to synopses in the case of writers new to the theatre. All will, eventually, be read.

Open Air Theatre
Regent's Park, London NW1 4NP   ☎01–935 5884

Contact *Ian Talbot* (Artistic Director)

Shakespeare and revivals only, except for summer lunchtime children's theatre (which in 1987 has been specially commissioned).

The Orange Tree Theatre
45 Kew Road, Richmond, Surrey TW9 2NQ   ☎01–940 3633

Contact *Sam Walters* (Aristic Director)

One of those just out of London fringe theatre venues good for new writing, both full productions and rehearsed readings. New plays have included *Four Attempted Acts* (winner of the Giles Cooper Award) and *A Variety of Death Defying Acts*, both by Martin Crimp; *Be There in the Many*, Rod Beecham, and *Winter*, David Mowatt. In 1987, they presented the première of Fay Weldon's *The Hole in the Top of the World*. Apart from a usual two or three new plays a year, there is an annual week of Rehearsed Readings. Prospective playwrights should bear in mind, however, that unsolicited mss are read in one great blitz every late spring/summer. Those submitting scripts in the early autumn could be in for a long wait.

Orchard Theatre
108 Newport Road, Barnstaple, Devon EX32 9BA   ☎0271 71475

Contact *Nigel Bryant* (Artistic Director)

FOUNDED 1969. Plays appealing to a wide age range, which tour some 60 or 70 cities, towns and villages through Devon, Cornwall, Dorset, Somerset, Avon and Gloucestershire. Programme includes classics, new adaptations, outstanding modern work, musicals and newly commissioned plays on West Country themes: *The Cuckoo*, Jane Beeson; *Sedgemoor*, John Fletcher. 'A large proportion of our work is concerned with the history, literary traditions, legends and present day life of the region. Unsolicited mss are read, but are usually unsuccessful simply because the theatre is committed to several commissioned new plays at any one time.'

Oxford Playhouse Company
Beaumont Street, Oxford OX1 2LW   ☎0865 723238

Contact *Richard Williams*

A touring company generally playing to a middle-class audience, with plays like *Travesties*, *Hamlet*, *Dr Faustus*, new works like *Airbase* and adaptations like *Tris-*

tram Shandy. Unsolicited mss welcome. Produce at least one new play or new adaptation a year.

Paines Plough

123 Tottenham Court Road, London W1P 9HN   ☎ 01–380 1188

Contact *Nichola Mitchell* (Readers' Panel Co-ordinator)

Produce nothing but new writing. Recent plays have included *Thatcher's Women*, Kay Adshead; *Pinocchio Boys*, Jim Morris. They receive around six unsolicited mss a week, and reports are made by the Readers' Panel on everything that comes in, though this can take two or three months.

Palace Theatre, Watford

Clarendon Road, Watford WD1 1JZ   ☎ 0923 35455

Contact *Claire Burns* (Artistic Director)

Try to get a new play or adaptation into each season's schedule. Recently these have included Edna O'Brien's *Madame Bovary*, and Tim Prager's musical *Spin of the Wheel*. In the previous season they premiered Michael Frayn's new adaptation of *The Seagull*. Policy on new writing, though generally positive, is under review at the time of going to press, with Claire Burns' appointment in July 1987.

Pardic Theatre Company

The Village Theatre, Maxwell Drive, East Kilbride, Scotland G74 4HG
          ☎ 035 52 48669

Contact *Jeff Parkes* (Artistic Director)

'We have never done any new plays, nor have we ever been sent any... East Kilbride is a hard nut to crack, theatrically speaking.' Past productions include *Educating Rita, Same Time Next Year, Private Lives, Jane Eyre.* Unsolicited mss are nevertheless welcome.

Pentameters

Three Horseshoes, 28 Heath Street, London NW3   ☎ 01–435 6757

Contact *Leonie Scott-Matthews*

Occasional plays and poetry readings. Very interested in new plays ('we've been a new writing theatre since 1968') but no resources to deal with an influx of scripts, so send letters and synopses first. Broad minded in terms of subject matter and style – 'it's not just Soho Poly working class angst... we've even put on farce, which isn't supposed to work in fringe venues, but it does.'

Permutt-Hadley Productions Ltd
6 Denmark Street, London WC2H 8LP   ☎01–836 3317

Contact *N. Ranceford-Hadley*

Touring and West End musicals and plays. Unsolicited mss not welcome.

James Perry Productions
1F Morpeth Terrace, Westminster, London SW1P 1EW   ☎01–828 2203

Contact *James Perry*

FOUNDED 1956, James Perry Productions is a small company which exists solely to handle the work of James Perry.

Plantagenet Productions
Westridge Open Centre, Highclere, nr Newbury, Berks.   ☎0635 253322

Contact *Dorothy-Rose Gribble*

Westridge Open Centre is mainly a music venue, and Plantagenet Productions no longer a touring company. New writers have proved unpopular with audiences at Westridge, and recitalists, when they do include new work, usually do so by invitation. No unsolicited mss.

Players' Theatre
Villiers Street, Strand, London WC2   ☎01–839 3256

Contact *Dennis Martin* (Director)

Present Victorian music hall entertainment, researched largely from sources like the British Library. No market for playwrights here.

Playfare Productions
1 Hogarth Terrace, London W4   ☎01–995 0065

Produce plays for children, both classics and fairy tales, for ages 4–14, which are written by a regular team, who know Playfare's needs. No interest in new scripts from other sources.

Polka Children's Theatre
240 The Broadway, London SW19 1SB   ☎01–542 4258

This Wimbledon theatre is interested in receiving scripts suitable for children of all ages, but principally 5–7 and 8–11. Looking for 'scripts that don't talk down to them.' Varied subjects and styles – often use plays based on existing stories, folk tales or novels. Plays which need a cast no larger than 5–7 people particularly welcome.

Q20 Theatre Company
Ivy Lea, Fyfe Lane, Balldon, Bradford, West Yorks BD17 6DP   ☎0274 591417

Contact *John Lambert*

Produce shows mainly for school and community venues. Particularly interested in plays for children. Q20 write a lot of their own material, and haven't the resources to pay professional contributors. Write initially with ideas.

Quill Theatre Productions
247 Norwood Road, London SE24 9AG   ☎01–674 1050

Contact *Ann Parnell McGarry* (Artistic Director)

Quill exist to produce new work, and suffer enormous gaps in their production schedule when, as is often the case, decent new work can't be found. Writing can be set in any period, as long as it offers fresh insights and relationships are strongly and authentically represented. 'Originality of approach is the most important thing.' In the market for serious work, fast witty comedies, musicals and children's. Finished scripts are preferred to synopses, unless someone wants to try out 'a truly brilliant idea'.

Rainbow Productions
64B Fitzjohn's Avenue, London NW3 5LT   ☎01–794 6916

Contact *Tim Webster*

Fringe theatre for fringe venues: 'We're an occasional company made up of professional actors and directors who produce work when not doing other things...' Past productions have included *DHL* (about D. H. Lawrence), Richard Hoggart; *Dada Play* and *Handkerchief of Clouds*, Tristan Tzara. No unsolicited mss – they won't be read; but letters and synopses will be.

Michael Redington
10 Maunsel Street, London SW1P 2QL   ☎01–834 5119

Contact *Michael Redington*

Recent West End productions have included *Breaking the Code*, Hugh Whitemore; *Mr and Mrs Nobody*, Keith Waterhouse. Interested in new work but unsolicited scripts not welcome; new plays generally come to him by way of contacts in the business – 'you always get to hear about the good things...'.

Royal Court Theatre (English Stage Company Ltd)
Sloane Square, London SW1   ☎01–730 5174

Contact *Michael Hastings* (Literary Manager)

The English Stage Company was founded in 1956 to put on new plays by, among others, Arnold Wesker and John Osborne. Today the Royal Court is one of the principal venues for new writing in England. Strong scripts on topical/radical issues are considered. The Literary Department deals with up to 2000 plays a year.

Royal Exchange Theatre Company

St Ann's Square, Manchester M2 7DH ☎061–833 9333

Contact *Michael Fox* (Literary Manager)

FOUNDED 1976. The Royal Exchange has developed a New Writing Policy, which they find is attracting a younger audience to the theatre. They produce English and foreign classics, modern classics, adaptations, as well as new musicals and new plays by young dramatists like Jeff Noon and Iain Heggie. The Royal Exchange receives up to 500 scripts a year, which are read by Michael Fox with a team of readers. Only a tiny percentage is suitable, but opportunities also exist for rehearsed readings, workshops and consultation on new work of promise. Currently there are two writers-in-residence, and a number of plays are commissioned each year. **The Corn Exchange**, their planned second theatre, will present limited seasons of new plays and experimental productions. See also *Competitions:* the **Mobil Playwriting Competition**.

Royal Shakespeare Company

Barbican Centre, London EC2Y 8DS ☎01–628 3351

Contact *Colin Chambers* (Literary Manager)

The literary department at the RSC, headed by Colin Chambers, receives around 500 unsolicited mss a year. 98 per cent of these are totally unsuitable. But the RSC is interested in new work: **The Pit** in London and **The Other Place** in Stratford are new writing venues, and roughly a quarter of the company's total output is new work. This, however, is generally commissioned, and unsolicited offerings from unknowns are rarely successful. Bear in mind that they are *not* interested in straightforwardly biographical plays (they get an awful lot of Lives of Elizabeth I) or singlemindedly topical writing, and have no use for reworkings of Shakespeare. They don't generally welcome musicals, and particularly not rewritings of *Kiss Me Kate* or *Les Misérables* (these have arrived by the sackful of late). There is, they find, a tendency among playwrights to assume that because the RSC have done a play once, they're in the market for more of the same. Usually the reverse is true, and it's wise to check whether a subject has been covered previously before submitting mss. The RSC doesn't generally hold rehearsed readings and workshops – their 'Early Stages' series (held early in 1987) is unlikely to become a regular event.

Scottish Theatre Company

37 Otago Street, Glasgow G12 8JJ ☎041–339 8777

Contact *Jill McGregor* (Assistant to Artistic Director)

Surprisingly, not really in the market for new plays: 'we don't get that many scripts because writers know we can't usually afford to put on new work'. They do however take up new plays once they've had a successful airing elsewhere. Other than that, their programme rests on the revival of both Scottish and international work: *Ane Satyre of the Thrie Estaites, The Wallace, Mary Stuart* (for the Edinburgh Festival) and a production of *Galileo* among them.

7:84 Theatre Company, Scotland

31 Albany Street, Edinburgh EH1 3QN ☎031–557 2442

Contact *John Haswell* (Associate Artistic Director)

Interested in scripts 'that show an awareness of reality in the 1980s, with particular reference to working-class life in Scotland, and the varied culture that this implies'. Past productions have included *Men Should Weep*, Ena Lamont Stewart; *There is a Happy Land*, John McGrath; *The Incredible Brechin Beetle Bug*, Mat McGinn; *The Albannach*, adapted by John McGrath.

Stanley Sher Enterprises Ltd

28 Oakhampton Court, Park Avenue, Roundham, Leeds LS8 2JK ☎0532 731348

Contact *Stanley Sher*

FOUNDED 1962. Produce plays for a family audience: pantomime and popular theatre, plus children's productions. Unsolicited mss welcome.

Soho Poly Theatre

16 Riding House Street, London W1P 7PB ☎01–580 6982

Contact *Tony Craze* (Script Consultant)

A new writing theatre, which presented its first revival for some years in 1987. The system for dealing with unsolicited mss is as follows: scripts go out to a team of readers, those they find interesting are passed on to Tony Craze, who invites writers of promise to his Writers' Workshops. An expansion of the Workshop programme is under way; in addition, there is an annual fortnight-long workshop especially for young writers (**Blueprint**, held each Easter). The theatre produces around six shows a year. Recent plays have included *Releevo*, David Spencer (winner of the Verity Bargate Award 1986) and *The Last Waltz*, Gillian Richmond.

SRO Productions Ltd

c/o Freedman Panter Associates, 2nd floor, Russell Chambers, The Piazza, Covent Garden, London WC2E 8AA ☎01–240 9891

Contact *A. Stirling*

Produce theatre aimed at Everyman: past productions include *Once a Catholic, Candida, A Nightingale Sang, The Streets of London, Born in the Gardens, Beecham, Are You Now Or Have You Ever Been?* Unsolicited mss welcome. 'Delighted to read new or experienced authors; particularly the former, who must write the play as they wish to express themselves, not in the way which they think will be most acceptable to budget-conscious producers – we can always tailor the cloth later!'

Barrie Stacey Productions

Third Floor, 4 Denmark Street, London WC2H 0LA ☎01-836 4128

Contact *Barrie Stacey*

The company exists primarily to produce the work of Barrie Stacey himself, e.g. *A Little Bit of the Other* in early 1988. This has been the case for the last three or four years. Very occasionally use work by other writers, e.g. *A Bedful of Foreigners* in 1986. Letters and synopses preferred to scripts.

Stoll Moss Theatres Ltd

Cranbourne Mansions, Cranbourne Street, London WC2H 7AG ☎01-437 2274

Contact *Louis Benjamin*

One of the most influential theatrical empires, with 12 theatres including the Globe, Lyric, Apollo and Queens in Shaftesbury Avenue. These tend to be the theatres which host straight plays, whereas Her Majesty's and the Palladium tend to be musical venues. Recent plays have included *Up on the Roof*, and *The House Of Bernarda Alba*. Less recently, *Singing in the Rain, Barnum*, and *La Cage Aux Folles*. Mr Louis Benjamin comments that after some years as theatre managers, in which other producers brought their own shows into Stoll Moss theatres, the group is now about to move into a new phase. This will mean a return to production, and a policy, still in the planning stage, of considering all kinds of subjects and treatments: 'the size of our operation means we are likely to have a slot for anything which interests us'. The policy will be to read everything, and to reply thoughtfully 'rather than sending a bland rejection note'. Well constructed synopses and letters are more likely to be considered than finished mss: 'we are looking into the possibility of commissioning plays where we consider the talent merits it...' Though letters/scripts should be addressed to Louis Benjamin, they are passed on to one of his staff for consideration.

Swansea Little Theatre Ltd

Dylan Thomas Theatre, Maritime Quarter, 7 Gloucester Place, Swansea W. Glam. SA1 1TY ☎0792 473238

Contact *Mrs F. Davies* (Secretary)

Produce Anglo-Welsh plays. Repertoire ranges from Shakespeare to family comedies. Include one new play each season as a matter of policy. A panel of readers/producers considers new scripts.

Bob Swash Ltd

44 Lonsdale Square, London N1 1EW ☎01-607 8291

Contact *Bob Swash*

In 1987, output included *One for the Road* and *Shirley Valentine* both by Willy Russell; and *Evita* on tour. New plays welcome – finished scripts only. 'We've found commissioning doesn't work ... interesting novelists rarely produce workable plays.'

H. M. Tennent Ltd
Globe Theatre, Shaftesbury Avenue, London W1V 7HD   ☎01–437 3647

Contact *Anne Rallsthorne* (General Manager)

London's oldest established theatre production company, and among the most prolific. Recent productions have included *A Month of Sundays*, Bob Larby; *Number
One*, adapted by Michael Frayn, and *Ducking Out*, adapted by Mike Stott. Haven't
produced work by new writers for some time, but do try out new plays and hope to
encourage playwrights of promise. Very interested to read new work of all kinds.

Theatre Clwyd
County Civic Centre, Mold, Clwyd CH7 1YA   ☎0352 56331

Contact *Toby Robertson* (Artistic Director)

Lively theatre company with a policy of genuine encouragement as far as new
writing is concerned. All scripts are passed on to an in-house reader – scripts are
preferred to synopses and ideas. Open minded on subjects – musicals and children's
are considered. In the 1987 season, new work has included *Barnaby And The Old
Boys*, Keith Baxter, and *Self Portrait* by Sheila Yeger.

Theatre of Comedy Company
219 Shaftesbury Avenue, London WC2H 8EL   ☎01–379 3345

Contact *Leslie Lawton* (Artistic Co-ordinator)

Founded three years ago to produce new work, and regard themselves as a good bet
for new plays, though in those three years most of the new work has been by Ray
Cooney, one of the most prolific and successful of West End comedy writers. Interested in strong comedy (but not farce) in the widest sense – Chekhov comes under
the definition. No unsolicited mss (there's a serious backlog of scripts) but letters and
synopses are considered.

Theatre Projects Associates Ltd
14 Langley Street, London WC2H 9JH   ☎01–240 5411   Telex 27522

Contacts *Philip Talbot, Pamela Hay*

West End and touring shows. Past productions have included *Edward II, Richard II,
She Stoops to Conquer, I'm Not Rappaport, Cabaret, Fiddler on the Roof, A Little Night
Music*. Unsolicited mss welcome, provided they are 'well written and interesting'.

Theatre Royal Stratford East
Gerry Raffles Square, London E15 1BN   ☎01–534 7374

Contact *Jeff Teare* (Associate Director)

Lively east London theatre catering for a very mixed audience, both local and
London-wide. A good bet for new work – unsolicited mss are welcome 'and we read

them – eventually!' Produce new plays, musicals, classics, youth theatre, plus local community plays/events. Hosts to the London Young Playwrights Festival, and its workshop.

Tigerwise Theatrical Management
71 St Georges Square, London SW1V 3QN   ☎01–828 3349

Contact *Anthony Smee*

Perhaps best known as concert promoters/musical managers (they handle the touring drumming groups Kodo and Samul Nori). Although they admit to also acting as producers, are not keen to specify of what. 'We will consider anything, including straight theatre, musicals and children's . . .' No unsolicited mss; letters and synopses in the first instance.

Traverse Theatre
112 West Bow, Grassmarket, Edinburgh EH1 2PD   ☎031 226 2633

Contact *Linda McKenney*

The Traverse is well known as a venue for new writing in Scotland; indeed has a policy of putting on nothing but new work, preferably by new writers. They also have a strong international strand in their scheduling. Recent productions have included *Kathie and the Hippopotamus*, Mario Vargas Llosa; *Kora*, Tom McGrath; and two plays by John Clifford, *Losing Venice* and *Lucy's Play*. Linda McKenny heads a reading panel whose task it is to sift through the many unsolicited mss the theatre receives. Unsolicited scripts welcome.

Andrew Treagus Associates Ltd
18/19 Warwick Street, London W1V 5RB   ☎01–734 4274   Telex 263899

Contact *Andrew Treagus*

Produce shows for a London and provincial audience 'used mainly to commercial fare', from large-scale musicals to small-scale straight plays. Unsolicited mss are welcome. Policy of encouraging new writing with possible play readings, or fringe productions of their work.

Trends Management
54 Lisson Street, London NW1 6ST   ☎01 723 8001

Contact *Jamie Phillips*

Theatre production is just one facet of their work (also act as an agency and as costumiers). Product on the light entertainment side – particularly revues and pantomime. Provide most material for these themselves; shows like *Sweet Charity* and *Palm Beach Revue*. No unsolicited mss.

Triumph Theatre Productions

Suite 4, Waldorf Chambers, 11 Aldwych, London WC2B 4DA   ☎ 01–836 0187

Contact *Duncan Weldon, Robert Selbie, Peter Wilkins*

A major producer of West End and touring shows, mostly revivals but with a regular output of new work. Recent productions have included co-producing *Kiss Me Kate* at the Old Vic, *Caught in the Act*, but also new work like *Melon*, Simon Gray; *A Piece of My Mind* Peter Nichols. New work tends to be by established playwrights, but the company are always on the look out for talented newcomers. They receive a great many unsolicited mss 'and we read them all'. Letters and synopses preferred in the first instance.

Tynewear Theatre Company

Newcastle Playhouse, Barras Bridge, Newcastle upon Tyne, Tyne & Wear NE1 7RH
☎ 091–232 3366

Contact *John Blackmore* (Artistic Director)

Tynewear produce a great variety of work: classics, hardhitting modern drama, and musicals rub shoulders in their seasons. All scripts are read and assessed, though this can take some time, as there is no literary manager as such. Generally three playwrights a year are commissioned by the theatre; these are usually people known to them, whose work they have previously produced. Particularly keen on scripts of direct relevance to the local audience. Occasionally also run writers' workshops, and may establish a competition in the near future. Past productions have included *Death of a Salesman, Who Killed Hilda Murrell?, The Gambling Man*, and a Geordie musical, *Tight at the Back*.

Umbrella Theatre

The Basement, 46 Compton Avenue, Brighton, E. Sussex BN1 3DS
☎ 0273 775354/25528

Contact *Debbie Hall*

Theatre for a 'discerning, intelligent and adventurous' audience. Particularly interested in new writing from abroad, and also welcome translations/scripts in their original language. Past productions have included *Angel Knife*, Jean Sigrio (Belgium); *On the Ruins of Carthage*, René Kalisky (Belgium); *Joseph and Mary*, Peter Turrini (Austria) and *Cabaret Camique*, based on the work of Pierre-Henri Cami (France). Unsolicited mss welcome.

Charles Vance

83 George Street, London W1H 5PL   ☎ 01–486 1732

Contact *Charles Vance*

In the market for small scale touring productions and summer season plays, although they haven't done much lately, as Charles Vance has been busy editing *Amateur*

Stage. In 1985, tours of *Jane Eyre* and *Mr Cinders*, and 4 pantomimes in 1986. Don't commission plays, and tend in any case not to do new work, though writing of promise stands a good chance of being passed on to someone who does: 'the chances of it actually being produced by us are very slim'.

W & J Theatrical Enterprises Ltd

51a Oakwood Road, London NW11 6RJ ☎01–458 1608

Contact *W. D. Robertson*

Represent actors and comedians as theatrical agents, direct farces and write and direct pantomimes. Unsolicited mss are welcome.

Watermill Theatre

Bagnor, Newbury, Berks RG16 8AE ☎0635 45834

Contact *Jill Fraser*

The Watermill occasionally put on new work. Recent new plays include *The Killing Time* by Euan Smith (who has written for them before) and in 1985, Fay Weldon's *Woodworm*.

Westminster Productions Ltd

Westminster Theatre, Palace Street, London SW1E 5JB ☎01–834 7882

Contact *Hugh Steadman Williams* (Artistic Director)

FOUNDED 1961. Encourages new writing 'which explores fundamental spiritual and moral values in a contemporary and relevant context'. Have produced 28 West End productions/co-productions, five feature films and three video dramas, plus school productions. Plays range from children's/family shows like *The Lion, The Witch and The Wardrobe* to classics like *An Inspector Calls*, plus good new plays. An outline or synopsis in the first instance is essential.

Whirligig Theatre

14 Belvedere Drive, Wimbledon London SW19 7BY

Contact *David Wood*

Produce one play a year, which tends to be a musical play for children, for primary school audiences and weekend family groups. All new mss should exploit the theatrical nature of children's tastes. Previous productions have included: *The Plotters of Cabbage Patch Corner*; *The Ideal Gnome Expedition*; *The Gingerbread Man*; *The Old Man of Lochnagar*. David Wood may offer a writing course in the near future, in conjunction with the **British Theatre Association**.

Michael White

13 Duke Street St James's, London SW1Y 6DB   ☎01–839 3971

Contact *Michael White*

Contributions are passed by Michael White to a script reader for consideration. Recent productions by this high output company have included *On Your Toes, Chorus Line* and *The Mystery of Edwin Drood*. Unsolicited mss are welcome – 'we read everything'.

US Publishing

Publishing – American Style

A successful book in the UK makes money; a successful book in America makes a fortune.
This thought should provide comfort to authors who might otherwise deplore the growing American influence in publishing; an influence made evident this last year by the takeover of **Cape, Chatto and Bodley Head** by the US giant, **Random House**, the shift of the power base at **Penguin** from London to New York and the acquisition of **ABP** by **International Thomson** (A Canadian company, but don't let that fool anyone).

The strengthening of the trans-Atlantic connection will undoubtedly lead to more books aimed at the main English reading market. But what type of books? A random survey of US publishers and agents suggests that writers who aim to bridge the great divide should apply their talents to:

- Historical novels with plenty of well researched detail. Scotland of the Bonny Prince is always popular.
- Thrillers and detective stories.
- Steamy family sagas. The buildup of interest in *Destiny* came first in America.
- Biography – as long as the subject is well known in America. Better still if he can be mistaken for an American.
- Science fiction.
- Horror – the more horrible the better.
- Espionage. But Cambridge deviancy is wearing thin.
- Books about royalty. Accuracy not essential.
  Do not hold out any hope for:
- Literary novels – unless they have an American setting or the authors have appeared on numerous coast to coast chat shows.
- Biographies of British politicians – even if they did meet President Kennedy.
- Children's books in which Popsy Wopsy meets the Snowman. The Americans do this sort of thing so much better.
- Books on self-improvement and how to make a million in business. If there is anything left to say on this subject, the Americans have already thought of it.

If in doubt ask Jeffrey Archer who knows the secret of scooping the American market. His books are everywhere. On a TWA trans-Atlantic flight, five Americans were reading Archer books and three of the copies were hardbacks. No greater compliment can be paid to an author.

Given a suitable product, a UK author may feel bold enough to go over the heads of the British publishers and appeal directly to their American counterparts. But in most cases it is easier and more cost effective to start on home ground. All but the tiniest publishers (and agencies) have links with the States and are as keen as their writers to secure a good American sale.

The following list of American publishers is by no means exhaustive. But it does give a fair range of publishers who are likely to be interested in general fiction and non-fiction.

For a full listing, consult *Writers' Market*, published by **F. & W. Publications**, 9933, Alliance Road, Cincinnati, Ohio 45242 at $21.95.

Abingdon Press
201, 8th Avenue S., Box 801, Nashville TN 37202   ☎0101 (615) 749 6403

Trade Books *Michael E. Lawrence* **Reference/Academic Books** *Carey J. Gifford* **Church Resources** *Leslie Pomeroy*

Publishes fiction – children's books only. Non-fiction, religious – lay and pro- fessional, children's religious books and academic texts. Average 100 titles a year. Approach in writing with synopsis only.

Harry N. Abrams, Inc. (Subsidiary of Times Mirror Co.)
100, 5th Avenue, New York NY 10011   ☎0101 (212) 206 7715
Telex 23–4772   Cable ABRAMBOOK

Editor-in-chief *Paul Gottlieb*

Publishes art, nature, science, outdoor recreation; no fiction. Average 65 titles a year. Submit completed mss (no dot matrix).

Academic Press
Orlando, Florida 32887   ☎0101 (305) 345 2000

Part of **Harcourt Brace Jovanovich**

Addison-Wesley Publishing Co. Inc.
General Books Division, Jacob Way, Reading MA 01867   ☎0101 (617) 944 3700
Telex 94–9416   Cable ADIWES

Publisher *Ann Dilworth*

Publishes biography, business/economics, health, how-to, photography, politics, psychology and science: also 'tools for living' books re finance, health, education and parenting 'by people well-known and respected in their field.' No fiction. Average 50 titles a year. Approach in writing or phone call in first instance, then submit synopsis and one sample chapter.

University of Alabama Press
Box 2877, University AL 35468

Director *Malcolm MacDonald*

Publishes academic books only. 40 titles a year.

Amacom
135 W. 50th Street, New York, NY 10020 ☎0101 (212) 586 8100

Publishing division of *American Management Associations*. **Contact** *Robert Kaplan*

Publishes management books.

Arbor House
235 E. 45th Street, New York NY 10017 ☎0101 (212) 599 3131/687 9855
Cable ARBORPUB

Editor-in-chief *Ann Harris*

Publishes fiction, romance, science fiction, fantasy, adventure, suspense. Non-fiction – autobiography, cookery books, how-to, self-help; including Americana, art, business, economics, health, history, politics, psychology, recreation. Non-fiction, approach editors in writing in first instance, Fiction, write or submit synopsis and sample chapters.

University of Arizona Press
1615 E. Speedway, Tucson, AZ 85719 ☎0101 (602) 621 1441

Director *Stephen Cox*

Academic non-fiction only – particularly with a regional-cultural link. Average 40 titles a year.

Methuen Inc
Associated Book Publishers Inc.
Box 5657, Scottsdale AZ 85261–5657 ☎0101 (602) 837 9388

Editor *Ivan Kapetanovic*

Publishes wide range of school text books and bibliographies, including non-fiction translations. Average three to four titles a year. No length requirement for mss, but artwork/photos should be submitted as part of package.

Atheneum Publishers
115 5th Avenue, New York NY 10003 ☎0101 (212) 614 1300

Editor-in-Chief *Thomas A. Stewart*

Publishes general trade material – politics, history, cookery, sports and general non-fiction. (Not less than 40,000 words.) No fiction. Write or submit synopsis and sample chapter.

Atlantic Monthly Press

8 Arlington Street, Boston MA 02116 ☎0101 (617) 536 9500
Cable LANTICMON BOSTON

Editor-in-Chief *Harold Evans* **Editor-in-Chief** (children's books) *Amy Meeker*

Publishes fiction, general, children's, poetry. Non-fiction – general. Average 50 titles a year. Approach in writing, submitting sample chapter (especially fiction).

Avon Books

1790 Broadway, New York NY 10019 ☎0101 (212) 399 1384

Editor-in-Chief *Susanne Jaffee*

Publishes general fiction and general non-fiction, including children's books, no textbooks. Average 300 titles a year. Submit synopsis and first three chapters (fiction).

Ballantine/DelRey/Fawcett Books

201 E. 50th Street, New York NY 10022 ☎0101 (212) 751 2600

Executive Editor (science fiction/fantasy) *Owen Locke* **Trade Books** *Joelle Delbourgo* **Senior Editor, Ballantine** *Ann La-Farge* **Senior Editor, Fawcett** *Barbara Dicks*

Publishes fiction – general fiction, science fiction and fantasy. No poetry. Non-fiction – general. (Mss not less than 50,000 words.) Average 700 titles a year.

Bantam Books Inc.

666 5th Avenue, New York, NY 10103 ☎0101 (212) 765 6500
Cable BANTAMBOOK NY

Vice-President/Publisher/Editor-in-Chief *Linda Grey* **Vice President/Editorial Director – Adult Fiction and Non-fiction** *Steve Rubin*

Publishes general fiction and children's books. No poetry. General non-fiction. No queries or unsolicited mss.

Beacon Press

Beacon Street, Boston, MA 02108 ☎0101 (617) 742 2110 Cable BEAPRESS

Director *Wendy J. Strothman*

Publishes general non-fiction. No fiction, poetry or children's books. Average 32 titles a year. Approach in writing or submit synopsis and sample chapters to **Editorial Assistant** *Nancy Lattanzio.*

Beaufort Books Inc.
9 E. 40th Street, New York NY 10016 ☎0101 (212) 685 8588

Editor-in-Chief *Susan Suffes*

Publishes fiction – mystery, thriller, contemporary and literary novels, including translations from French (no science fiction or first novels). General non-fiction. Average 40–50 titles a year. Write or submit complete mss (fiction). Write or submit synopsis and three sample chapters or completed mss (non-fiction).

Berkley Publishing Group (Publishers of Berkley/Berkley Trade Paperbacks/Jove/Charter/Second Chance at Love/Pacer; Ace Science Fiction)
200, Madison Avenue, New York NY 10016 ☎0101 (212) 686 9820

Editor-in-Chief *Nancy Coffey*

Publishes general fiction, including young adult. Non-fiction – how-to, inspirational, family life, philosophy and nutrition. Average 900 titles a year. Submit synopsis and first three chapters (for Ace Science fiction only). No unsolicited mss.

University of California Press
2120 Berkeley Way, Berkeley, CA 94720

Director *James H. Clark*

Publishes non-fiction, generally by academics. Also fiction and poetry, but only in translation. Average 200 titles in 1986. Preliminary letter with outline preferred.

University of Chicago Press
5801 South Ellis Avenue, Chicago, IL 60637 ☎0101 312 702 7748

Publishes academic non-fiction only.

Chronicle Books
1 Hallidie Plaza, San Francisco CA 94102 ☎0101 (415) 777 7240

Senior Editor *William LeBlond*

Publishes no fiction. General coffee table books. Average 35 titles a year. Write or submit synopsis and sample chapters.

Citadel Press
120 Enterprise Avenue, Secaucus NJ 07094 ☎0101 (212) 736 0007

Editorial Director *Allan J. Wilson*

Publishes only fiction translations. Biography, film, psychology, humour and history. No poetry, religion or politics. Write initially, before submitting synopsis and three sample chapters.

Contemporary Books

180 N. Michigan Avenue, Chicago, IL 60601   📞0101 312 782 9181

Editors *Nancy Grossman, Shari Lesser*

Publishes general non-fiction, professional and school test preparation, adult education books and sports.

Coward McCann Inc.

200 Madison Avenue, New York, NY 10016   📞0101 212 576 8900

Publisher *Phyllis Grann*   **Editor-in-Chief** (children's) *Refra Wilkin*   Part of the **Putnams Publishing Group**.

Publishes general books, children's, religious, biography, mystery, history. Major fiction publisher.

Crown Publishers Inc.

225 Park Avenue South, New York NY 10003   📞0101 212 254 1600

IMPRINTS
Include **Clarkson Potter, Arlington House, Harmony** and **Julian Press**.

Publishes non-fiction only: Americana, animals, art, biography, children's, cookery, health, history, hobbies, how-to, humour, music, nature, philosophy, photography, politics, psychology, recreation, reference, science, self-help and sport. Average 250 titles a year. Preliminary letter essential.

Jonathan David Publishers

68–22 Eliot Avenue, Middle Village, NY 11379   📞0101 (718) 456 8611

Editor-in-Chief *Alfred J. Kolatch*

Publishes general adult non-fiction, including cookery, self-help and sport. Average 25–30 titles a year. Approach in writing in first instance.

Dell Publishing Co. Inc.

1 Dag Hammarskjold Plaza, New York, NY 10017   📞0101 (212) 832 7300
                              Telex 23–8781 DELL   Cables DELL PUB

IMPRINTS
Include **Dell, Delacorte Press, Delta Books, Dell Trade Paperbacks, Laurel Delacorte Press** books for young readers, **Candlelight Books, Yearling** and **Laurel Leaf**

Publishes (Make sure query is directed to right department.) Fiction: *Delacorte* – top-notch commercial fiction. *Dell* – mass market paperbacks, rarely original fiction, sagas, romance, adventure, suspense, horror and war – especially interested in submission for *Candlelight Ecstasy* line. *Delta & Dell Trade* rarely interested in original non-fiction, publishes in trade paperback, guides, humour, modern society. *Yearling and Laurel Leaf* children and young adults. Average of 500 titles a year. Unsolicited mss: do not send mss, sample chapters or art work; do not register, certify or insure your letter; send only a four-page synopsis with covering letter stating previous work published or relevant experience.

Dodd, Mead & Co.
79 Madison Avenue, New York NY10016

☎0101 (212) 685 6464   Cable DODD NY

Managing Editor *Chris Fortunato*   **Director of children's books** *Jo Ann Daly*

Publishes fiction – mysteries, romantic suspense; non-fiction – biography, popular science, sports, music. Very rarely poetry, children's books. Average 200 titles a year. Write for permission before submitting mss to editorial department (60,000–100,000 words for adult books, 1500–75,000 for children's books).

Doubleday & Co. Inc.
Department AA-M, 245 Park Avenue, New York, NY 10167

☎010 212 984 7561

Can only consider ficton for mystery/suspense, science fiction and romance. Send copy of complete ms (60,000–80,000 words) to **Crime Club Editor, Science Fiction Editor** or **Starlight Romance Editor.**

Dow Jones Irwin
1818 Ridge Road, Homewood IL 60430   ☎0101 312 798 6000

Editor-in-Chief *Richard J. Staron*

Publishes non-fiction only, on business and financial subjects. Write with outline. Average 100 titles a year.

Farrar, Straus and Giroux Inc.
19 Union Square W., New York, NY 10003   ☎0101 212 741 6900

Children's Editor *Stephen Roxburgh*

Publishes fiction picturebooks and novel for children and young adults. Limited number of non-fiction titles. Submit synopsis and sample chapters (artwork/photographs as part of package).

David R. Godine
Horticultural Hall, 300 Massachusetts Avenue, Boston, MA 02115

☎0101 617 536 0761

Publishes fiction and non-fiction. Photography, art, history, natural history, children's, and poetry.

Greenwood Press
Box 5007, Westport, CT 06881   ☎0101 203 226 3571

Publishes non-fiction reference books, professional books in business and law, scholarly books (the *Praeger* imprint). Average 600 titles a year. Preliminary letter essential, with synopsis and sample chapter.

Grove Press Inc.
10 E. 53rd Street, New York, NY 10022   ☎0101 212 207 6900

Contact *Fred Jordan*

Publishes general fiction and non-fiction.

Harcourt Brace Jovanovich
Orlando, Florida 32887   ☎0101 305 345 2760

Publishes fiction and non-fiction. Non-fiction: educational, textbooks, biography, travel, children's, science travel, current affairs, history. Also poetry.

Harper & Row Publishers Inc.
10 E. 53rd Street, New York, NY 10022   ☎0101 (212) 207 7000

Managing Director *Katherine Kirkland*

Publishes general fiction, including historical and suspense. General non-fiction – no technical books. Average 300 titles a year. No unsolicited queries or mss.

Harvard University Press
79 Garden Street, Cambridge, MA 02138 ☎0101 (617) 495 2600   Telex 92–1484

Editor-in-Chief *Maud Wilcox*

Publishes non-fiction. Only scholarly non-fiction. Average 120 titles a year. Free book catalogue and mss guidelines.

D. C. Heath & Co
125 Spring Street, Lexington MA 02173   ☎0101 617 862 6650

Editors-in-Chief (College division) *Bruce Zimmerli*; (Lexington books) *Robert Bovenschule*; (School division) *Roger Rogalin*

Publishes textbooks, professional scholarly, and software. Textbooks at college level in all subjects. Average 300 titles a year. Preliminary letter essential.

Hippocrene Books Inc
171 Madison Avenue, New York, NY 10016   ☎0101 212 685 4371

Publishes general non-fiction, and reference books, particularly strong on maps and travel guides. No fiction.

Holiday House Inc.

18 E. 53rd Street, New York, NY 10022   ☎0101 (212) 688 0085

Editorial Director *Margery Cuyler*

Publishes children's general fiction and non-fiction (pre-school to secondary school). Average 35–40 titles a year. Submit synopsis and three sample chapters or complete ms, without art work.

Houghton Mifflin Co.

2 Park Street, Boston MA 02108   ☎0101 (617) 725 5000
Telex 94–0959   Cables HOUGHTON

Editor-in-Chief *Nan A. Talese*

Publishes general fiction, including poetry. General non-fiction, including how-to and self help. Average 110 titles a year. Approach in writing in first instance.

University of Illinois Press

54 E. Gregory, Champaign, IL 61820   ☎0101 217 333 0950

Editorial Director *Richard L. Wentworth*

Publishes both fiction and non-fiction. Fiction: ethnic, experimental, mainstream. Non-fiction: scholarly and reference books – particularly in the humanities, and Americana. Average 75 titles a year. Letter first.

Indiana University Press

10th & Morton Streets, Bloomington IN 47405   ☎0101 (812) 337 4203

Director *John Gallman*

Publishes fiction and scholarly non-fiction. Average 90–100 titles a year. Approach in writing or submit synopsis and (in case of non-fiction) sample chapters.

Alfred A. Knopf Inc.

201 E. 50th Street, New York NY 10022   ☎0101 (212) 751 2600

Senior Editor *Ashbel Green*   **Children's Book Editor** *Ms Frances Foster*

Publishes fiction (of literary merit). Non-fiction: including books of scholarly merit. Published 218 titles in 1985. Submit complete ms (fiction – 30,000–150,000 words). Write in first instance for non fiction (ms should be 40,000 150,000 words).

Lerner Publications Co.

241 First Avenue North, Minneapolis MN 55401   ☎0101 612 332 3345

Publishes books for children and young adults. Medical, music, art, remedial reading, maths, science, economics, history and general picture storybooks.

Little, Brown & Co. Inc.
34 Beacon Street, Boston MA 02108   ☎0101 (617) 227 0730   Telex 94–0928

Contact *Editorial Department* (Trade Division)

Publishes contemporary popular fiction as well as literary fiction; limited poetry list – usually by recognised poets. Non-fiction: how-to, distinctive cookbooks, biographies, history, science and sports. Average 100+ titles a year. Mss accepted only from published authors. Write or submit synopsis and sample chapters for both fiction and non-fiction – including art-work in the non-fiction package.

Longman Inc.
95 Church Street, White Plains, NY 10601   ☎0101 914 993 5000

Publishes primary, secondary, tertiary and professional textbooks. No trade, art or children's books. Average 200 titles a year.

Louisiana State University Press
Baton Rouge LA 70803   ☎0101 (504) 388 6618

Associate/Executive Editor *Beverly Jarrett*

Publishes no fiction. Non-fiction: scholarly studies, especially Southern studies, French, jazz. Average 60 titles a year. Send s.a.e. for ms guidelines.

Lyle Stuart Inc.
120 Enterprise Avenue, Secaucus, NJ 07094   ☎0101 201 866 0490/212 736 1141

Editor-in-Chief *Mario Satori*

Publishes both fiction and non-fiction: 'coffee table books', biography, how-to books, humour, illustrated and self help. Average 100 titles a year. Unsolicited mss not considered – write in first instance. Strong, even controversial ideas welcome.

MIT Press
28 Carleton Street, Cambridge, MA 02142   ☎0101 (617) 253 1693

Acquisitions Co-ordinator *Christina Sanmartin*

Publishes no fiction. Non-fiction: technologically sophisticated books including computers, sciences, engineering, economics, architecture, linguistics and philosophy. Average 100 titles a year. Submit synopsis, academic resumé and sample chapters.

McGraw-Hill Book Co
College Division, 1221 Avenue of the Americas, New York NY 10020

☎0101 (212) 512 2000

Publisher, Social Sciences *Philip Butcher*   **Publisher, Business & Economics** *Joseph Marcelle*

Publishes no fiction. Non-fiction: college text-books (social, business and physical sciences); reference books (social, business and physical sciences).

David McKay Co. Inc.
2 Park Avenue, New York, NY 10016

☎0101 (212) 340 9800

Publisher *Richard T. Scott*

Average five titles a year. No unsolicited mss or proposals considered or acknowledged.

Macmillan Publishing Company
Children's Book Department, 866 3rd Avenue, New York, NY 10022

☎0101 (212) 702 2000

Publishes children's fiction and non-fiction. Average 130 titles a year.

Merrill Publishing Co
1300 Alum Creek Drive, Columbus, OH 43216

☎0101 614 890 1111

Parent company Bell & Howell   **Editor-in-Chief** (Education) *Ann Turpin*   **Editor-in-Chief** (College) *Franklin Lewis*

Education division publishes texts, workbooks and software for school level. College Division publishes higher level books and materials in humanities, business, maths, science and technology. Average 400 titles a year. Synopsis and three sample chapters.

University of Missouri Press
200 Lewis Hall, Columbia, MO 65211

☎0101 314 882 7641

Director *Edward King*

Fiction and academic non-fiction. Fiction, drama and poetry only considered in February and March of odd numbered years. Letter essential. Average 30 titles a year.

William Morrow and Co.
105 Madison Avenue, New York, NY 10016

☎0101 (212) 889 3050

Editor (Greenwillow Books – children's) *Susan Hirschman*   **Editor (Lothrop, Lee and Shephard – children's)** *Dorothy Briley*   **Editor (Morrow Junior Books)** *David Reuther*   **Managing Editor Quill (Trade Paperback)** *Allison Brown-Cerier*

Publishes fiction, including poetry. General non-fiction. Approach only in writing. No unsolicited mss or proposals, which should only be submitted through a literary agent (50,000–100,000 words).

New American Library
1633 Broadway, New York, NY 10019 ☎0101 (212) 397 8000

Editor-in-Chief *Maureen Baron*

Publishes New work and reprints. Average 350 titles a year. Approach in writing only.

University of New Mexico Press
Journalism 220, Albuquerque, NM 87131 ☎0101 505 277 2346

Director *Elizabeth C. Hadas*

Publishes scholarly and regional non-fiction only. No fiction. Average 50 titles a year.

University of North Carolina Press
Box 2288, Chapel Hill, NC 27514 ☎0101 919 966 3561

Editor-in-Chief *Iris Tillman Hill*

Publishes scholarly and regional trade books. No fiction. Particularly interested in American history and Southern studies. Average 50 titles a year.

W. W. Norton Co. Inc.
500 5th Avenue, New York, NY 10110 ☎0101 (212) 354 5500 Telex 12–7634

Managing Editor *Sterling Lawrence*

Publishes general adult fiction and general non-fiction. Average 213 titles a year. Submit synopsis and two or three sample chapters, for both fiction and non-fiction.

Ohio University Press
Scott Quad, Ohio University, Athens, OH 45701 ☎0101 (614) 594 5505

Acting Director *Holly Panich*

Publishes no fiction. General scholarly non-fiction with emphasis on nineteenth century literature and culture. Average 25–30 titles a year. Approach in writing in first instance.

University of Oklahoma Press
1005 Asp Avenue, Norman, OK 73019 ☎0101 405 325 5111

Editor-in-Chief *John Drayton*

Publishes non-fiction only: American Indian studies, Western American history, classical studies. Average 50 titles a year.

Open Court Publishing Co.

Box 599, LaSalle IL 61301 ☎0101 (815) 223 2520

Director, General Books *Dr Andre Carus*

Publishes no fiction. Non-fiction: scholarly books, mainly philosophy, psychology, religion, economics and science; also German and French non-fiction translations. Average 30 titles a year. Write or submit synopsis and 2–3 sample chapters and artwork/photos as part of package.

Pantheon Books

201 E. 50th Street, New York, NY 10022 ☎0101 (212) 751 2600

Contact Adult Editorial Department (28th Fl.)/Children's Department. (6th Fl.).

Publishes fiction: less than five novels a year. Some foreign fiction in translation. Non-fiction: political and social subject, emphasis on Asia, medicine, how-to books. Some children's books. Average 90 titles a year. Write in first instance re non-fiction, no mss accepted. No fiction queries accepted at all.

Pelican Publishing Company

1101 Monroe Street, Box 189, Gretna LA 70053 ☎0101 (504) 368 1175

Assistant Editor *Karen T. Leathem*

Publishes fiction: very limited requirement (including children's books); most interested in Southern novels (publish one novel in two years). Non-fiction: general non-fiction (especially Southern regional). Average 40 titles a year. Write and submit ms and artwork (non-fiction); submit synopsis and sample chapters (fiction).

Penguin Books

40 W. 23rd Street, New York, NY 1001 ☎0101 (212) 337 5200

Senior Editor *Nan Graham*

Publishes paperbound books: art, architecture, classical literature, fiction, history, children's books, mysteries. All unsolicited mss returned unopened. Proposals through agents only.

Persea Books Inc.

225 Lafayette Street, New York, NY 10012 ☎0101 212 431 5270

Editorial *Karen Braziller*

Publishes art, literature, poetry, academic and social sciences.

Plenum Publishing

233 Spring Street, New York, NY 10013   ☎0101 212 620 8000

Editor *Linda Greenspan Regan*

Publishes scientific and technical treatises, monographs, textbooks, journals, handbooks, translations of Soviet books and journals, clinical medicine.

Pocket Books

123 Avenue of the Americas, New York, NY 10020   ☎0101 212 698 7000

Publishes fiction: adult, mystery, science fiction, romance, westerns. Non fiction: history, biography, reference and general books.

IMPRINTS

Washington Square Press – high quality mass market; **Poseidon Press** – hardcover fiction and non-fiction. No unsolicited mss; write in the first instance.

Prentice Hall Inc. Business and Professional Books Division

Gulf & Western, Sylvan Avenue, Eaglewood Cliffs, NJ 07632

    ☎0101 212 592 2000

Publishes how-to, reference, self-help, and technical non-fiction, on business, economics, sport, law, accountancy, computing and education. Average 150 titles a year. Particularly interested in high level books which will sell well by direct mail marketing.

Princeton University Press

41 William Street, Princeton, NJ 08540   ☎0101 609 452 4900

Editor-in-Chief *Sanford G. Thatcher*

Publishes art history, literary criticism, history, philosophy, religion, political science, economics, anthropology, sociology and science. Also poetry, which is judged solely in competition (mss to *Robert Brown*). Average 140 titles a year.

Putnam Publishing Group

200 Madison Avenue, New York, NY 10016   ☎0101 212 576 8900

Editorial *Gene Brissie, Bernadette Ford, Patty Gauch, Neil Nyrer*

Publishes general fiction and non-fiction, including children's books. Particularly strong on history, literature, economics, political science, natural science. Major fiction publisher.

Quartet Books Inc.

Suite 2005, 2155 Park Avenue, New York, NY 10003   ☎0101 212 254 2277

Editor *Catherine Norden* Part of the *Namara Group*.

Publishes animal, biography, business, history, jazz, philosophy, photography, politics, psychology, sociology, and middle Eastern subjects. Particularly interested in coffee table and illustrated books. Fiction: literary, adventure, crime and feminist. Books must appeal to both US and UK markets. Outline and sample chapters for non-fiction books.

Raintree Publishers Inc.

310 W. Wisconsin Avenue, Milwaukee, WI 53202   ☎0101 414 273 0873

Editor-in-Chief *Russell Bennet*

Publishes fiction and non-fiction – usually on an 'outright purchase' basis. Non-fiction: children's and reference books on animals, health, history, nature, photography, and reference. Books for schools. Fiction: adventure, historical and science fiction. Synopsis and sample chapters in first instance.

Rand McNally & Co

PO Box 7600, Chicago, IL 60680   ☎0101 312 673 9100

Editor *Jon Leverenz*

Publishes children's, adult non-fiction, school books for all levels, atlases, maps and travel guides.

Random House Inc.

201 E. 50th Street, New York, NY 10022   ☎0101 212 751 2600

Publishes general fiction and non-fiction, plays, reference books, children's.

IMPRINTS
Include **Reader's Digest** and **IBM Computer Books**.

Rosen Publishing Group

29 E. 21st Street, New York, NY 10010   ☎0101 212 777 3017

Publishes non-fiction books for a young adult audience, on careers, personal subjects; also art, theatre, music and health.

IMPRINT
Pelion Press. Classical music and opera subjects. Average 45 titles a year. Write with outline and sample chapters.

Schocken Books Inc.

62 Cooper Square, New York, NY 10003   ☎0101 212 475 4900

Publishes general non-fiction (including reprints) Jewish studies, women's studies, cookbooks, history, social sciences and children's.

Scholastic Inc.
730 Broadway, New York, NY 10003   ☎0101 212 505 3000

Editor *Ann Reit*

Publishes teen fiction for girls: romance, historical romance, 40,000–45,000 words. Average 36 titles a year. S.a.e. for guidelines essential before submitting mss.

Charles Scribner's Sons
Children's books department, 115 5th Avenue, New York, NY 10003
☎0101 212 486 4035

Editorial Director *Clare Costello* (children's books).

Publishes fiction and non-fiction. Fiction includes adventure, fantasy, historical, humour, mystery, science fiction, and suspense. Send synopsis and sample. Non-fiction on animals, art, biography, health, hobbies, humour, nature, photography, recreation, science and sports. Write in first instance. Average 40 titles a year.

Simon & Schuster
Trade Books Division, 1230 Avenue of the Americas, New York, NY 10020
☎0101 212 698 7000

Unsolicited mss returned unread. Fiction and non-fiction, through agents only. Publish general adult fiction and non-fiction. No textbooks, specialised, poetry or plays.

Stanford University Press
Stanford, CA 94305   ☎0101 415 497 9434

Editor *William W. Carver*

Publishes non-fiction only. Scholarly works in all areas of the humanities, social and natural sciences, plus more general interest, middle brow academic books. Average 55 titles a year. Write in first instance.

Stein & Day Publishers
Scarborough House, Briarcliff Manor, NY 10510   ☎0101 914 762 2151

Publishes adult fiction (quality), and general non-fiction. No technical, textbooks, children's. No unsolicited mss – preliminary letter essential. Average 100 titles a year.

Sterling Publishing
2 Park Avenue, New York, NY 10016   ☎0101 212 532 7160

Contact *Sheila Ann Barry*

Publishes non-fiction only: 'alternative lifestyle', games/puzzles, how-to books, health, home medical, business, cookery, hobbies, children's humour, occult, pets, photography, recreation, self-help, sports, technical, collecting, wines and reference. Average 80 titles a year. Write in first instance enclosing sample chapter list, synopsis and two sample chapters.

Taplinger Publishing Co

132 W. 22nd Street, New York, NY 10011   ☎0101 212 741 0801

Editors *Ms Bobs Pinkerton, Roy Thomas*

Fiction and non-fiction hardbacks. No children's. Fiction: serious and contemporary. Non-fiction: art, biography, calligraphy, history, theatre, general trade books. Write in first instance. Average 75 titles a year.

IMPRINT
Crescendo: music books.

Temple University Press

Broad and Oxford Streets, Philadelphia, PA 19122   ☎0101 215 787 8787

Editor-in-Chief *Michael Ames*

Publishes scholarly non-fiction only. American history, sociology, women's studies, health care, philosophy, public policy, and religion. Average 35 titles a year. Authors generally academics. Write in first instance.

Time-Life Books Inc.

777 Duke Street, Alexandria, VA 22314   ☎0101 703 838 7000

Editor *George Constable*

Publishes non-fiction general interest books only; usually heavily illustrated and originating in-house. Rarely consider unsolicited mss. Average 40 titles a year.

Times Books Inc.

201 E. 50 Street, New York, NY 10022   ☎0101 212 872 8110

Editorial director *Jonathan B. Segal*

Publishes non-fiction only: business, economics, science and medical, biography, history, women's issues, cookery, current affairs, self-help and sports. Unsolicited mss not considered. Letter essential. Average 45 titles a year.

Universe Books

381 Park Avenue, S. New York, NY 10016   ☎0101 212 685 7400

Editorial director *Louis Barron*

Publishes non-fiction only, on animals, antiques, art, architecture and design, ballet, crafts, economics, history, linguistics, music, nature, performing arts, politics, reference, science and social sciences. Also some biography, health and how-to. Monographs on specialist subjects in arts and sciences. Average 45 titles a year. Synopsis with two to three sample chapters.

Van Nostrand Reinhold Co. Inc.
115 5th Avenue, New York, NY 10003   ☎0101 212 254 3232

Publishes technical and scientific, business, medical, arts, crafts, design, aeronautical, marine, energy, photography, reference, encyclopaedias and handbooks.

Vanguard Press Inc.
424 Madison Avenue, New York, NY 10017   ☎0101 212 753 3906

Editor-in-Chief *Bernice S. Woll*

Publishes fiction and non-fiction. Fiction: adventure stories, experimental fiction, humorous, mystery, and literary. Non-fiction: all general and popular areas. No coffee table books, reference or technical. Average 20 titles a year.

Viking Penguin Inc.
40 W. 23rd Street, New York, NY 10010   ☎0101 212 337 5200

All unsolicited material is returned unopened. Proposals through established literary agents only.

IMPRINTS
Viking, Penguin, Viking Kestrel, Puffin, Stephen Greene, Frederick Warne.

Walker & Co
720 5th Avenue, New York, NY 10019   ☎0101 212 265 3632

Contact the Submissions Editor.

Publishes fiction and non-fiction. Fiction: adventure, mystery, romantic suspense, regency romance, historical romance, spy/thriller, westerns, science fiction and fantasy. Non-fiction: Americana, art, biography, business, histories, how-to books, children's, science, history, medical, psychiatric, music, nature, sports, parenting, psychology, recreation, reference, popular science, self-help. Average 150 titles a year.

Warner Publishing Co.
666 5th Avenue, New York, NY 10103   ☎0101 212 484 2900

Editor *Nancy Neiman*

Publishes fiction and non-fiction, both hardcover and mass market paperbacks.

University of Wisconsin Press
114 North Murray Street, Madison, WI 53715   ☎0101 608 262 4298

Acquisitions Editor *Barbara Hanrahan*

Publishes academic non-fiction only. Complete mss only.

Yale University Press
302 Temple Street, New Haven, CT 06502 ☎0101 203 432 0960

Publishes academic books.

Professional Associations

The Arts Club

40 Dover Street, London W1X 3RB   ☎01–499 8581

Membership secretary *Mrs Ridgway*

Subscription assessed individually   Town, £300 maximum
Country, £145 maximum

FOUNDED 1863. Some connection with the arts necessary for membership, which is only available by application with two sponsors.

The Arts Council of Great Britain

105 Piccadilly, London W1V 0AU   ☎01–629 9495

Chairman *Sir William Rees-Mogg*

In 1987 the annual grant dispensed by the Arts Council stood at £136 million. From this fund the **Arts Council** supports arts organisations, artists, performers, and others: grants can also be made for particular productions, exhibitions and projects. Grants available to individuals are detailed in the free Arts Council folder *Awards & Schemes* 1987/8.

Drama director *Ian Brown*   New writing is supported through *Theatre Writing Allocations* (contact the department for more details).   **Literature director** *Kate Marsh (acting)*   Apart from subsidising organisations like Book Trust and the Poetry Society, support is also given to little magazines and small presses, and a limited number of direct grants are offered to writers.

Arts Council of Northern Ireland

181a Stranmillis Road, Belfast BT9 5DU   ☎0232 381591

Literature Officer *Michael Longley*   **Drama Officer** *Dennis Smith*

The Association of Authors' Agents

c/o 4th floor, 26–28 Bedford Row, London WC1R 4HL   ☎01–405 6774

Secretary *Linda Shaughnessy*

FOUNDED 1974. Membership voluntary. The AAA maintains a code of practice, provides a forum for discussion and represents its members in issues affecting the profession.

ABSA (Association for Business Sponsorship of the Arts)

2 Chester Street, London SW1X 7RB ☎01–235 9781

A national independent organisation established by the business community, concerned with both the concept and practical details of business sponsorship of the arts, and to represent sponsors' interests. Though ABSA has not yet been involved in the commercial sponsorship of a 'purely literary work', other aspects of writing come up, and writers interested in getting involved in some way should send for *Sponsorship Manual* (£5 including p&p).

Association of Independent Producers

17 Great Pulteney Street, London W1R 3DG ☎01–434 0181

Contact *Matthew Crampton* **Subscription £75 p.a.**

FOUNDED 1976. Membership open (there are many writer members). Benefits include: an information service, a regular magazine, information packs on various aspects of production, and a free copy of the *Independent Production Handbook*.
Offers information about production, how to get in touch with producers etc. The general aims of the association are to encourage production of films and to broaden the base of finance and exhibition.

Association of Little Presses

89a Petherton Road, London N5 2QT ☎01–226 2657

Subscription £7.50 p.a.

FOUNDED 1966. Membership offered to individuals who run small presses; associate membership is available to other interested people or groups. Over 80% of all new poetry in Britain is published by little presses and magazines. ALP also publishes information booklets; *Poetry and Little Press Information, Getting Your Poetry Published* (over 32,000 copies of this sold since 1973) and the *Catalogue of Little Press Books in Print*, plus a regular newsletter. A full list of Little Presses (some of these, like Bloodaxe Books, are now sufficiently established and successful to be considered in the mainstream of the business) is available from ALP, or from the *Oriel Bookshop*, price £1.25 inc. p&p (see **Welsh Arts Council**).

Authors' Lending & Copyright Society

7 Ridgmount Street, London WC1E 7AE ☎01–580 2181

President *Lord Willis* **Secretary General** *Janet Hurrell*
Subscription £5 (Free to members of the Society of Authors, Writers' Guild)

Independent society which collects payments on a non-profit basis due to authors for collective rights in the areas of reprography, certain lending rights, private and off-air recording and simultaneous cabling rights. Open to both authors and their heirs.

Book Trust (formerly the **National Book League**)
Book House, 45 East Hill, London SW18 2QZ ☎01–870 9055

Director *Martyn Goff* OBE Subscription £25 p.a.

FOUNDED 1925. Benefits to members include a Lending library of books about books, the Book Information Service (which also provides a free service to the public) and access to the Centre for Children's Books. This centre acts as a bridge between those who produce books and those who read them, with a comprehensive collection of every book published in the last 24 months. **Book Trust** runs Children's Book Week. Other aspects of its work include organising touring exhibitions, the administering of 14 literary prizes, including the Booker (see *Competitions and Prizes*), and the carrying out of surveys which are then published. Book Trust publications include books about books, writers, prizes and education: a free list with order form is available from Book House. *Booknews*, quarterly, is free to members.

BAFTA British Academy of Film and Television Arts
195 Piccadilly, London W1V 9LG ☎01–734 0022

Director *A. J. Byrne* Ordinary subscription £75 p.a.

FOUNDED 1947. Membership limited to 'those who have contributed creatively to the industry'. Facilities for screening, discussions; encourage research and experimentation; lobby parliament, make annual awards.

BASCA (British Academy of Songwriters, Composers and Authors)
148 Charing Cross Road, London WC2H 0LB ☎01–240 2823

Contact *Marilyn Worsley* Subscription from £11.50 p.a.

FOUNDED 1947. The academy offers advice and support for both established and aspiring songwriters. Issues standard contracts between publishers and writers. Benefits of membership include the quarterly magazine, and assessment of beginners' work.

British Amateur Press Association
78 Tennyson Road, Stratford, London E15 4DR

Subscription £4 p.a.

A non-profit-making, non-sectarian society founded, in 1890, to 'promote the fellowship of writers, artists, editors, printers, publishers and other craftsmen. To encourage them to edit, print and publish, as a hobby, magazines, books and other literary works'. Also aims to create a spirit of healthy ambition and friendly rivalry among its members. Not an outlet for writing, but a fraternity providing contacts and support for the non-professional, professional.

British American Arts Association
49 Wellington Street, London WC2E 7BN ☎01–379 7755

Director *Jennifer Williams*

The senior organisation addressing the problems of transatlantic cultural exchange. It offers advice and counselling in all arts disciplines, runs a conference programme, and takes on special projects. Emphasis is on the non-profit sector. **BAAA** is not a grant-giving organisation.

British Copyright Council
Copyright House, 29–33 Berners Street, London W1P 4AA ☎01–580 5544

Works for international acceptance of copyright and acts as a lobby/watchdog organisation on legal and professional matters, on behalf of the trade. An umbrella organisation, which does not deal with individual enquiries.

The British Council
10 Spring Gardens, London SW1A 2BN ☎01–930 8466 (literature)

☎01–636 6888 (drama/film)

Staffed in eighty countries worldwide, the brief of the British Council is to promote a wider knowledge of Britain and the English language abroad, and to develop closer cultural links between those involved in the arts here and abroad. The British Council also supports overseas tours by dramatic companies, publishes papers on ELT and cultural subjects, and distributes English books abroad.

British Film Institute
127 Charing Cross Road, London WC2H 0EA ☎01–437 4355

Membership £25.25 (includes Monthly Film Bulletin)/£15;

Associateship £9.70 (plus concessions)

FOUNDED 1933: committed to the development of the art and appreciation of film and television. Runs the **National Film Theatre** and the **National Film Archive** in London, and funds film theatres in the regions, as well as supporting the making of new films, video and television largely through the *Regional Arts Associations*, but also through direct grants.

British Guild of Travel Writers
28 Oakfield Road, Finchley, London N3 2HT ☎01–346 3772

Chairman *Peter Hughes*   **Secretary** *Robin Mead*   **Subscription** £25 p.a.

The professional association of travel writers and editors, which aims to serve its membership's interests professionally and act as a forum for debate/meetings. Meet MONTHLY. The guild is represented on the BTA, and its members (c. 120) qualify for travel concessions and other benefits.

British Science Fiction Association
33 Thornville Road, Hartlepoole, Cleveland TS26 8EW

Membership Secretary *Jo Raine*   Subscription £7.00 p.a.

For both writers and readers of Science Fiction and Fantasy. Publishes *Matrix* (news), *Focus* (fiction), *Vector* (criticism), *Paperback Inferno* (paperback and magazine reviews). Also offers creative writing groups, a Science Fiction lending library and magazine chain, and an information service.

British Screen Finance
22 Southampton Place, London WC1A 2BP   ☎ 01–831 7561

Contact *Colin Vaines (script development)*

Took over from the now defunct **National Film Finance Corporation.** A private company aided by government grant. Current members of the consortium are Rank, Cannon and Channel 4. Chief executive Simon Relph says that BSF are 'prepared to look at wonderful scripts' if they come in. Their more usual work, however, is the support of existing film projects in need of backing. In exceptional cases, **BSF** will help put the other elements of a movie together, if it believes in a script strongly enough. Not interested in ideas; finished scripts only. Supports five or six films a year.

British Theatre Association
The Darwin Infill Building, Regents College, Inner Circle, Regents Park, London NW1 4NS   ☎ 01–935 2571

Director *Jane Hackworth-Young*   Subscription from £15 p.a.

FOUNDED 1919. Though the **British Theatre Association** is a membership organisation, the Play Library, the most comprehensive in the world, is open to all. Benefits of membership include the reference and lending sections of the library, a unique theatre information service, records, tapes and training courses. Publishes *Drama* magazine.

British Theatre Institute (incorporating Drama and Theatre Education Council)
c/o NCA, Francis House, Francis Street, London SW1

The British Theatre Institute was founded in 1971. In 1976 it called a conference of educational bodies which led to the formation of DATEC, the **Drama and Theatre Education Council.** The two joined forces in 1982. Because of this merger the BTI places particular emphasis on education and training. It also acts as a resource office and consultant on all aspects of theatre and drama education. Subscriber members include both individuals and organisations.

Campaign for Press and Broadcasting Freedom
9 Poland Street, London W1V 3DG ☎01–437 2795

Subscription £7 p.a. (plus concessions).

Broadly based pressure group, working for more accountable and accessible media in Britain. Advises on right of reply and takes up the issue of the portrayal of minorities (incorporating CARM, the Campaign Against Racism in the Media). Members receive *Free Press* (bimonthly), discounts on publications and news of campaign progress.

The Critics' Circle
c/o The Stage & Television Today, 47 Bermondsey Street, London SE1 3XT
☎01–403 1818

President *David Nathan*   **Honorary General Secretary** *Peter Hepple*

Subscription £8 p.a.

Membership by invitation only. Aims to uphold and promote the art of criticism (and the commercial rates of pay thereof) and preserve the interests of its members, who are professionals involved in criticism of film, drama, music and ballet.

Educational Television Association
King's Manor, Exhibition Square, York, YO1 2EP ☎0904 29701

An umbrella organisation for individuals and organisations using television for education and training.

The English Association
1 Priory Gardens, Bedford Park, London W4 1TT ☎01–995 4236

Secretary *Ruth Fairbanks-Joseph*.

FOUNDED 1906 to promote understanding and appreciation of the English language and its literature. Activities include sponsoring a number of publications and organising annual sixth form conferences. Publications include *English, Year's Work in English Studies* and *Essays and Studies*.

Federation of Broadcasting Unions
c/o BETA, 181–185 Wardour Street, London W1V 4LA ☎01–439 7585

Contact *Paddy Leech*

Unions involved in the **FBU** include **Equity**, the **NUJ**, and the **Writers' Guild**.

Federation of Film Unions
11 Wardour Street, London W1V 4AY ☎01–437 8506

Represents unions involved in film production, including the **Writers' Guild** of Great Britain.

Film & Video Press Group
81 Dean Street, London W1V 6AA

Contact *Peter Cargin*

A professional association for editors, journalists, and freelance writers in the audio-visual media.

Gaelic Books Council (An Comann Leabhraichean)
Department of Celtic, University of Glasgow, Glasgow G12 8QQ   ☎041–339 8855

Chairman *Professor Derick S. Thomson*

FOUNDED 1968. Encourages and promotes Gaelic publishing by offering publication grants, commissioning authors, organising competitions, advising readers and providing practical help for writers.

Independent Film & Video Makers Association
79 Wardour Street, London W1V 3PH   ☎01–439 0460

Subscription £12 p.a.

FOUNDED 1974. Practical help and advice on script development and funding, for its writer members.

Independent Programme Producers Association
50–51 Berwick Street, London W1V 3RA   ☎01–439 7034

Director *Paul Styles*   **Subscription** new members £86.25 p.a.

FOUNDED 1981 to protect and advance the interests of independent producers; has a membership of 400. General meetings, seminars, on all aspects of production, general and production advice, plus close consultation with Channel 4. IPPA Bulletin, every 2 months. The association is funded by subscriptions and by a 0.5% fee levied on members' production.

Independent Publishers' Guild
147–149 Gloucester Terrace, London W2 6DX   ☎01–723 7328

Subscription £25/£30 p.a.

FOUNDED 1926. Membership open to independent publishers, packagers and suppliers, i.e. professionals in allied fields. 220 members in the year 1986/7. Regular meetings, conferences, seminars, and a small publishers' group.

Independent Theatre Council
Old Loom House, Backchurch Lane, London E1 1LU   ☎01–488 1229

The management association and representative body for small and middle scale theatres (up to around 250 seats) and touring theatre companies. They negotiate contracts and have standard agreements with **Equity** on behalf of all professionals working in the theatre. Currently they are negotiating with the **Theatre Writers' Union** and **Writers' Guild** for a contractual agreement covering the rights and fee structure of playwrights writing for the 'fringe' theatres.

Institute of Journalists

Bedford Chambers, Covent Garden, London WC2E 8HA   ☎01–836 6541

General Secretary *John Hart*   Subscription £45–£125 (by assessment)

FOUNDED 1884. An independent trade union and professional association for writers, broadcasters and journalists in all media. Affiliation available to part time or occasional practitioners. Employment register, freelance division, legal advice.

The Library Association

7 Ridgmount Street, London WC1E 7AE   ☎01–636 7543

Chief Executive *George Cunningham*

The professional body for libraries and information specialists, with 25,000 members. The library (reference only) has a good range of books relevant both to library and publishing matters; both it and the bookshop are open to all.

London Screenwriters' Workshop

20 Jeffreys Street, London NW1 9PR   ☎01–482 0527

Subscription £12 p.a.

FOUNDED 1983. A means of contact, discussion and practical help for film and television writers. Meetings, monthly seminars, script workshops. Also acts as a pressure group for funding improvements in the industry.

The London Writing Rooms

Farringdon House, 105–107 Farringdon Road, Clerkenwell, London EC1R 3BT
☎01–278 7879

FOUNDED in 1986 on the American model to provide an office environment for writers. Desks cost between £20 and £28 a week. For this you get your own key (for 24 hour, 365 day access), the use of a small kitchen and a phone for outgoing calls only. Positive press coverage and the general bustle of the place since its launch attest to a desire among many writers for a businesslike, even punitive environment in which to work.

National Union of Journalists (NUJ)
Acorn House, 314 Gray's Inn Road, London WC1X 8DP

☎01–278 1812 (freelance division)
Main office 01–278 7916   Telex 892384

Subscription £104 p.a. (freelance)

TRADE UNION. Responsible for wages and conditions agreements which apply across the industry. Advice and representation for its members, as well as administering disputes, unemployment and other benefits. Publishes *Freelance Directory* and *The Journalist*.

The Newspaper Society
Bloomsbury House, Bloomsbury Square, 74/77 Great Russell Street, London WC1
☎01–636 7014

President *Graham Parett*   **Director** *Dugal Nisbet-Smith*

Organisation for the provincial morning and evening/provincial and London suburban weekly newspapers.
At the same address **Guild of British Newspaper Editors President** *Keith Parker*; **Newspaper Conference** (a Newspaper Society organisation primarily concerned with newsgathering facilities in London for the regional press) and the **Young Newspapermen's Association** for young newspaper executives. **Hon Sec** *Caroline Leigh*.

Office of Arts and Libraries
Great George Street, London SW1P 3AL   ☎01–270 5929

Among its more routine responsibilities, the OAL funds the British Library, and is responsible for the new library project at St Pancras. It is also responsible for funding to the **Arts Council** and the **Regional Arts Associations**.

PEN
7 Dilke Street, London SW3 4JE   ☎01–352 6303

General Secretary *Josephine Pullein-Thompson* MBE

English PEN is part of **International PEN**, a worldwide association of writers which fights for freedom of expression and speaks out for writers imprisoned or harassed for criticising their governments or publishing other unpopular views. Founded in London in 1921, **International PEN** now consists of 79 centres in 58 countries. **PEN** originally stood for poets, essayists and novelists, but membership is now open to all writers. A programme of talks and discussion is supplemented by the publication of a twice-yearly Broadsheet.

The Penman Club

175 Pall Mall, Leigh on Sea, Essex SS9 1RE   ☎0702 74438

Subscription £7.25 first year; £5.25 thereafter

FOUNDED 1950. International writers' society, offering free criticism of members' work, general advice, and use of writers' library.

Performing Right Society

29–33 Berners Street, London W1P 4AA   ☎01–580 5544

Collects and distributes royalties arising from live and recorded performances of members' music.

The Personal Managers' Association Ltd

Redfern House, Woodside Hill, Chalfont St Peter, Bucks SL9 9TF   ☎0753 887393

President *Peter Dunlop*   **Secretary** *Alison Shelley*   Subscription £100

An association of artists' and dramatists' agents (membership not open to individuals). MONTHLY meetings, for exchange of information, discussion, and acts as a lobby when necessary. Applicants screened. Maintains a code of conduct. A high proportion of Play Agents are members of the PMA.

Player Playwrights

1 Hawthorndene Road, Hayes, Bromley, Kent BR2 7DZ

Subscription £4 p.a.

FOUNDED 1948. A society for newcomers to play and television writing. Weekly meetings in central London. Run-throughs of members' work are staged, and a discussion follows.

Playwrights Co-operative

117 Waterloo Road, London SE1   ☎01–633 9811

FOUNDED 1981. Has evolved a process of script development – a sequence of readings, discussions and workshops. Also story conferences, rehearsed readings, critical and professional advice, workshops held in London venues, and help in getting the final script produced. Since its inception, an average of 34% of the scripts which have been through the Co-Op have ended in production. Only the talented are accepted for membership; the rest can become 'Playwrights Co-Op Subscribers'.

Playwrights' Workshop

22 Brown Street, Altrincham, Cheshire WA14 2EU   ☎061–928 3095

Honorary Secretary *Robert Coupland*   Subscription £2 p.a.

FOUNDED 1949. The society meets monthly in Manchester, and aims to support playwrights of all kinds interested in furthering their work. Guest speakers on all aspects of the theatre. Annual one-act play competition. Past members include Michael Dines and Harry Kershaw.

The Press Club

76 Shoe Lane, London EC4A 3JB ☎01–353 6207

Subscription £27.60–£66.70 (plus entrance fees)

FOUNDED 1882. Membership is open to both men and women in journalism, publishing and allied professions.

Publishers Association

19 Bedford Square, London WC1B 3HJ ☎01–580 6321–5

Chief Executive *Clive Bradley*

The national trade association (see also **The Scottish Publishers Association**) with over 500 member companies in the industry. Very much a trade body. Writers with queries are referred on to **The Society of Authors** or **Writers' Guild**. Publishes the *Directory of Publishing*, in association with **Cassell**. Also home of the Book Marketing Council, whose task it is to promote books and boost their sale, by running promotions like 'Brit Wit' on a regular basis.

The Romantic Novelists' Association

20 First Avenue, Amersham, Bucks HP7 9BJ ☎02403 7202

Secretary *Dorothy Entwistle*

Membership is open to published writers of romantic novels or of two or more full-length serials, and also to publishers, literary agents, booksellers and librarians. Meetings are held in London and speakers are often arranged. *RNA News* is published quarterly and issued free to members. See *Literary Prizes and Awards* for details of *Romantic Novelists' Award/Netta Muskett Award*.

The Royal Literary Fund

11 Ludgate Hill, London EC4M 7AE

FOUNDED 1790, the fund makes grants available to authors and their dependants in financial need on a stringently discretionary basis.

Royal Society of Literature

1 Hyde Park Gardens, London W2 2LT ☎ 01–723 5104

President *Sir Angus Wilson* Subscription £20 p.a.

FOUNDED 1823. Membership (limited to 300) by application to the secretary with 2 sponsors. Fellowships are conferred by the Society on the proposal of two fellows. Benefits of membership include lectures and poetry readings in the Society's rooms. Recent lecturers have included Melvyn Bragg, Helen Gardner, Francis King and Dilys Powell. Presents the **Royal Society of Literature Award**, and the **Winifred Holtby Memorial Award** (see *Literary Prizes and Awards*).

Royal Television Society

Tavistock House East, Tavistock Square, London WC1H 9HR 01–387 1970/1332

Subscription £22 (full UK member)

FOUNDED 1927. Covers all disciplines involved in the television industry. Provides a forum for debates and conferences on technical, social, and cultural aspects of the medium. *RTS Television Journalism Awards* are presented each February. Also runs a TV writing course.

Scottish Arts Council

19 Charlotte Square, Edinburgh EH2 4DF   031–226 6051

Literature Director *Walter Cairns*

The council's work for writers (defined as those whose work can command a fee, and who have a track record of publication) includes: *Bursaries* considered twice yearly; *Travel and Research Grants* considered three times yearly; *Writing Fellowships*, posts usually advertised; *International Writing Fellowship* organised reciprocally with the Canada Council; *Writers in Schools and in Public* – a list of writers willing to participate in the schemes is published. Also publishes lists of Scottish writers' groups, awards and literary agents.

Scottish Poetry Library Association

Tweeddale Court, 14 High Street, Edinburgh EH1 1TE   031–557 2876

Director *Tessa Ransford*   **Membership £7.50 p.a.**

A comprehensive collection of work by Scottish poets in Gaelic and English, plus the work of international poets. The benefits of becoming a member include a newsletter, and regular catalogues. Can provide lists of publishers, magazine outlets for writing, workshops. A postal service is also offered, for which there is a small fee.

The Scottish Publishers Association

25a South West Thistle Street Lane, Edinburgh EH2 1EW   031–225 5795

Director *Lorraine Fannin*   **Publicist** *Alison Harley*

The Association represents over fifty Scottish publishers, from multinationals to very small presses, in a number of capacities, but primarily in the co-operative promotion and marketing of their books. The *SPA* also acts as an information and advice centre for both the trade and general public. It publishes seasonal catalogues, membership lists, a detailed directory of members, and provides its membership with a regular newsletter. The *SPA* represents its members at international bookfairs, provides opportunities for publishers' training, and carries out market research.

Scottish Society of Playwrights

37 Otago Street, Glasgow G12 8JJ   ☎041–339 1787

Secretary *Charles Hart*   Subscription £20 p.a.

FOUNDED in 1973 by a group of playwrights, the society acts as a pressure group for playwrights, negotiates contracts with management, and provides a basic retyping and photocopying service for its members. Full membership is open to anyone who has had a play professionally produced on stage, television or radio.

Sean Dorman Manuscript Society

Union Place, Fowey, Cornwall PL23 1BY

Subscription £3.50 p.a. (after £1.50, 6 months trial period)

FOUNDED 1957. The Society trains its members in all branches of writing by co-operative methods, so avoiding the expense of writing schools. Typescripts are circulated in postal criticism folios, read, and returned with a wide range of opinions. Technical folios, in which markets and writing techniques are discussed, are also circulated.

The Society of Authors

84 Drayton Gardens, London SW10 9SB   ☎01–373 6642

General Secretary *Mark le Fanu*

Annual subscription £50 or £45 by direct debit

FOUNDED 1884. **The Society of Authors** is an independent trade union with some 3500 members. The Society advises on negotiations with publishers, broadcasting organisations, theatre managers and film companies; takes up complaints and pursues legal action for breach of contract, copyright infringement, etc. Along with the **Writers Guild,** the Society has played a major role in advancing the Minimum Terms Agreement for authors. Among the Society's publications are *The Author* (a quarterly journal) and *Quick Guides* to various aspects of writing. Other services include a pension fund and a group medical insurance scheme. Authors under 35, who are not yet earning a significant income from their writing, may apply for membership at a lower subscription of £32.

Society of Women Writers and Journalists

2 St Lawrence Close, Edgware, Middlesex HA8 6RB

Honorary Secretary *Olive Macdonald*

Subscription Town £15, Country £12, Overseas £9

Lectures at monthly lunchtime meetings. Also offers advice to members, seminars, etc. Journal *The Woman Journalist* issued three times a year.

South Bank Board: Literature Office
South Bank, London SE1 8XX   ☎ 01–921 0906 (literature)

Literature director *Moira Dooley*

A new feature of the South Bank complex is the recent appointment of Moira Dooley whose aims are to 'create a strong presence for literature on the South Bank'. Her brief covers all aspects of writing, and hopefully a venue within the Royal Festival Hall will be established for readings of literature, poetry and plays, plus workshops, and festivals. A writer in residence may be appointed. Other plans are at the committee stage at the time of going to press. Additionally, in Spring 1988, the National Poetry Library will move to the South Bank.

Television History Centre
42 Queen Square, London WC1N 3AJ   ☎ 01–405 6627

Co-ordinators *Sharon Goulds, Marilyn Wheatcroft*

Home of the television history workshop, the history centre 'provides a range of resources, materials, information and assistance to help people record their own history'.

Theatre Writers' Union
Actors Centre, 4 Chenies Street, London WC1E 7EP   ☎ 01–631 3619

Subscription £20 p.a.

Represents all writers working in the theatre, negotiates for terms and conditions, encourages new writing and presses for its further funding.

Translators' Guild Ltd
c/o 26–27 Boswell Street, London WC1N 3JZ

Membership is restricted to those who have passed the translator's examination in technical, scientific, commercial or social science fields. Also offer affiliation and student membership. Benefits include listing in an index which specifies the skills and languages of each member.

Welsh Arts Council
Museum Place, Cardiff CF1 3NX   ☎ 0222 394711

Literature director *Meic Stephens*

Funding available for little magazines, writers on tour and through competitions; but 'owing to financial strictures, bursaries and residencies have been temporarily suspended'. However, there are still ten annual prizes of £1000 available. *Oriel*, the

Welsh Arts Council bookshop, offers critical advice to writers – 'for a small fee' (☎ 0222 395548).

Drama director *Roger Tomlinson*

Funding is 'tight', and most of the work of the department is concerned with theatres and touring companies. Of particular interest to writers is the *Theatre Writing Scheme*, with awards to commissioning bodies who operate outside the main stream.

Welsh Books Council (Cyngor Llyfrau Cymraeg)
Castell Brychan, Aberystwyth, Dyfed SY23 2JB ☎ 0970 4151/3

Contact *Alun Creunant Davies*

FOUNDED 1961 to stimulate interest in Welsh literature and to support authors. The Council distributes the government grant for Welsh-language publications, promotes and fosters all aspects of both Welsh and Welsh interest book production. Its four departments, Editorial, Design, Publicity and Marketing, and Wholesale Distribution Centre offer central services to publishers in Wales, and writers in Welsh and English are welcome to approach the Editorial Department for advice on how to get their manuscripts published. *Book News From Wales/Llais Llyfrau*, quarterly, includes book lists, reviews, and articles on various aspects of Welsh writing and publishing.

Women In Entertainment
7 Thorpe Close, London W10 5XL ☎ 01–969 2292

A pressure group for women involved in the entertainment industry.

Writers' Circles
A nationwide network of writers' circles (hundreds of them, too many to list here) exists, designed to provide an informal atmosphere of mutual help and constructive criticism for writers of all grades. Your **Regional Arts Association** (see p.419) can usually provide a comprehensive list of those in your area.

Writers' Guild of Great Britain
430 Edgware Road, London W2 1EH ☎ 01–723 8074

General Secretary *Walter J. Jeffrey*
Annual subscription 1% of that part of the author's income earned in the areas in which the Guild operates, with a minimum of £30 and a maximum of £480.

A trade union, affiliated to the TUC, representing writers in film, radio, television, theatre and publishing. The Guild advises on all aspects of writers' agreements and leads the way in campaigns for minimum terms for writers working in film, radio and theatre. Along with the **Society of Authors**, the Guild has played a major role in advancing the Minimum Terms Agreement for authors.

Yr Academi Gymreig
3rd floor, Mount Stuart House, Mount Stuart Square, Cardiff CF1 6DQ

☎ 0222 492064

FOUNDED 1959 to encourage writing in Welsh. Membership by election. Publishes *Taliesin*, books on Welsh literature and an English/Welsh dictionary. English language section for Welsh writers in English, and those who write on Welsh themes.

Regional Arts Associations

Council of Regional Arts Associations
Litton Lodge, 13a Clifton Road, Winchester, Hants SO22 5BP   ☎0962 51063

Literature Secretary *Geoff Swallow*

CoRAA is a service organisation for the corporate needs of the 12 regional arts associations of England (Scotland and Wales have their own Arts Councils, and are not regionally split in this way). 'Increasingly the RAAs are becoming development agencies for the arts in the regions, and policies develop not only in response to regional demand, but also to develop new initiatives in areas of perceived need, and these – aside from the broad objectives of all RAAs – will vary from region to region.' As well as offering advice and practical help in the form of direct funding, the associations often also initiate arts events, such as touring theatre. Associate membership is offered to individuals; rates vary regionally.

DIRECT GRANTS FOR WRITERS
While most of the RAAs designate part of their budget for allocation direct to writers, this is often a minor proportion, which new or aspiring authors and playwrights stand little chance of receiving. Money is more readily available for the professional, though because of the emphasis on community access to the arts in many of the associations, this is often allocated to writers' appearances in schools etc, rather than to support the writer at the typewriter. It is generally accepted, too, that funding is more accessible to novelists than to playwrights. Direct grants are made to writers of fiction because, usually, there is confidence that the work will be published. The grant or bursary is regarded as an investment of sorts. But for playwrights publication is rarely the end result. Funding is more likely to go into the creation of workshops and performance, to bring along a play and help shape it for public consumption: ''The present structure is as much about performance skills as writing skills,'' one drama officer remarked, ''though just how the RAAs should be directing these funds has become one of the burning questions of the year.''

Buckinghamshire Arts Association
55 High Street, Aylesbury, Bucks HP20 1SA   ☎0296 434704

Literature Officer *Pat Swell*   **Drama Officer** *Margaret Hurd*

Founded only 3 years ago, BAA has a 'special relationship' with **East Midlands Arts**. Particularly supportive of ''poetry, the novel and short stories, biographies, memoirs, local history, story telling and children's books''. Organises creative writing courses, such as 'So you want to be an Author?', also operates 'Book the Writer', a subsidy scheme for writers to meet their public. Financial assistance can be applied for by writers, dramatists, publishers, small presses, magazines, poetry promoters, community bookshops.

East Midlands Arts
Mountfields House, Forest Road, Loughborough, Leics LE11 3HU ☎0509 218292

Literature Officer *Lynne Hapgood*   **Drama Officer** *Moira Sutton*

Covers Leicestershire, Nottinghamshire, Derbyshire (excluding the High Peak District) and Northamptonshire. A comprehensive information service for writers includes an extensive *Writers' Information Pack*, with details of groups and societies in the region, publishers and publishing information, a list of regional magazines which offer a market for work, advice on approaching the media, on unions, courses and grants. Also available is a directory of writers, primarily to aid people using their 'Writers' Visits Scheme', and in establishing 'Writers' Attachments'. 'Writers' Bursaries' (about 5 a year) are granted for work on a specific project – all forms of writing are eligible except for local history and biography. Writing for the theatre can come under the aegis of both Literature and Drama. A list of writers' groups is available, plus *Literature Newsletter*, and the free mazagine *Steppin' Out*.

Eastern Arts
Cherry Hinton Hall, Cambridge CB1 4DW   ☎0223 215355

Literature Officer *Laurence Staig*   **Drama Officer** *Richard Hogger*

Covers Bedfordshire, Cambridgeshire, Essex, Hertfordshire, Norfolk and Suffolk. Policy emphasises access for all in as wide an area as possible. As a self-styled arts development agency, great stress is placed upon the support of individuals, particularly in the interests of literature in the community. On the drama side, greater emphasis is placed on the creation of a structure to support the playwright – by means of adequate workshops and performance opportunities, rather than direct grants, though a small fund exists for the commissioning of work. Closely involved with the *Royal Court Young People's Theatre Writing Festival*. The *Visiting Writers' Scheme* subsidises visits by professional writers to schools and other organisations (and includes many household names). Can also supply lists of literary groups, societies and workshops in the area, plus details of residential creative writing courses.

Greater London Arts
9 White Lion Street, London N1 9PD   ☎01–837 8808

Literature Officers *Laurence Baylis, Vuyiswa Ngqobongwana*   **Drama Officer** *Anna Stapleton*

Awards and bursaries to individual writers are not currently offered by GLA, though this is under review. Applications are encouraged for projects which support the availability and awareness of contemporary literature, such as book and maga-zine distribution and representation, promotion and marketing schemes, and book fairs. Grants are also available for readings, performances and workshops involving creative writing of all kinds, as well as one-off film projects. **London Poetry Sec-retariat** subsidises appearances by published creative writers, whether poets, writers of fiction, dramatists, essayists or biographers. **Writers in Schools** subsi-dises the cost of bringing writers into contact with students of all ages.

Merseyside Arts
Bluecoat Chambers, School Lane, Liverpool L1 3BX   ☎051–709 0671

Literature Officer *Anne Gray*   **Drama Officer** *Shea Connolly*

Merseyside Arts covers Merseyside, part of Cheshire and part of West Lancashire. Presently no direct grants or bursaries are offered to individuals, writers included. Project grants, totalling £100,000 in the year 1987/88, can bring monies to writers indirectly. These go to fund existing projects and to establish new ventures **Merseyside Arts** feels it would like to involve itself with, and can include literature and drama projects. Similarly with fiction – grants are made towards publication, but direct to publishers, and not to writers. Residencies and the 'Writers Round Merseyside' scheme are also offered. Playwrights can find help in the form of sup-port for rehearsed readings, commissions etc. The question of how new, and par-ticularly young, writers should be supported is currently under review.

North West Arts
4th floor, 12 Harter Street, Manchester M1 6HY   ☎061–228 3062

General Arts/Literature Officer *Liz Mayne*   **Drama Officer** *Ivor Davies*

Covers Cheshire, Greater Manchester, Lancashire (except West Lancs) and the High Peak of Derbyshire. Financial assistance to a great variety of projects and schemes, including *Lancaster Literature Festival* and creative writing courses. Grants are made to both professional writers and dramatists. A Readers' Service is offered to any writer living in the region who submits original unpublished material at a time when funds are available. Writers should send their work with s.a.e. and postcard with name etc. for filing purposes. The *Writers in the Community* scheme subsidises writers' fees and travel expenses, when addressing societies etc. Have just launched a new literature magazine, *The Word is Out*.

Northern Arts
9–10 Osborne Terrace, Jesmond, Newcastle upon Tyne NE2 1NZ ☎091–281 6334

Literature Officer *Jenny Attala*   **Drama Officer** *Sheila Harborth*

Northern Arts covers Cleveland, Cumbria, Durham, Northumberland, and Tyne and Wear, and was the first regional arts association in the country to be set up by local authorities. Supports both organisations and writers, and aims to stimulate public interest in artistic events. Offers grants for published writers to release them from work or other commitments for short periods of time to enable concentration on specific literary projects. A separate scheme operates for playwrights by the *Northern Playwrights Society*. *Northern Arts* make drama awards to producers only. Also fund writers' residencies, magazines and publishing, as well as assisting financially the *Arvon Foundation, Lumb Bank writing courses*.

South East Arts
10 Mount Ephraim, Tunbridge Wells, Kent TN4 8AS ☎0892 41666

Literature Officer *Charmian Stowell*   **Drama Officer** *Charles Hart*

South East Arts covers the counties of Kent, Surrey and East Sussex. The Literature panel 'aims to create a high public profile for contemporary writing, and to encourage aspiring writers' to develop their skills'. Information, advice and training opportunities are offered to writers. Arts centres and other organisations, independent presses and writers' groups are among the recipients of direct funding. *Writers' Information Pack* available for £1.50 from the literature department.

South West Arts
Bradninch Place, Gandy Street, Exeter EX4 3LS ☎0392 218188

Literature Officer *Sheila Squirrell*   **Drama Officer** *Renée Smithens*

SW Arts covers Avon, Cornwall, Devon, much of Dorset, Gloucestershire and Somerset. 'The central theme running through the Association's constitution is development . . . increasing, improving, encouraging, advancing and co-ordinating.' The literature policy aims to promote a healthy environment for writers of all kinds and to encourage a high standard of new writing. The programme includes residential courses, residencies, and writers in education. There is also direct investment in small presses, publishers and community groups. Literary festivals, societies and arts centres are encouraged. 'Although *South West Arts* cannot act as a literary agency or offer subsidy for work in progress, we do on occasion sponsor special awards, such as the *TSB Peninsular Prize*.' (see *Prizes*)

Southern Arts Association
19 Southgate Street, Winchester, Hampshire SO23 9DQ ☎0962 55099

Marketing and Literature Officer *Keiren Phelan*   **Drama Officer** *Fiona Ellis*

The literature panel decides on funding for fiction and poetry readings, festivals, magazines, bursaries, a literature prize, publications, residencies and attachments. A third of the budget in 1987/88 will be spent on writers in education.

West Midlands Arts
82 Granville Street, Birmingham B1 2LH ☎021–631 3121

Literature/Drama Projects Officer *David Hart*

Covers Herefordshire, Worcestershire, Shropshire, Staffordshire, Warwickshire. 'Our policy is to contribute to the process whereby good writing, in the main by living writers, is made accessible to readers and to help provide opportunities for aspiring writers.' The *Writers in the Community Scheme* pays half the fee for writers' visits. Commissions to a professional writer to produce work are also made, though publication grants are made to publishers only, never writers. The Reading Service charges £5 and reports fully on short pieces of work – such as sample chapters of a novel. Also support 2 local literature festivals: The *Birmingham Readers' and Writers' Festival* and the *Shrewsbury Poetry Festival*. Lists of publishers of fiction and poetry in the region, national publishers of poetry, magazines in the area, and contacts for writing courses are available. No lists of writers' circles. Publish *People to People* magazine.

Yorkshire Arts
Glyde House, Bradford BD5 0BQ ☎0274 723051

Literature Officer *Jenny Barraclough*   **Drama Officer** *Chrissie Poulter*

'Libraries, publishing houses and the education service all make major contributions to the support of literature. Recognising the resources these agencies command, *Yorkshire Arts* actively seeks ways of acting in partnership with them, whilst at the same time retaining its particular responsibility for the living writer and the promotion of activities currently outside the scope of these agencies.' There are a limited number of bursaries available for writers: other funding goes to the *Arvon Foundation* at Lumb Bank the *Live Writing* scheme, which subsidises projects involving professional writers and students at all levels; and awards to independent publishers. Also offer support for literature in performance, such as the *Ilkley Literature Festival*, and live poetry events.

Library and Research Facilities

There are a large number of specialist libraries throughout the country, many of them belonging to professional or other associations. The most comprehensive guide to sources of specialist information is the *ASLIB Directory of Information Sources in the United Kingdom* published by Aslib, the Association for Information Management, in two volumes: *Volume One: Science, Technology and Commerce* and *Volume Two: Social Sciences, Medicine and the Humanities*. These books are available at all public reference libraries and are indexed by subject matter to enable the user to locate the library or other information source required.

Another useful publication is the *Guide to Government Department and Other Libraries* published by the British Library and again available at public reference libraries.

Writers in London and the Home Counties should enquire at their local library about the London and South Eastern Library Region (LASER) which is a co-operative organisation designed to improve public library facilities. Libraries throughout the LASER area have special collections of books allowing each library to cater for a specific subject and so preventing unnecessary duplication across the region. For example, a writer wishing to research American Literature would find the special collection at Tower Hamlets of interest. Similarly, Kensington specialises in biography, Hackney in optical instruments, and Redbridge in Public Health. Arrangements can be made at any of the LASER scheme libraries to borrow the book or books a writer may need for particular research. The current location of each special collection is detailed in the *Directory of London Public Libraries*.

The following list of libraries is therefore far from exhaustive.

The British Library Association Library
7 Ridgmount Street, London WC1 7AE ☎ 01-636 1544

Open 9.00 am to 6.00 pm Monday, Wednesday, Friday; 9.00 am to 8.00 pm Tuesday and Thursday. (NB From mid-July to mid-September opening hours are 9.00 am to 6.00 pm Monday to Friday.)

Open access for reference (loans are to members of the Association only). Provides British and foreign reference material on librarianship, information science and related subjects. Has special collections of historical library annual reports and theses on librarianship.

The British Library Business Information Service

25 Southampton Buildings, Chancery Lane, London WC2A 1AW   ☎01–323 7979

A resource facility for those engaged in all aspects of business, an invaluable reference source for specialist journalists.

The British Library India Office Library and Records

197 Blackfriars Road, London SE1 8NG   ☎01–928 9531

Open 9.30 am to 6.00 pm Monday to Friday; 9.30 am to 1.00 pm Saturday.
Open access for reference purposes. Long term use and loans to members only.

Contains an extensive stock of printed books, prints, drawings, photographs and manuscripts relating to Indological and modern South Asian studies. Large collection of manuscripts in Arabic, Persian, Sanskrit and Tibetan languages. A *Guide to the India Office Library* by S. C. Sutton is available to aid researchers.

The British Library Map Library

Great Russell Street, London WC1B 3DG   ☎01–636 1544 Ext. 265

Open 9.30 am to 4.30 pm Monday to Saturday.
Access by British Library Readers' Pass or Map Library Day Pass.

A collection of over a million charts, globes and maps, with particular reference to the history of British cartography. Maps for all parts of the world at wide range of scales. Special collections include King George III Maritime Collection and Topographical Collection, and the Crace Collection of maps and plans of London. Also satellite pictures of all areas of the world.

The British Library Manuscripts Department

Great Russell Street, London WC1B 3DG   ☎01–636 1544 Ext. 340

Open 10.00 am to 4.45 pm Monday to Saturday (closed Public Holidays and second week of November).
Access to reading facilities by Reader's Pass.

A useful publication, *The British Library: Guide to the catalogues and indexes of the Department of Manuscripts* by M. A. E. Nickson is available (£1.95) to guide the researcher through this vast collection of manuscripts dating from Ancient Greece to the present day. Approximately 85,000 volumes are housed here.

The British Library Music Library

Great Russell Street, London WC1B 3DG   ☎01–636 1544 Ext. 420

Open 9.30 am to 4.30 pm Monday to Friday.

Special collections include the Royal Music Library (containing several autographed scores by Handel) and the Paul Hirsch Music Library. Also a large collection of printed music, British and foreign.

The British Library Newspaper Library

Colindale Avenue, London NW9 5HE   ☎01–200 5515

Open 10.00 am to 4.45 pm Monday to Saturday. Last issue of newspapers 4.15 pm.
Admission by British Library Reader's Pass or Newspaper Library Reader's Pass
(available from and valid only for Colindale Avenue).

English provincial, Scottish, Irish, Commonwealth and foreign newspapers from
c.1700 are housed at this library. London newspapers from 1801 and most large
weekly periodicals are also in stock. (London newspapers pre-dating this period are
housed in Great Russell Street.)

The British Library Official Publications Library

Great Russell Street, London WC1B 3DG   ☎01–636 1455 Ext. 234/235

Open 9.30 am to 4.45 pm Monday, Friday and Saturday; 9.30 am to 8.45 pm
Tuesday, Wednesday and Thursday.

Provides access to current and historical official publications from all countries, plus
publications of intergovernmental bodies. Also House of Commons Sessional Papers
from 1715, UK legislation, current UK electoral registers and up-to-date reference
books on the social sciences with special emphasis on law.

The British Library Oriental and Printed Books Department

14 Store Street, London WC1E 7DG   ☎01–636 1544 Ext. 612

Open 9.30 am to 5.00 pm Monday to Friday; 9.30 am to 1.00 pm Saturday.
Closed on Sundays and Public Holidays and in the week preceding the last complete
week of October.
Access to Oriental Reading Room by special pass.

A comprehensive collection of printed volumes and manuscripts in or related to the
languages and cultures of North Africa, the near and Middle East and all of Asia.

The British Library Reading Room

Great Russell Street, London WC1B 3DG   ☎01–636 1455 Ext. 324/325

Open 9.00 am to 5.00 pm Monday, Friday and Saturday; 9.00 am to 9.00 pm
Tuesday, Wednesday, Thursday.
Closed Sundays and Public Holidays and for the week following the last complete
week in October.
Admission by reader's pass. (A leaflet, *Applying for a reader's pass* is available for
guidance).

A large and comprehensive stock of books and periodicals relating to the humanities
and social sciences is available for reference and research which cannot easily be
done elsewhere. There are also exhibitions on literary and historical figures and a
permanent exhibition on the history of printing and binding. Telephone enquiries
are welcome.

The British Library Science Reference and Information Service

25 Southampton Buildings, Chancery Lane, London WC2A 1AW   ☎01–405 8721

Open 9.30 am to 9.00 pm Monday to Friday; 10.00 am to 1.00 pm Saturday.

The national library for modern science and technology providing an invaluable resource facility for technical journalists. Telephone enquiries are welcome.

HERTIS The Hertfordshire College Library and Technical Information Service

The Hatfield Polytechnic Library, PO Box 110, Hatfield, Herts AL10 9AD

☎070 72 79678

Open 8.45 am to 9.30 pm Monday to Thursday; 8.45 am to 7.00 pm Friday; 10.00 am to 1.00 pm Saturday; 12.00 to 5.00 pm Sunday. During vacation period the library is open from 9.00 am to 5.00 pm Monday to Friday. (These times are for the Hatfield Library only, other HERTIS libraries have varying opening times.)
Access to reference material at all HERTIS libraries is open to the public.

The HERTIS group is served by Hatfield Polytechnic and twelve other colleges of further education which combine to provide a resource facility on engineering, computing, humanities (with particular reference to South East Asia) social and business studies as well as building, agriculture, horticulture and art and design.

Holborn Library

32–38 Theobalds Road, London WC1X 8PA   ☎01–405 2705

Specialises in Business, employment and law with over 35,000 items in stock.

Liverpool City Libraries

William Brown Street, Liverpool L3 8EW   ☎051–207 2147

Open 9.00 am to 9.00 pm Monday to Friday; 9.00 am to 5.00 pm Saturday.
Access to all the Libraries is open to the general public.

Arts and Recreations Library (Ext. 33). 50,000 volumes covering all subjects in the arts and recreation.

Commercial and Social Sciences Library (Ext. 29). Business and trade directories plus all UK statutes and law reports. Serves as a depository library for UNO and EEC reports.

General, Religion and Philosophy Library and Hornby Library (Ext. 31). Contains stock of 68,000 volumes, 24,000 maps plus book plates, prints, and autograph letters. Special collections include Walter Crane and Edward Lear illustrations.

International Library (Ext. 20). Open shelf and reserve stocks on language, literature, geography and history. Special interest is the collection on British history with much on politicians and statesmen. 20,000 copies of British, American and European plays plus language tapes in twenty languages.

Music Library (Ext. 49). Extensive stock relating to all aspects of music; includes 128,000 volumes and music scores, 18,500 records and over 3,000 cassettes. Special collections include Carl Rosa Opera Company Collection and Earl of Sefton's early printed piano music.

Record Office and Local History Department (Ext. 34). Printed and audiovisual material relating to Liverpool, Merseyside, Lancashire and Cheshire together with archive material mainly on Liverpool. Some restrictions on access, e.g. 30-year rule applies to archives.

Science and Technology Library (Ext. 7). Extensive stock dealing with all aspects of science and technology including British and European standards and patents.

London Borough of Camden Information and Reference Services
Swiss Cottage Library, 88 Avenue Road, London NW3 3HA   ☎01–586 5989

Open 9.30 am to 8.00 pm Monday to Thursday; 9.30 am to 6.00 pm Friday; 9.30 am to 5.00 pm Saturday.
Over 60,000 volumes and 600 periodical titles.

London Library
14 St James's Square, London SW1Y 4LG   ☎01–930 7705/6

Open 9.30 am to 5.30 pm Monday to Saturday (late opening Thursday to 7.30 pm); closed Sundays

Annual membership fee £70

One of the best general libraries in the country with over one million volumes, most of which are available on loan. Members are allowed to take out 10 volumes at a time or 15 volumes if they live outside London. Particularly strong in European languages, but stock excludes science and technology, medicine and law.

National Library of Scotland
George IV Bridge, Edinburgh EH1 1EW   ☎031–226 4531

Open 9.30 am to 8.30 pm Monday to Friday; 9.30 am to 1.00 pm Saturday.
Closed Map Room at 5.00 pm Monday to Friday; library on public holidays.
Access to Reading Rooms and Map Rooms for research not easily done elsewhere via ticket.

A collection of over four million volumes. The library receives all British and Irish publications. Large stock of newspapers and periodicals. Many special collections including early Scottish books, theology, polar studies, baking, phrenology and liturgies. Also large collections of maps, music and manuscripts including personal archives of notable Scottish persons.

National Library of Wales
Aberystwyth, Dyfed SY23 3BU   ☎0970 3816

Open 9.30 am to 6.00 pm Monday to Friday; 9.30 am to 5.00 pm Saturday and general holidays.

Access to Reading Room and Map Room by reader's ticket available on application.

A collection of over three million books which include large collections of periodicals, maps and manuscripts. Particular emphasis on the humanities in foreign material, and on Wales and other Celtic areas in all collections.

National Sound Archive
29 Exhibition Road, London SW7 2AS   ☎01–589 6603

Open 10.00 am to 5.30 pm Monday to Friday (late opening Thursday to 9.00 pm).
Open access to library.
Listening service (by appointment) 10.30 am to 5.30 pm Monday to Friday (late opening Thursday to 9.00 pm).

Northern Listening Service at British Library Document Supply Centre, Boston Spa, West Yorkshire.
Open 9.15 am to 4.30 pm Monday to Friday.   ☎0937 843434

An archive of over half a million discs and over 35,000 hours of tape recordings including popular music, oral history, drama, wildlife, selected BBC broadcasts and BBC Sound Archive material.

Sheffield City Libraries
Central Library, Surrey Street, Sheffield S1 1XZ   ☎0742 73411
Archives ☎0742 734756

Open 9.30 am to 9.00 pm Monday to Friday; 9.00 am to 4.30 pm Saturday.
Open access to the public, but prior arrangement should be made for consulting archive material.

Stocks Fairbank collection of maps, draft plans and surveying books, together with mss collections and parochial records relating to the area.

Arts and Social Sciences Reference Library   ☎0742 734747–9

Open 9.30 am to 9.00 pm Monday to Friday; 9.00 am to 4.00 pm Saturday.
Open access to all for reference purposes.

A comprehensive collection of books, periodicals and newspapers covering all aspects of arts and the humanities (excluding music).

Audio Visual and Music Library ☎0742 734733

Open 9.30 am to 8.00 pm Monday to Friday; 9.30 am to 4.30 pm Saturday.
Open access for reference purposes, loans with tickets.

An extensive range of books, records, scores etc. related to music. Also a video cassette loan service.

Business Library ☎0742 734736–8

Open 9.30 am to 5.30 pm Monday to Friday; 9.00 am to 4.30 pm Saturday.
Open access for reference.

A large stock of business and trade directories, plus overseas telephone directories and reference works with business emphasis.

Local Studies Library ☎0742 734753

Open 9.30 am to 5.30 pm Monday to Friday; 9.00 am to 4.30 pm Saturday.
Open access for reference use (advance notice advisable). ·

Extensive material covering all aspects of Sheffield and its population, including maps and taped oral histories.

Science and Technology Reference Library ☎0742 734753

Open 9.30 am to 5.30 pm Monday to Friday; 9.00 am to 4.00 pm Saturday.
Open access for reference.

Extensive coverage of science and technology as well as commerce and commercial law. British patents and British and European standards with emphasis on metals. (Sheffield also houses the *World Metal Index*.)

Sheffield Information Service ☎0742 734764

Open 9.30 am to 5.30 pm Monday to Friday; 9.00 am to 4.30 pm Saturday.

Full local information service covering aspects of the Sheffield community.

St Pancras Library
100 Euston Road, London NW1 ☎01–278 4444

Open access to general public.

Extensive stock of books, periodicals, maps and pamphlets with emphasis on social science, technology and science.

BBC Data Enquiry Service
Room 3, The Langham, Portland Place, London W1A 1AA ☎01–927 5998

BBC Data has an extensive library of materials relating to broadcasting and other media, as well as current affairs, the arts and sciences. This exists as an essential resource for BBC staff, but non-BBC researchers are able to make use of many facilities on a modest fee-paying basis. Where appropriate, BBC Data provides free assistance to *bona fide* libraries.

British Film Institute
127 Charing Cross Road, London WC2H 0EA   ☎01–437 4355

Open 11.00 am to 9.00 pm Tuesday and Wednesday; 11.00 am to 6.00 pm Thursday and Friday.
Closed Monday.
Open access for reference (regular users are expected to become BFI members).

A vast library of books, pamphlets, newspaper clippings, scripts and other memorabilia relating to the cinema and all its aspects (including video and television). Also stills and posters.

Commonwealth Secretariat Library
10 Carlton House Terrace, Pall Mall, London SW1   ☎01–839 3411 (Ext. 233)

Open 9.15 am to 5.15 pm Monday to Friday. Open for reference by prior arrangement only.

An extensive reference source mainly concerned with trade and production in the Commonwealth and its relation to the development of individual countries.

European Communities Commission Information Office
Abbey Buildings, 8 Storey's Gate, Westminster, London SW1 3AT ☎01–222 8122

Open 2.00 pm to 5.30 pm Monday to Friday.
Open access for reference.

Reference works on the European Community, plus copies of all EEC publications.

Fawcett Library
City of London Polytechnic, Old Castle Street, London E1 7NT   ☎01–283 1030

Open 1.00 pm to 8.30 pm Monday (during term time); 10.00 am to 5.00 pm Monday (during vacation); 10.00 am to 5.00 pm Tuesday to Friday.
Open access to non-Polytechnic members on payment of annual fee: £5.00 (full-time students £2.50) or one-day fee: £1.00

The leading library for feminist studies and research into all other aspects of women's history with emphasis on social sciences and the humanities. Contains extensive stock of books, pamphlets, photographs and archive materials. All loans are arranged via the British Library.

Foreign and Commonwealth Office Library
Sanctuary Buildings, Great Smith Street, London SW1P 3BZ   ☎01–212 9663

Open 9.30 am to 5.30 pm Monday to Friday.
Open access for reference purposes.

An extensive stock of books, pamphlets and other reference material on all aspects of socio-economic and political subjects relating to countries covered by the Foreign and Commonwealth Office. Particularly strong on official Commonwealth publications and legislation.

The French Institute (Institut Français du Royaume-Uni)
17 Queensbury Place, London SW7 2DT   ☎01–589 6211

Open 11.00 am to 8.00 pm Monday; 11.00 am to 6.00 pm Tuesday to Friday; 10.00 am to 1.00 pm Saturday.
Open access to reading room, but loans are to members only.

Annual membership £9.00; Students and OAPs: £6.00

A collection of over 70,000 volumes mainly centred on cultural interests with special emphasis on the French language.

Italian Institute of Culture
39 Belgrave Square, London SW1X 8NX   ☎01–235 1461

Open 9.30 am to 5.00 pm
Open access for reference.

A collection of over 20,000 volumes relating to all aspects of Italian culture. Texts are mostly in Italian, with some in English.

Book Trust
Book House, 45 East Hill, London SW18 2QZ   ☎01–870 9055

Centre for Children's Books, Children's Reference Library
Open 9.00 am to 5.00 pm Monday to Friday.
Open access for reference only.

A comprehensive collection of children's literature and related books and periodicals. Houses the Linder Collection of books and drawings by Beatrix Potter.

Mark Longman Library
Open 9.00 am to 5.00 pm Monday to Friday.
Open access for reference to non-members.

A comprehensive reference source on aspects of book production and bookselling and their history. Almost 10,000 volumes in stock, taking in printing and binding as well as literary criticism and biography. Special collection: the Perez Collection of over 12,000 bookplates.

Press Association Library
85 Fleet Street, London EC4P 4BE   ☎01–353 7440 (Ext. 55)

Open 8.00 am to 11.00 pm.

The editorial library of the PA is intended mainly for staff use, but researchers can acquire photocopies of specific press cuttings at a fixed rate from the **Special Reporting Department** (Ext. 100).

United Nations London Information Centre
20 Buckingham Gate, London SW1E 6LB   ☎01–630 1981

Open 10.00 am to 1.00 pm and 2.00 pm to 5.00 pm each Monday, Wednesday and Thursday.
Open access for reference.

A full stock of official publications and documentation from the United Nations and its major agencies worldwide.

Westminster City Libraries
Central Music Library
160 Buckingham Palace Road, London SW1W 9UD   ☎01–798 2192

Open 9.30 am to 7.00 pm Monday to Friday; 9.30 am to 5.00 pm Saturday.

Extensive coverage of all aspects of music, including books, periodicals and printed scores.

Fine Arts Library
Central Reference Library, St Martin's St, London WC2H 7HP   ☎01–798 2038

Open 10.00 am to 7.00 pm Monday to Friday; 10.00 am to 5.00 pm Saturday.
Open access for reference only (notice required in certain cases).

An excellent reference source for fine arts and crafts and related subjects. Also houses the Preston Blake collection of works by and about William Blake.

Medical Library
Marylebone Library, Marylebone Road, London NW1 5PS   ☎01–798 1039

Open 9.30 am to 7.00 pm Monday to Friday; 9.30 am to 5.00 pm Saturday.
Open access for reference.

Books, pamphlets and periodicals covering all aspects of medicine and the health services.

Westminster History and Archives Department
Victoria Library, 160 Buckingham Palace Road, London SW1W 9UD

Open access for reference.

Comprehensive coverage of the history of Westminster and selective coverage of general London history. 18,000 books, together with a large stock of periodicals, prints and photographs.

Copyright

High on the list of writers' worries is the question of copyright (literally, the right to copy). If I create a potential best seller, who is to say that somewhere between my typewriter and the finished product, the manuscript will not be purloined by an unscrupulous rival and reproduced as his own work? To achieve his purpose the villain need only refashion my material. This could be achieved very quickly. A really smart operator might even beat me to the starting post, claiming that I was the plagiarist.

It can and does happen; if rarely in such dramatic circumstances. More common than the straight steal of a new work is the paste and scissors job based on out-of-print books and articles or unpublished manuscripts. In broadcasting there are frequent complaints of rejected proposals re-emerging under other names. It is a foolish writer who does not take steps to protect his copyright. There is one certain way of doing this. Send a copy of your manuscript to yourself by registered post, then deposit the package and the dated receipt at a bank or other safe place. This way lies security.

A copyright notice appears in the front of most books. In its simplest form this is the symbol © followed by the name of the copyright owner and the year of first publication. The assertion of copyright may be emphasised by the phrase 'All rights reserved', and in case there are any lingering doubts the reader may be warned that 'No part of this publication may be reproduced or transmitted in any form or by any means without permission'.

But this is to overstate the case. It is perfectly legitimate for a writer to quote from someone else's work for 'purposes of criticism or review' as long as 'sufficient acknowledgement' is given. What he/she must not do is to lift 'a substantial part' of a copyright work without permission. Unfortunately, there is little agreement on what constitutes 'a substantial part', since the 1956 *Copyright Act* does not define the term. Legal precedents suggest that the quality of the 'part' and its value to the user must be taken into account as well as its length in determining whether it is 'substantial'. This explains how, in one case, four lines from a thirty-two line poem were held to amount to 'a substantial part'. On the other hand, even a 'substantial' quotation from a copyright work may be acceptable if a reviewer or critic is engaged in 'fair dealing' with his subject. But no-one should be surprised to hear that 'fair dealing' is another of those terms which is open to legal interpretation.

Circumstances may require a writer to consider surrendering his copyright. This happens most frequently with newspapers and magazines where freelances can be equated with permanent staff who generally consign copyright as part of their terms of employment. In deciding whether or not to comply with a request for more than first rights to publication, a freelance should consider the long term value of his contribution. If it is a straightforward news item destined to perish with the issue in which it appears then there is little point in making a fuss. But a lengthy feature on an ever-interesting topic might qualify for numerous reprints in other publications at home and abroad. In this case, the writer should follow the advice of the NUJ and other professional bodies and hang on to copyright for dear life; or alternatively only give it up in return for a payment substantial enough to compensate for lost royalties or fees.

A trick to look out for is the payment cheque which can only be cashed after the recipient has countersigned over words which grant rights to the issuing company. Don't sign unless you understand and accept what you are signing.

Script writers are another group who can lose out on copyright almost by default. Television and radio usually acknowledge the right to repeat fees but it is as well to read the small print on any contract. Just a few years ago the contracts department of one of the independent television companies tried to argue me out of copyright by claiming 'there are no plans to repeat the series'. Happily, I was practised enough to know that circumstances can change very rapidly. The series *was* repeated, twice.

As far as it is possible to tell, script writing for non-commercial videos such as company training courses or advertising features almost always requires the surrender of copyright to the client. As this is a fast expanding source of income, it is likely that the writers' organisations will have more to say about it in the years ahead. But to be fair, a writer who is working to order, that is, using material provided and turning it into presentable shape has a slender claim to copyright.

The same argument applies to sponsored books where the client, usually a company, pays directly for a document of record, a volume celebrating an important anniversary, for example. The writer may think it essential to stick by the principle of retaining copyright come what may, but there is no question that this may exclude him from a prosperous sector of the market.

To rush to the other extreme, copyright should never be renounced as a condition for entering a competition. Unscrupulous organisers of literary jamborees have been known to demand copyright in return for the chance of winning a miserable prize. Every writer is entitled to seek recognition but it is always wise to check that the price is not too high.

What does copyright cover?

In Britain copyright protection lasts for fifty years from the end of the year in which the author dies. For a published work of joint authorship protection runs from the end of the year of the death of the author who dies last. The fifty year rule applies to all written work including letters.

There is no copyright in a title. But when a title is distinctive and clearly identified with the work of a particular author, that author may be able to obtain an injunction and damages if the title, or something very close to it, is used by another writer. The question is, how close is close? Of recently published titles, Sally Beauman's block buster novel *Destiny* was thought by one critic to imply a link with the television soap opera, Dynasty. But to this extent, most popular literature is imitative and no reader is likely to be deceived into thinking that the two creations are the same. But if you are planning to write the fictional diaries of a pimply teenager, a title like *The Secret Diaries of Adrian Pole* will almost certainly get you into trouble with Sue Townshend.

There is no copyright in an idea or the bare bones of a plot. Many of those who protest that radio or television have stolen their brilliant idea for a situation comedy centred on a launderette or an old folks' home or whatever, can show nothing to support their claim except a brief letter to the head of comedy. Few ideas are original and, as any producer will confirm, the same ideas crop up time and time again. To have a reasonable claim to copyright the proposer of an idea must provide a full synopsis and sample material.

The terms of copyright outlined so far extend to all the member countries of the Berne Union. But the United States, which is outside the Berne Union, goes further. The *US Copyright Act* of 1909 provided for two separate terms of copyright, a period of twenty-eight years from publication followed by a renewal period of a further twenty-eight years. A new copyright act, which came into force in January 1978, made changes in the duration of copyright protection and set out rules for the transition of existing works.

Copyrights registered before 1950 and renewed before 1978 were automatically extended by the new act until December of the seventy-fifth year of the original date of registration. This meant that all copyrights in their second term were extended for nineteen years. But copyrights registered after 1950 and before December 1977 had to be renewed. The repercussions continue to this day since a work published in 1960 must be renewed before 31 December 1988 (1960 + 28) in order to obtain protection for the full seventy-five year period. Renewal forms can be obtained from the Register of Copyrights, Library of Congress, Washington DC 20559.

Works created after the new law came into force are automatically protected for the author's lifetime, and for an additional fifty years after the author's death.

Unwillingly to Court

The Law of Libel

Libel is a thriving business, a source of wealth for lawyers and not unusually for plaintiffs. Those who pay out are writers, publishers and their insurance companies.

In this country it is very easy to libel someone. If half of what was written in the United States about famous people was reprinted here, the courts would be over-flowing until the end of the century. Every journalist has his/her private list of crooks and charlatans who he would dearly like to expose. But fear of retribution in the form of a long and expensive court case in which the odds are heavily in favour of the plaintiff is a powerful deterrent.

The litmus test for libel is to ask, 'Would the words complained of tend to lower the plantiff in the estimation of right thinking members of society?' This begs the question as to who is a 'right thinking' person, but, without getting bogged down in semantics, assume that he/she is in the conventional mould.

It may be that the defendant did not intend libel. No matter. All that the plaintiff need show is that the statement would be understood by reasonable people to refer to him. There is a clear warning here for fiction writers not to venture too close to real life. It may seem a neat idea to introduce friends and neighbours into a story – it is so much easier to describe people you know – but if one of them is cast as a villain and recognises himself, albeit in an unlikely role, then a solicitor's letter will surely follow.

Names, too, can be a trap for the unwary. If a novel features a corrupt Member of Parliament, a financier who swindles his tax or a vicar with an obsessive interest in choirboys, it is as well to check that the names given to these characters do not correspond to flesh and blood people. Often, the more unlikely the name, the greater the risk. You may think you are on safe ground when you relate the dubious practices of the Rev. Harbottle Tiddles Grimston, but rotten luck dictates that as soon as the book is in print, a curious coincidence will be drawn to your attention. With such an unlikely name it is difficult to argue that you have acted unwittingly. The problem is accentuated by the sure knowledge that much of what appears in novels does relate to real life, even if the writer is not immediately aware of it. It is extraordinary what can be dredged from the subconscious. One well-known writer recalls the awful embarrassment of realising, too late, that the name of the leading participant in his steaming sex saga happened to be that of his fiancée. He avoided a libel action but she sent back his engagement ring.

In book publishing it is the biographers of contemporary or near contemporary figures who tread the narrowest line. To state a known fact about an individual, that he behaved deviously or dishonestly, for example, may raise questions about his friends, associates or family which they feel bound to contest. A film star who was famous for his stories of licentious adventurers, usually with the wives of other film stars, was never so much as challenged by his victims. But when he died and his biographer got to work, the writs began to fly.

Where a libel has been committed unintentionally or 'innocently', it is possible to alleviate the consequences by an 'offer to make amends'. This usually involves a published apology and a settlement of costs. Otherwise, unless it can be established that a statement, however defamatory, is true in substance and fact (a difficult trick to pull off), the defence against libel will probably turn on the assertion that the words complained of are fair comment on a matter of public interest.

This is where the wheel turns full circle because writers, who are themselves inclined to rush to law when they feel aggrieved, often hear the 'fair comment' defence from reviewers who have savaged their work. The perimeters of 'fair comment' are wide enough to protect the essence of free speech, so that, according to precedent, 'However wrong the opinion expressed may be in point of truth, or however prejudiced the writer, it may still be within the prescribed limit'. In other words, it is one thing to argue that a person's views are lunatic but quite another to assert that he is a lunatic.

Every writer is responsible for his own work. But this should not mean that when he makes mistakes he has to carry the can all on his own. The Press and broadcasting media invariably give full backing to their contributors (in most cases they have to because they assume copyright). But traditionally book publishers are reluctant to share the risk of libel. A typical contract includes a warranty clause which entitles the publisher to be indemnified by the author against any damages and costs resulting from a libel action.

It has been argued that the warranty clause is a necessary deterrent against greedy litigants who would see the prospect of winning higher damages from a company than from an individual writer. But most publishers take out insurance to cover this possibility. It is surely not too much to ask that the protection should extend to authors – particularly when they are tackling controversial subjects.

At the very least, the author should make sure his contract does not allow for unlimited liability. In 1972 David Irving whose book *The Destruction of Convoy PO17* had been the subject of a successful libel action, was in turn sued by his publisher Cassell who sought to recover the libel damages and costs they had paid out. The claim was for £100,000. But fortunately for Irving he had taken the advice of the Society of Authors to amend his contract. He was liable only for breaches of his warranty that the book was free of libel unknown to the publisher. Irving argued that Cassell knew all the relevant facts before an action was brought. In the end, Cassell did not proceed with the claim.

This and many other fascinating and instructive cases are fully documented in David Hooper's chronicle, *Public Scandal, Odium and Contempt* (Secker & Warburg, 1984). Hooper concludes that the time has come to reform the law of libel which 'can be very uncertain in operation, extremely expensive in practice and unduly technical in application'.

Sadly, but predictably, politicians do not put changes in the libel law high on their list of priorities.

Tax and the Writer

"No man in this country is under the smallest obligation, moral or other, to arrange his affairs as to enable the Inland Revenue to put the largest possible shovel in his stores.

The Inland Revenue is not slow, and quite rightly, to take every advantage which is open to it . . . for the purpose of depleting the taxpayer's pockets. And the taxpayer is, in like manner, entitled to be astute to prevent as far as he honestly can the depletion of his means by the Inland Revenue."

Lord Clyde. *Ayrshire Pullman v. Inland Revenue Commissioners*, 1929.

Value Added Tax

Value Added Tax (VAT) is a tax levied at a rate fixed from time to time by the Government on:

(a) the total value of taxable goods and services supplied to consumers.
(b) the importation of goods into the UK.
(c) certain services from abroad if a taxable person receives them in the UK for the purposes of their business.

Who is taxable?

A writer resident in the UK whose turnover from writing and any other business, craft or art on a self-employed basis is greater than £21,300 annually, or exceeds

£7250 in one quarter, must register with HM Customs as a taxable person. A writer whose turnover is below the quarterly and annual limits may apply for voluntary registration and this will be allowed at the discretion of Customs. A writer whose turnover is below these limits is exempt from the requirement to register for VAT, but may apply for voluntary registration.

A taxable person pays VAT on inputs, charges VAT on outputs, and remits the amount by which the latter exceeds the former. In the event that inputs exceed outputs, the difference should be repaid by HM Customs and Excise.

Inputs

A writer's inputs are goods and services that are supplied and used in the course of working. They are taxable at the standard rate or at the zero-rate or they are exempt. A writer pays VAT on those items or services which are taxable at the full rate but not on those which are zero-rated or exempt. The writer who is registered as a taxable person will be able to offset the VAT thus paid against the VAT that should be remitted to Customs.

Taxable at the standard rate	*Taxable at the zero-rate*	*Exempt*
Advertisements in newspapers, magazines, journals and periodicals	Books	Rent
	Newspapers	Rates
Agent's commission (unless it relates to monies from overseas, when it is zero-rated)	Periodicals	Postage
	Lighting	Services supplied by unregistered persons
	Heating	
Accountant's fees	Coach, rail and air travel	Subscriptions to the Society of Authors, PEN, NUJ, etc.
Solicitor's fees		
Agency services (typing, copying, etc.)		Wages and Salaries
Stationery and typewriters		Insurance
Artists' materials		Dividend Income
Photographic equipment		Taxicab Fares
Tape recorders and tapes		
Hotel accommodation		
Motor-car expenses		
Telephone		
Theatres and concerts		

NB This list is not exhaustive. The Treasury has the regulatory power to zero-rate, to exempt or to tax at the standard rate all or any of the categories. If in doubt consult your local Customs VAT Office.

Outputs

A writer's outputs are taxable supplies and services which are supplied to publishers, broadcasting organisations, theatre managements, film companies, educational institutions, etc. Such services are supplied in the form of licences to publish, produce, perform or broadcast the works, and in the form of labour for revision, rehearsal, proofreading, lecturing, appearances, etc. A taxable writer must invoice, i.e. collect from, all the persons, either individuals or organisations, in the UK for whom supplies have been made, for fees, royalties or other considerations plus VAT. He/she should be paid the total sums, i.e. fees, etc. and the VAT at the standard rate. An unregistered writer cannot and must not invoice for VAT. A taxable writer is not obliged to collect VAT or royalties or other fees paid by publishers overseas or others overseas for supplies.

Remit to Customs

The unregistered writer charges no VAT and therefore should have had none passed on to him/her from publishers, etc. The taxable writer adds up the VAT which has been paid on taxable inputs, deducts it from the VAT paid on outputs and remits the balance to Customs. If more VAT has been paid out on inputs than has been received on outputs he/she is entitled to claim a repayment of the difference from Customs at the end of the month in which the deficit occurred. Business with HM Customs is conducted through the local VAT Offices of HM Customs which are listed in local telephone directories, except for tax returns which are sent direct to the Customs and Excise VAT Central Unit, Alexander House, 21 Victoria Avenue, Southend-on-Sea, Essex SS99 1AA.

Accounting

A taxable writer is obliged to account to Customs at quarterly intervals on 31st August, 30th November, 28th February and 31st May. Accounts must be completed and sent to the VAT Central Unit within 28 days of the accounting date. It should be noted that only invoices are necessary to complete a VAT return, not receipts. A writer is held responsible for ensuring that the VAT that has been invoiced is, in fact, paid.

Registration

A writer will be given a VAT Registration Number which must be quoted on all VAT correspondence. It is the responsibility of the writer to inform those to whom he/she makes supplies, of their taxable status and Registration Number. A writer who would not normally be required to register as taxable may, on receipt of a single large payment, for example in respect of film rights or a paperback edition, find that the quarterly or annual turnover has risen above the limits and is liable to register. If the local Collector is satisfied that he/she will not turn over more than £21,300 in the next 12 months they may be permitted to continue unregistered. If not they must register and remain so until two complete years have passed during which the value of outputs has been below £21,300 annually. They may then de-register.

Voluntary Registration

A writer whose turnover is below the limits may apply to register. If the writer is paying a relatively large amount of VAT on taxable inputs – agent's commissions, accountant's fees, equipment, materials, or agency services, etc. – it may make a significant improvement in the net income to be able to offset the VAT on these inputs. An author who pays relatively little VAT may find it easier, and no more expensive, to remain unregistered.

Fees and Royalties

A taxable writer must notify those to whom he/she makes supplies of the Tax Registration Number at the first opportunity. One method of accounting for and paying VAT on fees and royalties is the use of multiple stationery for 'self-billing', one copy of the royalty statement being used by the author as the VAT invoice. A second method is for the recipient of taxable outputs to pay fees, including authors' royalties, without VAT. The taxable author then renders a tax invoice for the VAT element and a second payment, of the VAT element, will be made. This scheme is cumbersome but will involve only taxable authors. Fees and royalties from abroad will count as payments for exported services and will accordingly be zero-rated.

Agents and Accountants

A writer is responsible to HM Customs for making VAT returns and payments. Neither an agent nor an accountant nor a solicitor can take this over, although they can be helpful in preparing and keeping VAT returns and accounts. Their professional fees or commission will, except in rare cases where the adviser or agent is himself/herself unregistered, be taxable at the standard rate and will represent some of a writer's taxable inputs. An agent's commission in respect of zero-rated fees and royalties received from abroad is not liable for VAT.

Income Tax – Schedule D

An unregistered writer can claim some of the VAT paid on taxable inputs as a business expense allowable against income tax. However, certain taxable inputs fall into categories which cannot be claimed under the income tax regulations. A taxable writer, who has already offset VAT on inputs, cannot charge it as a business expense for the purposes of income tax.

Certain Services From Abroad

A taxable author who resides in the United Kingdom and who receives certain services from abroad must account for VAT on those services at the appropriate tax rate on the sum paid for them. Examples of the type of services concerned include: services of lawyers, accountants, consultants, provisions of information and copyright permissions.

Income Tax
What is a professional writer for tax purposes?
Writers are professionals while they are writing regularly with the intention of making a profit; or while they are gathering material, researching or otherwise preparing a publication.

A professional freelance writer is taxed under Case II of Schedule D of the *Income and Corporation Taxes Act 1970*. The taxable income is the amount received, either directly, or by an agent, on his/her behalf, less expenses wholly and exclusively laid out for the purposes of the profession. If expenses exceed income, the loss can either be carried forward and set against future income from writing or set against other income which is subject to tax in the same year. If tax has been paid on that other income, a repayment can be obtained, or the sum can be offset against other tax liabilities. Special loss relief can apply in the opening year of the profession. Losses made in the first four years can be set against income of up to three earlier years.

Where a writer receives very occasional payments for isolated articles, it may not be possible to argue successfully that these are profits arising from carrying on a continuing profession. In such circumstances these 'isolated transactions' may be assessed under Case VI of Schedule D of the *Income and Corporation Taxes Act 1970*. Again, expenses may be deducted in arriving at the taxable income, but, if expenses exceed income, the loss can only be set against the profits from future isolated transactions, or other income assessable under Case VI.

Expenses
A writer can normally claim the following expenses:

(a) Secretarial, typing, proofreading, research. Where payments for these are made to the author's wife or husband, they should be recorded and entered in the author's tax return, or (in the case of a married woman her husband's tax return) as earned income which is subject to the usual personal allowances.

(b) Telephone, telegrams, postage, stationery, printing, maintenance and insurance of typewriter, dictation tapes, batteries, office requisites and other equipment used for the profession. (See also (m).)

(c) Periodicals, books (including presentation copies and reference books) and other publications necessary for the profession, but amounts received from the sale of books should be deducted.

(d) Hotels, fares, car running expenses (including repairs, petrol, oil, garaging, parking, cleaning, insurance, licence, road fund tax, depreciation), hire of cars or taxis, in connection with
  (i) business discussions with agents, publishers, co-authors, collaborators, researchers, illustrators, etc.
  (ii) travel at home and abroad to collect background material.

(e) Entertaining foreign customers or prospective customers, e.g. publishers from overseas.

(f) Publishing and advertising expenses, including charges for proof corrections, indexing, photographs, etc.

(g) Subscriptions to societies and associations, press cutting agencies, etc. incurred wholly for the purpose of the profession.

(h) Premiums to pension schemes such as the *Society of Authors Retirement Benefits Scheme*. For contributors born in 1934 and later, the maximum premium is now $17\frac{1}{2}\%$ of net earned income. Higher limits apply for those born before 1934.

(j) Rent, rates, lighting, heating, water, cleaning, etc., the proportion being determined by the ratio which the number of rooms used exclusively for the profession bears to the total number of rooms in the residence. But see note on *Capital Gains Tax* below.

(k) Accountancy charges and legal charges incurred wholly in the course of the profession including cost of defending libel actions, damages in so far as they are not covered by insurance and libel insurance premiums. However, where, in a libel case, damages are awarded to punish the author for having acted maliciously the action becomes quasicriminal and costs and damages may not be allowed.

(l) TV and video rental (which may be apportioned for private use), and cinema or theatre tickets, if wholly for the purpose of the profession, e.g. playwriting.

(m) Capital allowances for equipment, e.g. car, TV, radio, Hi-Fi sets, tape and video recorders, dictaphones, typewriters, desks, bookshelves, filing cabinets, photographic equipment. Allowances vary in the Finance Acts depending upon political and economic views prevailing. At present they are set at 25%. On motor cars the allowance is 25% in the first year and 25% of the reduced balance in each successive year limited to £2000 each year. The total allowances in the case of all assets must not exceed the difference between cost and eventual sale price. Allowances will be reduced to exclude personal (non-professional) use where necessary.

NB It is always advisable to keep detailed records. Diary entries of appointments, notes of fares and receipted bills are much more convincing to the Inland Revenue than round figure estimates.

(n) Gifts to charitable bodies are allowed, subject to certain conditions, provided they are reasonable in amount and for a cause connected with the donor's professional activities. Tax relief is also available for three years (minimum) covenants to charities.

Capital Gains Tax

The exemption from Capital Gains Tax which applies to an individual's main residence does not apply to any part of that residence which is used exclusively for business purposes. The effect of this is that the appropriate proportion of any increase in value of the residence since 6th April 1965 can be taxed, when the residence is sold, at the maximum rate of 30 per cent (at present).

Writers who own their houses should bear this in mind before claiming expenses for the use of a room for writing purposes. Arguments in favour of making such claims are that they afford some relief now, while Capital Gains Tax in its present form may not stay for ever. Also, where a new house is bought in place of the old one, the gain made on the sale of the first study may be set off against the cost of the study in the new house, thus postponing the tax payment until the final sale. For this relief to apply, each house must have a study, and the author must continue his/her profession throughout. On death there is an exemption of the total Capital Gains of the estate.

NB Writers can claim that their use is non-exclusive and restrict their claim to the cost of extra lighting, heating and cleaning so that no Capital Gains Tax liability arises.

Can a writer average-out his income over a number of years for tax purposes?

Under Section 389 of the *Income and Corporation Taxes Act 1970*, a writer may in certain circumstances spread over two or three fiscal years lump sum payments, whenever received, and royalties received during two years from the date of first publication or performance of work. Points to note are:

(a) The relief can only be claimed if the writer has been engaged in preparing and collecting material and writing the work for more than twelve months.

(b) If the period of preparing and writing the work exceeds twelve months but does not exceed twenty-four months, one-half of the advances and/or royalties will be regarded as income from the year preceding that of receipt. If the period of preparing and writing exceeds twenty-four months, one-third of the amount received would be regarded as income from each of the two years preceding that of receipt.

(c) For a writer on a very large income, who otherwise fulfils the conditions required, a claim under these sections should result in a big tax saving. If his/her income is not large he/she should consider the implication, in the various fiscal years concerned, of possible loss of benefit from personal and other allowances and changes in the standard rate of income tax.

It is also possible to average out income within the terms of publishers' contracts, but professional advice should be taken before signature. Where a husband and wife collaborate as writers, advice should be taken as to whether a formal partnership agreement should be made or whether the publishing agreement should be in joint names.

Is a lump sum paid for an outright sale of the copyright or part of the copyright exempt from tax?

No. If a writer is resident in this country, all the money received from the marketing of his/her literary work, by whatever means, is taxable. Some writers, in spite of clear judicial decisions to the contrary, still seem to think that an outright sale of, for instance, the film rights in a book, is not subject to tax.

Is there any relief where old copyrights are sold?

Section 390 of the *Income and Corporation Taxes Act 1970* gives relief "where not less than ten years after the first publication of the work the author of a literary, dramatic, musical or artistic work assigns the copyright therein wholly or partially, or grants any interest in the copyright by licence, and:

(a) the consideration for the assignment or grant consists wholly or partially of a lump sum payment the whole amount of which would, but for this section, be included in computing the amount of his/her profits or gains for a single year of assessment, and

(b) the copyright or interest is not assigned or granted for a period of less than two years."

In such cases, the amount received may be spread forward in equal yearly instalments for a maximum of six years, or, where the copyright or interest is assigned or granted for a period of less than six years, for the number of whole years in that period. A "lump sum payment" is defined to include a non-returnable advance on account of royalties.

It should be noted that a claim may not be made under this section in respect of a payment if a prior claim has been made under Section 389 of the *Income and Corporation Taxes Act 1970* (see section on spreading lump sum payments over two or three years) or vice versa.

Are royalties payable on publication of a book abroad subject to both foreign tax as well as UK tax?

Where there is a Double Taxation Agreement between the country concerned and the UK, then on the completion of certain formalities no tax is deductible at source by the foreign payer, but such income is taxable in the UK in the ordinary way. When there is no Double Taxation agreement, credit will be given against UK tax for overseas tax paid. A complete list of countries with which the UK has conventions for the avoidance of double taxation may be obtained from The Inspector of Foreign Dividends, Lynwood Road, Thames Ditton, Surrey KT7 0DP or the local tax office.

Residence Abroad

Writers residing abroad will, of course, be subject to the tax laws ruling in their country of residence, and as a general rule royalty income paid from the United Kingdom can be exempted from deduction of UK tax at source, providing the author is carrying on his profession abroad. A writer who is intending to go and live abroad should make early application for future royalties to be paid without deduction of tax to HM Inspector of Taxes, Claims Branch, Magdalen House, Stanley Precinct, Bootle, Merseyside L69 9BB. In certain circumstances writers resident in the Irish Republic are exempt from Irish Income Tax on their authorship earnings.

Are grants or prizes taxable?

The law is uncertain. Some Arts Council grants are now deemed to be taxable, whereas most prizes and awards are not, though it depends on the conditions in each case. When submitting a statement of income and expenses, such items should be excluded, but reference made to them in a covering letter to the Inspector of Taxes.

What if I disagree with a tax assessment?

Income tax law requires the Inspector of Taxes to make an assessment each year calculating the amount of income tax payable on the "profits" of the profession.

Even though accounts may have already been submitted the assessment can quite possibly be estimated and overstated.

The taxpayer has the right of appeal within 30 days of receipt of the assessment and can request that the tax payable should be reduced to the correct liability which he must estimate as accurately as possible. However, if he/she underestimates the amount, interest can become payable on the amount by which he/she underpays when the correct liability is known.

What is the item "Class 4 N.I.C." which appears in my tax assessment?

All taxpayers who are self-employed pay an additional national insurance contribution if their earned income exceeds a figure which is varied each year. This contribution is described as Class 4 and is calculated in the tax assessment. It is additional to the self-employed Class 2 (stamp) contribution but confers no additional benefits and is a form of levy. It applies to men aged under 65 and women under 60. Tax relief is given on half the Class 4 contributions.

Anyone wondering how best to order his/her affairs for tax purposes, should consult an accountant with specialised knowledge in this field. Experience shows that a good accountant is well worth his fee which, incidentally, so far as it relates to matters other than personal tax work, is an allowable expense.

The information contained in this section is adapted from The Society of Authors *Quick Guides to Taxation* (Nos. 4 and 7) with the kind help of A. P. Kernon.

Through the Technology Barrier on a Word Processor

There are signs that the writer's turbulent love–hate relationship with the word processor is entering a more realistic phase. Against the sound of tinkling glass (another machine hurled through the window by a frustrated operator) there is a growing murmur of appreciation from those who have learned to master the beast. Meanwhile, the silent majority are slowly getting used to the idea of technology in the study but still wonder if the word processor is really for them.

An encouraging factor is the recent fall in prices brought about by the launch of the Amstrad PCW 8256 and 8512. Where once the investment in a word processor was £1000 plus, today a perfectly adequate machine can be had for a few hundred pounds. Even so, in assessing the value of a word processor it is as well to begin with the economics of writing technology. An occasional writer who deals in ordinary sentences which are not interposed by complex diagrams may find that his/her needs are fully ratified by the familiar typewriter or even by pen and paper. But if writing is a full time career, a business, then time is well spent looking at what the word processor has to offer.

To be worthy of the name, a word processor must have the following bits and pieces:

(a) a micro-computer
(b) a keyboard similar to that of a typewriter
(c) a visual display unit (VDU) which looks like a small television set
(d) a printer – either daisy-wheel or dot-matrix. A daisy-wheel is a metal or plastic disc shaped like a daisy with a letter embossed at the end of each petal. They come in different typestyles but are interchangeable on the same printer. Dot-matrix printers use tiny needles to create letter shapes so it is not necessary to change the printing head to create, say, italics or foreign language symbols. Dot-matrix printers are essential for graphics.
(e) a disk drive so that work can be stored

These items comprise the basic 'hardware'. But the operator also needs 'software' – a program to enable the computer to carry out instructions. This may be carried on a built-in chip or loaded from disk or cassette. A system with these components is capable of carrying out tasks beside word processing – keeping a record of accounts, for example. But holding to the main purpose of our word processor, to make the task of writing less arduous, what can it achieve?

The operator uses the keyboard as a typewriter. The words that are typed are displayed on the screen but are not printed until the command is given by pressing the appropriate key. This means he/she can easily correct mistypes, add or delete words, reverse the order of paragraphs, rereverse the order of paragraphs, in fact, make just about any change without a single recourse to Tippex.

At any time, the computer can be instructed to print a copy of what is on the screen or store the text on disk ready to be summoned whenever it is needed. Fresh copies of what has been written are available, without limit, at the press of a button.

So far, we have discovered at least two virtues of the word processor. For anyone who can use a typewriter it is the most efficient way of getting words on to paper. But it also offers valuable storage space. Work in progress but not needed immediately can be kept on disk. The word processor offers the chance to do away with those bulky files. Yes, it is possible to lose what you have written by mishandling the machine in some way. But an error of this sort is less likely than losing part of a manuscript down the back of a cabinet or inadvertently throwing it out with the waste paper.

It then follows, does it not, that he/she who operates a word processor can save money by doing without secretarial help? Well, not necessarily. A good secretary is more than a typist. It is quite possible to end up investing in a word processor *and* a secretary while finding that neither have enough to do.

As with money, so with time. It is unwise to make hasty conclusions on savings. There are many writers who claim that the word processor enables them to pack much more into the day. Equally, the critics point out the tendency to use the machine when less cumbersome if more conventional practices, like jotting down notes or scribbling a short letter would serve just as well and take far less effort. The message seems to be, beware of an obsession with gadgetry.

Some writers report how much easier it is to start the day with a machine instead of staring at the blank sheet in the typewriter. But they are not too sure about the effect on their style. The word processor has been known to bring on serious attacks of verbosity. Alternatively, it can foster excessive caution, the feeling that what is on the screen must be word perfect before it slips away into the memory bank. This may lead to an unattractive economy of words which judged by the reader can border on incomprehension.

What is needed is better training so that owners have a clearer understanding of the potential of their word processors. The more reputable dealers offer instruction as part of the package but it would be useful to check out the standard of training before deciding on a purchase. A straight blow-by-blow runthrough of the technical manual is not particularly helpful. There are several other important questions to ask before you decide to part with your money.

- Are the available programs suitable for your purposes? This is a good way to start because programs that run on one system may not run on another. So, for example, if you are a technical or educational writer whose work includes charts and diagrams, make sure your prospective word processor offers this program facility.

Satisfied on this point go on to ask:

- Does the word processor system have sufficient memory? Most programs are designed for business people who write letters and reports, not books with chapters of four thousand words or more. When the system cannot file more than a limited amount of text at once there is the risk of accidentally losing freshly created work.
- Does the VDU show you all that you need to see? Some systems can only show lines of forty characters.
- Does the print-out come with double spacing? Not all do, as many professional writers have discovered to their horror.
- Is there a word count facility?
- Does the system offer automatic pagination?
- Does it search and replace, say, a change of name throughout a manuscript?
- Is there an adequate after sales service?

If there is a satisfactory answer to all these questions and you decide to gamble on technology bear in mind that this is only the beginning of the adventure. The cybernetic experts are already working on a machine which will warn the operator when he/she is making a grammatical or spelling mistake. Soon after that we can expect a word processor which responds to dictation and, no doubt, makes the coffee at the same time. Maybe the days of the secretary are numbered after all.

Literary Prizes and Awards

General

Angel Literary Prize

The Angel Hotel, Angel Hill, Bury St Edmunds, Suffolk ☎0284 3926

Contact *Caroline Gough*

This Award is intended to stimulate interest in, and support for, writers in East Anglia. Two prizes are given, one for a work of fiction, one for a work of non-fiction. Books must have been published between October and September and written by authors living and working in East Anglia.
Prize £1000 and £500

Astra Prize for Medical Writing

(see *Academic* p. 463)

James Tait Black Memorial Prizes

University of Edinburgh, Department of English Literature, David Hume Tower, George Square, Edinburgh EH8 9JX ☎031–667 1011 (Ext. 6259)

These prizes, one for biography and one for fiction, were instituted in 1918 in memory of a partner in the publishing firm of A & C Black Ltd, and since 1979 they have been supported by the Scottish Arts Council. Each prize is awarded for a book published in Britain in the previous twelve months.
Prize £1000 (each)

Previous winners include: Biography, D. Felicitas Corrigan (*Helen Waddell*) Victoria Glendinning (*Edith Sitwell*); Fiction, Angela Carter *Nights at the Circus*; Paul Theroux *The Mosquito Coast*.

Boardman Tasker Memorial Award

56 St Michael's Avenue, Bramhall, Stockport, Cheshire SK7 2PL ☎061–439 4624

Founded in 1983, this award is given for a work of fiction, non-fiction or poetry whose central theme is concerned with the mountain environment and which can therefore be said to make an outstanding contribution to mountain literature. Authors of any nationality are eligible, but the book must have been published or distributed in the UK for the first time between 1 November and 31 October of the year of the prize.
Prize £1000 (May vary at Trustees' discretion)

Bridport Arts Centre Creative Writing Competition
Arts Centre, South Street, Bridport, Dorset ☎ 0308 27183

A competition for poetry and short story writing, plus sometimes a category for plays. Unpublished work only, written in English.
Prizes £1000 each; £500 & £250 for runners up.

Katharine Briggs Folklore Award
Derek Froome, Hon. Publicity Officer, The Folklore Society, 3 Broom Rd, Hale, Altrincham, Cheshire ☎ 061–928 1165

An annual award for a book receiving its first British publication in the previous calendar year which has made the most distinguished non-fiction contribution to folklore studies. The term folklore studies is interpreted broadly to include all aspects of traditional and popular culture, narrative, belief and folklore arts.
Prize £50 plus engraved goblet.

British Film Institute Book Award
Wayne Drew, British Film Institute, 127 Charing Cross Road, London WC2H 0EA
☎ 01–437 4355

For a book on film or television which is both innovative and accessible with a lively approach to the media.
Award £1000 Annual
Previous winners include: Michel Ciment *John Boorman*; Richard Schikel *D.W. Griffith & the Birth of Film*

Cheltenham Prize
Cheltenham Festival of Literature, c/o Town Hall, Cheltenham, Glos. GL50 1QA
☎ 0242 521621

As part of the Cheltenham Festival, an author is chosen by a leading literary reviewer from his year's reading.
Prize £250

The Duff Cooper Memorial Prize
The Viscount Norwich, 24 Blomfield Road, London W9 1AD ☎ 01–286 5050

An annual award for a literary work in the field of biography, history, politics or poetry, published in English or French during the previous 24 months. Financed by the interest from a Trust Fund commemorating Duff Cooper, first Viscount Norwich (1890–1954), the prize has two permanent judges, the present Lord Norwich, and the Warden of New College, Oxford, and three others who change every five years.
Prize £250 approx.

Rose Mary Crawshay Prize

The British Academy, 20–21 Cornwall Terrace, London NW1 4QP ☎01–487 5966

Founded by Rose Mary Crawshay in 1888, this prize is given for a historical or critical work by a woman of any nationality on English literature, with particular preference for a work on Keats, Byron or Shelley. The work must have been published in the preceding three years.
Prize £600 (or 2 prizes of £300 each)

Isaac Deutscher Memorial Prize

c/o Lloyds Bank, 68 Warwick Square, London SW1V 2AS

An annual award in recognition and as encouragement to outstanding research in the Marxist tradition of Isaac Deutscher to the author of an essay or full scale work published or in manuscript. Entries should be submitted by 1 May each year.
Award £100

Christopher Ewart-Biggs Memorial Prize

31 Radnor Walk, London SW3

An annual award to a writer of any nationality whose work contributes most to peace and understanding in Ireland or to co-operation between members of the European community. Works must have been published in the year of presentation and written in either English or French.
Prize £2000

Geoffrey Faber Memorial Prize

Faber & Faber Ltd, 3 Queen Square, London WC1N 3AU   ☎01–278 6881

Established in 1963 as a memorial to the founder and first chairman of Faber & Faber, this prize is awarded in alternate years for the volume of verse and the volume of prose fiction judged to be of greatest literary merit published in the UK in the preceding two years. Authors must be under 40 at the time of publication and citizens of the UK, Commonwealth, Republic of Ireland or South Africa.
Prize £500

Fawcett Society Book Prize

Rita Pankhurst, 46 Harleyford Road, London SE11 5AY   ☎01–587 1287

An annual award to the author of a book (alternately fiction and non-fiction) which has made a substantial contribution to the understanding of women's position in society today. All works submitted for the Prize are placed in the Fawcett Library at City of London Polytechnic.
Prize £500

Sir Banister Fletcher Award

Mrs Ridgway, Secretary, The Authors Club, 40 Dover Street, London W1X 3RB
☎01–499 8581

This award is financed partly by the income from a trust left by the late Sir Banister Fletcher, who was President of the Author's club for many years, and partly by the Arts Council of Great Britain. It is presented for the best book on architecture or the fine arts published in the preceding year.
Award £200

Glenfiddich Awards

11a West Halkin Street, London SW1X 8JL

A series of awards to writers who have contributed most to the civilised appreciation of food and drink through articles or books published in the UK. Also covers radio and TV programmes.
Award £750 plus Glenfiddich Trophy.
Also category awards of £100 plus gold medal; £100 and Glenfiddich Malt Scotch Whisky.

Martin Luther King Memorial Prize

John Brunner, National Westminster Bank Ltd, 7 Fore Street, Chard, Somerset TA20 1PJ

An annual award for a literary work (including poetry, plays and TV or film scripts) reflecting the ideals to which Dr King dedicated his life, published or performed in the UK during previous calendar year. No enquiries answered without s.a.e.
Prize £100

Kraszna-Kransz Award: Best Book on Photography

John Chittock, OBE, Kraszna-Kransz Foundation, 37 Gower Street, London WC1E 6HH
☎01–580 2842

For the book making the most original and lasting contribution to the art and practice of camera media. Details subject to annual announcement.
Prize £5000

Lakeland Book of the Year

Cumbria Tourist Board, Ashleigh, Holly Road, Windermere LA23 2AQ
☎096–62 4444

An annual award for the best book or booklet on any aspect of Cumbria and the English Lake District published in the year ending mid-May.
Award £100

Sir William Lyons Award

Jean Peters, The Guild of Motoring Writers, 2 Pembroke Villas, The Green, Richmond, Surrey TW9 1QF   ☎01–940 6974

An annual award to encourage young people in automotive journalism (including broadcasting) and foster interest in the motor industry. Entrance is by two essays and interview with Awards Committee. Applicants must be British and resident in UK, aged 17–23.

Macmillan Silver Pen Award

The English Centre of International PEN, 7 Dilke Street, London SW3 4JE

☎01–352 6303

An annual award, from nomination by PEN Executive Committee, for an outstanding novel written in English by a British author and published in the UK in the year preceding the prize.
Prize £500 plus Silver Pen.

Enid McLeod Literary Prize

Franco-British Society, Room 636, Linen Hall, 162–168 Regent Street, London W1R 5TB

An annual award for a full length work of literature which contributes most to Franco–British understanding. It must be written in English by a citizen of the UK, Commonwealth, the Republic of Ireland, Pakistan or South Africa and first published in the UK.
Prize £100

Arthur Markham Memorial Prize

Registrar and Secretary, University of Sheffield, Western Bank, Sheffield S10 2TN

☎0742 78555

There are six categories for work specially written for this annual prize: short story, essay, poem, group of poems, prose account, first chapter of a novel on a given subject announced annually. Candidates must be manual workers at a coal mine or have been injured when so employed.
Prize £200

Somerset Maugham Trust Fund

The Society of Authors, 84 Drayton Gardens, London SW10 9SB   ☎01–373 6642

The annual awards arising from this Fund are designed to encourage young writers to travel and to acquaint themselves with the manners and customs of other countries. Candidates must be under 35 and submit a published literary work in volume form in English. They must be British subjects by birth only.
Award £1000 – £2000 (each)

MIND Book of the Year – The Allen Lane Award

MIND, 22 Harley Street, London W1N 2ED   01–637 0741

This annual award, inaugurated in 1981 in memory of Sir Allen Lane, is given to the author of the book, fiction or non-fiction, which furthers public understanding of mental illness, published in the current year.
Award £1000

Mitchell Prize for the History of Art

(see *History* p.470)

Northern Arts Literary Fellowship

Northern Arts, 10 Osborne Terrace, Jesmond, Newcastle upon Tyne NE2 1NZ
                091–281 6334

Tenable at, and co-sponsored by the Universities of Durham and Newcastle upon Tyne for a period of two academic years.
Award £9000 p.a.

Northern Arts Writers Awards

Northern Arts, 10 Osborne Terrace, Jesmond, Newcastle upon Tyne NE2 1NZ
                091–281 6334

Awards are offered to established authors resident in the Northern Arts area on basis of literary merit and financial need. Application: spring/summer.
Award Variable.

Odd Fellows (Manchester Unity) Social Concern Book Award

Book Trust, Book House, 45 East Hill, London SW18 2QZ   01–870 9055

An annual award for the book or pamphlet of not less than 10,000 words within a specified area of social concern (varies each year). Entries must have been published in the current year in English and been written by citizens of the Commonwealth, Republic of Ireland, Pakistan or South Africa.
Award £1000

Catherine Pakenham Award

Managing Editor, London Evening Standard, 118 Fleet Street, London EC4P 4JT
                01–353 8000

An annual award found in 1970 in memory of Lady Catherine Pakenham, and given for a published or unpublished article (of up to 2500 words) or radio or TV script (but not short story) by women aged between 18 and 30 involved in or intending to take up a career in journalism.
Award £500
Previous winners include: Jaci Stephen (Standard); Sharon Maxwell (Cosmo-politan).

John Llewellyn Rhys Memorial Prize

Book Trust, Book House, 45 East Hill, London SW18 2QZ   ☎01–870 9055

An annual award for a memorable work of any kind by a writer who is under the age of 35 at the time of publication. Books must have been published in the UK in the year of the award, and the author must be a citizen of Britain or the Commonwealth writing in English.

Prize £500

Previous winners include: Elizabeth Jane Howard, V. S. Naipaul, Shiva Naipaul, Margaret Drabble.

The Royal Society of Literature Award under W. H. Heinemann Bequest

Royal Society of Literature, 1 Hyde Park Gardens, London W2 2LT

☎01–723 5104

Works of any kind of literature may be submitted by their publishers for consideration under this award, but only living authors are considered. Genuine contributions to literature originally written in English are sought, but preference will be given to publications which are unlikely to command large sales: poetry, biography, criticism, etc.

Award Amount varies.

Runciman Award

Book Trust, Book House, 45 East Hill, London SW18 2QZ   ☎01–870 9055

An annual award, instituted in 1985 by the Anglo-Hellenic League and sponsored by the Onassis Foundation, for a literary work wholly or mainly about Greece. The book may be fiction, poetry, drama or non-fiction and to be eligible must be published in its first English edition in the UK.

Award £1000

George Russell A. E. Memorial Fund Award

Bank of Ireland, Trustee Department, Head Office, Lower Baggott Street, Dublin 1, Ireland   ☎0001–785744 Ext. 2117

This award is made for a work of a literary character to a person of Irish birth normally resident in Ireland and under 35 years of age on 1 January of the year of the award.

Award £100 (Annual).

Ryman New Writers' Awards

PO Box 38, Chelsea, London SW3 3NL   ☎01–584 9594

Run by the Stationery Company.

Awards for previously unpublished writers in five categories: novel, short story, children's story, poetry and song lyric. Writers must be citizens of Great Britain and N. Ireland or Republic of Ireland. An entry fee is required.

Award £500 per category plus publisher's contract and minimum advance of £1000 (Annual).

The Saltire Society and Royal Bank Scottish Literary Award

The Royal Bank of Scotland plc, PO Box 31, 42 St Andrew Square, Edinburgh EH2 2YE   ☎031–556 8555

An annual award for a book on or about Scotland, or for a book with Scottish connections, not necessarily written by a Scot.
Award £1500

Scottish Arts Council Book Awards

Literature Department, Scottish Arts Council, 19 Charlotte Square, Edinburgh EH2 4DF   ☎031–226 6051

A number of awards are given to authors of published books in recognition of high standards in new writing as well as work of established writers. Authors should be Scottish, resident in Scotland or writing books of Scottish interest.
Award £750 (Bi-annual)

SCSE Book Prizes

L. Boucher, Chester College of Higher Education, Cheyney Road, Chester CH1 4BJ

Annual awards given by the Standing Conference on Studies in Education for the best book on education published during the preceding year – by nomination from members of the Standing Conference and publishers.
Prizes £500 and £300

André Simon Memorial Fund Book Awards

Tessa Hayward, 61 Church Street, Isleworth, Middx TW7 6BE   ☎01–560 6662

Two awards are given annually for the best book on drink and the best on food.
Award £1000

W. H. Smith Literary Award

Public Relations, W. H. Smith, 7 Holbein Place, London SW1W 8NR
                                         ☎01 730 1200 Ext. 5458

Annual prize awarded to a Commonwealth author (including UK citizens) published in English in UK in the preceding year, for the most outstanding contribution to English literature.
Prize £4000
Previous winners include: Doris Lessing, David Hughes, Philip Larkin.

W. H. Smith Young Writers' Competition

Public Relations, W. H. Smith, 7 Holbein Place, London SW1W 8NR

☎01–730 1200

Annual awards for poems or prose by anyone in the UK under the age of 17. There are three age groups. Sixty-three individual prize-winners have their work included in a paperback every year.

Prize £4000 (Total of range of prizes)

Southern Arts Literature Prize

Southern Arts, 19 Southgate Street, Winchester, Hampshire SO23 9DQ

☎0962 55099

This prize is awarded annually to an author living in the Southern Arts Region who has made the most notable contribution to literature during the year in published fiction, poetry or collection of short stories, or non-fiction. The 1986 prize was awarded for a novel.

Prize £1000

Marten Toonder Award

Literature Officer, The Arts Council (An Chomhairle Ealaion), 70 Merrion Square, Dublin 2, Ireland ☎0001–611840

A triennial award for creative writers.

Award £3000 (next: 1989)

TSB Peninsular Prize

Literature Officer, South West Arts, Bradninch Place, Gandy Street, Exeter EX4 3LS

☎0392 218188

An annual award for unpublished works of literature submitted by anyone who is resident in or who can demonstrate strong links with the region served by South West Arts (Avon, Cornwall, Devon, Dorset – except Bournemouth, Christchurch and Poole – Gloucestershire and Somerset).

Prize £1000 plus publication and £1000 advance on royalties.

Wandsworth All London Competition

Assistant Director of Leisure and Amenity Services (Libraries & Arts), Town Hall, Wandsworth High Street, London SW18 2PU ☎01–871 6364

An annual competition, open to all writers of sixteen and over who live, work or study in the Greater London Area. There are two categories, both for previously unpublished work, in poetry and the short story.

Prize £525 (Total for each class – to be divided between the top three in each category.)

Welsh Arts Council Prizes

Tony Bianchi, Welsh Arts Council, Museum Place, Cardiff CF1 3NX

☎ 0222 394711

Annual, non-competitive prizes are presented for works of exceptional merit by Welsh authors (by birth or residence) published in Welsh or English during the previous calendar year. There are five prizes for each language in the categories: poetry, fiction, non-fiction, literary criticism and young writer.

Prize £1000 (each)

Whitbread Book of the Year/Whitbread Literary Awards

Andrea Livingstone, The Booksellers Association of Great Britain & Ireland, 154 Buckingham Palace Road, London SW1W 9TZ   ☎ 01-730 8214

Publishers are invited to submit books for this annual competition for writers who have been resident in Great Britain or the Republic of Ireland for five or more years. The awards are made in two stages. In the first, nominations are selected in five categories: novel, first novel, biography, children's novel and poetry. One of these is then voted by the panel of judges as Whitbread Book of the Year.

Awards £18,500 (Book of the Year); £1000 (Remaining nominees).

Previous winners include: *Elegies*, Douglas Dunn (Poetry & Book of the Year); *Hugh Dalton*, Ben Pimlott (Biography); *The Nature of the Beast*, Janni Howker (Children's); *Oranges are not the Only Fruit*, Jeanette Winterson (First novel); *Hawksmoor*, Peter Ackroyd (Novel).

H. H. Wingate Prize

Book Trust, Book House, 45 East Hill, London SW18 2QZ   ☎ 01-870 9055

An annual award of two prizes (one for fiction, one for non-fiction) for the books which best stimulate an interest in and awareness of themes of Jewish interest. Books must have been published in UK in the year of the award and be written in English by an author resident in Britain, Commonwealth, Israel, Pakistan, Republic of Ireland or South Africa.

Prize £2000 (each)

Yorkshire Post Book of the Year Awards

Caroline Colmer, Yorkshire Post, PO Box 168, Wellington Street, Leeds LS1 1RF

☎ 0532 432701 Ext. 512

There are two annual prizes, one for a work of fiction and one for a work of non-fiction published in the preceding year. The larger prize is given to the book which, in the opinion of the judges, is the better of the final two.

Prizes £800 (first prize); £600 (second prize).

Yorkshire Post Art and Music Awards

Caroline Colmer, Yorkshire Post, PO Box 168, Wellington Street, Leeds LS1 1RF

☎0532 432701 Ext. 512

Two annual awards made to authors whose work has contributed most to the understanding and appreciation of art and music. Books should have been published in the preceding year in the UK.

Award £800 each – one for book on art, one for book on music.

Young Observer Teenage Fiction Prize

Sue Matthias, Young Observer, 8 St Andrew's Hill, London EC4V 5JA

☎01–236 0202

An annual award for the best full-length novel written in English for teenagers. The winning author must be a citizen of British Commonwealth, Republic of Ireland, Pakistan, Bangladesh or South Africa. Books must have been published between 1 July and 30 June.

Prize £600

Fiction

Angel Literary Prize

(See *General* p. 450)

James Tait Black Memorial Prize

(See *General* p. 450)

Booker Prize for Fiction

Book Trust, Book House, 45 East Hill, London SW18 2QZ   ☎01–870 9055

The leading British literary prize. It was set up in 1968 by Booker McConnell Ltd., with the intention of rewarding merit, raising the stature of the author in the eyes of the public and increasing the sale of the books. The announcement of the winner has been televised live since 1981, and all the books on the shortlist experience a substantial increase in sales. Eligible novels must be written in English by a citizen of Britain, the Commonwealth, the Republic of Ireland, Pakistan or South Africa, and must be published in the UK for the first time between 1 October and 30 September of the year of the prize. Entries are submitted only by UK publishers who may each submit not more than four novels within the appropriate scheduled publication dates. The judges may also ask for certain other eligible novels to be submitted to them. This has led to some controversy in recent years with publishers accused of 'holding back' obvious favourites in order to increase the chances of the prize going to one of their listed authors.

Prize £15,000 (Annual)

·Previous winners include: Kingsley Amis (1986), Salman Rushdie (1981), Paul Scott (1977), Ruth Prawer Jhabvala (1975), John Berger (1972).

The Constable Trophy

c/o Northern Arts, 10 Osborne Terrace, Jesmond, Newcastle upon Tyne NE2 1NZ
☎091–281 6334

An annual competition supported by the five Northern-based Regional Arts Associations for fiction writers living in the North of England for a previously unpublished novel. The winning entry may be considered for publication by Constable & Co., as may two runners-up.
Prize £2000 (First prize) & Trophy plus £1000 on acceptance by Constable & Co. in advance of royalties.

Mary Elgin Award

Hodder & Stoughton Ltd, 47 Bedford Square, London WC1B 3DP ☎01–636 9851

To encourage gifted new writers of fiction on the Hodder & Stoughton publishing list. No restrictions of age, sex or nationality apply, and writers need not be first novelists. Work to have been published or submitted to Hodder & Stoughton during the previous 12 months.
Award £50 (Annual)

Geoffrey Faber Memorial Prize

(See *General* p. 452)

Fawcett Society Book Prize

(See *General* p. 452)

Guardian Children's Fiction Award

(See *Childrens' Literature* p. 465)

Guardian Fiction Prize

Literary Editor, The Guardian, 119 Farringdon Road, London EC1R 3ER
☎01–278 2332

An annual award for a novel published by a British or Commonwealth writer, this is chosen by the Literary Editor in conjunction with the Guardian's regular reviewers of fiction.
Prize £1000
Previous winners include: Isabel Colegate.

The Hawthornden Prize

The Society of Authors, 84 Drayton Gardens, London SW10 9SB ☎01–373 6642

An annual award for a work of imaginative literature by a British subject under the age of forty-one published during the previous year.
Prize £750
Previous winners include: Robert Shaw, V. S. Naipaul.

Winifred Holtby Memorial Prize

Royal Society of Literature, 1 Hyde Park Gardens, London W2 2LT

☎01–723 5104

An annual award for the best regional work of fiction (or, in some cases non-fiction or poetry) written in English by a living citizen of the UK, Republic of Ireland or the Commonwealth, published in the year of the prize.
Prize £500

Emil Kurt Maschler Award

(See *Childrens' Literature* p. 465)

Sinclair Prize for Fiction

Book Trust, Book House, 45 East Hill, London SW18 2QZ   ☎01–870 9055

An annual award first made in 1982, this prize is sponsored by Sinclair Research Ltd and is for the best unpublished full length novel (not less than 50,000 words) of great literary merit and also of social or political significance. The book must be written originally in English and must be submitted by the author. Closing date for entries is 31 July. Entry form on request.
Prize £5000 plus publication by William Heinemann Ltd.

Welsh Arts Council Prizes

(See *General* p. 459)

Yorkshire Post Book of the Year Awards

(See *General* p. 459)

Non Fiction
Angel Literary Prize

(See *General* p. 450)

Best Book of the Sea Award

1 Chesham Street, London SW1X 8NF   ☎01–235 2884

This award was founded in 1970 and sponsored by King George's Fund for Sailors, and is given annually for a work of non-fiction which contributes most to the knowledge and/or enjoyment of those who love the sea. A second award may be given at the discretion of the judges for a work of outstanding merit.
Award £500; £250 (second discretionary award)

.Fawcett Society Book Prize

(See *General* p. 452)

Roger Machell Prize
The Society of Authors, 84 Drayton Gardens, London SW10 9SB ☎01-373 6642

An annual award for a non-fiction book on any of the performing arts, written in English, the work of one author and first published in the UK. This prize is sponsored by **Hamish Hamilton**.
Prize £2000

NCR Book Award
The Administrator, NCR Book Award, 206 Marylebone Road, London NW1 6LY ☎01-725 8244

The NCR Book Award was established in 1987 (first award to be made in 1988) for a book written in English by a living writer from Britain or the Commonwealth and first published in the UK. Publishers only may submit titles, limited to two per imprint. The award will cover all areas of non-fiction except academic, guide books and practical listings (such as cookery books). Titles eligible for the 1988 award must be published in the 12 months between 1 April 1987 and 31 March 1988, a short-list of four books will be announced in mid-April 1988. The aim of the award is to stimulate interest in non-fiction writing and publishing in the UK.
Award £25,000 (plus £1500 to each remaining short listed book).

Time-Life Silver PEN Award
English Centre of International PEN, 7 Dilke Street, London SW3 4JE ☎01-352 6303

An annual award, the winner being nominated by the PEN Executive Committee, for an outstanding work of non-fiction written in English and published in England in the year preceding the prize.
Prize £500 plus silver pen.

Welsh Arts Council Prizes
(See *General* p. 459)

Yorkshire Post Book of the Year Awards
(See *General* p. 459)

Academic
Astra Prize for Medical Writing
The Society of Authors, 84 Drayton Gardens, London SW10 9SB ☎01-373 6642

Awarded for a medical textbook written and published in the United Kingdom in the year preceding the award.
Prize £1000 (Annual)

Times Educational Supplement Schoolbook Award

Book Trust, Book House, 45 East Hill, London SW18 2QZ ☎ 01–870 9055

An annual award for the most outstanding schoolbook in the category specified for the year, either a single book for use in class or a representative book from a series.
Award £500

Biography/Autobiography

Joe Ackerley Prize

English Centre of International PEN, 7 Dilke Street, London SW3 4JE

☎ 01–352 6303

Commemorating the novelist and autobiographer, J.R. Ackerley, this Prize is awarded for a literary autobiography, written in English and published in the year preceding the award.
Prize £500 approx.

James Tait Black Memorial Prizes

(See *General* p. 450)

Nelson Hurst & Marsh Biography Award

Mrs Ridgway, Secretary, The Authors Club, 40 Dover Street, London W1X 3RB

☎ 01–499 8581

A biennial award (odd years) for the most significant biography published over a two year period by a British publisher.
Award £2000

Children's Literature

Hans Christian Andersen Awards

IBBY British Section, Book Trust, Book House, 45 East Hill, London SW18 2QZ

☎ 01–870 9055

The only international prizes for children's literature. Two prizes are awarded to the author and illustrator whose work has made a lasting contribution to children's literature.
Award Gold medals (Biennial – even years)

The Carnegie Medal

Library Association, 7 Ridgmount Street, London WC1E 7AE ☎ 01–636 7543

Presented for an outstanding book for children written in English and first published in the UK during the preceding year. This award is not necessarily restricted to books of an imaginative nature.
Award Medal

The Children's Book Award

Martin Kromer, 22 Beacon Brow, Bradford BD6 3DE   ☎0274 575301

For the best work of fiction suitable for children up to fourteen years, published in the given year.
Award Certificate

The Children's Book Circle Eleanor Farjeon Award

Jill Coleman, Secretary (Children's Book Circle), A. & C. Black, 35 Bedford Row, London WC1R 4JH   ☎01–785 7291

This award, named in memory of the much loved children's writer, is for distinguished services to children's books either in this country or overseas, and may be given to a librarian, teacher, publisher, bookseller, author, artist, reviewer, television producer etc. at the discretion of members of the Children's Book Circle.
Award £500

The Kathleen Fidler Award

c/o The Book Trust, 15A Lynedoch Street, Glasgow G3 6EF   ☎041–332 0391

For a novel for children aged 8–12, to encourage authors new to writing for this age group. The work must be the author's first attempt to write for this age range.
Award £500 plus possible publication by Blackie.

Guardian Children's Fiction Award

Stephanie Nettell, 24 Weymouth Street, London W1N 3FA   ☎01–580 3479

For an outstanding work of fiction for children by a British or Commonwealth author, first published in the UK in the preceding year, excluding picture books and previous winners.
Award £500 (Annual)
Previous winners include: Ann Schlee, Joan Aiken, James Aldridge.

Mary Vaughan Jones Award

Welsh National Centre for Children's Literature, Castell Brychan, Aberystwyth, Dyfed SY23 2JB   ☎0970 4151

For distinguished services to the field of children's literature in Wales over a considerable period of time. This triennial award will next be presented in 1988.
Award £600 plus silver trophy.

Emil Kurt Maschler Award

Book Trust, Book House, 45 East Hill, London SW18 2QZ   ☎01–870 9055

For 'a work of imagination in the children's field in which text and illustration are of excellence and so presented that each enhances, yet balances the other'. Books published in the current year in the UK by a British author and/or artist or someone resident for ten years are eligible.
Award £1000

The Other Award
c/o Childrens' Book Bulletin, 4 Aldebert Terrace, London SW8 1BL

☎01–582 4483

Children's books of literary merit that children will enjoy and which are progressive in their treatment of ethnic minorities, the sex roles and social differences are eligible for this honorary award. Books should be published in the period 1 July–30 June.

Parents Magazine Best Book for Babies Award
Book Trust, Book House, 45 East Hill, London SW18 2QZ ☎01–870 9055

An annual award for the best book for the under-fours (babies and toddlers) published in Britain in the year ending 31 May.
Award £1000

Ryman New Writers' Award
(See *General* p. 456)

Signal Poetry for Children Award
Nancy Chambers, Thimble Press, Lockwood, Station Road, South Woodchester, Stroud, GL5 5EQ ☎045–387 2208

This award is given annually for particular excellence in one of the following areas: single poet collections published for children; poetry anthologies published for children; the body of work of a contemporary poet; critical or educational activity promoting poetry for children. All books published for children published in Britain are eligible regardless of the original country of publication. Unpublished work is not eligible.
Award £100

Smarties Prize for Children's Books
Book Trust, Book House, 45 East Hill, London SW18 2QZ ☎01–870 9055

Established in 1985 to encourage high standards and stimulate interest in books for children, this prize is given for a children's book written in English by a citizen of the UK or an author resident in the UK, and published in the UK in the year ending 31 October. There are three categories: 6 and under; 7–11 and innovation. An overall winner from these categories is chosen for the Grand Prix.
Prizes £8000 (Grand Prix); £1000 (Other categories).
Previous winners include: Ray Marshall & John Bradley (Innovation); Susanna Gretz (Under 7s); Jill Paton Walsh (Over 7s & Grand Prix).

The Tir Na N-Og Award
Welsh National Centre for Children's Literature, Castell Brychan, Aberystwyth, Dyfed SY23 2JB ☎0970 4151

An annual award given to the best original book published for children in the year prior to the announcement. There are two categories: the best Welsh book and the

best English book with an authentic Welsh background.
Award £500 (each category)

Christian

Collins Biennial Religious Book Award

Sarah Baird-Smith, William Collins Sons & Co. Ltd, 8 Grafton Street, London W1X 3LA ☎01–493 7070

A biennial award given for a book which has made the most distinguished contribution to the relevance of Christianity in the modern world, written by a living citizen of the Commonwealth, the Republic of Ireland or South Africa.
Award £2000

The Winifred Mary Stanford Prize

Hodder & Stoughton, 47 Bedford Square, London WC1B 3DP ☎01–636 9851

This biennial award (even years) is open to any book published in the UK in English which has been in some way inspired by the Christian faith, and written by a man or woman who is under 50 years of age at the time of publication. Literary merit is a prime factor in consideration for the award, but the subject may be from a wide range including poetry, fiction, biography, autobiography, biblical exposition, religious experience and witness. Submission is invited, from publishers only, of books published in the two years prior to the award which is presented at Easter.
Prize £1000

The Universe – The Catholic Newspaper – Literary Prize

The Universe, 33/9 Bowling Green Lane, London EC1R 0AB ☎01–278 7321

An annual award for the book which best supports and defends Christian values – the theme alters each year. Any book written in English and published in Britain or the Republic of Ireland in the year of the Award is eligible.
Prize £500

Crime

John Creasey Memorial Award

Crime Writers' Association, The Press Club, Shoe Lane, London EC4A 3JB

Founded in 1973 following the death of the crime writer, John Creasey, who founded the Crime Writers' Association, this award is given annually for the best first crime novel published in the preceding year.
Award £1000 plus magnifying glass.

Crime Writers' Association Fiction Award

Crime Writers' Association, The Press Club, Shoe Lane, London EC4A 3JB

Two prizes awarded for the best crime fiction published during the preceding year..
Award £1000 plus gold-plated dagger; £500 plus silver-plated dagger.

Crime Writers' Association Non-Fiction Award
Crime Writers' Association, The Press Club, Shoe Lane, London EC4A 3JB

An annual award for the best non-fiction crime book published during the preceding year.
Award £1000 plus gold-plated dagger.

Essays
Alexander Prize
(See *History* p. 469)

David Berry Prize
(See *History* p. 469)

E. Reginald Taylor Essay Competition
Hon. Editor, *Journal of the British Archaeological Association,* Institute of Archaeology, 36 Beaumont Street, Oxford OX1 2PG

An annual prize, in memory of the late E. Reginald Taylor FSA, for the best unpublished essay, not exceeding 7500 words, on a subject of archaeological, art historical or antiquarian interest within the period the Roman era to AD 1830. The essay should show original research on its chosen subject, and the author may be invited to read the essay before the Association. In addition, the essay may be published in the *Journal* of the Association if approved by the Editorial Committee.
Prize £100

First Work
Author's Club First Novel Award
The Authors Club, 40 Dover Street, London W1X 3RB ☎01–499 8581

Contact *Mrs Ridgway (Secretary)*

Instituted in 1954, this award is made for the most promising first novel of the year. Entries for the award are accepted from publishers, and short stories are not eligible. All books must be published in the United Kingdom.
Award £200 plus Silver Mounted Quill.

Samuel Beckett Award
Faber & Faber, 3 Queen Square, London WC1N 3AU ☎01–278 6881
Jointly sponsored by **Channel Four**, the **Royal Court Theatre** and **Faber & Faber**, this award aims to give support and encouragement to new playwrights at a crucial stage of their careers. Two prizes are given, one for a first play for the stage and another for a first play for television. There is also the possibility of publication by .Faber.
Prize £1000 (each category)

David Higham Prize for Fiction
Book Trust, Book House, 45 East Hill, London SW18 2QZ   ☎01–870 9055

An annual award for a first novel or book of short stories published in the UK in the year of the Award by an author who is a citizen of Britain, the Commonwealth, the Republic of Ireland, Pakistan or South Africa.
Award £1000

The Times/Jonathan Cape Young Writers Competition
Jonathan Cape, 32 Bedford Square, London WC1B 3EL   ☎01–636 3344

This annual award is given for a first work of fiction or non-fiction written in English by an author under the age of thirty.
Award £5000 plus publication by Jonathan Cape.

The Betty Trask Awards
The Society of Authors, 84 Drayton Gardens, London SW10 9SB   ☎01–373 6642

These annual awards are for authors who are under 35 and Commonwealth citizens on the strength of a first novel (published or unpublished) of a traditional or romantic (rather than experimental) nature. The awards must be used for a period or periods of foreign travel.
Award £12,000 plus up to five awards of £1000 each.
Previous winners include: *Winter Journey*, Ronald Frame.

Yorkshire Post Best First Work Awards
Caroline Colmer, Yorkshire Post, PO Box 168, Wellington Street, Leeds LS1 1RF
   ☎0532 432701 Ext. 512

An annual award for a work by a new author published during the preceding year.
Prize £600 plus £400 for the runner-up.

History/Historical Novels/Romance
Alexander Prize
Royal Historical Society, University College, Gower Street, London
WC1E 6BT   ☎01–387 7532

Awarded for an historical essay of not more than 6000 words. Competitors may choose their own subject for their essay, but must submit their choice for approval to the Literary Director of the **Royal Historical Society**.
Prize Medal plus £100

David Berry Prize
Royal Historical Society, University College London, Gower Street, London
WC1E 6BT   ☎01–387 7532

Awarded for an unpublished essay on Scottish history within the reigns of James I to James VI, not exceeding 10,000 words. Candidates may select any subject from the

relevant period, providing it has been submitted to and approved by the Council of the Royal Historical Society.
Prize £100 (Triennial – next 1988)

Historical Novel Prize in Memory of Georgette Heyer

The Bodley Head, 30 Bedford Square, London WC1B 3RP   ☎01–631 4434
or
Transworld Publishers Ltd, Century House, 61–63 Uxbridge Rd, London W5 5SA   ☎01–579 2652

Founded in 1977 in memory of the celebrated historical novelist, this is an annual prize for an outstanding previously unpublished historical novel.
Prize £2000

Mitchell Prize for the History of Art

The Lady Vaizey, 24 Heathfield Terrace, London W4 4JE   ☎01–994 7994

There are two annual prizes, one to the author of an outstanding original contribution in English to art history assessed in terms of scholarly, critical and literary merit, and the second to the most promising first book fulfilling the same criteria. Books should have been published in the 18 months preceding presentation date in USA or UK.
Prize $10,000 and $2000

Romantic Novelists Association Major Award

Mrs Eileen Huckbody, 2A Rye Walk, Ingatestone, Essex CM4 9AL   ☎0277–352 964

Annual award for the best romantic novel of the year, open to non-members as well as members of the **Romantic Novelists Association**. Novels must be published between 1 January and 31 December of the year of entry.
Award £2000

Romantic Novelists Association Netta Muskett Award

Mrs Eileen Huckbody, 2A Rye Walk, Ingatestone, Essex CM4 9AL   ☎0277–352 964

The award is for unpublished writers in the field of the romantic novel who must join the **Romantic Novelists Association** as Probationary Members. Mss entered for this Award must be especially written for it.

The Betty Trask Awards
(See *First Work* p. 469)

Whitfield Prize
Royal Historical Society, University College London, Gower Street, London
WC1E 6BT   ☎01–387 7532

An annual award for the best work on English or Welsh history by an author under
forty, published in the UK in the preceding calendar year.

Plays
Verity Bargate Award
The Soho Poly Theatre Club, 16 Ridinghouse Street, London W1   ☎01–580 6982

Contact *Patrick Cox*

To commemorate the late Verity Bargate, founder and director of the **Soho Poly
Theatre Club**, this award is presented annually for a new and unperformed play.
The Soho Poly also runs an annual young writers course to encourage young play-
wrights.
Award £1000 (plus publication by Methuen)

Bridport Arts Centre Creative Writing Competition
(See *General* p. 451)

Bristol Old Vic & HTV West Playwriting Award
Playwriting Award, PO Box 60, Bristol BS99 7NS   ☎0272 778366

This award, initiated in 1987, is open to any author, amateur or professional, over
the age of eighteen and resident in the British Isles. Along with the cash prize there is
a trophy and the possibility of production on the stage or television.
Award £2000

Radio Times Drama Awards
BBC Publications, PO Box 1AX, 33 Marylebone High Street, London W1 1AX
                                                        ☎01–580 5577

Biennial award (even years) for an original work for either radio or television not
previously performed in public. Each entry to be supported by a sponsor experienced in production. Details of awards are announced in *Radio Times* in January.
Award £6000 in each category
Previous winners include: Peter Ransley.

Radio Times Radio Comedy Awards
BBC Publications, PO Box 1AX, 33 Marylebone High Street, London W1 1AX
                                                        ☎01–580 5577

Biennial award (odd years) for an original 30-minute script capable of being
developed into a series. Each entry to be supported by a sponsor experienced in
comedy drama. Details of awards announced in *Radio Times* in January.
Award £3500

John Whiting Award

The Drama Director, Arts Council of Great Britain, 105 Piccadilly, London
W1V 0AU ☎01–629 9495

Founded in 1965 to commemorate the life and work of the playwright John Whiting (*The Devils, A Penny for a Song*), this award is made annually to a playwright. Any writer who has received during the previous two calendar years an award through the Arts Council's Theatre Writing Schemes or who has had a premiere production by a theatre company in receipt of annual subsidy is eligible to apply.
Prize £3500

Poetry

An Duais don bhFiliocht i nGaelige (Prize for Poetry in Irish)

The Arts Council (An Chomhairle Ealaion), 70 Merrion Square, Dublin 2, Ireland
☎0001–611840

Contact *The Literature Officer*

Awarded for the best book of poetry in the Irish language published in the preceding three years.
Prize £1000 (Triennial – next 1989)

Arvon Foundation International Poetry Competition

Kilnhurst, Kilnhurst Road, Todmorden, Lancashire OL14 6AX ☎070–681 6582

Founded in 1980, this competition is for poems written in English and not previously broadcast or published. There are no restrictions on the number of lines, theme, age of entrants or nationality.
Prize £5000 (First Prize Biennial – odd years)

Alice Hunt Bartlett Award

The Poetry Society, 21 Earls Court Square, London SW5 9DE ☎01–373 7861

This award is given to the living poet the Society most wishes to honour and encourage. Special consideration is given to newly emerging poets, as merit warrants. The author must submit a volume of poetry containing no fewer than 20 poems or 400 lines. In the case of translations, the original poet must also be alive and the prize is shared equally between poet and translator.
Award £500

Bridport Arts Centre Creative Writing Competition
(See *General* p. 451)

British Airways Commonwealth Poetry Prize

The Arts Librarian, Commonwealth Institute, Kensington High Street, London
W8 6NQ ☎01–603 4535 Ext. 269

An annual prize, sponsored by British Airways, for a published book of poetry by an author from a Commonwealth country including the UK. Entries in non-English

officially recognised languages are accepted with a translation.
Prizes £5000 & £2000 plus four regional awards of £1000.

Cholmondeley Awards
The Society of Authors, 84 Drayton Gardens, London SW10 9SB ☎01–373 6642

In 1965, the Dowager Marchioness of Cholmondeley established these non-competitive awards, for which submissions are not required, for the benefit and encouragement of poets of any age, sex or nationality.
Award £3000 (in total, usually divided)

Denis Devlin Award
Literature Officer, The Arts Council (An Chomhairle Ealaion), 70 Merrion Square, Dublin 2, Ireland ☎0001–611840

Triennial award for the best book of poetry in English by an Irish poet, published in the preceding three years.
Award £1000 (next – 1989)

Geoffrey Faber Memorial Prize
(See *General* p. 452)

Prudence Farmer Award
New Statesman, Foundation House, Perseverance Works, 38 Kingsland Road, London E2 5BA ☎01–739 3211

For the best poem to have been published in the *New Statesman* during the previous year (July to July).
Award £100

Greenwich Festival Poetry Competition
25 Woolwich New Road, London SE18 6EU ☎01–317 8687

A biennial award for an unpublished poem in English of up to 50 lines by anyone over the age of sixteen.
Prize £1000 (Total prize money)

National Poetry Competition
The Poetry Society, 21 Earls Court Square, London SW5 9DE ☎01–373 7861

Run in conjunction with BBC Radio 3, this is now the major annual poetry competition in Britain. The prizes are each awarded for an unpublished poem of less than 40 lines by anyone over the age of 16 who lives, works or studies in the UK or Republic of Ireland. There is an entry fee of £2 per poem, and a maximum entry of ten poems per writer. Further details and entry form available on receipt of an s.a.e.
Prizes £2000 (First prize); £1000 (Second prize); £1500 (Third prize); plus smaller prizes.
Previous winners include: Andrew Motion.

New Poetry
c/o English Centre of Internatioinal PEN, 7 Dilke Street, London SW3 4JE
☎01–352 6303

Poets are invited to submit six poems for publication in an anthology produced jointly by Quartet and PEN. Publication is biennial alternating with NEW STORIES. S.a.e. for further details.

Outposts Poetry Competition
Howard Sergeant, 72 Burwood Road, Walton-on-Thames, Surrey KT12 4AL
☎0932 240712

Annual competition for an unpublished poem of no more than forty lines.
Prize £1000 (approx.)

Ryman New Writers' Award
(See *General* p. 456)

Signal Poetry for Children Award
(See *Children's Literature* p. 466)

Dylan Thomas Award
The Poetry Society, 21 Earls Court Square, London SW5 9DE ☎01–373 7861

An annual award given in alternate years for poetry and short stories, established in 1983 to commemorate Dylan Thomas and encourage the two forms in which he made his outstanding contribution to literature. This is open to all published writers in the UK (all entrants must have had poetry or short stories published within two years of submission). Entries must include published work, but unpublished work may also be included.
Prize £1000

Ver Poets Open Competition
May Badman, Haycroft, 61/63 Chiswell Green Lane, St Albans, Herts AL2 3AG
☎0727 67005

An annual competition for unpublished poems of no more than 30 lines written in English.
Prizes £100, £50, plus two prizes of £25.

Wandsworth All London Competition
(See *General* p. 458)

Welsh Arts Council Prizes
(See *General* p. 459)

Mary Wilkins Memorial Poetry Competition

Birmingham & Midland Institute, 9 Margaret Street, Birmingham B3 3BS
☎021–236 3591

An annual competition for an unpublished poem not exceeding 40 lines, written in English by an author over the age of 15 and living, working or studying in the UK. The poem should not have been entered for any other poetry competition.
Prize £200 (total of four prizes)

Reference

Bejam Cookery Book of the Year Award

Public Relations Department, Bejam, Honeypot Lane, Stanmore, Middx HA7 1LE
☎01–951 1313

Awarded for the best cookery book published in the UK between 1 September and 31 August. Particular emphasis is placed on originality of recipes, practical instructions, well-written and interesting text, health awareness and attractive presentation.
Award £2500 (plus commemorative gift)
Previous winners include: Carol Bowen *Versatile Vegetables*, Miriam Polunin *The New Cookbook*.

Bimco-Lloyd's List Maritime Book Prize

26–30 Artillery Lane, London E1 7LX
☎01–247 9461

For the best unpublished manuscript on operational, commercial, technical, financial or legal aspects of any sector of maritime industries and services.
Prize £15,000 Swiss Francs (More than £5000)

Times Educational Supplement Information Book Awards

Literary Editor, Times Educational Supplement, Priory House, St John's Lane, London EC1M 4BX
☎01–253 3000

There are two annual awards made for Best Information Books, one for the age range 10–16, and another for children up to the age of 9. Books must have been published in Britain or the Commonwealth in the year preceding the award.
Award £500 (each category)

Science Fiction

British Science Fiction Association Award

The Award Administrator, c/o The British Science Fiction Association, 7 The Thicket, Whitenap, Romsey, Hampshire

Annual awards are given in four categories: Best Novel, Best Short Fiction, Best Media Presentation, Best Artist, for work first published or presented during the preceding year.
Award Trophy.

Short Stories
H. E. Bates Short Story Competition
Leisure & Recreation Department, Northampton Borough Council, Guildhall, Northampton ☎0604 34734 Ext. 459 or 460

Named after the late H. E. Bates, one of the masters of the short story form, this competition is for short stories of 2000 words maximum. Any writer resident in Great Britain is eligible, and there are categories for children under 11 and under 16. *Prize* £50 (First Prize)

Bridport Arts Centre Creative Writing Competition
(See *General* p. 451)

Catherine Cookson Cup
Mary Monk, 7 Harlequin Gardens, St Leonards-on-Sea, East Sussex TN37 7PF

For a short story of not more than 2500 words on any subject. There is a £1 entry fee. *Prize* £150 plus cup.

London Newspaper Group Short Story Competition
The Editor, London Newspaper Group, Newspaper House, Winslow Road, London W6 9SF ☎01–741 1622

Established two years ago, with a total prize value of £5000. Top prize varies according to the year's sponsor – in 1987 it was the £3500 18-carat solid gold Mont Blanc fountain pen. The competition runs over a year – stories are published weekly, with a prize each month for the 'editor's choice'. All published stories go into the final competition, which is usually judged in December. Details of the 1988 competition now available.

Katherine Mansfield Menton Short Story Prize
The English Centre of International PEN, 7 Dilke Street, London SW3 4JE
☎01–352 6303

A triennial prize (next awarded in 1987) for a volume of short stories written in English by a British, Irish or Commonwealth writer, published in the UK in the preceding three years.
Prize £10,000 French francs.

New Stories
c/o English Centre of International PEN, 7 Dilke Street, London SW3 4JE
☎01–352 6303

Publication of short stories, not exceeding 10,000 words in an anthology produced jointly by Quartet Books and PEN. Publication is biennial alternating with *New Poetry*. S.a.e. for further details.

Ryman New Writers' Awards
(See *General* p. 456)

STAND Magazine Short Story Competition
Stand Magazine, 179 Wingrove Road, Newcastle upon Tyne NE4 9DA
☎091–273 3280

Biennial award (odd years) plus one year subscription to magazine for a short story written in English and not published, broadcast or under consideration elsewhere. *Prize* £1000 plus prizes of cash and one year subscription to Stand magazine.

Tom-Gallon Trust
The Society of Authors, 84 Drayton Gardens, London SW10 9SB   ☎01–373 6642

A biennial award is made from this Trust Fund to fiction writers of limited means who have had at least one short story accepted. Authors wishing to enter should send a list of their already published fiction, giving the name of the publisher or periodical in each case and the approximate date of publication; one published short story; a brief statement of their financial position; an undertaking that they intend to devote a substantial amount of time to the writing of fiction as soon as they are financially able to do so; a stamped addressed envelope for the return of the work submitted.
Award £750 (last award: 1986)

Wandsworth All London Competition
(See *General* p. 458)

Translation
The John Florio Prize
The Translator's Association, 84 Drayton Gardens, London SW10 9SB
☎01–373 6642

Established in 1963 under the auspices of the Italian Institute and the British–Italian Society, this prize is awarded biennially for the best translation into English of a 20th Century Italian work of literary merit and general interest and published by a British publisher in the two years preceding the prize.
Prize £500

Scott Moncrieff Prize
The Translators' Association, 84 Drayton Gardens, London SW10 9SB
☎01–373 6642

An annual award for the best translation published by a British publisher during the previous year of French 20th Century work of literary merit and general interest. *Prize* £1000

Schlegel-Tieck Prize

The Translators' Association, 84 Drayton Gardens, London SW10 9SB

☎01–373 6642

An annual award for the best translation of a German 20th Century work of literary merit and interest published by a British publisher during the preceding year.
Prize £2000

Travel
Thomas Cook Travel Book Awards

Book Trust, Book House, 45 East Hill, London SW18 2QZ

☎01–870 9055

The annual awards are given to encourage the art of travel writing in two categories: (a) best travel book, and (b) best guide book published in the current year.
Awards £2000 (a) £1000 (b)

London Tourist Board Guide Book of the Year Award

London Tourist Board, Public Relations Manager, 26 Grosvenor Gardens, London SW1W 0DU ☎01–730 3450

An annual award for new or substantially revised guidebooks mainly on London published between 1 June and 31 May. Two categories: General Guide and Specialist.
Award Gift and certificate.

Shiva Naipaul Memorial Prize

The Spectator, 56 Doughty Street, London WC1N 2LL ☎01–405 1706

An annual competition for the writer best able to describe a visit to a foreign place or people; for the most acute and profound observation of cultures and/or scenes evidently alien to the writer. Submissions must be unpublished and no more than 4000 words.
Prize £1000 plus publication in The Spectator.

Grants/Fellowships
Aosdana Scheme

The Arts Council (An Chomhairle Ealaion), 70 Merrion Square, Dublin 2, Ireland ☎0001–611840

Contact *The Literature Officer*

Aosdana is an affiliation of creative artists engaged in literature, music and the visual arts, and consists of not more than 150 artists who have gained a reputation for achievement and distinction. Membership is achieved via competitive sponsored selection. Members are eligible to receive an annuity for a five-year term to assist them in pursuing their art full time.
Award IR£5000 (Initial annuity)

Arts Council of Great Britain Writers' Bursaries

Arts Council of Great Britain, 105 Piccadilly, London W1V 0AU   ☎01–629 9495

Contact *Literature Director*

A small number of bursaries are available to poets and novelists of outstanding literary achievement needing financial assistance for the research or writing of their next book. Open to British and non-British subjects resident in England.
Award Amount varies according to need

The Authors' Foundation

The Society of Authors, 84 Drayton Gardens, London SW10 9SB   ☎01–373 6642

The Authors' Foundation makes grants annually to writers whose publisher's advance is insufficient to cover the costs of research involved. At present, preference is given to non-fiction. The author should make application to the Foundation in a letter giving details, in confidence, of the advance and royalties, together with the reasons for needing additional funding.

Bursaries in Literature

Literature Officer, The Arts Council (An Chomhairle Ealaion), 70 Merrion Square, Dublin 2, Ireland.   ☎0001–611840

Awarded to creative writers (fiction, poetry, drama) to enable concentration on or completion of specific projects.
Award £1500 – £6000

Eastern Arts Writing Fellowship

Establishment Officer, University of East Anglia, University Plain, Norwich NR4 7JT   ☎0603 56161

Awarded to a writer of established reputation in any field for the period of the Spring and Summer term. The duties of the Fellowship are discussed at an interview. It is assumed that one activity will be the pursuit of the Fellow's own writing. In addition, the Fellow will be expected to take part in some of the following activities: a) contributing to the teaching of a formal course in creative writing or running a regular writers' workshop on an informal extra-curricular basis; b) being available for a specified period each week to advise individual students engaged in writing; c) giving an introductory lecture or reading at the beginning of the Fellowship; d) organising one or two literary events involving other writers from outside the university; e) making some contribution to the cultural and artistic life of the region (e.g. by public lecturing or reading). Applications for the Fellowship should be lodged with the Establishment Officer by 1 October each year.
Award £2000

E. C. Gregory Trust Fund

The Society of Authors, 84 Drayton Gardens, London SW10 9SB ☎01–373 6642

Awards of varying amounts are made each year for the encouragement of young poets under the age of thirty who can show that they are likely to benefit from an opportunity to give more time to writing. Open only to British born subjects resident in the UK.
Award £15,000 (Total)

Francis Head Awards

The Society of Authors, 84 Drayton Gardens, London SW10 9SB ☎01–373 6642

Designed to provide grants to established British authors over the age of 35 who need financial help during a period of illness or disablement.

Macaulay Fellowship

Literature Officer, The Arts Council (An Chomhairle Ealaion), 70 Merrion Square, Dublin 2, Ireland ☎0001–611840

To further the liberal education of a young creative artist. Candidates for this triennial award must be under thirty years of age on 30 June, or thirty-five in exceptional circumstances.
Award £3000

Oppenheim John Downes Memorial Trust

5 Breams Buildings, London EC4A 1HL

The trust offers grants to writers and artists of all descriptions who are unable to pursue their vocation by reason of their poverty. Applicants must also be British by birth and of British parents and grandparents.
Award £50 – £1500 (Variable)

The Margaret Rhondda Award

The Society of Authors, 84 Drayton Gardens, London SW10 9SB ☎01–373 6642

This triennial award (next given in 1987) is intended as a grant-in-aid for a woman towards the expenses of a research project in journalism.
Award £300

The Royal Literary Fund

144 Temple Chambers, Temple Avenue, London EC4Y 0DT

The Fund helps published authors and their families when in financial need. For further details, write for application form.

Southern Arts Literature Bursaries
Southern Arts, 19 Southgate Street, Winchester, Hampshire SO23 9DQ
☎0962 55099

Discretionary annual bursaries may be awarded for periods of up to one year to authors of published poetry or fiction resident in the Southern Arts Region.

Travelling Scholarships
The Society of Authors, 84 Drayton Gardens, London SW10 9SB ☎01–373 6642

Annual, non-competitive awards for the benefit of British authors to enable them to travel abroad.
Award £1000 (each)

West Midlands Arts Creative Writing Attachment
Brunswick Terrace, Stafford ST16 1BZ ☎0785 59231

A scheme which provides a grant for an arts, community, educational or other organisation in the West Midlands Region to establish a creative writing attachment. The grant is paid direct to the writer, who can be a practising writer of poetry, prose, journalism, etc. Payment is for a part-time six month attachment.
Award £8000 p.a. (pro rata)

Yorkshire Arts Association Literary Awards
Literature Officer, Yorkshire Arts Association, Glyde House, Glydegate, Bradford BD5 0BQ ☎0274 723051

Application for annual bursaries from the Yorkshire Arts Association are invited from writers who are living, working or studying in the region. A number of bursaries are awarded to assist a writer's development and to encourage recognition of the writer's work. Preference is given to work where the creative imagination is the major element, but the Literature Panel will consider local history, biography and social history.
Prize £250 (each)

As We Go To Press . . .

Publishers

Aurum Press bought by the **Really Useful Group**, the production company for Andrew Lloyd Webber musicals.

Robert Royce Ltd bought by **Cassell**. Robert Royce joins Cassell board as development director.

Book Publishing division of **J. M. Dent** bought by **Weidenfeld**.

Robert Maxwell (BPCC) buys minority stake in **Elsevier**.

Thorsons announces a move into the general market. The new **Equation** imprint will cover a broad range of non-fiction subjects. Around 50 titles are planned for 1988.

A new imprint for environmental titles, **Green Books**, is set up with backing from Friends of the Earth, 6 titles planned for 1988. Address: Ford House, Hartland, Bideford, Devon EX39 6EE (☎ 02374 621).

Allen Lane, The Penguin Press to be revived as a hardback imprint within Viking.

Christopher Helm Publishers Ltd (see **Croom Helm**) can be found at Imperial House, 21–25 North Street, Bromley, Kent BR1 1SD ☎ 01–466 6622. They publish gardening, horticulture and botany, natural history and ornithology, travel books, film, media and general titles. **Editorial heads** *Christopher Helm, Joe Hemmings* and *Richard Wigmore*. Around 50 titles planned for the 1987/88 season.

Allison & Busby, recently saved from extinction by **W. H. Allen**, will remain intact as an imprint, though it's now to be found in the Allen empire in Hill Street.

Magazines

Best, a new sister magazine to German giants Grüner & Jahr's best selling *Prima*, with a similar cocktail of practical information and entertainment, has been launched. Same address as *Prima*, and with the same editor. Different telephone number though: ☎ 01–245 8847.

From the **International Publishers Association**, a new quarterly journal called *Rights* aimed at 'strengthening free authorship and independent publishing'. (Subscription £35 p.a. IPA, Avenue de Miremont 3, 1206 Geneva, Switzerland.)

Liz Tilbens becomes editor of **Vogue**.

Prizes

To celebrate her 45 years membership of **International PEN**, novelist Rona Randall donates a prize of £100 for a short story of not more than 2000 words written by a member of the English Centre.

A new prize for **Scottish Writer of the Year**, worth £5000 (the McVitie's Prize) is announced by the sponsor, United Biscuits. All writers born or now working in Scotland are eligible.

It has come to our notice that the **Vivian Ellis Prize** is for lyricists, as well as composers of theatre music/musicals, and the two should apply jointly. Started in 1985, it's an annual competition; the closing date in 1988 is the end of March. First prize £1000. Entrants must be under 30, and the work entered not professionally performed. Contact the Administrator, Eileen Stone, at the Performing Right Society, 29–33 Berners Street, London W1P 4AA. ☎01–580 5544.

London Weekend Television have announced a new live drama competition: 'as a television company closely involved with drama, we're anxious to see live theatre thrive'. Total prize money £37,500, to be divided into 1st, 2nd and 3rd prizes, to help stage 3 plays judged to be outstanding by a panel of 'distinguished judges'. The competition is open to producers, producing theatres and rep. companies, rather than playwrights direct. The deadline for 1988 is likely to be the end of September. More details from: Michael Hallifax, LWT Plays on Stage, South Bank Television Centre, London SE1 9LT ☎01–261 3434.

Agents

Alec Harrison of **Alec Harrison & Associates** died in August 1987.

Index